SHANNON STRIKES AGAIN

SHANNON STRIKES AGAIN

- *The Ringer*
- *Murder With Love*
- *With Intent To Kill*
- *No Holiday For Crime*

by Dell Shannon

Nelson Doubleday, Inc.
Garden City, New York

CONTENTS

SHANNON STRIKES AGAIN

THE
RINGER

Threefold the stride of Time, from first to last!
Loitering slow, the Future creepeth—
Arrow-swift the Present sweepeth—
And motionless forever stands the Past.
                    —Schiller, *Sentences of Confucius*

What seest thou else
In the dark backward and abysm of time?
                    —*The Tempest,* Act I, sc. 2

CHAPTER 1

Mendoza came back from lunch at one-thirty, and in the lobby of the big Police Facilities Building ran into Lieutenant Goldberg waiting for the elevator.

"They keeping you busy, Saul?" he asked idly.

"So-so," said Goldberg, bringing out the inevitable Kleenex. "As if I hadn't enough on hand, Auto Theft coming asking cooperation. So we overlap some, let them do their own damn routine." The elevator landed and they got in; Mendoza punched the button for Goldberg's floor. "They've been after this hot-car ring for months, and the Feds sniffing around too on account of the interstate bit. That Van Allen." Goldberg snorted. "We've all got our own troubles."

"*De veras,*" agreed Mendoza absently as Goldberg left the elevator. He punched the next button and stepped out upstairs. In the Homicide office, Sergeant Lake was gloomily contemplating a paperback book titled *How To Stay Slim.* "Anything new in?" asked Mendoza.

"Well, Jase just picked up that Sam Chase. He and John are leaning on him—don't know if they're getting anywhere."

"Him," said Mendoza. It didn't much matter whether they got Sam Chase to open up and sing a pretty song; his prints had been all over the handbag rifled of about eleven bucks, last Friday night, after a mugger had jumped the old lady from behind on her way home from the market. The old lady had been knocked down hard enough to brain herself on the sidewalk, which was why Homicide instead of Robbery had been looking for Chase. Chase had a record back to age fourteen.

Mendoza dropped the black Homburg on his desk and went down the hall to look into the interrogation room where Jason Grace and John Palliser were leaning on Chase. They were both looking pleased;

they left Chase huddled in the chair looking miserable and came over to Mendoza.

"At least he's got just enough sense to realize we've got him nailed for it by those prints," said Grace. "He came apart when we broke that to him."

"And this time he may get a real sentence," said Mendoza, "if it'll be a charge of involuntary manslaughter—all we can hang on him."

"On that I'll take no bets," said Palliser sardonically. Grace only brushed his narrow moustache, as dapper as Mendoza's, and his chocolate-colored face wore a cynical, sad expression.

Chase sat up a little and said, "Can I have a cigarette?" Palliser gave him one, lit it. Chase was a thin, unhealthy-looking fellow, not very big, with a pasty complexion and china-blue eyes under nonexistent eyebrows. He was twenty-nine, and he'd done little stretches here and there, as a j.d. and afterwards: six months, nine months, a year on probation. He looked at the three plainclothes detectives and said, "I been thinking. It's kind of an accident you got me for that—and there's that damn guy livin' high on that job he pulled last week. Things ain't fair, you know?" He looked aggrieved. "Jesus knows he'd be the first one open his jaw about me, shoe on the other foot. I guess I'll tell you."

"That'd be nice, Sam," said Grace gently. "What job? What's your pal's name?"

"Guy. I said. Guy Godfrey. I never did but one job with him, we aren't exactly pals. He did this job up in Hollywood—busted in a dame's apartment. I ran into him inna bar and he was telling me, see."

"And what was the job you pulled together, Sam?"

"Well," said Chase nervously, "it was his idea. And it was him did it. I mean the— Well, Jesus, the old lady'd seen both of us when we busted in, she'd reckanize us, see? And *that* was Guy's idea too. I said so all right, it's his idea, he does it. He says, we're in it together. So," said Chase lugubriously, "we ended up playin' a hand of blackjack, loser do the old dame, see."

"Well, I will be damned!" said Grace. They looked at each other.

"You never know," said Mendoza, "when the rabbit's going to jump out in front of you. *Caray,* I thought that one was dead."

"Mrs. Reiner," said Palliser. "That thing over on Constance Street, back in April. Be damned."

"I never heard the name," said Chase sadly. "I guess that was her. But it was Guy—"

That one they hadn't had any leads on at all, and it had got shoved in Pending nearly six weeks back.

"That hand of blackjack laid out on the kitchen table always did bother me some," said Grace now. "I had a little hunch it was something like that. So the loser took on the job of strangling Mrs. Reiner, was that it, Sam?"

"Well, it didn't matter how— And Guy lost the hand," said Chase hurriedly. "I didn't know nothing else about it—"

Mendoza laughed. "What odds do either of you give that Guy'll say the same thing?"

"That long a gamble I don't take," said Palliser. "I've got house payments to make these days." He went out to start the machinery for a warrant on Chase, and Grace took Chase off. When he'd deposited him at the jail he'd have a look in Records for Godfrey.

Mendoza wandered back to his office, called Wilcox Street precinct and asked Sergeant Barth if they had had an apartment break-in last week, in that territory. Barth said, with a vengeance, thirtyish divorcée living alone had surprised the burglar, got beaten up, and was still in a coma with a skull-fracture. "You don't say," said Mendoza, reflecting that it might have been Godfrey who accounted for Mrs. Reiner at that; he seemed to be disposed to violence. This count of violence on Chase was the only one that showed. "We've probably just found out for you who did it. An erstwhile pal came apart. I'll let you know the details when we get any ourselves."

"And not to sound ungrateful," said Barth, "but we've got a thing up here we're thinking about handing over to you. We've been going round and round on it, no smell of a lead at all, just a big fat mystery. Maybe you bloodhounds down at headquarters are smarter."

"Well—June," said Mendoza amiably. "Things a little slow at the moment. The nice weather. I don't mind taking a look at it for you. What is it?"

"A mystery," repeated Barth. "Which we do so seldom see. I think I'll pass it on in person. We're kind of busy up here with this gang of kite-flyers going around town." The precinct stations weren't neatly divided up into the different bureaus; those detectives took whatever cases came their way. "I'll see you sometime," said Barth, sounding harried. "G'bye."

Mendoza put the phone down, lit a cigarette, and ruminated on the cases Homicide had on hand to work.

Chase had cleared up the mugging for them; and they'd now haul all the material on Mrs. Reiner out of Pending and try to nail this Godfrey on that, along with Chase. The blackjack game had bothered Mendoza too; it was nice to have that explained; but just how much evidence there might be— The confession, of course, according to any smart lawyer Chase and/or Godfrey got, would be a nasty invention on the part of the brutal cops. However.

There were other cases in Pending too, all of which would probably stay there.

Somebody, last Thursday night about midnight, had held up Mr. Roy Manfred as he was closing his small liquor store on Third Street, and either because Manfred had put up a fight, or for no reason discernible, had shot Manfred dead. They had picked up some nice latent prints on the front door which belonged to a small-time pro named Lester Gumm, and of course that was frustrating. Gumm was off parole from his last sentence, and there was no reason he shouldn't walk into a liquor store and buy a six-pack of beer; he lived in a room just around the corner on Hartford Avenue. And of course that was just what he said he'd done: gone in and bought some beer, and that was how come his prints were on the door. It could be true: there was a fifty-fifty chance. If he'd shot Manfred, he'd got rid of the gun; they'd never tie that to him.

Then there was Carolyn Katz. She'd been a waitress at a small café, and had an apartment in an old place on Westlake Avenue. Last Tuesday night, a week ago today, she had come home from a movie about eleven o'clock. Other tenants on the first floor had heard screams and come out to investigate; but too late to save Carolyn's life. She hadn't been raped, she hadn't been robbed, but she'd been beaten severely enough to die of a skull-fracture next day. And that X might have been any mugger or, take your choice, any rapist, in Records—or not in Records.

Or it just possibly might have been someone who knew her who had a reason to want her dead.

There was the usual unidentified body found on Skid Row. Nothing much for Homicide to work.

There was the rather ambiguous case of Rose Plaidy, retired schoolteacher, Negro, widow without family, found dead in her own little house on Twenty-third Street, thus far of unknown causes. Wait for the autopsy report.

There was a flyer out from the F.B.I. on one of their Ten Most Wanted men, Lloyd Arthur Jenkins, a long record of violence, thought to be in California.

There was a rather funny little thing that probably wasn't anything for Homicide, but it was a sudden death and they had to look. An usherette—in fact the sole usherette—at a little movie-house on Main that ran exclusively Mexican movies. She had apparently fallen from the balcony and broken her neck. She hadn't any reason for visiting the balcony, so the manager said, and so they were taking a second look. Hackett and Higgins were out on that.

Glasser was asking questions around the apartment on Westlake; Landers and Piggott were asking Carolyn Katz's friends about discarded boy-friends and so on. That could have been a private kill; it wasn't very likely.

Mendoza yawned and lit another cigarette. Without much doubt, as these things died on them, or got solved and tied up, there'd be other cases coming along. But the pace was a little slower than usual, which figured—the first week of a nice warm (but not too warm) June. And, thank God, the heavy cold which Higgins had brought back from his unwilling sojourn in the mountains last April had run its course through the office and nobody was out on sick leave.

Praise heaven for small favors, he thought. . . . That was funny, Chase coming out with the answer to the Reiner murder, just like that. . . . The other curious case shoved in Pending, last month, William Moberly with a knife in his chest and fifty bucks in his pocket, in the rest room of the Greyhound Bus station, probably they'd never have the answer on that one.

The inside phone buzzed and he picked it up. "Seventy-seventh Street think they've got that Jenkins spotted in a bar," said Sergeant Lake tersely.

"So let them go pick him up," said Mendoza. "Do they want us to come hold their hands or what?"

"Do I pay attention?" asked Mr. Carlos Hernandez, shrugging violently. "Me, I'm a married man, I got my family, I don't go noticing girls I hire here. Only two girls. At a time. To take the money, show people inside the theater. These girls, *Dios.* They're lazy little good-fornothings mostly. This one, I don't know nothing about her. Named Luisa Fantini, is all. Italian. She only worked here two weeks, about."

The two big men stood looking at him: the twin bulks of Sergeants Hackett and Higgins, the two senior sergeants at Homicide. They'd worked together a long time, and they didn't have to use words to communicate. They were silently agreeing that Mr. Hernandez was probably an honest man telling them all he knew.

"How did you happen to hire her?" asked Hackett.

Hernandez shrugged more. "Other girl walks off job, I put ad in the paper. The Fantini girl answers it. It's part-time, you unnastand, we open at six—six to two A.M. but the usherette's here only till nine, I pay her five bucks for three hours, and it's not worth it. I guess I don't bother with another girl. Listen, are the customers that dumb they can't find seats for themselves? Do we get that many customers?"

"Do you know if she had another job somewhere?" asked Higgins.

"No. Maybe the ticket-girl would know. I guess they'd talk sometimes, maybe inna ladies' room after work. Yes, I got her address. Ticket-girl is pretty good girl, worked here nearly a year, Annie Sanchez. It's Antonio Avenue—I got it wrote down somewheres."

They were using Hackett's screaming-red Barracuda; they left the theater and got into it where it was parked in the yellow zone in front. "Why the hell," asked Higgins, "are we jumping the gun on this, Art? It looked as if this Fantini girl just fell over the balcony. All by herself. We haven't seen the autopsy report yet."

"So we're making work for ourselves," said Hackett. "Luis just said it looked funny, because she wasn't supposed to be up in the balcony at all. No, he didn't say he exactly had a hunch about it, but—it does look a little funny, George."

"Funny hell," said Higgins roundly. "She was off work at nine. She met a boy-friend in the lobby and they went up to the balcony to neck."

"And the boy-friend pushed her over the rail?"

"They could have been drinking," said Higgins. "They could have been high on Mary Jane or H. You know these run-down old houses, Art. The place wouldn't be crowded, not by a long shot. There probably weren't a dozen people in the place—and half of those drunk, sleeping it off, and the rest neckers. And she fell over and he panicked and ran."

"Well," said Hackett. "I don't know. It looks as if she went over after the place was closed, because she wasn't found till next morning when Hernandez came in."

"You know these places, Art! Maybe nobody noticed her land. I say, wait for the autopsy report."

"Which makes sense," agreed Hackett. He sat back and lit a cigarette with no move to start the engine. He didn't ask Higgins how the family was because he knew. Higgins the confirmed bachelor, humbly falling for Bert Dwyer's widow, had finally got her to marry him and acquired the secondhand family; and these days they were all looking forward to the firsthand family due in October, and maybe the Dwyer kids Steve and Laura even more thrilled about it than Higgins.

"The one we ought to be working," said Higgins suddenly, "is that Katz thing."

"Not a smell of a lead," said Hackett through a yawn. "We probably never will have."

"You sound like Matt."

"I tell you what it is, Tom," said Piggott as they waited for Mrs. Ruth Sneed to open her door, "it's just one of those things we'll work our legs off on, and never turn up a smell. The devil going up and down inciting to mischief."

"There's a lot of that going on all right," said Landers, and automatically reached for his badge as the door opened. "Mrs. Sneed?"

"Why, yes—you're *police?* Oh, about *Carolyn!* Oh, dear me. Come in, come in. I don't know how I can help you at all, but anything I can do—"

It was just a chance that Carolyn Katz had been killed deliberately, or accidentally, by somebody she knew; that was the only reason they were asking questions of people she'd known. They hadn't got anything at all to bear out that idea, and they didn't get anything new from Mrs. Sneed.

The picture that emerged, reinforced by the photographs taken of the corpse, was of a not-very-pretty, not-very-interesting young woman: a rather dowdy young woman who didn't have any steady boy-friends, or date much at all. She'd attended a Reform temple on Hill Street, but hadn't mixed socially with any of the other regular attendants. She'd been a reliable employee, said the manager of the small café where she'd been a waitress. The other two women working there said she never talked much about herself, had been a little standoffish—or perhaps shy. Reserved.

Everybody Landers and Piggott had talked to had said, Wasn't it terrible what had happened, these awful muggers and sex-fiends—and had asked discreetly, Had she been raped?

She hadn't been. And there had been thirty-four dollars in her handbag, dropped beside her. And that might be because he'd been scared off, by the other apartment people coming out, hearing her screams: he might have meant to rifle the handbag, and not had time. Or he might have meant to kill Carolyn for some private reason.

Landers was beginning to doubt that. When they'd wasted nearly an hour hearing much the same things from Mrs. Sneed they'd heard from everybody else who'd known Carolyn, he said so to Piggott. And Mrs. Sneed had known Carolyn somewhat better than anyone else they'd seen: she had worked at the café with her before she got married, five years back, and they had "kept up." Mrs. Sneed struck both Piggott and

Landers as another one like the Carolyn they'd heard about: a plain, uninteresting woman with not much to offer.

It didn't seem very likely that anyone had felt strongly enough about Carolyn Katz to care whether she lived or died.

"Just the mugger after her bag," said Piggott as they got into Landers' Corvair. "Or, take your choice, the rapist. Most of 'em don't care what the girl looks like—just so it's female."

" 'S right," said Landers. "And it might have been any of a thousand guys around town."

"No lead," agreed Piggott.

But they both knew where they went from here, on Katz. Look in Records for the similar M.O.'s—and on a thing like this there'd be literally hundreds of possible choices—and start the routine on it. The boring legwork.

They sat thinking about that, dispiritedly. Landers sighed and said, "I think I've still got a little spring fever, Matt. I just don't feel like doing the damn legwork. Who's going to miss Carolyn Katz?"

"Now that's no way to look at it," said Piggott seriously. Piggott was an earnest fundamentalist Free Methodist, if he was also the perennial pessimist. "Equal in God's sight, you know."

"Oh, sure, sure," said Landers hastily. "I just hope the lieutenant isn't feeling all eager on any of this piddling stuff we've got to work, to put us doing the overtime."

"Well, tomorrow's my day off anyway," said Piggott. "Lucky to get Wednesday for a change, choir practice and all. You have a date?"

"Tomorrow night," said Landers. He started the engine. "Might as well go back and do a report on this—handful of nothing." He laughed suddenly, shook his head at Piggott's inquiring look. He was thinking about his date.

Landers had taken out quite a few girls in his time. Of course, he had a little problem there: for whatever genetic reason, he had one of those faces that would look about twenty-one until he was a grandfather, and he was nearly resigned by now to having witnesses tell him he didn't look old enough to be a cop. Mrs. Sneed just now hadn't said it, but he'd seen the words, as it were, trembling on her lips.

Still, he'd known quite a few girls, and he was scarcely the innocent he looked. And some of the nice girls he'd known had been impressed because he was a plainclothes detective, and attached to Homicide at that. They just didn't know, he thought ruefully, how utterly unglamorous, how drearily undramatic, the job could be. The thankless and frequently boring job.

At least, he thought—looking forward, with an eagerness he'd never thought he might feel for a girl, to tomorrow night—at least this girl would never make that fundamental mistake. . . .

He'd been out with her three times in three weeks, the three weeks since they'd met.

He'd gone down to Records to check out a pedigree with the computer there, and he'd run into her quite literally, coming round a row of file-cases with a pile of manila envelopes in her hands. Papers scattered, and Landers apologized, bent to help her gather them.

"Never mind, they're all out of order now," she said philosophically. "There are still quite a lot of things computers can't do, that's what they keep us around for."

"You're new here," said Landers, looking at her. Sergeant O'Brien came up behind him and clucked at the mass of untidy papers.

"These damn bloodhounds," he said. "They don't understand paper work." And Landers was so bemused he didn't even try for a retort on that. "She's new all right. Miss O'Neill. Detective Landers, Homicide."

She wasn't anything like any of the female officers Landers had ever noticed before. She didn't, even in her neat navy uniform, look like a policewoman at all.

"I've been at Hollenbeck," she said briskly, giving him a friendly nod. And Landers never remembered afterward whether he'd said a polite Hello or How-do-you-do.

She must be over twenty-one, but he couldn't guess how much. She was only about five-three, and slim; and she had very thick, very curly, very flax-blonde hair in a neat short feathery cut, and, astonishingly, navy-blue eyes. He didn't discover that until the third time he looked at her. He'd never known anybody could have navy-blue eyes.

He'd taken her out to dinner three days later. They got along, they were the same kind of people. They laughed at the same things; and they both felt the same way about being on the force. He told her how he'd got fed up, still in uniform, only four years in then, and how that good cop Bert Dwyer had talked him into trying for rank. And how Dwyer had, later, died under the bank-robber's bullets.

She said, "You must have made rank early."

"Damn it, I'm older than I—well, I was five years in. I was twenty-six." And that was damn young to make Detective, as she knew; she just nodded.

She told him about herself, a little humorously. "Of course Mother couldn't know I'd grow up to join the force—I was named for her best friend, she was killed in an accident just before I was born—but honestly, what a name for a lady cop! Phillipa Rosemary—I'm Phil to all my friends." Her parents lived in San Diego, where her father was a pharmacist; she had a married sister in San Francisco.

Landers guessed you couldn't exactly call Phil O'Neill pretty; she had a nose that turned up, and a sprinkling of freckles on her white skin, and her mouth was really too big; but she was, well, Phil. A direct sort of girl, and you'd always know where you stood with Phil. She wasn't like any other girl he'd ever known at all.

It was really too soon to start thinking it could be anything serious— Landers guessed it was too soon. But, anyway, he was looking forward to seeing her again tomorrow night. To picking her up at her apartment on Kingsley Drive in Hollywood, Phil not in uniform but neat as ever in a pretty light-colored dress, high heels only bringing her blonde head up to his chest, and some perfume that smelled like lilies. And going out to Frascati's or that Hofbrau place on Sunset, for a drink and a leisurely dinner.

It was, he thought, an important sort of thing—that they laughed at the same kind of jokes.

Right now, go back to the office and get this damned report typed up. The handful of nothing on Carolyn Katz.

It was half-past four. Let the night men prowl around Records pulling the pedigrees on similar M.O.'s.

At about the same moment, Lieutenant Goldberg was feeling annoyed. "Look," he said, "it's your business, not mine. All right, I see the point, but we've got cases to work too, you know."

Captain Martin Van Allen of Auto Theft just scowled at him. He was a big stocky man going bald, with an incipient paunch and a very rudimentary sense of humor. "So it was this Sergeant Betts who picked Horace up before. I've seen Horace's pedigree, naturally. I want to hear what Betts can tell me about him. When'll Betts be back?"

"How the hell should I know?" said Goldberg. "He's out on this hotel burglary. He'll be back in his own good time. What can he tell you but what's in the record?"

"He's talked to him—I haven't. Horace has been picked up once before, after you laid a charge on him—as a dauber."

Goldberg sighed. He wasn't much interested in Auto Theft, or even the grand-scale ring which, so Van Allen said, was stealing cars wholesale and ferrying them back east in disguise, to be sold to the honest dealers. Jack Horace was a small-time thief; so he had a prior record as a dauber—a fellow hired to repaint stolen cars—Goldberg couldn't have cared less.

"We've got a hot tip he's in with this ring," said Van Allen. "The Feds are on it too, you know."

"So I'll let you know when Betts shows up," said Goldberg. He sneezed and reached for Kleenex.

Mendoza wasn't, if the truth was told, much interested in any of the very routine things Homicide had on hand. He agreed with Landers and Piggott that Carolyn Katz had probably been a very random kill. They'd see what showed on the autopsy reports on the Fantini girl and Mrs. Plaidy. He didn't have any hunches about those at all.

And he had entirely forgotten Goldberg's mention of that hot-car ring. Nothing to do with Homicide, anyway.

He went home early, to the house on Rayo Grande Avenue in the Hollywood hills, and as he garaged the long black Ferrari beside Alison's Facel-Vega, he found both redhaired Alison and Mrs. MacTaggart in the back yard. All four cats, he discovered, were huddled on the back porch watchfully. The shaggy dog Cedric sat at the foot of the back steps.

"Oh, Luis," said Alison. "You're early."

"You'll be wanting a dram to whet your appetite," said Máiri MacTaggart automatically, turning for the house.

"¿Qué ocurre?" asked Mendoza, kissing Alison. "You all look as if you're waiting for the bomb to drop."

"¡Qué disparate!" said Alison. "It's only—well, in this climate—"

There was a sudden gray-white flash and flurry in the alder tree, and Cedric barked. A too-well-known voice whistled shrilly, Yankee Doodle came to town—coroo, coroo—AWK!

"¡Porvida!" said Mendoza. "Don't tell me that obnoxious mockingbird is back again—"

"In this climate, amado," said Alison resignedly, "they nest three times a year, you know. He's building another nest. And dive-bombing the cats."

And the twins erupted from the back door. "Daddy, Daddy, el pájaro comes back! El pájaro he bites Bast on la grupa—" Johnny.

"Daddy, el pájaro making la casa all pretty for his esposa! Mamacita say, la esposa have little niños pretty soon—" Teresa.

"¡Dios!" said Mendoza. "Why I ever got embroiled in all these domesticities—"

"You know," said Alison despairingly, "they'll be three in August.

They've got to get Spanish and English sorted out before they start school—"

"*¡Vaya!*" said Mendoza. "I think I need that drink."

Hackett went home to his Angel, and Higgins to Mary and Bert Dwyer's good kids, only now beginning to feel they were all truly his. Palliser went home to the house on Hillside Avenue, and he still didn't altogether approve of Roberta going back to teaching for a year to help on the payments, but they could delay starting a family that long. Jason Grace went home to his Virginia in the house in Leimert Park. They were hoping against hope, still, to start a family some day. Tomorrow, Piggott would be off, and take his nice girl Prudence Russell out to dinner before they both went to choir practice.

And if Policewoman Phil O'Neill was looking forward to tomorrow night and her fourth date with Tom Landers, nobody but herself knew about it.

But as time moved forward inexorably, the trap set by Fate was waiting to snap shut.

CHAPTER 2

On Wednesday morning the autopsy reports on both Luisa Fantini and Rose Plaidy were waiting on Mendoza's desk. By the time he'd glanced at both of them Hackett and Higgins had drifted in.

"So now we know," said Mendoza. "Who else is in? You'd all better hear about this." Hackett brought Landers and Palliser into the office; Piggott and Glasser were off, and Grace hadn't showed up yet.

Mrs. Plaidy had died, quietly, of an embolism. That inquest was scheduled for tomorrow, and the verdict now foregone. But Luisa Fantini hadn't died so easy.

Dr. Bainbridge estimated the corpse's age as between twenty and twenty-four. Not *virgo intacta* but had never had a child. No indication of any chronic disease or addiction. Cause of death, a broken neck, apparently brought about by the fall. There were visible dark manual bruises—he had clipped photographs to the report—on the tops of both shoulders and the neck.

"So somebody shoved her over," said Higgins.

"Or," said Hackett, "she was struggling with him and fell over backwards."

"Either way it adds to violent death," said Mendoza. "Bainbridge says she was twelve to fourteen hours dead when he first saw her—that was ten A.M. on Monday or thereabouts."

"And," said Landers thoughtfully, "this is Wednesday. Haven't any relatives shown up?"

"We don't even know where she lived," said Hackett. "She'd only worked at that theater a couple of weeks."

"Well, you know the routine—motions to go through." Mendoza lit a new cigarette. "Somebody must know something about her. She wasn't living on that five bucks a day, either."

There was also the routine on Carolyn Katz. But as they all got up to start the day's work, in various directions, the office door opened and stocky Sergeant Barth of Wilcox Street came in. He clutched a bulky manila envelope to his chest.

"Morning, Mendoza. Said we'd be turning this one over to you."

"Your mystery," said Mendoza. "O.K., Tom, you and John go sniff round Fantini, see what you can turn up. I'll brief you on this later on. Sit down, Barth. You know Art Hackett—George Higgins. What's your mystery?"

"It's a funny one," said Barth. "When you come to look at it close." He opened the manila envelope. "About all we've got for a week's work on it is the photographs and a lot of statements that add up to nothing. Or, I should say, the mystery." Mendoza picked up one of the 8 x 10 glossy photographs and looked at it: a very candid shot of a corpse. The corpse was a woman, lying on her back on a carpet in front of an upholstered couch. A dark-haired woman, quite impossible to say whether she'd been good-looking or not, the face dark with blood and features battered. She wore a dark dress twisted and pulled up above her knees as she'd fallen. There was blood on the carpet: the one eye visible in this photograph was wide with surprise. "Harriet Hatfield," said Barth. "Age forty-seven, and as far back as we looked, absolutely nothing showing on her but the picture of the respectable upright matron." He picked out another photograph. "This is what was used, the lab thinks." Close-up of a wrought-iron poker, a miniature shovel from a matching set of fireplace tools. "Blood and brain tissue on both. And the handles too rough to take any prints at all." He sat down.

"So, the mystery," said Mendoza.

"Short and sweet," said Barth. "It's just—funny, Mendoza. What do I want to say, no shape to it. Here's Harriet Hatfield. There's plenty of money, not millions but substantial. Her husband Howard is the head chemist for Hollywood Girl Cosmetics—big firm, you know it. Owns stock in the company. Doing fine, but by the house, all we've turned up, they weren't throwing it around—just living well, you know. It's a big house, not new, up on Castaic Drive in Nichols Canyon. Class, you know, but not ostentatious. Harriet belongs to a bridge club, she goes shopping, she gives little dinner parties—sometimes she and the husband go to a show together. Quiet old-fashioned kind of family. Three kids. John, the boy, is eighteen. In his first year at Pepperdine College, lives on campus, comes home some weekends. Linda, twenty-one, is in her first job as steno in a big lawyers' office in Hollywood—she lives at home. The oldest girl, Catherine, is twenty-four. She works at an exclusive dress shop in Beverly Hills, and I do mean exclusive. Shop owned by an old friend of her mother's, a Wilma Tanner. She's a designer, if that's the word—trademark Tanya Creations. Sold only in this shop. You get the picture?"

"Vaguely. *¡Adelante!*"

"So, Catherine comes home about six-thirty a week ago Monday night and finds that." Barth gestured at the first photograph. "And we come running to start the routine. I'll just give you a general breakdown on what showed—or didn't. The statements are all in there. First, nobody had been home all day but Harriet. Catherine left at eight o'clock that morning, Linda at eight-thirty, her father about the same time. Now, there was quite a lot of valuable stuff in the house. Mrs. Hatfield had jewelry valued at around ten grand, and Hatfield has a cash-box in his desk with a wad in it all the time—about two thousand, he said. And nothing was missing. The house hadn't been ransacked—all shipshape. Nothing even out of place except in the living room." He nodded at the photograph. "Second, when we got the autopsy report the time of death was estimated at between one and three P.M., but the neighbors hadn't heard any disturbance at all, no screams or bangs. Thirdly—"

"Private motive?" said Hackett, jumping to conclusions. "If it was a break-in for loot and she surprised him, he wasn't scared off by the screams to bring neighbors. Neighbors close?"

"Well, those are big lots, but the nearest house isn't more than sixty feet away from the living-room windows of the Hatfield house—some of which were open. And it's a quiet neighborhood. Mrs. Brownlee next door was home all day. She didn't hear a thing, she says, and the dog didn't bark once. She says the dog always barks at strangers anywhere around."

"And," said Higgins, "dogs having better ears than we do, the dog would have heard any screams or struggle."

"I suppose," agreed Barth. "Anyway, we can write off the casual burglar just on that. He'd have known he had time to go through the house. So we started to look at everybody the Hatfields knew. The way she got it—the doctor said, at least a dozen blows—looked as if somebody didn't like Harriet much. But there was just damn all." He put out his cigarette. "She was a nice woman, everything we got. Family all broken up. A nice family, seems like. Perfectly harmless, kindhearted woman. We talked to all the women she knew best. She wasn't a gossip. She wasn't a snob. She was, by everything we heard, a nice kind generous woman without an enemy in the world. And then we dug a little deeper and came up with Howard Hatfield's girl-friend. Ex, that is."

"Ah," said Mendoza interestedly.

"And it fizzled out like—like stale champagne," said Barth mournfully. "He's fifty, not bad-looking. He was embarrassed we'd found out about it. It was two years ago. Girl on the make, receptionist in the company office. He said he'd been a damn fool, she'd flattered him was all, but he'd come to his senses after a couple of months and ended it. His wife hadn't known about it at all. And it couldn't have anything to do with this. And it couldn't, that I can see."

"Girl wanting him back? His money, that is?" said Higgins. "Or putting the bite on him?"

"Why?" asked Barth. "He'd have seen his wife didn't know. We looked the girl up. One Bobby Sarsfield. She's got a good job as receptionist for an actors' agent on the Strip, and he's keeping her on the side. Very well, if you want to know—apartment on Sunset. Why the hell should she hark back to a brief affair two years old with fifty-year-old Howard? He says he hadn't seen her since. I believe him."

"Well, I don't suppose you stopped looking there," said Mendoza.

"Where else is there to look? They know the neighbors—the Brownlees one side, the Rockhams the other—but not very well. Say hello when they notice each other, that's it. The neighbors say they're nice people, no noisy parties, the young people polite. Brownlee's an attorney—they've got two married daughters and grandchildren. Rockham's a stockbroker, big firm in L.A.—he's sixty-four, she's sixty-two, and he's got a heart condition and she's got high blood pressure. Not that there was any reason, we *looked*," said Barth. "Both Brownlee and Rockham at their offices as usual all day. The Hatfield kids—" he sighed. "Nice polite people, all broken up over Mother getting killed. John is a bright boy—studying engineering. We looked back to when he started first grade and there's not a hint of anything against him. Ditto for the girls. Bright, nice girls."

"Boy-friends?" asked Mendoza, leaning back with his eyes shut.

"Sure," said Barth. "Linda's got a couple of fairly steady ones. Peter Webster, Fred Hoiles. Both from much the same kind of family. Both upright respectable young fellows in good jobs, no black marks. The Hatfields liked them both. Catherine's going steady with Owen Hartigan, and the Hatfields liked him too. He's interning at Hollywood Community, a clean record."

Mendoza's long nose twitched. As usual, he was fastidiously dapper in silver-gray dacron, with snowy shirt and discreet silk tie. He straightened the tie absently and fiddled with his gold cuff links. "This is a little mystery, *de veras*. Of course, say it was a casual break-in, she surprised him, and he grabbed up what was handy to knock her out—"

"And battered her face in with a dozen blows? Nobody could have thought the house was empty—she'd been out to the market earlier and her car was left in the drive."

"Oh, really? Well, what I was going to say," said Mendoza doubtfully, "was that if it happened like that, she could have screamed at least once and if he thought anybody had heard—"

"You've got no out there," said Barth. "We went all round on this too. We thought, say it was a nervous j.d. pulling his first job—even so, it's a very outside chance. That's an old house, and there are a lot of bushes and trees all round it. The natural thing for the casual burglar to have done, if it had happened like that, would've been to dodge into a bedroom, the back porch, even outside behind the bushes, to see if anybody had heard anything. And nobody had—which thirty seconds' wait would have told him. I don't think she had time to make a sound at all, Mendoza. And anyway, the casual burglar—or the nervous j.d.— wouldn't have been such a fool as to try the daylight burglary with her car there in plain sight in the drive."

"And a pretty little puzzle that is, all right," said Mendoza. "I don't see—"

"You're welcome to it," said Barth. "I'll lay a bet you'll be hiding it away in Pending after you think it over."

"Any ideas?" Mendoza asked when Barth had gone.

"I'd like to see those statements," said Hackett slowly, rubbing a thoughtful hand over his jaw. "There's got to be a loophole, Luis—you know as well as I do murders get done for damn little reason sometimes—"

"That was what I thought," contributed Higgins. "Somebody right outside, she'd maybe had a little fight with. It could be. Some hairtrigger character—the gas-station attendant giving her the wrong change, or—" he paused.

"And there is the old saw, *de mortuis*," said Hackett. "All these people telling the Wilcox Street boys, sure, she was a saint on earth. Maybe—"

"Look, Arturo, Barth and his boys are experienced cops too. You think they didn't take that into account? Think of it?" Mendoza brushed his moustache the wrong way and back again. "It's just a funny little mystery, *seguramente que sí*."

"So we go back and cover the same routine all over again?"

"You never know, something may show up the second time round," said Mendoza meditatively.

*   *   *

The ticket-seller at the Mexican movie house, Annie Sanchez, wasn't too much help to them at first. She was a nice honest girl and sorry, she told Landers and Palliser, she didn't know any more to tell them. They'd found her at home, an old turn-of-the-century house on Antonio Avenue the other side of the yards, and she told them they were lucky to stop by just then, she'd usually be at work but she'd had to take Mama to the doctor's this morning.

Fat, placid Mama Sanchez sat and rocked on the porch, beaming at them, and benevolently offered them a little glass of wine.

"No, thank you, Mrs. Sanchez," said Palliser. "We just want to ask Miss Sanchez a few questions—"

"No harm, a little glass good wine. You fellows, a plenty hard job you got, such times, these terrible *ladrones* all over. Do you good. I get—"

"No, really, thanks very much but we're not allowed—" They finally got that across to her and she looked astonished.

"Not allowed a simple little glass nice homemade *vino?* A terrible job you got, you poor fellows. I feel sorry in my heart for you. Try to catch the *ladrones,* terrible, and not even a little glass good wine." She shook her head.

"Mama—" The girl was a little embarrassed. "I guess they'd like to talk to me private. You know the doctor said you better keep your leg up—" Mama was gently urged into the house. "But if it's about that Luisa, I don't guess there's much I could tell you, at that. She only worked at the theater a couple of weeks, I didn't know her, to say *know.*"

"Well, did you talk with her much at all?" asked Landers. "She ever say anything about a boy-friend, her family?"

"Well, no, she never," said Annie. "Now wait a minute. I just remembered that—it'd be about the first week she was there, I saw her meet somebody when she went off at nine o'clock. Yes, a man. I didn't pay much notice, I mean why should I, she was pretty, I guess a lot of fellows might've been after her. I was waiting for Jimmy—Jimmy Cortez, we're engaged, he usually walks me home nights. All I could say, this fellow Luisa went off with, he was kind of tall. I didn't see him real good, didn't hear her call him anything. She never said anything about him."

"Do you know where she lived?" asked Palliser.

"Sure. I wouldn't, only she happened to say when we were in the ladies' room together once. She said she could walk to the theater, it was

only a couple of blocks from Boyd. Oh, and that time too, she said—"
Annie thought. "I don't know why she did, it hadn't nothing—anything—to do with what we'd been saying—I just remembered that too. It
was funny. She was combing her hair—she had real nice hair, you know,
blacker'n mine, and shiny as could be, she must've washed it nearly
every day—and she wore it long, just tied back like—and she said, Gee,
it sure was good to get let alone, nobody at her day 'n' night, where'd
she been, what'd she done, and all like that. I thought it was a funny
thing to say," said Annie earnestly, "because, gee, what'd a person *feel*
like without somebody to care where you went and what you were
doing or feeling? A family? But Luisa—well, I guess she was only about
twenty, and she didn't seem very—very grown-up like. Like a kid."

"Do you know if she had another job? She couldn't be getting along
just on what she made three hours a night at the theater?" asked
Palliser.

Annie shook her head. "Doesn't seem as if, but I don't know. Like I
said, I work nine to five at Kress's over on Broadway—I'm saving like I
can for when Jimmy and me get married. But Luisa never said about
that. She was kind of a funny one."

They went back to Palliser's Rambler and drove up to Boyd Street. It
wasn't a very long street and they started out with the two houses that
advertised *Rooms* with signs in front windows. They got the right one
on the second try.

Mrs. Baumgartner said indifferently, "Fantini, yeah, that was the
name she said. Eyetalian. Little dark girl, an' I thought maybe no better
'n she should be. But why in time are cops around? She do something?"

"She's dead," said Landers.

"Dead? Well, if that don't beat all," said Mrs. Baumgartner mildly.
"She couldn't've been more 'n twenty or so. What? Yeah, she'd been
here about a couple weeks. I don't know nothin' about her atall. She
paid me twelve bucks a week for the room, all I'm interested in—o'
course if she'd brought *men* in, anything like—but she never."

"Did she say where she'd moved from?" asked Landers.

"Nope, why should she? Why, yeah, I s'pose you can look at the
room, you want. I never noticed she didn't come back, last couple o'
nights. I don't bother climb the stairs no more."

They went upstairs and looked at Luisa's room, at the rear of the old
house. The house hadn't been thoroughly cleaned in a long time, and a
vague smell of dust, mice and old wood hung over it. The room Luisa
had rented for the past two weeks was about nine by ten. There was a
painted wooden bedstead with a thin mattress, worn sheets, a cotton

blanket and bedspread. There was a painted chest of drawers, a straight chair, a braided rug covering a patch of the old pine floor, and a small cardboard wardrobe in one corner.

In the wardrobe, perhaps two dozen dresses crowded together on hangers: some long evening dresses, more bright prints and revealing chiffons and silks. A dozen pairs of high-heeled shoes tumbled on the floor of the wardrobe. In the chest, a jumble of new-looking lingerie, mostly black lace and nylon.

"I'll be damned," said Palliser suddenly. He'd been going through the bottom drawer of the chest; he straightened. "Look at this, Tom."

Landers looked. On Palliser's palm, a little strip of brown paper. The kind of little strip banks used to fasten sizable sums of bills together, usually with a notation of the amount on the outside. There was a notation on this little strip, in ballpoint print. *$1000*, it said simply.

"I'll be damned!" said Landers. And then he said, "So—all these clothes—most of 'em look new. And the rest of it—shoes and underwear. So, had she used up the thousand bucks and that was why she got a job?"

"What kind of a job, for God's sake?" said Palliser. "Five bucks a night? And how do we know how many grand she had? That she didn't still have how many of these wads fastened with the brown paper?"

"Then why the job?" asked Landers.

"Suitcases," said Palliser suddenly. "She must have had suitcases." They looked, and found three suitcases stashed under the bed. Two were old, brown leather bags, old-fashioned; the third was a smart new airplane-weight aluminum case. And that one had a little tag in one corner of the lid, *Fraser's Sporting and Leather Goods,* it said, *Bakersfield, Calif.*

"Well, a lead of sorts," said Palliser. He shook his head at the strip of paper. "This is a funny one, Tom. A thousand bucks cash. They always use these little strips for cash, don't they? Did she land here from Bakersfield two weeks ago?"

"We ask Bakersfield," said Landers, "if they know her. Or if this store knows her."

"I don't suppose a photo of the corpse would be very much like her alive."

"We have to go through the motions," said Landers. "Come on." They put a seal on the door and started back for headquarters.

They had to go on looking for answers on Luisa Fantini; by the autopsy report that was a homicide, of whatever degree.

* * *

Mendoza had sent Hackett and Higgins up to Castaic Drive in Nichols Canyon, to talk to Harriet Hatfield's neighbors again, and then to her friends; they had read the statements by then. As Hackett said, there was always the *de mortuis* bit; but Barth would know that too.

And right now Mendoza was thinking that *de mortuis* didn't enter into Wilma Tanner's orbit. Maybe it was instinct that had led him to Wilma Tanner first.

She was a big woman, buxom but not fat, with brown eyes and salt-and-pepper hair and a good-humored mouth. She didn't look any younger than her age, which would be about Harriet's age, but she was neatly dressed in discreet navy blue, with makeup as discreet. The eyes, which normally might hold wit and amiability, looked at him sadly and rather anxiously.

"None of us can make any sense out of it at all, Lieutenant," she said. She had taken him from the very plush, very feminine, very expensive-looking front shop of Tanya Creations (gold-veined marble walls, Victorian décor, and subtle fluorescent lighting) to what she called her office, a cluttered little room with a large desk taking most of the space, large ashtrays and two comfortable chairs. "Cathy's out to lunch—she takes the first hour," she said absently. "I suppose you'll want to see her too." She looked troubled. "It's just—a thing that couldn't happen, Harriet getting killed like that. Only it did." She lit a cigarette before he could snap his lighter, and sat back and blew a long stream of smoke. "Such a nice girl, Cathy. And I think quite talented—reason she wanted to work with me." She cast an experienced glance at Mendoza. "You look as if you can see farther through a millstone than most, as they say. That other officer—well. I knew Harriet all her life, Lieutenant. We went all through school together—from kindergarten on up. If anybody knew Harriet—!" And her eyes were honest and frank on him. "I know what you have to think. Was there some personal reason? But there's nothing—just nothing."

"We have to ask," said Mendoza. "And hope we'll get straight answers, Mrs. Tanner."

"Yes. Miss," she said. "I took my maiden name back after the divorce." She passed one strong spatulate hand over the salt-and-pepper hair in its severe cut. "They're such a nice family," she said. "Harriet was—it's a terrible word for it—nice. An ordinary nice woman, Lieutenant. Ordinary—that's a wrong word too, but what else can I say? Tell you? That other officer—he said you'd decided it couldn't be just a burglar, I don't know why, that seems to me the only way it could have been. He kept asking personal things about Harriet, but—" She made an impatient gesture. "Silly. So silly. Harriet was—was just a nice decent woman with a nice family she loved, and they loved her." She wouldn't have known about Howard Hatfield's brief lapse. "She'd done her best to bring up the children well, and they're all good kids. Responsible. Reliable. They didn't always have so much money, when the children were small, you know—Howard started out as just one of the staff chemists with the company. They had to be careful, and save—Harriet was a good manager. And Howard saved to buy some stock in the company, and got promoted—" She put out her cigarette. "How many thousands of American families like them, Lieutenant? Harriet—Harriet was my friend, and it sounds—priggish?—but she was a good woman. Honest. Gracious. Kind. A good wife and mother. I—maybe it's not such a good idea for a woman to be really interested in a profession, a career. I know in my case, that was what broke up the marriage—what it amounted to, I was just more interested in the job than in Brian." She grimaced. "But Harriet never wanted anything but what she had, you see? It was her only interest—take good care of her family, her home. I'm afraid I was rude to that other officer, Sergeant somebody—asking about other men—just silly! So silly. Harriet—"

"I see," said Mendoza. He got the nuances from people always, and he was seeing Harriet Hatfield, at a little remove. Not an intellectual: an intelligent enough woman: domestic: a good wife and mother, probably.

Wilma Tanner opened her big leather purse that she'd dropped on the desk, and fumbled at a bulging billfold. "I don't know if you've seen a picture of her," she said. "That's Harriet."

Mendoza looked with interest at the color snapshot. It was a fairly close shot of three people seated on a couch: a man and two women. "Howard and Harriet," said Wilma Tanner, "and Linda." The man had a thin intellectual face, thin brownish hair, rimless glasses, a rather miserly-looking mouth. The girl Linda was blonde, the ash-blonde hair that would turn mousy in a few years, an insipidly pretty girl. Harriet Hatfield (he remembered that battered bloody face) had had a roundish face, medium brown hair in a simple style waved off her brow, friendly blue eyes; she seemed to have kept a good figure.

"My God," said Wilma Tanner, "if Rabbie had still been alive—! It was the first thing I said to Howard when—"

"Rabbie?"

"Their old collie—he just died last month. They'd meant to get a new puppy, but not right away—"

And the Brownlees' dog next door hadn't barked. Mendoza felt frustrated. A door opened and shut, and Wilma Tanner said, "That'll be Cathy. You want to see her, I suppose."

Thirty seconds later Mendoza stood up to face a tall, slim, very dark girl dressed very smartly in, probably, a Tanya Creation. She had an unusual face, not quite pretty but arresting: high cheekbones, large dark eyes under sharp-arched brows, a wide mouth made for smiling. "Miss Hatfield," he said.

"I just don't know what more any of us can tell you," she said. Tears came into the dark eyes. "It just seems impossible—Mother. The other man—who talked to us before—he said, not a burglar, because nothing was stolen, but—there just isn't anything more to tell you—"

Mendoza was still feeling frustrated when he dropped into Federico's for a very belated lunch and ran into Hackett. "What's happened to Jase, by the way? I haven't laid eyes on him today."

"He's chasing down that Guy Godfrey. I left George to go see a few more of Harriet's lady friends. So far, it all checks out just the way Barth made it. You get anything?"

"*Nada.* Or rather more than I want," said Mendoza. "I saw this Tanner woman. And Howard."

"I had," said Hackett, "another thought about Howard. If he once took up with the extracurricular girl-friend, why not another? Or three?"

Mendoza sat back and grinned sardonically. "I may have you beat by a few years, Arturo—"

"Six."

"—But that just means I've had more experience. I read Howard Hatfield like a first-grade primer, *amigo.* The all-business, all work and no play, dead serious fellow. I'd have a guess he's slightly more ignorant about females than the average man in the street, and I would also have an educated guess that that was the only time he stepped off the straight and narrow."

"About that kind of thing I trust your judgment, boy."

"I'd also have a guess that the girl—what's her name, Bobby Sarsfield —isn't a very subtle piece of goods. She wouldn't have to be to gather in Howard. Don't they say it's a dangerous age? He—"

"*Cuidado, compadre.* You're not far off it yourself."

"*¡Vaya al diablo!* I'm the exception that proves the rule," said Mendoza with dignity.

"What about her?" asked Hackett.

"Harriet? *Impossible.* From all I gather—and Wilma's an honest woman, she wouldn't cover up. Not when it's murder. It's a little mystery, that's all. Funny." Mendoza started on his steak sandwich. Hackett sighed and drank black coffee.

"There's still the routine to do. Covering the same ground. Waste of time."

"I don't know. The second time round—" Mendoza poured himself more coffee absently. "Did I tell you that damn mockingbird is back? Building another nest, *Dios*."

"You and your livestock," said Hackett.

Landers had typed a follow-up report on Luisa Fantini while Palliser sent the indicated teletype up to Bakersfield. A query to the lab told them that no photograph was available of the corpse's face. "Why the hell should we have taken one?" asked Scarne. "So you want one now? We haven't got anything to do up here, of course, but run around taking special shots for Homicide. All right, all right, I'll see what I can do for you. Say by three, O.K.?"

They went out to lunch, and when they came back a teletype was waiting from a sergeant up in Bakersfield. Luisa Fantini was not in their records. If L.A. would send up a photo, inquiries would be made at the sporting and leather goods shop. They hung around waiting for the photo, and Grace came in towing a sullen Guy Godfrey, so they helped to lean on him, and as might have been expected got nothing useful at all.

Chase was, said Godfrey with varied obscenities, talking through his hat. He didn't know nothing about that break-in up in Hollywood. He knew even less about the murder of Mrs. Reiner and the blackjack game. He drew them a graphic outline of Sam Chase's lineage, personal habits, and probable fate. After a while they got tired of him; they'd try him again later. They would probably never make the charge stick, and have to let him loose. Which meant that nobody would get tried for Mrs. Reiner.

By then the close-up photo of Luisa Fantini's dead face was waiting; not a very good one, but it should be recognizable to anyone who'd known her. She had been a good-looker: the regular small pert features suggested that in life she had been gay, sparkling; and maybe, as Annie had said, not quite grown-up.

Landers and Palliser went out again, armed with copies of the photograph, after wiring one up to Bakersfield. They went out on the tiresome legwork, asking all around that rooming house, all around that theater, in bars and restaurants and stores, if anybody had ever seen this girl, with somebody or alone.

Landers asked the questions with half his mind a few hours ahead in time. To when he'd be parking in front of the apartment house where Phil O'Neill lived, in a clean shirt and his best suit, to pick up his girl in a pretty dress and the perfume like lilies, and take her out to dinner. He wasn't really much interested in Luisa Fantini, or how she had come to fall over that balcony. There was just a faint curiosity at the back of his mind about that little strip of bank paper.

At five-forty-five he landed back at headquarters and met Palliser just coming into the lobby. "You get anything?"

"Not one glimmer. You?"

"Nothing. A great big blank. Of course it could be a better picture."

Just as the elevator door swung back silently, three men came up beside the two men from Homicide. They were all strangers to Landers and Palliser. The big balding stocky man they had seen around the building: neither of them knew his name, nor that of the plainclothesman with him, but both, to any cop, wore the familiar aura of fellow police. The third man was different. His right wrist was cuffed to the left wrist of the second officer. He was a thin man about forty, with small pebble-gray eyes and a long sharp nose. He looked unhappy.

The five men got into the elevator. Palliser looked at the big man politely. "We're Eight," he said.

"Four."

Palliser punched the Four button. "If you ask me," he said to Landers, "it'll get tossed in Pending eventually."

"Probably," agreed Landers absently.

The thin man peered round at them. He looked surprised. "Oh," he said, "so you dropped on him too. That one." He gave Landers a sly half-grin. "Cops smarter 'n you thought, hah?"

"*What?*" said the big man. He turned and looked at Landers.

"Well, that's him, dint you know?" said the thin man. "Him. The one I tole you about, Cap'n. One o' them runnin' the whole thing, them hot cars."

"What?" said Landers.

The thin man said, "He's the one the other guy called Speedy. I tole you. How'd you pick him up so quick?"

CHAPTER 3

The twins' baths had been supervised, and promises extracted for two
Just-So stories before bed—"*El Gato* all by himself!" insisted Johnny,
Terry trying to outshout him on demands for *el elefante pequeño*—and
Mendoza had just taken his first sip of coffee when the phone rang
down the hall.

"Don't tell me," said Alison.

Mendoza swore mildly and went to answer it. "Mendoza."

"Lieutenant—" Sergeant Thoms, and he sounded peculiar. "You're
not going to believe this, but—and my God, there's an I.A. man listening
to this call, for God's sake—and they took Tom up to—well, Palliser
went with—but—"

"Take a deep breath and start from the beginning, Bill. What the hell
is I.A. doing sniffing round my office? . . . *¿Quién?* . . . *¿Cómo dice?*
¡Jesus y María! What the hell—*Tom?* You're not making sense—*¡es
ridículo!* What? Did—"

"This damn Van Allen, he's Auto Theft, stranger to me, of course he
doesn't know Tom—and the Feds are in on it, and the damn I.A. men
took them all upstairs, but Palliser said to call you—"

"I should think so indeed. *¡Es imbécil! ¡Allá voy—*I'm on the way!"
Mendoza slammed down the phone and made for the bedroom after his
hat. Twenty seconds later he tripped over their shaggy dog Cedric slurping water from his bowl on the back porch. The Ferrari roared to life
and backed violently down to the fork of the circular drive.

"Just like being married to a doctor," said Alison resignedly.

"Ah, well," observed Mrs. MacTaggart, "there's one thing about a
nice plain stew, *achara*—you can hot it up time after time without spoiling it. I daresay he'll be wanting it when he comes back."

* * *

Mendoza came past the door labeled *Internal Affairs* fast and found John Palliser sitting in a chair flanked by a grim-faced man at a desk. "What the holy hell is all this about, John? Where's Tom?"

Palliser opened his mouth and the man at the desk said, "Uh-uh, Sergeant. We keep it all formal."

"Formal be damned!" said Mendoza angrily. "You home-grown Gestapo—"

"Now, now." Another man came in from an unmarked door at the side of the office. "You needn't call names, Mendoza. We've got a thing here and we'll work it according to Hoyle, just to be sure. And you know that as well as I do."

"You're holding one of my men—"

"For good and sufficient reason," said Captain Macklin gently. "This could be quite a thing, Mendoza. You haven't heard all the details yet."

"Details be damned, the thing's ridiculous."

"I said it's crazy," said Palliser. "Just crazy."

"We've got to be sure," said Macklin. "You know that."

Mendoza dropped his hat on the desk and brought out cigarettes, gave one to Palliser, lit one himself. "So I'll hear your Goddamned silly evidence," he said sharply.

"An eyewitness—"

"*¡Vaya por Dios!* Any cop with a year's experience knows what that's worth!"

Macklin looked a little annoyed. "Identification of a ranking detective as a—"

"Which is the reason, isn't it?" Mendoza took him up. "All the trappings— Where have you got Landers?"

"You know how we operate, Mendoza. This Horace has fingered two other fellows he says will back him up. Some of Van Allen's men are out hunting them right now. We don't want Horace to lay an eye on Landers again until it's in a regular lineup. Sometime tomorrow, with luck. Lieutenant Wright and Southey are in there questioning Horace now—"

"My God," said Palliser suddenly, "I never called Robin—"

"Is the sergeant allowed to phone his wife, Macklin?" asked Mendoza. "You don't tell me. So very damn careful we have to be to inform the pros of their rights—who's in there representing Detective Landers?"

"Well, this has caught us all on the jump—"

"Aren't you right. One side, I'll sit in on this. You show Sergeant Palliser a phone he can use. And I'll see Landers when I've heard the ins and outs of this—this farce." Mendoza walked past Macklin and opened the closed door.

It was thirty minutes later that the scene he'd interrupted was resumed. The three I.A. men, Van Allen, and three Feds had looked at him in annoyance, but admitted he had a right to some background. It was Van Allen who gave it to him, baldly.

"This hot-car ring. It's been a going concern for months—we've had cooperation from Philly and New York and Chicago and St. Louis, where the cars got spotted. By what we turned up—and the Feds—it's based here. The cars heisted, by men hired for the job, late model Caddys, Imperials, Chryslers, Lincolns—repainted, fitted with new plates and registration, and ferried back east. Sold to the honest dealers, and one hell of a job it's been to trace those we've spotted. Philly thinks they've spotted a drop there. We've been looking at everybody here with a pedigree in that line, and we spotted the garage last Monday by putting a tail on this Jack Horace—he looked hot for it, he's been hired as a dauber before. Durfee's Garage over on Virgil. Al Durfee's in Records too—ours, and downstairs as a strong-arm man for a gambling house Gardena shut down five years back. So we pick up Horace, and he comes apart and fingers two others—Rodney Dunne and Bill Byron—they're two who've been heisting the cars, Horace doing the repainting. We were bringing Horace in to get a formal statement from him when he recognized your boy right off. He just said, 'So you picked him up too.' Just like that." Van Allen eyed Mendoza truculently. "He wasn't two feet away from him. And I wouldn't say this Landers is a nonentity who'd be hard to remember."

"*¡Vaya!*" said Mendoza to himself. "But it's ridiculous, for God's sake! Landers—he's been at Homicide for five years, since he made rank —I know him inside out. It's—"

One of the I.A. men, Southey, spoke up: a tall dark serious fellow. "Lieutenant," he said, "we'd expect you to speak up for one of your men. But you don't *know*. We don't know. It's not very often we get a man on this force going wrong, but it does happen, if once in a blue moon. And when it does, we want to find out. That's what we're here for, Lieutenant."

Mendoza met his eyes angrily. "We know why you're here, damn it." Internal Affairs—

And one of the Feds looked at his watch and stood up. "We're interested in the ring, boys, so anything you get on that—but I guess the rest of this is your own private fight." He collected the other two with one glance and they filed out quietly.

Internal Affairs, LAPD: the first department of its kind: police to watch police. This was a crack force, and they wanted to keep it that way. Internal Affairs, keeping its careful eye on the personal and professional behavior of LAPD men, occasionally got a little puritanical: maybe that was only to be expected. Most of its work lay in investigating charges on the police by the citizenry: in an average year they might look into a couple of thousand such complaints, and find maybe eight or ten valid, and issue official reprimands to that many officers. As Southey said, it was a very rare occurrence for an LAPD man to turn out a bad cop or something worse. The last case like that Mendoza could remember had been twenty-three years back when he was just a rookie: a bunch of officers at the Valley Station pulling the burglaries on off time. That had been quite a thing: a nine days' wonder in this force.

Something turned up, I.A. had to look—just in case.

They didn't, thought Mendoza unreasonably, have to be so damned serious about it. As if Landers—Landers of all men—

Palliser hadn't seen Landers since they were shepherded up here, until the desk-sergeant grudgingly led him into an anteroom down the hall and indicated that he could use the phone there. Three sides of the anteroom were paneled: the fourth was glass from waist-high to ceiling, and as Palliser picked up the phone he heard tapping and turned to see Landers on the other side of the glass. Landers was looking tremendously relieved to see him; he also looked rather wild, tie pulled loose. All these rooms would be soundproofed; Landers just gestured at him imploringly. Was he locked in there? Palliser wondered. He gestured back inquiringly.

Landers was scribbling in his notebook. He held it up. A phone number in large print, and below, *Call and apologize—can't make date.*

Suddenly Palliser felt absurdly relieved, for no reason. It somehow made all this seem more mundane: just a missed date with a girl. He nodded violently, copied down the number. He was conscious that Landers was watching him as he called Roberta and made a hurried explanation. She said resignedly she'd expect him when she saw him. Dialing the other number, Palliser looked back to the glass: Landers had disappeared. Had they taken him somewhere else?

He hadn't given Palliser any name: when a cool contralto answered the phone, Palliser said, "I'm—er—calling for Tom Landers, Miss—uh.

Something's come up, he can't make your date, and he says to apologize—"

"Oh," said the contralto. "Something broke all of a sudden?"

"What?" said Palliser. "Well, no, it's—" he was craning his neck looking for Landers on the other side of the glass: what were they doing with him in there? "It's sort of involved, we're stuck up here in I.A.—" He wasn't paying much attention to what he did say, and he wasn't prepared for the naked shock and astonishment as the contralto caught him up sharply.

"*I.A.? Tom?* Who is this? What on earth do those obnoxious do-gooders think Tom—"

"What? This is Sergeant Palliser, Miss—"

"O'Neill. Sorry, you didn't know. I'm down in Records, Sergeant. I suppose you can't tell me what's going on."

"I don't think I'd better." What was Landers doing, dating a female officer?—though she did sound, well, female.

"If not before, I'll get the story on the grapevine tomorrow. Listen, Sergeant—do you have any idea when he might get away?"

"No. I don't— No."

"Well, you tell him to come round here if it's before midnight."

"I will if I see him," said Palliser uneasily.

"I told you straight all I know," said Jack Horace. He looked at them stubbornly, stolidly: big beefy Van Allen, the three I.A. men, Mendoza. A silent uniformed sergeant took shorthand notes. "I ain't so sorry you dropped on me, no lie, on account I didn't like that Rosso guy. He could be a mean one, I figure. About the other one, the other mastermind you picked up, I couldn't say—I only saw that one like maybe three-four times. Rosso was the one came around, look over the cars in, bring the new plates. You didn't ask questions with that guy. Do what you're hired for, that's it. I'm hired to paint the heaps, I don't ask about the operation, but I can guess this 'n' that. The heaps went back east, I know that much—how I woulden know. There'd be guys back there to take 'em, hafta be. But all I know is, Rosso was the guy here. The guy in charge. And that other one."

"About that one, Jack," said Southey. They hadn't told him anything, naturally: but he sensed dimly that something new and important was going on, different cops questioning him; he looked wary. "The fellow you recognized—or thought you did—in the elevator. Was—"

"Oh, that's him all right," said Horace. "I only saw him that three-four times, like I say, but I had it figured he's maybe the contact for the back east setup. Rosso arranged for ever'thing here, payoff for the heaps, and the paintin' an' the new plates. But from just talkin' on the quiet like with the other guys—like Dunne and Byron I tole you about— it was the other one come move the heaps out, with a couple other guys I don't know nothin' about, see. I figure he's the one knows the drops back there, sets up the shipments, see. I kinda think—I don't *know*, but just somethin' Rosso said to him once, I got it in my head the money come from some operators back east, see. Harder to trace the heaps way across country."

"O.K.," said Southey casually. "You know that other one's name?"

"Nope. Don't you? You got him. Like I say, he only come by—while I was inna garage, workin' on the heaps—that three-four times. With Rosso. No, I don't know Rosso's front name. I just heard Rosso call the other guy Speedy, a coupla times."

Southey offered him a cigarette. "You had a pretty good look at him, though—when you spotted him right off just now."

Horace looked from one to the other of them as if he suspected a trap. "Well," he said, "he's got a face you'd kinda remember, don't he? First thing I noticed about him—this Speedy—he looks so awful young. Younger than I guess he is, because it seems, way he acts and talks, he's been around awhile. Around period. Not a kid. But he looks young. And the long jaw on him, and the way his hair grows straight back—and his eyebrows real straight, don't curve like most people's—well, yeah, I reckanized him easy."

"Remember when you saw him the last time? At the garage?"

"Sure. It was last Friday afternoon about five. He was only there about ten minutes. In the office with Rosso."

"All right, Jack." Southey got up. He said to Van Allen cryptically, "On ice. Solitary. See what shows tomorrow." Van Allen grunted and put a hand under Horace's arm and led him out.

"And just what the hell is that worth?" asked Mendoza hardly.

"Well, you know what it might be worth," said Macklin. "Just like the man said, Landers wouldn't fade into a crowd. He's over average height, and he's—noticeable, in a kind of way, because he does look younger than he is. And how many men do, Mendoza—that much younger than their real age?"

"*¡Por Dios!*" said Mendoza. "I don't understand this—" He brushed his moustache back and forth angrily. Horace had come out with that so unhesitantly, so readily. "So what now?"

"We wait to pick up these other witnesses Horace fingered. He says they saw this Speedy too. Can probably make him. Meanwhile, Horace doesn't see anybody but the jailer. When we get Dunne and Byron, we hold the lineup with Landers, see what they say."

"The cards all neatly stacked, heads you win, tails we lose," said Mendoza. "If they say yes, you believe them. Eyewitness evidence from the pros."

"Not necessarily," said Southey. "But it would kind of weigh down the scale, wouldn't it? Then, we look further."

"You might," said Mendoza acidly, "have a look at Landers' record as well. Just to throw in the wild card. And now I'll see him."

Landers said, "I just can't take it in, that's all. It's crazy. How the hell could this—*me?* I know they say everybody's got a double, but—"

"That's got to be the answer, Tom," said Palliser forcefully. "Somebody like you. Looking enough like you that— Look," he turned to Mendoza, "what this Horace said, it was in that garage he saw the fellow. Maybe not very good light. And anybody Tom's height and build—with dark hair and—"

Mendoza didn't say it wasn't quite so simple as that. Looking at Landers there, in a rumpled gray suit and loosened tie, he kept hearing the echo of Horace's voice: *he looked so young, younger than he is.* That, probably, was the first thing anybody would notice about Tom Landers. The fresh complexion, the misleading ingenuous look of youth. When he spoke, in a good baritone voice, and you looked twice at his dark eyes, you saw he was older: was, in fact, thirty-one. But at first glance you noticed that young look.

"Where were you," he asked Landers abruptly, "at five o'clock last Friday afternoon?" By the grace of God, Landers out questioning a witness, typing a report in the office, out on something with another man, this whole thing knocked down flat right then.

"Friday?" said Landers. "Friday's my day off." He thought. "Let's see, I went out to pick up some stuff at the market—that was earlier. I guess I'd have been just starting to fix dinner, I was going out and then I got interested in a book—"

"*¡Mil rayos!*" said Mendoza.

"But, my God—I can't *understand* it," said Landers. "I just can't—"

He was still saying it to Phil O'Neill an hour later, pacing the living room of her neat small apartment. She'd given him a drink he disposed of in three swallows, and insisted on fixing him a healthy sandwich; he felt a little less hollow after that. She was curled on the couch in a starched blue housecoat, her blonde head shining in the lamplight, and listening to him.

"—A lineup!" he said. "Me! To see if these Goddamned small-time pros can identify me—me!—as one of the masterminds of this damn hot-car ring! I swear to God, this is just a nightmare I'm having—it can't be real. My God, they told me—told me not to leave town, and not to report to the office tomorrow—just stay home! Me! I wouldn't like to bet they haven't got a tail on me!" He stopped in front of her looking white and shaken.

Phil uncurled herself and took the glass from him. "You need another drink." He followed her to the kitchen while she measured Scotch, added water and ice cubes. "They say everybody's got a double. But—" She handed him the glass, studying him seriously.

"But? My God, you don't think—"

"No, I don't think, idiot. But I can't understand it either." She sounded puzzled. "It's not as if you—well, had an *ordinary* face."

"That sort of sounds like a lefthanded compliment," said Landers with a forced smile. "Once seen never forgotten?"

"Well—" she considered. "Something like that, anyway. I don't understand it at all."

Landers took a swallow of his drink. "And, my God," he said suddenly, "don't I know I.A.! They'll be poking around in my history back to first grade, and likely questioning Mother and Dad— My God, what could I tell them? I'm in trouble with the law? Me, a ten-year cop?"

"You'd better call them anyway," said Phil practically. "Warn them. It's Fresno, isn't it?"

"But I just can't understand any of it," said Landers. "It doesn't make sense, Phil."

"It doesn't seem to make much. If there's anything I can do—you know my vacation starts Saturday." But her eyes were still puzzled and—was it speculative?—on him.

For the first time since this nightmare had started, Landers stopped feeling surprised and angry, and began to feel a little frightened.

Mendoza went home, to be fussed over and fed by Máiri MacTaggart, and blew off steam at Alison.

"It is simply impossible, that's all. Landers, I ask you, *cara!* He made rank at twenty-six, there's not a mark on his record, he's an efficient, reliable, experienced man. And this shifty little pro saying— ¡Porvida! But how the hell—"

"You're either saying too much or not enough," said Alison, watching him. "What bothers you, Luis?" She stroked the tangle of two cats on her lap, Sheba and Nefertite, automatically. Bast the matron was coiled on the sectional, and the miniature lion El Señor brooded to himself on the credenza.

"Well, damn it," said Mendoza, "he's not a man you would forget if you'd seen him a few times. And that Horace saying—he sounded so damn positive, and it's just not possible. I need a drink."

Inevitably, El Señor reached the kitchen ahead of him for his ounce of rye in a saucer. Mendoza swallowed rye, swore at the glass, and went down the hall to call Hackett and then Higgins. They both said the same things, after initial indignant exclamations, about nearsighted pros and the damn suspicious I.A. men.

"But, you know, Luis—" said Hackett.

"I know, I know. Rather a distinctive fellow in his own way. But—"

"But when you come to think, Luis—" said Higgins. "He isn't just an ordinary-looking guy, Tom. I should think—" He stopped, and Mendoza could see him rubbing his prognathous jaw.

There wasn't any more to say about it then.

Before looking at the reports on his desk on Thursday morning, Mendoza called Southey. The other witnesses, Dunne and Byron, hadn't been picked up yet; but Van Allen was planning a raid on that garage this afternoon. Nobody there knew that Horace had fingered them; with luck they'd pick up most of the ring's employees; with more luck, Rosso. Whoever he was.

"You'll let me know," said Mendoza. He started to go over the reports, and all of them came in at once—Hackett, Higgins, Grace, Palliser, Glasser, Piggott. The rest of them had the gist of the story from Palliser, but they wanted to kick it around, and the same things got said. Piggott concluded gloomily that it was just more of the devil's machinations against honest men. Hackett and Higgins were both supposed to be off, but aware that the office would be a man short, had come in voluntarily.

"Look, boys," said Mendoza at last, "it's wait and see right now. What Auto Theft gets on that raid—what the other witnesses say. It's a bastard and I don't like it any better than you, but there it is. And there's work to do, damn it."

By chance, the first report he picked up was signed by Landers: a follow-up report on Luisa Fantini. Like all Landers' reports, neatly typed and correctly spelled. Landers the efficient and reliable. . . . At the moment, Mendoza wasn't interested in how Luisa Fantini had come to fall over the balcony. But there'd been that inquiry to Bakersfield—

He went out and asked about that. Bakersfield had sent a reply overnight. The sporting and leather goods shop vaguely remembered, in the person of a clerk, a girl who might have been Luisa Fantini coming in to buy a suitcase, maybe two, three weeks or a month back. If it had been Luisa, she must have paid cash for it: a search of checks accepted by the shop for the last month didn't turn up her name.

Which said nothing at all.

There was also Harriet Hatfield. Just how had Harriet Hatfield, that ordinary matron, good wife and mother, come to be battered to death in her own living room?

Mendoza asked Sergeant Lake to fetch some coffee, and sat back over it and ruminated. He could just see—only just—a possible answer on Harriet Hatfield. Barth had said, and they had agreed, that the time of day, the time of death, and the undisturbed valuables, ruled out the casual break-in. Maybe not, thought Mendoza. Suppose it had been the j.d.—from the neighborhood or not—pulling the break-in on impulse. Maybe supporting a habit. If so, jittery and easily panicked. One like that, maybe riding a little high, might conceivably have battered Harriet Hatfield to death, the unnecessary violence a mark of the breed, and then fled in panic without attempting to take any loot, afraid the noise had been heard. It was just conceivable.

Only why hadn't the dog next door barked?

And if it had been one like that, no way to go hunting him. Unless they found one like that living in the neighborhood. There hadn't been any strange prints in the house. . . .

Mendoza stabbed out his cigarette, his mind inevitably going back to Landers. He felt guilty at even speculating—he could not believe in that so-confident identification—but there was the hard fact: not exactly an ordinary face, Landers'.

"But," he said suddenly aloud, "but— *¿Qué sé yo?* Talk of fantastic— but it could be—"

Down in Records, Phil O'Neill was feeding information into a computer. She hoped that if she looked busy and brisk, the sergeant would assume she was working on some legitimate request from upstairs and not bother to check.

She had put together all of the salient physical features of Thomas Michael Landers, as they appeared on his official description. The computer supposedly would present her, eventually, with the names of any individual males in L.A.'s records who matched the description. It was a place to start.

Caucasian, male, five-eleven, one-sixty, hair black, eyes brown, thirty-one, complexion medium, appendectomy scar, no marks. Details of education, exam-scores, didn't matter.

The computer muttered to itself for some time and presently handed her nine names. The pedigrees varied from burglary to narco dealing to rape.

All nine men had mug-shots on record. Phil went and looked them all up.

Not one of them bore any faint resemblance to Tom Landers.

Descriptions, she thought, staring into space, didn't really say much: could be misleading. Even the precise police-type descriptions. You could, for instance, describe Phil O'Neill and her sister Kitty in much the same way: they were both small and blonde, Kitty only two years older at twenty-seven; blue eyes, fair skin, appendectomy scars and tonsils out and straight noses and that awful tendency to freckles—but they weren't really alike at all. Not to anybody who knew them. They didn't even look much alike, and Kitty was more like Dad—impulsive and given to sudden enthusiasms—while Phil O'Neill, however deplorably, was an intensely practical and common-sensible female.

It was funny about genes, thought Phil vaguely.

Hackett, worrying about Landers, had gone out again to look some more at the Hatfield thing. He had had, belatedly, the same idea about it that Mendoza had, and he did the patient legwork all through that neighborhood up there, looking for the hypothetical j.d., possibly with the habit. He got nothing. Most of the residents were older people; few young people around. But the more he thought about it, the more convinced he was that that was the only possible answer; and it needn't have been a j.d. from around there. Just anybody with a habit, looking for the wherewithal to support it; and that was a neighborhood of big expensive homes. Where the loot might be had.

But of course there was nowhere else to go on that idea. Harriet Hatfield, even as Barth had predicted, would probably end up in Pending.

He came back to the office at a quarter of twelve and found Jason Grace feeling frustrated about Guy Godfrey and indignant about Landers. They'd never nail Godfrey for that, said Grace; all they had was Joe Chase's statement, worth nothing, and they'd had to let Godfrey loose. And what the hell was going to happen about Landers? "I know we've got to realize these I.A. men don't *know* him," said Grace, brushing his dapper moustache in unconscious imitation of Mendoza, "but anybody who knows him—my God, of all the crazy things—"

"Crazy is the word," said Hackett. "Where's the boss, Jimmy?"

"Arguing with I.A. on the phone."

"I seem to remember Seventy-seventh thought they'd spotted that Jenkins the Feds have got fliers out on—what was that?" Jenkins was a known double killer, which was why the fliers had come to Homicide.

"False alarm. Maybe it was him—he'd gone by the time they got there." The phone buzzed; Lake manipulated plugs. "Headquarters, Homicide . . . O.K., sit on it, somebody'll be there . . . New body. The Spring Hotel over on Temple. Probably natural death."

"Oh, hell," said Hackett. "I'll take it. If George calls in, tell him I'll meet him at Federico's at one."

"I just don't understand it," said Grace complainingly as Hackett went out. "Positive identification of Tom—it's out of *Through the Looking Glass*, Jimmy. Of course, this cheap little pro—have they tested him to see if he's got twenty-twenty vision, I wonder. It's got to be a crazy mistake of some kind."

"Let's hope to God," said Lake seriously. "The damn I.A. men always so quick to jump the gun." Mendoza came out of his office looking annoyed, and asked if anything new was in. He looked more annoyed to hear about the new body and Guy Godfrey.

"More paper work. And that Goddamned Macklin—"

The phone buzzed. "Headquarters, Homicide . . . Right away! O.K. —Spring and—we're on it . . . Bank job," said Lake tersely. "Spring and Ninth. The guard jumped one man—squad car's there now."

"¡Condenación! All right, come on, Jase."

Higgins and Palliser were just getting out of the elevator down the hall, so they went along too.

CHAPTER 4

They got to the bank about the same time as the Feds—Mendoza had finally got round to having a siren installed in the Ferrari. There wasn't, as it turned out, much for them to do at the bank: the guard had jumped the lone heister and a couple of male tellers piled out to subdue him. He was sitting in a chair behind the railing labeled *New Accounts*, surrounded by the heftiest bank employees, one of them brandishing a gun. One of the Feds took that away promptly; it was an old .45 automatic with a full clip.

The bank-robber looked at all the law men and said despondently, "It was tryina do a job alone, that's where I went wrong. I shouldn't never've tried it. But I don't know nobody out here."

And the Feds took a second look at him and were pleased. The bank-robber was Lloyd Jenkins, on the run from a murder rap in Chicago. It wasn't the first time he'd killed—he'd hit more than a dozen banks, with a little gang of pals, through the Midwest, and once shot a bank guard—but the Chicago rap was first degree. He had caught his best girl with another boy-friend and shot them both, back in March.

When the guard heard who it was he'd jumped, he looked ready to pass out.

L.A. couldn't hold Jenkins; there'd be extradition. They stashed him in the Alameda jail. The Feds went back to whatever they'd been doing, and the Homicide men went to Federico's for a belated lunch.

Everybody but Mendoza ordered pre-lunch drinks. The waiter brought Mendoza black coffee with the others' drinks, took orders efficiently. Mendoza lit a cigarette and said, "I've had one of my far-out ideas, boys."

"A hunch?" Grace cocked his head.

"No hunch. Just an idea. That Horace"—Mendoza looked meditatively at his coffee—"came out with all that so pat. So prompt. Drop the coin and click-click, out comes the confident identification."

"What's in your mind now?" Higgins swallowed Scotch and water.

"Could it be a frame? A deliberate frame? Horace knowing what Tom looks like, primed with that description? By somebody?"

"Who for God's sake would want to frame Tom?" asked Palliser blankly.

"That I couldn't guess at. It's just a thought."

Palliser drank bourbon and shook his head. "I don't see it. I'd like to buy it, because it could be the only logical answer, but—I was there, you know. When that Horace first spoke up. If I'm not a genius, I don't think I'm all that stupid either, and all I can say is, that sounded damn —spontaneous."

"Sometimes they're good actors," said Higgins. "I'd like to buy that too, Luis. It struck me that it was all—like you say, pat. Rehearsed? I'll say this much. I wouldn't bet I could just tell somebody, for instance, what one of you looks like, even a detailed description, and trust him to pick you out of five or six men. Unless the rest were all midgets or something. But it'd be very damn easy for anybody to describe Tom so he'd be picked out right away."

Palliser and Grace stared at him. "Now that never struck me," said Grace. "But you are so right. How'd you describe John here, so a stranger might recognize him? Any tall dark fellow in his thirties 'd fit that description. But Tom—"

"And you know," said Mendoza dreamily, "that was the very first thing Horace said. He said that was what he noticed first—he looked so young, this guy. The first thing any—mmh—third party would have told him about Tom Landers."

"But—" Palliser thought. "But look, how does this hot-car thing tie in? Why all of a sudden, in the middle of something that isn't Homicide's baby, the frame—if it is? Not even Horace knew Auto Theft was going to drop on him, on that. What the hell would anybody in on that deal know or care about Tom Landers?"

"I couldn't say," said Mendoza. "I just say it could be, that's all. And then, you know—the pros don't get picked up every time on the same count."

"Which means what?" asked Palliser.

"Oh," said Higgins. "Yes. Well, we can ask Tom—"

"Ask him what?" asked Grace.

"About somebody maybe he picked up once—on something to do with Homicide—who nursed a little grudge on him," said Mendoza, regarding the steak sandwich set in front of him. "Who may now be—what story am I building, George?—just maybe—"

"Yes," said Higgins thoughtfully. "Who may now be, say, in competition with this Rosso—whoever he is—in dealing in hot cars. Who may have got to Horace—and possibly these two pals of his, he seems to have parted with their names a little fast, didn't he?—killing two birds with one stone. Put Rosso out of business and frame Tom at the same time. Like all your stories, it's a little bit complicated, and the pros aren't, very, as a rule. But it *could* be. And if it is, Tom will likely remember who might have laid any threat on him, for what."

"Or didn't," said Mendoza. "Just nursed the grudge." He poured himself more coffee. "I'll commit myself this far. If Dunne and Byron make the positive identification, all as confident as Horace, I'm going to have triple doubts that that's for real. Damn what I.A. may think, that would say to me it's a frame."

"I might think so too," said Higgins. "But damn it, Luis, how many times do we hear it? I'll get you, cop. And how many times do they do anything about it?"

"There's always the exception that proves the rule. . . . Have you got anything on that girl, John?"

Palliser sighed. "A cooperative witness," he said, "who gives us nothing at all—or not much."

There was the routine to be done, cases to be worked. They still didn't know much about the Fantini girl, and Palliser had been out most of the morning armed with that photograph, looking for anything on her. He had started on the premise that if she had met a man once after work at the theater, she might have done so often, and they might have gone to one of the bars or cheap restaurants on up from there.

At a bar five blocks up Main from the theater, he finally struck pay dirt.

"Her," said the bartender, glancing at the photograph. "Yeah, sure I seen her in here. That's a hell of a picture of her, though. She's a lot prettier 'n that."

"Did she come in alone or with somebody?" asked Palliser.

"Why, she come in with Duke, acourse. She's Duke's new girl."

"I see," said Palliser. "And who's Duke?"

"You said you're a cop? Neither of 'em done anything, have they?"

"Not that we know of," said Palliser truthfully. "Who's Duke?"

"Well, he's a guy. Just a guy, comes in here sometimes. Duke's O.K., he works downa street at the men's store. What? Well, I don't know his right name, everybody calls him Duke account he's a sharp dresser. Duke Wagner."

Palliser went down to the men's store, a cheap little place with a couple of gaudy sports-coats in the window, and asked for Duke Wagner. The owner looked at his badge, did a little fawning, and told Duke he could take whatever time the officer needed, we had to cooperate with the force, didn't we?

He talked to Duke over a muddy cup of coffee in the drugstore on the corner. Duke Wagner was a little too good-looking and a little too conscious of it: the Greek profile under wavy blond hair; he was tall and well-built, in a gay plaid sports-jacket, a flashy tie. He had a very winning smile. Not one to be satisfied with the cheap men's store on Main Street, thought Palliser: he'd have ambitions. On the make, but very cautious of his own skin. Ambitions toward TV?

Wagner turned a frank gaze on him and answered questions readily. "Luisa, sure, a good kid," he said. "She's only been here a little while. I met her in Dinty's bar one night. Oh, maybe three weeks back. She's a real looker, you know? Yeah, sometimes I'd meet her at that theater and we'd have a few drinks."

"When did you see her last?"

"Oh, last Saturday it was, why?"

"If you'd been going around together, didn't you expect to see her in the next few days after that?"

Wagner looked a little flustered. "No," he said. "No, I didn't. I—why all the questions, anyway? I don't get it, Luisa hasn't done anything, has she?" Palliser showed him the photograph. Wagner stared at it and asked, "What—what's wrong with her? This picture—she sick or something?"

"Or something. She's dead, Wagner."

"Dead!" said Wagner. He went a sickly gray. "How can she be dead? Luisa—what happened, how—"

"Never mind," said Palliser. "Just answer a few questions, Mr. Wagner. Did you have a date with her after Saturday night?"

Wagner shook his head blindly. "No. No. I—tell you how it was. I—it sounds funny, maybe, but it's how it was. Luisa—well, sure, I picked her up that night, she's a looker, maybe an easy lay—you know how you do. But, see, we get talking, we kind of thought about things the same way, and we felt—I got to explain how it was—kind of friendly. How we're both out to get somewhere, you get me? This crummy neighborhood— old Jackson and his cheap little store, my God, sixty-five bucks a week— Look, I picked her up for the usual reason, but it was funny—

after a while we felt just friendly, you get me. Like, sympathetic." He tasted the word on his tongue, experimental. "Like that. Luisa told me about herself. You want to hear that?"

"I would. What did she tell you?"

"Well, see, she was raised on a farm way up north, I think she said outside San José someplace. Her pa was awful strict, you know how some of these Italians are, they seem to think kids belong to 'em, order 'em around however they want—not just Italians I don't mean, old-country people like that sometimes. He'd beat her too, beat up on her and her ma and the other kids. Anyway, there wasn't never any money, he's a kind of miser, and she has to work like a dog all the time, and so she ran away. She stole some money out of her pa's pants one night and ran away. Came here on the bus, and she's got ambitions, see, she was going to get somewheres however she can. Poor kid, she was only twenty, my God. How did—"

Palliser took that with a large grain of salt, thinking of that little brown strip of paper from the wad of cash. "I see. And how was she planning to get somewhere?"

Wagner was silent. "It's not so easy for a girl, you got to sort of make allowances," he said at last. "I—well, I tell you all I know. If some bastard hurt her some way— Well, I tell you, see, she was looking for some—some guy loaded, to make up to. Like that. I said I'd meet her, a couple times, we'd have a couple drinks—but a lot of nights, she'd get all dressed up and hit places uptown, looking for the rich guys. She told me some about it."

"I see. What luck had she had?" asked Palliser.

"Well, not the kind of deal she was after. See, she'd bought herself some nice clothes with her pa's money she took, she was real class when she got dressed up. Sure, she met up with the eager johns, but it was the permanent deal with somebody really loaded she wanted, not the one-night stands, she wasn't that kind of girl," said Wagner earnestly. "But last Sunday afternoon, I only saw her a few minutes, I met her on the street. She told me—" he shook his head. "She was all lit up, sort of sparkling—excited, you know?—she said, night before she'd met up with a real high-class guy, not so young maybe but he looked like a good deal for her. It was at some bar out on Beverly, something to do with gypsies the name was—no, she didn't say what the guy's name was. Just that it looked like a good deal. She was going to meet him that night. And that's all I could tell you. I never saw her again."

Palliser thought. If that was so, and it rang true, he didn't think Luisa would have revealed her shabby background by taking the john to Boyd

Street. Pretty evidently, by all that, she'd been posing as the high-class call-girl. If she'd made a deal with the john, it would be at his place, or some hotel. He foresaw more legwork around the bars uptown, and sighed.

He passed that on to Mendoza at lunch; Mendoza didn't think much of Luisa's sad tale of an ill-used childhood either, but they'd ask San José anyway. The rest of it rang a little truer.

After lunch Palliser looked in the phone book for bars on Beverly Boulevard. He didn't find any gypsies mentioned, but he did find the Tzigani Room, so he drove out there to show the photograph and ask questions. It was just open, but frustratingly, of course, the bartender and waiters on duty after nine P.M. weren't there now. And that probably meant some overtime tonight.

He went back to the office and began to type up a report on what Wagner had told him.

Piggott and Glasser were doing the dogged routine on the Carolyn Katz case. They had looked in Records for the pedigrees of men picked up on similar assaults, and gone out to look for the first batch of those that showed. It was boring and unrewarding, because even when they found those men and brought them in to question, very few of them could produce alibis, and there was no evidence at the scene to link to anybody.

Up to noon they had found and questioned three men from the list. All of them denied knowing anything about Carolyn Katz, none of them had alibis for the relevant time, and any of them could have done it but there was just no evidence.

"You know, Henry," said Piggott over a drugstore sandwich, "I think it'd be a shortcut if we just put this thing into Pending right now. We'll never get anywhere on it."

"I wouldn't doubt you're right, Matt," said Glasser. "But we have to work it some, after all."

"That thing about Tom—it's crazy. Just crazy. I wondered if it could be a frame," said Piggott, his thin dark face morose.

"How the hell? What I heard, what the Lieutenant said, this pro claimed to recognize him right off. Oh," said Glasser. "Oh, I see what you mean. Somebody could have described Tom to him—"

"When he acted so positive, way I heard it. Bearing false witness," said Piggott. "It's almost got to be, Henry, because Tom—well, we've both worked with him awhile."

"Yeah," said Glasser. "That's so, Matt. I'd take an oath he's as straight as they come. But this Auto Theft deal—how the hell could anybody mix Tom in with that? Setting up a frame?"

"I don't know. But I do know that the devil is—like the minister was saying just last Sunday—full of wile and subtleties. All too true, Henry. And always watching for ways to catch the honest men."

"Well, I'll tell you one thing," said Glasser thoughtfully. "If I.A. goes after Tom, to try to break him, the Lieutenant—as they say, Matt— will be neither to hold nor bind. Like a tiger after those damn suspicious do-gooders."

A gleam of slightly unchristian satisfaction showed in Piggott's eyes. "Oh, that he will, Henry, that he will. And more power to him."

Mendoza had been fidgeting around the office ever since he'd come back from lunch; he knew I.A. probably wouldn't be calling until at least three o'clock, but you never knew—and with Van Allen's raid on that garage— He sat swiveled around looking out over the view across the city, the Hollywood hills a blur on the horizon this slightly overcast day, and smoked too many cigarettes.

A new body turned up on a park bench in MacArthur Park. Palliser had just finished typing a report, and went out to look at that. At three o'clock Hackett came in and said he'd come round to agreeing with Barth that Harriet Hatfield posed a real mystery. Seeing that Harriet and everybody connected with her looked so upright and respectable.

"You're unsold on the hopped-up j.d.?" asked Mendoza inattentively.

"On account," said Hackett, "of the dog. I got to thinking about that dog, Luis. The Brownlees' dog next door. Call it fifty feet between the two front doors, and the back yards adjoin each other. Ornamental wooden fence and a hedge between 'em." He sank his big bulk in the chair beside the desk. "Dogs," he said, "are funny. If you didn't know. Breeds."

"¿Y qué?"

"Well, I just got to thinking about the dog. And I went and saw Mrs. Brownlee. The dog is a Dalmatian."

"So?"

"They're not barkers," said Hackett, "as a rule. She said the dog always barks, just once or twice, at strangers anywhere near. To let her know the stranger's around. Well, George said dogs have better ears. The dog would probably have heard any stranger—intruder—on the property next door. And barked. The dog was in the Brownlees' back yard all afternoon."

Mendoza swiveled around and looked at him. "Q.E.D.?" he said softly.

"Well, call it ninety percent yes. The dog didn't bark."

"So it wasn't a stranger next door? You're telling the story, Art."

"It's kind of logical to say so, isn't it?" said Hackett reasonably. "It was somebody who'd been to the Hatfield house before. Somebody the dog next door knew was—all right. But how could it be, Luis? Such damned upright people— Oh, well, I know that says nothing really. But—"

The inside phone rang and Mendoza snatched it up.

"Lieutenant?" Southey. "We've got Dunne and Byron—and a couple of others. We're ready to set up the lineup now."

"I'm on my way," said Mendoza tersely.

They were being even more careful on this than they ordinarily would be on arranging the completely equitable, fair showing. The lighted platform up there in front was isolated from the darkened space here, and this area was soundproofed: no word spoken here could be heard by the men on the platform.

And Macklin was saying rather fussily now, "This is quite irregular, Mendoza, I hope you realize that. Ordinarily no outsider would be allowed to be present with the witnesses—and you can stay only if you give your word to remain absolutely silent—the witnesses will not be influenced in any—"

"All right, all right! But I'll hear this at first hand, Macklin. Speaking of influence—"

"Are you accusing—"

"I'm not accusing you Nice Nellies of anything but jumping to conclusions," said Mendoza irritably. "Have you taken the trouble to glance at Landers' record?"

"We've seen that, yes," said Southey. "You know we don't jump to conclusions, Lieutenant. We just want all the facts in."

"Facts," said Mendoza, unconsciously stating one of his deepest convictions, "mean damn all when you're dealing with human people."

A grunted expletive turned him around to face Van Allen. The Auto Theft captain looked slightly contemptuous at that overheard remark; there was unconcealed dislike in his eyes on Mendoza's beautifully-tailored silver-gray dacron suit, the gold links and heavy gold ring.

"So here they are," he said.

The two men with him were rather typical of the pros cops saw a lot of. They weren't unintelligent or even without skills: just lazy. They'd rather get it the easy way. Both of them had pedigrees of theft, break-ins, shoplifting. The job they had just been picked up for must have been one of the easiest they'd ever had: hopping cars on order, getting paid for ferrying them to the Virgil Street garage.

Dunne was twenty-six, a weedy young man with a too-small mouth and hard eyes. Byron was much bigger, sandy, a little too fat, trying for an arrogant swagger.

Southey gestured, and the uniformed man who had come in with Van Allen herded the two over to the other side of the room. "What did you get?" asked Southey quietly.

"Four of them," said Van Allen. "The little guys—like these. The other two hired to hop the cars too. Six new shorts in for processing. This Rosso wasn't there." He looked like an angry bull.

"Durfee?" asked Southey.

"Or him either. Damn it, it was just the odds," said Van Allen. "We might have dropped on the whole ring—it was just the way the ball bounced."

"Coincidence!" said Mendoza, and laughed. "It doesn't enter your head that that might say Rosso and Durfee knew the whistle had been blown, and made tracks to cover?"

"It was just the way the ball bounced," repeated Van Allen doggedly. "These four we picked up know we've got the goods on 'em. They've got no reason to shut up on anything—not when they know Horace's already split. No, for God's sake, they haven't laid eyes on Horace, natu-rally. I told 'em he'd fingered them and they came apart. They give us Rosso too. Just the name. Description of sorts. I never asked one ques-tion about the other one, but they told me there is a second man. The other two never saw him. These two give us just what Horace did—the second man wasn't there often, at the garage. When he was, usually at night, in the office with Rosso. And usually just before a shipment moved out. These two started to tell me what they knew about him, I stopped 'em."

Careful, so careful to be fair, thought Mendoza sardonically.

Southey nodded and went over to Dunne and Byron, Macklin beside him. "Now I want you to listen carefully," he told them in his quiet voice. "You're going to look at a number of men up there in the light. All we want is for you to tell us whether you've ever seen one of them before. If you have, we'll ask you some questions about that. If you haven't, that's just too bad. But we'd like you to be very sure about it, you understand?"

Both men nodded jerkily. "All right," said Southey. There were chairs down there in front of the platform; he led them there. Mendoza sat down directly behind Dunne; Southey and Macklin flanking the two, Van Allen behind Mendoza.

The light on the platform brightened suddenly. A uniformed man came out first, and after him, rather slowly, a file of eleven men. I.A. leaning over backwards, thought Mendoza: eleven men, all of a general type.

Landers was the sixth man in line. All the men were between five-ten and six feet. They were all dark, or darkish. They were all clean-shaven. They were all in the late twenties or early thirties. They were wearing suits and white shirts. And Mendoza knew who they'd be, too. Men on the force, men picked as that general type, possibly a couple of prisoners from the Alameda jail. In silence they filed onto the platform, in silence stood there.

And in that file of men, for the one reason, Tom Landers stood out. He looked, at first glance, so much younger than any of the rest.

Dunne moved suddenly. He said, "That's him—the other guy. Isn't he the one, By?"

"Don't consult with each other," said Southey in the darkness, "please."

"Yeah, that's him," said Byron. "He was in the office with Rosso once, I brought in a heap. I never heard what his name is, but Jack told me—"

"That's right," said Dunne. "I only saw him twice, but he's a guy you'd remember."

"Which one?" asked Macklin. The men in line stared straight ahead; under the light Landers looked pale.

"The sixth one," said Dunne. "Sixth man in from the left. I reckanized him soon's I saw him, on account he looks so young. Not as old as I guess he is, but I wouldn't know how old he is."

"That's right," said Byron instantly. "You'd spot him easy, on that account. Even if you only saw him once like I did."

And Mendoza said loudly, "*¡No faltaba más!* All dovetailed nice and neat—as if I needed any more convincing it's a Goddamned frame!"

Macklin turned on him furiously.

They wouldn't let him see Landers alone; at least it was Southey who stayed in the room with them.

Landers was looking angry again now, and that was a good thing. "Listen, Lieutenant, a lot of good it does to say it, but—"

"Skip that," said Mendoza. "We haven't got much time. I think this is a frame, Tom, and if so we're going to find out all about it—"

"Excuse me, you won't be allowed to do any investigation in this matter," said Southey. "It's I.A.'s business."

"I've been on this force, for my sins, twenty-four years this month, Lieutenant," said Mendoza icily, "and as a rule I decide what's my business and what isn't. At the moment you're an observer only. Tom, I want you to think back and try to come up with anybody—anybody at all—who might have any reason to set a frame on you."

"Well, but offhand I can't—"

"I don't want offhand. Think about it. Motives are sometimes damn small. Now in the meantime these—officers," said Mendoza, "are going to be questioning you hot and heavy. As a fellow officer—"

"Detective Landers is suspended from duty," said Southey.

"Temporarily," said Mendoza between his teeth. "Now you're not guilty of anything so they're not going to find any evidence. So you're going to cooperate with them any way they ask."

"Sure," said Landers. "God knows they can look—for one thing, these operators must have been taking a lot of loot at that racket, and they're not going to find any attached to me."

"*De veras*. We're both feeling damned annoyed about this," said Mendoza, "as well as—mmh—surprised—"

"That you can say again."

"—And you might feel even more damned annoyed at some of the personal questions they're going to be asking you. I just want you to remember something, Tom. We swear at I.A. and sometimes we laugh at it—but this is the top force anywhere—and you come to admit it, I.A. is one of the reasons. If we have got a bad one carrying a badge, we want to know."

"And amen to that," said Landers seriously. "All right. I know that. I just can't figure this at all, but there's got to be some logical answer. A frame—I don't know."

"And, damn it, other things to work," said Mendoza. "But we'll be in touch, boy. We'll find out what's behind this damned farce—" Southey cleared his throat and Mendoza's grin tightened. He gripped Landers' arm. "Whatever the hell *is* behind it. You just mind your manners with these fellows."

Landers gave him an anxious smile. "I'll do that. Thanks, Lieutenant."

*   *   *

And he had known what to expect, in a general way, but if Mendoza hadn't said all that to him, he might have lost his temper. As it was, he hung onto it tight; he cooperated, remembering what Mendoza had said.

He gave them his bankbook, his keys. He told them how he spent his money, what he saved, that no, he didn't have a safe-deposit vault. He explained the florist's bill they found when he emptied his pockets; he was surprised to see it still there—flowers for his mother's birthday last month. They asked him about girl-friends, and it was the queerest damned thing, he had to stop to think to remember the last girl he'd dated before Phil O'Neill. He didn't mention her name at all, afraid to get her in trouble with him.

They asked him the hell of a lot of personal questions, all right, but he went on hanging onto his temper. The fact that three men had identified him as a pro crook he'd just stopped thinking about: that was just nightmare, an impossible thing. There must be a logical explanation somewhere, but that was just too much to think about right now. He clung to the facts he knew: he wasn't guilty of anything, so there'd be no evidence for them to find, no ill-gotten loot, no secrets.

With the impersonal, inexorable voices going on at him, Landers kept his temper. He answered the questions. After a while he lost any impulse to anger, resentment; he was just concentrating on answering truthfully, fastening all his hope to what Mendoza had said.

He had no idea what time it was when Southey straightened and said to him formally, "As I told you, Landers, you're suspended from duty pending the outcome of this investigation. You are not to leave town. You'll hold yourself available for questioning at any time. Right now you're free to go home."

And Landers knew how the grapevine worked, too. Some version of this all through the headquarters building by now.

My God, how and why was all this happening to him?

They'd given him back his keys. Looking at his watch, he found it was ten minutes to nine. A few hours ago they'd taken a break, given him a sandwich and coffee; his stomach was growling now, but he felt faintly sick.

The Corvair had been dusted for latent prints. They had wiped most of the powder off, but he could tell.

He drove home, to the rather shabby apartment on Fountain where he'd lived ever since he'd come to L.A. and joined the force. The apartment had been searched and dusted too. Everything was in place, as he'd left it, but he knew that. He had never realized before what a feeling of—violation—that could give you, your private place looked over by alien eyes. By searchers.

He felt empty, but he didn't want to go out to a restaurant, and he didn't have the energy to make a sandwich or put a TV dinner in the oven.

He went out and got back into the Corvair, and he'd driven up Fountain to Normandie and turned left there before the thought entered his mind: was he wearing a tail?

To bring Phil into this Goddamned mess—

He slowed and pulled in to the curb, watching the rearview mirror. Cars passed him, apparently unconcerned. Landers thought tiredly, yes, and make some obvious maneuver to shake off the possible tail (*him*, with a tail!), just double the suspicion in their minds—

After debate, he went down to Ardmore. That was a side street, empty at night. No cars turned after him; he parked, but no lights showed in the mirror.

He turned back to Normandie, down to Melrose, and down that to Kingsley.

She came unhurriedly at his ring to open the door. She was wearing the starched blue house-robe, primly high at neck, full around her ankles, and it showed her slim neat figure. Her short blonde curls shone in the light.

"I shouldn't have come—"

"Well," said Phil, surveying him calmly, "one good thing may come of all this mess, now I take a look at you. You look at least five years older already, you realize that? You also look as if you'd been through a wringer. Have you had anything to eat?"

"I don't remember—a sandwich a while ago—"

"I've got creamed chipped beef left over. Whole wheat toast. Asparagus or Italian beans. But I think," said Phil, "you need a good stiff drink first."

CHAPTER 5

The corpse on the bench in MacArthur Park looked to Palliser like one of those things that might create more than paper work. The ambulance was waiting when he got there; the squad-car men holding off a little knot of curious people. The interns said the man had been dead at least eight hours; presumably he'd been taken for a sleeping bum until somebody sat down beside him.

He was an elderly man, and his clothes looked expensive, a gray suit, white shirt, new shoes. The interns said it looked like an overdose of some kind, at first glance. There wasn't a thing on him but an empty prescription bottle in his breast-pocket, and that bore only a doctor's name: Dr. William Bartlett, an address in Beverly Hills. Palliser let the interns take the body, and drove out to Beverly Hills.

Dr. William Bartlett had his own smart little clinic building, and the offices were closed on Thursdays.

Great, thought Palliser. He went back to headquarters and typed up a report. He had, belatedly, realized what Landers had: damn that ridiculous identification, there wasn't going to be any evidence for I.A. to find on Landers, so it would be O.K., just—as the Lieutenant was saying—the attempted frame that fell apart.

And he'd be doing some overtime tonight, so he went home a little early, to the house on Hillside Avenue that was too big for them now. He told Roberta about the frame. "It'll be a tempest in a teapot," he said. "Naturally there won't be any evidence on him, it'll blow over. But I wonder what was behind it."

His lovely dark Robin gave him a rueful smile. "You've given me something new to worry about now. Besides all the trigger-happy thugs. Your own private watchdogs jumping on you for any little thing."

"Well, not just any— I suppose they have to look, damn silly as it is to anybody who knows Tom. But it'll be all right in the end," said Palliser. "Rough on Tom for a couple of days, that's all."

At nine o'clock he went out again, to the Tzigani Room. The Tzigani Room was attached to a new and large and expensive-looking chain motel, and it was crowded. Palliser was patient, and a harried head-waiter, impressed by the badge, cooperated. The ninth waiter Palliser talked to, looking at the photograph of Luisa, said he wouldn't like to get anybody in trouble.

"Do you know her?" asked Palliser. "This is police business, Mr.—"

"Smith," said the waiter surprisingly. All the waiters were dressed in somebody's idea of gypsy attire, tight black trousers, white shirts with billowing sleeves, and red silk ties. This one was swarthy enough to look the part. "George Smith. Look, it isn't like the manager lets B-girls in here, but people behave O.K., how do you throw 'em out? For all I knew she was stayin' here."

"All right, when did you see her? With somebody?"

"She was in Friday and Saturday nights last week," said Smith reluctantly. "I didn't say anything to the head. Why should I? She was a pretty girl, she was dressed nice, nothing too sexy or—you know. Blue lace dress she had on, nice dress, and a kind of white cape across her shoulders—and she acted O.K. How should I know she didn't know the guy before?"

"Who?" asked Palliser.

"Well, Mr. Silverman. He's stayin' here. He's kind of regular, he'll be here—stayin' here I mean—maybe a couple of weeks every three, four months."

"Is he still here?"

"Look, you don't need to tell him it was me told you? I don't want no trouble—we aren't supposed to talk about the guests—well, that's him in the corner booth, but—"

Mr. Harold Silverman, looking at the badge, was a little flustered. "Police?" he said. "Why the hell are police interested in me?" He was a big man about forty-five, not a bad-looking man, with thick curly gray hair and a Brooklyn accent. "Why you asking?" He wore two diamond rings.

"You know this girl, sir?" asked Palliser, holding out the photograph. Silverman looked at it.

"What's this about?" he asked in a quieter voice.

"The girl's dead."

"Dead? That little— Well, I will be good and Goddamned," said Silverman blankly. "So that's why— How? What happened to her?"

"It looks as if she was murdered. You did know her?"

Silverman looked shocked. "Oh, my God. I hope to God you're not going to connect me—the papers—my God, Jacob would have a fit. So that's why she never showed. I'll be damned."

"If you'd just tell me what you know about her—"

"Sure," said Silverman almost absently. "Buy you a drink? Well, I guess I'll have another. My God, this shakes me. In the midst of life, all right."

Silverman was the high-class john Luisa had picked up on Friday night. He was partner and chief salesman in a big jewelry-manufacturing company in New York; he was fancy-free, divorced, with plenty of money to spend, and Luisa had looked like a real fun girl to him. He had about a week's worth of business to finish up in L.A., after which he proposed that they spend a couple of weeks in Acapulco; meanwhile, he'd get her a room at the motel. "That is," he said to Palliser, "I'd give her the money to. They're particular, they don't put up with funny business." She'd been supposed to meet him for dinner at seven-thirty on Sunday night, but she hadn't. He didn't know where she lived, any way to get in touch with her; he'd been mad about it. She sure looked like a girl you could have fun with. . . .

Palliser thought about that autopsy report. Luisa dead maybe as early as eight o'clock that night, falling over that theater balcony: or shoved over. Why had she missed keeping her date with her high-class john?

And Silverman, mad at being stood up, had gone out and picked up another girl along Hollywood Boulevard. Had gone back to her apartment with her. "I don't know if she'd say, Sergeant—I don't figure she's a pro, and—"

It didn't matter. Silverman was alibied by waiters here up to nearly ten on Sunday night. Palliser asked Silverman to come to headquarters in the morning to make a statement. "My God, this isn't going to come out in the press? I want to help you guys, Sergeant, but—"

"No, sir, it's just for our records."

It was, however, funny. Luisa on the make for a john with money, so when she found one she stood him up. Why?

Mendoza was wakened just after dawn by faint and then more definite sounds from the alder tree in the yard.

Coroo, coroo. Awk. Yankee Doodle came to town came to town— AWK!

That damn mockingbird. The cats were huddled at the foot of the king-size bed. El Señor got up and walked over his mother and sisters to stare out the window. A sudden flash of gray-white beyond that: the mockingbird was up early, intent on his nest-building.

Mendoza pulled the sheet over his head. Alison was sound asleep. It was no use; he was awake for good. Half an hour later subdued sounds from the kitchen galvanized the cats into action. El Señor, standing on his hind legs, rattled the doorknob until he tripped the latch, and all four cats vanished down the hall toward Mrs. MacTaggart and breakfast. . . . Five minutes later the mockingbird began to scream raucously, and an amiable bark informed Mendoza that their shaggy dog had been let out into the yard. Three minutes after that, the twins erupted down the hall shouting.

Alison sat up. "Why on earth did we, *amado?*" she asked sleepily. "Get into all this?"

"It was strictly your idea," said Mendoza.

He landed at the office at ten minutes to eight. The grapevine had, of course, carried the tale of I.A.'s investigation to every office at headquarters, and the night men Schenke and Galeano had hung around to ask him what went on. "I think it's a frame," said Mendoza, "and a fairly crude one too. But there'll be no evidence for I.A. to find. I only hope to God they'll come to the same conclusion."

"Those guys briefed to identify Tom?" asked Galeano. "Who'd try a thing like that? Without any more to back it up—"

"As I said, crude," said Mendoza. "We just wait and see what shows."

It had been a quiet night: nothing new for Homicide. He read Palliser's report on the body in MacArthur Park: nothing to do on that until they got the body identified through that doctor.

When Hackett and Higgins came in at eight-fifteen, he beckoned them into his office with a crooked finger. "You two are on special detail. I want Al Durfee—if possible, before I.A. gets hold of him. I'd like Rosso ditto, but that's a little more difficult."

"Just a little more, the man says." Hackett looked at him. "Are you just pining for a vacation, *amigo?* You're not careful, you'll find yourself alongside Tom on suspension. So you want Durfee. If we find him, and fetch him back to master like good dogs, you know what's going to happen?"

Mendoza grinned. "*Pues sí.* We may lose part of the ninth floor when Southey and Macklin explode. I'll take the risk. I'm just a dedicated officer trying to help out those dedicated I.A. men, that's all—business is a little slack here for once and I'm just being helpful, turning my two

senior bloodhounds onto Durfee. You find him, we'll send him up to
I.A. like good boys."

"Straight up, I don't think," said Higgins.

"Well, after I've had a talk with him," said Mendoza, shutting his
eyes and leaning back in his desk-chair. "It's not that I don't have—
mmh—faith in these dedicated I.A. men. Not at all. They're cops too.
But they're not, at the moment, operating on the premise that there's
been a frame, and I feel they might be *muy cortés* to Mr. Durfee. Such
little gentlemen they are."

Hackett laughed. "I don't know Durfee. You think a little less politeness might open his mouth wider?"

"Es posible. When and if you pick him up, you two savage-looking
cops can stand over him and tell him, we know all about the frame,
come on, who put you up to it. Etcetera. I'd just like to hear what that
might produce. We can always say," said Mendoza placidly, "that we
couldn't get through on the phone, or something."

"I keep having this feeling," said Hackett, "that we might end up getting suspended too. You know how touchy I.A. is. And that's up in the
air, we haven't found him yet. And I.A. and Auto Theft are both looking for him too. And Rosso."

"If you run into any of them," said Mendoza, "you can just look surprised and say, What a coincidence. The sooner you start to look the
sooner you may get results. *¡Vamos!"*

Higgins and Hackett looked at each other and went out resignedly.

Mendoza hadn't said it to them; and he wouldn't have to say it to any
other man in the office, because they'd see it for themselves once they
thought about it. They had said, after the first little shock, I.A. mount-
ing an investigation and Landers suspended from duty, that it would
blow over: frame or mistake or whatever, there'd be no evidence for
I.A. to find on Landers, no illicit loot or a tie-up to pros—so it would
fizzle out. When they thought it through, as Mendoza had, they'd see
that it couldn't.

There the ugly little fact stood: three pros, presumably with no personal ax to grind, had identified Tom Landers positively as the second
operator running a hot-car ring. So, no solid evidence, I.A. couldn't ask
for his resignation, couldn't do a thing to him. No proof. But there the
mark would be—forever a question mark. And so, when the chance for
promotion came, Landers—who had passed the sergeants' exam with the
top grade—would be passed over. Probably passed over from now on.
The LAPD didn't promote officers with question marks on their records.

If this couldn't be definitely proved to be a frame—or of course a mistake—it would hang like a Sword of Damocles over Landers the rest of his professional life.

And there were the current cases, legitimately Homicide's business, to be worked. Harriet Hatfield. Carolyn Katz. The Fantini girl. That new body.

Mendoza swore softly to himself, took up his hat and went out to the anteroom, where Sergeant Lake was gloomily studying *How To Stay Slim.* "I'll check in by noon, Jimmy."

Palliser had gone out looking for that doctor in Beverly Hills; Piggott and Glasser were doggedly pursuing their hunt through Records for Carolyn Katz's killer, and Grace was in court covering the inquest on Luisa Fantini. Nobody but Sergeant Lake was in the office when Lieutenant Carey of Missing Persons came in and said he'd got that new corpse identified for them. A description had been sent down to his office yesterday.

"The people called in yesterday morning. I didn't see the description until an hour ago, it rang a bell so I called them. They've just identified him at the morgue. One Wilson Guilfoyle, address in Beverly Hills. I gather he'd been going a little senile—he was nearly eighty, had had strokes. It looked like suicide?"

"I couldn't say," said Lake. "Palliser was on it, and he's out."

"Damn," said Carey. "Well, if he calls in or comes back, let him know, hah?"

He had just gone out when Harold Silverman came in, looking nervous, looking curiously around the Homicide office, and said Sergeant Palliser had asked him to come in to make a statement.

Lake hadn't any idea what that was about; he felt a little indignant at Palliser; but he'd just noncommittally asked Silverman to sit down when the outside phone buzzed and it was Palliser.

"Anything up, Jimmy? I've got that body identified, the doctor—"

"Yes, so has Carey. You needn't have gone chasing off. And a Mr. Silverman's here wanting to make a statement."

"Oh, hell, I'd forgotten him," said Palliser. "I'll be in in twenty minutes."

Both Auto Theft and I.A. had been before them—long before them—in Records. The grapevine stretched to Records too, and Sergeant O'Brien eyed Hackett and Higgins curiously; but he didn't make any comment. He produced the pedigrees without question and Hackett and Higgins looked at them.

Albert Joseph Durfee didn't have too long a pedigree or too bad a one. He had a little j.d. record of hopping cars; after that, nothing until he was twenty-seven and charged with grand theft—he'd stolen some expensive tools from the garage where he was working. He was a skilled mechanic. He'd got into law trouble again five years later, a burglary charge dropped for lack of evidence. Then, his arrest for assault at that gambling house where he'd apparently been an unofficial bouncer. That was all. He was now forty-seven, and from somewhere since five years back, he'd got hold of the money to start buying the garage on Virgil. His mug-shot showed a heavy-jowled man with a sullen mouth and heavy eyebrows.

"Suppose we do find him?" said Higgins. "He looks like a tough customer, Art. Could you get the truth out of him at all? Even our Luis?"

"No bets," said Hackett. There was a recent address—he was only off parole since last year—on Second Street past Hoover.

Rosso, of course, was another thing. None of the witnesses in that case knew his first name, or said they didn't. As they'd all said too that he was a mean customer, all business, it was only natural they hadn't known. There were fifteen men named Rosso in the current LAPD Records; it took a while to get particulars on them. When they did, it turned out that six of them were presently incarcerated here and there, from Atascadero to the county jail, on various counts. Four of the others looked like very small-time pros by their records. Three others had done time for embezzlement, rape, and forgery, which somehow didn't sound close to operating a hot-car drop. The last two, however, sounded quite possible. Victor Rosso, forty-seven, had done time for fencing, possession of stolen goods. Paolo Rosso, forty, two arrests and one charge on receiving stolen goods. There had been a man charged with him on that, one James Herbert Saunders, and just to be thorough they looked him up too.

And looking at Saunders' pedigree, Hackett said, "I'll be damned. Does this say something, George?"

Saunders was described, five years back, as Caucasian, male, twenty-four, five-ten-and-a-half, one-seventy, complexion medium, hair dark brown, eyes blue, no marks.

"You're thinking, an honest mistake," said Higgins, looking at that. "On the surface, vaguely like Tom. He's got brown eyes but who notices that close? I think we go looking for these birds, Art."

"Durfee first."

On their way out of Records they passed a good-looking little blonde in neat uniform, making for the computer. "Getting some cute junior officers these days," said Hackett idly.

Mendoza, with an effort putting Landers at the back of his mind, had gone to see Howard Hatfield again. There wasn't, he had decided yesterday, anything at all in that little lapse of Howard Hatfield's, to tie up to this murder. He had decided that after ten minutes' talking with the shallow-eyed pseudo-redhead Bobby Sarsfield in a plush office on the Strip. She hadn't remembered Hatfield's name at first; she didn't like cops, but she wasn't smart enough to have faked that.

Hatfield was in his office on the top floor of the three belonging to Hollywood Girl Cosmetics, in a tall building on Wilshire Boulevard. He polished his glasses slowly as he answered Mendoza; he looked older and graver than when Mendoza had first seen him only a few days ago.

"It's the little things that one notices," he said with a twisted smile. "I—we never thought about it, at least I suppose the girls—but, the house all run smoothly, the marketing done, dinner waiting when we— And now, well, the girls both working, they do their best, but—Harriet was always a little house-proud, as they say. Kept things just so. And a—a good cook." He was silent, and then he said, "It's just a terrible mystery. We can't imagine what could have happened—why. That other man—Sergeant Barth—he explained why you don't think it was just an ordinary burglar, but I just don't know what other explanation there could be."

"Mr. Hatfield, did you and your wife discuss most things together? What I'm getting at, if she had had a quarrel, an argument, with someone—a personal disagreement—do you think she'd have told you about it?"

Hatfield looked surprised. "Why, I imagine so—I'd have heard about anything like that. It would have been unusual—Harriet wasn't a—a secretive person. But anything like that—it'd be impossible. Someone she knew—Harriet didn't—didn't have arguments with people, Lieutenant. She was—easygoing. And nobody would—" He put his glasses on, looking at Mendoza curiously, incredulously. "I'd been very busy," he said suddenly. "We're bringing out a new line in the fall, and I'd had a good deal of overtime work here. But I'd surely have heard of anything like that. Harriet—you can't be thinking—"

"We don't know, Mr. Hatfield. We're just asking."

"Her friends—most of her women friends, I know their husbands— we'd entertain them—dinners, Sunday lunch." He looked at his clasped hands. "All just ordinary nice people, Lieutenant. Beth and Tom Lederer—the Novaks—the Townbridges— You can't be thinking—"

Mendoza had seen Hackett's report on those people. Hackett might look like the big stupid cop but he got nuances from people too. Those couples, closest friends of the Hatfields, were impossible, said Hackett. From Homicide's point of view. Ordinary people: Mendoza was tired of that word. And all of them, as it happened, were firmly alibied for the afternoon Harriet had been battered to death.

The children, he thought. The grown-up children. Was there possibly anything there? The girls had boy-friends. John in college: had he got in with some friends the Hatfields disapproved? Sniff around them, their personal lives.

The dog wouldn't have barked at any of the Hatfields' friends, coming frequently to the house.

He opened his mouth to ask Hatfield about the girls, about John.

Palliser took the statement from Silverman before he called Carey. By that time Grace had come back from the inquest, and went to sit in on the new one with him.

Mrs. Alma Swift and Mr. Wilfrid Guilfoyle, Junior, had still been in Carey's office making statements; they were voluble to the Homicide men.

"He'd been getting a lot more forgetful lately," said Guilfoyle earnestly. "Poor old Uncle Will. He realized it, and he minded like hell. Alma could tell you." Guilfoyle was about thirty, very natty indeed in pale fawn slacks, a sports-jacket with the faintest of brown shadow-plaids, a white silk scarf draped inside the jacket in lieu of a tie.

"Well, he had," said the woman. She was middle-aged, angular and plain, gray hair pulled back to a knot; she wore a long-sleeved black dress that gave the effect of a uniform. "I've been housekeeper for Mr. Guilfoyle for over twenty years and it was a terrible thing to see him failing like he had been since his last stroke. He always had such a sharp mind."

"I gather," said Palliser, "that Mr. Guilfoyle was—er—quite well off?" The doctor had said, filthy rich: very much the self-made man, and still wearing the pants, so to speak, if the strokes had slowed him down.

"Oh, yes, sir. But to think of him doing such a thing— Such a turn it gave me, when I went up with his breakfast yesterday morning and there was his empty bed!" She sniffed into a handkerchief. "To think of him—that other man, he said the doctors thought he'd taken an overdose of his heart medicine—the bottle—but I don't see how it could be,

Mr. Guilfoyle'd never do such a thing on purpose— And way downtown here—I just don't understand it!"

"Well, I suppose I'd better tell you this," said young Guilfoyle in a subdued tone. "It just didn't cross my mind that he meant anything by it, but— Well, you see, I live—lived with him, and I used to take him his coffee after dinner, he liked to sit in the library then, and"—he smiled— "you know, I'd talk with him, try to cheer him up. He was crotchety, poor old uncle, the way old people— And just a few times lately—I never said anything to you, Alma, because I never thought he really meant it—when I'd be settling him in his chair, get his footstool, he said to me life was getting to be a damn nuisance, he'd be better dead. Well, I tried to josh him out of it, but—"

"I see," said Palliser. "He knew that if he took all those tablets at once it would kill him? The digitalis tablets?"

"Oh, *dear!*" said Mrs. Swift, and burst into tears. "Oh, my dear goodness! Anybody'd know that, wouldn't they? But to *think* of him—poor old Mr. Guilfoyle—getting up in the middle of the night and—"

"That would be Wednesday night," said Palliser. "Did either of you hear anything? Anybody else sleep in the house?"

She shook her head. "He wouldn't *hear* of a nurse—the doctor said—but, to *think*—"

"Well, it seems a rather peculiar thing for him to do," said Grace in his gentle voice. "To go all that way from home to—instead of just quietly taking the overdose after he went to bed. And how did—"

"I thought about that," said Guilfoyle abstractedly. "Since you called —that other officer that is, and—we found it was uncle." He looked up at them earnestly. "You see, he wouldn't have wanted to make any—any unpleasantness in the house. It was one of the things he minded about getting old, having to depend on other people, being a—a care, you know. And he never would ask for help unless he had to—he was, well, considerate like that. You can say that, Alma."

"Oh, dear, that must have been it—yes, he was always so kind—it was just since his first stroke he'd got—a little difficult, and it fretted him so when he couldn't remember things—"

"Well," said Palliser, "but how did he get down here, Mr. Guilfoyle? There wasn't any money on him—"

"Oh, Mr. Wilfrid! Your *car!*" exclaimed Mrs. Swift agitatedly. "Do you—do you think—he *could?*"

"He might have," said Guilfoyle. "My car's missing from the garage at home. In the upset of finding uncle missing, I didn't discover it until—"

"Did he drive?" asked Grace.

"He hadn't in some time—about ten years—but he knew how, of course."

"Did he have access to your keys?"

"Well, I keep a spare set in the drawer of the chest in the front hall. He knew that. I—" Guilfoyle blinked. "I never dreamed he'd—well, how could we? But—"

"What's your car?"

"Oh, it's a Triumph—open sportster. I've got the license plate written down somewhere—"

"Thanks very much, sir, we'll have a look around," said Palliser. "You understand there'll have to be an autopsy."

"Oh, *dear!*" Mrs. Swift subsided into her handkerchief again. "That dear good man—"

A call to Traffic told them that the Triumph registered to Wilfrid Guilfoyle had been towed into the garage this morning after accumulating twenty-four hours' worth of overparking tickets. It had been parked on Park View Street, abutting one side of the park.

Palliser and Grace went down to look at it. It looked perfectly clean, and there was no suicide note left in the glove compartment or on the seat. They called the lab to come and give it a going over.

On the way back upstairs, Grace said, "You know, John—this fantastic thing about Tom. Even if they don't turn up any evidence, which they can't, there'd always be the—implication."

"I know," said Palliser heavily. "I saw that too. Damn it, Jase, the frame sounds just as fantastic—but what else could it be? They say everybody has a double, but coincidence I swallow just so far—a double for Tom showing up right here, out of the blue?"

"But a frame—" Grace was silent, brushing at his moustache. As the elevator started up he added, "But I really did not take to Wilfrid with his precious silk scarf."

"Neither did I, with bells on," said Palliser.

Mendoza had come back to the office while they were still downstairs, and asked if Hackett or Higgins had called in. "Nope," said Lake. Mendoza looked annoyed.

Five minutes later he was sitting at his desk neatly stacking the deck of cards and dealing himself a crooked poker hand when the phone buzzed at him. Lake said economically, "Tom." Mendoza picked up the outside phone.

"How're you doing, Tom?"

"Not so hot," said Landers. "I've been trying to think—what you asked me—I didn't get much sleep. But I can't come up with one damned thing. About a frame—that's got to be wild, Lieutenant."

"They were all so very damned—pat," said Mendoza. "Which is what put it in my mind. Sure, that's him—and coming out, excuse me, with the one salient point of your description which would be the first point anybody—" He had balanced the phone on his shoulder, was shuffling the deck: an honest shuffle this time, just to keep his hands busy on the cards. He always thought better with the cards in his hands.

"But it doesn't add," said Landers. "Look, Lieutenant. The only office I've been in, since getting into plainclothes, is Homicide. Not that that says anything, any department operates the same way. You said, a frame—somebody with a grudge on me. And, sometimes a very damn small motive will trigger a thing like that. And I guess you're right. But, how could any motive, damn what it might be, be aimed at me personally? Sure, we go doing the legwork alone, we've never got enough men —but on a charge, on questioning witnesses, there's always at least two of us on it. Isn't there?"

Mendoza's hands paused on the cards, ready to start dealing a hand. "¡Demonios!" he said to himself. "And of course you're quite right. Me, the veteran the damn press is so fond of calling me—missing the trees for the wood. But—"

"Even if, for God's sake," said Landers, "you want to hark back to my days riding a black-and-white, it was all in Seventy-seventh and Central divisions where there's two men to a car. If anybody's got a grudge on me from then, he's also got a grudge on twenty men I rode with as partners—or, in Homicide, any man I ever worked a case with, which is all of 'em."

"¡Caramba!" said Mendoza vexedly.

"It's no help, I just thought I'd pass it on. Do you still think—"

"I don't know what I think, Tom. Just that there's got to be an answer, a sane answer, somehow." Mendoza began to deal the honest, random hand of poker.

"Even if they can't find any evidence—just those damned eyewitness identifications—"

"There's an answer, damn it. I'll find it," said Mendoza; and stared at the hand he had dealt himself.

Random chance. Ace, king, queen, knave and ten of hearts. A royal flush.

Good omen? He said, "Don't fuss, *amigo*. Matt would tell you that force-for-good is always active on the side of virtuous men."

Landers laughed rather forlornly. "I don't know that I'm all that virtuous, Lieutenant."

CHAPTER 6

It was nearly noon but Mendoza wasn't thinking about lunch. He had, again following in the footsteps of I.A., seen the pedigrees of Byron and Dunne. Byron's only relative was an uncle in Camarillo; Dunne had a family, over in Boyle Heights.

Mendoza went to see whoever was home. He found a slatternly middle-aged woman who told him at length it was just misery and grief, try to raise kids, no thanks from them you get, and if it wasn't the damn kids bringing the fuzz down on a respectable woman it was the old man. "Lyin' in there right now drunk again, and more fool me to stick around atall."

He found, a little more to the point, Rodney Dunne's kid brother Jerry, who already had a pedigree started at seventeen. Auto theft, shoplifting. Jerry answered questions sullenly. Yeah, he'd known a little about that job Rod was on, heisting shorts for a ring of some kind. Easy money. Rod never said no names, the guys running it, only that the top guy looked sorta mean.

"The top guy. He said there was more than one?"

"Yeah. I guess. First he thought it was just the one guy and then another one showed, like he was in it with the other one."

And just why he'd wasted time getting that— Mendoza swore, heading the Ferrari back for North Broadway. The vague thought had just crossed his mind, if it was a frame, had there been a second man in that racket at all? Really?

If Durfee and Rosso had known the ring was fingered—or was going to be fingered— Or if somebody else had fixed Horace to finger it— Conceivably the frame (given somebody with the grudge on Landers) had been a bonus: side money.

It was something to think about.

* * *

Landers hadn't started to think about lunch when a Sergeant Slaney of I.A. came to fetch him in for another bout of questioning. They rode all the way down to headquarters in silence, Landers in the back seat. By the time the car turned into the parking lot Landers was burning with resentment. The damn I.A. men seemed to have turned the phrase around: guilty until proved innocent.

Upstairs, Southey and Macklin wasted no time on the formalities. They sat him down in a chair, the inevitable uniformed man taking notes, and Southey held out his hand palm up. "Your key?" he asked conversationally.

Landers stared at the key on the square palm. It was a long, thin, flat key, silvered metal. "No," he said. "That looks like— No, it's not mine."

"That's funny," said Macklin. "It was on the shelf in the closet of your bedroom, Landers."

Landers said flatly, "That's impossible. I never saw it before. I don't—"

"You told us," said Southey, "that you don't rent a safe-deposit box."

"No, I don't. I don't need one, why would I? I don't have any valuables to—"

"Such as cash," said Macklin. "You say this isn't your key. Then what was it doing in your bedroom closet?"

"I never saw it before," said Landers, feeling confused. "I don't know how it could be. I don't—"

"On the closet shelf," said Southey. Landers looked from one to the other of them—Macklin big, broad-shouldered, dark, Southey slighter with a thin face and very shrewd blue eyes. "There wasn't anything else on the shelf except a Colt .22 revolver and some ammo for it. In a box."

"That's all I thought was on the shelf," said Landers. "I use that sometimes when I go home—target practice, my father's got a gallery in the basem—"

"Your home's in Fresno?"

"Yes—no, I live here. My parents live in Fresno. I—"

"Your father's a veterinary surgeon with his own hospital there. And your sister, Mrs. Jean Kelvey, also lives in Fresno."

"Yes." God, if they'd been nosing around up there—upsetting the family—

"And you don't know anything about this key?"

"No, I don't. You ransacked the place," said Landers, "so you know
—or ought to guess—that I don't use that shelf in the closet, damn it. I
don't own a hat, and I've got nothing to put there, no reason to use it. I
stashed the extra gun there because it was out of the way."

"You ever have a nickname?" asked Macklin.

"Not that I remember." And as he said that, a funny vague memory
stabbed him: there had been a name, a funny pet name, his mother had
used to say in fun when he was very small, but he couldn't remember
what it was.

"Never been called Speedy?"

"No, for God's sake. Why would I be?"

"People pick up some funny nicknames sometimes, that's all. This
key—"

"I never saw it before."

But he knew what that damned key was: the key to a safe-deposit
box in a bank vault. Mendoza said, a frame: had it been carried that
far, had that key been planted on him? What possible reason anyone
could have—

When they finally told him he could go, he had to take a bus back to
Hollywood. He collected the Corvair and went out to the nearest coffee
shop for lunch.

Lieutenant Robert Southey felt academically sorry for Landers.
Those positive identifications were not evidence, of course; it remained
to be seen whether any solid evidence would show up. Macklin liked
the key; Southey, thinking all round the thing, didn't much. It didn't
strike him as a very likely place to keep a single key, not even on a
chain: a key you might be using rather often. The key had been pushed
way to the back of that shelf, where even a man as tall as Landers
would need a kitchen stool or ladder to reach it.

Landers' Corvair wasn't in the apartment lot or in front. (He had
finished paying for it a year ago, they knew now; he wasn't in the habit
of running up bills, and at the moment he didn't owe anybody anything;
and he hadn't been throwing any cash around.) Southey rang the bell of
the first right front apartment where the manageress lived. This was one
of the first apartments that had gone up on Fountain Avenue, twelve or
fifteen years back, when the new modern ones began to be built. Scattered along here still were the old shabby garden-courts, the equally
shabby four-family places dotting this long narrow street that snaked
through Hollywood; but this was a newer Spanish-style building.

"Oh, it's you again," said Mrs. Burgess. They'd showed her the search warrant yesterday, and she didn't much like them.

"Just a few more questions," said Southey. "You told us that Landers has lived here for nearly ten years?"

"That's right."

"That must be nearly as long as this place has been up."

"It was built in nineteen fifty-seven," she said shortly. "I've been here since it opened."

"So you can tell me who rented that apartment before Landers."

"Well, what on earth you want to know that for—I s'pose I can look. I keep records." She didn't ask him in. He waited on the step until she came back and said, "I remember him now—Mr. Kenneth Lowry. He was here about two years. Just like Mr. Landers, nice quiet young man, no trouble, rent on the dot. He worked at a theater somewhere, he ran that projection machine, they call it. He left when he got married."

Southey thanked her and went back to his car. He met Captain Macklin for lunch at an unobtrusive bar and grill out on Third that specialized in steaks. Macklin was a teetotaller and already halfway through a T-bone; Southey ordered one to match and a Scotch-and-water first.

"Foley came in just after you left," said Macklin. "It's a model the Security-Pacific banks use for safe-deposit boxes. He left a copy with them, they'll try to trace it for us. Hell of a job."

"There may be a shortcut," said Southey. "All right, he's lived there ten years—we could see he doesn't use that shelf. Bachelor living alone—it was damn dusty. As if nobody'd been near it in weeks. That key could have been left there, by accident or loss, by another tenant years ago. I know you're supposed to turn 'em in when you give up the safe-deposit box. People don't always bother, and anybody can lose a key. Anyway, I got the name of the tenant before. He was a projectionist—may still be—if so, we can probably trace him through the union."

"I can hope you're right," said Macklin. "Landers has got a very clean record. I'd hate like hell to find out he's gone wrong. But how do we get round those damned positive identifications, Bob?"

Southey shook his head. "I've got no ideas on that," he said soberly.

There wasn't much Palliser and Grace could do about the Guilfoyle thing until they got the autopsy report and a lab report on the car. They had by default gone back to Luisa Fantini; both of them thinking about Landers but not mentioning that.

Since they hadn't been in on the Fantini thing at the beginning, after lunch they went back to the office and looked at the first reports Landers had written and the lab photographs of the corpse *in situ.*

One thing struck them both at once. "What was she doing in the theater like that?" asked Palliser. "She was supposed to meet Silverman at seven-thirty, and it looks as if she was all dressed up for that." The photographs of the sprawled slender body on the dusty thin old carpet of the theater aisle showed it wearing a black-lace-and-chiffon evening gown, low cut front and back. The gown had crumpled around her where she fell, pulled up to show twisted slim legs in sheer smoke-gray stockings, high-heeled black patent pumps. A little velvet clutch-bag lay near the body.

Palliser rummaged and came up with the list: contents of bag, comb, powder puff, costume gold compact containing such-and-thus brand of face powder, neutral-beige tone, one brand-name lipstick labeled True Persimmon, one ten-dollar bill. Jewelry from body, one costume pearl necklace, value about three bucks, one ditto pearl ring, one costume gold bracelet, one pair pearl stud earrings.

"She was all dressed for her date," said Palliser. "A seven-thirty date. By the autopsy she didn't go over that balcony until eight or later. And come to think, what brought her to the theater that night? From what we've heard, she'd walked off the job. She'd have got dressed in her room, wouldn't she?"

Grace brushed his moustache. "Funny, all right. But she was a good-looking girl, John. Probably attracted men like flies. Jealous boy-friend? You said Wagner sounded on the level. Sympathetic, as he said. She'd found the high-class john, good luck to her. But—"

"So he did. She hadn't been here very long, if she bought that suitcase in Bakersfield not more than a month back. Of course the jealous boy-friend could have followed her. Wagner said she told him, from somewhere around San José. There's no tracing her back on that—too vague."

"Um," said Grace. "But what was she doing in the theater that late? Nothing in Tom's reports on that?"

"Not a damn thing. Of course we've found out all this since. I think we go talk to Hernandez again."

They found Hernandez in the manager's office at the theater; it was just open, at two o'clock. Another girl than Annie Sanchez was in the ticket-booth, which they ought to have known; Annie had told them she had a regular job.

"Well, I thought it was a little funny myself," said Hernandez. "I told one of the policemen that—I think I did. I think one of the men that come first, in the car, but I couldn't swear— She hadn't come in the night before, see. To work. This Fantini girl. I asked Annie if she'd said anything to her, but she hadn't. So I figured she'd just walked off the job. These girls. I don't bother with another one—just the girls to sell tickets. It's not worth it. And then next morning, I come in like usual, place all dark, the house I mean, but the lights on in the lobby so's I can see my way, I spot something down there—so I look, and there she is. My God, dead. And all dressed up like for a party. I couldn't figure it. I don't figure it now."

They exchanged exasperated glances. The flustered Hernandez, babbling that to a uniformed man who had probably said, Save it for the detectives; and no detective hearing it at all.

And it looked all the funnier, of course.

They said they wanted to talk to the girl selling tickets. "So go ahead, so long as you don't stop her taking the money. She wouldn't know nothing, she never laid eyes on the Fantini girl, far's I know."

But she had. Her name was Nita Valdez and she was a very young seventeen, in her first job and conscientious. She was a nice girl, respectful to police officers, and she said to them in a soft, frightened voice, "I wondered if maybe I ought to tell. Mr. Hernandez or somebody. Because it was so terrible—poor, poor Luisa, an awful sad life she had, and to die like that—it was awful, wasn't it?"

"You knew her?" asked Palliser.

It all came out in her gaspy little voice. Luisa had come round to the theater one afternoon, just after she'd started to work there Nita guessed, and said who she was so Nita'd let her in. She said she'd left her compact in the ladies' room that time—but, they could read between the lines, Nita naively worshiping the glamorous Luisa, the credulous admirer, and Luisa would have basked in that. Enjoyed telling the dramatic tale and getting the sympathy, the admiration.

"It was just awful," said Nita. "She hadn't any mother or father, just this awful old uncle who beat her and made her work like a slave—and he didn't give her enough to eat either. What? Oh, it was a farm someplace over by El Centro, I seem to— But she was so brave, you know, she ran away from him, but she didn't have any money and—and she met this man and she thought he was going to give her a job, but it turned out he was"—Nita blushed—"you know, he wanted her to do bad things—and she ran away from him too, and finally she got here and—"

"That's interesting," said Palliser. Luisa had told fancy stories.

"And she was *nice* to me—she was just so nice, like a—like a princess, she was so beautiful—and I guess she saw I liked her—and I didn't think anything about it only then—" suddenly Nita started to cry. "I thought—maybe I ought to tell—"

"About what? Nobody's going to do anything to you, miss," said Grace softly. "She wanted to go in the theater daytimes? Why?"

"Oh—oh—oh!" sobbed Nita. "She said—she said the people where she had a room weren't honest—and there wasn't a good lock—and she was afraid they'd steal—and she had a—a—a hiding place inside the theater—oh—oh—oh—"

Palliser and Grace looked at each other. "For what, Nita?" asked Palliser. "What did she have to hide that was worth stealing?" The remnants of a wad of cash?

"I—don't—know," wailed Nita.

"Or where the hiding place was?"

She just sobbed, shaking her head.

"So, a little work to do," said Grace sadly. It was a good-sized theater. There was no point in turning the current customers out, starting a search now. Anybody might have stumbled on Luisa's cache in the five days since her death; or she might have cleaned out whatever was there. Or, of course, her killer might have taken it. But just in case, they would look. Tomorrow morning when the theater was closed.

"Rope the lab in on it," said Palliser tiredly. He didn't think Luisa Fantini was any great loss. But it was Homicide's business to work the cases, whoever the victims had been.

Hackett and Higgins had spent a completely profitless day looking for Al Durfee. It was, they agreed, adding insult to injury that wherever they went, both Auto Theft and I.A. had been before them. "Oh, more cops," the owner of Dick's pool hall on the corner up from that garage had said. "Tell you whatever I can, like I told the other cops, but I don't know much about him."

Durfee had come in there sometimes for lunch, to play a few games with anybody else in. Everybody had thought the garage was a legit business. Durfee seemed like a nice enough guy.

They tried all the likely places near the garage, where Durfee might have been known, and then they split up with the short list of Durfee's known pals listed in his pedigree. They met at Federico's at one-thirty for lunch and compared notes. They had only found two of the pals, both also with pedigrees, both on parole, and both of them claimed not to have laid eyes on Durfee in weeks.

"But I heard this and that," said Higgins, after a preliminary swallow of his drink. "Durfee's a gambler—"

"I heard the same thing," said Hackett. "And according to this guy, anything goes with him—the ponies, poker, whole works. And what's that worth in locating him, George? He's long gone, if you ask me. Either he was tipped off about the raid or lucky in not walking into it— he's on the run, and God knows which direction."

"By what we've heard," said Higgins, "that ring was operating for months. They must have been taking a nice piece of change out of it, Art. Maybe it was burning a hole in Durfee's pocket."

"Oh," said Hackett. "Vegas?"

Higgins shrugged. "Or Reno—Mexico City. Do no harm to ask 'em to take a look around for him. And what do you bet Auto Theft and I.A. both already have?"

"Well, just in case they haven't, we will. Meanwhile, I suppose we go on making bricks without straw, to convince Luis we're earning our keep."

"Is that one of his for-real hunches—the frame?"

"I don't think so. It's—the wrong shape for a frame," said Hackett. "Or—I don't know . . . He's going to get himself in trouble with I.A., if he goes on horning in like this."

"That won't worry him," said Higgins amusedly. "Point is, he's going to get all of us in trouble too."

"And I can't say that'd worry me," said Hackett, "if we turn up something to get Tom out of trouble."

After lunch they went, as the only place left to go, to the place on Second Street where Durfee had rented a room. Either Auto Theft or I.A. had put a seal on the room door; that couldn't be helped, but it was annoying. No knowing what had been in the room, leads to Durfee's other pals, whatever. At least they did know he wasn't driving his own car: the Ford registered to him had been in the garage. They talked to the woman who owned the house, Mrs. Blessing, a fat benevolent-eyed old lady who said, "Oh, you're policemen too. About poor Mr. Durfee. Seems like he was just born to trouble, that man."

That was one way to look at it. "When did you see him last, Mrs. Blessing?" asked Hackett.

"Why, let's see, it was sometime on Thursday afternoon. I was out at the side watering the roses when he come out with a suitcase, but I didn't pay much mind to that, just thought he was going off for the weekend like he's done before. Then when the other policemen came— my, my, the things that poor man gets led into!" She looked at Hackett. "You put me in mind of my boy, sir—he's a big one like you, takes after his dad, and nice blue eyes like yours too. That first policeman come askin' questions"—she sniffed—"I sort of took against him, some reason. Real abrupt-like he was—" That would be Van Allen all right, thought both Hackett and Higgins—"and I figured, he's so interested in poor Mr. Durfee, let him go look how he pleases. Putting a great big wax seal on that door! As if to say I'd go snooping in other folks' things! But you been real polite. Why don't you go see Mis' Durfee?"

"What? His wife?"

"Well, ex. But she's a nice lady, she feels sorry for him, getting in trouble all the time. It was when they split up and he moved in here, she come to me and says, now you just let me know, he gets to hittin' the bottle or in some fix, see? And I said I would. Once or twice, last year, he got behind on the rent and I called her and she come right around and paid me. You like to go see her?"

"Er—yes, ma'am, we would," said Higgins. "You didn't mention this to the other officers?"

"I did not. Let 'em find her theirselves, they want. But I'll tell you. She's right over on Grattan Street. Mrs. Alice May Durfee. I even got her phone number," said Mrs. Blessing, beaming at Hackett.

In the Barracuda, Higgins said, "Just like the moral maxims say, Art, politeness does pay off."

Hackett smiled fondly on the slip of paper with Alice May's address. "At least we've stolen a march on I.A."

Mendoza got home in the twilight, to the usual uproar just increased by Cedric in the back yard barking at the alder tree and the mockingbird madly using the remaining light to carry twigs nestward, breaking off to dive-bomb Cedric. Inside, the twins were bathed, powdered, and pajamaed, and descended on Daddy like twin hurricanes, clamoring to be read to.

"¡El Gato! ¡El Gato, Daddy! Read los cuentos 'bout El Gato and—and—and El Rinoceronte!" Johnny clutched his tie.

"¡No Rinoceronte! ¡El elefante pequeño!" Terry yanked on his collar excitedly.

"¡Bastante!" said Mendoza. "Quiet! Let go of me, monstruosos, or I'll have no breath to read anything! ¡No me molesten!"

Alison and Mrs. MacTaggart hastened to the rescue, tripping over cats. "Now Daddy's tired, let him have his dinner in peace—¿comprenden? Be good now—you can have los cuentos after a while—"

"And the man will be needing a drink to whet his appetite—" Mrs. MacTaggart hurried to the kitchen, hotly pursued by El Señor intent on his drink of rye.

"I thought you said something," said Mendoza to Alison over breaded veal chops, creamed potatoes, and Mrs. MacTaggart's special scones with her own jam, "about using one language or the other until they learn the difference."

"Don't nitpick," said Alison. "After the day we've had, with that damned mockingbird—and the twins watching his every move, and Cedric convinced he's a burglar and barking at him—¡Dios!" She smoothed her hair absently. After six months of letting it grow, she'd got impatient coping with it, and these days looked like the Alison he'd first known, the red hair in a short feathery cut, and very becoming too. She was, for once, wearing the two-carat solitaire diamond earrings he'd given her for her birthday last August. He reflected a little ruefully that it took some time for the people—like both of them—who'd grown up minus much money, to get used to having it. . . .

But with *los cuentos* duly read and the twins hopefully drifting to sleep, he paced the living room worrying about Landers. "It's a bastard," he said. "Damned if you do, damned if you don't. So I.A. doesn't come up with any evidence, there are still those damned identifications. All right, so pat, so glib, but—there."

"And what do they say?" asked Alison tartly, looking up from where she was rubbing El Señor's shamelessly exposed fat stomach. "You're not thinking simply enough, *amado*."

"*¿Qué es esto?*"

"The trappings," said Alison. El Señor uttered a querulous comment; he liked his stomach massaged, the harder the better. "This Horace—he takes a glance at Landers, and there's some superficial resemblance to this crook, so Horace comes out with that, so they picked him up too. And comes the reaction, and at second glance Horace sees it isn't the crook, but it is a cop. And he's naturally pleased to get a cop in trouble, so he goes on saying it is too this crook."

"And I wish it was just so simple," said Mendoza. "The flaw in that reasoning, my love, is that there are also Dunne and Byron. And Horace was very much incommunicado until after they'd made the positive identification too."

"Oh," said Alison. "Oh. I didn't— I see what you mean."

Higgins went home and with an effort paid attention to his second-hand family, Bert Dwyer's kids. Laura had a new piano piece to play for him, and Stevie—now with the brace off and the limp almost gone—had just finished *The Man Without a Country* and was enthusiastic about it.

"Gee, that's an awfully great book, isn't it, George? You ever read it? I'm going to ask the teacher if I can do a report on it instead of that awful old thing she gave me."

"It's a good book, Steve."

"You know I just can't hardly wait, George," said Laura. "For the baby. It's a whole four and a half months more, Mother said. Before we'll *know*—I mean, if it's David George or Margaret Emily."

"I know, Laurie. It won't matter really."

And after dinner, with the kids settled down to homework, Mary's gray eyes on him. "You're fussing about this thing."

"Damn it," said Higgins, "can I help it? If they don't turn up any evidence—still the damn implication, on his record. Luis saying, a frame. I wonder. If Durfee didn't know they were fingered—and what the hell his ex-wife might give us, if we do find her—"

"Since a couple of months ago, George," said Mary tranquilly, "when you got away from those three toughs with nothing worse than a cold, I've been convinced that just lately Providence is being a little more alert about looking after the good guys. Something will turn up."

"And I hope to God you're right," said Higgins.

Hackett went home, to Angel concocting a new recipe, and four-year-old Mark imitating a jet plane, and his darling Sheila, these days navigating somewhat less like a candidate for A.A., and worried aloud about Landers. "Luis saying a frame—it doesn't smell that way to me. Like Palliser said, how could Horace come out so damn spontaneous— but what else could it be, for God's sake?"

Angel gave him a quick glance, her mountain-pool eyes sympathetic, and said briskly, "Don't bring the office home, Art. Have you weighed today?"

"I'm down three pounds," said Hackett gloomily.

"Well, maybe some benefit to worry," said Angel. "Don't pull pussy's tail, Mark! Now, if he's innocent, surely something'll turn up to say so—"

"And I hope to God you're right," said Hackett.

Phil had called Landers at six o'clock. "It's very forward of me," she said coolly, "but I think you need cheering up. I could bear to be taken to dinner."

He took her to the Frascati's out on Sunset. He told her about his latest session with I.A. "This damn key," he said. "I never *saw* it before. *I* don't know where it came from. Shelf in my closet, they said—of all the damned things, I never use it for anything, but don't I know how they read that! The damn key could have been there since I moved in, but they'll say, well, I've lived there ten years, how could I have missed it?"

She had made him drink a double Scotch. She looked at him consideringly there opposite her, at one of the outdoor tables on the terrace. She was slim and neat in a sleeveless blue cotton dress with a full skirt, little pearl earrings, high-heeled white sandals. She said, "You said you've got a sister. Any cousins?"

"What?" asked Landers, surprised. "Well, a couple. Why?"

"Nothing really," said Phil. "That key—you know, I think that Lieutenant of yours is all wrong. I don't think it's a frame at all, Tom."

"What? It sounds crazy, sure, but when the Lieutenant said—"

"Mmh," said Phil. "The great Mendoza. With his crystal ball. I've heard. Even geniuses have off days." She sipped her martini; the waiter came up and she said she'd have the herb omelette, please. Landers ordered a steak without consulting the menu. "My vacation starts tomorrow," said Phil.

"Oh. Yes. You—going anywhere?" asked Landers with an effort.

"I don't know. I think so," said Phil absently. "I rather think I am . . . I've just got a new car, did I tell you?"

CHAPTER 7

Landers had called Mendoza overnight and told him about that damned key. "When I got home last night, Mrs. Burgess came over—the manageress. She said one of the same men who searched the place had come asking about the last tenant. But my God, that'd be ten years back, Lieutenant—how could—"

"And who was it?" asked Mendoza.

Landers told him. Looking at the scribbled note on his desk, on Saturday morning, Mendoza thought about those so-careful and thorough I.A. men. They had this key linked to Landers, and they were going to follow that up through every channel, checking back with the banks—the banks just as precise and a damned lot slower—and only after every avenue had been explored would they possibly start to think about another explanation.

Mendoza thought it might be helpful to take a little shortcut here.

This and that had turned up overnight: reports on his desk. A prostitute strangled over on Temple, probably by a customer. A knifing in a bar on Main. A new unidentified body on the Row. He shoved the reports aside and hauled out the five telephone directories. Various people liked to accuse him of having the tortuous mind: once in a while it went somewhere more directly.

In ten years, of course, Kenneth Lowry might have moved to New York, or died. It was just worth a first cast.

There were nine Kenneth Lowrys and fourteen K. Lowrys in the phone books. Mendoza started phoning. He had only the one question to ask; it wouldn't take long. Hackett looked in, and Higgins, and then Palliser; he waved them off impatiently.

He found the right Kenneth Lowry on the nineteenth try, at an address in Seal Beach. Rather he found Mrs. Lowry, who said yes where everybody else had said no. She also asked questions, but reluctantly told him where to locate Lowry—the Drury Art Studio in Long Beach.

Mendoza got his hat and told Rory Farrell, sitting in for Lake, that he probably wouldn't be back that morning.

On the way down on the freeway he wondered whether the Drury Art Studio produced real pornography or plain nudes. It turned out to be a prosaic project of conservationists which turned out nature studies and wild-life documentaries. Kenneth Lowry, in his mid-thirties, balding, with myopic eyes behind horn rims, was very surprised to see him.

Mendoza took shortcuts. "The apartment on Fountain Avenue. Before you were married, Mr. Lowry."

"That's a while back," said Lowry. "We've got three kids now. What about it?"

"Did you rent a safe-deposit box at a bank then?"

"What *is* all this about?" asked Lowry. "Police—well, it's beyond me why you're asking but I'll play. No, I didn't. I didn't have any reason to. But—"

"But?"

"Well, for God's sake, talk about ancient history," said Lowry. "I had a key to my father's box. We both had access to it, that is. Yes, then—when I lived there."

"Still have it?"

"No. Dad died just after Ruth and I were married."

"What happened to the key?"

"I—" Lowry stopped. "Well, I hadn't remembered that till just now. There was the usual red tape to go through—probate and so on—a seal on the box. I didn't keep it on, we weren't living in Hollywood. But when they asked for the keys back, I could only find Dad's."

"Yes," said Mendoza. "So you could. You kept it separate from your other keys. A key you didn't use often."

"I don't think I ever did use it—it was just a—a convenience, in case Dad was sick. Yes—"

"What did you keep on the closet shelf in that apartment, Mr. Lowry?"

"What?" Lowry looked confused. "Why—how should I remember?—oh, I guess I'd stash summer things there in winter, and—"

"Yes." Let I.A. get all the details. Eventually the bank would identify the key. Save I.A. some time and effort. "I'm sorry, Mr. Lowry, but I'll have to ask you to come back to headquarters and make a statement."

"What? What in God's name is all this? Look, we're *busy*, we're just cutting this thing—"

"I'm very sorry," said Mendoza. "This is important too, Mr. Lowry. You're a good citizen—all we can do is apologize for asking you. But a man's career is—mmh—in danger."

"Oh, hell," said Lowry, shrugging. "Be kind of interesting to see the inside of that place up there, at that."

He didn't see much of it. Mendoza took him up to the Internal Affairs office and marched him in on Lieutenant Southey while the uniformed sergeant in the anteroom protested. "All right, Southey," he said briskly, "here's a shortcut for you. Mr. Kenneth Lowry, former tenant of Landers' apartment. That safe-deposit key you turned up probably belonged to his late father's safe-deposit box, and between you and the bank you can sort it out and identify it. Thus unlinking Landers with the key."

"Look here," said Southey angrily, "what do you think you're up to, Mendoza, interfering with this investigation? You've got no business—"

"Why, I'm just being neighborly and helping you boys out a little," said Mendoza.

"Damn it, you're interfering and it's a breach of regulations as you damn well know!" said Southey. Macklin came in the open door wearing a scowl; he had obviously heard that exchange.

"If you want to get included in this investigation we can oblige you, Mendoza. You know you're to keep strictly hands off on I.A. matters—"

"And you don't know me well enough, Macklin, to know that I don't sit and twiddle my thumbs when one of my men is in trouble!" said Mendoza hardly.

Southey opened his mouth, shut it, and said, "Sergeant."

"Sir."

"Would you—er—take the witness out, please. If you'll just wait a few minutes, Mr. Lowry— So, you're implying that we'd try to railroad a man, Mendoza? You're accusing us of bias and covering up evidence, by God? That charge we can take right to the top—and I've heard this and that about you stepping outside the rules too—" They were both glaring at him.

"Now let's stop calling names," said Mendoza with a thin smile. "I'm not accusing you of one damned thing. All I'm saying to you, and occasionally the fact needs underlining, is that you watchdogs are so damn chary of showing any bias, you tend to lean over backward to avoid bias toward the cops. May be salutary in a general way. You're not going to tell me that you were even thinking about former tenants until you'd bloodhounded that damn key back to the factory that made it. So I took a shortcut for you. There's Lowry to unlink Landers with the key —use him." He turned on his heel. "You needn't bother to say thanks."

"I wasn't planning to," said Southey. "And you can damn well keep your nose out of this from now on, Mendoza!"

"Just until I find you dragging your heels again, *amigo*," said Mendoza. He went down to his own office and called Landers to tell him the key had got itself explained away. "Where is everybody?" he asked Farrell.

"Palliser and Jase took everybody someplace to search a theater," said Farrell.

"*¿Cómo?* What the hell's all that about?" Mendoza hadn't seen Palliser's overnight report.

"I couldn't say," said Farrell comfortably. "They had a warrant, and I think they turned out some lab men too."

"*¿Y después?*" said Mendoza. "What next?" He started to read reports.

It wasn't, as theaters went, a large one, but as a place to be searched there was a lot of it: some thirty-five rows of seats on the main floor, divided into three sections by two aisles, and the main lobby, offices and cubbyholes and cupboards, the area behind the curtain and screen. And they hadn't any idea of what they were looking for.

"We know she told whoppers," said Grace at the outset. "This could be just another one, John. A hiding place in the theater—I ask you! What kind of valuables could she have had? All right, that little strip of bank paper, the thousand bucks cash. Luisa wasn't an idiot—she wouldn't hide that in here, instead of stashing it in her handbag to keep an eye on it. And no sign of cash, maybe she'd spent it all."

"It doesn't sound very likely, the rigmarole you said she gave Wagner and then this Nita," contributed Higgins dubiously.

"Then why did she want to get into the theater at odd times?" said Palliser. "I know it sounds silly, but this isn't such a hot part of town, George. If she had something valuable, she just might have found a handy cache for it somewhere here—and checked up on it now and then."

"So we go wild-goose hunting," said Piggott. "Well, it's more interesting than all the boring legwork on Katz. Where do we start?"

Nobody had any ideas on that. "Check the ladies' room first," suggested Palliser; but that proved to be fruitless. It was a bare tiled place, three toilet-cubicles, no possible hiding place. They fanned out into the theater, starting with the front row of seats.

"Wild goose you can say," said Grace to Palliser. "She wouldn't have dared leave anything—like what?—in the body of the theater. A public place, people coming in, fiddling around with the seats—"

But they looked. With the house lights all on, Hernandez watching interestedly. They looked everywhere there was to look, and turned up a lot of dust and nothing else. Hernandez told them the place was swept out twice a week. "People are pigs," he said. "The things the janitors find—" But there certainly weren't any valuables anywhere here now.

Palliser took time out for a cigarette and Higgins came to join him. "As if we needed any more exercise," he said.

"Wait a minute," said Palliser. "The balcony—she was up in the balcony. Late for her date."

"So you said."

"She was going to move into Silverman's motel—probably the next day. She hadn't packed her clothes yet. But she had apparently walked off this piddling job. Hadn't come to work. Had she come here to pick up what she'd cached away? Maybe followed by X? And anyway—if she did have a hiding place here, it seems more logical it might have been up in the balcony. I wouldn't think many customers here use it."

"You're right," said Hernandez promptly. "We don't get a full house often. Kids wanting to neck pick the last row of seats."

"So let's try the balcony." They moved the hunt up there, and went on training flashlights under seats, turning up seats, for some time without finding anything.

"She wouldn't have taken the risk," Grace was saying again, when one of the lab men stood up and his flashlight swung an arc around, up the wall, before he snapped it off.

"Hold it!" said Palliser sharply. "Hold—we're damn fools. The balcony was searched after she was found—"

"Well, we looked around," said Scarne, "sure. But—"

"That door's got to be left unlocked by law." Palliser went over to it: the door leading to the fire escape. He shoved the heavy bar down, the door opened, and sunlight streamed in. They looked, the lab men crowding up.

A little steel platform, and the stairs going down to the right. And lying on the platform just outside the door, a cardboard box: a shoebox. Palliser bent and looked at it. "That won't take prints," said Scarne. Palliser bent to pick it up; it resisted, and he found that it had been bound with twine to the open steel strip of the landing. He cut the twine carefully, preserving the knot, and straightened. He took the box top off.

Something had been Scotch-taped to the bottom of the box, and violently pulled away. While he contemplated what was left, Higgins took the box top.

"McKellar's Fine Shoes, Lompoc, California. So both the tales she told were phony."

"Yes," said Palliser absently. A piece of Scotch tape, in the bottom of the box, still held a good-sized piece of brown paper— "Manila envelope," he said. He worked the tape loose.

Caught inside the wedge that had been a corner of an envelope were two more triangular bits of paper. One was tinged faintly pink and showed part of a rather fancy engraved border. The other was stiffer paper, heavy and thick, and bore an ornate letter T in black print.

They stared at the pieces. Higgins said, "You know something? I think that pink thing could be a corner torn off the pink slip on a car."

"But what the hell?" said Palliser blankly. "Luisa's valuables? And somebody killed her for them?"

"Whatever they were," said Grace.

Hackett had been feeling—he had cast around for a word and come up with one. Redundant, he thought. This Hatfield thing. It was there, it had to be looked at; and it was annoying in at least two ways. First, there was Landers; they were all a lot more concerned about Landers than anything else, though (and that was annoying too) they had to keep hands off and let I.A. do the investigating. Though if an idea occurred to Mendoza about where to look, that wasn't going to stop him. Second, the Hatfield thing was annoying because it was so meaningless— so shapeless.

Hackett had gone back over ground Sergeant Barth and the men at Wilcox Street had already covered, looking for something overlooked, and had found nothing. Luis had said, what about the Hatfields' grown-up children?—these days, kids getting into bad company, something like that—but that had been off the top of his mind. If he hadn't been thinking about Landers, he'd have known that Barth would have covered that.

Barth and his minions had checked everything they could check. The Hatfields' grown-up children were reliable, responsible young people. Catherine's fiancé, Owen Hartigan, had a clean record, would begin practice next year after finishing his internship. Both girls had good reputations; the Hatfields had never disapproved of any boy-friends; both girls were working in apparently congenial jobs among upright people. The boy, John, had a clean record too, and seemed to be a good student at his engineering course.

In a way, of course, thought Hackett, the dog next door made it into a kind of locked-room puzzle. What the evidence of the non-barking dog said (shades of Sherlock Holmes) was that whoever had battered Harriet to death was known to the dog: had visited that house next door before and been admitted freely. At least an acquaintance, if not a friend.

At which point, checking back on all the statements and reports Barth had turned over, Hackett had a sudden brain-wave. With his mind half on Landers, he had been idly thinking back over cases they had all worked together, and quite suddenly remembered that messy one—the child murders—and heard an echo of Mendoza's voice talking about the familiar strangers. Really strangers but not thought of as such by many children—or adults.

He sat back and lit a cigarette and thought. Laundry truck drivers. Bakery trucks. Fuller Brush men? Milkmen? In neighborhoods like that, the milkmen might come round to collect at civilized times of day —or did they? Anyway, someone like that was possible. A familiar figure, known, coming to the house on legitimate occasions, so the dog not barking.

Grasping at straws, he thought. He went out to the Barracuda in the lot, got on the freeway and drove up to Castaic Drive in Nichols Canyon.

Hatfield wasn't at home, presumably still busy over Hollywood Girl Cosmetics' new fall line. Everybody else was: the boy home for the weekend. Harriet had been buried at Forest Lawn nearly ten days ago.

"It isn't that we can blame you for—not finding out," said Catherine rather bleakly. She had ink on her fingers, a smear on her chin; she wore a smart blue smock over blue slacks. She wanted to be a designer, he remembered. A very pretty girl, in an unusual way: so dark, and oddly Slavic flat-planed cheeks. "I know it can't be—simple."

The other girl was dressed to go out; she excused herself in a thin voice when the doorbell chimed. A clean-cut young fellow appeared, shaking hands with John, respectful to Hackett; a terrible thing to happen, he said earnestly, Mrs. Hatfield such a nice person.

When they had left, John Hatfield said to Hackett, "Of course you don't get over a thing like this—just so soon." He shook his head. "You come home and—just without thinking—you expect Mother to be there like any time. And then you remember."

"Yes, I know," said Hackett. A nice family. And what with the dog next door, no shape to the sudden death striking here. "I've got just a few more questions, if you don't mind."

"Anything we can tell you—"

And except for one small thing, he got nothing at all. They didn't send things to a laundry: had a washer and dryer. Mother hadn't bought from a bakery truck, she went to a bakery down on Sunset. She didn't buy things at the door. (Habit, thought Hackett: they hadn't always had money, she'd got into the habit of thrift, and things bought at the door were usually a little more expensive.) She did buy eggs from a man who had his own chicken ranch in the valley, because they were so much better than the eggs at the market. But neither of them knew which day he usually came, once a week.

"But she'd been getting eggs from him for years," said Catherine. "You can't possibly think—"

"Well, I don't know, Miss Hatfield. We just like to check everything," said Hackett. He thought irrelevantly that it was odd how children turned out. Mark probably going to be as big as he was, and luckily Sheila had got Angel's eyes and—but you never knew. If that was a photograph of Harriet Hatfield on the table beside the door, she'd been a nice-looking woman, but only her youngest daughter resembled her at all. Catherine so dark, and the boy square-jawed, sandy-haired—possibly more like the father. "I'd just like to—do you know his name?"

"It's an ordinary name," she said. "Smith—Robertson—no, I don't. But I think Mrs. Brownlee takes eggs from him too, she'd know. But you can't possibly be thinking—"

Hackett thanked her and went down the curving front walk to the street: no sidewalks up here. There was a car in the Brownlees' driveway. He started up that walk, and as he stepped onto the porch the dog barked inside. It was a single amiable bark that said, "Stranger," that was all. Hackett felt unreasonably annoyed at the dog.

Mrs. Brownlee welcomed him in with surprise and pleasure. She was as amiable as the dog, an elderly overfed Dalmatian, who came sniffing at Hackett's shoes wagging his tail. Mrs. Brownlee was a plump blonde with dangly bracelets and rather foolish china-blue eyes, and she told him eagerly that she'd just remembered something. "I don't suppose it could be anything to do with what happened to Mrs. Hatfield—of course that was a burglar or even worse, the terrible people running around these days—but that other officer said it was important to tell you everything we remembered, whether it seemed important or not—because after all you men are *trained* to see what is important—"

"Yes, Mrs. Brownlee. If you could just tell me, I think you buy eggs from—"

"But then I thought twice," she plowed on, "and, well, naturally I don't know anything about criminals, but everybody reads mysteries, don't they, and I should think those authors have to write about things the way they really are—*which* is why I was so glad to see you here again, in fact if you hadn't come I'd just about decided to call and tell you—not you personally I mean but the police—because what I thought was, you see, if it *was* a burglar murdered Mrs. Hatfield, which seems to be the only way it could have been, then it could be she was—the way they say it—*casing the job*." Mrs. Brownlee paused impressively.

"What?" said Hackett. "Who?"

"This woman. I just remembered it yesterday, and I'd thought it was queer at the time, but I never thought it might be important until I got to thinking about it again. Yesterday. And I thought—"

"What woman? If you'd just tell me what you remembered from the beginning," said Hackett patiently.

"Oh, certainly. I couldn't be sure of the day when I first saw her, but it was about three and a half weeks back. And of course I don't know if that was the first time she came. Or how often she did come. Only, I just remembered *that* too, that first time I saw her, Captain didn't bark, so she'd probably been there before. I saw her twice, that's all, and I thought it was a little funny then—Mrs. Hatfield had a woman come to clean, twice a month, but her I know, Mrs. Rawlins, I have her myself and besides she drives a Chevrolet—"

"Mrs. Brownlee, if you'd— What was funny about it?"

"Why, she was walking. She came up the street walking, and we're quite a way up the hill here. Practically everybody's got a car now, don't they? It looked queer, you see—because she wasn't from anywhere around the neighborhood, I'd have seen her before, and she was on foot, and she must have walked all the way up from the boulevard—or farther. There's a bus-stop there," said Mrs. Brownlee vaguely.

And what was this? "You saw her twice. She went to the Hatfields'?"

"Yes, that's right. The first time was about one o'clock, I was watching out for the mail. The next time—oh, it was about a week later, I think, or not quite so much, I was just going out to get my hair done, and I always have a three o'clock appointment so it'd have been about a quarter to. She just rang the bell and Mrs. Hatfield let her in."

"Could you describe her?"

"Oh, let's see now, I'm not very good at that—I didn't see her close to —but I'd guess she was about medium height, and thin—not very well dressed, I just got that *impression*—I couldn't say how old at all. She walked as if she was tired, but my goodness, anybody would be after climbing that hill, walking—"

Hackett regarded her with veiled exasperation. He couldn't imagine what this odd little jigsaw piece might add to the case; it was probably extraneous.

"And it just occurred to me—if it *was* a burglar—that she could have been an accomplice, *casing the joint*," said Mrs. Brownlee, "and so I thought I'd better tell you—"

And so who was Jane Doe? An old acquaintance fallen on hard times, Harriet dispensing private charity? Or—

He thought he would lay the odd jigsaw piece before Luis. But first—

"So I asked Catherine and John," he said to Mendoza, "and they didn't know who it could have been. So I went and asked Hatfield at his office and he didn't know either. So you can ruminate on it and produce a hunch."

"*Extraño*," said Mendoza. "I scarcely think, Arturo, that Jane Doe was a burglar's moll casing the joint."

"Neither do I. But who was she?"

"I haven't the slightest idea," said Mendoza. "For a change, you can try your deductive powers on what the rest of the boys turned up on Luisa Fantini," and he told Hackett about that funny little find.

"A pink slip. Also *extraño*," said Hackett.

"And I think," said Mendoza, making a steeple of his long hands on his desk, "having looked at it, a legal document of some kind. That kind of paper."

"Luisa's valuables," said Hackett, and yawned. "Have we got anywhere on the Katz thing?"

"*En ninguna parte*. I told Matt to shove it in Pending—he and Glasser were looking overworked. At least we've got Tom unlinked from one piece of trouble," and he told Hackett about that.

"And you needn't tell me what names the I.A. boys called you. Are you still thinking, a frame?"

"I don't know," said Mendoza abstractedly. "Damn it, it could be just as simple as Alison said—malicious mischief—get a cop in trouble, fun and games—if only Horace hadn't been incommunicado. . . ." He got up abruptly. "*¿Qué significa eso?*" he said to himself. "There was that time Tom had his pocket picked and the stupid jailers wouldn't believe he was a cop. Yes, making assurance doubly sure. I suppose you can find something to do, Arturo. I'm going down to the jail."

* * *

What Hackett found to do was more follow-up on yesterday's little break. He ran into Higgins doing the same thing.

They had heard about Alice May Durfee, the sympathetic ex-wife who had kept tabs on former hubby, from Mrs. Blessing, yesterday; but they hadn't found her yet. She rented a single apartment at the Grattan Street address, but none of the other tenants knew much about her or where she worked. The night men had gone over to try again at ten last night, with no luck.

She wasn't home now, at three-thirty on Saturday afternoon. Hackett and Higgins asked around the shops up the street on Olympic Boulevard, but no one seemed to know her. They were ready to head back for the office when a shabby maroon VW turned into the curb in front of the apartment house and a buxom hennaed female got out of it.

"Somehow," said Hackett, "that looks like Durfee, female version." He loped after her. "Mrs. Durfee?"

"Well, I don't use the name no more," she said, turning. "You're fuzz. I s'pose about Al." She sounded resigned.

After listening to her for three minutes, they took her back to the office in Higgins' car. Mendoza was just back; he was sitting at his desk looking annoyed, shuffling the cards. He left the hand he had dealt lying there while he listened to Alice May.

She was pushing fifty and looked it; she wasn't caring, and she was forthright, emphatic. "So Al's a wrong one," she said. "No reason I can see either, he's a good mechanic, get jobs easy. But he gets into things— no willpower, no guts. I don't know but what it's a little bit my fault, which is the reason I"—she shrugged—"looked after him some. You could put it. See, I work hard and I was lucky. I got my own beauty parlors—two of 'em now, I don't say the classiest like on Wilshire Boulevard, but I hire good operators and I do real good. I finished paying off the mortgage on my first place now, own it clear, so it's all profit, except for taxes. I do all right. I guess Al sort of felt it, me doin' better than him. I knew he'd been in trouble when we got married, but I thought I could straighten him out. More fool me." She got a cigarette out of her capacious shabby handbag and Hackett lit it for her. "Thanks. Real gentlemen you fellows are. He was O.K. the first couple years, got a good job all steady. Then, boom, he went—in with the old racket again. I gave him another chance. He's a nice guy, Al. And I guess it was lucky we never had any kids. But the next time, I see it's no go. You get me."

"We get you," said Mendoza. "So you divorced him."

She sighed. Her blunt, not unhandsome middle-aged face was incongruous under the perfectly arranged hennaed hair. "Yeah, I did. I didn't like to. And I felt sorry for him. He's an unlucky guy. A gambler for one thing, he's got a dollar in his jeans he'll bet on anything—and an unlucky gambler."

"Most are," said Mendoza, and Hackett muttered under his breath, present company excepted.

"Yeah, that's so. Anyway, I guess you're interested in this latest thing. I never knew the ins and outs, what kind of racket it was, until Al come to see me—"

"When?"

"Four o'clock last Thursday afternoon," she said promptly. "I suspected he was in a racket of some kind again, most likely something to do with cars. He's good with cars. He come barging into my place—this is my first place, on Hoover, I work there, the other shop's on Beverly and I got a good girl to manage it, right on her toes and better be too, I'm particular about service—he come barging in asking for travel money. I took him in the back—he'd never dared come in my shop before, so I knew it was serious." She smoked fast, and bit her orange lipstick. "If you're goin' to say, helping a fugitive, I can't help it. He told me these guys had been running a racket out of his garage and he didn't know it. He said the fuzz had come down, just then, and he had to go on the run."

"Did you believe him, Mrs. Durfee?"

"My name's Beauchamp," she said. "My maiden name. It sounds classier, don't it? It's spelled with a *p* and all but you say it like Beecham . . . I don't s'pose I did, no. But I—was married to him, Al's the only guy ever— I know he's no good, but—the poor guy just can't seem to help himself, you know? He said he'd got cleaned out in a poker game down in Gardena the week before. That, I believed."

"So?" asked Mendoza.

"So I gave him two hundred bucks. You'll think I'm a damn fool. Maybe I am."

"Few people," said Mendoza, "haven't been damn fools at this and that time. He was—mmh—taken by surprise, the fuzz descending on the garage?"

She stared at him. "That he sure was, mister. He said he hadn't known about the racket, that was just a tale for me—damn fool Alice May, always the right side o' the law, *which* he knew. But he was caught with—well, he didn't have any notion the fuzz even suspected anything, way he talked. He'd been out shooting some pool, came back to find the place lousy with cops. So he ran. To me."

"For travel money. He couldn't even get his car—it was in the garage," said Mendoza. "Where was he heading and how?"

She shrugged again and stabbed out her cigarette. "Would I know? Just away. And you want him. You're never going to make him any different, but— If you want a guess, he headed for Vegas or Reno. He said something about a guy named Ricky, they didn't pick up either. Maybe they went together. Maybe this Ricky had a car. I don't know."

"Oh, really," said Mendoza. He looked at Hackett. "I think, Art, that you and George will now escort Mrs.—er—Miss Beauchamp up to Internal Affairs, also informing Captain Van Allen, and explain that we— mmh—just stumbled across her by pure coincidence—"

"I can hear what Macklin will say," said Hackett.

". . . and that we're just being cooperative. Knowing they'll be interested."

"I think it might be more to the point," said Higgins, "to explain that Art's bonny blue eyes prompted Mrs. Blessing to open up to him. She took a notion against Van Allen."

"For valid reasons," said Mendoza, looking amused. "¡Vamos! And my compliments to Lieutenant Southey."

CHAPTER 8

"Damn it," said Mendoza, pacing the living-room floor, "the hell of it is, no guarantee there wasn't a mix-up at the jail. And jailers have tongues too. Added to which, there's a grapevine in jail just as much as at headquarters, and anybody could have known that Horace—" He caught Sheba as she leaped for him from the back of the sectional; she scrambled up on his shoulder.

"You're not making much sense," said Alison, who was trying to read while Bast washed Nefertite on her lap.

"But, damn it, even so," said Mendoza, "even granted that—all Dunne and Byron could have known was that Horace had fingered a cop. Not which cop."

"Which you said before. *¡Bastante!*" said Alison as Bast and Nefertite started to wrestle. "Enough is enough—off! But, Luis—"

"*¡Demonios!*" said Mendoza. "What I would give for an hour alone with Dunne and Byron!"

"Those I.A. men are detectives too."

"Granted. And I do not imply, if you were wondering, that being little gentlemen they wouldn't press that pair too hard. But they're leaning over backward not to show bias—they always do. And at the moment they're concentrating on Tom. Which I know is just the wrong place. Hell! If I could have a free hand to question those two, lean hard enough on them, with Art and George to make faces and scare them— By God, could they have been primed? They both came out with that so damned—spontaneous."

"*Amado,* you know he's completely innocent, so—"

"Pure hearts protected by guardian angels?" Mendoza laughed. "It doesn't always work out that way, *cara.* I wish to God it did. And I might as well stop wishing, on those two—don't I know it, nobody but I.A. allowed to talk to them."

"You'll wear out the carpet. Worrying never helps."

"That's a constructive piece of advice," said Mendoza irritably. The shaggy dog Cedric came in licking his hairy chops, and Sheba left Mendoza in one bound to invite him to play; Mendoza laughed. "All right, we just hold good thoughts on it . . . but I wish to God I had a hunch on it. . . ."

No hunches came to him. As he opened the window before getting into bed, there came a faint sleepy voice from the alder tree. *Yankee Doodle came to . . . AWK.* "My God," said Mendoza, "we're stuck with that bird for life. I told you so."

Sunday is just a day to cops. Theoretically Mendoza was supposed to have it off; in practice he seldom did. He was in his office, immaculate in silver-gray dacron, as usual at eight-fifteen. Everybody was in except Piggott, who would show up after church.

Glasser went out on the strangled prostitute. Hackett was still mulling over the funny thing Mrs. Brownlee had given them on the Hatfield case. Higgins was discussing Luisa Fantini with Grace and Palliser; Palliser had teletyped an inquiry up to Lompoc yesterday afternoon. That wasn't a very big town; if she had come from there somebody on the force should know it.

"I'll tell you what did come to me," said Hackett. "Mrs. Brownlee said she only saw this woman twice, coming to the Hatfield house. And the dog didn't bark. So I think she must have come a couple more times, and been let in. But what for, and who was she?"

"I don't see any possible way to find out," said Mendoza, "when the family didn't know. . . . And you know, Art, the fact that Al Durfee was taken by surprise by—mmh—Van Allen's raiders argues that his employers were too. Rosso and—er—Speedy. So it wasn't a fingered job."

"So?"

"So, I said, if it's a frame on Tom, maybe a side bonus as part of putting Rosso and Company out of business. But it doesn't look that way."

"But Horace could still have made the mistake, and then stuck to it out of—malice, the way you said. Only Dunne and—" Hackett sighed and lit a cigarette.

"I talked to Tom last night," said Higgins. "He's feeling low. The trouble is, it's all so up in the air I don't see how I.A. can get anything to say a definite yes or no."

"Sword of Damocles," said Mendoza absently. Sergeant Lake came in and said they had a new body—woman out on Severance Street. Hackett and Higgins went out on that resignedly. One of the many annoyances of police work is that, not only being never finished, it necessarily leads men from one piece of routine to another before any conclusion is reached.

Grace was just saying, "That thousand dollars Luisa had—or probably had—did she swipe it somewhere? And whatever else she had in that—" when a uniformed man came into the anteroom and handed Lake two manila envelopes.

"Autopsy and lab reports," said Lake, handing them over. "Guilfoyle, who's that?"

Palliser snatched one and handed the other to Grace. "Hold your breath, Jase. Did we have a joint hunch?" He opened the report.

"I'm the one has hunches around here," said Mendoza. "What kind was this?"

"On Wilson Guilfoyle, poor old fellow going senile—only according to his doctor not as senile as some people may have wanted to— Oh, boy," said Palliser. "It was a hunch all right, Jase. Listen to this. 'Immediate cause of death'—well, it was the overdose of digitalis tablets all right—'indication is that tablets were dissolved in black coffee, to the approximate amount of two cups, two to four hours prior to death. Deceased had eaten a meal consisting of beef, potatoes, green vegetable and vanilla pudding approximately five hours prior to death—' "

"And the lab gives us something too," said Grace pleasedly. "Some dandy latent prints on the steering wheel, gearshift and light-knob of that Triumph. Not the corpse's."

"My God, is he that much of a fool?" said Palliser.

"What are you talking about? I'm supposed to know what goes on around here," complained Mendoza.

"You'll find the gist of it in my reports," said Palliser. "Come on, Jase!"

The house in Beverly Hills was an old one, a big one, on a generous plot of ground, in an older section of town. It was defiantly old-fashioned, with a porch round the front and one side, and dormer windows, and a pane of colored glass in the wide front door. As they climbed the steep wooden steps, Palliser said, "But why the hell did he take him all the way downtown?"

"Maybe that will emerge," said Grace.

The housekeeper, Mrs. Swift, opened the door to them, again in her decent black long-sleeved dress. "Oh!" she said. "Oh, Mr. Wilfrid was going to call you—to find out when we can have the—poor Mr. Guilfoyle's— Oh, come in." She forgot to shut the door, staring at them.

"Is Mr. Guilfoyle Junior here?"

"Why, yes, sir, he is. He's just having breakfast—if you'll come—"

"Just a moment, Mrs. Swift," said Palliser. "You've been here a long time, you said. I wonder if you know anything about the money. Old Mr. Guilfoyle's money—and what money young Mr. Guilfoyle has."

She stared at him. "Why, yes, sir. There isn't any secret about that. Mr. Wilfrid was Mr. Guilfoyle's only relative since his brother passed on some years back. Mr. Wilfrid's father. He didn't have near as much as Mr. Guilfoyle, but it's in trust for Mr. Wilfrid, Mr. Guilfoyle managed it. And of course I suppose his own money will come to Mr. Wilfrid."

"I see," said Palliser. "That's very interesting. And did Mr. Guilfoyle and Mr. Wilfrid get along well together? Any quarrels, differences of opinion?"

"Well—" she stared at him, looking a little confused. "Of course Mr. Wilfrid's young, and my Mr. Guilfoyle was old—set in his ways you might say. He'd go on at Mr. Wilfrid about—well, he didn't like some of his friends, and—things like that, but it was just—" She looked from one to the other of them, surprised and disturbed.

"Very natural, in fact," said Grace.

"Well, yes, I guess so."

"So we'll see Mr. Wilfrid," said Palliser.

He was in the old-fashioned breakfast-room, drinking coffee and smoking a cigarette, and he was again very natty in pale fawn slacks, a blue-green shadow-plaid sports jacket with a faintly green-tinged silk scarf tucked negligently between the lapels. He looked up. "Mr. Wilfrid, it's the police officers, they—"

"You really are pretty stupid, aren't you, Guilfoyle?" said Palliser. "And you must think we're pretty stupid. You might at least have taken the trouble to put his fingerprints on the steering wheel and a few other relevant places."

"What?" Guilfoyle went muddy gray, staring at them.

"It all looked so easy," said Palliser, "didn't it? I don't know your routine here, but we'll be finding out." He turned on Mrs. Swift. "I think Mr. Guilfoyle took his coffee after dinner in the library, didn't he? And you cleared away the meal and probably didn't see him again before he went to bed?"

She put a hand to her mouth. "Why, yes, sir, that's—he hated so to be helped, and he could get to bed by himself—"

"In fact, not at all senile," said Grace, "if he did forget things now and then. So you brought him his coffee, Mr. Guilfoyle, only you'd gone upstairs first and got his digitalis tablets and dissolved them in it—"

Guilfoyle sprang up so suddenly he knocked over the chair. *"What is this?* You can't—you damn nigger, walking in and saying—"

"If we're calling names there might be a couple for you too," said Palliser. "Deliberately killing an old man who trusted you. I don't—"

"Killing?" said Mrs. Swift in a muted shriek. *"No—"*

"I don't know whether your prints are on record anywhere, but with the evidence we have we'll be taking them, you know, and I rather think they'll check out as identical with the prints on the wheel—and other places—in your Triumph. As the last one to drive it. What about it, Mr. Guilfoyle?"

"No, I—we told you how he— He'd threatened to kill himself, I told you how—"

"Unfortunately you seem to be the only witness to that," said Palliser. "And it was easy—up to a point. He passed out rather soon after drinking the coffee. This is a big house, and you weren't afraid that Mrs. Swift would hear anything and wonder. I think—considering all that shrubbery shielding the drive from the street out there—you ran your car down the drive and just carried him out to it. He wasn't a very big, heavy man. If he had any wallet on him, you took that, tucked the medicine bottle in his pocket, and off you drove downtown to MacArthur Park. It'd be a deserted area by ten o'clock—no trouble getting him in, leaving him on the bench. Why, Mr. Guilfoyle?"

"Why—why— There *wasn't* any reason for me to— No, you're all wrong, I—"

"Oh, my God!" said Alma Swift, and sank into a chair and started to cry.

"I didn't mean why about that," said Palliser. "We can guess why you did it. He disapproved of some of your habits, and it was possible— seeing that he was far from senile—that he wouldn't have left you any money at all." Guilfoyle had both hands over his eyes; he rocked to and fro. "But why MacArthur Park? Why ferry your uncle's body all the way down there?"

"I think maybe I can answer that," said an interested voice behind them. Palliser and Grace turned. A big man in a rumpled gray suit, a man with a face as craggy as Higgins', came a few steps into the room. "Captain Ward, local force. You're LAPD? That's very interesting, what you were saying. Excuse me—the door was open, I just walked in. I've got a warrant for Mr. Guilfoyle's arrest."

Palliser introduced himself and Grace. "Charge?"

"Narco possession." Guilfoyle suddenly made a wild dash past them for the hall, and Ward collected him handily. "Just for that, I think we use the cuffs."

"Listen, you can't do this to—"

"You'll be surprised," said Ward, and added, "Somebody ought to do something for the lady." They looked, and Alma Swift had fainted ungracefully onto the floor. Grace went to find the kitchen and a glass of water.

They sorted it out at the Beverly Hills police station, with Wilfrid in a temporary detention cell. "I guess that's half your story," said Ward. "We know Wilfrid—and the old man knew that too, because last year we got Wilfrid on five counts of D.-and-D. within about six months. He's been running with a few unsavory characters on our beat—"

"Fags?"

Ward shrugged. "Your guess as good as mine. He knows some. Most of them he knows are users. We can have a guess he is too, if not all the way hooked or he wouldn't still be going for the liquor. But knowing Wilfrid, and the old man, we'd have taken a long hard second look at the situation if the old man had just been found dead in bed. Which I suppose Wilfrid guessed. He must have figured you boys downtown are maybe too busy to take much notice of one more corpse."

Grace grinned. "That's possible."

"I'll say this," added Ward. "The old man was a character, not much education but a smart fellow in his time, and I happen to know that a couple of months ago he hired a private shamus to watch Wilfrid. It'd be kind of poetic justice, wouldn't it, if he'd already made a new will and cut Wilfrid out? You think you've got him solid on a murder first?"

"It looks pretty good," said Palliser. "If the prints in the car are his, and I'd take a bet."

"That's the hell of a thing," said Ward. "Just get him out of the way, hell-bent for the money. I'll keep my fingers crossed that the old boy had cut him out."

They took Wilfrid back to L.A. headquarters and tried to get something out of him, after reading him the piece about his rights; but he just turned sullen and silent. After a while they took him down to the jail and came back to apply for the warrant. They would get a search-warrant for the house; there might be some evidence there, and they'd requisition Beverly Hills' records on him. The D.A. didn't, by law, have to show motive in a murder charge, but it was always nice to be able to show one.

By that time it was twelve-thirty and they went up to Federico's for lunch.

Southey phoned Mendoza at noon. "Thank you so much for Mrs. Durfee," he said icily.

"Quite welcome. We thought you'd find her interesting."

"We did. To a point. I'd be more interested in hearing about the strange coincidence which caused Homicide to stumble across her."

"It's a long story," said Mendoza.

"I'll bet," said Southey. "How many times do I have to tell you—"

"Don't bore me," said Mendoza. "You careful boys trying not to show bias—the wrong direction. Such gentlemen. I'll lay any amount you name you haven't done any serious leaning on those witnesses yet, to get the slightest glimmer as to whether they're lying—"

"We are not mind-readers up here."

"Oh, for God's sake! Any five-year man in uniform can make the educated guess about that!"

"We all have opinions," said Southey, his tone dropping in temperature by the word. "You will keep your paws off this business, I told you."

"Yes, I know you did," said Mendoza. "I remember it distinctly. I presume you've got fliers out on Durfee to Vegas and Reno."

"You can presume what you damn well like," said Southey, and hung up.

They all landed there at the same time—Hackett, Higgins, Piggott, Palliser and Grace—and took the big table at the front of the room near the hearth. They were starting to hear about Guilfoyle when Mendoza came in, sweeping off the black Homburg, and joined them.

"I.A. is annoyed at us," he said.

"Do we look surprised?" said Hackett. "At least John and Jase have tied up something." They heard about that one while everybody but Piggott had pre-luncheon drinks.

"Nothing in about Luisa," said Higgins, finishing his. "That's almost as—as shapeless a thing as Hatfield. I think we'll end up with both of them in Pending."

"The devil," said Piggott, "is getting around these days. Making mischief. That Katz girl—not a pretty girl, or very smart maybe, but she didn't deserve to die like that. And there wasn't a smell. It could have been anybody we looked at out of Records—"

"Or somebody making mischief for the first time," said Grace.

"And there is now the new one," said Hackett, settling his bulk more comfortably; the chair creaked. "Oh—the low-calorie plate," as the waiter came up. "Damn it, I was up two pounds this morning . . . Mrs. Anna Shaw. Over on Severance Street—one side of an old duplex. It looks like—run of the mill. Par for the course. She was sixty-nine, a widow, lived there with her daughter, Wanda Shaw. Middle-aged spinster. Daughter was out at a movie last night, came home about eleven, took it for granted Mama was asleep—she usually went to bed about nine-thirty. Didn't find out anything had happened until this morning. Mama dead in bed, place ransacked, back door forced. Not much gone, but there wouldn't have been much there. Daughter's a salesclerk at Bullock's. What's gone, a portable TV, old lady's watch and a little jewelry, odds and ends."

Mendoza grimaced. "*¿Qué más?* The little lout's doing what comes naturally. Mama made a little noise, he biffed her one?"

"Looks like. Daughter was all broken up. If only she'd looked when she came home—but she didn't want to disturb the old lady, just put on enough lights to get to her own room." Higgins put out his cigarette with a sigh. "Not that it'd have made any difference—the interns said the old lady probably died right then. Knocked over the head with our old friend the blunt instrument."

"So, another little job just like the one you stashed in Pending yesterday, Matt. Back to Records for the M.O.'s," said Hackett. "But on Harriet Hatfield, Luis—"

"Don't mention the name to me. There is just nowhere to go on that. As for locating your Jane Doe—" Mendoza shrugged and sat up as the waiter approached. "Food. I am starving."

Hackett looked balefully at his low-calorie plate. "But I'd like to know the answer on Harriet. What the hell could have been behind that?"

"I'm a little more interested, Arturo, in what the hell could be behind this fantastic thing about Tom."

They kicked that around awhile, but they'd said all there was to say about it. They were all feeling frustrated at the necessity to keep hands off and let I.A. handle it. Even with Mendoza not giving a damn about what I.A. said, there wasn't anywhere for them to go looking, to show it was a frame, a mistake, about Landers.

And to put the thing on the lowest basis, it left Homicide a man short.

*   *   *

When Palliser and Grace came into the anteroom at one-thirty, Lake handed Palliser a teletype.

"From Lompoc," said Palliser. "They don't know her either. Luisa."

"But that box—well, of course, I suppose she could have picked up a shoe-box anywhere. Or could she? Could she, John? That's not a very big town. What would be the odds on some outsider buying a pair of shoes in Lompoc and then landing in L.A. close enough to Luisa that she came by the box? Somehow? It wasn't a very old box."

"The box for her valuables. In the hiding place in the theater," said Palliser. "That was a damn silly sort of thing to do, Jase, you know? Just out on that fire escape. She was a scatter-brained sort of female. On the make, but—doing what comes naturally."

"And she hadn't been at that rooming house very long, but you know, we never tried to catch any of the other roomers home to ask questions. She also seems," said Grace, "to have been a talkative female. She just might have let something out to one of the other roomers. Something other than her whoppers."

"And it is Sunday," said Palliser. "Let's go and ask."

At the house on Boyd Street, they talked to the owner, Mrs. Baumgartner, again, but she didn't know anything about Luisa. She rented out six rooms in the house, and four of the roomers were in.

Mr. James Turner, recovering from a hangover, told them frankly he'd have liked to make time with that girl, but she'd turned up her nose at him. He'd seen her a dozen times maybe the while she lived here— Mr. Turner was out of work and not too concerned about hunting a new job while he was getting unemployment compensation. He said airily, what the hell, some girls fell for his line and some didn't, there it was.

Mrs. McSorley, fat, sixtyish and woolly-minded, said she hadn't noticed the girl much. Not to notice.

Miss Lila Weaver, prim and mousy and notably nervous of anything male, told them in a near-whisper that she'd never spoken to that girl, a real fast sort of girl she'd looked, and it only showed how right she'd been, that girl ending up murdered.

Miss Cora Foley, however, told them something they hadn't known. It didn't lead them anywhere and in fact it was no use to them at all in finding out what had happened to Luisa Fantini, but it was interesting.

Miss Foley was a hard-eyed blonde about thirty, a waitress in a cheap restaurant on Main, and she told them in a brassy voice that she didn't poke her nose into other people's business. "Do unto others," she said, waving her hands in the air to dry the garnet nail-polish she'd been applying when they knocked at her door. "I only noticed that girl a coupla times, she had the room right acrost, you know. I'm out a lot, and it wasn't no skin off my nose what she was doin' or not. I don't think she had a job, though, not right off, she'd come 'n' go different times, when I was here to notice. What the hell? But one thing I can tell you."

"What's that, Miss Foley?" asked Grace.

"Well, the one time I seen her close, I was just goin' out one night—she hadn't been here long then, I don't think, maybe a week. I had the evening shift and I was just leavin' like I say, when she come out of the room acrost. And the only reason I noticed, hall's usually dark but my door was still open, so there was some light. All dressed up she was, nice clothes she had, classy, and she never said nothin' to me or I to her, but she had her hand on the door to shut it and I saw the ring she had on. I useta go with a guy worked in a jewelry store, I know a little bit. And that ring, it had a pretty good-sized di'mond in it."

"Is that so?" said Palliser. "Can you describe it?"

"Oh, I only saw it a second, and off she goes. It was a gold ring—yellow gold, I mean—and it had just the one di'mond. Maybe almost a carat di'mond."

"Well!" said Palliser. He looked at Grace. Something new, but what did it tell them?

Landers was feeling terrible. A big part of it was being at such loose ends. One thing you could say about police work, you might not get rich at it and you might be in a good deal more danger of sudden death or injury, but it kept you busy. For ten years he had been very busy at it, in uniform in a car, and then at Homicide, at least eight hours a day and sometimes a good deal longer; and it felt very queer to get up in the morning, shave and dress and then have no place to go.

Suspended from duty. They had a queer and nasty flavor, those words. Him. Who'd always just tried to be a good cop on this top force.

The daytime programs on TV were impossible, except for a couple of old movies he'd picked up. You couldn't read all the time.

I.A. hadn't come near him again; he kept expecting the polite summons, the same silent contemptuous sergeant to ferry him downtown, the questions.

The damn watchdogs in I.A. just taking it for granted, for God's sake, that those damn small-time pros were telling the truth? *That's the one, that's him, the one they call Speedy.*

Like asking when you stopped beating your wife.

At least the Lieutenant had cleared up that damn business about the key.

Aware that probably I.A. would go nosing around up in Fresno, he had finally called his father last night. He'd said it was just some inter-departmental red tape, not to worry. But of course he'd had to talk to his mother too, and he'd never been very good at covering up things from her.

At noon on Sunday, he called Phil's number; maybe she'd take pity on him and go out to dinner again. But the phone rang emptily in his ear until at last he hung up.

Phil, on vacation, going off somewhere to enjoy herself. Well, what did Tom Landers matter to her? Nothing, obviously.

Feeling very sorry for himself, Landers switched on the TV and watched a so-called comedy hour without smiling once.

Phil O'Neill had a new car; she'd only had it for three months. It was a little bright-green Gremlin, and she had set out in it bright and early on Sunday morning with a bag in the storage-space under the flip-up rear window. She took the freeway through what used to be Dark Canyon Pass over to the San Fernando Valley, and made time up to the Ridge Route. By noon she was pulling into Bakersfield.

It was a good deal warmer in these inland valleys, even in June; she was glad she had put on the new green silk-jersey sheath, low-necked and sleeveless. She had lunch there, and got on the road again. There wasn't much traffic, even on Sunday, and she made good time.

At three-forty-five she came into the outskirts of Fresno. She stopped at a drugstore and consulted the phone book. Elm Street. But just out of curiosity she drove down Union Boulevard first, past a rambling gray stucco building. *Fresno Small Animal Clinic, Dr. John Landers.*

The house on Elm Street was big and old-fashioned, two-storied, set back from the street with two tall maple trees in the front yard. And there were people sitting on the front porch, and a car in the drive.

Phil had not, however, spent four years as a junior officer in the LAPD without losing any shyness she'd ever had. She parked the Gremlin at the curb, got out and marched up the front walk. The four people on the porch watched her coming with surprised interest, the sun bright on her blonde curls.

"Dr. Landers?"

"That's me." The tall lanky gray-haired man rose from the wicker rocking chair. "Can I do something for you, miss?"

Phil divided a brisk friendly smile among them, as interested as they were if she didn't show it, and for a different reason. Dr. Landers was square-faced, more fair than dark complexion, hazel eyes. Mrs. Landers —a faint look of Tom there; she had a long face, dark eyes, crisp short hair still almost black; and she had kept a good slim figure, and her wide mouth smiled at Phil. The girl would be Jean; more definitely like Tom, a thin face, lively dark eyes, humorous mouth. The fair young man would be her husband, Bob Kelvey; Phil thought Tom had said he had his own TV repair shop.

"I'm a friend of Tom's," she said. "I'm on the force too. I came—"

They were hospitable, friendly. They urged her to sit down, and Mrs. Landers brought her a glass of lemonade. They asked questions, interested in her. "Tom called just last night," said his father. "Never mentioned you though, Miss O'Neill. I couldn't make head or tail of what he said—about somebody coming to ask questions. I wondered—"

"And did somebody?" asked Phil.

Mrs. Landers leaned forward. "Tom never could fool me. I thought then he was in some kind of trouble. Do you know anything about—"

"Yes," said Phil soberly. "He's in quite a lot of trouble, Mrs. Landers. Anybody who knows Tom knows it's a lot of silly nonsense, but—well, you see, I.A.—Internal Affairs—has to investigate it. His Lieutenant is furious—"

"Mendoza," said Dr. Landers. A little brief smile touched his steady eyes. "We've heard a lot about that one. What's this all about, Miss O'Neill? Are you from this Internal Affairs department?"

"Heavens, no. I'm just a lowly clerk down in Records. And—a friend of Tom's. You see—"

"That I do see," nodded Mrs. Landers. "And I must say his taste is improving. That last girl he was dating—well, she sounded to me like a little cat—which I shouldn't say, I like cats personally."

Phil laughed. "Well—I've only been at headquarters about two months, we don't really— But anybody who knows Tom—"

"And I refuse," said Jean Kelvey in a warm voice, "to call you Miss O'Neill. I've got a little hunch we'll all be knowing each other better."

Phil explained apologetically about the impossible Phillipa Rosemary. "But that isn't why I came—" and she flushed a little at Jean's mischievous smile. "You see—I'll explain how it happened, and you'll see what a—well, a mess it is, for Tom—these three pros identifying him as one of the operators of a hot-car ring—which is ridiculous but you can see—"

"What damn nonsense is this?" exploded Dr. Landers.

"Tom?" said Kelvey incredulously. "Why, that's the most damn silly—"

"I never heard anything so silly in my life!" said Jean.

"Well, of course it is. But three witnesses—you can see I.A. has to look—"

"Of all the *damned* ridiculous things—"

"Jean," said her mother in a troubled voice.

"Well, it is! Tom? Why, a thing like that—they could discharge him from the force—and you all know he never had any other ambition all his— You don't mean anybody *believes* that?" Jean stared at Phil.

"Well, it has to be looked into, you can see. You know we are the top police force in the world—"

"Which is exactly the reason Tom wanted—"

"Now let's calm down here," said Dr. Landers, "and listen to what Phil has to say. I think she's got something to say."

"You may think it's fairly harebrained," said Phil. "I said his Lieutenant is furious, and saying it's a frame, and I suppose the other men at Homicide are too. But from all I've gathered, the witnesses are—call it simple. Ordinary pro louts. So I just had the thought that maybe the whole thing was—simple."

"How do you mean?" asked Jean.

"Just," said Phil, "a mistake. Only Tom isn't just ordinary-looking. So I came up here to ask you to—tell me something. Show me something."

"Anything we can do, if it's to help Tom. What things?" asked Mrs. Landers curiously.

Phil smiled at her. "Some family history," she said, "and—if you have any—some family photographic albums."

CHAPTER 9

About eleven-forty Sunday night the two men riding the black-and-white on that beat, Ferris and Hart, got sent over to an apartment house on Westlake Avenue, to an assault of some kind. They found a weeping young woman and a little crowd of aroused tenants on the first floor, most of them in nightclothes. They were greeted with relief and excitement.

"—Tried to *assault* me!" sobbed the young woman. "Just came up and grabbed me and if it hadn't been for Mr. Gebhart hearing me scream—"

"You all right, miss?" asked Ferris. Her dress was torn but otherwise she didn't look much harmed. "You don't want an ambulance? Well, can we have your name?"

"No, I'm all right—I got away from him and he just ran. I'm Mary Ridgeway, I live in four-oh-five. But I can tell you who he was—and Mr. Gebhart saw him too—"

"That I did," confirmed Mr. Gebhart mushily. " 'Scuse me—get my teeth—"

"Say," said Hart suddenly to Ferris, "there was that homicide right here last week, you remember? Another assault, only the girl didn't get away. Maybe the Homicide dicks'll be interested in this, Bob."

And Mary Ridgeway shrieked, *"Carolyn Katz!* Oh! Do you think *he* could've been the *one?* And he just grabbed me— Oh, Mr. Gebhart!"

"There, poor girl," said the manager, less accordion-like with teeth in, "it's all over now."

So on Monday morning they found that report waiting from the night shift, a note signed by Sergeant Galeano. "Identified attacker William Royce, resident apartment building. No record with us. Not at apartment up to 3 A.M. Employed Weideman Interiors Wilshire Boulevard."

"Well, if that isn't a funny one," said Glasser, looking at it. "Just after we throw Katz in Pending, maybe a break. I suppose we go see Royce, if we can find him."

And Piggott said, "An interior decorator, committing an assault? But we'd better check him out, Henry."

Mendoza was already in; as Piggott and Glasser went out past the open door of his office, he was saying to Hackett, "All I'm saying, Arturo, is that we haven't done one damned thing on this Rosso, and I'd lay no bets that I.A. is—yet—and I think—"

"—Get us all suspended from duty," said Hackett exasperatedly.

Weideman Interiors had a whole new building to itself in a smart block of Wilshire; inside the double plate-glass front door, it presented a rather kaleidoscopic panorama of styles, displayed in chopped-off sections. Victorian blood-red plush gave abrupt way past a gilt railing to Moorish tile and Spanish wrought-iron furniture; next to that a chintzy Down East bedroom abutted on an ultramodern bar in zebra stripes. Neither Piggott nor Glasser was impressed.

A brisk dark woman in black harlequin glasses and a tight black sheath covering an emaciated frame came up to them. "I can help the gentlemen?" she asked.

"You can," said Glasser. "Mr. William Royce. We understand he works here. Is he here now?"

"Oh, Mr. Royce. He is here, but I'm afraid he's not at all well. A migraine headache. Mr. Burns has him resting in his office—"

"Isn't that a shame," said Piggott. "I'm afraid we'll have to disturb him." They produced their badges simultaneously, and the emaciated lady let out an ungracious squawk.

"Police? Mr. Royce? Whatever do the police—"

"Which way?" asked Glasser.

William Royce, when they found him sitting on a black plastic couch in the manager's office, looked at them wanly. "I knew she'd tell," he said. "I knew—but I—but I—there wasn't anything to do but come to work—as usual—and all I wanted—" He was a weedy little man with no chin, weak pale eyes, and a thin reedy voice. He looked about twenty-five and actually was thirty-two, they were to find. He described himself as a commercial artist, but didn't look very successful at that either: employed here as a mere copier of other men's work. They told him they wanted to talk to him, and he said he supposed so, and they read him the piece about all his rights and took him back to headquarters.

Higgins was just coming out of the sergeants' office and Royce shied back at sight of him as if he'd been a sidewinder.

"Like a witness?" asked Higgins genially.

"It won't do any harm," said Glasser.

But as it turned out, Royce came apart almost as soon as they asked him anything. He admitted he'd been the one last night, but it wasn't an assault, he said drearily. He looked at them standing over him in an interrogation room and he said, "Girls don't like me. They laugh at me. I never had a girl-friend. They laugh at—how I look. But I'm like anybody else inside! I—I'd—just like—to have—a—girl-friend. And Mary's a pretty girl—she came home just ahead of me last night and—and—and all I wanted to do was kiss her! She might've let me—that was all I wanted—but she screamed as if—as if—"

"Royce," said Piggott tiredly (it took all a man's time to keep up with the machinations of the devil), "what about that other girl, last week—Carolyn Katz? Did you want to kiss her too?"

Royce looked down at the floor. He said, "She—she wasn't so pretty. You see, I thought—I thought maybe she was like me. Like me. Wanting—friends, and not—not having any. Because she wasn't pretty, or so awful young. I—thought—maybe she wouldn't mind. If I—kissed her. When she didn't expect it. That was all—I ever—meant to do."

"And so what happened when you tried?" asked Glasser very gently.

Royce looked up at them slowly. "She," he said, "she—it was all— you don't understand how I felt. Her. Not pretty, but—if she was—a girl —who'd let me—I thought— But she screamed and screamed and screamed—as if I was a monster of some kind—her, a girl like that! As if I was a *monster*—and all I wanted—just like any human being, but she—" He pounded one fist on his knee, just once. "I—wanted to hurt her, then. Acting as if I was a *monster*, when all—"

That was about all the coherence they got out of him; it was probably enough. They got it down and he signed it in silence and Piggott took him down to the jail while Glasser started the machinery on the warrant.

It was funny, clearing up the Katz thing so unexpectedly.

"Have any guesses as to whether they'll stash him away in Atascadero?" asked Piggott.

"Probably they will," said Higgins. "If he isn't legally nuts he's heading that way. And at that you can feel a little sorry for him. At least that's one off our minds."

*   *   *

Hackett had argued with Mendoza to no avail. "I.A. will be hunting this Rosso eventually, Luis—and Auto Theft. Very much their job, and they're cops too. Who knows whether they got any prints in that garage as leads?—we've got nothing. All I say—"

"And all I say is," said Mendoza, "you came across a couple in Records who just might be this boy. Follow them up as you can and see what you get."

"Listen," said Hackett, "I know we're all concerned about this, but there are other things on hand—and I.A.—we never got a statement from the Shaw woman yesterday, she was too upset, and sometime today we've got—and there's Luisa—"

But he didn't get to any of their legitimate business until after lunch. Meanwhile he did a lot of tiresome legwork looking for both those possible Rossos out of L.A. Records. Both addresses noted were out of date, and neither was in a neighborhood where the residents particularly liked cops; he did some asking around and got nowhere at all. But he was feeling better about Landers' thing now: the I.A. men weren't fools, and those witnesses had admitted they'd only seen this Speedy a few times. When the principals were hauled in, Durfee and this Rosso, they'd probably give it away that the identification was a mistake. The idea of a frame was too fantastic; it had to be a simple mistake—some superficial resemblance. It was damn tough on Landers but sooner or later it would get cleared up.

And he was a good deal more curious, if possible, about what was behind the Hatfield murder than about the death of Mrs. Anna Shaw— the violent lout breaking in for the little loot—but there was always the paper work to do. After lunch he and Higgins went over to the duplex on Severance Street, and found Wanda Shaw listlessly straightening up the shabby living room, and asked her to come in to make a statement.

"Anything you say," she said. "It seems kind of heartless to be dusting and all, as if nothing had happened, but Mother liked things kept tidy." She was a thin drab of a woman in her forties, with a drooping mouth and defeated-looking tired eyes. She came along silently, in Higgins' car, and upstairs in the sergeants' office they gave her the chair beside Hackett's desk, brought her a cup of coffee. "You're very kind," she said. "What do I have to do?"

"Just tell us again, for the record, what happened when you came home on Saturday night, Miss Shaw—and then about Sunday morning."

"Oh. All over again? Well, you heard how it was. I don't go out nights hardly at all, Mother doesn't—didn't like being left alone. Besides, working all day— Well, I fixed her supper and had mine and did the dishes before I went out, to the movie, and she had her radio right beside the bed—she had her supper in bed, she hadn't been feeling so good that couple of days—poor Mother, she had a lot of troubles—"

"Yes, just take it easy, Miss Shaw."

"Oh!" she said. "If I'd only looked, when I came home! If I'd only just put on the kitchen light, I'd have seen into the living room and noticed the television gone—but I never thought—it was late—" She bowed her head in her hands.

Hackett was taking notes, and looked up at movement to find Mendoza in the doorway regarding Wanda Shaw interestedly. He drifted in and sat down behind her at Palliser's desk.

"I never *thought* to!" she said piteously. "I knew Mother'd be asleep—and any little noise disturbed her, I didn't want to—and I was going right to bed myself, had to be up at six to fix her breakfast, she liked—So I just put on the light in the service porch a second to see my way into the hall—I know the house, of course, we've lived there thirty-two years—and I went into my room and shut the door and—and went to bed, and all the time poor dear Mother was lying there—lying there—" She sobbed into her hands. Higgins pushed the coffee cup toward her.

"Just take it easy now. Drink your coffee. You heard the doctor say she was already— There wasn't anything you could have done if you had—"

"No, but it's just the *idea*. She was always so afraid of burglars, you see. I was always careful to keep the doors locked—but that back door, I guess it isn't a very good lock, old one—I never thought— Oh, when I think of poor Mother there—"

They took her through the relevant details, times and items missing from the house, and Higgins started to type up a statement. He had it ready for her to sign in twenty minutes, and they called a squad car to take her home. "You're very kind," she said again vaguely. "I suppose you'll do your best to find out whoever it was that—"

"Yes, of course we will, Miss Shaw." The uniformed man ushered her out, and Hackett cocked his sandy head at Mendoza, who was sitting back in Palliser's desk chair with his hands clasped across his flat middle. "And did you find that piece of routine business edifying, *compadre?*"

Mendoza stood up and automatically straightened his tie, yanked down his cuffs. "*Piense antes de hablar,*" he said pensively. "I'm always telling Alison that marriage has ruined my well-known talent for women, but maybe I've retained a little at that."

"Meaning what?"

"I'm not too sure myself. And—"

"Don't ask me about Rosso. If either of the possibles in our Records is the one Auto Theft's after, he's long gone. And as if you need reminding, we've got legitimate work to do."

"I saw Henry's report on that whore. Nobody's going to find that X."

"No loss," said Higgins. "But there's still the Fantini girl—"

"And Hatfield. If you want to know, Harriet Hatfield is haunting me," said Hackett. "I've been round and round on it, and there's just nothing. Nothing to say who or why. Such a damned ordinary woman, Luis. And you stand there maundering about Rosso."

"I wasn't."

"You were going to. Look, when and if they do catch up to him and Durfee, it'll all come unraveled. It's got to. They—"

"I'd like to hear the reasoning on that, Arturo."

"Well, for one thing they'll have no remote idea that these underlings have fingered a cop. I.A. being so good at keeping secrets, the press hasn't heard even a rumor. When Durfee and Rosso are picked up, you know how I.A.'ll handle it—the casual intimation that they've also got the number two man, and the casual lineup—and Durfee and Rosso both saying, Hah, that ain't either him, any of those guys."

"Which had also occurred to me," said Higgins.

"Oh, yes?" said Mendoza. "Hey presto, the other three made a little mistake, and I.A. and Auto Theft swallow that right off. It doesn't cross their minds that Durfee and Rosso could be protecting an accomplice—"

"But—"

"The press," said Mendoza, "doesn't have a monopoly on news, *amigos*. There's a grapevine everywhere. A lot of our pigeons offer the info to the other side too—and you both know as well as I how uncanny the grapevine can be. Would you take an oath that it's absolutely impossible—wherever Durfee and Rosso are—that they could have got the word about Horace and the other two fingering the cop? By mistake or whatever? So, would it work quite that way? If I.A. or Van Allen picks up Durfee and Rosso? Wouldn't they be pleased to tell I.A., Sure, that's the guy, that's Speedy."

Hackett massaged his jaw. "You're not exactly a Pollyanna today, Luis. I hadn't seen it quite that way, but—"

"But there's no *evidence*," said Higgins. "Nothing but these identifications—and from who, for God's sake? Three louts of—"

"So they couldn't ask for a resignation on that," said Mendoza. "You know how it'd be. Forever on his record. Sword of Damocles."

"Goddamn it," said Higgins. "There ought to be something we can do—"

The sergeant attached to Internal Affairs who had been sent up to Fresno was a fifteen-year man named Kurt Wengel. He was by nature a thorough and careful man, and he had been briefed by Lieutenant Southey in all the details.

He got to Fresno on Saturday morning, and found a middle-class motel and checked in. In what was left of the morning he located the principal of the high school and politely bullied him into opening the school records to him. Sometimes things showed up in school records that pointed out latent tendencies.

He didn't find much of interest in Tom Landers' school records. Beyond the fact that Landers had been better in English than math, and had taken two years of Latin with a C average, there wasn't anything in the records to offer Wengel a lead.

He tried the school library next—school wouldn't be out for two weeks and the library was open to students studying for final exams—and found, after search, a class yearbook of the year Landers graduated from high school.

Looking through that, he found a couple of items which interested him very much. When he left the high school, mindful of I.A.'s eternal rule of discretion—a rule kept mostly out of fear of harming the innocent—he drove five miles up the road and found a pay phone to call Lieutenant Southey.

"I haven't had a chance to work at that angle yet, Lieutenant, the athletic record. Tomorrow. But another little thing showed. In this yearbook, there was a kid named Rosso in the same class."

"You don't tell me," said Southey.

"That's right. Charles Vincent Rosso. Same age as Landers. The phone book lists a John Rosso, only one, so maybe it's the same family. It could be that this Rosso had been a school pal, and showed up again down there on the bent, and inveigled Landers into—"

"That could be," said Southey. "We should know about Rosso, with any luck, sometime. We picked up quite a lot of prints in that garage. Durfee's, and some unknown—the Feds are checking to see if they know them."

Wengel drove back to Fresno. He'd only been transferred to I.A. five years ago, after a stint in Bunco, and he often thought that of all dirty jobs a cop came in for, I.A. offered the dirtiest—checking up on fellow cops. It wasn't very often at all that they found a man on this force guilty of anything really bad; but this thing right now was shaping in Wengel's mind as the worst that could happen—a cop going wrong with a vengeance, on the bent with pro crooks.

He had copied down some names from that yearbook, other boys in that graduating class; but he went to look up what he could find about Rosso first. The John Rosso listed in the phone book was a farmer outside of town, living in a prosperous-looking big white farmhouse. He looked askance at Wengel's representation of himself as checking up for Social Security records (all the governmental bureaucrats' snooping provided cops with some useful cover these days) and told him his boy Charles was working in the city. San Francisco. He was with a brokerage there. Oh, yes? thought Wengel. Story for the home folks?

He found some of the other names from his list in town, starting out again on Sunday. Some of those boys had left town. One had a garage, another an insurance business, another was a teacher in an elementary school. And so on. He went on looking, asking questions; he explained his questions by introducing himself as a statistician working on a thesis, and as cover he asked questions about other people in that class too. He was a patient, thorough man, and by Monday afternoon he had built up a picture of Tom Landers, that many years ago, which wasn't going to be much help to Lieutenant Southey.

It didn't tell them anything they hadn't known, for Landers' record was just fine up to now. So was his record all this time ago. None of it said that Landers hadn't recently been tempted by the easy money to joining this Rosso—old school pal or not—in the hot-car operation.

It didn't even say much that Landers and Rosso had known each other casually. It wouldn't have been a very big graduating class—not like a high school in the city—and most of them would have known each other. But late Monday morning he came across, in his dogged search, Mr. Fred Barker, who was the pharmacist-owner of a drugstore on the main street and had also been in that graduating class.

Mr. Barker was a tubby little man already losing his hair, a garrulous little man pleased to reminisce at the drop of a casual question. Wengel told him his sister was thinking of taking a teaching job at the high school, and led him on from there. . . . "Landers?" said Barker at last. "Oh, sure, know the whole family. Been here a long time, they have. Doc Landers, he's got the biggest animal hospital in the county, good man I guess. . . . Yessir, I was at school with their boy—lessee, Bob, Bill, Tom, that's him. His sister's a mighty pretty girl but she never had any time for me—married to Bob Kelvey she is, no kids yet—" And Wengel eventually got him around to school athletics. Somebody had told him, he said, that this Landers had been pretty good at— "Oh, sure," said Barker. "Me, I was never any good at athletics any kind, no coordination—but Landers was a track man—kind of a star that last year in high when we beat Dinuba at the meet—"

"Oh," said Wengel. "Track man, was he? Pretty fast?"

"Oh, I guess so, kind of a star you could say—"

"Did he ever get called Speedy?"

"Why, uh, I don't know but what he might have," said Barker. "Like I say—"

Wengel was a good man, but in keeping with his plodding habits of routine, he completely lacked any imagination; and it never crossed his mind that Barker was just a fat little man who had been an unhappy fat boy in high school, with few friends, and hadn't really known Landers at all, then or now. As far as Wengel was concerned, Barker was an important witness. He noted down that conversation to relay to Southey.

He got round to the family on Monday afternoon. They seemed like nice people, he thought sadly. Dr. Landers was at his hospital, but Mrs. Landers was home, a nice-looking woman, and Mrs. Jean Kelvey was there too, and a friend of hers, a pert-looking little blonde who hadn't much to say, but then she probably didn't know much about Landers if she was just the sister's friend and lived here.

He had by then looked up the family. What he was looking for, of course, was the possibility that there had recently arisen some pressing need for money. He didn't find anything like that; both the elder Landerses seemed to be in good health, the hospital was doing well, Bob Kelvey's store was doing well. There'd be somebody looking down in L.A. to see whether Landers had contracted any gambling debts or other expenses which might have led him into temptation.

It was very likely that Landers had told the family something about this; Wengel didn't use much camouflage with them. He didn't expect anything useful from the family, and he didn't get anything; if the family knew anything about Landers getting led into a crooked setup, they wouldn't be telling Sergeant Wengel.

The women had evidently been doing some housecleaning or furniture-arranging. Funny, when they must be worried about Landers.

He went away to find a phone and report to Lieutenant Southey.

"Well!" said Jean. "I suppose that's your man from I.A."

"With a vengeance," said Phil.

"Exactly like a Prussian officer," said Jean indignantly. "Asking if Tom likes to gamble! Asking—"

"Well, they have to investigate," said Phil.

"Now, Jean," said Mrs. Landers. "If Phil's idea is at least halfway sensible, we'd better get on with it. The last time I saw your Grandmother Borman's album was when I put it away after Father died—I think it's in that old sewing chest in the attic. I seem to recall it's behind that old wardrobe trunk, and why I didn't give that to the salvage years ago I'll never know—"

They climbed stairs, Jean still muttering about Wengel, "—All he needs are the dueling scars—honestly, asking *such* questions about—"

Phil smiled at their backs. Nice people. They wouldn't hear of her going to a motel, there being plenty of space in the old house. And they had both been interested in the idea, which was so simple—as Phil said apologetically—that it was really no good going to the men in I.A. with it. Or even the Homicide men. Even if they'd pay any attention to a junior officer from Records. "I should think not," Mrs. Landers had said at once. "Men do tend to have such complicated minds, don't they? But I don't think it's harebrained at all, Phil—it won't do any harm to *look,* anyway."

Phil had spent last evening with Jean going over some rather modern family albums. Dr. and Mrs. Landers' wedding pictures, Jean and Tom as babies, children. A few older photographs. "That's my aunt Mary Brennan—Father's sister—and that's Father of course—and John's grandfather—"

They were all nice-looking people, but Phil frowned over the photographs. The only one that gave her pause was Mrs. Landers' aunt, Mary Brennan. There was just a look—

And later on, over a second album, "That's my grandfather, Robert Pitkin. A fine-looking man, wasn't he? We always said Tom— Oh!" Mrs. Landers stared at Phil excitedly. "He *does,* doesn't he?"

"He does indeed," said Phil. Robert Pitkin, photographed in sepia probably around the turn of the century, was a tall thin serious-looking young man in very proper Victorian dress, including a flowered silk waistcoat. He had a long droopy moustache, a long jaw, rather prominent cheekbones and brooding dark eyes.

"I never noticed it so clearly before," Jean had said, crowding close to peer at the print. "But I haven't looked at these for ages—Tom's the spitting image of him, Mother, if he had a handlebar moustache! That's extraordinary—"

"Not at all," said Mrs. Landers. "My own grandfather, after all. He married a Margaret Gorman, they had two children— And of course—"

"Yes," said Phil. "And that's your side of the family. Tom looks a little like you, you know."

"More like me—boys generally do take after mothers," nodded Mrs. Landers. "I used to call him—my goodness, I hadn't thought of that in years! But you think it might be on my side. Well, there are a couple of old albums, some tintypes in them—as old as that—I cleared out when Father died. I think they'd be up in the attic."

And now they were up in the attic of the old house, looking. The sewing chest came to light behind the coffin-like wardrobe trunk, and the albums were unearthed.

"They're filthy—don't you touch them till we take them down and wipe them off. These are both Father's, I'm pretty sure—but older things in them too. I should have said, of course Grandfather was a Junior. Robert Pitkin Junior, and his father—"

"Mother!" said Jean suddenly at the foot of the attic stairs. *"Great-aunt Serafina!"*

"Good heavens, yes! I expect she'd have the Lord knows what, back to Year One. But Jean, you know how she is. If she took a notion to Phil—but she'd just as likely not, you know how she feels about modern girls, and—"

"Great-aunt Serafina?" asked Phil.

"My dear Lord, that woman!" said Mrs. Landers in exasperation. "I expect most families have a difficult relation or two, but she is a cross to bear. She's eighty-five this year, and I swear I think she's too mean to die. She won't go to a rest-home—heaven knows she's got the money, her father left her half the land and she owns four farms outside of town—and she won't admit she's not fit to live alone. All we can do is check on her every day or so to see she hasn't fallen and broken something— Well! You see, that's just what I was about to tell you—my great-grandfather, Robert Pitkin Senior, went beyond the pale, as I gather his family felt, and actually married an Italian Catholic girl—"

"Oh," said Phil. "That's where the dark eyes come from."

"I suppose so. A Maria Arnoldo, she was. We don't know anything about her family, I expect they cut her off entirely, and it'd have been back about eighteen-seventy-five anyway. I—"

"Where?" asked Phil interestedly.

"Oh, San Francisco. Great-grandfather came out from Iowa as a young man, for the gold I expect, but he ended up keeping a hotel in San Francisco. Anyway, they had three children—my grandfather Robert Junior, and Serafina, and Jean Ellen, but she died as a child. It was the reason—and I hadn't thought of it in years," said Mrs. Landers,

"Tom being so dark as a baby, I used to call him my little *bambino,* just in fun. . . . Serafina never married, and she's been a cross to us for forty years—of course with all that farm income she never had to *do* anything—creeping about that musty old house over on Maple Street getting smaller and meaner and more suspicious of everybody by the day. *But—*"

"*And* more Italian," said Jean. "Her mother filled her with all these notions, you see, noble Italian heritage, and she goes on and on—"

"But," said Mrs. Landers, "if it's photographs of that side of the family we're after, she's got scads of old relics tucked away, I couldn't guess what all—things of her mother's and—"

"But you know how she is!" said Jean. "She'd never let *us* see half of what she's got stashed away—"

"Well, we'd better figure out a way," said Phil. Suddenly Great-aunt Serafina's hoarded relics became a castle of treasures to be stormed by hook or crook.

The autopsy report on Anna Shaw came up at five-thirty Monday afternoon. For once Dr. Bainbridge, not besieged by too many corpses, had got on the ball. He sent a note along with the report, and Hackett handed it to Higgins with raised brows.

"Suggest you see lab report in re furniture at scene," Bainbridge had scrawled. "Bedside table right of bed. Also photographs of scene *in situ.* Deceased's nightgown saturated with tea. Trust you or lab dusted teapot."

"Now what the hell?" said Higgins. They hadn't got a lab report on Shaw yet; those boys took their time. And this was such an open-and-shut thing—he and Hackett had already had a desultory look through Records for the similar M.O.'s, if you could say there was much M.O. about this.

Hackett got on the phone to the lab and was patient. "At least you can give us something, Duke. What about the bedside table on the right? . . . Oh? . . . Well, what does that say? Nothing. All right, all right, send up a report sometime. . . . There was blood on it," he relayed to Higgins.

"The bedside table? And so what?"

"Bainbridge," said Hackett, "is occasionally cryptic. Like our Luis."

After dinner, with the kids settled down to homework, Brucie the Scottie asleep at Mary's feet as she did some mending, Higgins said suddenly, looking up from the new *American Rifleman,* "You know, it's frightening. That's what I've been thinking—it just came to me, Mary. About Tom. A thing just—out of the blue. If a thing like that can happen to Tom, it could happen to any of us. It scares me, all of a sudden."

Mary's gray eyes smiled at him. "Not you, George. Nobody could ever mistake you for anybody else."

He laughed ruefully. "Maybe not. But—coming all of a sudden, like— *My God!*"

Mary jumped. "What?"

And after a long pause Higgins, on his feet, said abstractedly, "She was in bed, you see. All tidily tucked in. That was what—"

"Bringing work home," said Angel. "I know you're all fussed up about Landers, Art, and I can't blame you there, but it's no good worrying. And the rest of your puzzles will either get solved in time or end up in Pending."

"Easy to say," said Hackett. "I tell you, that Hatfield thing is haunting me. I have the definite feeling that this Jane Doe comes into it somewhere, but of course there's no possible way to go looking for her. . . . I only hope to God those I.A. men are as smart as they think they are. Luis saying—and damn it, he's only too right. And they don't know Tom. Personally. Damn impersonal, in fact, the damn lean-over-backwards *investigation*—"

"Hasn't he had any hunches?" asked Angel.

"I think," said Hackett slowly, "he's unsold on the idea of a frame. I don't see how it could be myself—and yet— It has got, you know, to have been a personal motive on Harriet Hatfield—the way you've got to read it. Hasn't it? Whatever was behind it. The way her face was battered in—a dozen blows at least, Bainbridge said—and it would be a wrought-iron hearth set, too rough to take prints. It looks like the sudden impulse, sudden loss of temper—but what the hell could have triggered it, on Harriet—" He stopped with his mouth open. He said, "My good God in heaven."

Angel looked up from her magazine. "Inspiration?"

"Ins—" said Hackett in a hollow tone. "My God. I thought we'd had our spate of offbeat ones for the year. The blood on the—the tea—and I saw the damn lab photographs of that—she was in bed, all the way in, the covers—and the teapot— Oh, my God!" He plunged for the phone. "I'd better call George—"

"The teapot?" said Angel blankly.

CHAPTER 10

"Well, I did wonder," said Mendoza, regarding the lab photograph of Anna Shaw's body and the bedroom it lay in.

"He wondered," said Hackett. "Two hundred years ago he'd have been burnt for a warlock."

"But, my God, that woman—" Higgins shook his head. "It looked so run of the mill—"

"Oh, you'd have noticed something wrong when you took a second look at the photographs," Mendoza consoled them.

"So what's it all about?" asked Grace interestedly. He'd been off yesterday and hadn't heard about the Shaw case at all. Palliser was off today. Hackett started to give Grace a break-down on it.

"Suppose you go and ask her to come in for a few questions, George," said Mendoza.

Higgins took Grace with him. They found Wanda Shaw at the shabby house; she told them Mr. Seward had said she could take a week off. She rode back to the headquarters building in listless silence, and it wasn't until they settled her in a chair beside Mendoza's desk and she noticed him there, slim dapper cynical-eyed Mendoza, watching her, that small fear came into her eyes.

"Miss Shaw," said Mendoza formally. "I'm afraid you didn't tell us quite all the truth about how your mother died, did you?" He offered her the box of cigarettes.

"Thank you, I don't smoke," she said. She looked up at him directly: the other men might not have been there. "You know, don't you? I always heard—the police here are—smart about things. But I thought—I suppose I was stupid, and so you know."

"We'd like to hear the truth, Miss Shaw."

"I expect you would," she said. She looked ghastly: no makeup on her sallow complexion, her graying brown hair lifeless and uncurled, clothes shabby and drab. She seemed to realize that suddenly, and flushed. "I'm sorry, I must look awful—I usually keep up, do my hair and all, the store, you know, you've got to—but I just haven't bothered, not going in. Since." She was silent, picking a piece of lint from her sleeve, and then she said without looking up, "If you've got to hear about it, you'd better hear the truth. It was just the last straw. The last. That was it. If I can explain it—if there could be any explaining it." Her voice was flat and tired. "The Bible says honor thy father and mother, and I did—I did try. Pa took a lot of the care of her before he passed on, that was more than ten years ago. But since, I tried—it was my duty and I did it. There's no other relatives, I was all—all there was. And you have to be patient and kind with old people, maybe you'll be like that some day. I *tried*. But—" she stuck there, making a hopeless gesture, and Mendoza urged her on with soothing murmurs. Higgins was taking notes.

"I don't like to say it but she was difficult. It was hard. I work all day, I have to, earn money to live on—for her too. And she knew that, but she always kept on, why couldn't I come home fix her dinner at noon. And why couldn't I be home to fix her supper at six, she liked it early. And half the time when I'd fixed it, she'd decide she wanted something else so I had it to do over. And massage her back, and I couldn't wash her things at the laundromat, the machines tear things to pieces, I had to do all those by hand, and be careful— And only get this brand or that of everything there was at the market, only she'd forget, and say I got the wrong one, have to change it. I don't suppose," said Wanda Shaw painfully, "that I'd ever have had a chance to marry anybody anyway, but she wouldn't have let me. She said so. Child of her own body, and all the terrible time she had *having* me, I had to take care of them. And her after Pa passed on. And get her in and out of the tub, and she had to have that Lilac Dawn talcum and it costs twice as much— And most nights she'd have me up, just after I'd got asleep, massage her back or make her a cup of tea. She never stirred out of the house, so of course she couldn't sleep. Oh, I sound complaining, and I shouldn't. It was my duty. But, you see, I was tired," said Wanda. "I was so tired. Just trying to keep up with—with the ordinary things, it was difficult. I'd be just starting to wash my hair, it'd be Wanda do this, do that. Or washing out my own things—trying to keep my nails nice, something like—she'd have to have the pillow turned over or— I was tired," she said to Mendoza. "It was my duty, but I was so tired."

"Yes, Miss Shaw," he said gently.

"And it isn't once a year I go to a movie, but it was the new Disney one, you see. I wanted to see it. It was a comedy, and I thought—it'd do me good to see it. And it was all *arranged*—for two weeks she knew I was going to see it, since I knew it was coming. And I felt good that night, when I got home. About going out, and the movie. I knew I'd have to hurry, the second show goes on at nine-ten, it's the Strand up on Alvarado, I'd have to take the bus, about a ten-minute ride. And I hurried, I fixed her supper and she said the egg wasn't done enough so I fixed another, and I had some toast and things while she was eating, and washed the dishes, and made her tea. She liked it by itself, a whole pot, after supper, and I was all ready to leave when I took it in—it was already after eight, I don't get home till about a quarter of seven. And when I put the tray down—she looked at it and she said—she said, Wanda, I think I'd rather have green tea tonight—and she *knew*— Have to boil another pot, I couldn't get the right bus—to make the second showing—"

"Yes, Miss Shaw?" said Mendoza.

"And all of a sudden, I guess I just lost my temper. Because she *knew* how I'd looked forward— And it was—such—a—little thing," whispered Wanda Shaw miserably. "Just—a—movie—I wanted—I didn't realize what I'd done until—until I'd done it. I hit her with the teapot, she fell out of bed against the table and—"

They exchanged glances. "And when did you think of trying to cover up what you'd done?"

She shook her head. "I don't know. I sat there for a long while. I couldn't realize—what had happened. That she was dead. But she looked terrible there, it wasn't nice, her there on the floor. I was used to lifting her, I put her back in bed. And then I thought, suppose—suppose I had gone to that movie. Nobody'd know if I had or hadn't, we don't know the neighbors. And while I was gone—"

"Yes. What did you do with the portable TV, the other things you said were taken?"

"Oh, those. I put them behind Pa's trunk in the garage. We sold the car after Pa died," she said absently.

"We'll ask you to sign a statement," said Mendoza, and she nodded.

"It's funny, I'm not sorry you found out, and I had to tell you." Suddenly she looked at him with a timid smile. "I—I just thought of something. They'll put me in jail, won't they? In a cell?"

"Why, yes—until—"

"All by myself?" she said. "Alone? And I won't have to stand on my feet eight hours a day? Just alone in a cell, with *nothing to do?*"

"Well—"

"Oh," said Wanda Shaw, and her smile turned radiant. "I expect I'll go to hell for what I did, but you know, right now, that jail sounds just like heaven to me."

"I really thought we'd had enough of the offbeat ones," said Higgins. "I'll be damned. But you can feel sorry for the poor woman at that."

"People," said Grace. "They do come all sorts, boys. What makes life interesting." He had taken her down to the Alameda facility; the warrant was applied for. Subject to the D.A.'s approval, involuntary manslaughter. She might spend five years in; a jury might give her less, but it had been her own mother. As Higgins said, speaking purely physically.

"I'd still like to know," said Hackett to Mendoza, "what rang bells in your head, you just looking at her yesterday."

Mendoza grinned. "And listening. Experience gained from old sins, boy. The females who go throwing dears and darlings and poor sweets around are usually—to, mmh, use the vernacular—strictly from Siberia. And Wanda didn't strike me as usually given to overemphasis. That poor dear Mother just rang a small bell."

"Oh!" said Hackett. "Well, if you're at loose ends I wish to God you'd go out and have a hunch about Harriet Hatfield. That is still bugging me, with bells on."

Mendoza stood up and straightened his tie. Quite suddenly—they had both seen it happen to him before—he was all lit up, on top of the world. It always affected him like a stiff drink, a thing like this: Mendoza seeing right to the truth of some little puzzle, the X-ray vision. And he was still fussing about Landers, too, but he couldn't help the extra adrenalin shooting through him, the essential egotist Mendoza clearing up the little problem with a flick of his mind. He clapped Hackett on the shoulder.

"So you want the answer on Harriet, Arturo? Well, by God, I'll go and look—I might just pull it out of a hat for you." He took up the black Homburg and went out, clapping it on at a rakish angle.

"And, you know, he just might," said Higgins amusedly. "When he's in that mood—"

Hackett laughed. "Let's hope he does, George. Besides the Fantini girl—and I can't say I really care who shoved her over the balcony— Harriet's the only real mystery we've got on hand."

There was, however, plenty of the routine work to do. The court calendars were full, and only today was an inquest being held on Carolyn

Katz; Piggott was covering that: the D.A.'s office had reports on Royce
by now and would handle that as they pleased, full evidence or an open
verdict. Business had stepped up a little for Homicide. The body yesterday was for pretty sure a natural death; just the paper work on it; but a
new one had turned up overnight, looking like a suicide, out on Beverly; Grace had gone to cover that, after looking at the lab photographs and Schenke's overnight notes on it.

Just before lunch, there was a messy hit-run over on Third, and
Hackett went out with Higgins on that. They had lunch before going
back to type reports, and it was a quarter to three when Sergeant Lake
looked in the door of the sergeants' office and said tersely, "Goldberg,
wanting the boss."

Hackett picked up the inside phone. "What's up, Saul?"

Goldberg sneezed. "Just being neighborly. I thought Luis'd like to
know they've picked up Durfee. I ran into Van Allen just now and he
let it out and then tried to—er—pledge me to secrecy. He—"

"The hell you say. When and where?"

"Reno, this morning. He's just been fetched in and they're setting up
a lineup with Landers now."

"Hell!" said Hackett, slammed down the phone, beckoned Higgins
and ran. "Jimmy, you any idea where the boss is?"

"Nary a one. Don't you?"

"Damnation—he was going out on Hatfield but—" Hackett grabbed
for his notebook. "Try the house, Jimmy," and he read off the number.
But there was no answer there. He had Lake call Wilma Tanner's shop
in Beverly Hills.

"Why, yes, the Lieutenant was here," said Miss Tanner's deep voice.
"In fact he took Cathy away, but she's back now and—"

"Miss Tanner, did he happen to tell you or Miss Hatfield where he
was going from—"

A hiatus while she consulted with Catherine. "No, he didn't, I'm
sorry."

"Can't be helped—thanks," said Hackett. "Jimmy, if he comes in tell
him where we are. We'd better get down there fast, George—you know
he'll want to cover this."

When they came into the soundproofed room beneath the brilliantly
lighted platform, and up to Southey and Macklin, the I.A. men nearly
snarled at them.

"May I ask how you got wind of this?" asked Southey.

"A little bird with allergies named Saul Goldberg," said Van Allen grimly. "Which I'll remember."

"So that's Durfee," said Hackett. The man standing a little apart, with a uniformed man beside him, looked very much as he'd imagined Durfee might, from his mug-shot. He was big and burly, with an incipient paunch, and by his face he wouldn't have a very high I.Q. In fact, a stupid lout, thought Hackett in satisfaction. Either way Durfee should give the show away. If he didn't know about the other identifications, he'd deny Landers; if he did, he was too dumb to tell a plausible lie.

"All right," said Southey sourly. "You're here, you can stay. No talking to the witness."

"Offhand," said Hackett, "I can't think of anything I've got to say to him." He and Higgins took chairs to the right and behind the two I.A. men and Durfee.

"What's this all about, anyways?" asked Durfee. "Who'm I s'posed to look at?"

"Just tell us if you know any of the men up there, when they come in. If you've ever seen one of them before," said Southey.

"Well, O.K., but I don't get—"

Just as the room darkened further, somebody slid quietly into the chair beside Hackett. "Luis—thank God! I hoped you'd—"

"Wait for it," said Mendoza. The men began to file onto the platform up there, led by a uniformed man. Landers, in a gray suit and rather rumpled tie, was the fifth man in line.

There was silence from this little group in the dark; Al Durfee would have a slow mind. Then out of the dark his voice rose, holding complete and open astonishment, utter incredulity.

"I wouldn't 'a' *believed* it!—by God, I can't believe—anybody so Goddamn—can't take it in—"

Southey and Macklin jumped up; all at once there was confusion and noise. Mendoza made one lunge and pulled Southey away from Durfee and took Durfee's burly shoulder in an iron grip. "All right, what were you going to say next, Durfee?" he snapped. *"What?* Tell me! Anybody so close to looking like Speedy—was that it? Anybody so Goddamn like him? Tell me!"

Durfee pulled away, looking around wildly. Macklin yanked Mendoza off him. "Let go of that man, damn you! Goddamn it, you know the rules! By God, if you lay a hand on me I'll break you—"

And Hackett had seen Mendoza like that before too, and he dragged him back from Macklin by brute force. *"¡Bastante, amigo!* Suppose you ask Durfee the same question, Macklin! Just what did he mean and what was he going to say next?"

"None of you has any business here—" began Southey coldly, and Mendoza pulled away from Hackett and resettled his jacket.

"You haven't a hope of convincing me of that," he said hardly. "Ask the question, Lieutenant! You're supposed to be a smart cop. Ask Durfee the question!"

And all the while the line of men stood motionless up there on the lighted platform, staring straight ahead.

Southey and Macklin looked furious, but they were caught in front of the witnesses from Homicide. Southey turned to Durfee, who stood head down, sullen, a bewildered big bull confused by the red flag. "Well, Durfee? What did you mean? Do you know one of those men up there?"

After a moment Durfee seemed to make up his mind. He raised his head slowly, licking his lips, looking at each of them in turn. "I ain't sayin'," he muttered. "I ain't sayin' a thing. I got a bad memory for faces."

Southey cast a look of veiled triumph at Mendoza. "Come on, you're among friends," he said genially. "You know we've nailed you for this caper. Wouldn't you like to see your emp—"

"Careful, Lieutenant," said Mendoza. "You're leading the witness."

Southey compressed his lips. "You know those men up there can't see or hear you, Durfee. *Do you know one of them?*"

Durfee shook his head blindly, stubbornly abiding by the decision he'd made. "I ain't sayin'."

Mendoza let out a long breath that was half a sigh. For once in his life, Hackett had an urge to practice a little third degree. Durfee was a big bull, and bullheaded, but he knew something—maybe the whole answer here, and he might come apart if—

They went around on the merry-go-round a few more times before Macklin lost patience and told the sergeant to take him away.

"And don't we know what the famous imagination has put in your head now," said Southey.

Mendoza got out a cigarette. "Now look," he said in an unexpectedly mild tone. "We're supposed to be on the same team. We're both supposed to be interested in the truth, not winning points for our respective sides. You're not a fool, Southey, and you heard what Durfee said, looking at that line. He is a fool, which we both know. And I'd really like you to tell me just what else he might have meant by that. He couldn't believe anybody could look so much like—Speedy? Very probably. He—"

"For God's sake! You don't even know he was looking at Landers!" said Macklin.

"I really wish you wouldn't drag your heels so hard," said Mendoza very softly. "And don't try to tell me this is none of my business. *Por favor,* don't. I've got a little reputation around this place, friends, do I need to remind you?"

"Reputation for—"

"And if that man from my office has gone wrong, I really ought to have known it. He's my business, if you like. Will you tell me if you've identified Rosso?" Mendoza finally lit the cigarette.

"Yes, we have—" Southey consulted mutely with Macklin and shrugged. "We got some latents in the garage, the Feds made them for us. He's Gustavo Rosso, native of Brooklyn, time done back there for fencing, last picked up in San Francisco, twice, for auto theft. He's on P.A. from Quentin on another fencing charge."

"Well, well, well," drawled Mendoza, "isn't that interesting! Now, Mr. Bones, will you answer the sixty-four-dollar question and tell me just how a busy Homicide officer—we do get kept quite busy in the general way, you know—happened to get together with a pro crook last heard of in Quentin? A crook whose latest known beat was 'Frisco? That's quite a little trick Landers pulled there."

Southey said repressively, "We've turned up a little suggestive evidence in his home town. And that's all I'm going to tell you, Mendoza." He turned for the door; Macklin and Van Allen followed.

Mendoza stood rocking a little, heel to toe. *"Hagar sus apuntas—* stakes down and wait for the throw," he muttered. "Tell me what else he was going to say."

"Nothing else, obviously," said Hackett. "Somebody like Tom—the hell of a lot like him. Is that what he meant?"

"I took it that way," said Mendoza. "And damn it, that makes it all the more complicated. Coincidence? *¡Condenación!"*

"He wasn't acting," said Higgins. "Not that one. But I see what you mean."

"Rosso sounds just a little bit smarter," said Hackett.

"De veras."

"And you got that point over—how the hell could Tom have met up with a character like that?"

"I hope," said Mendoza, "that Southey is as smart as he ought to be.

Well, we wait and see. And we'd better get back to our own stamping ground." They started for the elevators down the hall.

"Did you have a hunch on Harriet?" asked Hackett, punching the button.

Mendoza contemplated his hat. "I don't know. I really don't know what I have got on Harriet, Art. Or if I've got anything. That's been a queer one all the way. It still looks queer. And as for what I have got—*Demonios,* I suppose there could be a dozen plausible explanations—the trouble is, I can't think of any. . . ."

He had not expected to find anyone at home in the house in Nichols Canyon; he had gone straight to Wilma Tanner's shop in Beverly Hills. He didn't think Hatfield, or the girl Linda, had much imagination. It was nearly twelve then, and he asked Catherine to have lunch with him. "You take the first hour, I remember. There's just a few things I'd like to talk to you about."

"Well—" She'd looked a little puzzled, a little wary; he put out some of his charm and she thawed. By the time he'd got her settled at a table at Frascati's, in the pleasantly dim dining room, and ordered her a martini, she was talking freely.

"I'm just trying to get a few new ideas, Miss Hatfield. We're finding this one a difficult case to sort out. You may think I'm asking you some funny things, but I'm supposed to be the detective, after all."

"Whatever I can tell you to help—"

"You all told us that your mother hadn't had—so far as you knew—any arguments or quarrels with anyone, any difficulty of any kind, oh, say in the month before she was killed. If she had had, the family would probably have heard about it?"

She nodded. "Of course. Mother wasn't—secretive. But she didn't quarrel—"

"No. Your father had been busy at his office. He told me that possibly she wouldn't have mentioned any little difficulty to him, knowing he was busy."

"Y-yes. That's true. But there couldn't have been—"

"Miss Hatfield," said Mendoza, finishing his rye, "I'd like you to think about this and take your time answering it. In the month or so before her death, do you remember your mother saying or doing anything —oh, unusual, or at least unusual for her? Something out of the ordinary?"

She didn't answer for a moment, and then asked, "Why?"

"Usually," he told her, "the motive for a murder isn't very important. That may sound strange to you, but it's so. Once in a while it is important. I think if we could find out what the motive for your mother's murder was, we'll be a lot further on."

She was an intelligent girl. "I see. Well, I can tell you something, only whatever it means—" She shrugged. "Daddy and I couldn't make head or tail of it, it was just—funny. It wasn't until after the second thing that I thought of the first one, and it might not mean any more to you than it does to us, Lieutenant. I'd just told Wilma about it this morning and she couldn't make it out either."

"What, Miss Hatfield?"

"Well, I'll tell you how it happened, Lieutenant. We've been starting to—to go through Mother's things—" She swallowed, blinked, and went on. "And I was looking through her dressing-table drawers, you know, sorting out things Linda or I might use, and I found my birth certificate in the top drawer. Right in the middle of her handkerchiefs, all folded up."

"Your—" Mendoza didn't know what he'd expected; it certainly wasn't that.

"It was funny. I showed it to Daddy and he was surprised too, he said he'd thought it was at the bank. In the vault, with the other things like—oh, their marriage certificate, and the deed to the house—the other birth certificates. Linda's and John's. He said Mother must have got it out for some reason, but why she would have—"

"She hadn't mentioned it to you?"

Catherine shook her head. "It was just—a funny little thing. It's just an ordinary birth certificate. And it was then I remembered the other thing, I'd thought that was funny at the time too, but it went right out of my head afterward—"

"And what was that?"

She finished her drink and turned the glass around on its little paper doily. "Well, it was about, oh, six weeks ago. I came home about the usual time—six-thirty—and Mother was in the kitchen. Johnny was at school of course, it was the middle of the week, and Linda was meeting Bob for dinner, so we'd be alone. Mother said Daddy'd called that he'd be late—she was drinking a cup of coffee at the table, and I sat down to have one too. You see, Lieutenant, Mother wasn't—I mean, she was always open, she said whatever she had to say right out. Which was why it was—funny. We were just sitting there and all of a sudden I realized she was staring at me, and I said—you know how you do—was my face dirty or what— And she looked at me so *queerly,* all I can describe how it was, and she said, 'Of course you're dark, dark eyes and all, but I always said you took after my father's side of the family.' And I said, what on earth did she mean, but she just shook her head and—and got up and went into the living room, and later on she just said she'd been looking at some family pictures. It was—queer," said Catherine.

Mendoza stared at her. And just what did that mean, if anything? He couldn't make head or tail of it either. But he'd asked for anything out of the ordinary.

"Miss Hatfield, do you mind letting me see that birth certificate?" he asked abruptly.

"Why, no, it's still at the house." He drove her up there after lunch, and she gave it to him.

And looking at it, he still hadn't a glimmer as to what that might mean. As she said, an ordinary birth certificate. Catherine Marian Hatfield, born 11 A.M., April 24, 1947. Lawrence Maternity Clinic, Western Avenue, Hollywood. Father Howard John Hatfield. Mother Harriet Anne Hatfield. Legitimate. Weight seven pounds six ounces.

Perplexed but automatically obeying training, he copied down the data and thanked her.

And no hunch came to him on Harriet Hatfield.

"Damn it," he said to Alison, finding her in the back yard as he drove in, "it just gets more muddled. Wait till you hear. They've picked up Durfee and—"

"Muddled you can say!" exclaimed Alison. Bast, ambling up to greet him, jumped and snarled as *el pájaro* swooped to peck her rear end. Cedric came galumphing from the back porch barking madly, and Sheba dabbed hastily at a new hole in the dahlias and ran for shelter on the porch with Nefertite and El Señor.

"*Yankee Doodle came to town!*" came the war cry from the alder tree. The twins erupted out the back door with Mrs. MacTaggart in vain pursuit.

"*¡Mil rayos!*" said Mendoza. "You'd think I'd be entitled to some peace and quiet when I come home—"

"And a man of your advancing years too," said Alison.

He smacked her accurately on the indicated spot. "You'll find out how advanced! *Caray*"—as the offspring landed on him—"let me get my breath! All right, all right, *los cuentos* after dinner, but get off me now, I've had a tough day, *niños*—"

*   *   *

Phil was feeling partly a fool and partly a traitor; she reminded herself that it was all for a good cause.

It had been Jean's idea. "Of course if she finds out she'll raise hell," she had said inelegantly, "but she might not. She probably doesn't go pawing over things every day. If all we want is to look at, well, whatever's there, I could smuggle it back before she knew. I've got a pretty good idea where to look. A few times when she was in a good mood she's brought out things to show me—I never paid much attention, but the family things, photographs and like that, she got out of this old chest in her bedroom. Now you collect antiques, Phil."

"I do?"

"Definitely. Great-aunt Serafina has a house full of antiques—marble-top commodes and whatnots and horrible little iron footstools and heaven knows what. I wouldn't give two dollars for the whole lot, but you," said Jean firmly, "are fascinated by antiques. You are a friend of mine from—from, well, the city—she won't ask which. And you want to see her antiques. But you can't do it in that dress, you'd better have one of mine, it'll hit you below the calf and Great-aunt Serafina will approve a nice modest girl. And I'm going to leave you there to admire the antiques while I do some shopping for Mother. Only I'll sneak back in while you hold her in the living room—excuse me, parlor. Double parlors," said Jean, "and a black marble mantel."

"Goodness," said Phil. "No antiques in her bedroom?"

"I devoutly hope not," said Jean. "You just hold her in the parlor. Admiring the fretwork on the plate-rail and the black marble. Oh, and she's got a stuffed bird under a glass dome, and her brother's collection of seashells."

And right now, Phil was saying admiringly, "And not a crack in the marble, Miss Pitkin—it's in beautiful condition," and feeling rather sorry for half-senile old Serafina, a little bent figure in black dusty ankle-length clothes, the cracked old voice, the snaggle-toothed smile. People could live too long. And at the same time, unwilling fascination kept returning her eyes to Serafina's wrinkled old face. Her brother, Robert Pitkin Junior, in that photograph—if Tom had a moustache, his spitting image, said Jean. And here was Serafina, age blurring what must have been at least a characterful face in youth—a long dark face, with high cheekbones and straight bars of brows, and dark eyes. It was her father who had married the Italian girl, and for some reason Latins didn't go gray very often; the brows were still black and the thinning hair in unfashionable pinned-up braids was black too.

"This was my dear mother's," said the broken old voice, "the only

thing she brought from her old home when she married. The only thing.
I can tell you like pretty things—"

"It's beautiful," said Phil gently. It was a hurricane lamp, an ornate
thing typical of the period, clear glass with an etched design and
prisms dangling from the candle-holder it fitted.

"It's old—old. She married my father in eighteen-eighty-two," mumbled Serafina. "I was named after her mother—"

Phil felt as if she'd been here for days, but it couldn't be over an hour
since Jean had breezily banged the front door and called good-bye. She
cast around for something else to say about the marbletops, the mantel,
the stuffed bird, and Serafina said suddenly, clearly, "Of course she
came of a very aristocratic Italian family. I remember—remember her
telling me—often—her mother's family, all noble—"

Jean appeared suddenly in the front hall. "Here I am to take your
visitor off, Great-aunt. Had a nice time? Lovely things Great-aunt has,
don't you think?"

"Lovely," said Phil.

Serafina suddenly turned on both of them. "Come bothering at me,
you young chits, making fun—I won't be bothered! You're young Jean,
you and your short skirts and lipstick—I won't be bothered! Go away!"

"Yes, Great-aunt," said Jean soothingly.

"For heaven's sake," said Phil as they hurried down the front walk,
did you find anything? I never expected to have to play Little Theater
when I had the harebrained idea—" They got into Jean's car and she
started the engine hastily.

"She'll boil me in oil if she finds out—but I think I got something interesting." A block away she parked at the curb and opened her large
straw bag. "Here you are."

Phil sorted out musty old papers, photographs. A very old, stiff sheet
of paper, with onionskin sheets protecting it: *Contract of Marriage*—she
spelled out the Latin slowly, dredging her memory. Robert A. Pitkin.
Maria Anastasia Arnoldo. It wasn't a civil certificate; Phil laughed.
"Look at this—Maria was a good churchwoman, she got him to be married by a priest. *Fr. Jesus Salvador Alvarez.* And—"

A large sepia photograph, names on the back in a fine spidery brown
ink. Three folded sheets of delicate old paper, a hand barely legible
now, the words not English, but she could make out the heading: *Rancho de la Vergine, Soledad, Cfrn., 18 octubre 1888.*

And a birth certificate. Or were there birth certificates that long ago?
In the seventies and eighties, San Francisco a hamlet. Phil unfolded the
brittle paper carefully. A baptismal record. Maria Arnoldo had, per-

haps secretly, properly had her son baptized in the Church. The Church of the Good Shepherd, San Francisco, November 23, 1883, Fr. Patrick O'Hanlon Moriarty—

Phil let out a long sigh. "This might help a lot, Jean."

The trail leading to San Francisco now. Though there was also—

CHAPTER 11

Hackett got into the office first on Wednesday morning, and found Sergeant Lake reading a teletype. "Relayed," he said, handing it to Hackett. "Sent up from Missing Persons just after six last night."

"Yes," said Hackett, reading it. "Carey was notified about the body, of course." It was a teletype from the sheriff of Santa Barbara County; an Antonio Camparo, local rancher, had reported his daughter missing, known to be in Los Angeles—Luisa Fantini. "So if she was married, how come the husband didn't report her?"

Lake shrugged. Mendoza came in, a little late, and looked at the teletype. "Well, well. She seems to have got missed a little late in the day." He went down to Communications and teletyped the news about Luisa up to the sheriff.

When he got back, everybody was in. It was supposed to be Piggott's day off but he had come in to be on hand if anything broke on Landers, and if business wasn't as hot and heavy as it sometimes was, they were still a man short. Hackett and Higgins had, for a wonder, got a pretty good description of that hit-run car yesterday afternoon, and all garages had been alerted to be on the lookout for it; it had probably sustained some front-end damage.

Grace, Palliser and Piggott heard the gist of what Al Durfee had come out with and agreed rather savagely as to what he'd meant. "Those damn watchdogs, just like you say, leaning over backwards—" said Palliser.

"They can't make a charge stick," said Piggott without conviction. But Piggott was always a pessimist.

But the business came along to be worked. The D.A.'s office issued a summons to Mendoza to present himself at once. Grace was saying he didn't like some funny things about this suicide, and went out on that again. The inquest on Anna Shaw was called for this afternoon; somebody would have to cover that.

A new call came in at ten-fifteen, one of those tiresome things making paper work for the Homicide office: accidental death on a construction site close in downtown. A scaffolding had slipped, or somebody been a little careless, and there was all the paper work to do, an inquest. Higgins went out to get the information on that, passing Mendoza just coming in. Mendoza was looking annoyed.

"What'd the D.A. want?"

"He doesn't like the idea of calling it involuntary manslaughter on Anna Shaw," said Mendoza. "He's making it murder second."

"And who argues with the D.A.?" said Hackett; and that was when the uproar commenced.

Confused loud voices out in the anteroom, shouts and angry sounds—Mendoza and Hackett went out to see what was up.

"Now quiet down, Mr. Camparo—just simmer down and let's—" And a little wiry dark man was shouting half in impassioned Italian at Carey and a third man who was just scowling back.

"Please be quiet, Mr. Camparo—just calm down and let's try to make sense of this—"

"He let my Luisa get killed—you show me my poor little Luisa there dead, flat, ice-cold—this *bastardo,* this son-a-bitch, why I marry my Luisa with him but I think he make good husband—I tell him—"

"*¡Silencio!*" said Mendoza sharply. "What the hell is this all about, Carey? You—quiet down—*¡Bastante ya! ¿Comprenden?*" The wiry man subsided, directing a fierce glance at them all. "All right, come in here."

"This is Mr. Camparo," said Carey in Mendoza's office. "As you gather. He—they landed on me half an hour ago. They've just identified your corpse. This is Joe Fantini, her husband. Lieutenant Mendoza—"

Camparo sketched a half bow. "How do. 'Scuse I am mad, say loud things—my little Luisa—" Fantini, who was a dark topheavy-looking young fellow about thirty with immense shoulders and short bowed legs, just grunted. "It seems that Mr. Camparo didn't know Luisa had left her husband until yesterday. His sister—"

"That Rita," Camparo interjected, "she don't never like Luisa, she likes make stink, bad gossip, scandal, however! She tells me—and Joe has a letter, she says, Luisa never comin' back—and I go to Joe—"

"Why they all got to mess in my business, Goddamn it," broke in Fantini with a snarl. "So she's gone, and good riddance! I'm better off 'thout her, an' old man Camparo ain't goin' to—"

"Why else I marry Luisa with you?" shouted Camparo, in a sudden fury again. "She's bad, fast, naughty girl—in her thoughts only, I keep a good eye on, catch her sneak off with boys even in little children's school—better she's married young to good steady fellow, keep her safe! And you—you Joe! Better oughta you beat one like that, she talk back to you, won't work! How you act? How? You call her few names, is all—women don't understan' names! You use your fists, she wouldn't 'a' run off—"

"Damn it, I'm sorry she's dead, but what the hell could I do?" He appealed to the Homicide men, as unconsciously dramatic as Camparo. Both of them were in stiff city suits, obviously unaccustomed wear; they looked uncomfortable. "So she goes off, but I got work to do on my farm, I'm not about to—"

"Farm! Farm! Why else I marry her to you?" shouted Camparo. "Good land you got from your papa, good place—good steady husband, you keep the eye on this naughty girl—but what you do? You beat her good, scare her, she be nice girl, nice wife! You, you get her killed dead —some low-life down here kills her, you lettin' her run off—an' you say to me—"

"Now, look," said Mendoza, "let's get some order here. Jimmy! Mr. Camparo, if you'd just wait outside a few minutes, we'll talk to you presently." Camparo was still gesturing and shouting when Lake gently urged him out.

"Damn it," growled Fantini, "what the hell I let that ol' bastard drag me down here for—between him and Rita, nag, nag, nag— So all right, Luisa's dead, do I do any cryin'?" He glowered at them. "I was a damn fool let the old man talk me into marryin' with her—a damn pretty girl but no sense, an' a bad heart she had too."

"When did she leave you, Mr. Fantini?" asked Hackett.

"Who looks at calendars? Three weeks, a month. Listen, so it's over, finished, she run into trouble down here and got killed. So I pay for a funeral. I got work to do on my place—"

"Did you quarrel with her, was there some immediate cause for her leaving?" asked Mendoza.

"What? No, no, she just went off. Do I pay attention to what she says, complain, nag, I don't listen. Damn that Rita! I told you so, told you so, bad girl, bad wife—so she was, she didn't hafta rub it in day 'n' night! So I'm sorry for what happened, Goddamn it, what else do I say? Goddamn Rita, has to go tattle to the old man an' he goes up like a rocket—you heard him." Fantini stood up.

"We heard him. Sit down, Mr. Fantini. Just a few more questions. You had a letter from your wife? What did she say?"

"Nothin'. Nothin', just she's gone for good, don't expect see her no more."

"And was there a return address on it?"

"What? No. No, I just seen it come from L.A. So what? I'm sick of her complain, complain, all the work, no fun—I'm not about to come looking, drag her back."

"You didn't report her missing?"

"Look, mister, she's grown-up, she can do what she wants. Why should I?"

"Did she have any money? Did she steal some from you when she ran away?" asked Hackett. "Like a thousand bucks?"

Fantini stiffened, his back to them. "How'd—now where'd I get a thousand bucks?"

"From the bank," said Mendoza, "with a little strip of paper around the roll with a note on it saying how much was there."

Fantini whirled on them, his face convulsed. "You— Nobody knew—"

"*¡Ya está!*" said Mendoza softly. "What a pity John isn't here—he did most of the spadework on it." Hackett looked amused and opened the door to glance out.

"He's just in," he said laconically, and beckoned, and Palliser came in looking curious. "We're just about to hear the whole story on Luisa."

Fantini was still staring at Mendoza. His muscular throat worked; suddenly he reached up and tore loose the stiff collar and tie. "You— you don't know," he muttered. "You try to trap me—I don't tell no lies, get in trouble—I never seen her again. She went off and I never seen her after. I don't know what money she—"

"The bank will tell us, you know," said Mendoza. "That you took out that thousand bucks in cash, Joe. What was it for?"

"I—I—you don't—"

"And why did you come back, Joe?" asked Hackett. "Walking into the trap?"

"That ol' devil!" spat Fantini suddenly, venomous. "Between him an' Rita— *It was all done with!* It was finished! I hadda be such a Goddamn fool, leave that letter around so's Rita seen it—I got work to do, I don't aim come back—but that stubborn ol' devil, he—"

Mendoza looked slightly amused now; the wiry little Camparo evidently the stronger character. "There was also," he said, "or I think there was, the pink slip on a car—"

"And that legal document," said Palliser, looking interested. "What was that thousand bucks for, Fantini?"

Fantini was glowering at the floor. "Land—land, that other field, 'n'

Pancho he say cash—" His voice was absent; he looked up at them and suddenly his voice went high. "Goddamn that sneaky little bitch! Goddamn her! Nothin' but trouble, since the day I first laid eyes on her—an' that ol' bastard knowin' it, he pass her off on me! I shoulda *knowed* better! Me buyin' the little bitch a di'mond ring, her makin' cyes and me a damn fool as much as— But at least I got over it!" He had been on his feet pacing; now he wheeled and pounded an impotent fist on the wall, furious. "She runs off, I'm glad see her back, but that Goddamn little bitch, she takes my cash an' the certif'cate on my new truck I just paid for an' the *deed to my land*—an' she says, she writes, take another thousand bucks to give 'em back—that bitch, that bitch—"

"And so what did you do, Joe?"

"Goddamn, I got to get 'em back—I come to get 'em back! What the hell else would I do?" he asked chokingly, beyond any fear or discretion. "Sure there's an add-ress—she wanted more o' my money! She didn't get it, by God! I—"

"What she did get was a broken neck," said Hackett. "How, Joe?"

"You think you know so Goddamn much," said Fantini.

"We might guess," said Palliser. "She'd spent the thousand on clothes mostly, and a couple of weeks' room and meals. But she hadn't picked up a sucker with real money, so she took the piddling job, as little work as she could do, to pay her room rent awhile longer. She tried for some more money from you before she met the rich john. And I think you caught her just as she was leaving that night—leaving the house on Boyd Street—to keep her date. Didn't you? Maybe in the street, so nobody there ever saw you. I think—"

"Mmh, yes," said Mendoza, eyeing Fantini, "just enough superficial cunning to make the try for—er—your valuables, and cover up a little afterward. You told her you'd pay her the money. So she took you to the theater, didn't she? It'd make her late for her date, but the john was eager, and the prospect of another thousand bucks was worth it. She told you to wait five minutes and come up the fire escape—"

"My God, of course!" said Palliser. "Annie Sanchez never saw him—"

"And she pushed that door open and—"

"Just out there that dirty ol' place, inna box—*my proppity!* Anybody mighta picked it up—her laughin' at me—" Fantini smacked one big fist into his palm. "Oh, Holy God, I shoulda took that ol' devil's advice an' beat up on that one first week I married her! I shoulda—I was so Goddamn mad I didn't know what I was—I went for her, just to get that box —*my proppity*—an' we sorta fell back through that door—"

"And not a soul in the balcony," said Palliser. "She was little and thin, and the handful of people in the dark down there wouldn't have heard or seen. You sent her over before you realized, didn't you? And then you remembered the diamond ring, and went down and took that back too."

Fantini stopped talking and turned to face the window. After a moment he said in helpless fury, "I hadda let that ol' bastard bully me, come down *look* for her—up like a rocket, he hears she's— It's all *his* fault, that ol' son of a bitch Camparo! It's all *his* fault!"

"My God," said Palliser, "and we haven't warned him about his rights—you know what the bench would—"

Mendoza laughed mirthlessly, eyes on Fantini's back. "It's a toss-up whether he'll give us that in a statement all over again after the warning. But at least we know. Take him down to jail, John. We'll set up the machinery for a warrant."

And then they had a wild free-for-all out in the hall when it penetrated Camparo's head that Joe was the one who'd killed Luisa. He was raving hysterically when a couple of officers from First Aid got there and gave him a shot and took him away.

They were all ready for lunch then, and Grace and Piggott came in as they were leaving. They heard about Luisa, and Grace said seriously it was an object lesson. They were all sitting round the big table at Federico's then, and the rest of them looked at him and asked what he meant by that.

"Not many people," said Grace, "get deliberately murdered, unless they've asked for it some way."

"Well, I won't say Joe did it deliberately," said Palliser. "Malice aforethought."

"No, but she had sort of invited it, hadn't she?"

"The Katz girl didn't," put in Piggott.

"But if anyone ever did invite it," said Higgins, "it was Anna Shaw. That poor damned Wanda—"

"And that wasn't deliberate either," said Mendoza, "whatever the D.A. thinks. And if Harriet Hatfield asked for it, I'm damned if I see how."

"No hunch?" asked Hackett.

"Nothing in the crystal ball." The waiter came up and Mendoza ordered a steak sandwich. They ordered all round, and Hackett looked martyred and gloomily said he'd have a salad.

"And at that, the calories even in oil dressing—Jimmy's found a new one. Low protein only. He says he's lost five pounds on it. But damn it, I'm out and around all day, I've got to keep up my strength—"

"I want to talk with you sometime about this suicide," said Grace. "I don't much like it. But meantime, I've been thinking about that Durfee." He brushed his moustache. "By what you said, that was—you might put it—straight from the heart. What he meant was, he couldn't believe anybody was so much like this Speedy. So I've got a simple mind."

They all knew that. "You've got an idea?" asked Hackett.

"Well, a smidgen of one. They've got computers downstairs. Suppose we add up everything about Tom that's—er—purely physical, and feed a computer with it. See if we've got anybody listed who conforms to the same description."

"Now that is an idea," said Hackett, unaware that it had already been attempted, before Phil had an even simpler idea.

"Is it?" Mendoza cast an ironic glance at Grace. "I don't suppose any of us upright American citizens are just too sure what ancestry might show in our pedigrees beyond a few generations back. Just on the —*disculpeme*—face of it, Jase, lighten your complexion three shades and darken mine ditto, we'd sound very damned similar on an official description."

Palliser looked from Grace to Mendoza. "By God, you would. That never struck me before, but—you're both about five-ten, one-sixty, medium, black hair, moustache—"

"And if you," added Mendoza, "were an inch shorter, John, you and Tom would sound alike. Five-eleven—you're six feet even, but what's an inch?—dark hair, long jaw, clean-shaven—"

"I've got hazel eyes."

"And as for Art and George here—"

"No," said Higgins. "I have it on authority from my wife that nobody could ever mistake me for anybody else." They laughed and surveying his craggy face agreed. The twice-broken nose, prognathous jaw, and high forehead were landmarks that would hardly be duplicated in another countenance. "I only hope the baby takes after Mary," added Higgins thoughtfully.

The waiter came up with a big tray and Mendoza put out his cigarette. "You never know how heredities will act. One of the twins taking after Alison and—genes are peculiar." And then suddenly he half-rose, upset his empty coffee cup, and said loudly, "*¡No puede ser! ¿Qué es esto? ¿Y pues qué?* But what the hell could—"

"I think," said Hackett, "he's having a hunch at last."

*   *   *

If it was a hunch, Mendoza didn't know what it might mean. All he knew was the direction it sent him.

At three o'clock he found the Lawrence Maternity Clinic and Emergency Hospital out on Western Avenue. What it might have been like twenty-four years ago was impossible to say; now it occupied nearly a square block, a rambling building of gray stucco evidently added on to from time to time. Inside the double front doors was a square lobby, a counter partitioned off to make a small office-area behind it. An efficient-looking uniformed nurse inquired how she could help him.

Mendoza produced the badge and introduced himself, which flustered the nurse considerably. "Oh! What—what do you want here? Did you say *Homicide?*"

"That's right. I don't quite know myself," said Mendoza. "I think for a start—" He was really groping in the dark—"I'd like to look at some of your records a while back—1947."

She repeated the date incredulously. "Why, that's years and years—I don't believe Dr. Lawrence—"

"You do keep records that far back?"

"Why, of course, sir, the doctors are most particular. We have records of every patient the clinic has ever— But I'm afraid I don't know— I'd better fetch Mrs. Headley." Mendoza had upset routines; she was annoyed but curious.

She brought him an authoritative older woman who asked him severely why he wanted to examine their records. "A little something came up in a case," said Mendoza vaguely. "Obstetric records. Nineteen forty-seven. If you could—"

"Really!" she said. "I think Dr. Lawrence had better hear of this—"

Dr. Lawrence couldn't have been over thirty, and he regarded Mendoza with more excited curiosity than annoyance. "Homicide!" he said. "What on earth are you after here, Lieutenant?"

"I'm not sure. If I could just see the records, Doctor? For nineteen forty-seven?"

"Well, I'll be damned," said Dr. Lawrence. "That's quite a long time back. And I don't know whether you'll find 'em just as orderly as they should be." He grinned at Mendoza cheerfully. "My uncle started this place in nineteen forty-five, it had hardly got going yet by nineteen forty-seven. His idea was to provide reasonable obstetric care at minimum costs, and he started on a shoe-string—my God, nineteen forty-seven, there'd have been about fifteen beds and three nurses. Good doctor, you know, but rather a vague old boy—he still is. And where the hell records as old as that would be kept— Oh, well, Headley'd know. She always knows everything, she's been here since the year after that, come to think, nineteen forty-eight."

It took even Nurse Headley nearly half an hour to dredge up for Mendoza a dusty file-case full of alphabetized filing-cards: records of all the patients of that young, small clinic of all those years back. Strictly a maternity clinic then: evidently expanded since to offer other services. (Yes, the Hatfields young people then, without much money, saving as they could; this place licensed and operated by an M.D., so safe, but less expensive even then than a regular hospital.) These days there'd be more than one doctor on duty, a whole staff of nurses, office help.

There were not much more than a hundred and fifty patients on file for that year. The elder Lawrence still in private practice on the side then, while he tried to build up his clinic? Probably.

Mendoza shuffled through the cards, looking for dates.

He came up—groping in the dark, following the blind prompting at the back of his mind—with five names.

Ida Welcome (Mrs. Robert).

Ruth Hillyard (Mrs. Theodore).

Vera Kaufman (Mrs. William).

Jessica Manyon (Mrs. Kenneth).

Harriet Hatfield (Mrs. Howard).

All five of those women had had babies on the same day, April 24, 1947. The births ranged from 6 A.M. to 10:50 P.M.

All the babies had been legitimate: three boys and two girls.

Four of the births had been normal deliveries, one a breech.

And one of the babies had been stillborn, one of the girls.

Mendoza looked at his notes. Just what the hell did that say? Nothing at all.

But, annoyingly, he felt that it ought to say something to him.

Hackett, Higgins and Mendoza had all called Landers last night to offer him assurances that I.A. couldn't possibly make a charge. What Durfee had come out with—and what Rosso might come out with, if and when they picked him up—and in any case it was damn farfetched to suppose that Landers could have teamed up with one like Rosso or Durfee. Which I.A. could see.

But Landers was as much aware of some of the facts of life as they were, and he reflected glumly, on Wednesday night, just what the future might hold. Even if I.A. couldn't dredge up any solid evidence—which they couldn't, of course—the implication would be there, forever on his record. And so if he got any promotion at all, it would be slow and reluctant.

He sat there in the living room of the little apartment, on Thursday morning, and thought about it. With cold logic and a little knot of absurd fear at the pit of his stomach, he thought.

He'd never had another ambition. He'd gone to a junior college two years after high school, marking time; he'd taken a liberal arts course, and the one evening course offered in Police Science. After he'd come down here and joined the force he'd taken evening classes at Hollywood High, and passed the exams in Police Science II, III, and IV. He'd passed the detectives' exam and he was up to take the sergeants' exam again the next time round. He'd felt confident of passing that. But it would do him no good at all if this mark on his record would get him passed over for promotion.

He didn't know any other job. He'd never been much good with his hands, at anything manual; it had disappointed his father that he didn't want to follow his own profession, but Landers would have been no good at that. If he was going to be stuck in Detective rank until retirement age, he'd better resign now and get into something else. But what?

Of course there was only one answer to that: private-eye work. And he wouldn't like it. A man on the LAPD had something behind him, making him a little taller: pride, integrity, principle. A standard to live up to. A private eye was just a paid snooper.

And Landers was suddenly filled with a kind of furious and astonished anger, pushing away any other feeling. That the casual little lie could suddenly, like this, threaten to destroy him. Everything he had.

And Phil, he thought drearily. There'd been Phil. He'd started to think, the only girl he'd ever really feel like— But jobless, starting in somewhere else, how could he—? He'd thought maybe she'd felt—

But she hadn't, obviously, because she'd gone blithely off on vacation without even calling to say good-bye. Or good luck.

Phil got to the outskirts of San Francisco at noon on Thursday, having started out at dawn. The traffic slowed her down toward the city. And in San Francisco, of course, was Kitty: Mrs. James McCaffrey. Phil debated about it: easier to find a motel; but in spite of some differences, they were sisters. Phil drove west to Kitty's apartment and announced herself meekly.

And of course Kitty was all questions and speculations. Phil told her firmly she was on private business.

"I'll bet," said Kitty. "Whose?"

"Private LAPD business," said Phil, which was nearly true.

"Yah!" said Kitty. "A four-year junior officer the Chief sends on a delicate mission four hundred miles. And why you ever wanted such a job—What really attractive male would be interested in a lady cop?"

"You'd be surprised," said Phil, which was a mistake and started the questions all over again. "Now stop it, Kitty—I just want a bed and dinner and breakfast—and no interference! And I haven't asked about Jim."

"He's in Portland for the company. So I'm footloose and free—where are we going?"

"No place. I am going out," said Phil. "After I've had a shower and changed my clothes."

"Lady cops are no fun," said Kitty.

"I'm not here for fun," said Phil.

She looked in the phone books and as she'd hoped, found the Church of the Good Shepherd still there. If it was, of course, the same one. Not in the city, on the outskirts down the peninsula. Quite a way from the San Francisco of eighteen eighty-three—or earlier, she thought doubtfully. But she got back in the Gremlin and drove down there after lunch, and was slightly reassured by the main building: it was old, very old, with later additions tacked on.

She parked and went in; the suburb had grown around the old place, which must have once had more extensive grounds. The church, dim and cool, seemed to be deserted, but at length she came across a robed figure near the pulpit; her heels clattered on the tiles as she went down the aisle.

"May I help you, miss?" He turned to show her a gentle aquiline face, strongly Spanish in the liquid dark eyes and mobile mouth.

"I hope so." She smiled at him and introduced herself, explaining. If they could find church records that far back, trace the family—she showed him the ornate Latin marriage contract, the baptismal record.

"Dear me," he said, "that is some time ago, Miss O'Neill. But of course the church was keeping such records then when the civil authorities were not—San Francisco a very small town then, you know." Phil said yes and that was why she'd come to the church. "Yes, indeed. We should have records beyond that—we started, you see, as a small mission here in the years long before the gold was found. I beg your pardon, I should—I am Father Jaime Suarez. Now let us look and see what we can find. Of course we were very fortunate in the earthquake and fire—this far out of the city, we had some damage, I understand, but negligible. I think the records prior to nineteen hundred would be—perhaps we had better consult Father Rodolfo, he is more familiar—"

In the end, they found a few tantalizing items which helped Phil not at all, or very little. Among the earliest records of the church, they found a notation in a foreign-looking fine Latin script, the record of a marriage sanctified between Paolo Arnoldo, age thirty, and Serafina Maria Corpofretta, age twenty; that was dated 1851. Later on, 1861, there was a baptismal record for Maria Anastasia Arnoldo. And 1853, 1855, 1859, baptismal records of Luigi, Pietro, Matteo. Baptismal records of Maria's brothers, sisters? The Italian surname—so many people from all over flocking into northern California in the years after 1849—it might be no relation at all, but the dates would be about right, thought Phil. Serafina must have been born in 1831, then.

And then, nothing. Also at that period, people had drifted.

But it was disappointing. Phil asked about current records.

"Ah—looking for the same surnames? Well, we can look, but I'm afraid we have all too few parishioners these days."

In the current records appeared one Roberto Arnoldo, and Father Rodolfo could tell her something about him. A businessman, he said, living in Palo Alto. Two children—the record listed their baptisms. Phil didn't think Roberto was going to be any use to her, but she thanked the priest warmly.

She answered Kitty absently over a very good dinner—Kitty was domestic and a good cook—until Kitty said she'd shake her in a minute. "And don't tell me you're not mooning over some man! If ever I knew the signs—"

"I do not," said Phil in a dignified voice, "moon over men, and of all the vulgar phrases—"

"At least I got a rise out of you. Who is he? *What* are you doing here? I have the definite feeling you're up to something exciting and if you don't let me in on it—"

"It's *private*," said Phil; and relented. "Honestly it is, Kitty, but if it works out all right I'll tell you afterward. Because—oh, it's *got* to work out all right! His whole career—don't I know those boys at I.A.!" And she didn't know what had been going on down there—whether they'd picked up those other men, what they might have said about Tom. . . .

"Promise? God-strike-me-dead promise?" The remembered childish phrase set Phil laughing.

"Solemn. Only—it's got to be all right. I know it sounds perfectly harebrained—but Jean and Mrs. Landers didn't think so—"

She sat up in the guest bedroom after Kitty had gone to bed and studied the faded old sepia photograph . . . to be hoped Great-aunt Serafina hadn't discovered the rape of her dear mother's relics and caught Jean to boil her in oil. . . . But it had to be that side of the family, she thought. By all the evidence.

There were six people in the stiffly-posed photograph. Were they posed leaning on something, for the exposure of two or three minutes? But the faces, faded, were fairly clear.

The queer voluminous clothes of the middle eighteen-hundreds. Full skirts, high necks, tight sleeves: tight trousers, high collars, all very formal. They had the look, these people, of people uncomfortably dressed up in unaccustomed clothes to have their photograph taken. The photograph was mounted in a very worn, scuffed cardboard frame, and on the lower left of that appeared in ornate, once-gilt print the legend *Walton Studio, New York City.* On the back someone had written the names, the ink dried brown and faint. *Luigi Corpofretta, Maria, Pietro, Serafina, Leo, Tomaso.* (So Serafina had named three of her children for her brothers and sister.)

And Papa, dignified in his formal clothes, with the long sweep of moustache, had the high cheekbones, the straight bars of brows, the dark piercing eyes. The children, in these terrible clothes—Serafina looked most like him, but there was a look there in the boys, too—just babies, two or three at the most, but—

These would be—she worked it out—the parents of the Serafina who had married Paolo Arnoldo: and Serafina Arnoldo had been the mother of Maria who married Robert Pitkin Senior. This was the Serafina Great-aunt Serafina was named for. An influx of immigrants from everywhere, in the eighteen-thirties and -forties: this family, having its picture taken, could have been just off the boat.

And heading for California when? After the gold rush, of course. Like Robert Pitkin, who ended up keeping a hotel in San Francisco. But a few people got rich on the gold and then—

Other gold in California, thought Phil. She got out of bed and took out of her overnight case the brittle old letter. Rancho de la Vergine, Soledad, 1888. A long time ago. When that letter was written from the ranch of the Virgin, Soledad would have been three saloons, an assayer's office and a stage change, and all about it was the rich golden land, much of it virgin land, to be filled with the good crops—vineyards for the wine, grain and fruits—and for the cattle, the great herds of cattle—not then the white-faced meek Herefords of today, but tough range-cattle and some longhorns from the south. . . .

The letter was in Italian and she couldn't read it. It began *Mia cara Maria,* and ended, *con amore, tuo fratello Pietro.* She could work that out from Latin: with much love, your brother Pietro. Evidently if the rigidly orthodox parents had cast Maria off for marrying a Protestant, at least one brother had kept in touch with her.

Phil wondered, a successful brother? Owning his rancho? Passing it on to a son? Because people drifted, but sometimes they stayed put too.

It was such a very simple idea she'd had, she thought, that it sounded a little scatterbrained . . . only there had to be something in it, because —Tom's whole career—

Phil switched off the light. Tomorrow, she thought, crossing her fingers superstitiously, tomorrow. . . . Soledad wasn't far down the coast; and 1888 was a long time ago, but—

It had to come out all right, because Tom—

CHAPTER 12

On Thursday morning Grace and Palliser were waiting for Mendoza when he came in. "This suicide," said Grace plaintively. "We'd just like an opinion, Lieutenant."

"I saw your report on it. What's wrong with it?"

"Nothing exactly," said Palliser. "It's suicide all right, bathroom door locked inside, wrists slashed. But why? There just wasn't any reason—a young fellow, good health, good job, no debts to speak of, no girl trouble. It looks—"

"If you say funny," said Mendoza, "I'll turn around and go home. You've worked homicide detail long enough to know that people don't need reasons to do funny things. If you're sure it's a bona fide suicide, do the paper work and forget it."

"That'll be you," said Palliser to Grace. "I'm going down to the jail with Higgins to try to get a formal statement from Joe Fantini."

Higgins had come in, day off or not. I.A. was still hunting for Rosso, and might pick him up any time. Or, of course, not at all. Piggott came in just in time to meet Carey; Carey had a sobbing female in tow who'd just identified the latest corpse. He'd been, by the autopsy, a long-time user of the hard stuff, but evidently somebody would miss him. Resignedly, Piggott steered her to a chair and started to ask questions and take notes.

When Hackett came in late, having mowed the back and front lawns after breakfast, he found Mendoza sitting at his desk playing with the cards. He had run his fingers through his hair, and with a disarranged few locks over one eye, the rest untidily on end, a cigarette in the corner of his mouth, and the cards riffling through his hands, he looked—as Hackett told him—like a riverboat gambler of the old South. "Sideburns," said Hackett. "All you need. What's bothering you besides Tom?"

"Damn it," said Mendoza to himself, "what the hell has that got to do with it? Hunch be damned—I'd have some inkling what a hunch was saying to me. I haven't. I've just got the irrational feeling that it's something to do with what happened to Harriet. And I don't know what. I can't imagine what it could have to do with it."

"What are you talking about?"

Mendoza squared the pack, shuffled, cut, and turned up the king of hearts. Shuffled and cut and turned the same card. Meditatively he said, "Ida Welcome. Ruth Hillyard. Vera Kaufman. Jessica Manyon. Talk about irrelevant." He shuffled and cut and looked at the king of hearts.

"And who are they and what have they got to do with Harriet? That one really—"

"I don't know. Nothing," said Mendoza, "nothing at all. They just happened to be in the same place with her at the same time, once."

"Well, I've known you to go off on some wild goose chases, but that—"

"I know," said Mendoza. He squared the deck and looked at it. "¡Condenación! And not a whisper out of I.A.—or the grapevine. They'll never get anything else on that at all, Art. And we know where that leaves Tom." He picked up the pack and began to stack it from left to right hand, methodically. He cut and put down the ace of spades. Shuffled, cut, laid down the ace of hearts. And again, ace of clubs, and again, ace of diamonds. Hackett said that was very pretty but it solved no puzzles. "Doesn't it?" said Mendoza. "The trouble with working puzzles from our end, Arturo, just as it is the trouble about sitting in a game with a stranger—which comes to the same thing—is that you never know when there might be an extra ace floating around." He laid down the pack and turned his palm to show Hackett a second ace of hearts.

"If I.A. should ever get any solid evidence on you," said Hackett, "you've got another trade to fall back on."

Mendoza laughed and got up. "Don't ask me where I'm going or why, boy. I'm groping in the dark. Harriet haunts me too. And this is such a damned irrational thing—but I think I'll sniff round the edges and see if anything faintly interesting shows up." He took up his hat and went out, leaving the cards scattered on his desk.

In the anteroom, Lake said, "Hold it," as Hackett came past. "The desk downstairs."

Hackett sat down at his desk and picked up the inside phone. The desk sergeant downstairs passed on a name and address. There had been an alert out to all garages in the county on that hit-run car: they had (they hoped) a fairly good description of it, either a Chrysler or Dodge or Pontiac, dark green, late model. By what the lab had come up with, it had a broken right headlight and possibly a dented right fender. A garage-owner in Chatsworth had just called in on that, said it was possible he had the car right there now.

Returning mild thanks that this wasn't three months later in the middle of a heat wave, Hackett drove out to Chatsworth, which was forty miles through traffic even on freeways, and introduced himself to Bill Godsden, the garage-owner.

"Look," said Godsden, "I don't like tellin' the tale on anybody, but I don't know this guy and it said in the news about that hit-run—a kid killed, wasn't there, and his ma hurt bad?"

"Six-year-old. The woman's still in intensive care," said Hackett.

"Yeah. Terrible thing. You gotta be careful in downtown traffic, can't make time. Anyway, this guy brings this heap in, just says fix it up, don't ask no estimate or nothing. Which I think is a little funny, and when I come to look—"

Hackett looked and saw what he meant. Smashed headlight, couple of dents in the right fender about child-height. He told Godsden to leave the car alone, the lab would be up to tow it in for examination. The car, a two-year-old Chrysler, was registered to Gary B. Raye at an address in Brentwood. Mr. Raye had probably figured that Chatsworth was far enough away that nobody out there might have heard of the hit-run. Mr. Raye had figured without the LAPD.

Hackett asked, "Did he say how he'd done the damage?"

"Told me his wife ran into the garage door."

Hackett got back into the scarlet Barracuda and started for Brentwood.

Mendoza didn't know what he was groping for in the dark at all. He just had a vague feeling that there was something there to grab if he could only catch hold of it.

Four completely irrelevant women. To each other, and certainly to Harriet Hatfield. In the same place, by chance, for a few days twenty-four years ago.

It was in the cards none of them lived here any more.

He had idled along Wilshire in the Ferrari, with no destination in mind; now he found a public lot, walked up to a drugstore on the corner, and proceeded to find out about that. They could all still be here: none of them might be. He looked in all five phone books, and found Kaufmans, Hillyards, a few Welcomes and more Manyons. That one was easier than the rest: the book listed a Jessica Manyon at a Santa Monica address. Of the others, going by initials he made six calls without answers and reached four Mrs. Kaufmans before finding the right Vera Kaufman in La Crescenta. Eventually he identified Mrs. Ida Welcome in Pasadena, Mrs. Hillyard in Tujunga. Suspiciously and curiously they confirmed their presence, those years ago, at that place.

Telling himself he was seven kinds of a fool for wasting time like this, Mendoza went out to the Ferrari again, poorer by several dollars in quarters and dimes, and got on the valley freeway for La Crescenta.

Mrs. Vera Kaufman had, in twenty-four years, turned into a grossly fat matron. She was slightly flattered by a visit from a police-officer, but utterly bewildered as to why he had come. So was Mendoza. She showed him a portrait of her son Paul, who had been born there that twenty-four years ago and was now in the Marines.

Being in the general area, Mendoza headed for Pasadena and Mrs. Ida Welcome. It was a neat white frame house with a green lawn in front. Mrs. Ida Welcome was glisteningly black and had a jolly smile. She offered Mendoza a cup of coffee—"I was just about to have one myself and I don't have any truck with instant, it's real coffee, sir"—and just as complete bewilderment as to what he wanted. Yes, her eldest boy had been born at that place, that was Jim, he'd just got married last year and Mrs. Welcome would be a grandmother pretty soon now.

Neither Mrs. Kaufman nor Mrs. Welcome had known Harriet Hatfield, since, or then, or lately. And of course there was no reason why they should have, every reason why they wouldn't have, and he really didn't know why the hell he was wasting time like this.

He drove back into the San Fernando Valley for Tujunga. Academically he thought what time had done to these five women, impersonal and careless time. The gross Mrs. Kaufman: jolly Mrs. Welcome probably not much changed, Harriet Hatfield risen a little, the husband making money, buying a house in a fashionable area.

Time had been unkinder to Ruth Hillyard. He found her in an ancient sagging house on the back of the lot, the front house nearly as dilapidated with a *For Rent* sign in the yard. There was no attempt at greenery; a half-full garbage can stood by the front step of the rear house, and children squabbled noisily in a yard nearby.

Ruth Hillyard, presently opening to his knock, was obviously suffering from a hangover. She looked at him blearily, once a nice-looking girl, now with raddled complexion and permanently bloodshot eyes. "Oh, you're the one called. What the hell police want of me—" She let him into a dusty, dirty living room, offered him a drink, without apology said she'd have one herself anyway. And why the hell he was here—

"Oh," she said, "that place. Yeah. Lessee, that was Charlie. Sure. The first one. I had three altogether, worse luck, though I wouldn't absolutely swear Charlie was Theo's, but that's water under the bridge and anyways I was married. No thanks from the kids. Charlie's off in the Navy and Doreen had t' get hitched last year and God knows where Lou's got to." She yawned. "Boy, I got a head. Sure you won't have a drink? You're kind of cute for a cop."

Feeling as annoyed at himself as he ever had, but still gripped by the vague conviction that there was something here to be groped after, Mendoza drove down to Santa Monica, stopping on the way for lunch at The Fox and Hounds. When he found the address listed for Jessica Manyon, it was the left rear unit of a dreary old court in the oldest section of town. His repeated ring at the bell finally brought response from the neighboring unit. The front door there opened and a cautious eye rolled at him; apparently reassured, she opened the door to reveal herself as an elderly thin woman in a gray ankle-length bathrobe and that article of Victorian respectability—Mendoza had never seen one before and was fascinated—a mobcap.

"Were you wanting Mis' Manyon? She's never at home this time o' day—she works. At Robinson's Beverly Hills, in handbags. . . . Oh, you're welcome, I'm sure." Her eyes were curious on him.

He drove back to Beverly Hills, parked the Ferrari in the huge lot of that huge store, and went into the ultra-smart sophisticated atmosphere of Robinson's. Consulting a directory, he found Handbags listed as on the First Level, and wandered up and down aisles until he found the right counters. A very Parisian-looking blonde was being waited on by the only clerk visible, a thin rather haggard-looking woman in correct department-store-clerk black and pearls; she just missed being smart. A check was being offered, there were murmured requests for identification. The blonde decided not to be offended.

Mendoza fingered a large emerald-green cobra bag with a brass buckle. If that was Jessica Manyon, she didn't look as if she had ever harbored any maternal emotions. Very much all on the surface: a facade, but the clerks in smart places like this usually were that type— And he was an absolute fool, running around looking at these women: these irrelevant women, nothing remotely to do with Harriet Hatfield or her sudden death.

"May I help you, sir?" She glistened at him, but impersonally, even absently.

"Miss Manyon?" said Mendoza.

She was surprised, thrown off stride. "Why, that's my name—how—"

"Never mind," said Mendoza, coming to a decision: talk about wild geese! "My wife just happened to mention you might help me—her birthday—I'll take this." He thrust the cobra bag at her; Alison could always use another handbag.

She looked confused. "It's sixty-five dollars, sir—would it be cash or charge?"

From the days before the old man died and all the loot came to light, Mendoza had a deep and ingrained horror of charge accounts. He pulled out a checkbook hastily.

Since yesterday, of course (Palliser had expected it) Joe Fantini had been provided with a lawyer, and he had shut up like a clam. To repeated coaxings from Palliser and the standard tough-cop talk from Higgins, he stayed dumb. They gave up on him finally and by then it was time for lunch. They found Grace and Piggott ahead of them at Federico's.

"So ten to one," said Palliser, "we'll never get Fantini nailed for it. He never said such a thing to us, well-known corrupt police just telling lies about him. Why the hell didn't somebody warn him when he started to talk? He was so surprised it probably wouldn't have fazed him then."

"From what you said, he came apart too quick," said Grace. "What bothers me, we shouldn't have been so surprised. Natural sort of thing, husband murdering a two-timing wife."

Piggott said, "That's the trouble with this job, we see so much of Satan's work we get used to it."

"Where's Art?" asked Higgins.

"No idea. Wherever he is, probably ordering cottage cheese or green salad right now."

"And he'd tell you it's not funny," said Palliser mildly.

"More to the point," said Grace, "where is Tom? I tried to call him just now—he's not home. I wonder if the I.A. boys—"

Palliser said, "Don't spoil our appetites, Jase."

The same taciturn sergeant had called for Landers and driven him downtown in silence. Up in the I.A. office, he was shown into an empty interrogation room with four chairs and a table in it, an ashtray on the table, and nothing else. Now what? thought Landers. He lit a cigarette and went over to the one window: there was a nice view out over the city, this clear day.

The door opened and he turned, but it wasn't Southey or Macklin who came in: it was Al Durfee. Clad in unpressed tan jail-issue pants and shirt, he stared at Landers and Landers stared back.

After a moment, then, Landers got mad. The oldest trick known to professional manhunters, and they tried it on him! Did they think he was an absolute fool? If they did, then they were fools themselves and the last officers to call themselves pros or be in a position to investigate fellow cops. Bug the room and let both suspects in here alone to hear what they might say to each other! Landers felt that helpless rage rising again. The casual little lie— And he wouldn't know this was Durfee, officially he wasn't supposed to know Durfee—unless he was guilty with him; but Mendoza had told him privately that they'd picked Durfee up, what he looked like and what he'd said at that lineup yesterday.

That part of it, Landers wasn't even speculating on: coincidence, resemblance, whatever. And Durfee was dumb but he wasn't that dumb: he'd know they had unseen listeners here too.

Landers said conversationally, "You're Durfee. And for Lieutenant Southey's benefit, I don't know you because we were in a racket together, but because I had you described to me, and I guess Lieutenant Southey can guess by whom." He went over and stood in front of him where Durfee had sat down. "Who is he, Durfee? This fellow who looks something like me?" he asked sharply. "You know him—you don't know me—and you know us apart, don't you?"

Durfee never said a word, just glowered at him. "Damn it, you know who he is!" said Landers. He had an insane impulse to seize those bull shoulders, try to shake it out of this lout, this dumb brute with just enough sense to try to save himself a little time in jail. Durfee just an employee in that racket, and if they never picked up the two principals Durfee would get a lighter charge. "Damn it, tell me! You know I'm not him—this Speedy! It won't do you any harm to tell them so—" But it would, of course; and that was why Durfee was dumb. They could surmise (if they would, if they believed him that Landers wasn't Speedy) that he knew the other man's name.

Durfee growled at him and opened his mouth, only to say, "I ain't sayin' nothin'. Not nothin'."

Landers didn't try to talk to him again. Ten minutes later the sergeant came and led Landers out and told him he could go. Landers took a bus back to Hollywood, ate half a sandwich at a drugstore, and dropped into a movie-house showing old classics. When he came out three hours later and started home, he didn't remember anything about the movie at all except that just at the last the U.S. Cavalry had arrived to the rescue.

He wished he could think there'd be a last-minute rescue for Tom Landers.

Mendoza came home early, having forestalled Grace's effort to detail the funny suicide to him, and Hackett's to offer him a blow-by-blow account of how he'd picked up the hit-run driver. Mendoza came home to the house on Rayo Grande Avenue in the Hollywood Hills, and greeted his hostages to fortune very absently.

Mrs. MacTaggart told him he would have a dram to whet his appetite, and El Señor followed her kitchenward. Alison had been off on a day's painting trip and demanded opinion on the result, displayed on an easel beside the credenza. "I've missed the feel somehow—the light came out wrong—"

"I got you a new handbag," said Mendoza, handing over the package.

"Well, how very nice of you, *amado*—what prompted that?" She looked back at the little seascape. "Not at all what I intended, but this last batch of rose-madder I—*Luis!*" said Alison, having just come up with the sales-slip. "How dare you—*sixty-five dollars*—and it's real cobra—"

"Yes, and I thought it had cured me of an obsession," said Mendoza, "but it doesn't seem to have."

"It's beautiful—but *sixty-five*—" The cats appeared to be patted, and the shaggy dog Cedric; the twins were about to have their baths, and could be heard in noisy jollities down the hall. Mendoza swallowed the rye in three gulps, took off jacket and tie, went into the bedroom to hang both away, and came back to pace the living room. "What were you doing in Robinson's?" asked Alison.

"Chasing a wild, wild goose," said Mendoza. "An irrelevant wild goose. There is nothing in it at all—¡nada absolutamente!—and I thought I had put it out of my mind. Out. Irrelevant. Irrational. But I keep having the feeling—" He stopped short in the middle of the room and automatically caught Sheba as she leaped for him. She scrambled up to his shoulder. "Yeast," said Mendoza.

"*Yeast?*" Alison was investigating the handbag, and now said, "Well, of *all* things—talk about being modern—" The handbag was fitted out with, besides the usual mirror, a cobra-sheathed comb, compact, and handy pint-sized flask. She looked at him resignedly. "You didn't notice, I know. *Yeast?*"

"Working away," said Mendoza, "in the dark. My mind. Or mush-rooms," he added vaguely. *"I* don't know what the hell is there in my mind—"

"You're fussing about Landers," said Alison. "I know. If they—"

"Oh, Tom," said Mendoza. He wandered out to the hall, up to his little-used den, and sat down at the desk and brought out a pack of cards. Sheba fled.

"*¡Qué hombre!*" said Alison. "*¿Para qué?*—what's the use?" She went to the kitchen to put the finishing touches on dinner.

Summoned three times, Mendoza finally sat down to dinner with her and absently consumed wild rice, pot roast, browned potatoes, asparagus in Hollandaise sauce, a slice of Mrs. MacTaggart's special chocolate cake, and four cups of coffee. When Alison asked him if he wanted more potatoes, he said, "*¿Cómo?* I could look forever at it, there is nothing there—how could there be anything there?"

"I don't know. If you'd like to tell me about it, *amado*—"

He held out his cup for more coffee. "What set me off in this direction? Oh— *Ridículo*. Nineteen forty-seven, I ask you . . . and the dog, of course—"

Alison steered him back toward the living room. "I don't think you're in a fit state to read Kipling aloud tonight. You'd better—"

The twins, of course, had other ideas. Powdered and pajamaed, they corralled him at the living-room door. "*Los cuentos* now! Máiri said," announced Johnny firmly. "All about *El Gato* all by himself—an'—an'—*El Rinoceronte!* Daddy—*El Gato* first—don' listen to Terry, *niña tonta*—"

"Daddy—Daddy—*no Rinoceronte, La Ballena* swallows *el marinero! La Ballena,* Daddy—"

"Really, you know—" began Alison.

Johnny planted himself insistently on Mendoza's shoes and tugged at his trousers. "*El Gato!*" he shouted at the top of his lungs. "*El Gato* all by himself—an' *la mujer* makes *el pacto* with—*la mujer* more smart as *El Gato*—"

And Mendoza said, "*¡Diez millones de demonios desde el infierno!* Jane Doe! By God, Jane Doe!"

Alison rescued Johnny as Mendoza ran for the phone. As he ran, he brought up a few random thoughts from the yeast of his subconscious mind.

"Tired-looking—she was—and why not? But why—why the hell? Jane Doe—Santa Monica? But that store— Art? Meet you at the office in half an hour . . . I don't know. Something. Nothing. It's ridiculous, damn it, but— I'll see you."

Hackett had stopped telling him he was going senile by the time they came to the door of the shabby old duplex unit of the court in Santa Monica. They waited, Hackett shifting his bulk restlessly, and the door opened. There wasn't any screen door, and the little living room behind the woman in the doorway was lighted brightly. Mendoza, with his long sight, saw over her shoulder in there the large framed photograph on the table, and he let out a sudden deep breath.

"¡Ya está!" he said very quietly. "It was a hunch after all—only we didn't hold the extra ace."

"What is it?" Her voice sounded tired too. She snapped on the porch light, saw Mendoza first. "Oh, you were in the store— Yes?" His eyes led hers to his outstretched hand, with the badge in it. For a moment she didn't move. Then she turned and walked into the room, tacit invitation. They went in.

Hackett had just discovered the photograph. "But, my God," he said in naked astonishment, "that's—but it can't—"

Mendoza picked it up: a glossy eight-by-ten photograph in a silver frame. Holding it, he looked at Jessica Manyon. She had once been a pretty woman: fair complexion, brown hair, hazel eyes. Habit and necessity had kept her groomed, clean, neat, but her face was too thin and she looked older than she probably was.

She turned away from them, and then reached to the coffee table, took a cigarette from the box there. Mendoza flicked his lighter. "I think," he said, "you have something to tell us, Mrs. Manyon."

"I don't know your name."

"Lieutenant Mendoza—Sergeant Hackett. Central Homicide."

"Yes," she said. "And I can't imagine how you found me. But it really doesn't matter. It was just—the last thing of all the bad things, and I wasn't going to live with it any longer. I was going to the police tomorrow. So it really doesn't matter at all."

"Sit down, Mrs. Manyon. I have to inform you that you needn't talk to us if you'd rather not, and you are entitled to—"

"An attorney, yes. Don't be stupid. I'd decided to tell the police, and so it doesn't matter at all. You know, I never was superstitious, but I wonder now if there are—jinx people. If I'm a jinx to—everybody I touch." She looked at him reflectively. "The worst of this is, it's not only going to affect me. Innocent people too. But I suppose it's—impossible that it—shouldn't have to come out. All of it. Would you do me a favor, Lieutenant? You'll find a bottle of bourbon in the kitchen, if you'd make me a drink? I think it might help. Do have one—yourselves —if you'd like."

When he brought her the glass, she took a long swallow and put the glass down beside her. "A jinx," she said. "I wonder. I'll tell you just how it happened, and maybe you'll wonder too." And she found a small smile for Hackett, who was still studying the photograph. "That," she told him, "was my husband. Kenneth Charles Manyon. He was killed in a silly little accident on Christmas Eve, nineteen forty-six. He'd been all through the fighting in Europe, and then he came home—to be killed like that. He was twenty-six and I was twenty-five. We were expecting our first baby in April."

"Oh, yes," said Mendoza. "Yes, I see."

"Do you? After Ken was killed—I wonder if you can understand how much I wanted that baby. Something of Ken's. Of ours. We—we'd decided on names, Martha for a girl, Charles for a boy. Of course I got his insurance—he was still in the Army—and I came back here, I'd grown up here. It was home even though I was alone—my father died when I was twelve, and Mother the year before Ken was killed. There weren't any relatives at all. I came back here—and I went to Dr. Lawrence. I liked him, he was a good doctor, I'm sure of that. He'd just started his clinic—and—I went there—to have the baby. He—"

"Oh, yes." And Mendoza heard the echo of young Dr. Lawrence: *about fifteen beds and only three nurses.* Could you say, hurried and overworked nurses?

"And then—and then they told me—the baby was dead. Stillborn. I wanted to die—it wasn't fair. But you don't die, you go on because you have to. It seemed as if Ken had died all over again. But I—picked up the pieces, and I went on." She took another swallow of her drink. "I don't want to bore you, I needn't go into details. I got married again four years after that, but he was—no good. A drinker, a drifter. I divorced him, and I took Ken's name again. It—well, never mind. And I've had to work, of course, but it didn't seem worth the effort to—take courses, get a better job. It didn't matter. There wasn't anyone to care. And time went on—until about—six weeks ago. Funny. A day like any other day. When—she—came—to—my counter—to look at handbags." Her eyes were wide, blind now. "When I saw her—the first time—"

Mendoza reached over and took the photograph from Hackett. "When you saw Catherine Hatfield," he said, "and realized—" The photograph showed a good-looking young man in uniform; and uncannily, Catherine Hatfield was a latter edition of him. The same olive skin, straight nose with flared tip, dark eyes, wide smiling mouth, pointed chin, dark smooth hair.

"She was Ken's daughter!" said Jessica Manyon, and she still sounded astonished at that little fact. Her mouth was trembling. *"Our* daughter. I couldn't mistake—it was like seeing Ken young again—even his smile, one-sided—and—I knew—then I knew—"

The hurried, harried nurses, perhaps a couple of deliveries coming along at once, the doctor busy—or summoned and not yet there—and the little unforgivable mistake about the name. "It was Harriet Hatfield's baby who was stillborn," said Mendoza.

"Oh, my God," said Hackett.

She nodded tiredly. She swallowed more of the drink. "I knew. I—I could have been fired, but I couldn't help it—I had to know who—who she—who she *thought* she was . . . I just walked off—followed her. *My* girl—my daughter, that I'd never known, never known about—Ken's daughter. She went—to that shop." Only a couple of blocks from the big department store. "I went in, she was waiting on the customers. I pretended—I don't know how I did, I'd realized it but it was like being in a dream—I got her talking, I found out her name, where she—" She raised her head and there was stark misery in her eyes. "A *mistake*—just a mistake—all that time ago. And if it wasn't my fault—it wasn't theirs either —those people—all those years, she'd been their girl, they thought—I couldn't be so cruel as to tell her, right then—"

"So you went to see Mrs. Hatfield," said Mendoza gently.

"What else would I do? What else *could* I—" She looked a little wild; she took a deep breath, controlled her voice. "I called her—to be sure she was alone, and I tried to be—calm and sensible about it. I took Ken's picture—so she could see for herself— She didn't believe me, of course she didn't want to believe me, and at first I couldn't blame her— *but*— It's not as if I wanted *much,*" said Jessica Manyon desperately. "They'd had her—my daughter—all those years, and I'm alone, I haven't anyone. I said if I could just see her sometimes—if she could just know, and understand how I felt— But she—Mrs. Hatfield—she wouldn't agree to that. She was—I could tell—trying not to believe it, even after she saw Ken's picture, after— She wanted to go to that clinic and ask, but I knew there'd be nothing to find there—the mistake made—all that time ago, the doctor'd have found out then—if there was any record."

"Yes. You went to see her several times," said Mendoza, leaning to light her new cigarette. So the dog had seen her there before, and hadn't barked, next door. "You were seen walking up the hill."

She put a hand to her head. "The car went out on me last year—it

wasn't worth getting repaired. I can take the bus to work. Yes. I kept—
at the last I was pleading with her—I didn't care what I had to do—but
somehow, I had to get her—to say—it was only right, you can see that.
All that time she'd thought—her own daughter, and I couldn't—" She
was a woman of integrity; maybe this wouldn't have happened otherwise.

"That last day," she said, "if I can explain it to you—I was feeling—
desperate. She didn't want to believe me, and by then she'd just shut her
mind to it. She was—hard, because—I know now—she was frightened.
That was it, of course she was frightened." And of course the normally
open Harriet Hatfield hadn't told her family, her nice close-knit family,
anything at all about this. "She said—it just wasn't possible, and I
wasn't to bother her anymore—and I was just a—a fanatic with a queer
idea and she wasn't going to have me—upsetting her family." Jessica
finished her drink. "I'd been so sorry for her at first, you know. Any
woman would be. But I—when she said that, I—I tried not to be sorry
for myself, but sometimes—it's hard. And all I could think, right that
minute, was how she had—so much, so much, and things I'd never had—
and it wasn't right that she should have *my daughter* too, just because—

"I don't remember hitting her, you know. I'd tell you about it if I
did, but I don't. I remember—it was funny, I could only get out a whisper at her, wasn't I ever to have anything, when she had—and then—and
then, she was lying there—"

There was a little silence, and she looked up with a tired smile. "A
jinx," she said. "It wasn't her fault at all—Mrs. Hatfield's. But I suppose
I wasn't—seeing that very clearly at the time."

And then she asked, "Do you want me to come with you now?"

"I think he's got one of those things Socrates called his daemon,"
said Hackett to Angel. "He didn't really know there was anything there,
he just felt it. But, my God, those two poor women—and the girl—
Couldn't Hatfield or somebody sue that clinic for—"

"What good would that do now?" asked Angel soberly. "But I know
how she must have felt. And in a way, the worst still to come—"

"The press uproar, God knows. And I'm damn glad, my Angel, that
we can—identify ours so easy. Mark like me and Sheila with my
mother's hair and—" Even that didn't make her laugh. "I think I'll call
George," said Hackett.

Higgins came back from the phone and said seriously to Mary, "It's
a kind of relief. The kids. Stevie's going to look a lot like Bert, and

Laurie with your eyes and all. I hope the baby takes after you too—if it's a girl, I mean. But at least let's hope it looks like one of us."

"Why?" asked Mary, amused. "I'm keeping fingers crossed it isn't a girl. The worst spoiled brat in the state, between you and Steve. But why the sudden anxiety, George?"

"That Hatfield thing," said Higgins. "What a thing. That was Art on the phone. The damnedest thing you ever heard—"

"But, Luis!" said Alison, horrified. She sat up in bed, looking very fetching in a blue nylon gown, her red hair curling crisply, burnt flame in the bedside light. "What an awful thing—and with the press falling on it, new sensation, as they will—you don't know who to feel sorriest for. The girl, or—"

"My bet would go there." Mendoza stripped off his trousers, deposited his watch on the bureau tray. "To have that sprung on her all of a sudden—mmh, yes, you can sympathize with everybody concerned in this one."

"But I'll say something else." Alison hugged her knees, looking thoughtful. "If that girl's got any good stuff in her—or the Hatfield husband any common sense and kindness—they'll stay by the Manyon woman. The girl, anyway. Any woman would know how she'd feel."

"*Pues sí.* And I'm relieved to reflect," said Mendoza, buttoning his pajamas, "how much Johnny looks like you and how much Terry looks like my grandmother. Enough to give any parent a qualm or two—"

"*¡Bastante!*" said Alison. "Don't be silly. They're really terribly careful about that kind of thing, there's not a chance that—"

"Are you reassuring me for the past or the future?" Mendoza switched off the light.

"Now really, Luis— Well," murmured Alison, "of course they do say that children born to elderly parents are apt to be more intelligent—"

"Elderly!" said Mendoza. "*¡Gatita roja, mujer malvada,* miscalling me—"

CHAPTER 13

Phil was feeling frustrated when she headed out of Soledad north on Thursday evening. The trouble was, she thought, she'd got her mind so firmly fixed on historical records that she'd forgotten a few contemporary facts.

She'd got to Soledad at ten that morning, and thinking of those possible records down in black and white, had made for the courthouse. A motherly clerk had fallen easily for her tale of doing genealogical research for a history of the early state, and helped her look: and nothing had turned up at all. No records of wills, marriages, deaths, births, or anything with either of the surnames she was looking for. By two o'clock there wasn't anywhere else to look, and she sat in the car wondering where else to try, and thought of the local newspaper.

There was a public library; it had back files of the local paper, and she pored over them for some time, without success. What she was looking for, of course, was some evidence of one of those families being still around; but in all the years, she thought, even if there were any descendants here, the name might have changed.

And then it came to her what an idiot she'd been. Two ways. First, of course the important records would be at the county seat, which was Salinas. The second thought opened up wider vistas. When that letter from the Rancho de la Vergine was written, the fact that it was headed *Soledad* didn't mean a thing. In 1888, Soledad would have been the stage-junction, the place the letter was handed on for eventual delivery; and very possibly the only junction in a hundred miles or more. That rancho could have been anywhere in two or three big counties; she didn't think they'd got round to drawing county boundaries then.

Impatient at herself, she started north again for Salinas, not a long drive. She got there too late to do anything that day, checked into a motel and was up early on Friday only to find that the courthouse didn't open its doors until nine-thirty. She fumed over breakfast and was waiting when the custodian arrived.

Again she was lucky in finding a friendly clerk; in fact, she reflected later, it was luck that had sustained her all the way, not good sense. He was a little perky man named Oakes who reminded her of a robin. He suggested property transfers as the most likely fertile source— "Because of the surname of course, but that we can't be sure of, I can see—" but when nothing turned up, he said apologetically that before 1900 people had been very lax about such legalities—little enforced county authority. At any rate, there was no mention of the property known as the Rancho de la Vergine.

"Well, we needn't be so easily discouraged," said Mr. Oakes brightly. "Suppose we look at a little later period—"

Nothing turned up. Even until rather recently, Phil thought, with all the new rules and regulations, not every will got formally offered for probate. Property deed-transfers would be on record somewhere; not necessarily here. For all she could be sure of, that property could now, with boundaries drawn, be over in Merced County or up in Stanislaus County.

"Death certificates," said Mr. Oakes. "Marriage licenses—" But they were a rather recent requirement too, and Phil said absently that if the property had stayed more or less in the family, they had probably been Catholic. And thought about church records, not hopefully.

But it was another place to go, and also, church records (so divorced from state regulations) might go back a long way, if there were any. The only thing was, the church harboring them might be anywhere a good long way from Salinas.

Or would it? Phil thought about that. Back all those years ago, there probably wouldn't have been a church in Soledad, or for miles around there. What would there have been? A few Indian missions, priests traveling about? And Salinas was an old town too.

She debated about trying the old mission, but that was over toward Monterey and she wasn't sure it was open, or harbored any records. In the end she drove around and chose the oldest-looking Catholic church she found, which didn't look so ancient at that, and went in.

Here she found a brisk young redhaired priest who was instantly fired with interest in her search. "Fascinating, history," he told her enthusiastically. "People. Eighteen eighty-eight, you said, that'll be a while back, but let's think about it. No church here then, of course. The mission, the big one, that is, but St. Artemus had a small mission hereabouts, I seem to recall—that's us. Every Christian place then—few and far between, you know, Miss O'Neill—would send priests out on regular tours, a week or two weeks' journey around—marrying people, burying 'em, baptizing—that sort of thing. Necessary, with only a few men of the cloth in hundreds of miles, you see. Let's have a look at some of the early church journals." He unearthed these from a chest in a bright little room at the side of the church, and looked interestedly. And it was in that old journal, near the front of the tall old tome, that they came across two lines of Latin script recording the ceremony of marriage between Elena Ranulfo and Matteo Corpofretta of the "ranchero on the fork of the River San Joaquin near El Pináculo."

"Well!" said Father Murphy, interested. He translated that for her. "That gives you the location, anyway, Miss O'Neill. Of course in the last seventy-eight years"—the marriage was dated 1893—"the property may have changed hands a dozen times, or been broken up—and even if it hasn't, and any descendants are still around and still good church-members"—he chuckled—"they'll still hardly be dependent on traveling priests these days, any later records would—"

"But where was it, what do you mean?"

"Show you a map." He found a map of the state in a drawer, unrolled it. "Right here—here's where we are, and here's the San Benito Mountains, east and north of Soledad—and the Pinnacles National Monument. Your rancho'll be somewhere in that territory, or it was. There's a number of tributaries of the San Joaquin through there."

"Well." Phil looked at the map. And again she thought she'd been an idiot, wasting time. Not very big populations around there, Soledad or east of it. But of course she hadn't known a more precise location for the property. Now she thought that there should be a few old-timers who might, hopefully, remember old names and people and places.

It was only a little after two o'clock. She snatched a sandwich at a drugstore, got the gas-tank filled, and headed back for Soledad. She didn't stop there but found a secondary road leading east away from town.

Six hours later she was admitting she was lost. The road had led up into hills and more hills, empty and wild; presently a sign directed her to the National Monument. It occurred to her, discouragingly, that the original rancho might have been purchased by the government for the National Monument. Another road led her north through completely wild land, and when she came to one looking slightly newer and more promising, going east again, she took it, but it led her through more emptiness.

She drove on; she must come to some evidence of civilization some-time. It was full dark and she was nearly starving to death and watching the gas-gauge anxiously when around a curve of the hilly road she came suddenly on human habitation. A gas-station: a lighted café: four parked cars: across from the café a row of four houses.

"Thank heaven!" said Phil.

The woman in the café fed her on waffles and maple syrup and very good coffee, and said she guessed Phil could use her extra bedroom, no motels around there. To further questions she added that Captain Adam Watkins knew pretty well everything about these parts, his grand-dad had come here back in the seventies. Captain Watkins of the Highway Patrol—station just up the road, him and Corporal Fosdick was all there was but about all the law needed around here.

"Thank you very much," said Phil. "And I could eat another waffle, please."

Friday had been a somewhat hectic day for Central Homicide.

Mendoza had called Howard Hatfield at eight o'clock, asked him please to keep the family home. He had broken the story to them as gently and tactfully as possible, but of course it wasn't a story they could listen to calmly. He'd brought a policewoman with him, and that was just as well: the girl broke down and Hatfield was incredulous, bit-ter, angry, and breathing vengeance in turn.

The Hatfields were in for an unpleasant time. Unfortunately truth was not always pleasant. The press, casting around for new sensations, was going to fall on Harriet Hatfield, Jessica Manyon and the Lawrence Clinic as manna from heaven.

It would be, Mendoza reflected, only neighborly to warn young Dr. Lawrence—but before he got round to it, he was summoned to the D.A.'s office for a conference.

The D.A., having read the first reports on the Hatfield case, couldn't decide whether to call it murder first or second. Mendoza couldn't help him there. The warrant would be processed sometime today.

The inquest on Grace's suicide was scheduled for Friday afternoon, and Grace and Palliser were still wondering what was behind that one. "Waste of time," said Mendoza over a hurried lunch. "As long as you're sure it was suicide."

"Oh, that it was . . . I'm just curious," said Grace. "This Hatfield thing is making headlines. Those poor damned people."

But there wasn't anything Homicide could do to make it easier for the Hatfields. Homicide's business was getting at the truth, and sometimes the chips flew far and wide.

William Royce was up for arraignment today; Piggott could cover that, offering the brief evidence. The Hatfield thing, now entirely out of Homicide's hands, was annoying because every time a Homicide officer appeared in the main lobby the press was around him clamoring for more details.

They had still to get a formal statement from that Raye, the hit-run driver, and get that warrant through.

At six o'clock on Friday evening, just as Mendoza was thinking of going home, the D.A.'s office called and one of the prosecutors informed him that they were making it murder first on Jessica Manyon. "Always providing the psychiatric examination shows her to be competent."

Mendoza, hat in hand, went out to the anteroom talking to himself about psychiatrists and passed that on to Grace and Higgins, just leaving as Sergeant Thoms took over the switchboard. "Competent!" said Mendoza. "Would you take a bet that if they say she's neurotic they'll call it temporary insanity?"

Grace laughed. "Which has always struck me as about the silliest charge there is. Temporary insanity kind of like saying temporarily dead."

"*Exacto*. Silly is the word." And inevitably they were waylaid by reporters on their way out.

On the way home Mendoza thought about the silly phrase and muttered to himself. Jessica Manyon was sane, he thought; but everyone had a breaking point, and to some it came easier—or quicker—than others. If Jessica had had anything else—a live husband, another child, even an aged aunt—it could be that the little unforgivable mistake wouldn't have sent her to the breaking point.

But the thing in him, the part of Luis Mendoza that worried around and about any little puzzle like a dog with a bone, had settled down and was satisfied about the Hatfield thing, now. And as a result of that, it had started to worry and wrestle again with the puzzle about Landers.

On the one hand it was nothing, the casual lie or mistake built up into more than it warranted by the perennially suspicious I.A. men—or make that watchful. And on the other, of course—

Mendoza swore aloud, turning into the driveway. It wasn't quite dark yet, and as he came out of the garage a vigilant whistle greeted him from the alder tree: *Yankee Doodle came to town!*

"If that—creature—stays around here permanently," he said to Alison, "I wish to God one of you would teach him the rest of that tune."

"I know," said Alison. "Like waiting for the other shoe to drop."

Saturday started out even more hectic than Friday. At least no court-rooms demanded attendance, on a weekend, but business at Homicide had stepped up. June would be fading into July in a couple of weeks, and July with the first of the summer heat always brought a rise in the crime-rate. It hadn't gone over eighty last week; today it was edging up past eighty-five.

Another body had turned up in MacArthur Park, but not a mysteri-ous one. Hackett, coming back to type a first report on it, said tersely, "Kid about eighteen. Typical description. At a guess, the overdose, let the surgeon say if it's acid or H or speed. No I.D. on him." Before start-ing the report he sent a description down to Missing Persons.

Grace and Palliser had gone out to look at another corpse, but both of those were run-of-the-mill business, no problem for Homicide ex-cept creating the everlasting paper work. The second corpse was that of an elderly man horridly, but naturally, dead in a cheap room on Temple Street. He had hemorrhaged his life away on the thin flowered rug there; among other things in the room were papers identifying him as an outpatient at the General Hospital, so Grace and Palliser went around there to find out more about him.

Just before noon on Saturday a shocked and incoherent young Dr. Lawrence invaded Mendoza's office. "My God," he said, "what *is* this? I was away overnight—my sister's birthday—the press falling on—and Uncle nearly had a coronary—my God, but these things don't *happen!* It's just impossible—I tell you, these things don't—"

All Mendoza could offer him was sympathy.

And he was wrestling again with the problem of Landers, the impos-sible, handle-less answerless thing. Ordinarily he managed to control his temper with the brashest pressmen, but today a couple of them annoyed him considerably with some crude questions about Jessica Manyon. He came into Federico's feeling dangerous, and unprecedentedly put down a double rye.

It was just nicely warming his empty stomach when Lieutenant Southey came up to the table.

"Well, now," said Captain Adam Watkins comfortably, "not that I've laid eyes on many policewomen, you're about the fetchingest one I ever saw, Miss O'Neill. So you're just expecting me to answer questions without knowing why?"

"It's a complicated sort of story," said Phil apologetically, "and besides I don't want you to—get any preconceived ideas. I can only tell you it's about something terribly important and—and it involves a man's whole career."

"Well, I don't mind obliging you," said Captain Watkins. This little rural barracks of the California Highway Patrol had one room up and one down. The corporal slept upstairs when he was on duty; Captain Watkins had a comfortable ranch home of his own back in the hills, and a wife who worried about his meals when he was on shift away from home. Phil thought it was wasted effort; the captain had a little round paunch, a round rosy face, and shrewd blue eyes.

"You said you'd like to hear some gossip about local folks? Well, that's a thing old-timers like me do real good, Miss O'Neill—"

"Maybe there are families around who've been here for a long time," suggested Phil. "Since the seventies and eighties?"

"Some of 'em, sure," he said. There was a desk in this little office but the captain seemed to prefer his old rocker by the window to the swivel desk-chair. "You interested in any particular families? My grand-dad came here back in eighteen sixty-four, time he got out of uniform. First Virginia Rifles. I guess I know most of what there is to know about most local folks—besides bein' an old-timer I'm the law around here."

Phil didn't want to lead him directly. "There was a ranch," she said. "I don't know how big, or exactly where, but somewhere around here, and it was—" she started to say the name, and substituted, "owned by an Italian named Corpofretta. Pietro Corpofretta."

"Oh, them," said Watkins. "That old Fir Green ranch. I always did wonder how it came by the name, there aren't any firs on it as far as I remember." Eighty-three years, thought Phil, and the foreign-sounding name getting garbled; perhaps the descendants of Pietro not even knowing the language, American now, and not knowing what the name meant. "That place," said Watkins. He brought out his pipe and started methodically to fill it from an old pouch. "Old man Cris Corpofretta owns it now. It was a good workin' ranch when he inherited it from his dad. Around four thousand acres, call it. He's let it run down some. Doesn't run more than a couple of hundred head of cattle, and raises just about enough to grain 'em decent. That was one o' the biggest and best properties round here once. There was a tale—I recall my grand-dad telling that—that the first Corpofretta won the land on a horse-race. I don't know if that's so, but it's the kind of thing that used to happen when this country was young—Americans just coming in, you know." He puffed energetically, at last got the pipe lit. "Anyway, Cris came by it by marriage you could say. His great-uncle—he had the same name too—all he had was a daughter, and she couldn't take title to the land, acourse, so by all accounts—I heard that through hearsay, little before my time it was—he married her to her first cousin, that'd be Cris's grand-dad. This the kind of thing you want to hear, Miss O'Neill?"

"Just the kind of thing, please." But— "Does this one, the man who owns the ranch now, have any children for it to go to?"

"Well, I guess you could say that's the reason he's let the place go downhill," said Captain Watkins. "There isn't properly speaking anybody except the grand-kids, and no telling if either of 'em 'd want to work it. I expect Cris'll leave it to John Trebizond in the end. He's married to Cris's granddaughter Julia. Sure, Cris had a boy, just the one child, Matthew. He wasn't interested in the place, he turned out a city man—went away to college, and then the war came and Matthew joined up. He was killed at Anzio in the Second World War."

"Oh," said Phil. "Then he had children?"

"Yes, he did," said Captain Watkins. "He got married while he was in college, and he had two—a boy and a girl. Their mother used to bring them to Cris's ranch, summers. Till she got married again. Julia, she's the older of the two, she loves the place, a nice girl Julia is, she came back here to live with Cris and finish high school. The boy—Randal his name is, they call him Randy—well, he's a city man too."

"You said this Julia lives here—"

"Yep. Married to Johnny Trebizond, got two good boys, Johnny's in real estate over in King City. Could be the boys'll show some interest in the ranch, they get older, and Cris maybe'll leave it to them. Couldn't say. I don't figure he'd think about Randy at all."

"What about him?" Phil thought, he would be about thirty-three, thirty-four?

"City man like I say." Watkins contemplated his pipe. "We never saw much of him, since he used to come here summers when he was a kid, up to the time he was twenty-one, twenty-two. Since, he comes back to visit Cris every once in a while. Not so often, and no special time. Be here a week, a month, off he goes again. Very pleasant-spoken feller, and he gives out that it's when he's out of a job he turns up here—" Watkins cocked his head at Phil. "I been wondering about that, just lately. No real reason to. He's supposed to be a salesman of some kind. I can't say I've seen much of him—I'll just hear he's stayin' with Cris again, awhile, and then he's gone. I do know that Julia nor Cris never hear from him, one year's end to the other, till he turns up here—once in a long while."

"Oh," said Phil. Suddenly her heart started beating a little faster. "Did you say he's there now—at the ranch?"

"Didn't say, but he is. Sure enough. I heard it from Fred Whitehead just the other day, he's the rural-delivery driver. Old Cris never says much when he does come to town, but I got it figured he doesn't so much cotton to Randy landin' on him, even as often as he does which isn't often. City man," repeated Captain Watkins. "Doesn't turn a hand when he is there."

Phil stood up. "Captain Watkins, could you—could we drive out to this place and—maybe I could get a look at this Randy? That's all I want to do. It might—it just might be—terribly important, and help a lot."

"Well, I don't know why not," said Watkins easily. "I haven't been over that way in a spell, and the corporal can hold down the station. Isn't often I get the chance to take a pretty girl for a ride in my cruiser."

As they went out, Phil found she had, absurdly, crossed the fingers on both hands tightly.

Hackett came into the dining room with Higgins just in time to hear the loud raised voices down at the front of the room, and they both ran. Mendoza was swearing violently in Spanish; Hackett got there just in time to grab him as he swung on Southey.

"Insubordinate—" said Southey, white and furious. "You know I'll report this, Mendoza! You've no business inter—"

Mendoza told him what he could do with his report. "Goddamn it, Southey, you watchdogs have built this thing up out of nothing and you know it! You've got no damned reason to keep my man suspended and by God I'll expect you to—"

"On the contrary," said Southey, "we've turned up some evidence from his home town that he was once known by that nickname. We have the identi—"

"That's impossible," said Hackett and Higgins together.

"On the contrary," and Southey's voice was pure ice, "it is perfectly sound evidence. From a former school acquaintance of Landers', Fred Barker, and the more we turn up on this the more I—"

"For God's sake simmer down, Luis!" said Hackett. "Go away, Southey. Take your Goddamned meaningless little evidence on a man you don't know at all and get out of our sight—I'm not going to hold him forever."

Southey stalked off. "You needn't ruin the press of this jacket," said

Mendoza, and Hackett let him go. "What the hell, Art? They can't have evidence—on *Tom?*"

"It's some damned nonsense they've built out of nothing, it's got to be. What set you off at him?"

Mendoza laughed shortly. "A double rye and something he said about Tom. Never mind. But what the hell they think they've got—"

For once Hackett ate his low-calorie plate without martyred comment. They cut lunch short; afterward they got into the Ferrari and Mendoza drove up to Fountain Avenue.

They found Landers, in sports-shirt and slacks, gloomily watching an old movie on TV. He greeted them with apprehension. "What now?"

"That's what we'd like to know," said Mendoza. "The I.A. boys now tell us they've got evidence that you were once called Speedy. Back in school, up in Fresno."

"Oh, don't be ridiculous," said Landers. "I never picked up a nickname in my life, let alone a silly one like— Where'd they get that from?"

"One Fred Barker," said Hackett, sitting down. "Who is he?"

"Who? *Barker,*" said Landers, staring. "Oh, *him.* Oh, for God's sake! I just hope all their evidence is as worthless as that! Barker's a little fellow who never made friends at school—hanger-on, didn't know anybody very well. Or vice versa. Where he dreamed that up for I.A. God only knows, but anybody in town who knows me could tell you that's a lie."

"*¡Condenación!*" said Mendoza. "And by God, what I wouldn't give to turn up some real evidence to show them they've been chasing a mirage—and rub their noses in it well and good!"

"Amen to that," said Hackett. "And that'd be quite a trick, Luis."

"At any rate, that little piece of their so-called evidence we can scotch—and I really thought they were supposed to be better trained than that, taking hearsay for— But how to get you off the hook altogether—" Mendoza swore again.

And Hackett said rather heavily, "When the chips are all down, boy, I think somehow the deck gets stacked on the side of the good people."

"Go say that to Mrs. Manyon, Art," said Higgins quietly, "or Catherine Hatfield. Or Wanda Shaw."

"Oh, hell and damnation!" said Hackett angrily. "What else can we do about this, Luis?"

"Hold the good thought," said Mendoza dryly, "that what you just said holds true at least fifty percent of the time, Arturo."

*   *   *

And if any official prayers were put up on it, it was probably by Piggott, or possibly by Mrs. MacTaggart, who in her sojourn with the Mendozas had come to take a proprietary interest in the LAPD.

In any case, whether it was official prayers or Mendoza's flights of profanity, the answer walked into the Homicide office at seven-forty Saturday night.

Mendoza and Hackett were still there because just as they'd been leaving at six o'clock, a sergeant from Missing Persons had brought in a distraught middle-aged woman in tears. She had just, said the sergeant, identified the teen-age kid full of dope as her son. She sat in Mendoza's office and wept, and as she wept she talked.

"It was all the boys he went with—real bad boys—but he wouldn't listen, he wouldn't listen—they know it all, that age, they never believe anything bad can happen to them—it was the boys like that Chavez, and Harry Rodriguez, and Alfonso Real—they got him to taking the dope—he wouldn't listen, I tried to get him to listen to me, but—"

They wanted the names of any other users, pushers, sellers, and the night men weren't in yet. Sergeant Thoms called Alison and Angel; police wives get used to that sort of thing. They got the woman's name, which was Juanita Enriquez, and asked patient questions. By seven-thirty they'd got all she could tell them, which was quite a lot, including some addresses and the names of a few adults possibly selling the stuff. They called a squad car to take her home.

"I'd better pass this up to Callaghan's office," said Mendoza.

"I suppose," said Hackett. "Damn, I wish I could think of something constructive to do about Tom. Everything they've got—or think they have—is all up in the air, and don't tell me they don't know it! Those damn bloodhounds leaning over backward—"

Mendoza got up, frowning, and stretched. "*¡No es verdad!* The point is—incompatibility. If that's the word."

"Come again?"

"Incompatibility. They don't know Tom. We do."

"Oh. Yes," said Hackett. "But that's past praying for."

Mendoza picked up his hat, and Sergeant Thoms appeared in the doorway looking surprised. "Lieutenant—" He stood back, and a little pert-looking blonde came into the office. She wasn't exactly pretty, and she wasn't cute either because she had a pair of very steady sensible dark-blue eyes to offset the freckles on her nose and a new sunburn. She looked tired, and her green silk-jersey dress was wrinkled. "Lieutenant Mendoza?"

"That's me. What can we do for you?"

"I'm Phil O'Neill. Oh, I mean—" She fumbled in her bag and produced a badge. They looked at it, surprised. "I thought I'd better come to you. Because I.A. probably wouldn't listen to me at all. I'm just a clerk down in Records. I work the computer."

"Oh, you work the computer," said Hackett. "But what—"

"I'm doing it all wrong," she said. She shook her head, feeling one temple. "I'm still muzzy from driving—sorry. I'm a friend of Tom's, you see. And when this funny thing happened—well, of course it's awful, but to anybody who knows Tom it *is* funny—in a sort of way—and I just had an idea. I'm sorry, I just didn't think you'd listen to me, Lieutenant—of course Tom's told me this and that about you, the other men—but it wasn't even as if it was a hunch. It was just a simple little idea."

"About Tom and this funny thing?" asked Hackett.

"Well, yes. And my vacation was coming up, so I—"

"*Phil* O'Neill?" said Mendoza.

She blushed through the new sunburn. "Well, Phillipa Rosemary—only not for a junior officer LAPD. You can see that. And so I went looking—it sounded fairly crazy, but Mrs. Landers and Jean didn't think so, of course—"

"What," asked Mendoza, "was the idea about, Miss O'Neill?"

"Genes. I came as soon as I could. It was just about ten when— And it's nearly five hundred miles, but I made it in just over eight hours. And considering some of the roads before I got back on the coast highway— But we mustn't waste any time, Lieutenant," she said earnestly. "You're the one to take it up to I.A. and—and shove their noses in it. They still wouldn't listen to me."

"Take what? To I.A.? What do you—"

"Why, I've found him," she said. "I knew *in my bones* he had to be somewhere—but just as Mrs. Landers said, it was such a simple idea the men wouldn't even think about it—probably laugh your heads off. But I found him. And Captain Watkins is keeping an eye on him for us, and you'd better send him a teletype to arrest him—material witness will do to start—"

"Found who?" asked Hackett blankly.

"Oh, for goodness' sake, *men!*" said the pert blonde impatiently. "The one these idiotic witnesses thought they were identifying—the dead ringer for Tom—the real Speedy. His name is—"

CHAPTER 14

Mendoza stared at her for a moment and then let out a yell of exultant mirth. "*¿Parece mentira? ¡No me diga!* My God, do you mean— Oh, by God, but what a facer for those—" He leaned on the desk, laughing helplessly.

"And I think you ought to teletype Captain Watkins," said Phil urgently. "He couldn't arrest him just on my say-so, of course, but you— Not that I think he's likely to run, he hasn't an idea he's been spotted, I was very careful, but—"

"My God!" said Hackett. "My God—a ringer for Tom? But what—how'd you find—"

"Well, he'll startle you," said Phil. "I thought it *was* Tom ten feet away—of course they're fourth or fifth cousins, I haven't worked that out, but—we really had better get him nailed, you know—"

Mendoza pulled himself together. "Oh, by God, what a—by God, *how* I'm going to enjoy— Yes, Miss O'Neill. Yes, we had." He leaned down and planted a kiss on her freckled nose. "If I'd known there was a real detective working on it— Come and tell me where to teletype."

When they came back Hackett was talking excitedly with Galeano and Schenke. "No, that's all I—Luis took her to— Did you get him?"

"Captain Watkins is going out into the wilds to nail him right now," said Mendoza. "I've got the C.H.P. to say they'll fly him down tomorrow. Material witness. But what a—*Dios,* and wasn't it just the sudden scatterbrained idea a female would have, and then get it to work out just as— Oh, I can *hear* Southey and—" He collapsed again.

"I called Tom," said Hackett. He had also tried to get everybody else; but Higgins had taken the family out to see the new Disney, and Palliser was at a discount house with Roberta haggling for a new refrigerator. Everybody he had got had asked excited questions and castigated him for not knowing the answers. They demanded details from Phil now. "Tom said he'd be right down—"

Phil, overtaken by yawns after the long drive, told them about it sleepily. "It was just logical," she said. "Genes. And he takes after his mother's side and by the photographs quite a few of them looked a lot like Grandfather—no, it'd be Great-grandfather—and so I just went and looked. I knew *in my bones* that Speedy had to show up somewhere along the line. And—"

"Women," said Schenke. "Women! She knew! She just went looking—"

"*What* did you say his name is?" asked Galeano.

"Corpofretta. Randal—Randy. And when I heard from Captain Watkins—"

"I'll be damned," said Galeano. "In very rough translation, that's what that means."

"What?" said Schenke and Hackett.

"Speedy," said Galeano. "You could say. A rapid body. That's the damnedest funny one I've heard, but I bet that's how he came by that nickname."

They were still asking questions when a breathless Landers arrived to hear about it all from the start. "—Fifth cousins, I think," said Phil through a yawn. "And you might be twins. Well, brothers. Uncanny. Taking after Great-grandfather."

"What?" said Landers blankly. "What—you don't mean—I'll be eternally damned! All the while you've been chasing around looking—why, *Phil*—"

"On the scatterbrained idea," said Schenke. "I can't get *over* it. She just knew, so she went and looked and boom, there he was."

"And I'm starving, if anybody's interested," said Phil.

"I'll buy you the biggest steak available, Miss O'Neill," promised Mendoza.

"I don't want a steak," said Phil. "I want bacon and eggs. I've been thinking about bacon and eggs ever since I passed through Guadalupe at five o'clock."

"*¡Mi pobre niña!*" said Mendoza. "We'll find you bacon and eggs—" The phone buzzed on Sergeant Thoms' desk.

"Hassle over at the U.S.C. Medical Center," he relayed a moment later. "Sounds sort of confused—you'd both better go." Swearing, Schenke and Galeano went out. The rest of them took Phil up to a bar and grill on Wilshire and fed her bacon and eggs.

"Heavenly!" she said, buttering toast. "—And then there was Father

Murphy, he helped too, and of course Captain Watkins—I wonder if Randy's got a pedigree somewhere. It rather sounded like that—and I think Captain Watkins had started to wonder too. If he thought he was a little hot, he'd make tracks for Grandpa's isolated ranch in the hills—"

"I'd take a bet on that," said Mendoza. He and Hackett had been starving too, and for once Hackett hadn't counted calories, but absorbed a large T-bone and a pile of french fries, listening to the story of the hunt.

"That Italian girl way back there—it was just a kind of family joke!" said Landers. "Oh, I don't mean joke exactly, but you know what I—my God, my great-grandfather—it never crossed my mind there'd be relatives, but—"

"Italians," said Phil, "usually reasonably prolific. I knew— Oh, we've got to call Fresno! My heavens, if Great-aunt Serafina found out about—"

"What do you know about—" Landers stared.

"Goodness," said Phil, crumpling her paper napkin and standing up, "if Jean hadn't burglarized Great-aunt Serafina I'd *never* have found Speedy! And they'll be dying to know— Jean was so furious at that I.A. man, and he was rather Prussian—have you got any change? Go get some. There's a pay phone in the lobby—" She trotted off briskly and Landers went to get some change.

"Of all the damned far-out things!" said Hackett. "I'm going to be curious to see this Speedy. And—"

"You and Tom."

"And you know something, Luis? I think—"

"Oh, yes," said Mendoza, laughing. "Yes, indeed, Art. Tom's got quite a girl there, hasn't he?"

"—Fifth cousins," said Phil. "I think. Maybe even sixth. But it's just the way I guessed—genes. It's really no wonder—so many of the family seemed to take after that old man in the photograph. Oh, Jean, I'll send those back right away—if Great-aunt Serafina—"

"No!" said Jean excitedly. "Honestly? No, that's all right, Phil—she thinks she's mislaid them somewhere, I can just slip them back— Does he really look like Tom? I know you said it must be like that, but how queer—"

Landers thrust his head into the booth. "*I* want to talk to them."

"Yes, in a minute . . . Well, every family's bound to have one black sheep. The rest of the family sounded quite respectable. We think this Speedy may have a record somewhere—"

"I wouldn't be surprised," said Jean. "Phil, are you and Tom—"

"He's right here," said Phil hastily, "he wants to talk to you—"

"Yes, just a minute, here's Mother."

Phil handed the phone to Landers. When he hung up ten minutes later she was propping up the side of the booth, and he said he'd drive her home, she was dead on her feet.

"Don't think I could drive 'nother ten feet," she agreed. When he stopped in front of her apartment on Kingsley she was sound asleep and he had to shake her awake.

"Well, of all the queer things!" Alison sat up in bed, hearing all about it with fascination. "Not but what I don't see exactly how she reasoned. A thing any woman would think, and don't say scatter-brained, Luis. It's just as you were saying about the twins—perfectly logical that they should look like both of us, only different sides of the family—"

"Occasionally," said Mendoza, buttoning his pajamas, "women still astonish me."

"And really not surprising," said Alison, "that they should turn out so much alike—Landers and this Speedy, I mean—even in the fourth or fifth generation. The genes still there. Dormant or whatever."

"But to jump to such a conclusion right off the—"

"Not at all," said Alison. "She sounds like a very bright girl, Luis. Simply postulating a probable possibility."

"*¡Ay de mí!* But scatterbrained or not, the conclusion seems to have justified the—mmh—jumping. I'm going to be damned interested to see this fellow. And—*¡Santa María y José!*—how I'm going to enjoy shoving I.A.'s nose into this one!" He started to laugh again.

"It's just another illustration," said Alison with satisfaction, "of the old adage."

"*¿Cómo?*"

"Never," said Alison sedately, "underestimate the power of a woman."

She called Angel the next morning as soon as Mendoza had left and the twins, full of breakfast, were tearing around the back yard with Cedric in pursuit, the cats hiding under bushes, and *el pájaro* swearing at all of them from the now completed nest.

"Isn't this the most—"

"I was *fascinated* when Art told me. Of all the queer things—Mark, leave the pussy alone!—and yet you know, Alison, it was a perfectly logical sort of thing to think of—"

"Which I said to Luis. But they don't like things to be so simple. Not just Luis—of course he's got that complex mind to start with—but any of them, Angel. Men. A fairly complicated result, like Landers getting identified that way, they think it has to have a complicated reason. But this girl sounds very bright. She—"

"She sounds a dear. I want to meet her. Do you suppose she and Landers—"

"I haven't an idea. But when she went to so much trouble—"

"Mmh," said Angel. "I think so. And he certainly couldn't do any better, by what Art said. Oh, dear, they *are* looking forward to telling off those I.A. men! Art was up two pounds and he never even swore . . . Well, depending on when they *do* get married, I thought a shower —with everybody—"

"By all means," said Alison, and then began to laugh. "Really, Angel —speaking about jumping to conclusions—"

The hassle at the U.S.C. Medical Center had turned into quite a thing; Schenke hung around to outline it to Mendoza. A trio of juveniles riding very high on something had been brought in by an irate parent; as the parent happened to be very much a V.I.P., an internationally known entertainer—"In quotes," said Schenke rather disgustedly, and mentioned his name—he had not been turned away to the General. In the process of admitting the juveniles one of them had turned out to have a gun. One intern had been shot dead, a male nurse was in serious condition, and one of the uniformed men in the first car to get there had been shot in one hip. After the Homicide men got there—"He'd got up on the roof of one wing then, and he had a dozen boxes of ammo on him," said Schenke, "he'd just run wild"—he'd got Galeano in the shoulder and leg. Schenke would be sitting on night shift alone for a while; when he left Nick in the hospital, he said, they weren't sure if any bones were broken.

"These Goddamn idiots of kids," said Schenke further, angrily. Yes, they had got him; Schenke had put a bullet in his leg. "I'd rather have made it his head." The well-known entertainer was the sniper's father, and it turned out that the other two juveniles were the offspring of another V.I.P. from the same sophisticated milieu.

"And how very convenient," said Mendoza, sounding pleased.

"Convenient?" said Schenke. "With Nick in the hospital—"

"Maybe Art's right and the cards get stacked in our favor. *De veras.*

The press has still got the Hatfield thing, but this will—mmh—fill them with joy all over again. It should be very easy to squelch any stray rumors about suspicion of a ranking officer—especially when we've got Speedy to hand over to Van Allen. The bird in hand." Mendoza grinned; Hackett was excitedly relaying the story to the rest of them, out in the anteroom. "George, I'll let you and Art share the exquisite pleasure of telling the tale to I.A. John, you and Jase might find out whether Speedy has a pedigree with us." They had queried San Francisco on that overnight.

"—And," said Mendoza, sitting back at his dapper ease in the chair beside Captain Macklin's desk, "I think that sums up the explanation for your benefit, gentlemen. We all do make mistakes, and while it was entirely understandable that you should—given the initial rather outlandish reason—want to look into the matter, I should have thought," and he smiled slowly at them, "that you would know just a little more than is apparently the case about rules of evidence. In any case—"

"Be damned to that," said Macklin. He sounded suspicious. "I'll believe this rigmarole when I see it proved out myself! All you've got is this fool girl's word—what the hell was a Records clerk doing at—"

"On her own time," Hackett pointed out enjoyably. "And she rang the bell loud and clear, didn't she?"

"I'm not taking that without any more than you've given us!" said Southey sharply. "You were exceeding your responsibility in authorizing the arrest of this man—it's all extremely irregular, bringing in the Highway Patrol, for God's— You haven't an iota of evidence, and—"

Mendoza dropped a little of his suavity, crushing out his cigarette. He stood up. "Put up or shut up, Lieutenant. You can soon judge for yourself. The C.H.P. will be landing him at International this afternoon—"

"And Captain Macklin and I will meet the plane," said Southey.

Mendoza looked at him in silence for a moment. "Afraid I'd try to coach the witness? I might trust you to meet the prisoner, Lieutenant," he said gently, "if you promise to take along a couple of uniformed men from Traffic to make sure he doesn't get away from you between there and here."

"He'll be brought in," said Southey grimly, "and we'll see for ourselves if there's anything to this—tale—or not."

"And you'll arrange it all nicely according to Hoyle," pursued Mendoza, "with a lineup and the three witnesses. Detective Landers is quite ready to cooperate—just one more time, Lieutenant. Say four o'clock?"

"There'll be enough of us there to see fair play," added Higgins to that, and gave them his craggy grin.

The I.A. men didn't bother to say that they knew that. The men from Homicide came out, and Mendoza leaned on the wall and started to laugh again.

"By God, but it was worth—all the worry and fuss!" he gasped. "Their faces—and all because—all because a little blonde Records clerk —had an idea! *Dios,* the more you think of it—"

"I'll say one thing," said Higgins, grinning in sympathy. "By what you tell me, Tom's got something going for him in that girl. I'm damn curious to see this Speedy, but also that blonde. Pretty?"

Hackett considered. "Little," he said, "and dangerous."

"Dangerous?"

"Have any male wrapped around her little finger," said Hackett, "with him convinced it's just opposite." Higgins grinned again and said, That kind.

Phil didn't remember falling into bed. She woke up at one o'clock, hungry again, and made herself a healthy ham sandwich after a long shower. She was just finishing the sandwich when Mendoza called.

"We thought you were entitled to be present at the lineup I.A.'s arranging. Four o'clock."

"I'd love to," said Phil. "Did they say some terribly unkind things about me, Lieutenant?"

"Well, they claim to be gentlemen. They were annoyed, shall we say, by your unsolicited interference. And I hope, Miss O'Neill—you realize we've taken you on faith—that you weren't influenced by wishful thinking when you described Speedy."

"Oh, my," said Phil. "You just wait, Lieutenant." Her car was still parked down in the headquarters lot, she'd have to take the bus. . . .

When she came into the dimmed room with the bright-lighted platform at its front, a little crowd of men was already there. Even before Mendoza came up to introduce her, she recognized them from what Tom had said, various times. The men from Homicide he worked with. The two big ones, sandy Art Hackett, dark George Higgins with his ugly but somehow attractive face. The middle-sized dark fellow would be Matt Piggott, seeing the devil's hand everywhere, and maybe he was right. Dapper brown Grace, tall dark Palliser with his grave mouth.

Off to one side was Captain Van Allen of Auto Theft: it was queer to realize that this had all started as one of his run-of-the-mill cases.

The witnesses Byron and Dunne sat with a uniformed man beside them; Al Durfee sat between Macklin and Southey.

The two I.A. men had already seen the ringer, thought Phil; Mendoza had told her they had fetched him in from the airport; but their faces were wooden. Then the platform brightened up there, and they all watched as the line of men filed onto the platform in silence.

Landers was second in line this time. Three more men of the same general type, and then—

"*Jesus!*" exploded Byron and Dunne simultaneously. There was a little hushed murmur of incredulous profanity from some of the Homicide men.

Durfee stared up there and then slumped in his chair. Southey nudged him sharply. "What about it?"

"What do I say?" asked Durfee in a surly tone. "I didn't *believe* it— naw, it wasn't him, but it mighta been his twin—but I'm gonna say it ain't? Just to get a guy I don't know from Adam off the hook? And me further on the hook? I ain't no flat wheel."

"All right, so which one is the fellow you know as Speedy?"

"Well, that one, acourse," said Durfee reluctantly. "Now you got him, it's no skin off my nose. The one at the end of the line. But, jeez, you can see why I—"

It was queer seeing them together, thought Phil. She remembered the moment she'd first seen him—Captain Watkins casually hailing the old man, just cruising around, showing the pretty tourist the country, how's tricks, Cris—and the tall city-dressed man slouching up. It could have *been* Tom—and then she had seen the differences.

But up there, in line separated by three men, the likeness was uncanny—and yet they were unlike.

Corpofretta was the older by two or three years, but he had the same quality (was it freshness of complexion, the way the eyes were set, the mouth?) of looking young—younger than he was. There were the same features, harking so strangely back to that strong-featured man in the faded old photograph—high cheekbones, wide mouth, dark eyes, dark hair growing straight off the forehead, the straight bars of brows—

"God," said Dunne in the darkness, loud and incredulous, "you couldn't hardly tell which was which—but—"

But, with the other one, with Speedy, there was a weak cast to the mouth, an indefinable air of cheap arrogance. Seeing them together, anyone who knew either would know them apart, she thought; and that was queer too.

"Satisfied, Southey?" asked Mendoza. "Would you like to thank Miss

O'Neill for finding the missing jigsaw piece? Well, perhaps Captain Van Allen will."

And Southey said stiffly to the uniformed sergeant, "Will you go and ask—Detective Landers—to join us, please?"

Van Allen somewhat grudgingly let the Homicide men sit in on an initial questioning. By then they had Speedy's pedigree: a rather lengthy, if minor, pedigree all around the Bay area, and two counts from L.A. County with the sheriff's boys. B.-and-E., burglary, auto theft and fencing.

He shrugged at them: it was how the dice fell, he said. Almost worth getting dropped on to find out he had a double. He laughed at Landers and said that was a real hot one, all right—he'd got a big kick out of finding he could double for a cop. But close to, they were all seeing that they weren't really doubles: only at first sight, apart from each other.

"Rosso?" he said. "How should I know where he's lit out to? We come back and find the place lousy with fuzz—we took off. That's all I know. Whole operation shot to hell, and we musta had a dozen real sweethearts in ready to go—call it six, seven grand profit. Way the ball bounces. I figure I'm hot, I make tracks for the old man's place—good place to cool off, nobody knows about me up there." Or did know, he'd be adding to himself; he looked angry.

And later, "Sure, some guys call me Speedy. I don't know the lingo, all the Italiano to me's the name, but I remember Grandpa sayin' that— it's kind of what it means, see."

He was small-time, Randy Corpofretta; they left him to Van Allen.

"So, welcome back to the team," said Mendoza to Landers in the hall.

"And, my God, you don't know what a relief— But, damn it, you know what I've got to worry about now?" Landers laughed. "That damn pro lout is going to be passing himself off as me—now he knows about it—"

"Don't borrow trouble," said Mendoza amusedly.

"At least," Hackett reminded him philosophically, "I.A. knows about it too."

"There is that," admitted Landers. He'd looked around for Phil, but she had disappeared.

"Miss O'Neill," said Mendoza, "is a very understanding girl, Tom. She said she thought we'd rather have an all-male reunion, but you can take her out to dinner."

"Oh," said Landers. "Oh, yes, thanks."

"You know, Tom," said Hackett, "if you want my advice, you'll take out a permanent lien on that girl before somebody else does. If I wasn't an upright married man—"

"I had the same thought," said Palliser. "Not that I ever went much for blondes, but she's quite a blonde, isn't she?"

"And a smart one," said Piggott, "which they aren't always. Now you take redheads—" Maybe some day Piggott would get around to proposing to his redhead.

"You buy her a good dinner," Grace told him seriously. "She's earned it."

Mendoza clapped Landers on the shoulder. "Come on, boys—I'll buy drinks around."

They got waylaid by the press, but—even as Mendoza had predicted—the press hadn't an inkling about an upright detective getting confused with a pro; the press was agog with interest in the celebrities' offspring.

"We ought to go see Nick," said Mendoza as he and Hackett got into the Ferrari. "Do you know what he likes to read?"

"*Es muy extraño,*" said Hackett. "Detective novels."

They had Jessica Manyon's arraignment coming up, and Wanda Shaw's; the paper work on the other current cases to get through, and from now on as the heat built up business at Homicide would increase as it always did in summer. But the latest crisis was past, and Mendoza's daemon was for the moment at rest.

As he switched on the engine and the Ferrari roared to life, he muttered absently, "Eggs . . . So Alison said. A new batch. And if they turn out like their father— That damned bird deviling the cats—*¡Caray!* A man wants a little peace and quiet when he comes home—"

"If you really did," said Hackett, "you wouldn't have."

"Wouldn't have what?"

"Married the redheaded Scots-Irish girl."

"I mean, there's no way to say thanks," said Landers. "When I think of all the trouble you—"

"It was interesting," said Phil. "I'd sort of got my teeth in it by then."

"And where you got such a crazy idea to start with— Well, it was, Phil! My father said—"

"Oh, men. Your mother and Jean saw it right away. Naturally."

"And when I think of you tackling that awful old woman— Great-aunt Serafina," said Landers, "replaced the bogeyman for Jean and me as kids. Phoo! She is a terror—"

"No, she's not," said Phil. "She's just a lonely old woman who—who never had much, Tom, and she's jealous of the little she does have."

Landers looked down at her in silence. He'd brought her to Frascati's on Sunset Boulevard, the nice quiet place where you could be private and leisurely, and he'd enjoyed a meal for the first time in days. Phil looked very neat and cool and self-possessed in a blue cotton-lace dress and the high-heeled white sandals that still only brought her blonde curls to his chest.

"Well, I can't get over Jean," he said. "She used to be terrified of the old lady. You seem to have hit it off with Jean and Mother just fine."

Phil smiled and then canceled the smile primly. "Oh, well," she said vaguely, "your mother's just fine. I expect Jean can be a little—um, you know—bossy, if you're around her much."

"That's absolutely right," said Landers, gratified by her perspicacity. "I've often thought Bob's too soft with her—a very nice guy, but too easygoing, if you know what I mean. But what I wanted to say was, well, it was damn good of you, Phil—go to all that trouble, just on a hunch—that is, it was *my* trouble, and you needn't have—"

"It was interesting," said Phil again. "When I joined the force, I hoped eventually I'd be doing some real police work—but this was the first chance I had, really. If it wasn't exactly official."

"Yes, but—well, I'm grateful," said Landers. "For your having the crazy idea at all."

"Men," said Phil, and smiled at him.

"And you know something?" said Landers. He reached down and took hold of her left hand with his right, and put her cigarette out. "You smell nice—something like lilies—"

"Spring Jonquil, and I'm glad you appreciate it, it's four dollars an—"

"And I guess the boys gave me some good advice."

"Oh? Lieutenant—"

"And Art Hackett and Higgins and Palliser and— Come to think, they've all got wives, except Matt, and ought to know. I think maybe I ought to take the advice."

"What did they—"

"Come on," said Landers, dropping bills on the table and getting up, pulling her up with him. "Let's get out of here. I'll explain it to you in private."

MURDER
WITH
LOVE

Omnia vincit amor: et nos cedamus amori.
Love carries all before him: we too must
yield to Love.
—Virgil, *Eclogues, X, 69*

—But what a mischievous devil Love is!
—Samuel Butler, *Notebooks*

CHAPTER 1

Mendoza drifted into the Homicide Bureau about three o'clock of a hot Friday afternoon: hotter than they usually got in early August. The air conditioning was not on, and Sergeant Lake looked stickily uncomfortable at his desk by the switchboard.

"So you finally show up," he said. "They haven't got around to us yet."

"So I see," said Mendoza. Beyond the anteroom, across the big communal detective office, all but two of the tall windows were missing all their glass. "And I'm entitled to half a day off for once. Anything new gone down?"

Sergeant Lake opened his mouth and suddenly the building shook a little and swayed. "Damn it, they say we'll be getting these aftershocks for a month," said Lake uneasily. "And I don't feel just so happy sitting here this high up all day."

"Well, the building hasn't fallen down yet, Jimmy."

"Higgins went out on a new body, but it didn't sound like much of anything—another heart attack, probably. The autopsy report came in on that bum—you don't have to ask what it says. Matt and Jase are out looking for possibles on the heist, and I don't know where everybody else is."

Mendoza went into his office, yawning. As he sat down in his desk chair, the building moved slightly again and the desk slithered an inch or so away from him. "Damnation," he said mildly.

The men at Central Homicide, LAPD, had been busy at the usual humdrum routine up to last Monday; there hadn't been anything big or very baffling on hand, just the tedious routine of clearing up after violent death. They'd had the heist job, a bar over on Fourth, the bartender shot; and the inevitable suicide, and the old wino over on the

Row dead in an alley, and they had just cleaned up a hit-run. They had all gone home on Monday night, and the night watch had gone home by five-fifty Tuesday morning, and like ninety-five percent of the residents of L.A. County, were asleep in bed when a major earthquake occurred to Southern California. Later scientific estimates placed its epicenter out east of Newhall, but earthquakes are unpredictable in effect, and downtown L.A. being on a direct north-south line with the epicenter, destruction hit there too. A good many windows in the Police Building had been smashed, a few sidewalks buckled, a number of streets had been a shambles of broken glass from store-front windows, and over on Skid Row the old Midnight Mission, sheltering its usual collection of derelicts, had collapsed in rubble. Oddly enough there'd been only one casualty there: everybody had got out but one man when the roof fell in. The autopsy report was on Mendoza's desk now; he didn't look at it. He yawned again and lit a cigarette.

Out in the valley, of course, there had been devastation and disaster, and for forty-eight hours nearly every law man in the county had forgotten his regular job to help out on all that had to be done, from directing traffic down here to helping evacuate nearly a hundred thousand people from their homes to picking up looters in evacuated areas to ferrying people to the nearest civil-defense centers. But now things were getting cleaned up. The engineers had drained the reservoir and the dam was under repair, so all the evacuees had gone back home yesterday. The searchers had found the last of the bodies in the rubble of the two hospitals which had collapsed, and it was going to be a good long time before those freeways were in use again, where the overpasses had fallen down. Things were getting back to normal. Only, as usual after a major quake, they were getting the aftershocks, some of them registering respectably on the Richter scale, and the experts said they might go on for weeks.

Mendoza, finding himself tossed unceremoniously out of bed in Tuesday's pre-dawn, and hearing Alison's exclamation as she picked herself up from the other side of the bed, had been much occupied since; with things getting cleared up, he had taken most of today off. In fact, this was the first time he'd been to the office since Monday night—all hands had been needed in the disaster areas. Fortunately Hollywood was not in line with the quake's epicenter, and the house on Rayo Grande Avenue had only lost a few dishes and glassware.

Hackett came in looking hot and tired. "Jimmy said you'd finally shown up. Well, I don't blame you for taking some time off. They haven't got round to our windows yet, I see." Men had come on

Wednesday and carefully cleared away the shards of glass still in the frames, but they were probably replacing the windows one floor at a time; and this was a big building. "And do you know what I just saw in the *Herald?* Talk about insult to injury—the specialists are now saying that because this one was on the San Gabriel fault, there's still pressure building on the San Andreas and we could have another big one any time. My God."

"Yes, I saw that—encouraging," said Mendoza absently.

"And we'll never get anybody for that heist job. No special M.O., it might have been any pro hood in town."

"Also encouraging." But the only homicides occurring since Tuesday morning had been natural deaths—heart attacks, and one heat prostration.

At least they had Nick Galeano back with them, just this week, from his little siege in the hospital after he'd been shot up by a kid high on the acid.

Higgins wandered in and said, "Welcome back. Not that I blame you for taking some time off, Luis." He pulled his tie loose, got out a cigarette; he and Hackett together made the office suddenly smaller. "The new one's just more paper work—another coronary, looks like, and probably brought on by fright at these damn aftershocks. And do you know what those damn-fool experts are saying now? In the *Herald—*"

"We saw it," said Hackett. "Spreading alarm and despondency, if you ask me. Not, for God's sake, that anybody in my family is worried— Mark got quite a kick out of it, first one for him, and Angel just says, Fate. What is to be will be. Well, I suppose she's right at that."

"And Mary says the same thing," said Higgins gloomily. "Steve and Laura got a charge out of it too—their first one. And we didn't get any damage, but—" He massaged his prominent jaw. Mendoza and Hackett regarded him with idle amusement. Higgins the longtime bachelor, falling for Bert Dwyer's widow, had now some hostages to fortune to worry about: Bert's good kids, and the new baby due in October.

"God," said Hackett, "I wish it'd either cool off or our windows would get put back." It was obviously useless to pipe refrigerated air conditioning to offices minus windows. "We don't usually get it quite so bad in August—"

"I'll tell you something funny, Art," said Higgins. "It's always hot when we get a quake. Hotter than usual. I wonder if there's any connection."

"Well, one of the experts up at the planetarium—on TV last night—

seems to think it's a matter of the sun and moon being in direct alignment. There was an eclipse on Monday night, you know—"

Matt Piggott and Jason Grace came in and Grace said, "Have a nice morning off? Not that I blame you. We might as well throw that heist job in Pending, we'll never land on anybody with enough evidence." His chocolate-brown face, moustache as neatly narrow as Mendoza's, wore a pensive look.

"I said so," said Hackett.

"And aside from the paper work on the other bodies, business slow," said Piggott. "Everybody so scared by the quake they're sitting quiet at home, maybe."

"Waiting for the next one," agreed Grace. He lit a cigarette and strolled over to the windows, and Hackett told him nervously to stay away from there.

"One of these aftershocks could send you right out. I wish to God there *was* some legwork to do, I'd just as soon be on the street as up this high—"

"Fate," said Mendoza. "Trust your guardian angel, Art."

"And you can laugh," said Piggott, "but there are, you know. The guardian angels. Look at Higgins—and Tom, come to that." They thought about that; maybe there were. Higgins getting away from those three escaped cons, back in April, without a scratch; and Tom Landers' strange ordeal last June, when he'd got mistakenly identified as a pro hood. But Landers' guardian angel, you could say, had been pretty, trim, smart (in both senses) Policewoman O'Neill down in R. and I.

"How's Tom doing with that cute blonde?" wondered Hackett. "Anybody heard lately?" It was Landers' day off today.

"He's not," said Grace sadly. "His mind's made up all right, but she's a very sensible sort of girl, that one. Says they haven't known each other long enough to be sure. But she's still dating him, so maybe he'll get her to marry him eventually."

The inside phone rang and Mendoza picked it up. "Yes, Jimmy?"

"Things starting to move again," said Lake. "Shooting at a travel agency over on Spring."

"Right." Mendoza passed that on. "You can toss for it."

"I'll go," said Hackett at once. "I feel safer on terra firma." He got up.

Grace grinned. "In earthquake country—like the old joke says—there are times when the terra just isn't so firma."

"That does it," said Higgins. "I'll go too, with the third-rate vaudeville jokes floating around. And I don't like these damn windows any more than you, Art."

They left Mendoza yawning again. "And the elevators," said Hackett as he punched the button. "They can get jammed—"

It was the Acme Travel Agency, We Send You Better, and a little crowd had collected in the street outside, where the black-and-white was parked at the curb. Hackett and Higgins shouldered through the crowd to find another small gathering inside the building. Off to one side, one uniformed man was riding herd on half a dozen people and his partner was standing over two people sitting in a couple of the chairs lined at one side of the long counter—a sullen-faced dark young man and a sobbing blonde. There was a body on the floor on this side of the counter, with the colorful travel posters above it.

The second uniformed man came forward. "Very glad to see you, sir. Quite a little party here, by what we gather. It was the owner called us— Mr. Haskell—" He nodded at a scared-looking middle-aged man over there with three women, another man. "Seems this guy just walked in and started shooting. Here's his gun." He handed Higgins a big revolver. It was a Colt .45, empty now.

Hackett bent over the body. Another young man, a good-looking man, fair, well-dressed in a light-gray suit, white shirt, dark tie. He'd been hit in the body, at least a couple of slugs, maybe more, and he'd bled a good deal onto the patterned vinyl flooring.

"He just—he just walked in and started shooting—" The middle-aged man came forward hesitantly. "You more police? He—that one—" he nodded at the corpse, "he'd just come in, with the lady, his name was Gorton, he said they wanted plane reservations for Rome, and I was just— When this other one came in and just started shooting—no reason at all—and Ruby screamed, that's Ruby, she works here of course, I ought to say I own the business, it's my own business, my wife and I—only Marge went to the bank, thank God she wasn't here when— And he just started shooting, and—"

"All right," said Hackett, and stood up.

"There's an ambulance on the way, sir," said the other uniformed man. "All these people say they witnessed it, so we held 'em for you."

"So who's the marksman?" asked Higgins genially. The sullen young man didn't look up at him.

"Goddamn little bitch," he said. "It was her I ought to've shot. Her too. Just bad luck I didn't get her too." He was also a fairly good-looking fellow, dark and tall, with a pugnacious jaw, and well dressed.

"Damn little bitch—and my *partner*—my good old friend and partner! Rome, yet. With *my* wife—on *his* vacation! For God's sake, I ought to've—"

"So, what's your name?" asked Higgins.

"Oh, for God's sake. William J. Campden. He's Dick Gorton. For God's sake—Campden and Gorton, such buddy-buddy partners—for God's sake, in college together, and—"

The blonde emerged from her handkerchief, where she sat sobbing, and she was a very pretty blonde even with her eye makeup smeared over one cheek and her eyes red. She was, in fact, quite a dish for any male who appreciated the obvious. She had big brown eyes and a nice slim rounded figure, and her long flaxen hair waved shimmering past her bare shoulders, and she was wearing a very abbreviated white sundress and spike-heeled white sandals; her toenails were painted blood-red. She sobbed and hiccuped and said, "You big bastard! Killing Dicky! You weren't ever going to know anything *about* it—it didn't matter—you were supposed to think I was visiting Mother in Colorado Springs just like I told you! You wouldn't have known anything about— and you didn't need to *kill* him! You didn't—"

"So it's Fate," said Campden bitterly. "I just happen to leave the office early and stroll up to Benny's bar for a drink. Just in time to see my dear little girl-wife and my buddy-buddy partner—who I thought was up at Tahoe, where he said he was going—all cozily going into a travel agency arm in arm. *Rome* yet, the man says. My God. I wouldn't have known— Oh, you are a prize, Sandra. You really are."

"Well, you *wouldn't* have! And you didn't need to—"

"Mr. Campden, if you'd just—"

"Oh, hell," said Campden. He looked up at Hackett and Higgins. "It was just damn bad luck I had the gun on me. Or Fate. We keep it at the office, I was taking it home to oil it. And I've got a temper that goes off—as you could maybe guess." He sighed a long deep sigh. "So—he's dead. She's the one I should have— Little bitch Sandra. And me the innocent husband, never suspecting a thing."

"We weren't g-going till next month, he said Rome in September was w-wonderful—but I was so scared about the earthquake so he asked for his vacation early—and you had to see us, just an accident really— Oh, Dicky!"

"All right, Mr. Campden, up," said Hackett. "I have to explain all your rights to you," and he started to go through that ritual. Higgins was calling up more cars, to ferry the witnesses in to make statements.

The Central beat was getting back to normal after the earthquake: the irrational, the wanton, the senseless crime and violence.

By the time they got all the witnesses back to the office, Palliser had come in, so he and Grace and Piggott shared the job of getting the statements down with Hackett and Higgins. It turned out that Campden was a lawyer; he and Gorton had shared offices on Spring Street. Now it would be up to the D.A. what he wanted to call this, manslaughter or murder second or whatever.

They were still busy on that when Lake put through a call from Wilcox Street.

"Mendoza?" Sergeant Barth of that station in the middle of Hollywood. "We've got a thing here we want you on from the start. Whether you're busy down there or not."

"Not very, for once. What's up?"

"Well, it could be quite a thing—I'd just like the experts on it, Mendoza." Barth sounded abrupt and worried. "It's La Presa Drive up above the boulevard. Bring a lab team, hah? Right now."

"¿Cómo? Something important?"

"To us, yes," said Barth. "One of ours. Patrolman on our beat. No, he's not dead, but his chances don't look so good."

"¡Cómo! I'm on my way." Mendoza reached for his hat and started out. "Jimmy, I want a lab truck to meet me at this address." He passed it over. "Pronto. Seems business is picking up."

It was still very hot on the street, in late afternoon. The Ferrari's steering wheel was nearly too hot to touch. But at least the freeways downtown hadn't collapsed, and he made good time up to Hollywood.

La Presa Drive . . . Luis Mendoza had been a cop on this force for twenty-four years and had ridden a squad car awhile; he knew his city in and out. This was a quiet little backwater with some of the oldest streets, the oldest houses, in the hills above Hollywood. There were new, smartly fashionable areas up here but this wasn't one of them. The winding narrow streets off Outpost Drive had a faded gentility; the houses on them had once, thirty years ago, been substantial upper-class houses, many of them large, but time had run by and the moneyed people, the elite of Hollywood, had moved to newer fashionable residential areas.

When he found the house, around many curves of the narrow street, there were three cars parked in front, one a black-and-white. As he parked the Ferrari, the big mobile lab truck pulled up behind him and

Scarne and Duke got out of the front seat, with Marx and Horder climbing out the back.

It was a big old frame house, perhaps forty years old. Like most of the houses up here, it didn't have much yard around it: these were small lots carved from the hillside. It was painted white, it was two-storied, with a strip of lawn and a front porch. The front door was open and as Mendoza stepped to the porch Sergeant Barth appeared there—stocky, middle-aged, worried-looking.

"Mendoza, glad to see you. Now we've got a very funny thing here indeed. You'll want to talk to his wife, of course—she's at the hospital, naturally, went along in the ambulance—as long as there's any *chance*—but it didn't look too good. Well." Barth passed a hand across his face. "He's a good man, Mendoza. One of our bright young men. Kind to end up downtown as captain—a career man. Patrick Henry Logan."

"So what happened?" Mendoza glanced around the living room. It was large and rectangular, dim because the house faced north, and rather sparsely furnished: a long Naugahyde-covered couch, a few chairs, a long coffee table, plain beige drapes and carpet. Another plainclothesman and a uniformed man were bending over chalk marks at the other end of the room. A door there gave a glimpse into a den or dining room, to the right; to his left here, the square entrance hall had stairs leading up.

"There's no sense to it," said Barth angrily. "Look, Mendoza, he's a good man. He's got four years' service with us and he's passed the detective exam already. He'd be up for promotion when there was a hole left. He's twenty-six, married three years—his wife's name's Sally, she works part time at a dress shop down on Sunset. They haven't any family yet, and there's house payments, I suppose, car payments— *I* don't know. What I do know, I've talked to some of the other men he worked with, and there isn't anything showing—Logan and his wife get on fine, her father was a cop too, retired captain out of Hollenbeck—and Logan wouldn't, for God's sake, have any enemies—a very easygoing guy, doesn't get into arguments with people, very clean record with us—an ordinary fellow—well, not ordinary, an ambitious career man—but you see what I mean. There's just no reason—"

"All right, I've got Logan. What happened to him? And what do you want here, the full treatment?"

"But absolutely," said Barth. "For a start, this room, the den and the kitchen." Mendoza nodded at the lab men, who started unpacking their bags silently. "So, his wife doesn't work Fridays. He's on the swing watch, due in for briefing at three-thirty, start the tour at four. Riding a one-man car in central Hollywood. He'd have left home about three, to get down to the station and change into uniform. His wife said good-bye to him about a quarter of three when she went out to do some marketing. They've both got cars, yes. She came home about three-forty-five and found him. Up there." The chalk marks on the carpet were at the end of the room, just under a window; also bloodstains—quite a little blood had been spilled on the carpet, there and over by the door into the den.

"The call went down at three-forty-nine, Sergeant," said the uniformed man. "And I'll back that up, my God— Pat's a very mild guy, easygoing all right, nobody could have any reason to—"

"She called the ambulance, and us," said Barth. "Whoever it was, Mendoza, and whatever the hell it was, he'd been all but beaten to death. I don't know whether any weapon was used, there could have been—the interns said it was touch and go, and if there was any chance they had to get him in fast—one artery pumping blood—multiple skull-fractures, I'd guess, and probably internal injuries—"

"*Dios.*" Mendoza got out a cigarette and looked at it. "A career man, you said. So Logan is not just the average five-nine, a hundred and fifty or better."

"That's the damn point," said Barth, "or one of them. He's not. He's six-one, a hundred and eighty-five, and he's in top condition. He knows judo. Last week he ran into a pro heavyweight up on Fairfax and brought him in alone—hell, the man was drunk but still—"

"Mmh, yes," said Mendoza. "Yes. And he's an easygoing fellow who hasn't any enemies, as far as anybody knows. His wife— Well, of course you haven't had a chance really to question her yet."

"Not really, no. But she told us that. Nobody with any reason to—I only talked to her a minute or so, she naturally wanted to go with him in the ambulance, but she's a cop's daughter and a cop's wife, Mendoza, a level-headed girl—a nice girl—upset as all hell, you can see she's in love with him—and she'd know. Wouldn't she? About anybody with any reason to—"

"Mmh, yes," said Mendoza again. "But we all know, depressingly often there's no reason behind the violence. Some people don't need reasons. *¿Cómo no?* See what the lab can pick up. At least we can narrow down the time—between two-forty-five and three-forty-five. Did any of the neighbors see anything, a car or— Mmh, indeed, six-one, a hundred and— You know, Barth, that says to me that it could have been more than one X. Jumping him. Because—" He looked around the room, where Marx and Horder were efficiently dusting every surface for latent prints and Scarne was taking photographs—"Logan would have put up a fight, just attacked by one man—even unexpectedly. There'd have been more mess in here, furniture knocked over, and so on."

"That just occurred to me before you got here," said Barth. "But for God's sake *why?* Who? Why Logan? Because it looks as if it was a personal grudge of some kind, beating him up like that, and there'd be no reason—"

"Reasons and reasons," said Mendoza absently. "Some people don't need much reason. I suppose the wife hasn't had a chance to look around for anything missing."

"Burglars?" said Barth incredulously. "At three o'clock in the afternoon? Up here? And beating him nearly to death?"

"Posible. If only just. In any case, we want her to look. And there won't be much traffic up here at any time of day. We ask the neighbors whether they saw a car, anybody on foot, anybody near this house. A car is more likely. We can, of course, look at his reports over the last couple of weeks, what and who he ran across on the job—" Mendoza met Barth's disgusted expression and grinned sardonically.

"I thought you were supposed to be an expert. For God's sake, Mendoza! A uniformed man riding a quiet beat in Hollywood?"

"Inverosímil, yes—very unlikely. Not one of us who hasn't heard it— I'll get you, cop—but threatened men live long, so they say. But just now and then it does happen. We'll look and ask. But first we ask the neighbors—any of them who were home. There might be a shortcut here."

Owing to the winding street, not many near neighbors on La Presa Drive would have been in a position to observe anything near the Logan house; and only three of them had been at home at the crucial time. Any car passing up the street could have been heading for Castilian Way, or Oporto Place, other little streets farther up. What they got really didn't take them much further.

Mrs. Richard Fitch, who lived a block down from the Logans on La Presa, but in the nearest house to theirs—these were short blocks—was much shocked to hear about Patrick Henry Logan. She had been working in her front yard from about three to three-thirty, she said, and only one car had passed her going up the hill, and that car she knew. It was a red Mustang owned by young Jim Brinkman—the Brinkmans lived up on Oporto Place, her son Bob went to school with Jim.

Mr. Fred Nicholson, retired stockbroker, lived on Castilian Way, at the corner where La Presa crossed it. All he could tell them was that some time that afternoon a car had passed his house, "Like a bat outta hell," said Mr. Nicholson. "One o' these souped-up jalopies, sounded like—no, I didn't see it, and I couldn't tell you what time it was exactly, somewhere around three, I guess. I was out in the kitchen getting a can of beer out of the refrigerator—my God, we don't usually get this kind of heat in August—and it *could* have turned on La Presa but I just couldn't say." Mr. Nicholson was a widower and lived alone. "Like people said to me"—he was garrulous, pleased to have visitors—"after Agnes died, I ought to sell the house, get an apartment—but it's been home for thirty years, I know it's too big for a man alone, but it's home—where Agnes and I lived thirty years. I stayed on. And tell you one thing, never so much as a crack in the plaster last Tuesday, it's a hell of a lot better built than these jerry-built new apartments. . . . Logan? No, I don't know him— I'm sorry, I wish I could help you more, but—"

Mrs. Claudia Franks answered Mendoza somewhat distraitly. She lived in a pink stucco house across the street and down the hill from the Logans. She was a big blonde woman in her forties, corseted and very neat in a tailored navy dress, discreet makeup, and she looked at the badge and said to Mendoza, *"Police?* But what on earth— Well, I'm expecting an important telephone call, if it won't take much time—of course I want to cooperate with— What? A car? Well, yes, I've been home most of the afternoon, mostly in the living room here, but I don't— Yes, I did hear a couple of cars go by. It's pretty quiet up here as a rule, you notice— But of course I didn't go to look out, why should I? Well, yes, one of the cars was kind of loud, like one of those little four-cylinder things, but I didn't see it. Why?"

"Do you know the Logans, across the street?"

"Why, of course," she said. "Such nice young people, and Mr. Logan—" A phone shrilled somewhere and she said, "Oh, that'll be—I'm sorry, you'll have to excuse me—" And she shut the door precipitately.

And of course that told them nothing. Nothing at all. A noisy car heading up (possibly) La Presa Drive. Young Jim Brinkman. Well, talk to him, but—

When Mendoza started home at six-thirty, Patrolman Logan was still alive—but only just, in Intensive Care at the Hollywood Receiving Hospital.

What had happened to him, and why?

Mendoza came out of the garage; at this time of year it was still light, and a vigilant voice assailed him from the alder tree. *Coroo, coroo—*

YAWK!—Yankee Doodle came to town! That damned mockingbird— and Alison said it was nesting again.

He came in the back door to find his household looking much as usual. Their shaggy dog Cedric was slurping water from his bowl, and Mrs. MacTaggart was busy over the stove, while all four cats—Bast, Sheba, Nefertite and El Señor—were weaving round her legs reminding her that this was their usual dinnertime if anybody remembered. Alison, red hair in disarray, was supervising the twins' supper.

"Honestly!" she said, as the twins erupted at him shouting. "Johnny— Terry—*¡bastante!* Come back here and finish your pudding— Honestly, Luis, it is maddening. I got a man to come and look at the driveway—" The driveway, last Tuesday morning, had sustained a large crack down its middle. "But he can't come to fix it until next week."

"As long as it gets fixed eventually," said Mendoza, kissing her. "Things getting settled down to routine again—we've got a new one. A peculiar new one . . . *Pues sí,* Terry, I'll read to you—let me catch my breath, *niños!* And come to think—"

"And of all things," said Alison, "those experts are saying now that this quake was on the San Gabriel fault so the San Andreas is still under pressure and another one could happen any—"

"I saw it, I saw it," said Mendoza. "So encouraging, yes."

CHAPTER 2

On Saturday morning when Mendoza called the hospital, Logan was still hanging on, still unconscious. Mendoza and Hackett went over there at nine o'clock; the wife was still there, and they wanted some opinions from the doctors too.

"I don't know why he's still with us," the chief surgeon told them. "We're not saying yet he'll make it. There were four skull-fractures, one arm and shoulder broken, stab wounds in the chest, and a femoral artery severed—we've been pumping blood into him since he was brought in."

"God," said Hackett. "Stabbed—any other weapon used, you think?"

"Probably. Nobody made those dents in his skull with a fist. He's got a very sound constitution, of course. My God, who'd do such a thing?— some personal grudge, was it?"

"Anybody's guess," said Mendoza, "so far."

Sally Logan was sitting where she'd been all night, in a little waiting room at the end of that floor. She'd be a pretty girl ordinarily, dark-brown hair, blue eyes, a nice figure; but her eyes were red and she looked very tired and her plain blue cotton dress was rumpled. There was a man with her, a man perhaps sixty, burly, with curly gray hair and a weatherbeaten face. He eyed Mendoza and Hackett and said, "They got Central on it right off. Just as well. I'm Royce—at Hollenbeck up to last year." Sally Logan's father. "What the *hell*—I just don't understand it, who'd want to hurt Pat?" He looked very angry.

Sally Logan told them wearily that Pat's parents lived in Pittsburgh; she'd wired them and they were flying out. "Now, Mrs. Logan," said Mendoza, "we don't like to bother you at a time like this, but there are questions we've got to ask—"

"Sure there are," said Royce. "Trouble is, there aren't any answers.

No enemies. Nobody with any grudge on him. No recent trouble of any kind. Pat—"

She sat up and looked at the men from Homicide. "That's right. There's nothing I can tell you," she said steadily. "Nobody who could have any reason to want to hurt Pat. It's c-crazy. Hurt him like *that*. I'd know if there was, and there just wasn't . . . I'm sorry, I'll try to— Yes, he'd tell me about anything like that, we always tell each other everything. Anything different, or funny, that happened on his tour, you know, or— But he hadn't been on regular tour until—day before yesterday. Tuesday and Wednesday he'd got sent out to Valley, the civil-defense people—"

"You're doing no good sitting here, Sally," said Royce roughly. "I've told you. When you've answered all the questions, you're going home to bed. We'll hear any news fast enough."

"We'd like you to look through the house, Mrs. Logan, check to see if anything's missing."

Royce glanced at Mendoza. "Berserk burglar? Doped up? That's possible, I suppose."

"There wouldn't be anything—valuable—to steal," she said. "Pat might have had ten or twelve dollars on him, not any more. Yes, I see. All right. But just for *that,* to—"

Mendoza shrugged at Royce, who got up and urged her to her feet. Pat Logan had had nine-eighty-seven on him, still in his billfold when they undressed him at the hospital. Barth had checked at Wilcox Street: Pat Logan's uniform and regulation Police Positive .38 were just where they should be, in his locker there.

"So?" said Hackett when Royce had led the girl out.

"It looks as if we'll need the crystal ball for this one, Arturo." Mendoza lit a cigarette. "Just a peculiar thing with no shape to it."

"I wonder about that Jim Brinkman Mrs. Fitch mentioned. You never know where a lead will show."

"*De veras.* I'm still thinking, especially after what we heard from the doctor, a couple of X's. To do such a job on him, and he was hardly a helpless victim—he'd have put up a fight, and he doesn't seem to have." Logan's right knuckles grazed and bloody, that was all. One of the first blows knocking him out?

"I'd buy that," agreed Hackett. "In fact I'd say it's obvious." He slid his bulk into the Ferrari behind Mendoza. "I wonder—"

"Inspiration struck you?"

"I don't know," said Hackett. "I'll think about it before I say."

*　　*　　*

Downtown everybody was in except Lake; it was his day off, and Rory Farrell was sitting on the switchboard.

There'd been a new body—just a kid, said Glasser, over the report: with the kit on him, all the equipment for mainlining the H. Piggott had gone out with him on it, and said now, "Back to Sodom and Gomorrah, I swear. He couldn't have been eighteen—these idiotic kids conned that there's no harm in it—the devil getting around these days."

Nothing else had turned up. They had got the statements from Campden, Mrs. Campden and six other witnesses to the shooting yesterday and there wasn't any more to do on that until Campden came up for arraignment. Palliser, Grace and Landers were just sitting around, listening with interest to the details on Logan. They agreed, more than one X. But who, and why?

"And Echo answers," said Mendoza. "Where's George?"

"Down the hall after coffee. I guess," said Grace, "everybody is still staying home waiting for the next quake."

As if it had been awaiting the word, the building moved uneasily, and the floor was momentarily unsolid under their feet. "The Lord," said Piggott gloomily, "bringing down destruction, and I'm just surprised it wasn't sooner and more."

"I don't *like* these damn aftershocks," said Glasser.

Higgins came in looking annoyed. "These damned aftershocks," he said. "I spilled half my coffee just then." He drank from the paper cup. "What'd you get at the hospital?"

Hackett started to tell him. There was no sign of any work done on the windows yet, and the hot morning sun struck through brightly: the office was already stifling.

"Lieutenant," said Farrell, looking in. "New one. Sheridan Hotel up on Grand."

"So, I'm the lieutenant—let some of my minions go and look at it," said Mendoza. Patrick Henry Logan, that good career cop—

Landers and Palliser went out to look at it. Tom Landers was feeling a little moody these days. He'd finally met the right girl, his very smart Policewoman Phil O'Neill—Phillipa Rosemary, only not, as she said, for an LAPD officer—but little blonde Phil O'Neill had a great deal of common sense. Hadn't known each other long enough, she said briskly and sensibly. And she'd got to know his family up in Fresno when she was playing his guardian angel last June, and there was his sister Jean deviling at him, when are you and Phil getting married—and his darling Phil acting so damned *sensible*—

Well, she went out with him, and by God eventually he'd get her, Landers vowed to himself.

"Business picking up a little," he said as they got into Palliser's Rambler.

"Maybe. I hope not too hot and heavy," said Palliser. "I've got a muscle pulled or something in my shoulder—" He felt it. "They had me using a shovel over at the Mission most of Tuesday."

"That was a mess. Lucky only the one casualty. It'll seem funny to have it gone."

"We'll lose some city landmarks after this one, all right." The oldest houses in Los Angeles, over on Olvera Street, had sustained heavy damage; anybody's guess if they could be restored.

The Sheridan Hotel was not the classiest hostelry in town. It was an old tan-brick building, and as soon as they entered the lobby they both noticed the ugly gaping cracks in the wall above the counter.

"She ain't gonna fall down right this minute," said the man behind the counter. "Patch it up a little, she'll be O.K. She come through the 'thirty-three one too. You more cops? Thought so. It's upstairs, second floor. Maid went in and found him. Seems he's registered here all right, but—"

"What's the room number?"

"Two-twenty."

They climbed uncarpeted worn stairs and found the room. A uniformed man was standing in front of the door with a frightened-looking Negro girl. "I'm Warner, sir. Miss Millie Weekes—she found him."

"Oh, my Lord!" she said. "I didn't know anybody had that room again—I just went in to check on the towels—oh, my Lord!"

"Little party here last night," said the patrolman. "I would guess."

They went in. This was an old hotel, the rooms shabby and cheap. The furniture was old and sparse—a double bed, a small chest of drawers, a rickety straight chair. Palliser and Landers looked around the room, looked at the corpse, and made some immediate educated guesses at what had gone on here.

The body was a man's body, a man not young, a big man with muscled shoulders and an incipient paunch. He was lying on his back on this side of the bed, and he was wearing only gray trousers and an old-fashioned sleeveless undershirt. There were bruises and blood on him, and also marks on his bare throat. He was cold. There were a few indications of a struggle: the worn rug scuffed up in one place, the lamp on the chest knocked over.

On the bedside table was a bottle of cheap Scotch three-quarters empty, and a glass. On the chest, a paper cup with a few drops of Scotch left in it. There was a package of paper cups on the bed. Ashtrays full of ashes and dead butts: in one, a crumpled pack that had held Lucky Strikes. Palliser turned over the ashes in the other tray with a ballpoint pen and said, "Detectives they call us. Sometimes we hardly need to be, Tom." The cigarette stubs in that ashtray were all stained with pink lipstick.

"And," said Landers, looking at that, "this kind of hotel, the very superficial cleaning—whatever the lab may pick up here could be useless. On the other hand, you could say not much finesse, if that's the word."

There was an old leather billfold lying on the bed beside the paper cups. Palliser flicked it open with the pen—the shiny worn leather might yield some nice latents—and there was a little folder of plastic slots for I.D. cards, photos. The first slot held a California driver's license for Christopher W. Hauck of an address on Melbourne Avenue in Hollywood. It was a four-year license, which said he had a clean record as a driver. He'd been forty-six when it was renewed last year.

They told Warner to stay on it, told the maid they'd want a statement from her, and went back downstairs. Landers called the office for a lab team. They questioned the clerk.

"Like I said, he was registered. Last night—I'd never laid eyes on him." He showed them the entry in the registry. A nearly illiterate hand had filled it in: *Mr. & Mrs. C. W. Hauck.*

"Oh, yes," said Palliser. "You didn't sign him in?"

"Nope. I go off at five. It'd have been Jim Glidden, he's the night clerk."

"Where'd we find him, you know?"

"Home asleep, I guess, this hour. Sure, his address'll be here somewhere—" The clerk found it: Judson Street over in Boyle Heights. They waited for the ambulance, the lab men, turned them loose on the room, and took the maid back to the office to get a statement.

When they came out to the street again, Landers to head for Boyle Heights and Palliser to Hollywood, there was a lone picket strolling up and down in front of the building. He had a long white beard and threadbare clothes, and his homemade sign proclaimed THE END OF THE WORLD IS NEAR—REPENT!

"I wonder if Matt's seen that," said Landers, and Palliser laughed.

"And I might add that we wouldn't have laughed at it at six A.M. last Tuesday."

"No," said Landers. That was a fact. And things were pretty much cleaned up down here now—except for all those empty windows in the Police Building—the glass swept from the sidewalks, the crumpled old Mission posted with *Unsafe* signs and awaiting the bulldozers; but out in the valley the engineers were still working to repair that dam, and it would be some time before work started on the freeways.

Jim Glidden finally answered his doorbell after Landers had leaned on it steadily for five minutes. It was an old apartment house in this down-at-heel section of the city, and Landers fully expected Glidden to be elderly and down-at-heel too, so he was a little surprised when Glidden did open the door—a fellow in his early twenties, slim and fair-haired and healthy-looking. He was yawning, tying an old terry bathrobe over pajamas.

"What the hell?" he said to Landers. "Don't tell me I got out of bed for a Fuller Brush man? What? A cop? A *cop?*" He stared at the badge. "You don't look old enough."

Landers was nearly resigned to hearing that; but Phil had reassured him that he'd aged at least five years over that queer affair last June. "It's for real," he said equably. "Like to ask you some questions, if you're the Jim Glidden who's night clerk at the Sheridan Hotel."

"That's me. Come in." He was still yawning. "I know it's not the Beverly Hilton—"

"Detective Landers."

"Sure. Sit down. But they do say, beggars can't be choosers," said Glidden. The apartment living room was rather bare of furniture but looked neat and clean; there was a bookcase full of books on one wall. Landers sat down on the couch and Glidden on a chair opposite.

"You aren't exactly what I expected," said Landers. "Not a very lucrative job. A dead-end job."

"But a night job," said Glidden, "where I can usually snatch a few hours sleep. I'm studying for the Bar, but it's a long haul and I'm earning my own way. Dad died last year, my mother works uptown, and the hotel job's very handy for my purposes, see what I mean."

"Oh," said Landers. "Well, last night a Christopher Hauck registered at the hotel. When, and who was with him?"

"And I am not exactly an idiot," said Glidden, cocking his head at him. "Yes. The manager laid that on the line when he hired me, and it wasn't any business of mine whether I liked it or not. It's a convenient job for me, as I say, and what the hell could I do about it anyway? I will say it wasn't just so often it happened—we get a lot of small-time salesmen, that kind of thing, people without much money but straight clients. Once in a while that—the obvious john with the girl-friend, but the manager says their money's as good as anybody's." He shrugged.

"So, Hauck? A girl with him?"

Glidden grinned. "The other way round, I'd say. He'd had a few but he wasn't high, he knew what he was doing. I'd never seen either of them before. The girl—" He thought. "About twenty-five, five-four, good figure, bleached blonde, she had on a dress that was just barely there—skirt up to her thighs, and a lot of costume jewelry. Yes, I'd know her again. Neither of them had any luggage, of course."

"That's very helpful, Mr. Glidden. We'll be asking you for a formal statement."

"Sure. Why? I mean, what happened to bring the cops around? Did he end up murdering her or something?" asked Glidden curiously.

Landers grinned at him. "The other way round, I'd say," he said dryly.

The address on Melbourne Avenue turned out to be a comfortable-looking old California bungalow on a quiet street. The woman who opened the door to Palliser was middle-aged, plump, comfortable-looking like her house, with gray hair and rimless glasses.

"Does Mr. Christopher Hauck live here?" Palliser brought out the badge. "I'm afraid—"

Her face changed. "Something's happened to him," she said quietly, "hasn't it? Come in. I'm his sister—I'm Reba Roberts. Yes, Chris lives here with me—I'm a widow, never had any family, and when Joe died we thought it was only sensible Chris should— Something's happened to him, hasn't it?" She sat down on the edge of a chair, staring at Palliser.

"I'm afraid so, Mrs. Roberts." He broke the news as tactfully as possible, making no implications, but the crude facts could hardly be glossed over.

"And I might have *known*," she said sorrowfully, angrily, harshly, cutting across his words. "I might have *expected* it. Chris running around after *women* all the time—and a man his age ought to have known better, but the ones like Chris don't change. Don't seem to learn anything. But to die like *that*—" She gave an involuntary sob and Palliser asked if he could get her a glass of water. "Thank you, sir—the kitchen—"

She sipped the water and wiped her eyes with a clean handkerchief. "It's a shock—of course it's a shock, did you say Sergeant? Police coming to tell me— Well, he was my brother, we grew up together, I can't but say he was a good brother to me—Joe didn't leave much, but Chris always made good money and he was generous, I've got to say. He helped out on the expenses, I don't know how I'd have managed to pay off the house, it hadn't been for Chris— What? He's a—he was a construction worker, Sergeant—a master carpenter, a good workman—he always made good money. He was good to me. But you couldn't talk to him—he never married, and he was always chasing round after—you know—loose women. Like that. I can't deny it. Like he was still just a young blade, know what I mean. I couldn't talk to him—he'd just laugh and say he's footloose and fancy-free, you're only young once and better love it up while you can. He always said it that way—better love it up while—"

"Would he have had much cash on him, Mrs. Roberts?"

"Probably," she said. "He liked to carry a good roll. He'd've got his paycheck yesterday—over four hundred dollars, two weeks' pay. He might have had it all on him, times he'd take it all in cash. . . . But to die like *that*—some little floozy he'd just picked up— Well, I suppose it's just as well we haven't any family to feel the disgrace, Sergeant. . . . I suppose I can't—make any arrangements—right away?"

"We'll let you know," Palliser told her gently.

So Chris Hauck, who should have known better at his age, had just been asking for it, he reflected on his way back downtown. Carrying the roll, picking up the floozy. But no floozy had beaten and/or strangled Hauck, obviously. Hauck, still loving it up. Asking for what he'd got.

The bearded picket was still in front of the building.

Mendoza, leaving Hackett typing a report, went up to Oporto Place to see Jim Brinkman. It was absolutely nothing, of course—only you never did know where a lead would turn up.

He didn't turn up any lead from Jim Brinkman.

Jim Brinkman was home alone in the old stucco house on the winding hillside street. He had just finished his first term at L.A.C.C., and during vacation was tutoring in math to get his grades up, he told Mendoza. He was an upright-looking young fellow, in contrast to the long-haired louts wandering around town in the dirty clothes. He was middle-sized, stocky, dark, and polite to a lieutenant of police, if bewildered.

He'd come home about three yesterday afternoon, sure, he said. From his math lesson. Straight home. And his mother had been home, she could say. They didn't know the Logans at all. And he didn't recall passing any other car on the way up the hill here—up Outpost he'd come, and then up La Presa to Oporto. It was a quiet neighborhood, not much traffic.

Mendoza came back to the Ferrari and said, "*¡Mil rayos!*" That had been an exercise in futility, as he might have known it would be. He went back to La Presa Drive and parked, and tried Mrs. Franks's pink stucco house; there were questions she hadn't been asked yet. But nobody answered the door: the pink stucco house was empty.

Frustrated, he drove back downtown and noticed the picket for the first time. He wondered if Matt had seen that yet. Upstairs, he found Palliser and Landers talking about the new body with Farrell, and heard the details on that one.

"Asking for it," said Palliser. "Loving it up, my God. But at least somewhere to go on this one."

"You hope," said Mendoza. He got the lab on the phone. "That hotel room—have you got anything useful?"

"You boys are always in such a hurry," sighed Duke. "I couldn't tell you yet. We picked up a lot of latents—a few good ones, more bad. It'll take a little work to raise any on that paper cup but we hope to eventually. And weed out any belonging to the corpse, yes. And analyze the lipstick. We're on it, Lieutenant, but we don't produce instantly. Tomorrow, maybe something definite." And that was what they always got from the lab.

"I wonder," said Mendoza, "if Matt's seen that picket downstairs." Palliser and Landers laughed.

"Yes, he did," said Farrell seriously. "And all he said was that children and fools speak the truth. And for God's sake, Lieutenant, will you stay away from those damn windows! One of these damn aftershocks could—"

A new call from Traffic at four-thirty turned out to be the inevitable accident. Higgins went out on it, and looked at it sadly. There was a sign posted prominently on the building—an old stucco apartment house on Temple—*Unsafe for occupancy*. The quake hadn't knocked it down but it was all ready to go. And Alfredo Reyes, entering the building, had put his foot through a rotten stair-board and brought down a wall on his head. Alfredo, who had been nineteen, had left a friend outside, who explained it all tearfully to Higgins and the patrolmen.

"Yessir, we see the sign—but it's Alfredo's old grandma, she lived here but they make ever'body leave—after the earthquake, see?—but it's her little bird, little canary—she was scared then, forgot it, but she wants her little bird—poor little bird, Alfredo just wanted get it for his grandma, she loves the little bird—"

Higgins felt depressed, taking the names, the address. He went back to the office and typed up the report and started home. As he turned into the drive of the house on Silver Lake Boulevard, his spirits rose a little. At least the house hadn't got one crack in its plaster, last Tuesday, and his family would be here to welcome him—the good kids Steve and Laura, his as well as Bert's now, and his lovely Mary, and the little Scottie Brucie.

They were. And to his question Mary's gray eyes laughed. "I'm fine, idiot. Only getting awfully tired of feeling like a pup tent, this far along. Well, I *do*. And looking like a horse—"

"You look," said Higgins fondly, "just fine."

Hackett went home and told Angel about Patrick Henry Logan. "A miracle he's still alive. And no rhyme or reason to it, you can see."

"There must be—you'll find it," said Angel encouragingly. "Dinner in twenty minutes—have you weighed today, Art?"

"I was two pounds down." Hackett fought a perennial battle against his metabolism and Angel's cooking. And four-year-old Mark and his darling Sheila belatedly discovered he was home. . . . Hostages to fortune, he thought, and him with all the seniority built up in earthquake-prone L.A.— But there were all those people who went right back up Mount Vesuvius to rebuild after an eruption—

Palliser went home and just grunted when Roberta told him she'd got the teaching job starting in September. He didn't so much approve of her going back to work, even for a year, to help with the house payments. "Don't go all *male* on me," she said. "You know it will be a help, John."

"Now, Robin. You know how I feel, that's all."

And quite without planning to, Matt Piggott surprised himself by proposing to Prudence Russell that night, and she said yes. His vacation was scheduled for next month. . . .

And Jason Grace went home to his Virginia and she told him the test had been negative again. They'd been hoping to start a family ever since they'd been married, but no luck. . . . "Don't fuss about it, honey," said Grace.

"Well, I can't help it, Jase."

*   *   *

"Now settle down, you two," said Alison firmly to the twins. "Yes, yes, *los cuentos*—your father'll read you—*the stories*," she added suddenly. "English, the stories. Spanish, *los cuentos. ¿Comprenden?* Oh, damn."

Mendoza laughed. "You get A for effort, *cara.*"

"But we've got to get them—untangled, Luis," said Alison, smoothing her red hair. "They haven't a notion of any difference between, and when they start school—"

"A couple of years yet, after all. *Pues sí,* I've got to agree with you, but—"

"If you'd just think what you're saying," said Alison, and to the solemn twins pajamaed and powdered ready for bed, *"Pues sí*—But yes. Two ways to say it, you see? Spanish—English."

"El cuento all about *el lobo*—he eat her all down!" said Miss Teresa with ghoulish satisfaction.

"The wolf," said Alison. "And it's eat her all up, Terry—"

"Down. *El lobo* with *dientes muy grandes!"*

"No *el lobo!"* shouted Master John. *"La bruja* burn up in *la estufa!"*

Mendoza rocked with laughter. "It is not funny," said Alison crossly. "We said we'd have to try—the English only, until they grasp the difference—"

The cats were elsewhere, napping after dinner. The shaggy dog Cedric was very much present, listening interestedly.

"And if you ask me," said Mendoza, "not that I go along with the head doctors, but this sudden thirst for blood—"

"Eat her all down," said Terry pleasedly.

"La bruja burn up *muy mucho,"* contributed Johnny.

"Very much," said Alison. "Very much, Johnny. Oh, for heaven's sake, Luis! That's silly—"

In pursuit of broadening the twins' literary horizon, last month, from Mother Goose and *Just So Stories,* she had unearthed a battered copy of Grimm from their heterogeneous collection of books, and that had been an instant hit.

"But don't they say, *achara,"* Mrs. MacTaggart had worried, "all those terrible ogres and killing, not right to frighten the mites so—"

"Nonsense," Alison had said robustly. "After all, Máiri, generations of children have been brought up on Grimm and Andersen and turned into quite normal adults—besides, don't they say too, relieving frustrations—"

And the wolf gobbling up Grandmother had been much appreciated, as well as the witch burned in the oven, but as to reaching any understanding about the difference between English and Spanish—well, the twins were not quite three, of course.

But something, as Alison said, had to be done.

"The wolf," said Alison now. "English, Johnny. *The wolf.*"

"He ate her all down," said Terry bloodthirstily, and giggled.

"All up, Terry."

"*La bruja—la bruja* all burn up—"

"The witch," said Alison. "English. The witch. Two ways to—"

Mendoza said, "*¿Donde irá a parar todo esto?* Talk about dilemmas, my love—"

"And you are being no help at all! Honestly!" said Alison. "Honestly! Now, Johnny, say it after me. The wolf. That's English. *El lobo*. That's Spanish. Two different—"

"Read about *la bruja*," demanded Johnny, thrusting Grimm at Mendoza. "She got all burned down in *la estufa*—"

"Burned up, Johnny."

"You are," said Mendoza, "fighting a losing battle, *cara*."

"Oh, for heaven's *sake!*" said Alison. "I'm just trying to—"

On Sunday morning, somewhat to the surprise of the doctors, Patrolman Patrick Henry Logan was still alive, and his pulse was just a trifle stronger. They weren't saying yet that he'd make it, but the odds had shortened a little. If by the grace of God he should make it, he could provide answers for all the questions eventually. But the doctors weren't being definite yet.

Just as they were thinking of lunch, the lab sent up a report: the lab usually got something for them in time, and it had turned up another X for them now.

"But they are so stupid," said Palliser. "The little pros at the bottom. I do get tired. That Hauck was asking for it—begging for it."

The lab had identified some latent prints from the used paper cup. They were in L.A.'s records. They belonged to one Linda Schnell, who had quite a little pedigree—soliciting, shoplifting, prostitution. She was Caucasian, twenty-seven, blonde and blue, five-four, a hundred and twenty, appendectomy scar, old record of V.D. at General Hospital; she'd been picked up last about four months ago, on a charge of shoplifting, thirty days in—the address then had been on First Street.

She wasn't there now.

"Nobody that size accounted for Hauck," said Landers.

"So she's got a boy-friend," said Mendoza. "Put out an A.P.B. on her, Tom." The continuous thankless dirty job—

CHAPTER 3

Nobody who knew George Higgins would have called him a sentimental man, but his rough-hewn exterior concealed a warm heart, and he had, late yesterday afternoon, called the Humane Society about that canary. The canary belonging to Alfredo Reyes's grandmother. He'd just got back to the office on Sunday after lunch when he got a call from a cheerful-sounding Mr. Ryan.

"Just thought you'd like to know we rescued that canary, Sergeant. Oh, yes, it was all right—hungry and thirsty, but it's perked up now."

So that had turned out all right—only not for Alfredo Reyes. Higgins put the phone down just as Sergeant Lake looked in and said tersely, "Call from Traffic. They've just found another body on Main."

Higgins swore; more paper work; and he and Grace were the only ones in, so they both went over.

This half-block of building, once small shops, along that stretch of Main, had been scheduled for demolition before the earthquake; the quake had done half the job. It had been a four-story building, and most of the roof was still there but inside ceilings had crumbled, floors given way, and part of the front wall had collapsed. The hard-hatted city engineer said to them, "Everybody knew the building was vacant—condemned six months ago. So nobody had a look around here until now." This afternoon, inspecting city property reckoned unsafe, they had; and there was another body. Half buried in the rubble of a fallen ceiling, inside one of the former shops.

"I suppose," said the other city workman, "he could have been a bum sneaked in here to sleep."

That, when they took a look at him, was probably what he had been. He was an elderly man, and his clothes were old and shabby. He had two dimes in one jacket pocket, and a broken wine bottle in the other: it had originally contained cheap muscatel.

Both Higgins and Grace could guess he'd never be identified. Just another derelict. The city would bury him and that would be that. Since Tuesday the known death toll from the quake had crept up day by day as more bodies were found; this would add one more.

They saw the body off for the morgue and went back to the office; Grace typed the report. No work was getting done on the windows on this floor yet, but they had noticed a crew working on those on the first floor. Eventually they might get back their air conditioning.

There had been an accident up on Olive, said Lake, with one D.O.A. —Piggott and Glasser had gone to cover that.

"Where's the boss?"

"Up at Wilcox Street."

Mendoza and Hackett were up at Wilcox Street to talk to some of Pat Logan's fellow officers before they went on shift. Mendoza had asked Barth to bring them in early, but he didn't know what they could tell him, and they weren't telling him anything new at all.

"There just couldn't be any reason for anyone holding a grudge on Pat—" That was the consensus. It seemed that Bill Roth and Mike Gomez knew Logan somewhat better than the others; they'd all been in the same class at the Police Academy four years ago, and at Wilcox Street since.

"He's an easygoing guy," said Gomez. "Well, hell, excuse me, Lieutenant, but you know all the tests a man has to pass before he can even apply for the job, on this force. We like to think, the real pros—us. There just couldn't be anything on the job behind this, Lieutenant. Have you heard how he's doing?"

"They're not ringing any bells yet," said Mendoza.

"I'd go along with Mike," said Roth. "But what else could have triggered it? The only thing I could figure, some hophead high on something, but—"

"But," said Mendoza, irritably rubbing his moustache the wrong way. It was a large But. None of the men could offer them anything more: Logan was a good cop, he and his wife got on fine, he liked his job, he was a likable, easygoing fellow.

"So, something right outside?" said Hackett on the way back downtown. "That crossed my mind, Luis. A thing like this so often at random—just chance that it was Logan. A couple of junkies hunting anything pawnable to support the habit—and running wild when they didn't find much loot."

"No," said Mendoza. "The house wasn't ransacked, Art. All right, it says nothing that that's an older neighborhood, not wealthy homes up there—the punks turn up anywhere. But he still had his billfold on him. Nobody had searched the house. They—I think it's got to be they—just came in and went to work on Logan. The front door was probably unlocked, that time of day—he'd have been just about to leave the house, probably, the time margin what it is. His car was still in the garage. Keys in his pocket."

"So what other answer is there?"

"I don't know," said Mendoza. "Damn it, it's just shapeless—it shouldn't have happened, there's no reason for it to have happened, only it did. I want to see his wife again, and by then the lab should be able to tell us if they picked up anything useful at the house. And if they haven't, I'll be damned if I can see where else to look, Art."

At the office, he called the hospital. Logan was still unconscious, but it began to look as if he might make it.

Landers and Palliser had gone down to R. and I. to have a look for known associates of Linda Schnell. They ran into brisk, neat Phil O'Neill, trim in her navy uniform: she was busy at one of the computers, but flicked a warm smile in Landers' direction. Waiting for the right cards to emerge from the slots in answer to their questions, Palliser said he could wish Landers good luck there. "A very smart blonde, Tom."

"And very damn practical," said Landers. "But I'll get her—eventually, I swear."

The computer turned up some names from their records—Angie Black, Julia Kurtz, Marian Henry. They looked, and their pedigrees read about the same as Linda's: the same charges, the fines, the thirty-day and sixty-day sentences. These were the drifters, the irresponsible, lazy ones who always lived hand to mouth, and used sex to earn money because it was an easy way. These days, a lot of them would be on welfare, but even the increased largesse the welfare board handed out now wouldn't buy all the liquor they wanted, all the fancy clothes—other things.

One of those women, Marian Henry, was in the county jail now on a thirty-day sentence for shoplifting. They drove out North Broadway to see her.

In jail, of course, she was clean and neat, and they wouldn't let her plaster on the makeup. She looked sullen and sorry for herself, in the plain tan dress, county issue to prisoners: she was a small dark woman in the mid-twenties, with heavy-lidded dark eyes. She said she didn't have any yen to talk to cops.

"You know Linda Schnell," said Palliser economically. "Know her pretty well, don't you?"

"And so what if I do? Can I have a cigarette?"

Landers gave her one, lit it. They were talking to her in one of the interrogation rooms; she slouched over to a straight chair. "Know where she's living now?"

"Why? You want her for something?"

"We'd like to talk to her," said Landers.

"So go find her. I'm not about to help the fuzz."

"Who's she been going around with lately, Marian?" They had a few names also from the computer, men Linda had lived with off and on—boy-friends. And the boy-friends had showed up in Records too, inevitably. Leo Farber: burglary, theft from the person, B.-and-E. Ray Wengel: burglary, narco possession, pimping. Harry Fordick: armed assault, assault with intent twice. And they had looked at the disposition of all those cases with resignation and frustration. The softheaded judges, the damn court decisions so careful of the criminal's rights while ignoring those of the upright citizenry to be safe in their homes. None of those men had served over six months in jail, on any one count.

"What about it, Marian?" asked Landers.

She shrugged at him. "I mind my own business. I wouldn't know. Linda's a pal of mine, I'm not about to help you pin anything on her."

"You might be doing her a favor by telling us about her boy-friends, Marian," said Palliser. "By what we can guess, at least one of them is a killer. He killed a man last Friday night—a john Linda'd picked up."

Her eyes narrowed on him. "Don't con me, cop. Linda wouldn't take up with nobody like—"

"So maybe she didn't know he was. Has she picked up a new boy-friend lately?"

She hesitated, looking from one to the other of them, her mouth tightening. "That's a come-on, you're tryin'a scare me some way. Linda—"

"Gospel truth, Marian. Anybody who kills once can kill twice. And it was a very messy kill, wasn't it, Tom? Fellow beaten and strangled, looked like—"

There was a long silence. "I haven't seen her in a while," said Marian

Henry finally. "I been here four weeks today, and I hadn't seen her, maybe a week before I got picked up."

"So, five weeks back, Marian—Linda had a new boy-friend?"

"She—no," she muttered unwillingly. "No, she knew him before somewheres—hadn't run into him in a long time, she said. She said he was a very nice guy, a real fun guy, she said."

"Oh, she did. And so what's his name?"

She put out her cigarette in the glass ashtray. "Foster. Foster Sterry. I never seen him, that's all I know."

"So I guess you can congratulate me," said Piggott, pushing the button for their floor.

"Congratulations, Matt," said Glasser. "That's good news. Time you settled down, acquired a family."

"And see who's talking."

"Well, I just never seem to meet a girl I'd want to settle down with. Maybe some day."

"We figured on getting married next month, when my vacation—"

"Good," said Glasser. "She sounds like a nice girl, Matt. Prudence. I like old-fashioned names like that."

The elevator landed and they walked down the hall. Two uniformed men were waiting for them at the door of the Homicide Bureau, with the three witnesses brought up from the scene to make statements. It had been a simple traffic accident, both drivers somewhat at fault, but the paper work went on forever. "If you'd just come in here, Mr. Hulbert," said Glasser, "I'll get your statement down for you to sign—"

Piggott was taking the two women into another room. Piggott, that rather lonely man, the upright fundamentalist, deserved a pretty, nice wife, and good luck to him.

Landers and Palliser went back to R. and I. to look for Foster Sterry. He wasn't there. At least by that name. No computer knew Foster Sterry.

"Computers," said Palliser, "are fallible. Sometimes the old-fashioned routine still pays off."

Landers translated that. "Put the word out to the pigeons that we're looking for him. And with the A.P.B. on Linda, it could be when we find her we'll find him."

They had shoved that heist job in Pending. There had never been any solid leads on it, anything like usable evidence. Now, it was dead. Now they had other things to do. They separated and went wandering around the Row, the streets around there, putting out the word that the cops were interested in one Foster Sterry. Half an hour's work, half a dozen men passed the word—the grapevine would take it from there.

Palliser ran into one of their more reliable informants coming out of a bar on Fourth Street—Joe Perez. Joe owned a hole-in-the-wall hamburger joint on Second; he had a small pedigree of petty offenses, not much.

"Foster Sterry?" he said, wrinkling his brow. "Don't ring no bells, Sergeant. I'll ask around. What I can tell you is about this bookie, see. Just showed up last week, started operations outta a pool hall just down from my place. I can put the finger on him for sure, Sergeant—"

Palliser took the name, the address. A lot of the unthinking citizenry might think that set of laws was unrealistic, and so it looked to be: legal to place a bet inside the track, illegal outside; legal to play draw poker only in towns where gambling was permitted (which meant, here, Gardena); illegal anywhere else. Some people would always like to gamble, and there'd always be gamblers to oblige them. What the citizenry didn't realize was that legal gambling was always linked up with the more unsavory things—the syndicate dealing in women, in pornography, in narcotics, the rackets generally.

Palliser went back to headquarters and passed on that information to Lieutenant Perce Andrews in Vice.

By three-thirty Mendoza and Hackett were up on La Presa Drive again. They found Royce there with Sally Logan, and a nice-looking older couple introduced as Logan's parents. They had all been about to leave for the hospital.

The men from Homicide listened to the expected repeated questions. Why did it have to be Pat? Why had it happened to Pat? They'd like to know too. Royce, the longtime cop, stood by jangling coins in his pocket restlessly.

"The doctor called a little while ago, they seem to think Pat's a little better—"

"Yes, we heard, Mrs. Logan, that's good news. We're all pulling for him to make it, you know," said Hackett. "Did you have a look around here for anything missing, anything—"

"That's just impossible," said Sally Logan. "No, of course there isn't. Dad and I both think there must have been more than one, because you could see there was hardly any struggle, and Pat would have— But there's nothing gone, and—"

Hackett followed Mendoza's glance round the living room, and sighed. A transistor radio sitting on the coffee table. A TV on its own wheeled stand in the corner. Possibly another radio in the kitchen. There probably wouldn't be much jewelry here, a young couple still with house payments, car payments, all the rest; but Sally Logan's mother was apparently dead, she might have a few pieces of jewelry from her. There would be clothes, the odds and ends pawnable. If the X's here had been a pair with the habit to support (the habit also increasing the likelihood of that savage random attack) there would have been things missing. The house would have been ransacked. Logan's money would have been taken.

And all that Royce would have seen, too. He was worried about Logan, evidently fond of his son-in-law; but he gave them a sardonic grin and said, "Just nowhere to go, is there? It couldn't be a personal motive, and it doesn't seem to have been even the random thing, the senseless thing we've all seen too damn often."

"Well, we haven't had a lab report yet. Could be they've picked up something to offer us a lead," said Mendoza.

"Always possible. Occasionally those boys pull rabbits out of hats. Let's hope they can here."

"Oh, there was one thing I remembered," said Sally suddenly. "After you talked to me before, Lieutenant—at the hospital. Of course it couldn't be anything to do with Pat's getting—but," and she attempted a stiff little smile, "I know cops, all right—you always want every last little detail."

"What's this, Sally? You remembered something that might—"

"It couldn't possibly tie in anywhere, Dad. But I suppose you'd better hear about it, Lieutenant. You see, we don't know too many neighbors up here—we're both busy, and it isn't a neighborhood where people —fraternize, which is all right with me—but of course we do know some people by name, and of course some of them know that Pat's on the force. Well, the Stanceys up the hill, and Mrs. Franks, and some others —you're friendly, say Hello, and Nice day, and like that. But anyway, what I'm getting to is that last Wednesday—yes, it was Wednesday, because they'd called Pat to come in early, everything was still in a mess out in the valley, the civil-defense people rushing around and all those people to be evacuated—they said to come in at noon. So it was about nine o'clock that morning, just after the office called, that Mrs. Franks came. I'd never exchanged more than six words with her before. Pat was upstairs shaving—"

"Mrs. Franks. That's the fat blonde across the street?" asked Royce.

"That's right. And I was just leaving the house myself," said Sally, "you know I work all day Wednesdays, so I didn't know anything about it until Pat got home that night—he told me then. He—"

"What did she want, Mrs. Logan?" asked Mendoza interestedly.

"Well, she didn't say much to me. She said she understood Pat was a police officer, and she was terribly worried about something and maybe he could give her some advice. I thought it was a little funny," said Sally, "but when Pat told me about it later, I—the poor woman. And rather a silly sort of woman, but you can't help feeling sorry for her—"

"He talked to her then?"

She nodded. "I went up and told him, and he was a little surprised too. I mean, she's an older woman and— But he said—he said—" Sally put a hand to her throat. "He'd just finished shaving, he was wiping his face—and his hair all on end—he just w-winked at me and said, went to show how the neighbors must appreciate the superior wisdom of cops—and he'd be right down—"

"But you weren't there when he talked to her, hon?"

"No, I said I left—I was late. I asked her to sit down, said Pat would come in a minute. I didn't hear about it until that night."

She faced them, a little bewildered, in the living room of the pink stucco house. She was not a very intelligent woman, or a very sophisticated woman: five minutes' conversation told Mendoza and Hackett that. She was, however, an honest woman, if shallow and sentimental, and she said, "But I don't understand why you're asking about it. What happened to Mr. Logan—just terrible, but it wasn't anything to do with us. With Donny. Mr. Logan—there's so much violence going on now, isn't there? People say, all the terrible TV programs. His wife's very pretty, and he was so kind and good. It was all perfectly awful and I've been terribly upset about it, but of course as Dr. Hopewell said it's best to *know,* and I never would have if it hadn't been for Mr. Logan. He was so kind, taking time to explain, you know."

"Explain what, Mrs. Franks? Why did you want to see Mr. Logan that day?" asked Mendoza.

"Why, it was Donny," she said. "My boy Donny." The living room of the pink stucco house told them, possibly, all they needed to know about Claudia Franks. It was painted pink too, with ruffle-bordered rose-colored drapes, fussy Victorian love seats and a French gilt desk, framed flower prints on the walls. "I've tried to make it up to Donny, for not having a daddy, you know. His daddy died when Donny was only two—this awful leukemia he had, just a young man. Of course he left me well enough off, I don't mean millions but comfortable, and I've tried to make it up to Donny. Anything he wanted—and he's always been a good boy—but—" A slight gasp— "I—I'd been worried about him. Just lately. I know a lot of young people get into trouble these days—you read in the papers—and these terrible drugs all around—Donny has his own car, of course—"

"How old is he, Mrs. Franks?" asked Hackett.

"Eighteen. He's just eighteen. And just lately I'd been worried—he'd be away till all hours and I wouldn't know where—and not answering when I asked, and sometimes he was so strange, not like himself—and cross— He—he—swore at me sometimes. You read in the papers how even good young people, from good families, get to taking these drugs—and I was frightened," she said. "I was frightened. He wasn't acting right. I didn't know what to do."

"And you thought of—mmh—Mr. Logan." Mendoza had made a steeple of his long hands; he watched her.

"Well, you see, I suddenly thought—a police officer would know more about that sort of thing. I was a little embarrassed—but a police officer, well, it's rather like a—a doctor, isn't it, and then I thought too, a man—sometimes mothers don't understand boys that age, however much they *love* them—but— And he was very kind," said Mrs. Franks. "So kind and helpful. He listened to me, and he asked me some questions—about how Donny'd been acting, you know. He explained there were symptoms that'd show, he said—was Donny very moody lately, and was he eating right, and did he wear sunglasses, and were his eyes blistered-looking, a lot of things like that— And it didn't seem possible but he said— My Donny!" She put a crumpled handkerchief to her mouth. "It was just how Donny had been acting—"

"He told you the boy was probably taking drugs?"

She nodded. "He asked—if we had a—a family doctor. Of course I've gone to Dr. Hopewell for years, and he took care of Donny since he was a baby—not that he was ever sick much, a big strong boy he's always been— Anyway, Mr. Logan said I should get him to examine Donny, and find out—and there were clinics and hospitals where—maybe they could cure him, if he was—"

Which had been quite proper advice from Patrolman Pat Logan. "He also told you something else," said Mendoza.

"Yes, he did. He said if—if we found out that Donny had been taking drugs, we—the doctor—ought to inform the police. But I don't know if Dr. Hopewell—"

"Mmh. You called the doctor," said Mendoza. And what did this rigmarole say? Wednesday: the day after the earthquake: two days before Logan was attacked. . . .

"Well, I was terribly upset—I'd been afraid, but what Mr. Logan said —about *symptoms,* and Donny acting just like he said— Yes, I called Dr. Hopewell. He doesn't have office hours on Wednesdays, I called him at home, we've gone to him a long time and I thought—in an emergency— And he did. He came right away."

"What time was that?"

"When I got back from talking to Mr. Logan. He said he had to be on duty at noon—it was about ten to eleven when I got home—"

Patrolman Logan, diverted from regular duty that hot Wednesday, working overtime helping out the civil-defense crews still digging out the bodies, helping evacuate the thousands of people in the path of that dam threatening to give way. "Yes?"

"Because Donny was there then," she said. "Just lately I never knew when he would be. Or where he was. I—I only found out in May he hadn't been going to school. And he'd gone out that morning before I got up. In his car somewhere. But he came home—it was funny, as if it was meant—just before I did. He was up in his room playing records— this terrible music the young people seem to like—not what I call music, but— And Dr. Hopewell said to keep him there, he'd come right away— and I don't know how I could have stopped him, Donny I mean, if he'd wanted to leave, but he was still up there playing records when the doctor came, and it was just terrible—" Suddenly she began to cry in an indecisive sort of way. "Calling me names and swearing—but I know it wasn't the real Donny, these awful drugs—Dr. Hopewell said—I was so thankful he was there to manage everything— And he had a terrible time with Donny, he called an ambulance and they had to—had to—he was fighting all of them—"

"I think we'd like to have a talk with Dr. Hopewell," said Mendoza gently. "Where do we find him, Mrs. Franks?"

They found Dr. Oliver Hopewell, irritated at being invaded by cops on Sunday, at home: a neat expensive modern house in Westwood. Dr. Hopewell was, probably, a very competent general practitioner with a good practice, and he recognized the necessity of cooperating with the police; he concealed annoyance and answered them readily.

"Of course the woman's a fool," he said brutally. "Indulged the boy every way, never attempted to discipline him, and there's a substantial income, I gather. Not that I know much about the boy—never much wrong with him physically—but, given our present social culture as we might say, maybe this was expectable." Dr. Hopewell was fiftyish, with a nakedly bald head and an unexpected little white beard like a billy goat's. He hunched his shoulders. "A scene, yes. I could see the boy was high on something—I called an ambulance in a hurry. I couldn't have handled him alone. As it was, we had a time getting him to the hospital—naturally I didn't dare risk giving him morphine or anything else until I knew what he had inside already. It turned out to be the Blue Angels. In the vernacular."

"Sodium amytal," said Hackett.

"But it could have been anything—as I needn't tell you. From speed to heroin to any of the barbiturates. My God, these *kids!*" said Hopewell. "Anything."

"We know. So?" said Mendoza.

Hopewell spread his hands. "What can I do? I didn't get much out of him. I might guess he's been the whole route, from the pot to H to the acid—oh, I know the jargon!" He laughed mirthlessly. "And I also know—as you gentlemen do—that it's largely futile, once they're hooked, to try for the permanent cure. But we have to try. Make the gesture. And Mrs. Franks, God knows, has the money for the deluxe attempt. I've got him in the Spencer-Evers Clinic in Huntington Beach. They deal exclusively with the addicts—on a private basis—and they're very good." He shrugged again. "I wouldn't take a bet on Don Franks, but for whatever good it'll do, they'll try."

"No, Doctor, neither would I," said Mendoza. "But didn't it occur to you that the local police might be interested in Don Franks? That—"

Hopewell stared at him. "Why? Oh—he hadn't any narcotics on him, Lieutenant. Naturally I made sure of that, and I searched his room at the house. That was after the ambulance came and the attendants had him under restraint. He was absolutely clean."

"And high on the Blue Angels," said Hackett. "Then."

"Naturally if I'd found any narcotics on him I'd have—"

"You might have assumed," said Mendoza, "that a user could give us the names of any suppliers. You should have contacted the precinct—"

"My God, Lieutenant," said Hopewell, "give you a few more names to chase up? With all of it, any of it, available almost anywhere—the suppliers on every high-school campus in town? I don't remember who said it— 'To understand the twentieth century is to come to grips with madness.' *I* don't know the answer. I can only try to help where I can."

"*Ya lo creo,*" said Mendoza. "And this was on Wednesday."

"That's right. Why? Well, I got there—to the Franks's house—about noon. Devil of a nuisance, of course, my day off—and by the time I'd seen him and called the ambulance and we got him under control, and I looked over his room, well, call it twelve-forty. I saw him checked in at the clinic at one-thirty. It's a good one, as I say, they try—"

"He's been there ever since," said Mendoza.

"Yes, of course. I said they specialize. The addicts of all kinds. The patients are very strictly supervised, yes."

Mendoza looked at Hackett. This unexpected new evidence, turning up the only smell they'd had of somebody who might harbor some grudge, some grievance, on Patrolman Logan. The apprehension and incarceration of yet another punk j.d. on dope. Would Don Franks have known that it was Logan, the cop just happening to live across the street, who had confirmed Mrs. Franks's fears and brought in the doctor? Probably—that would have come out in the little scene when the doctor first appeared. And the dope—of any variety—so often did spark off the senseless violence.

But Don Franks had been locked up at this clinic for addicts since Wednesday afternoon.

Their shapeless little mystery was still shapeless.

CHAPTER 4

Mendoza eased the Ferrari up the drive, carefully straddling the rather sizable crack opened by the earthquake, and into the garage alongside Alison's Facel-Vega. At this time of year it was still light at nearly seven o'clock, and most of his household was in the back yard. Bast and Sheba were sensibly sheltering on the back step; Nefertite was digging a hasty hole behind the chrysanthemums; and El Señor, uttering curses at the top of his half-Siamese voice, was making a run for the back porch while the mockingbird dive-bombed him.

The twins were shouting. *"El pájaro* bite Señor—Daddy, see *el pájaro—"*

"YAWK!" screamed the mockingbird, and got in a second hard peck on El Señor's rump before he bolted into the house by the cat door there.

"He's afraid El Señor steal *los niños* out of nest—Mama said—"

"Yes, yes, I see *el pájaro*—I don't know whether there are *los niños* in the nest, Terry—all right, Johnny, *los cuentos* before bed—"

"El lobo eat Grandmother all down," said Terry reminiscently.

Alison came out to rescue him. *"¡Bastante! El pájaro's* gone home, you two come in now. Tough day, *amante?"*

The shaggy dog Cedric went on barking furiously at the alder tree, whither the mockingbird had vanished.

"You've given up on the untangling?" inquired Mendoza.

"No, of course we can't. But it'll have to be done like regular lessons, you know, the deliberate effort made at it. Half an hour mornings and afternoons—like that. And how long do mockingbird eggs take to hatch?"

"I haven't the slightest idea. You said that creature's nesting again—the way he's attacking the cats—"

"Máiri doesn't know either. But I'm afraid there is a nestful of *los niños,* all right."

"I said we'd be stuck with him for life," said Mendoza. "And if you're conducting lessons, while you're at it you might try to teach him the other half of 'Yankee Doodle.'"

"Which is a thought," said Alison. She shooed the twins and Cedric into the kitchen, the other three cats preceding them. "I'll finish dinner, Máiri, you get these two settled down. Yes, yes, monsters, your father'll read to you—half an hour, mind, that's all—"

Johnny suddenly seized hold of Mendoza's trousers and began shouting at the top of his voice, "Rumple-rumple-rumple! *El villano* steal *el niño!* Rumple-rumple-rumple—"

"Now what in the name of guidness," said Mrs. MacTaggart, and gave him a vigorous spank on the bottom. He turned an angelic smile on her.

"We just got," said Alison, "to Rumpelstiltskin, Máiri. While you were at the market. . . . If you want a drink before coping with the monsters, Luis—"

"On general principles only." El Señor understood English and landed on the counter with a plaintive demand for his share; Mendoza poured him an ounce of rye in a saucer and their alcoholic cat lapped eagerly. Mendoza swallowed half his own drink and watched Alison meditatively as she got a big bowl of salad from the refrigerator. He was pleased she'd cut her hair; after six months of coping with it shoulder length, she'd had it cut again in the short feathery cut and looked like the Alison he had first known. The Alison who had, after too many years as the lone wolf, at last captured Luis Rodolfo Vicente Mendoza into the domestic scene—and who but a redhaired Scots-Irish girl could have done that?

"Out of the way," she said, coming past with the bowl.

"Who or what," asked Mendoza, "is Rumpelstiltskin?"

Alison stared at him. "You never had Grimm's fairy stories read to you?"

"Why?" he asked reasonably. "My grandmother'd probably never heard of them. Ask me anything about the pantheon of Aztec gods, but—"

"Well, maybe you'll improve your education along with the offspring's. Suppose you get out of my way and do so. With any luck they'll settle down in half an hour and we can have a peaceful meal."

Mendoza laughed, finishing the rye. "*¡Más vale así!* You reassure me, *gatita. Muy mucho,* as Johnny would say."

"Reassure you?"

"Because I was doing some thinking on the way home," said Mendoza. "About mother love."

"Prompted by what?"

"Mmh—this and that. Chiefly, I think, that. It's like apple pie and—and the circus and Disneyland," said Mendoza. "Nobody could possibly be against it. But, *Dios,* what havoc it can cause on occasion. The—mmh—wrong kind of mother love."

"You can explain it over dinner, please—I'm busy."

"I'm going," said Mendoza meekly and, pausing to hang up his jacket on the way, went to read Grimm to the twin monsters.

"What the hell kind of wild-goose chase are we on?" asked Higgins at nine o'clock on Monday morning. "This kid couldn't possibly have had anything to do with beating up Logan—he's been locked up since Wednesday afternoon."

"That's what I said," said Hackett, "until Luis pointed out that this whole Franks rigmarole was the only unusual thing showing up in Logan's immediate past." He was taking the Barracuda up the winding road carefully.

"Well, but I wonder just how unusual that was, Art—the citizen asking for advice. It's a funny thing, but even back when I was in uniform, you got it—the honest citizen taking it for granted that a trained cop would know what to advise—the boy getting into bad company, the girl taking up with a punk, Uncle Bill's taste for whiskey. And I'd think these days, with most people aware of the rise of crime and—"

"We can ask his wife if it had ever happened before—if it happened often. But the fact is, it is the only different thing that happened to him this last week, and we'll just look round it a little in case it could give us a lead."

"Oh, I see that, sure. I wonder if the lab turned up anything at the house."

"Any luck, we'll get a report today."

They found Mrs. Claudia Franks in a pink housecoat having breakfast. "I don't have to get up early," she said apologetically, "so I don't. I suppose I should. But it doesn't seem— And I've been so worried about Donny." She undoubtedly had been: the only thing in life she had to spend affection on, which she'd done not wisely but too well. "Dr. Hopewell said I shouldn't go out there—to that hospital— If I could just see him, know he was all right—but Dr. Hopewell said—"

They showed her the search warrant: always better to do the thing the legal way. She was surprised. "Oh, you can look anywhere you like, of course—but what did you think might be— Oh, do you think he had some of these awful drugs here? Oh—"

It was a big house for two people: three bedrooms upstairs, a big den and dining room on the ground floor. Don Franks's room was the right front one. Hackett and Higgins stood and looked around it for a minute before they made a move, and each knew what the other was thinking, and there wasn't any need to put it in words.

When Art Hackett was eighteen, his father had been making a fairly good salary at an office job in Pasadena, the main office of a market chain. They had an old but comfortable house in an oldish part of town; Hackett had his own room, but things had been a little tight that year because it was his sister Elise's third year in college, and even though she worked summers to help— He'd had a modest allowance, but since he was twelve he'd also held jobs, the paper route, cutting neighbors' lawns, the odd jobs to pick up extra money.

And when George Higgins was eighteen, he hadn't had it so good as that. His mother had died when he was twelve, and the year he graduated from high school, down in Santa Monica, his father had been killed in an accident. Higgins also had had the paper route, the odd jobs; and his father had had just about enough in the bank to pay for a funeral. Higgins had gone to work then as a common laborer, the only job he could get, at seventy per week.

She'd come panting up the stairs after them. "Oh, have you found anything? Is there—"

"Not yet, ma'am," said Higgins. "Could you tell us how much money Don might have, ordinarily? Did he have a part-time job, or—"

"Oh, no—nothing like that. He didn't need to— Of course he has his allowance, he has his car to run, and if he took a girl out— What? Fifty dollars a week, I—everything so high now—and if he needed any more he knew he just had to ask—I—"

Hackett got rid of her politely; she trailed down the hall looking back. Higgins shut the door. "My God," he said simply. "Two hundred per, just for existing. Just for taking up space."

It was a good-sized room, and expensively equipped. Transistor radio, a portable TV, stereo phonograph, a large collection of L.P. records in a rack. A mahogany bedroom set, old-fashioned and solid. A complete lavatory and wardrobe off the bedroom.

They started to look around. "What are we looking for?" asked Higgins. "Just the pills? But when he had that much for certain, he could buy a fix of any kind whenever he felt like it—"

"But they do like to be sure of the fix when the yen hits them," said Hackett, and added, "Well, well." Higgins came to look. In the top drawer of the bureau, under a pile of handkerchiefs, a new gun—a brand-spanking-new Smith and Wesson .38 revolver. "That cost something," said Hackett.

"Especially for Donny." Seeing that Don Franks was a minor and wouldn't be eligible for a gun permit, buying that under the counter he had paid something for it. And under which counter had he bought it?

They went on looking. They unmade the bed and turned the mattress over. They looked under the carpet, behind pictures and back of drawers. It wasn't until they got to the lavatory that they came across anything else.

There, in the stall shower, one of the square tiles moved under Higgins' hand. He got out his knife, pried at the edges; it yielded and he lifted it clean out. Something came with it. The underflooring had been cut out just below it, a space just enough smaller than the eight-inch-square tile that it fit into it solidly; and firmly lashed to the underside of the tile with electrician's tape was a length of heavy twine. At the end of that, as Higgins lifted the tile all the way out, was a sizable plastic bag tied on the other end of the twine.

"I think we just hit a jackpot," said Hackett. "Gimme—let's see." They started to empty the bag carefully on the lavatory floor.

Most of the expectable lot was represented—it was, as Hackett said, a mixed bag. Quite a collection of the pills—the uppers and downers, barbiturates, bennies, the crystals, the Blue Angels and Red Devils and Yellow Submarines—several decks of H, and of course a separate plastic bag full of marijuana.

Hackett and Higgins looked at each other. "Did you say a jackpot, Art?"

"I think," said Hackett, "we'd like to know the names of some of Don's pals, George. If she knows any."

"I'd take no bets on that." They started to pack it all back into the bag.

She didn't. She looked at them anxiously and said, "Well, a boy Donny's age, they're growing up, you know, they don't like families prying and asking questions, and you've got to remember that— I saw an article in a magazine once, about letting young people alone, respect their privacy—and besides Don doesn't like being asked things, where he's going or who with— I know he used to be good friends with Bob Vandermeier—the Vandermeiers lived just down the hill when Don was in junior high and he and Bob—"

"You don't know whether they're still friends?"

"No, I—well, it's not as if I didn't encourage him to bring his friends here, I did—we've got the nice sheltered patio and a barbecue and all—but he never seemed to want to. Not since he'd been in high school—had his car—well, you know boys that age. They're always coming and going. He—I didn't ask him any more," she said nervously. "That—that was one of the things that frightened me, you know. I tried to raise him to have some manners—but just lately, he—well, I don't know where he learned some of the language, and sw-swearing at me—just because—just because I *cared* about him, wanted to know where—worried about him—"

"What's the answer, Art?" asked Higgins in the Barracuda. "The hell of it is, you know, she just wouldn't believe you if you told her it's mostly her fault."

"I wonder if that's too easy an answer. Sure, not a good idea—anything Donny wants—the car—what was the car, I wonder—"

"I had a look in the garage while you were extricating us all polite. I don't somehow think Mrs. Franks drives a Mercedes sports model."

"No. But there are people who've survived the overindulgent raising and not gone off the rails. But it's not our job to philosophize, George."

"I'm speculating," said Higgins, "on something else. That's quite a cache of stuff he had stored away. I wonder what Luis got from the doctors at that clinic."

He and Hackett had worked together a long time, and they were basically the same kind of men; but also they were both experienced cops, and sometimes the shortcuts presented themselves to the experienced eye. They didn't have to spell out what was going through both their minds.

What Mendoza, going down to Huntington Beach to that private clinic, had got was just a little more suggestive.

He had called the hospital before he left the office. "We're just cautiously saying we think he'll make it, Lieutenant," said the doctor. "A minor miracle. His pulse is much stronger and it's possible he'll regain consciousness some time today or tomorrow. Of course the big question is, the extent of any brain damage."

Mendoza thought back to the time when Art Hackett had lain in a coma with the doctors saying the same thing. And Art had come through all right, which didn't say that Pat Logan would, and he knew what Sally Logan and the rest of them were feeling. *Pares o nones,* odds or evens—how the cards fell in the deal, he thought.

And of course Luis Mendoza had been brought up to believe that Something was in charge of affairs—and all of a sudden, now, dimly he wondered if Something was. When he came to think, the unexpected good luck (the guardian angels?) they'd been having lately—George getting away from those ugly thugs with a whole skin—and Landers getting taken off the hook by the belated discovery of the real X—

It was the way the cards fell. *Pares o nones.* . . .

They didn't let him in to talk to Don Franks. They had a rule of absolute isolation. But a scholarly-looking Dr. Faulkner talked to him readily about the case.

"I doubt very much whether he's really hooked, Lieutenant. No needle marks on him. No telling if he's tried the acid, but my guess would be—and I've seen too many addicts, more than I like to think about—my guess would be that he's experimented around with the pills, just for kicks, and that's about the extent of it. I haven't got him to talk much—beyond the usual complaints, complete with the obscenities, about the damn interfering fuzz, and Mama, and the doctor—"

"*Así, así,*" said Mendoza. "A free country, and everybody entitled to do his own thing and make his own decisions—nobody has a right to interfere with the beautiful souls seeking peace and love—"

"Oh, please, Lieutenant. Yes. But I did get one rather interesting thing out of him." The doctor adjusted his glasses. "We were running some tests, and I commented on the absence of needle marks—this was the first I'd noticed it—and he said, The H? Man, not him, he knew what that stuff could do to you. And then he shut up."

"*Interesante,*" said Mendoza. "In fact, you don't think he'd qualify as an addict? To anything?"

Faulkner said cautiously, "Well, you never can be sure, when they've gone so far as to experiment with any of it. But I don't think he's hooked on anything now, no. Once the sodium amytal was out of him he snapped back to normal—er—physically."

"Yes," said Mendoza. Physically. Most of the motive behind any addiction was not physical. A lot of reasons, or sometimes only one.

"So, have we got the other half of the story?" said Hackett.

"Very possibly." Mendoza straightened the desk blotter, brushed ashes off the polished wood; he sat back and lit a cigarette. It was very hot in the office; both Hackett and Higgins had pulled their ties loose. Some time the repair crews would get up as far as Homicide, to put glass back in their windows, and the air conditioning would get turned on. Some time.

Mendoza had passed on Faulkner's opinion to his two senior sergeants, and heard what they had to tell him. The office was quiet—doors open to the central corridor—except for the sporadic typing where Detective Jason Grace wrote a report in the big communal office across the hall. Palliser and Landers were out hunting known associates of Linda Schnell, and evidently Piggott and Glasser were out on something too.

"But it doesn't add up to anything for us," said Hackett. He readjusted his bulk in the chair beside Mendoza's desk and it creaked protestingly. Higgins had hoisted one hip to a corner of the desk.

"*Qué contrariedad*," murmured Mendoza. "What a disappointment for us."

Hackett looked at him suspiciously. "Well, it seems to me as if we'd been ferreting out a little suggestive evidence to hand over to Callaghan up in Narco. What led us to Don Franks?— Mrs. Franks's little heart-to-heart with Patrolman Pat Logan, last Wednesday morning—"

"Indubitably."

"—And aside from the fact that we've agreed it was a couple of X's who beat up Logan—how is he, have you heard?"

"They're saying he'll make it. No guarantee on the amount of brain damage. Same like you that time. But maybe his guardian angel is doing overtime."

"Thank God for that— A couple of X's who beat up Logan, neither of them could have been Don Franks, who's been incarcerated at that clinic since Wednesday afternoon. It was Friday Logan got jumped."

"All on the nose," nodded Mendoza. "The only reason we went looking at Don Franks—what, George?"

"Well, my God, he was the only one who showed who might have had a little grudge on Logan. Logan kindly explaining the symptoms of drug use to dimwitted Mama, who fetched the doctor in to haul Don off to the clinic. But—"

"And we now find that, A, Don isn't really hooked on anything. Just experimenting. And staying away from the H because he knows what that can do to you. And, B, he has a rather extensive cache of the hard stuff, representing quite a little investment, stashed away at home. Would either of you take any bets—"

"Well, for God's sake, Luis," said Higgins impatiently, "we're not idiots—of course we saw that! He was likely setting up as a seller, maybe a pusher—what you got from Faulkner just underlines that—"

"*Pues sí*. And consequently, George, all things being equal—"

"Oh, my God!" said Hackett suddenly. "But what fools—I just—"

And Sergeant Lake ran in. "Threatened shooting—black-and-white on the way—the McLaren Building on Wilshire, second floor—"

They all got up in a hurry. Mendoza snatched the .38 and a box of ammo from the top drawer; they met Grace in the corridor and ran. Hackett fell into the Ferrari after Mendoza, in the lot downstairs, and Mendoza switched on ignition and siren at once. Higgins and Grace dived into Grace's little blue Elva and tailgated the Ferrari out of the lot.

That building was a good forty blocks across town, one of the modern new office buildings just beyond MacArthur Park; the Ferrari's siren clearing the way, they made it at the same moment the black-and-white zeroed in from the opposite direction.

The crowd had begun to collect in the street.

A man came running out the front entrance of the building. "Police—thank God somebody called—shots fired, a lot of shots, just now, not two minutes ago! Up there somewhere—I was just getting into the ele—"

Mendoza gestured the uniformed men to the rear of the building with one savage movement; Higgins pounded after them. The rest of them ran into the building and up the marble stairs to the right. Whoever had called had said, second floor—

Up there, the whole corridor was in an uproar. Every door was open, people out in the hall, the more timid peering from doorways, asking questions, exclaiming—a woman screaming somewhere.

"Police? Up here—" They ran for that door, halfway up the corridor from the stairs, on the left side. The man there was very badly shaken; he was a tall, thin, nice-looking Negro wearing a doctor's white smock over dark pants, and he said, "In there—I think—the shots came from in there—I haven't been in, but Mrs. Stafford said—I haven't gone in—"

"I called," said a breathless voice. "I called you—I heard him—the door was open—" She was a diminutive blonde in a nurse's white uniform. "I told Dr. Blaise and he—but then all the shots—"

They went in with guns out. But a gun had spoken in there, and there wasn't any need for more guns.

It was an expensive modern office, as all those in this building would be. The gold lettering on the corridor door said *Dr. John Harlow, M.D.* There was a waiting room, heavily carpeted in beige pile, a beige couch and chairs, a long low fruitwood coffee table spread with magazines, several lamps, ashtrays. A glass panel to the left of another door: it was open, to show the receptionist's desk beyond, and the door was open to a short hall, other doors off that and at the end an open door.

Inside the door to the hall sprawled the white-uniformed body of a woman. A young Negro woman, bloody and still, the blood still widening slowly in a little pool beyond the body. "My God—" said Hackett.

The doors on either side opened on small examining rooms with the tables, the sinks, empty and sterile. The door at the end of the hall led to the doctor's office—a desk, thick carpet, chairs, fluorescent lighting—and more death. The man lay on his back, legs twisted, grotesque, in the middle of the room: he had on light gray trousers, a white smock, and a stethoscope still dangled around his neck, the slow stream of blood still running, staining it. The woman lay nearly across the threshold of a smaller room off this: a young woman, Negro, her blood still pumping from some artery—even as they came in, that suddenly stopped, and her body quivered once and was still.

For a heartbeat, they just looked. The woman had been young, pretty, well dressed: on this hot summer day, a jersey-silk sheath, cool blue; no stockings; medium-heeled white sandals. A big white patent handbag lay a few feet away from the body. The man had been hardly older, in his thirties: a tall man with regular chocolate-brown features.

"My God," said Hackett again.

The other man came in then behind them. "I didn't like to come in—she called you, we thought— *Oh, my God!* Dr. Harlow! It's—and his nurse out there—oh, my God!"

The woman in the hall stopped screaming abruptly.

"But Dr. Harlow—" The big Negro in the white smock looked at them dumbly. "Who'd do a thing like this? Who'd—"

Hackett said automatically, "You can identify the victims? May we have your name, please."

He nodded jerkily. "Colcannon. James W. Colcannon. My office—I'm a dentist, my office is right across the hall—I heard the shots, naturally I came—but Mrs. Stafford said— It's Dr. Harlow, yes, but who would do such a—"

Mendoza turned. "What about the two women? Can you tell us who they are, Doctor?"

He shook his head blindly. "The nurse—Dr. Harlow's receptionist, I think her name's Jenkins—"

Higgins and the two uniformed men came in. "Nothing," said Higgins. "He got clean away, Luis—we were just too late. Nobody in the parking lot—we can ask if anybody saw him come out, but there's not a smell there now. No telling even which way he went after leaving the building."

But there'd be places to ask questions: all the ground-floor offices, the buildings across the street. Mendoza said, "Keep these people out, for God's sake!" and the two patrolmen went to mount guard on the door to the corridor. "Art, we'll want a lab truck and an ambulance. Ask Bainbridge to come in person—he'd better see this from the start." Hackett went out in a hurry.

"But, everybody in the office," said Grace numbly. He holstered his gun. "The doctor, the nurse, the patient—" He went over and looked at the white handbag.

"But who'd want to do this to Dr. Harlow?" said Colcannon.

"Jase—" Mendoza came up beside him.

"It'll take prints, that patent, but—" Grace bent and pushed back the flap of the bag gently with one fingertip: the clasp was unfastened. He tilted it a little and a woman's blue leather billfold slithered out; they squatted over it, and Grace coaxed it all the way out with the tip of his pen, flipped the billfold open. On the left side, a plastic slot for an I.D. card, filled out in a neat hand. *Mrs. Ann Harlow,* an address in Leimert Park, *in case of accident notify Dr. John Harlow—*

"His wife," said Grace. "Harlow's. Why—"

"But Dr. Harlow," Colcannon was repeating, "Dr. Harlow so well thought of—such a good man—did a lot of charity work, I'd heard—who'd have any reason to—"

"Luis—" Higgins beckoned him. Mendoza went halfway down the hall; Higgins had the little blonde there. "Just tell the lieutenant about it, Mrs. Stafford. Mrs. Lilian Stafford, Luis, receptionist for Dr. Blaise down the hall—"

"Orthodontia and dentures," she said. "Two-fourteen. That's right. Oh, my God, are they all *dead?* It doesn't seem possible— I was—it was my coffee break, I only took ten minutes because we were busy—I went down the hall to the rest room, I was coming back, I—" She was excited, but she was a level-headed young woman and in control of herself. "I came past Dr. Harlow's office, the door was open just a crack and I heard him—a man's voice—he was saying, 'I'll kill all of you, I will too, I'll shoot you all'—and he sounded— And I ran back to the office and called the police right away and then I told Dr. Blaise and he'd started down here when there were all the shots—oh, my God, are they *dead?* I can't believe—"

"We'll want a statement from you, Mrs. Stafford." As well as from most of the other people here on this floor when it happened, and probably those on the ground floor too. This one was going to be a king-size mess to work, Mendoza foresaw.

The ambulance arrived downstairs, the interns coming in with a stretcher. "Hands off," said Mendoza. "The full treatment on this one."

People were still milling around in the corridor, the interns hanging around waiting, when Dr. Bainbridge bustled in with, coincidentally, Scarne and Duke of the lab behind him. "Give this one the eagle eye, boys," said Hackett. "Did we say business was slow, everybody waiting for the next earthquake? My God, the wholesale slaughter—"

And Scarne was aiming the camera, Duke phlegmatically dusting the desk, five minutes later, when they heard it. The little fretful whimper from somewhere—that other door off the office—beyond the woman's still body.

It was a compact little lavatory, white tile floor, commode, Pullman vanity washbasin, stall shower. It was in the stall shower that Jason Grace, rushing in just ahead of the other men, found it. Where Ann Harlow, perhaps hearing that threatening voice—*I'll shoot you all*—had hastily, fearfully, hidden her baby—before going to the door to her husband's office, where death had waited.

Grace picked it up almost reverently and said, "My God—my God, its mother must have—"

The baby had been asleep, just waked up to loneliness. As they were to find, Celia Ann Harlow, just three months old. She was fat and brown with big brown eyes and a dimple beside her rosebud mouth, and she had kicked off the pink blanket around her and she smiled up from Grace's arms and gurgled.

"My God," said Grace. "From now on I believe in the guardian angels. Everybody else in the office— But who? And why?"

CHAPTER 5

"But how did we miss him?" said Higgins savagely. "You heard what that fellow said—not two minutes ago, the shots—just as we got here, Luis! How did he vanish into thin air, whether he went out the front or back? This is a big building—"

It was an eight-story building, occupying nearly a full block with its large parking lot behind and to one side. The patrolmen and Higgins, running round to the rear, had found the parking lot nearly empty, at that time of day, and not a soul to be seen. Round the other side of the building, nothing. There were pedestrians passing, on Wilshire; then, realizing that something had happened, stopping to form a little crowd. But none of them had seen a man run out of the building.

They had called up three more cars—before Mendoza had called for a lab team and Bainbridge—and made a hurried search of the first three floors. In the lobby, a door to the basement (so the sign said) to the left of the entrance was locked; that was N.G., and of course for nearly a hundred percent sure he'd left the building at once. Only a couple of people on the third floor had heard the shots: everybody on the ground floor had, but the time element was against them there too. Nearly every tenant in the building was a professional of some kind: doctors, dentists, optometrists, a couple of lawyers—more doctors than anything else —and they didn't as a rule start office hours until ten. On the ground floor, where the bank of elevators took up half the corridor, the only offices occupied, at the rear of that long hall, had been those of a lawyer and another dentist; and by the time they and their office help had got out to the hall, to the front of the building, the gunman would have had time to get out that way without being seen.

Had had, in fact. By that time they had talked to Mrs. Myrtle Boggs, whose screams had welcomed them to the second floor. Mrs. Boggs had seen him go, and a lot of use she was to them. She'd been on her way up the hall toward the office of Dr. Edward Cunningham, gynecologist; she had a ten-thirty appointment. She had passed Dr. Harlow's office and was four or five offices up the hall—by what she could tell them—when she was paralyzed at the fusillade of shots.

"And I couldn't *move*, maybe twenty seconds, I was so scared—and I screamed—and I looked back because the shots came from back there—and I *saw* him! He came out that door—yessir, the door of that doctor's office—he came out running and he ran down the stairs—the front stairs —I saw the gun in his hand—and I couldn't stop screaming—"

They had asked her questions, and she'd tried to answer them. But she couldn't tell them much. They could hope after she'd calmed down a little she might remember more; but it wasn't surprising she hadn't seen more details. These corridors were lighted, but not all that well; and she'd been startled, confused; and she'd only seen his back.

"It was so *fast*—I don't suppose I saw him more 'n five seconds, and he was gone, down the stairs—well, it was a man, but I only saw his back, and the gun in his hand—he was running, and I couldn't even guess how tall he was or what clothes he was wearing—but he was the one, I saw him run out of that door and I saw the gun—"

Slowly, in Harlow's office, order was being brought from confusion. The baby had been taken over to Juvenile Hall pending the discovery of any relatives. Grace had gone out to the Leimert Park address to look for relatives, friends. Bainbridge had examined the bodies; photographs had been taken and, eventually, the bodies removed. The lab men were dusting everything they could see in here; the detectives kept out of their way, talking to other tenants in the building, hunting anybody who might have something relevant to tell them.

The other nurse in Dr. Blaise's office identified Harlow's receptionist: Mrs. Harriet Jenkins, and supplied an address and that of Bill Jenkins' employer. Palliser went over to break the news to him. Jenkins was a skilled mechanic, working at a big Cadillac agency on Washington; he came down to the morgue to identify the body before he broke down. "We were saving for the house—wanted to get the house all paid off, only reason she went back to work the last five years—she liked the doctor, a fine man—it was the house payments, reason she—"

The men at Homicide came up with answers most of the time; the one answer they never had was the one to that question, Why did it have to be—?

Bainbridge had said they didn't look like very big slugs, but at close

range any gun was deadly; had been here. He'd try to get them out at
once for Ballistics.

They got this and that, talking to the other tenants on that floor. "I
knew him—just casually," said Dr. Colcannon, calmer then. "To say
hello and nice morning, is all. He'd been here longer than I have. I was
busy with a patient when I heard the shots—and of course I didn't think
it could *be* shots—backfires or— It wasn't until, oh, five or ten seconds
later I realized it was shots, and came out through my waiting room—"
He hadn't seen the gunman. "Just the woman standing there and
screaming—"

The tearful pretty brown girl named Mary Ellen Rosden, from Dr.
Blaise's office, told them that Mrs. Jenkins had been her best friend's
aunt—her best friend Carla Jenkins. It had been Mrs. Jenkins had got
Mary Ellen interested in nursing. "That is, she was a graduate nurse,
but she was hired just as the receptionist in Dr. Harlow's office, he had
a regular nurse too, Mrs. Jenkins was just as glad to take that sort of
job, not on her feet so much—she liked Dr. Harlow—but who'd do such
an awful thing? When I think of that baby being there—"

The other nurse had arrived by then, to faint dead away at the news;
but, revived, she couldn't tell them much either. Everybody had liked
Dr. Harlow, nobody would have had any reason to—

Grace called in at twelve-thirty. "So what have you picked up, Jase?"
Everything had been printed then, and the lab men were gone, leaving
Mendoza and the others in occupation of Dr. Harlow's once immaculate office, now bloodstained and disordered, with a film of fingerprint
powder on most surfaces, and the furniture in disarray where they'd
moved it to get at awkward spots. Mendoza was sitting at Harlow's desk
going over the few solid facts they had with Hackett and Higgins.

"Nothing," said Grace. "Or nothing to give us any leads at all. There
aren't any relatives, period. I've got two neighbors, one on each side of
the Harlow house—Mrs. Gaster and Mrs. Pine. Mrs. Pine and her husband—who's an optometrist—about the same age as the Harlows, and
knew them better. In fact, well enough that she called her husband and
they've offered to make funeral arrangements, there being nobody else.
Both the Harlows were brought up in orphanages, there aren't any relatives at all. Harlow in a private orphanage back in Maryland, his wife in
a Catholic place in San Diego. They'd been so happy about the baby,
married seven years and given up hope of a family."

"Yes, Jase." And they all knew the Graces felt like that too. Mendoza lit a new cigarette. "No enemies, no recent trouble."

"Nothing. He was thirty-four, she was thirty-two, she'd taught art for a couple of years, gave it up when he'd got his practice established. He started out in general practice eight years ago, right in that same office. He had a fine reputation, everybody"—Grace sounded tired—"liked him."

"Yes. Why was Mrs. Harlow there with the baby, did anyone know?"

"Just chance," said Grace sadly. "Another random thing is all. Harlow had hospital rounds to make most mornings—he wouldn't have office patients scheduled until about eleven—"

The first appointment listed in the book had been at eleven-fifteen. "Yes. So?"

"—And Mrs. Harlow had been fussing about the baby. Mrs. Pine says, the least little thing—but you can see why she would, coming so late when they hadn't hoped— Anyway, she thought the baby had a little temperature, and she called her husband's office when she knew he'd be there, about ten-fifteen. And he told her to bring the baby right down —her name's Celia Ann, by the way—for him to check. Mrs. Harlow had her own car, it'll be in the lot down there—white Chevy Corvair five years old." He added the plate number. "Just chance that she was there. The Pines were close friends and they've never heard anything about any difficulties with patients, any quarrels or threats. But—"

"Mmh?"

"Nothing," said Grace. "Really. But the name sort of rang a bell with me—I seemed to remember my father mentioning Harlow—so I called to ask him." Grace's father was on the staff at the General Hospital. "He knew him, sure. Harlow interned at the General. Dad says he was a very good man, very competent. He'd tried to persuade him to specialize—said he had the makings of a very fine surgeon—but Harlow decided on general practice."

"Well," said Mendoza. "All of which gives us no ideas at all." He brushed his moustache the wrong way and back again. "Damnation. Could it have been just a nut off the street? That random? No, damn it, he must have known who he was threatening to shoot— Well, we've done what we can here. See what the lab picks up. See what Ballistics— We're going up to Federico's for lunch."

"So, I'll see you," said Grace.

At Federico's, waiting for lunch over preliminary drinks, they came to no conclusions except that this one was going to give them a lot of work.

"Take a look at all his patients," said Palliser with a sigh. "For somebody who—what? Thought he'd used the wrong treatment or something? At everybody he knew, for any trouble or—borrowed money, lent money? Was he a gambler, maybe, reneging on a deal?"

"Was he playing around with somebody's wife?" contributed Landers.

"I should doubt that, considering what Jase got," said Mendoza. "The Harlows seem to have been a perfectly respectable couple, all wrapped up in the baby they'd never expected to have. And that wasn't any kill over a gambling debt, John. This, if you want my considered opinion, was a nut. Pure and simple."

Grace came up to the table to hear that. "And that I'll go along with, Lieutenant. Perfectly respectable you can say. It's a nice house—colonial." Leimert Park, of course, and View Park where the Graces lived, were both very superior, well-groomed city areas where a considerable number of Negro professional people lived, with a few of the formerly wealthy white residents still scattered around. "She was a gardener—always puttering around her flowers, Mrs. Pine said. They were homebodies, didn't go out much—of course he had a busy routine—a few close friends, not socializers. He'd take a highball before dinner. She was Catholic, of course, but there wasn't any argument about it, he was perfectly agreeable the baby should be brought up in her church. They were just crazy about that baby, she said."

"Respectable married couple," said Hackett. "I had a thought, but it's a dead end."

"What?" asked Palliser.

"If he had white patients as well as black. Would he, Jase?"

"I should think probably—some, anyway. These days. Why?"

"Yes, I just thought if somebody with the funny notions got the idea that the stupid nigger doctor had given somebody the wrong medicine—but of course nobody like that would be going to Harlow to start with. Or, likely, anybody in such a family."

"Dead end," agreed Higgins. "We look at his patients and everybody he knew. My God, what a job."

"It's a shame about that baby," said Landers. "Cute little thing."

"That's so, Tom," said Grace. "A shame."

They checked in at the office at a quarter of two, and as they came in Lake looked up from his paperback. "Oh, John, you're to call this number. I don't know what about—a woman."

Palliser sat down at his desk, got an outside line and dialed. Presently a female voice answered, and he said, "This is Sergeant Palliser."

"Oh. This is Reba Roberts, Sergeant—you know, you're the one came to tell me—about Chris—the other day."

"Yes, Mrs. Roberts. I haven't checked, but I think the body—that is, you can probably claim it today or tom—"

"Well, I wasn't calling about that, but thank you, I guess I can make some arrangements—"

"Any funeral director will take charge for you, claim the body and so on."

"Oh. Well, what I wanted to ask was, when could I have Chris's car? I suppose you wanted to examine it and all, and of course there's no hurry, I don't drive, but—"

Palliser stared at the phone. "His *car?* He was driving—" But what idiots they had been not to ask—not to assume he had been. Practically everybody in L.A. had a car, or access to one. And Hauck, living in Hollywood, ending up at the Sheridan Hotel downtown— Both Tom and I slipping, thought Palliser. Tom had an excuse: he was in love. But I'm married to the girl, reflected Palliser with a mental groan. Supposed to be trained detectives, and a little thing like that— "We didn't know he was driving, Mrs. Roberts. We haven't got his car. Can—"

"What? Well, I certainly thought—then where is it?"

Palliser could have a good guess. It was in the possession of Linda Schnell, or Foster Sterry, or both. And they were two days late sending out a call on it. "Can you tell us the make and model, Mrs. Roberts?"

"Surely. I've got the license number too, had it written down in the phone book—mine, I mean—on account, well, you know I told you how Chris was—and if I ever had to— It's a Buick, a white sedan, he got it new six years ago. The license number is HNO 504."

"Thanks very much. I'm sorry about this, somebody should have asked you if he had a— Well, thank you."

"I'm sure I hope you find it, Sergeant. As I say, I don't drive, but I can get something for it, I suppose."

"We'll let you know," said Palliser. He then naturally sought out Landers across the room and asked him why they'd been such idiots. "We might have known he was driving. And damn it, you've got an excuse for acting like an idiot—"

"I have?"

"You're in love with that cute blonde. But I haven't—at least, I've got the girl all tied up legal—only she's off on this miserly kick. Going back to work to get the furniture paid off, damn it. I don't approve of working wives. But I can guess where Hauck's car is, can't you?"

"No," said Landers. "What I can guess is who's driving it. Seeing that it hasn't been hauled into the Traffic garage as abandoned on the street. We'd better put it on the hot list."

"I'll do it," said Palliser.

Of course there was quite a lot of the tedious routine to do on the Harlow shooting, even if no leads turned up. They had to get the formal statements typed up and signed, from everybody in that building who had told them anything pertinent; and one from Mrs. Pine, and Bill Jenkins. That would take time, but if they ever got any evidence on this killer, they had to have all that down in black and white for the D.A.

Meanwhile, of course, they had been deflected off the Logan case, off the Hauck case, the other things turning up to make more paper work if no mysteries. Palliser confessed his sin of omission to Mendoza, who told him everybody had moments of aberration. "At least you've got it on the hot list now. It may turn up your floozy and her boy-friend."

Piggott and Glasser drifted in about then and everybody asked where they'd been. "At a time when we needed every man—"

Glasser said indulgently, "well, you have to make allowances. He's just got engaged. I was on legitimate business. Nothing much—report to type. Old lady died in her sleep, apparently, apartment over on Virgil. Jimmy said something big was up when I called in."

They all looked at Piggott, who said with dignity he'd been out buying an engagement ring. "Though with everything a cop sees, I think maybe we're fools, try for the peaceful married life, maybe a family. With the devil going up and down— Well, she didn't want a diamond, I got her her birthstone—it's an amethyst, with some little diamonds each side—"

"Very nice," said Glasser benignly.

Palliser, Landers, Grace, Piggott and Glasser went back to the McLaren Building to fetch the witnesses in and get the statements typed up. "It just occurs to me," said Hackett, sitting down in the chair beside Mendoza's desk, "that when all this erupted, we were just making some educated guesses about something else."

Higgins had followed him in. He was looking grim. "I thought I'd check," he said. "I just called the hospital. On Logan. He's had a relapse. They thought he was going, about nine this morning, but he's still hanging on—just barely holding his own—he could pass out any time."

"My God," said Hackett. "When we thought—"

"So, all the more reason to catch up to the X's on that, boys. ¿Qué le parece?" Mendoza stabbed out his cigarette. "Where were we?"

"Deducing that Don Franks was setting up as a seller. With that hoard stashed away, maybe had been set up as a seller some time. But Franks couldn't have had anything to do with beating up Logan—"

"No. But reason it out. The unnecessary violence on Logan—why? No personal grudge that anybody knew of. The only unroutine thing Logan had done lately was to offer advice to dimwitted Mama Franks. Thereby getting Donny incarcerated. Incarcerated, Donny couldn't supply the fix for any of his customers, and that must have—"

"Annoyed them," said Hackett. "How did any of his customers know that it was Logan put the finger on Donny?"

"If they did, any of them—if that's the way it went—doubtless something will emerge as you go along," said Mendoza. "You might hunt up that Bob Vandermeier. Shortcuts. They were in junior high together, Vandermeier may still attend the same school as Donny."

"That had occurred to me," said Hackett.

Before he and Higgins left the office, however, the lab report came in. The lab hadn't picked up any useful latents at the Logan house, any strange prints. They had found two kinds of bloodstains—a lot of type O, which was Logan's, and a little of type AB, which was a fairly rare type. "That's funny," said Hackett, reading the report over Mendoza's shoulder. "We said if Logan got in a couple of blows, that was all—knocked out almost right away. Of course he might have bloodied a nose—"

"Or," said Higgins, "whoever had that knife was turned on and not noticing just where he aimed it."

"And that is also a thought," said Mendoza. "Suppose you go and look, *compadres.*"

"While you do what?"

Mendoza trickled smoke through his nostrils. "I have here," he said sleepily, "Dr. Harlow's case records. They look like fairly dull reading, but one never knows when something suggestive might show, or where. It's a place to start."

"And the hunch rising up to biff you between the eyes, let us hope," said Hackett.

Which sometimes the hunches did. Mendoza was sitting on the end of his spine, hands clasped across his flat stomach, eyes closed. "Symbolic," he said. "Very symbolic. Improving my education, Alison says."

"What's symbolic?"

"Rumpelstiltskin," said Mendoza. " 'Discover my name'— Mmh, yes. Reach in blind and hope the hunch hits you. *¡Vamos!*"

*   *   *

Hackett found Bob Vandermeier at three-forty-five, by the simple expedient of checking with Hollywood High School. Summer school was in session and a skeleton staff was there. Bob Vandermeier attended Hollywood High School, and his address was Briarcliff Road: another hillside street, a newer wealthy residential area.

Mrs. Vandermeier, small and dark, was frightened and indignant, police asking for Bob, and Hackett was patient, explaining—just questions about another boy at school—and she thawed under his big reassuring smile. "It isn't that I worry about him," she said at last, "I know Bob's all right—but dear Lord, these days can you be sure about anything? I'll get him, Sergeant—he's out back with the pup—he's starting her on her obedience lessons."

Bob Vandermeier was not a handsome boy, but he was reliable-looking: the only word for it. He had a round freckled face and steady blue eyes and close-cropped sandy hair and heavy shoulders: a big boy, mature-looking too. He sat on the couch opposite Hackett, with a leggy Great Dane pup at his feet, and listened to Hackett soberly.

"Don Franks," he said. "I'm not a pal of his anymore, Sergeant. *Sit,* Cleo. He's in trouble? I'm not surprised at that. He's really goofed off, the last couple years."

"In what line? I don't want to—" Hackett hesitated. "That is, if you feel—"

The boy smiled. "Make me rat on him? Sergeant, some of us have a little more sense than you might think. That's kid stuff, isn't it? If somebody's doing something wrong, illegal, it's only sense to see they get stopped. No, I didn't know Don was doing anything wrong, just suspected. He really got in with the wrong ones, first year in high—that was when we split up, way back there, so I couldn't tell you anything about him since, not that I know myself."

"Except that he was running with the wrong ones? Wrong which way? Who?"

"What do you think? The drug scene—the longhairs and beautiful people," said Bob. He looked down at the dog, the lines of potential grandeur blurred by puppyhood, the awkwardness of fast growth. He smiled. "It's kind of like Cleo here," he said. "Kind of. I mean, those kind, they're always talking about doing your own thing, what you want when you want, freedom, they talk about. But it's like Cleo here—just letting her do like that, she'd be the biggest nuisance you could have around, you know. All over the place— Well, you've got to teach 'em how to behave, how to handle themselves. So they're good for something, you know? That kind—I don't know how they figure—but they don't think just so logical. Besides going for the dope, which is just plain silly."

"So it is," said Hackett.

"I don't know that Don's gone in for that. But some of the kids he goes with—I could guess," said Bob. He scratched behind Cleo's ears reflectively and she grinned widely up at him. "Was he?"

"In a way," said Hackett. "Who does he run with?"

"Oh—I don't know any of them, just their names. I do know Ken Burkhart's been arrested once, something to do with drugs, I think. The others, I couldn't say. I wouldn't know all of the ones Don ran with. Jim Root, Marty Murphy, Ron Dolan, that girl—Kathy something—Cuthbert, Cathcart, something—and one they call Buck—I wouldn't know 'em all. Yes, they all go to Hollywood High—well, that is, or they did. You did know Don had dropped out, last semester? A couple of that bunch had too. At least, I had the same English class with this Murphy and the Kathy girl, and they hadn't showed up the last couple of months of the semester. And that's another thing, you know, Sergeant."

"What?"

"Well, they were both," said Bob, "so stupid in class. We're supposed to think that kind have got the answers to everything—them and their Do-your-own-thing whatever and whenever—when Murphy spells *hotel* with two *l*'s on a blackboard assignment, and doesn't know a comma from a semicolon?" Hackett laughed. "Well, I only got a B in that class," said Bob, "but I'd like to think I'm some smarter than that. It's like my granddad says—I think it's an old-country proverb—you got to learn to walk before you can run."

And it was reassuring to reflect that there were, hopefully, more teenagers like Bob Vandermeier around than the other kind. That was of no immediate help in locating these more recent pals of Don Franks's. By the time Hackett had seen Bob, the school staff had gone home. Tomorrow. . . .

Just before Mendoza left the office, the lab sent up a preliminary report on the Harlow shooting. The slugs had been examined by the Ballistics men: four in Harlow, three in Mrs. Harlow, two in Mrs. Jenkins. They had not been much damaged, and Ballistics had pinpointed the gun: a Harrington and Richardson nine-shot .22 revolver. Which was no surprise in one way: what they'd got, that X in and out fast, he wouldn't have had time to reload. A nine-shot: so, the gun emptied, the people dead, and every last thing they knew was that X was male. Seen from the back, running, gun in hand. Three people dead, why?

"It's beautiful, Matt," said Prudence.

"I suppose we've just got to have faith," said Piggott, holding her hand with the amethyst ring on it, "that there'll be ten righteous men to save the city. Satan going up and down—"

"Pessimist." She laughed at him. "There are always more good people than bad, darling."

"That is a fact," said Piggott more cheerfully.

Landers, feeling tired—thinking about that baby, and the Harlows, and Patrolman Pat Logan—God, like that time Hackett had lain between life and death—Landers took Phil O'Neill out to dinner at Frascati's. And Phil, looking impossibly cool and neat in such heat, smiled wisely at him and said she *was* making up her mind, when they'd known each other longer they could tell better if they'd get along.

"But, Phil darling—"

"Sentimental," she said. "Because I do not approve of divorce, Tom. And it's the little things that are important. Whether you're tidy or sloppy, or laugh at the same things, or—"

"We do."

"—Or believe the same things," she said vaguely. "Do you like beets?"

"No."

"That's good, I detest them. You're passing tests, don't fuss," said Phil sedately.

Palliser got home late, and over warmed-up stew regaled Roberta with the Harlow shooting. "Just nowhere to go—unless, of course, the boss has a hunch. And the cutest baby you ever saw. Jase saying, the guardian angel—maybe." He felt his shoulder. "Damn it, I've definitely done something to this shoulder—manning a shovel last week, of all—"

"I've been figuring," said Roberta inattentively. "With what I'll be earning, John—we can put all of it on the contract for the furniture and the new refrigerator—we could get the whole thing paid off in eighteen months, do you know that?"

"So all right." He looked up at her, his lovely dark gray-eyed Robin, slim and thoughtful. "We could. We said, a family—two anyway—and as far as I'm concerned—"

"Well, eighteen months isn't very long—"

"I'm not going to argue about it," said Palliser. "We don't have fights, do we?"

"No, darling. Ever. All I say—"

"Well, eighteen months," said Palliser with a sigh. "All right. Miser."

Sergeants Galeano and Schenke, on night watch, were desultorily discussing rival baseball teams when a call came through from the desk downstairs. They both went out on it. The call was clocked at ten-fifty; the black-and-white was sitting on it when they got there.

It was a mama-and-papa store, a little grocery and delicatessen, on Third Street. The ambulance came five minutes after they got there. There was a woman, elderly and fat, dead behind the counter where the cash register gaped open. And the shocked, shaken old man— "We was just about to close, we close at eleven—I'd gone into the back, we got our apartment behind the store, and Amy was just puttin' a new roll of tape in the register—I hear the bell go, customer come in, it wasn't quite eleven and— And then I hear Amy yell and the shot— But there wouldn't've been more'n fifty bucks— Amy—we was just about to close —Amy was puttin' a new tape— No sir, I didn't see anybody, time I got out—"

So there was something else for the day watch to work.

CHAPTER 6

Mendoza was annoyed on Tuesday morning to find that new one waiting to be worked; business picking up again; and one of the petty nuisances of police work was the necessity, as new things came up, of dropping one case before it was finished to deal with another.

He handed Schenke's report to Hackett; Higgins read it over his shoulder. "So we chase off on this? I want to track down some of those punks Franks knows. Have you called the hospital—how's Logan doing?"

"Just holding his own," said Mendoza. "And damn it, that William Campden is up for arraignment today, one of you'll have to be there."

"Anything we get on this we'll get from the lab," said Hackett, dropping Schenke's report on Mendoza's desk. "I think it's more important to locate these punks."

"Conforme, you can go hunt the punks." It was Grace's day off; they were a man short.

"What about Harlow?" asked Higgins.

"I'm on that—if there's anywhere to go on it. Call in, and *buena suerte."* And as they turned, "Hold it, what's this?"

"Autopsy report on Hauck—just came in." Sergeant Lake handed it over.

"So, if John and Tom are in yet—"

Hackett and Higgins started out to look for the punks.

Palliser came in feeling his shoulder, with Landers behind him. "Damn it, I've pulled a muscle or something, it's been getting worse the last few days. That picket's wandering around again, did you notice?"

*"No me diga—*I didn't." Mendoza looked out the door. "Oh, Matt—good. We've got a new one overnight—here's Bob's report. As Art said, anything useful we get on it we'll get from the lab, but it won't do any

harm to talk to the old man again—Jacob Durand. Wife Amy was
D.O.A., single shot. Ask if they'd ever been held up before, any neighborhood punks who might be likely."

"Will do." Piggott took the report.

"Did she like the ring?"

Piggott smiled. "She did. She tells me I'm a pessimist, saying what an
awful chance we're taking. Which I guess I am." He glanced at the report. "Little bit more of Satan's work, and the poor old woman— I'll
see if I can pick up anything."

Mendoza sat down to read the autopsy report, handed it over to
Palliser; it didn't hold any surprises. Hauck had actually died of strangulation, and of course that was a very easy way to kill somebody
whether you meant to or not, in the heat of the moment. He had a few
bruises making it look likely that he'd exchanged blows with somebody
just before he died. And he had been well past the legal point of intoxi-
cation. Time of death estimated as between midnight and four A.M. last
Friday night.

That told them nothing new. If Hauck's Buick was being driven anywhere around, it should be spotted eventually; but this was a big town
with a lot of cars on the streets, and Traffic patrol was spread thin.
Palliser and Landers agreed that there wouldn't be much percentage in
locating more of Linda Schnell's girl-friends; they knew she'd been in
that hotel room with Hauck, said Palliser, and what Marian Henry
said—

"*No hay tal,*" said Mendoza. "Details, details. Marian Henry's been
in the county jail for a month. She told you that about five weeks back
Linda was teaming up with an old boy-friend she'd just come across
again. Foster Sterry. We don't know anything about him. You've seen
Linda's record. Are you seriously convinced that in five weeks she
couldn't have forgotten all about Sterry and picked up with somebody
else, or picked up with a dozen other boy-friends? Aside from any johns
she may have rolled?"

"Well, when you put it like that," said Landers, "that's so, of course.
She could have. So we'd better find some more pals of Linda's, who've
seen her more recently, and ask."

"I think so," said Mendoza.

"Have you had any hunches on Harlow?" asked Palliser.

"*Nada.* Unless— Well, a couple of ideas. We'll see. . . ."

As Hackett and Higgins came up to the scarlet Barracuda in the lot,
the ground shifted slightly and rolled under their feet for ten seconds.

"These damn aftershocks," said Higgins. He looked up at the Police Building—and these days, of course, they were calling it Parker Center for that irascibly tough and high-minded and dedicated chief who had been largely responsible for making this the top police force anywhere—and shook his head. On this side of the big rectangular building, a crew on a scaffolding suspended from the roof was installing glass in the second-floor windows. "Well, progress. They may get to us a week from tomorrow. In this weather, my God." He got into the car.

"How's Mary?"

"Oh, fine. She says she's tired of looking like a dirigible. She looks fine," said Higgins comfortably. They did say, the older they were the harder they fell; and Higgins, fond though he was of the Dwyer kids, was looking forward to his own family. Hackett thought of Angel saying, if it turned out to be a girl, the worst spoiled brat in the country. Well, little girls—

The steering wheel of the Barracuda was almost too hot to touch.

"These punks, Art. How strong a lead is this?"

"Well, it could be a hot one, George. The way this Logan thing shapes up. God, I hope he makes it—he seems to be a good man."

"Yeah. Try the high school first for addresses."

At Hollywood High School, they got addresses for the kids Bob Vandermeier had named—Martin Murphy, Ken Burkhart, Jim Root, Ron Dolan; who Buck might be nobody knew. Hollywood High was a big school and took in kids from a wide area: the fashionable hillside places, the shabby streets of central Hollywood, and every sort of neighborhood in between. These days, it didn't seem to matter what kind of neighborhood the kids came from. The turned-on generation came from all kinds of backgrounds.

They looked for the nearest address first—Jim Root, Edgemont Avenue. It was one side of a duplex on an old block half single houses, half rental units. The woman who answered the door stared at their badges. She was a slight woman in a drab cotton dress, brown hair going gray, a thin face, and she said, "Jim? You want to see Jim? What's he done?"

"We don't know that he's done anything, ma'am," said Higgins. "We'd just like to talk to him."

"Well, you can't because he's not here. And I don't know where he is." She put a hand to her mouth: a hand calloused with hard work. "You try," she said tiredly, "you try. He's my only one—his father walked out on me when Jim was just a baby, I had to support us. I have —I've never been on the welfare, I've taken care of myself and Jim, and I tried to bring him up right. But you see how it was. I had to work.

Leave him alone. I saw he went to Sunday School—I talked to him. But a boy gets to be fourteen, fifteen, he gets away from you—it's like you don't know him at all no more. He got a job once when he was fourteen, fifteen—at a market—he never liked school much and he wanted to earn—but they wouldn't let him work, see. Said he wasn't old enough. *I* went to work awhile before I was fourteen. But—"

"I see. How long has he been gone?" asked Hackett.

She shook her head. "After that, he just seemed to—not care about anything. He was like a stranger. Saying and doing things—he wouldn't talk to me, listen to me. He'd go off a week at a time, I wouldn't know where— Only this time I guess it's for good. Like his dad walking out. Well, he's turned eighteen, you can say he's grown. He's been gone since the middle of May—I haven't laid eyes on him since. He went while I was at work—I work for the Ace Cleaning Company, they take contracts like for cleaning big buildings, offices. He took all but a few of his clothes and all the extra money I'd saved from the coffee canister, and I haven't seen him since."

"Well, thanks very much," said Hackett.

She just made a defeated gesture and shut the door. "I've just thought of another bad pun," said Higgins. "Root the rootless."

"More truth than poetry," said Hackett. "It's a sad thing to think, George, that eventually life is going to catch up to all these irresponsible louts of kids. You can't go on goofing off and getting away with it forever."

"What she said about his acting different—could be he's hooked on something."

"Or a lot of different things." They got in the car. They didn't wonder how Jim Root was managing to live. The turned-on kids, goofing off, crowded together sordidly in a rented room, relying on the petty theft, mugging, or more serious crimes for their basic necessities—which would involve a narco salesman.

The next address was for Ron Dolan, Yucca Street. It was another old place, a single house, and they waited nearly five minutes for an answer to the bell. When the door opened, they faced a little old lady, white-haired, thin and stooped, with thick-lensed spectacles riding low on her nose. She blinked up at the two big men, at their badges. "Police officers, ma'am. Does Ron Dolan live here?"

"Police—" she said. "Police? Ron? Why, what—what do you want—with Ron? He's my grandson. Ron wouldn't do anything wrong, officers. He's just a boy—he's only eighteen."

"Well, we'd like to talk with him, Mrs.—"

"Dolan, I'm Frances Dolan, I've brought Ron up and he's a good boy, officers. Why do you want to talk to him?"

"Excuse me, Mrs. Dolan, where are his parents?"

"They're dead," she said. "My only son—and his wife, they were killed in an airplane crash when Ron was five. I've brought him up and he's a good boy—"

"Well, if we could see him, please. Is he here?"

She let them in reluctantly, led them back to the kitchen, an old-fashioned square kitchen with the table in the middle. Ron Dolan was sitting there finishing breakfast—bacon and eggs, a smell of good coffee in the air. He looked at the badges, and he said, "What you want with me? I haven't done anything."

And Hackett and Higgins recognized him instantly. They'd both seen a lot of the punks, and they came all shapes and sizes, but certain things about them never altered. Ron Dolan was tall and thin, dark, with dark shifting eyes and a narrow chin, and he was neatly enough dressed in a blue shirt and dark pants. But the automatic sullen suspicion in his eyes and voice, the quick resentment-of-cops attitude before he even knew why they were there, told the story. His hair was down past his ears—probably all the old lady, dim and vague as she might be, would let him get by with; but he had a swashbuckling pair of sideburns.

"You happen to know where Jim Root is, Ron?" asked Hackett conversationally.

"No. I don't. I haven't seen him awhile." Ron's eyes moved once; he didn't change expression, but he had answered that too quick. He had, surprisingly, been expecting that question. Hackett and Higgins shared silent curiosity.

"What about Don Franks?"

"I haven't seen him either. No."

"Think hard," said Hackett.

"I don't have to. I don't know anything about it."

"I don't understand this," said Mrs. Dolan anxiously. "What do you think Ron's done? Ron's a good boy—" And both the Homicide men could read his impatient glance at her without an interpreter. The woolly-minded old woman, never any suspicion that Ron was anything but what she expected of a grandson, clean-cut-American-boy— Quite evidently she wasn't aware that he'd dropped out of school in the middle of last semester. He'd find it easy to get away with murder in this household, help himself to her money, tell her anything; and naturally he despised her for a fool.

"Did you know Don Franks is selling the hard stuff?" asked Higgins.

"I don't know anything." But he did; they read him like a book. This kind wasn't very smart, and all the more vulnerable because they thought they were.

And there wasn't anything they could bring him in on. Get a search warrant? On what grounds? Was he holding any dope? If he was, he'd get rid of it as soon as they were out of sight. But he knew something about Jim Root, and he knew about Franks. Did that say he was tied up to Root some way? On what?

They could go on talking to him, questioning him, for the next hour; they'd get nothing. They went out and sat in the Barracuda, aware that they were probably being watched. "He knows where Root is," said Hackett. "Doesn't he?"

"I think so. But so what, Art? That doesn't say that any of 'em has anything to do with Logan. It doesn't say that either Ron or Root was a customer of Franks's, even."

"No, it's up in the air. But if we're ever going to find out," said Hackett, "whether either of them has anything to do with Logan, it might be worth an hour's time to—er—beat the bushes to alert the hare."

"Come again?" said Higgins.

"Well, there's a Spanish proverb—*Más vale una onza de práctica que una libra de gramática.* More in one ounce of experience than a library of books. I guess you could say experience tells us this and that. George. About the ones like Ron. And whether Root, Franks or Ronny-boy had anything at all to do with Pat Logan getting jumped. Ronny-boy knows something about Root—and unless we are both wool-gathering, George, it's something cops would be interested in. *¿Cómo no?*—are you with me?"

"Right behind. You want to beat some bushes?"

"Just for kicks. The punks always think they are so smart, and they so very seldom are." Hackett glanced in the rearview mirror. "About a block up, George, is a drugstore on the corner. With, I hope, a phone booth. Call Wilcox Street and get a black-and-white up here. And arrange a tail for Ronny."

Higgins grinned. "What they call a catalyst." He slid out of the car. Hackett sat there and smoked a cigarette, watching the house, until he came back. Five minutes later the black-and-white drifted up and parked ahead of the Barracuda, and Hackett and Higgins got out to confer with the two uniformed men. The usual uniformed men: trim, clean-cut, alert-looking. This the top force anywhere.

"What's up, sir? You the Central detectives—on Logan? I'm Walsh-Gonzales."

"Little playacting, boys," said Hackett. "There is a punk in that house we're hoping to scare into doing something silly."

"It doesn't take an awful lot to do it sometimes," said Gonzales. "This punk had something to do with Pat getting beat up?"

"It could be. There'll be a plainclothes tail arriving to sit on him in about fifteen minutes," said Higgins. "You just sit here till the tail takes over. The punk won't notice the tail, of course, but I hope he's feeling nervous about all of us right now." He and Hackett delivered simultaneous sinister looks at the Dolan house, very open and obvious. Ron would be watching.

"Little playacting," said Walsh. "There's just one thing."

"What's that?"

"Well—" He looked at the two senior sergeants from Homicide, burly Art Hackett, massive-shouldered Higgins. "If the pair of you didn't already scare the punk, will he scare at all?"

Mendoza had found Dr. Harlow's records extremely dull reading. Dr. Harlow had had the usual run of patients any general practitioner would have: the chronically half-ill elderly people, young mothers, children, people of all ages with the aches and pains, the need for minor or major surgery. He had had a good-sized practice, a full daily routine. There was nothing at all exotic, unusual, or suggestive in the records; no sudden hunch hit Mendoza about the run-of-the-mill general cases Dr. Harlow had handled.

They hadn't finished getting all those necessary statements down yesterday by any means; Glasser and Piggott (after he'd seen Jacob Durand) would be fetching more witnesses in today. Mendoza, going out to ask about that, found Glasser just coming in with Mrs. Gladys Short.

"Good," he said. "I wanted to talk to you, Mrs. Short."

"Mr. Glasser said a statement—well, you told me yesterday—"

"Yes. You can do that later—right now I'd like to ask you some questions."

"Well, of course, if I can help any way, to find out who— It just doesn't bear thinking of," she said. "Dr. Harlow—and his wife, such a nice woman—and Harriet Jenkins. I never had such a shock in my life." She followed him into his office, sat down in the chair beside his desk; she fanned herself absently with a handkerchief. It was very hot in the office, the sun striking brightly through the glassless windows.

Gladys Short had been Dr. Harlow's other nurse: the one who actually served as a nurse. She was a plump woman, milk-chocolate color, about forty, with a normally round pleasant face now looking a little drawn, and intelligent eyes.

"Did you think," said Mendoza, "that if it had happened half an hour later, you might have got it too?"

"That was just one of the things I thought about, Lieutenant," she said quietly. "Yes. And all I can think—such a terrible thing, and just the Lord's mercy that poor sweet baby didn't get killed too—all I can think, a lunatic. Because—"

"Picking Dr. Harlow at random? You know, if you follow me," said Mendoza, "I could just buy that—if his office had been on the ground floor."

She stared at him for a minute and then said, "Oh. Oh, I see— because—he went to the trouble of—"

"Climbing the stairs. He didn't just want to shoot somebody. It was somebody specific. Had you been with Dr. Harlow long?"

"Since he opened his office. I worked at the General after I gradu- ated, but it's a rat race like they say. It's a good hospital, with a good staff, but it's big—and always busy. We got run off our feet half the time—"

"You know a Dr. Grace there?"

"Dr. John Grace? Why, yes, sir, he's chief of gynecology—a very nice man, a good doctor. Why?"

"No reason—his son's one of our bright boys in this office. You prob- ably met him yesterday. So—I'm going to ask you to think back and tell me anything, anything at all you can remember—"

She had, of course, denied that there *was* anything like that, anyone with a reason to have a grudge on the doctor. He laid out some persua- sive charm, and she said suddenly, "Well, there had been that Ainslie man. . . . I think it was around May—it'll be in the records. But a little thing like that—! Well, if you want to hear—"

A William Ainslie, coming in with an infected hand. Said he'd cut himself accidentally trying to get something out of a garbage disposal. Two fingers had been badly mauled. Dr. Harlow had done what he could, but in the end Ainslie had lost all but partial use of two fingers on his left hand, and he had threatened to sue the doctor. "It didn't come to anything, of course, because the doctor'd done all any doctor could do, and besides it came out that Ainslie hadn't gone to a doctor right away, he'd tried to take care of it himself until it got infected."

And, under prodding, she remembered the girl. A while before that— "I can't think what gets into these little fools—" A girl named Karen something, that would be in the records too. She'd come to see the doctor, just a teen-age girl, a new patient they'd never seen before, and been told she was pregnant. She'd evidently been very upset and scared —"You could see that. I'd have felt sorry for her, but for what she tried. And how she ever thought she'd get away with such a thing I don't know, but she told her father the *doctor* was responsible—that she'd gone to see him and he'd attacked her or something— There was quite a scene," said Mrs. Short indignantly, "we had the man creating an uproar, calling the police and all—honestly, that girl having the gall to—. But of course Dr. Harlow could show it wasn't true. He never saw a woman patient alone—at least, more than five minutes or so. Especially young ones. Doctors aren't fools, Lieutenant."

"No. Father a fool, or did he believe that?"

"Why—I don't know. He wasn't an educated man—terribly upset about the girl—he didn't make any formal charges, no, but I don't know whether he—maybe went on believing we were all lying, just to protect the doctor. Maybe—"

"Mmh. Anything else?"

And she thought, and suddenly began to laugh, and sobered. "Oh, dear, I just remembered that. Oh, the doctor did laugh so over that! He wasn't—wasn't a *solemn* man, but he was quiet, you know—serious. But he did laugh so over that. We all did. It was a little Chinese fellow—Kun Low Soo, I couldn't forget that name! You know, Lieutenant, most Orientals here now—well, most *people*—they're smart, city-wise people—but you get all sorts, and this little fellow could hardly speak English. He was a chef at some restaurant in New Chinatown, and he came in with his wife. A pretty little woman—she was pregnant. The doctor did all the usual things, you know, ran some tests and all—I seem to remember her blood pressure was low, and he prescribed some medication for that —and she came in every month for a checkup, and finally she went into labor and it was a little girl. No complications, everything went off just as it should—of course she'd had nine other babies, in about ten years we gathered. But the little man was simply furious!" Remembering it, she laughed again. "He came to the office the next day—he said the doctor had swindled him—nine worthless daughters his wife had produced, and this time he'd taken his boss's advice and brought her to a real doctor instead of a midwife, and a real doctor should have guaranteed that it was a son—he was furious! He really believed it, you know—I've never seen the doctor laugh so—"

Mendoza grinned. "*Ridículo,* yes—you can't yet make out the order, wanted, one male, live birth—as I know to my cost—"

"Oh, do you have all girls too?"

"One of each. Twin monsters. But—when was this?"

"Oh, just last June. But, Lieutenant—"

"An ignorant man. Really believing— Well, that's interesting," said Mendoza. "And something to look at closer."

"But you can't think—that silly little man would—do *that?* Shoot the doctor, and—just for *that,* no reason at all?"

"You said to me, a lunatic," said Mendoza. "Which means, somebody irrational. I could just see Mr. Kun Low Soo qualifying as irrational, Mrs. Short."

But just occasionally—possibly an effort on the part of the guardian angels to spur them on as good cops, reassuring them that the dedicated routine did pay off—occasionally something went right by the book, smooth as cream, just the way the manual said routine should go. And that could be very gratifying.

Hackett and Higgins came in, briefed Mendoza on their beat-the-bushes operation. Ron Dolan had taken off, with the tail after him, in a ten-year-old Ford, about half an hour after the tail had got in position. They'd waited round the corner to see that much. Sooner or later they should hear more.

Palliser and Landers had found another girl-friend of Linda's and were questioning her down the hall.

And at a quarter to twelve Duke called from the lab. "Sometimes we do all your work for you."

"So you do. What have you done now?"

"This heist job last night. No witnesses, piddling take, and a D.O.A. We went over the place, of course. Four nice clear latents on the cash register. Oh, and the gun was a Colt .22 of some kind, Ballistics says an oldie and beat up."

"The latents. Identified?"

"Oh, yes. Idiots they are," said Duke. "He must know they're on file. It makes you wonder."

"Sometimes it does. I have been wondering about the small-time punks," said Mendoza, "for twenty-four years, Duke—since you were in kindergarten. I haven't reached any conclusion yet. Who is the small-time punk, *¿por favor?*"

"Edward Hobart. Little pedigree, B.-and-E., petty theft, purse-snatching, attempted burglary. The usual counts, probation, et cetera. Twenty-three now, five-eleven, one-fifty, Caucasian, brown and blue, no marks. Last known address, Beacon Avenue. He lives—or did live—with his mother."

"*Vaya historia*," said Mendoza. "Thank you so much."

"No trouble, we just had to look," said Duke.

Mendoza passed that on. "My God," said Hackett, "doing what comes naturally. But no record of violence before?"

"There is that." Mendoza got up and looked across the hall. "Matt? You hear anything more from Durand than what Bob and Nick got last night?"

"That poor old soul," said Piggott. He came into Mendoza's office with a report in one hand. "I was just getting it down. They'd run that store for thirty years together. Harmless old couple—no family at all. No, Durand said they'd never been held up before, never had trouble with anybody in the neighborhood. He never saw the heist-man at all, he was back in their apartment while she was closing up. He just heard her scream, I suppose when the fellow showed her the gun—and then the shot. He—"

"Mmh," said Mendoza. "And Hobart's record—the little sneak thief, trying for something a little bigger than he'd ever done before—and possibly panicking when she screamed—yes."

"Oh, have we got him?" asked Piggott.

Mendoza brushed his moustache absently. "Seeing that Hobart's last known address is some sixty blocks away from Third Street, and that ordinary customers don't have any occasion to touch the cash register, I would say we have, Matt."

Hackett got a call just then from Wilcox Street, so he and Higgins went off to hear the latest on their catalyst. Palliser and Landers emerging from the sergeants' office, Mendoza asked them what they'd turned up.

"Nothing new," said Palliser. "Girl-friend of Linda's who saw her last Thursday tells us she's still going around with Foster Sterry. We sent an inquiry to the Feds, see if they know him."

"So now you can go look for Edward Hobart," said Mendoza, and filled them in on that.

"But my God," said Landers, "you would think some rudimentary *sense*—when he knows we've got his prints—"

"The Edward Hobarts don't have rudimentary sense," said Mendoza. He sat at his desk with the cards fluttering absently in his hands—Alison and the domesticities had ruined his poker game but he still thought sharper with the cards in his hands—and there were people who said Luis Mendoza had missed his calling, should have been a pro gambler. He thought about Dr. John Harlow, and William Ainslie, and that teen-age girl, and Kun Low Soo. . . . People to look at. People, coming all sorts, and you never knew what they might do. . . .

Occasionally, it worked out just the way it should, theoretically. The lab handing them the nice evidence; the pedigree on file; the address the right one.

At the shabby apartment, Mrs. Elmira Hobart told Palliser and Landers that Eddy was looking for a job. "He's engaged to get married," she added. "A nice girl, Julia is, and Eddy wants to get a job so as to marry her. She don't know about that little trouble he's been in— Eddy don't mean anything wrong, it's just, it's hard for him to hold a job—"

A gun? Oh, Eddy didn't have a gun. Eddy wanted to get married, he wouldn't be getting into more trouble, and he'd gone up to that employment place, the state one, about an hour ago. To try to get a job. They wouldn't tell Julia about Eddy getting in that little trouble, would they?

"Really, it makes me feel tired," said Palliser. "Not two cents' worth of common sense, Tom." He felt his shoulder.

"Well, what we get paid for," said Landers philosophically. As they came back to Palliser's Rambler, suddenly the earth gave under their feet, sickeningly, and for ten seconds was unsolid. "These damn aftershocks— Where is that agency? Olive, I think—"

They found Edward Hobart sitting patiently in a line at the California Employment Agency, and brought him back to headquarters to question. Mendoza sat in on that.

"I didn't mean to!" said Hobart in a high frightened voice. "I never meant to do such a thing! I'm awful sorry it happened—it was just—well, my God, I had to have some money, I had to—you gotta understand, I want to marry Julia, I just got engaged to Julia, and I needed some money. I wanted to buy her a nice ring and all, a wedding trip some place—"

"Where'd you get the gun, Eddy, and where is it?" asked Palliser.

"Why'd you pick the Durands' place?" asked Landers. "You couldn't have thought there'd be much loot there?"

Hobart licked his lips. He was unhealthy-looking, pasty-faced, otherwise not bad-looking. "I—I'd never tried anything like that before, a real holdup—" No, he was small-time. "I—I—I borrowed the gun—from a guy I know—I said I'd cut him in, but it was only forty-two bucks! I was—kinda nervous, try a real big place like a—a theater or a drugstore— people around—I—a little place like that, I thought easier— But when she yelled, I—I didn't mean to shoot off the gun! I don't know much about guns—it sort of went off, and—"

"So who'd you borrow the gun from?"

"I—a guy named Al. Al Koonz. I guess he's got a record. I didn't mean to—"

"But you did." The D.A. might call it manslaughter, or murder second; that wasn't up to Homicide.

"But it was just for Julia!" he said wildly. "I just wanted to get the nice things for Julia—oh, *Julia!*" He began to sob. "It was just because I love Julia so bad, I had to—have some money—and I couldn't get no job—"

"Love, in fact, in general," said Mendoza. Late home, he surveyed Alison sitting up in bed reading, the lamp turning her red head to flame; she had on a new topaz nylon nightgown. "You look very fetching, *enamorada.*"

"*Gracias.* Love?" said Alison.

"Love. It is a dangerous commodity," said Mendoza, "depending on who harbors it." El Señor, annoyed at being waked, uttered a few low curses from the tangle of cats at the foot of the bed. Mendoza yawned and began unbuttoning his shirt. "And of course Kipling always had the word for it, too." His strange enthrallment to Kipling was still puzzling his household.

"Love," said Alison. "*¿Qué es esto, amante?*"

"*Too much Ego in his cosmos,*" said Mendoza. "Really what it always comes down to."

CHAPTER 7

Hackett got home at six-thirty and said he hoped dinner was ready. "I've got to go back downtown—overtime. I'd have called and picked up something down there, but we have to wait for the lab to do a hurry-up job and I thought I might as well come home."

"We are flattered," said Angel. He slapped her behind and she yelped. "You don't know your own strength, Tarzan." Mark bounded up precipitately, hearing Daddy's voice, and Sheila came tottering holding up her arms.

"And how's Daddy's own Sheila?" Hackett picked her up.

"She is a nuisance," said Angel. "Been under my feet all day, and pulling the cat's tail—"

"Now, Angel—"

"Well, I have to do something to counteract your spoiling her, Art. Yes, you do. Yes, I know she's just a baby—it's the principle of the thing. Men." She smiled at him. "What's the overtime? Is that going to be a black eye?—for heaven's sake— And how's that patrolman doing?"

"Holding his own. That's the overtime—fingers crossed—I think. And if so, just for that— Well, the jungle gets junglier all the time, my Angel. George and I have been sitting on it most of the day, waiting for something to jell, and it finally did, so—the overtime."

"You've *got* them?" Angel's mountain-pool eyes sparkled with most unchristian pleasure.

"Fingers crossed," said Hackett again.

"Dinner in ten minutes—pot roast and brown potatoes, Italian beans and green salad with Roquefort—not for you—"

"I'd like some peas for a change."

"Four times the calories."

"Damn it, I know. Well—"

"How'd you drop on them, darling?"
"Well—"

They had waited round the corner, having ostensibly driven away from the Dolan house, until the tail arrived and the black-and-white departed. The tail was a nondescript, youngish man in a shabby suit, with an inconspicuous dark sedan several years old and very dusty. He got out of the car, having parked on the opposite side of the street, set a briefcase down on the grass near the curb, and got out a clipboard. He spent some time apparently checking addresses, and finally backed into the car, feet planted on the ground, door open, and industriously accomplished some paper work on what looked like order blanks. A salesman doing his tedious job, obviously.

They had hoped he wouldn't have to wait long, and he didn't. About fifteen minutes later Ron Dolan came backing out the drive in an old blue Ford. The tail finished his pen work, gathered in the briefcase, shut the door and slid under the wheel. In thirty seconds the two cars vanished, turning at the next intersection.

"And let us hope he is really good," said Higgins. And that was at eleven o'clock, or thereabouts. They kicked it around for a few minutes —it was really all up in the air, not what either of them would call a good solid lead at all—until Hackett suddenly swore.

"By God, George, we're slipping. The quake scared us out of any wits we— You know what? The Vandermeier boy said one of those, Ken Burkhart, had an arrest record."

"And we never checked it out."

In the interests of saving time—and there was no telling when the tail might report in, with what, and probably their home office could use them on some job if this one didn't pan out—they went back downtown, and called R. and I. for the record on Kenneth Burkhart.

They were just briefing Mendoza about it when the package came up —and that was a little surprise. There were two of them. Kenneth Burkhart senior, Kenneth Burkhart junior. And both had pedigrees. The one, long and bad; the other, short and suggestive.

Hackett looked at them and said, "Not exactly surprising—but what a— I wonder how the boy escaped being made a ward of the court. Some mix-up, I suppose. But what a—"

Kenneth Burkhart senior was now forty-seven years old. He had a pedigree with the LAPD, the L.A. Sheriff's Department, and the Pasadena Police Department, and it started thirty-four years ago when he was thirteen, picked up with some other kids for vandalism. It went on, attempted assault, public drunkenness, B.-and-E., attempted burglary, burglary, robbery from the person, armed robbery. He'd served time— the latest time, in Quentin for six years; he was on P.A. right now. He'd got off on other counts, technicalities, insufficient evidence; he'd only served twelve years altogether. But he was, by the record, the very typical pro hood—allergic to work, partial to the bottle, and picking up what he could how he could. The P.A. report tagged him as a widower, made no mention of the son. Some mix-up in the record?

Kenneth Burkhart junior was now eighteen. He'd first been dropped on, four years ago, for attacking a younger boy on a school playground with a knife. And who had he been living with then?—the record said, Probation to guardian. Then, attempted B.-and-E., grand theft auto, and more recently narco possession—Mary Jane.

"Such an old, old story," said Hackett. Higgins, reading, just sighed and lit a cigarette. He'd just finished looking at that record when Sergeant Lake said, "Art—Wilcox Street."

Hackett listened, said tersely, "We'll be up. Yes, O.K., I see that. . . . The tail called in. He'll be reporting to Wilcox Street, we'd better go up and sit on it. Oh, get Burkhart's address—same as the kid's? —I just wonder—"

The tail's name was Bill Knowles and he was supposed to be good. He'd called in at one-fifty. Ron Dolan had driven around aimlessly for a while— No, not trying to shake the tail, he hadn't a clue he was wearing one—and stopped at a McDonald's for a coke and sandwich. He had then taken off again and ended up at a single house on Genesee Avenue. He'd rung the doorbell and gone in, and come out a few minutes later with another kid about his age, and they'd driven off—both in Dolan's car—and when Knowles called, they were sitting on a bench in the first picnic-ground area in Griffith Park up from Riverside Drive, just talking. The car parked a little way down the hill. He'd stick with them, call in when he could. . . .

"Ronny-boy scared the fuzz knows something," surmised Hackett. "Who'd he pick up?"

"By the addresses we got from the school, Martin Murphy," said Higgins.

"Well, well. It's not very far from here. Let's see if there are any more Murphys home."

It was a modest house, a California bungalow, on a quiet street in central Hollywood; the yard was well kept up, with a green lawn, flowering shrubs round the porch. The woman who answered the door was nice-looking if not young—once very pretty, brown-haired, brown-eyed, with discreet makeup, a neat housedress, a pleasant contralto voice.

"Mrs. Murphy?"

"Why, yes—" She stared at the badges, and her face whitened, and she said, "Something's happened to Jim! Oh, what—"

"Your husband? No, Mrs. Murphy, it's your son we'd like to talk to you about. Your son Martin."

"*Marty?*" she said. "*Police?* Well, this is just crazy—Marty's never been in any trouble with the— That's impossible! Marty's a well-raised boy, this is a good home, we go to church regular—"

"May we come in, Mrs. Murphy?"

She let them in reluctantly. "You aren't saying you think Marty's done anything? Anything wrong? It's just impossible, that's all—"

"Where is he, by the way, do you know?" asked Higgins in his deep voice.

She looked at him angrily. "Well, of course I know! If that isn't just like the cops, try to make out— Of course I know! He's gone somewhere with the Dolan boy—"

"The Dolan boy. You know him?"

"Well, of *course*. They've been all through school together— Ron's a nice boy, good manners, a good home. Like Marty. *What* do you think—"

"Know where they've gone? When to expect him back?" asked Hackett.

"Oh, for heaven's sake! They're not children, they're both eighteen and it's vacation—I can trust Marty—"

Which told a story, and a too familiar one to cops. Too many parents, trusting the kids, and not exactly kids, of course—you didn't check up on an eighteen-year-old the way you did on a five-year-old. Naturally.

"*What* do you think he's done? It's just silly, but—"

"We don't know that either of them has done anything, Mrs. Murphy," said Hackett. "He just—showed on the edge of something."

"Well, you can just show yourselves out of my house—trying to say Marty's in police trouble! Crazy—"

On the way back to Wilcox Street Hackett said, "But it is natural, you know—that age, they're practically grown up—or should be—and if the parents have never had any reason to suspect the dope, anything else, it wouldn't cross their minds—you don't check up on kids that age like toddlers—"

"Yes, yes," said Higgins. "Words of one syllable. And isn't that the reason the speed's so popular?" The speed—Methedrine—produced a short-term high that wore off without many revealing symptoms; the kids innocently attending a record party, a picnic at the beach, and back to normal by the time they came home.

It would be quite a shock for the Murphys—as it had come as a shock to God knew how many other parents across the nation—if it turned out Marty was mixed up in something like that.

They sat in the detective bureau at the Wilcox Street precinct and waited for Knowles to call. "My God, it is *hot*," said Hackett. This was an old precinct house, and lacked air conditioning.

One of the Hollywood detectives said, "You're just spoiled, based down there at headquarters. The nice central air conditioning—"

"Not," said Higgins, "this last week. The quake broke most of our windows."

"Well, for God's sake, I hadn't heard about that. But we've been busy. Tuesday and Wednesday they had me helping the civil defense evacuate people—with nineteen things to do here and all the paper work—"

"That so? We were downtown digging up that mission for bodies—"

They were still exchanging reminiscences of the quake when Knowles called in at three-forty-five. "They're back in town," he said. "They made a phone call from the park, that is, Dolan did. They're now at a bowling alley on Fairfax, just watching the play. I'm here too. . . . Oh-oh."

"What's up?"

"Nothing—one of these aftershocks, didn't you feel it? Funny. Well, I'll call in when I can."

He didn't, until four-thirty, when Hackett and Higgins were feeling as if they'd wasted the whole day. A while before, they had called the hospital; Logan's pulse was a little stronger, they were told, and he seemed to be getting restless. "That's a good sign," said Higgins.

"You would know?"

"I would know, boy. Since that week we spent fussing about you, assaulted just the same way and all those damn doctors saying gloomily, Even if he lives he may never recover his mind. That," said Higgins, "was quite a week, Art. What with that multiple killer running around loose, and the abortionist—"

"Yes, I've heard. What—"

"Well, I was just thinking," said Higgins, "we have been busier than we are now. Feeling more harried, if that's the word. Come to think, we've only got a couple of fairly tough ones to work— Of course Harlow—"

"Don't say it, don't say it," begged Hackett. "So we congratulate ourselves, only a few things on hand, just inviting the tough ones to come at us hot and heavy! What *I* remember out of the dim past is saying one morning, all in the most innocent way, that it was a little boring to have business so slow—and, wham, we got the funny king-size tough ones turning up all at once."

Higgins chuckled sleepily, loosening his tie further. "Those coffins . . . I don't think it's right, you know—keeping people jittery. All the stuff the papers are running, pressure still building on the San Andreas, we could have another one any time. . . . That picket was up by the Plaza this morning."

"Sometimes," said Hackett, "I almost agree with Matt. All we see at the bottom, George—a wonder the Lord has held His hand this long."

They were both feeling tired and useless by the time Knowles called again. The whole day wasted. This had been no kind of lead at all, and they had probably wasted their own time, and Knowles's, following it up.

And then Knowles called. "I only hope this may say something to you, Sergeant." Knowles, out on the street, driving, was very tired and hot too. "They met another kid at the bowling alley, and they've come up to an address on New Hampshire—old apartment building. They've all gone in. I don't know which apartment yet."

"*¿Dónde estamos ahora?*" said Hackett, surprised.

"What?"

"Excuse me—now and then I go to echoing the boss. What the hell? Wait a minute—George, what's the address on the Burkharts?"

"New Hampshire—old part of town—why?"

"Now I do wonder," said Hackett. "Thanks, Knowles, I think we'll be over."

"If you want a relief for me, you'd better set it up with Sergeant Barth—"

"We'll see," said Hackett. He relayed that to Higgins, who rubbed his jaw and thought it over.

"Ronny is worried about cops calling. He picks up Marty, they have a private talk in a private spot and make a phone call. They pick up— who? And why? And is it anything to do with us at all? Young fellows in summer vacation, just roaming around."

"Well, I wondered if that was Jim Root they picked up. Let's go see."

"But we've got nothing, Art. No reason even to ask them any questions. About what?"

"Maybe something will emerge," said Hackett vaguely.

Something did. By the time they got to the New Hampshire Street address, they found a black-and-white just pulling up to the curb, the uniformed driver getting out. As they got out of the Barracuda, Knowles came out to them from the apartment entrance—an old tan-brick apartment.

"Sergeant—there's been a fuss of some kind going on—I think it's our boys, by the voices—not a fight, just an argument of some kind—second floor up there. Neighbor across the hall has complained three times, and I guess just called the law—"

Hackett ran to catch the patrolman. "This could be our business, we'll come in with you." The patrolman looked surprised, looking at the badges, and then curious.

The argument was still going on, a blurred cacophony of raised voices, obbligato to a blaring TV, beyond the door of the second-floor apartment. A couple of neighbors in the hall, looking indignant. The patrolman pounded on the door, got no response to his announcement of police officers, so he and Hackett hit it together.

The usual shabby, shoddy living room of a cheap apartment this vintage. A paunchy middle-aged man in undershirt and shorts looked blearily up at them from where he watched the television, a can of beer in one hand. The voices came from the bedroom, only now understandable.

"For Jesus' sake, Ken, *listen* to me! *Do* something, Marty, he's gotta —he's the one—"

The patrolman pushed the door open. "Now break it up—quiet down —police!"

The three on their feet whirled and froze to a little tableau.

"Club meeting?" asked Hackett. "What about, boys? Do we need a password to get in?"

Ron Dolan, a hefty, redhaired kid who might be Marty Murphy, a nondescript dull-looking kid, sandy-haired, who might be Jim Root. They looked at the law breaking in on them, and just for a breath Dolan and Murphy looked very frightened, and then the heavy secret sullenness shut down on all their expressions.

"You can't do anything to us," said Dolan. "We haven't done anything. You been—*following*—that's police brutality—you can't—"

"Well, you've been creating a disturbance," said the patrolman briskly. "That'll do for a reason to look you over."

"And I think," said Higgins pleasedly, "there'll be another reason." He walked over past the three and looked at the fellow sprawled on the unmade bed.

That one looked up at him and said muzzily, "Who're you?"

"Nemesis," said Higgins, who remembered this and that from English Lit in high school. "You'll be Ken Burkhart."

"Ken—for God's sake—" screamed Dolan desperately.

Burkhart was feeling no pain. He was coasting now—just nicely high, not quite incapable but turned on just right, with all his inhibitions comfortably blocked off and feeling fine, just fine. He was a big fellow, dark and thick-chested, with a hairy torso visible because all he had on was a pair of shorts. He grew a heavy beard and he hadn't shaved in a few days.

He giggled up at Higgins, and he said, "Tell 'em—go 'way. Don't bother—come back t'morra. Can't be bothered now—'bout tha' cop. The pig. Beat up—on the pig, tha's good. Zowie—did a job—on tha' one."

"Ken!"

"Hell of a fun thing—but tell 'em—go 'way now. T'morra—talk about the pig—"

Higgins looked at Hackett; they wore identical grim smiles. "And isn't that interesting," said Knowles behind them; unconsciously he balled one fist and caressed it with his left hand.

"It looks as if we haven't wasted the day after all, Art," said Higgins.

In the course of shaking the five down before bringing them in, they had a look at the old Chevy registered to Ken Burkhart, in the garage behind the apartment; and in the trunk they found a homemade sap, the thick end of a baseball bat wound with electrician's tape. It had stains of some sort on the business end. There was also a bloodstained T-shirt and a switchblade knife, also stained.

Kenneth Burkhart senior gave them more trouble than the kids. He was half drunk and had no clear idea what cops were doing there, why, or what was going on. When they took his beer away and told him to put on his pants, a shirt, he lunged out at random and gave Hackett the makings of a nice shiner before Higgins and the patrolman got hold of him.

They filed the kids out ahead, and he blinked at them and said, "The kids—you droppin' on the kids—what the hell? Them pills, stuff—what the hell, *I* like a few drinks, what the hell if the kids take a li'l ride on—Fuzz! Ever' time a guy turns around, damn fuzz—"

"That's right," said Hackett, feeling his eye, "we're the world's worst spoilsports, always ruining somebody's good time."

At headquarters they handed the sap, the knife and the shirt to the lab and demanded a hurry-up job. The thugs who had assaulted Pat Logan they wanted to nail hard and fast, with every piece of solid evidence they could turn up.

"Amen," said Duke. "We'll get right on it. We ought to have something for you by eight o'clock, say."

Hackett found Mendoza and brought him up to date. "The luck going our way for once, Arturo, I'll sit in on this."

So they were all back there at seven o'clock, to try for a voluntary statement from one of them. They pried at Ron Dolan first: the weakest link, said Mendoza. But weak characters are also frequently very obstinate characters, and Dolan was terrified by then but he wouldn't say a word. It was probably the first time he'd ever been caught up to, to face any sort of retribution; and he didn't know how to face it except by denying that it was happening. He just went on shaking his head and saying, "No—I don't know anything about it—no—"

Ken Burkhart junior was unfit to question; he'd been sent over to Central Receiving to be sobered up from whatever he was high on.

So then, after a while, they tried Martin Murphy, and he was frightened too but he was smarter than Dolan and he wasn't parting with a thing, not even *Don't know nothing about it*. The punks—such big men until they were caught up with.

At seven-thirty Barth had called from Wilcox Street. They had, he said, the panicky parents calling, on Martin Murphy—wanted to report him missing—and before that, Dolan's grandmother. Having informed them that the boys were in custody, they now had a pair of belligerent Murphys creating a disturbance, demanding to be told chapter and verse, demanding to see the boy. Hackett relayed that to Mendoza, where Sergeant Thoms sat minding the switchboard, and Mendoza grinned, took the phone from him, and said, "Barth? Stall them half an hour longer and we'll be ready for the indignant citizens. Rescuing Junior from the stupid and/or brutal cops."

"You've seen a vision in your crystal ball?" muttered Hackett.

"I think," said Mendoza, "we pin our faith on our infallible men of science." Duke came in just then and he added, "*¡Tanto bueno por aquí!* Preserve calm, Barth—you won't get sued for false arrest this time. . . . So what have you got for us?"

"Just what you want," said Duke pleasedly. "The shirt has got blood on it, about four days old. It's type AB mostly, some type O. The knife —we can tell you the manufacturer, the retail outlets where it's sold—but more to the point it has got Ken Burkhart's prints on the handle and type O blood on the blade."

"*Muy lindo,*" said Mendoza.

"The sap has got blood on it, all type O."

"Thank you so very much, *compadre,*" said Mendoza. "And now we will ask some more questions and find out just what did happen."

"You are so optimistic," said Hackett. "We know more or less what happened, Luis—but if they're not talking, is this enough for a case? A lot of people have type O blood. It's a first count on Murphy and Dolan, and nothing really ties them in—"

"We've seen Murphy and Dolan. Third boy," said Mendoza. He took the lab report from Duke.

Jim Root wasn't nearly as bright as the other two (Ken Burkhart's potential intelligence they would judge when they'd seen him minus the dope). He faced them there in the interrogation room warily; he said, "I haven't done nothing—you got no reason bring us in like this. So what if Ken was turned on? We wasn't—and—we didn't know what he was talkin' about—"

"Oh, didn't you?" Hackett stood over him and he looked nervous. Hackett might intimidate anybody by mere size: and add George Higgins alongside him, anybody might look nervous.

Mendoza, slim and dapper and elegant as always, even at this end of a day, looked at him contemptuously. "We have quite a lot of nice evidence here, Jim, even if we can't expect you to grasp just how solid it is. Laboratory evidence, if you know what that is, Jim. There was Pat Logan's blood and somebody else's on that T-shirt. The knife has Ken's fingerprints on it—you do know about fingerprints, Jim?—and Pat Logan's blood on the blade. The sap—"

And Root burst out, "That——cop! That——pig! Oh, my God, it was Ken—never 've did it except we was all turned on some and Ken said— *It was all that——cop's fault!*"

Bob Schenke took it down in shorthand as it came out of him, and he probably didn't realize it was being taken down, and he probably wouldn't have cared.

"What the hell," he said dully. "It gives you a lift. Things a real drag —no bread, always gettin' fired off any job you get—Ma always at me— I get fed up. I moved in with Ken. His old man don't care— What? I only got a job part-time, that bowlin' alley, yesterday—boss at me all 's morning—"

(They were to find that when Ken Burkhart's mother died, her sister had been named guardian, Burkhart senior in Quentin then; she'd washed her hands of the pair of them and moved out six months ago.)

"What? That cop—that *pig*—Don was the seller, see? The seller we knew—he was the contact. For anything—Mary Jane, speed, barbs, whatever—I and Marty and Ken and Ron, I don't know who else bought from him— But that day, we knew about that damn cop because Ken 'd gone home with Don to make a buy, see—met him some joint in town, and he wanted some stuff—he went back to Don's place, get it—and he was still there, Don took some speed then, about all Don ever did turn on with, I guess—and he was still there, Don puttin' records on and all—when he hears the old dame—onna phone. Hears her say how that cop—that *pig*—tole her about—about—"

Pat Logan blowing the whistle on Don, and Mama calling the doctor.

"He was the seller!" blurted Root in remembered panic. "He had the stuff—for a price—we didn't know no other contact—and when you need it, you need it bad, man— Ken got out, but he saw that ambulance come —take Don off somewhere— He was the seller! That Goddamn cop—it was all his fault! If he hadn't— What?"

"You thought it over for a couple of days—without anything to turn on with—and decided to beat up on the cop in revenge?" Mendoza's tone was gentle.

"What? I—I—it was just—I don't know! That Goddamn cop—no call interfere like that—do your own thing, nothin' to do with him—Goddamn— Only Ken made another contact, he won't say who—but he got some speed— I don't know what day, Thursday, Wednesday, what's with the day—Friday, yeah, yeah—we got to thinkin' about that *cop*—no call interfere— You know something? You know something, Don he got a kick outta livin' acrost the street from a pig! A real charge he got— So we knew— And the door wasn't locked—we just went in there. I—had— that—sap. We made— Well, he was a real tough guy. Only, they was four of us, see? He knocked Ken down—and he hit me, my nose started bleedin'—that was my shirt—but— We thought he was dead, we left him— Is he dead?"

"You had better start praying," said Higgins, "that he isn't going to be."

"But it was all his fault! Goddamn cop, if he hadn't—"

If he hadn't, they all thought, been doing his job. The way a trained LAPD man should.

Before he went home, Mendoza called the Logan house, and got Royce.

"The punks," said Royce tiredly. "The junkies. For that reason—can we call it a reason, Mendoza?"

"No. *Ya lo creo. ¿Quién sabe?* We've got them. To charge, on the evidence."

"And what will they get?" said Royce. "If Pat dies—"

"God forbid. I know. Assault with intent, and the first count for three of them, and with one of these damn softheaded judges— What's the hospital saying?"

"Doubletalk. His pulse is better, he's getting restless— That is a good man, Mendoza, a good cop, and these Goddamned irresponsible little punks—full of dope—" Royce uttered a literal growl. "By God—"

"Doing their own thing. *Too much ego*— Well, we've got them. The assault with intent, at least."

And he went home to Alison. Quite often he wondered just what the hell he was doing still down here, at the thankless dirty job, after the old man died and there'd come to light all the gilt-edged stock and real-estate deeds. The money for the luxuries, for Luis Mendoza and now Alison and their hostages to fortune—

Higgins said to Mary, "Will you tell me why I picked this job? Talk about the bottom of things—the muck in the gutter! Those damn irresponsible lazy *louts*—"

"Because you're a responsible, honest, upright man," said Mary.

"Because I'm an idiot," said Higgins.

"Well, you've *got* them, at least."

"Which will be a fine consolation for Sally Logan if Pat Logan should die—or end up a permanent invalid."

"Which will *not* happen," said Mary. "Because I think there are guardian angels, George."

"I can only hope you're right."

"I'm right," said Mary serenely. "Since you got away from those thugs, George, I have all sorts of faith in the guardian angels."

CHAPTER 8

On Wednesday morning, with Piggott and Glasser off and Grace back, there was still a good deal of cleaning up to do on the punks. The inevitable paper work had to be finished and sent in the right directions; and they had to bring Don Franks into it too, get a statement from him if possible.

"The punks," said Grace, hearing about that. "At least let's hope they'll be out of circulation for a while."

Mendoza called the Huntington Beach clinic and was told that Franks had been discharged. The sometime user, not a hard addict; no reason to keep him. He called the Franks's home and Mrs. Franks told him yes, Donny was there. "So," said Mendoza, "suppose you chase up and get him, Art. See what we can get out of him, anyway." Hackett and Higgins would be busy most of today finishing that one up legally.

"And what are we doing on Harlow?" asked Grace. Landers drifted in and followed him into Mendoza's office. Palliser, Sergeant Lake said, had already been in and gone, on a call from Traffic.

"I did a little legwork on that myself yesterday," said Mendoza, "with no luck at all. I didn't find anybody I wanted to see. Maybe you two will today." He told them what Mrs. Short had remembered; she had identified the names in the doctor's records, and there were addresses. "I know they're no motives at all, to the rational mind. But whoever did that wholesale shooting—"

"True," said Landers. "As you've said before, it depends who has the motive. I could just see a little thing like these triggering it—except for the Chinese fellow, which is just silly. But the only thing that does occur to me—if anything like that was going to start X shooting up the doctor's office, wouldn't it have been right then? Not a couple of months later?"

"And I'd say so too," said Grace.

"I don't know," said Mendoza, smoothing his moustache absently. "Again, it depends who. Somebody brooding over something? All I do say is, these are the first possible leads we've got on Harlow, people who had, or thought they had, some grievance on him. We'd better look at them."

"I see that." Landers got up. "So let's go do some legwork, Jase."

"And even if we didn't have to," said Grace, "we wouldn't be any more comfortable here, would we? There was a crew working on the third-floor windows when I came in." It was very hot in the office, and the occasional gust of wind sweeping around the tall building, this high up, blowing papers around, didn't improve any tempers.

"Toss you for which car," said Landers, and won the throw. "So you drive. Just as well, that thing's starting to nickel and dime me to death. New battery last year, and now it needs a lube job and a new tail pipe, and it's been eating oil— And who can afford a new car?"

"Especially if you're going to get married," said Grace. They got into the elevator.

"That's another thing. Damn it, Jase, I always thought blondes were supposed to be scatterbrained flibbertigibbets with no common sense. Common sense! That girl's got her head screwed on so tight— We haven't known each other long enough, it's better to be safe than sorry, and besides she likes her job and doesn't want to stop working— But I'll get her eventually, I swear I will. She is," said Landers, "quite a blonde."

"So I hear." Grace grinned at him. They got into the little French racer, the bright blue Elva, in the lot. The picket with his white beard and homemade sign was patrolling Temple Street today. "Before we go looking for these people, Tom, there's something I want to check out at that office building."

"Sure. What?"

"Well—"

The call from Traffic in Hollywood had been relayed downtown just this morning. It had been called in to Wilcox Street as the Traffic shifts changed last night, before the night watch at Homicide had gone home. Chris Hauck's car had been spotted in the parking lot of a third-class nightclub on Fairfax Avenue. And Palliser, heading for Hollywood now, was cussing out loud and wondering why the hell it hadn't been staked out. The call sent out on it must contain the information that it was wanted in connection with a homicide—

Actually, he found out at Wilcox Street, it didn't. Once in a long while even the efficient LAPD goofed, and whoever Sergeant Lake had talked to in Communications had just put the plate number on the hot list, period. The patrolman who spotted it was riding a tour alone and couldn't do anything but report to the station, which he had, at twelve-thirty. And Wilcox Street had a night watch too but as it happened the call on the hot car had come in at the same time as a rather spectacular accident happened, a four-car crash on the boulevard with two dead.

"I'm sorry as hell," said Captain Garden contritely when they'd sorted it out. "Sometimes these things— And of course it might just have been abandoned there—"

"What a hope," said Palliser gloomily. He went and looked, of course, and of course this morning the nightclub's parking lot was as bare as a desert. Palliser said several other things to himself, heading back downtown.

At least his shoulder felt better. He'd stopped at First Aid before going home last night, and a nurse with hamlike hands had manipulated it and made some adjustments, it felt like, to his spinal cord; and Roberta had got out the deep-heat massager. . . . That was another thing, thought Palliser. Robin going back to work. He did not approve. They were getting by all right on what he made—the house payments heavy, but they could make it, it wasn't necessary for her to go back to teaching. Get into the habit, he reflected now, feeling depressed, and she'd keep putting off any family—he could hear her—just another semester, John, until we get the furniture paid off— Women!

And where the hell were Linda Schnell and her boy-friend? The car parked in Hollywood last night, but were they still driving it? The word was out to the pigeons—maybe some time something would turn up. Of course Chris Hauck had asked for it, and probably wasn't much loss, but the case had to be worked.

"What occurred to me," said Grace, "after I thought about it, was that door. The door to the basement. Higgins and the patrolmen were searching the building—well, that is, looking around for any sight of him because it was barely minutes after the shooting, by what we heard. And that door was locked, but I wondered if it had been."

"Had— Oh," said Landers.

"If it wasn't, and just locked itself when it got slammed—I'd just like to know," said Grace, "whether it had been locked, and if there's another way out of the basement."

"As usual, having the simple mind, you think of the simplest thing."

"And that would be pretty simple."

They parked in the side lot of the McLaren Building and went in. There was a building superintendent; they'd seen him on Monday too but hadn't taken a statement because he hadn't seen or heard anything, he'd been on the top floor examining a recently vacant office for needed renovations. His name was Enoch Shepard, and he was in his office on the ground floor: a cubbyhole with a desk, a couple of chairs. He was a big broad black man about fifty, with rimless glasses, and he listened to Grace's questions and said, "I see what you're after, sir. That basement door? That hood—whoever it was—killing all those people. Terrible. I couldn't believe it, I heard about it first. But—"

"What's in the basement? Who'd go there?"

"Odds and ends. We hire a company to come and clean—floors, windows, rest rooms, all like that. But you stop to think, a big building like this, little things needing fixing all the time. Venetian-blind cords, light bulbs needing to be put in, washers in faucets, toilets getting stopped up, all sorts of little things. I hire a fellow, part-time job, to come in and do that—help me, that is. Him and me's the only ones 'd be going to the basement, we keep supplies like that there. And toilet paper and towels for the rest rooms, and so on. But I hadn't been to the basement that morning myself and Freeman hasn't got a key. Wait a minute, now, there's an extra key to that door always hangin' right here—" He pointed to the wall beside the door. "Master key for every floor, key to the basement, to the elevator housing. But Freeman isn't here, mornings —comes in at one o'clock. Dick Freeman. He's got a regular night job, likes to earn extra."

"And the basement door was locked." Grace and Landers exchanged glances. Even if X had somehow known about that key to the basement —it wouldn't have been any use to him, for the pursuit had been fairly hot, if he had detoured to get that key ten to one he'd have been collared by the patrolmen. And it was a very unlikely thing for a fleeing gunman to do, dive into the basement. It was absently that Grace asked about another door out of the basement and was told that there was a back door giving on the parking lot.

"That's N.G.," said Landers when they'd thanked Shepard and started back to the car. "But now we know, anyway. Where do we go now?"

"Looking for William Ainslie, who got a couple of fingers mashed in a garbage disposal."

*　　*　　*

They found Ainslie after some trouble. He wasn't at his apartment on Vermont, but when they checked with the manager to ask if he still lived there, he offered them a lead. "Mr. Ainslie? Oh, yes, sir, he does. But he's usually out mornings. If it's important you'll probably find him at the Whitman Recording Studio on Santa Monica."

"That's where he works?"

"Oh, no, but he goes there to do his practicing. We couldn't have that in the apartment, you see. He's a musician, Mr. Ainslie, plays with a very popular combo, the best nightclubs."

They found the Whitman Recording Studio, went in and asked. "I think he's here," said the improbably flaxen-blonde receptionist. "I'll ask Joe—" She got Joe on an inside line. "Oh, I thought— Well, yes, I saw Mr. Feldman come in but how'd I know—" And presently she told Grace and Landers, "He was here, he'll be back, they don't know when, but his agent came to see him and they went off somewhere— I'm sorry, I don't know exactly when he might be back."

"There are days like this," said Grace philosophically. "Now, this teen-age girl who tried to throw the doctor to the wolves to convince Daddy she hadn't either been a bad girl—"

"Karen Lightner. Down on Geraldine Street."

And that was a backwater, and what they found there might or might not be suggestive. Mrs. Carol Lightner, small and brown and meek-looking, said, "He won't like it, your coming to ask. He just don't care to talk about it. We've always been respectable folk." Reluctantly she revealed that her husband was home; he worked nights, was a night watchman at a big warehouse. "He won't like you coming," she said.

He didn't. He was a big beefy man, and when she led them out to the back yard of the little frame house, he was carefully trimming the hedge between this and the next yard. The house and the yard were small, but very neat. There was a patch of lawn here, and flower beds. And Henry Lightner didn't like their arrival at all, but he went into the house with them and answered questions.

"I'm a deacon in our church," he told them. "I always been a religious man and I respect the law, officers. We never had but the one child, and I figured we'd raised her in the right way, like the Book says. It's been a grief to us. I don't like talkin' about it."

"We understand that, Mr. Lightner," said Grace in his soft voice, "but we have to ask you a few questions. We—"

"Why? Has that man done somethin' else?"

"Do you mean Dr. Harlow?" He grunted. "Did you believe your daughter when she told you the doctor had—er—raped her?"

Lightner was silent, and then he said very reluctantly, "I reckon—when I heard all them others say, them nurses and— I reckon I believed her right off, but I got to say I—I just don't see how a man like that—educated and all, makin' a lot of money—why he'd do such a thing—I don't know what to think, and that's all I can say."

"Henry," said his wife timidly, "you know what she said—later on—"

"I know she lied to us. She was raised to know better. She lied to us once we know, she maybe lied other times." He shook his head.

"She said—after that doctor could show it wasn't like she said—she said some boy at school had—you know. But that wasn't so either because—" She faced Grace and Landers miserably, twisting her hands together. "Because later on her friend Mona—Mona Wilson, she was just cryin' her eyes out, couldn't b'lieve it, a good girl she is—she tole us her own brother, he heard fellows talkin' at school, 'bout how Karen—Karen—oh, we couldn't b'lieve it but— How she went with a lotta different boys, and—" She began to cry.

"Mr. Lightner, where is your daughter now?" asked Grace. The episode with Dr. Harlow (and how stupid could the girl be?—she hadn't gone to him until she was pregnant, and his records would show that) had happened last January.

Lightner said heavily, "I don't care to talk about it anymore, officers. It's a shut book. I been prayin' for her, all I can do now, and I reckon my duty to do." He got up and went out of the room.

"She—she's dead," whispered the woman. "She had a miss, that time, lost the baby. But 'long last month, I guess—she found out—and she went to one o' these nasty women do such things, girls in trouble—and she got sick from it and she died. Last week over in the big hospital."

"Thanks very much, Mrs. Lightner," said Grace gently. They went out to the Elva. "What do you think, Tom? That says a little to me. Last January—but just last week, the girl's death bringing it all back. He'd like to think that somebody outside was responsible for—"

"Setting Karen's feet on the downward path," said Landers thoughtfully. "Yes indeedy, Jase. There may just be something here."

"We'll lay it in front of the boss, maybe he'll see something about it in his crystal ball. Meanwhile—" It was only ten-thirty; they drove back to the Whitman Recording Studio.

This time they found their man. "Studio Three," the blonde told them, and they hunted down several corridors, found the door.

"You the cops looking for me?" He turned from the big orchestra-sized marimba: a nattily dressed young man, a little darker than Grace and clean-shaven, and obviously a successful young man. His light-gray suit was sharply tailored, his tie real silk, he wore a flashy diamond ring on his right hand and a gold watch on his left wrist. He was a good-looking man, the same lean regular features as Grace, but his eyes were restless. "Bill Ainslie—me. What do cops want with me?"

Grace introduced themselves. "So sit down—shoot," said Ainslie. He sat on the piano bench—this cluttered studio room was littered with musical instruments, music stands, tables piled with sheet music—and Grace and Landers found a couple of folding chairs.

"You went to a Dr. John Harlow," began Landers, "with an infected hand—and you—"

Ainslie looked suddenly disconcerted and concerned. He thrust his left hand into his jacket pocket. "Harlow?" he said. "Yes, that's right. This same Harlow who—" The press had had modest headlines about the wholesale shooting, and several ministers had based sermons on the theme of the miraculously preserved baby. "It *was* him?" asked Ainslie in a subdued voice. "That got— Yeah, the same address—my God, what a thing. What a thing! His wife, the nurse—and that baby—the *Herald* had a cut of her, cute little tyke. My God—" And he sat up suddenly and said, "For God's sake! You—are you thinking—*me?* Bill Ainslie? A thing like—oh, my God!"

"You—er—made a little fuss," said Grace. "Threatened to sue the doctor—"

"Oh, my God!" said Ainslie rather wildly. "Listen, I—well, of course it's all *right,* I can prove where I was. When it happened. Monday morning—well, of course I was right here, and so was Les—Les Morton, he's the bandleader, and part of the time Lee McHugh was too—going over some new arrangements—up to noon."

"They'll say so?"

"Sure they'll say so. But listen, I've got to tell you how it was—I know I acted like a damn fool that time, but it was— Well, damn it!" He took his left hand out of his pocket and held it out. The third and fourth fingers had healed crookedly, with visible scars on the back of the hand, the fingers obviously stiff and useless. "You see, I'm a musician, my hands— Well, it was a *thing.* I had to train myself—thank God I'm not a piano player is all!" He shuddered, and shrugged. "I'm the drummer—drums, marimba, xylophone—so it could've been worse. But —I know I was acting like a damn fool, but I was just so mad—and I ought to say, Harlow was nice about it. He could've been mean, but he wasn't. And I calmed down, I apologized and—my own damn-fool fault—"

"How come you didn't go to a doctor right off, when it happened?" asked Grace.

"Oh, for God's— Look," said Ainslie, "look. I was at this dame's. She's married, her husband's a gorilla. And she's fixing drinks in the kitchen when she drops her damn ring down the garbage disposal by accident—she's not a very smart dame, boys—and my God, I'm fishing for it when she accidentally flips the switch—and I nearly got out in time, but—" Both Landers and Grace were grinning. "Look, my God, I'm dancing round the kitchen dripping blood all over like crazy, and she's having hysterics when, my God, her husband walks in the front door! She thought he was out of town at a match—he's a pro heavyweight. Well, I tell you, I'm long gone out the back door, hand and all, so he doesn't know who was there—but he knows somebody was on account of the blood—and my God, they're always dropping in at the Kit-Kat Club, that's where we're playing right then, and if he sees me sporting a bandage—! I'm not exactly famous for being backward with the girls—" Ainslie gestured, and added, "It wasn't funny, boys. I could've got clobbered—that gorilla—"

"How'd you pass it off?" asked Landers amusedly.

"I told Les I had the flu. By the time I finally went to the doctor, thank God that gorilla *was* out of town. For a while. And I've had to train myself, hold the stick in three fingers. But—"

But it wasn't Ainslie, completely rational Ainslie, who had shot up Harlow's office.

"Con qué estamos con esto," said Mendoza. He leaned back in his chair at the big table at Federico's and swallowed straight rye. "The autopsy report came in—on the Harlows and Jenkins. Nothing in it, of course. We know what they died of. All healthy specimens, no indication of any addiction, alcoholism, et cetera. Quite respectable corpses."

"Which we also knew," said Hackett. He and Higgins had had a busy morning on all the paper work. Grace and Landers had just come in and joined them to report their morning's labors.

Mendoza finished the rye and said thoughtfully, "That Lightner. I just see what you mean, Jase. That's human nature—we see a lot of it. Looking for the scapegoat. Love—a dangerous commodity, yes. . . . The girl was well brought up, as the phrase goes, and shouldn't have stepped off the straight and narrow voluntarily. How much was it due to the strict upbringing that she did, or do any of you go along with the Freudian notions?"

"Your age is showing, Luis," said Hackett. "You don't keep up with progress and a changing world. The head doctors themselves don't go along with Freud any more, not all of 'em anyway. The puritanical up-bringing maybe sends A straight into a brothel, B into a nunnery, and C to Z into perfectly normal adult lives. Human nature."

"Yes," said Mendoza. "But when Lightner found out, how tempting to think that some evil male had given her a shove. The first tale she told was the one on Harlow—and it could be that, emotionally as they say, Lightner does believe it."

"But nobody could, when you think it over," said Landers. "She didn't lay eyes on Harlow until she was pregnant—" He stopped.

"Oh, didn't she? That's not what she told Papa."

"Of course not," said Grace slowly. "Of course it wasn't. However she happened to go to Harlow—maybe picked him out of the phone book—she told Papa the reason she went to him was because he was the one *did* it, made up to her and lied about not being married and se-duced her. And—"

"And then she dies just last week—post-abortion septicemia," said Landers. "Could be he started brooding on it again, convinced himself it was all Harlow's fault? It could be, but—"

"I think, just to be thorough," said Mendoza, "we look at Mr. Lightner harder and closer. He doesn't sound the type to be talking free and loud about it—could be he's a brooder. So, where was he on Mon-day morning? Does he own a gun or have access to one? If so, does it happen to be a Harrington and Richardson nine-shot .22?"

"We'll look," said Grace.

"There is also, of course, Kun Low Soo."

They all laughed. "Scraping the bottom of the barrel," said Higgins. "That's just stupid."

"*Alla vá,*" said Mendoza. "As stupid as shooting three people to death in public."

"A way to look at it," said Grace.

Hackett sighed at the low-calorie plate as the waiter served them. "At least we're getting the paper work out of the way on these punks. That Don Franks. . . . Do you know, it hadn't struck me, but we hadn't laid eyes on him until today. Providing the leads, really the one behind the whole caper."

"And what kind of punk is he?" asked Landers. "Not that we can't guess."

"Too smart," said Hackett and Higgins together. "Laughing at us and saying he wasn't stewing," added Hackett, "probation all he'd get,

Mama with a high-priced shyster, and what the hell, pretty soon it'd all be legalized anyway, the hard stuff too—and why not?"

Landers looked at his steak sandwich. "That picket was out again."

"I noticed him," said Mendoza. "Yes, and when that happens—¡Dios me libre!—we can all happily go mad together. . . . We'll look hard at Lightner, Jase."

"And you always say," said Higgins, "we clear up one thing, we're apt to clear up another. Things going by threes. Has—"

"You're just inviting trouble, George," said Hackett. "It also works out that you clear up one thing, right off the bat three other things show up to work."

"Don't be superstitious. Donny annoyed me," said Higgins, "is all. Because for one thing he is very probably right—Mama will retain the high-priced mouthpiece, and with all the legal doubletalk—"

"Mother love," said Mendoza, "mmh. And there is the proverb, Sin hijos y sin celos, no hay de consuelos."

"And that means what?" asked Higgins.

"Without children and without jealousy, no affliction. . . . Not that I'm troubled with jealousy," said Mendoza, "being sufficiently egotistic. But I began to believe that as soon as those twin monsters appeared on the scene. But maybe I am improving my education at that." He poured himself more coffee. "Human nature. . . . There's a very basic sort of symbolism there, you know. Interesting. Encouraging."

"Where?" asked Grace.

"Oh, the fairy tales. Grimm. All the fairy tales." Mendoza lit a cigarette. "The basic, primitive, bedrock convictions of mankind expressed in them—just as in the mythology. ¿Cómo no? And it's very encouraging that whatever vicissitudes occur to the heroes and heroines, in the end everything comes out all right. The wolf who ate Grandmother getting his comeuppance, and—"

"Encouraging, hell," said Hackett, "it's wishful thinking. And if I had a dime for every time I had to read that story to Mark—"

"And," said Mendoza, "the wicked stepmother and stepsisters getting their just punishment and— The twins are a little young to appreciate it, but I appreciate 'The Fisherman's Wife.' Basic convictions of mankind, which we can say must be rooted in experience, that in the end right triumphs and evil is punished. Mmh, yes—Rumpelstiltskin—'Discover my name—'"

"Has anybody," asked Higgins, ignoring him, "called the hospital?"

"They're sounding just slightly more hopeful," said Mendoza abstractedly.

"So, fingers crossed that we get the punks only on a charge of assault with intent."

Palliser, having a busy day, was unaware that Hackett was being an unwitting prophet about new ones coming along. He was just feeling harassed.

He'd got back to the office in time to take a new call—everybody else in was busy on the paper work, on questioning Don Franks, then—and Sergeant Lake said no, there hadn't been any pigeons calling in. Damn it, thought Palliser, Linda and her boy-friend were somewhere—with the car showing up in Hollywood last night—for ninety percent sure they were driving Hauck's car.

The new one was nothing but the promise of more paper work. The kind of thing cops in any big city saw, carbon copies whether New York or Los Angeles, Miami or Portland. The young woman dead in a third-rate hotel room, sediment in the bathroom glass, note propped on the bureau: he doesn't love me, I'll show him how much I love him, good-bye. Palliser looked at it sadly, irritably, resignedly.

The paper work, the lab work, all to add up to just another suicide. There was identification on her, the family to contact: in this case in Des Moines, Iowa.

By the time he'd typed a report on it, it was getting on for noon. He went out for a sandwich and a malted milk (feeling momentary sympathy for Sergeant Lake whose years of sedentary labor at the desk these days had him counting calories and comparing bitter notes with Art Hackett) and came back to find that one of their pigeons had called in. In re the A.P.B. on Linda Schnell. The pigeon didn't know where she was, but passed on the information that maybe Mae Gallio might know. The address was Breed Street in Boyle Heights.

Palliser went over there to see if Mae was home. She was. He hadn't looked, but he could guess, a similar record to Linda's—frosted dark hair, lavish eye makeup, a psychedelic-print pantsuit. She was, however, clean at the moment and hadn't any objection to talking to the fuzz. And none of Linda's other pals they had talked to had been able to tell them her latest address—the Lindas moved around—but Mae Gallio could.

"A place on Darwin," she told Palliser. "Rooming house. She hadn't been having such good luck lately—it can be a drag, you know?—she was down, way down, last time I saw her. What?"

"You know Foster Sterry? Her latest boy-friend?"

"I don't know," she said. "Never heard the name. But she was moaning about all her bad luck lately. Got behind on the rent and all."

After prodding at her some more, Palliser went on to Darwin Street, which was a very tired-looking area of old L.A., and found the rooming house where Linda Schnell had had a room for, he learned, about the last three months. It was the kind of rooming house which housed a lot of the Linda Schnells. Its owner, a slatternly elderly woman, told Palliser pithily that what roomers did was their own business, she couldn't care less as long as she got the rent on time, and she couldn't say anything about Linda Schnell—she didn't pay notice to roomers coming and going, but that one, Room Four upstairs, she'd moved out last Sunday with all she had, one suitcase. She didn't know if there'd been a man with her, or if there was a car.

Palliser swore to himself. Well, the Lindas drifted.

And there was this Harlow thing—and Logan— They had been busier, but he felt a little harried. He had, from the pals of Linda's he'd talked to, the names of a few favorite hangouts of hers—the Black-and-White Bar on Fourth, the Ace-High on Grand—but where was the manpower to stake those out?

And he said to Lake, disgustedly, "Just for one like Hauck! The middle-aged Lothario who ought to have had better sense. Asking for it, picking up the floozies, flashing the roll—"

"Well, Matt would say, equal in the sight of God," said Lake seriously. And plugged in and said, "Central Homicide, Sergeant Lake . . .O.K. Oh? What's the— Got it."

"Don't tell me, something new," said Palliser.

"That's just what, John. West Kensington Avenue, up by Echo Park. A body, yes."

It was the body of a woman, in a bathtub in an elderly, neat and ordinary apartment: an eight-family unit. The body had been identified: a Mrs. Rhoda Fleming. Apparently beaten.

Her son-in-law had found her. He was a tall, thin, dark young man in his twenties, and he said to Palliser, agitatedly and volubly, what he'd been saying to the patrolmen— "Rosie couldn't raise her on the phone, she's been worried, her mother I mean, Rhoda—we always call her Rhoda, a nice woman, a respectable woman, she works of course, Rosie's father died four years ago—Rosie and I been married three years this month—Rhoda worked at this gift shop in Hollywood, a nice place on Sunset—"

Palliser called in for a lab team.

"But my God, officer, my God, how could it have happened? Is she drowned? A heart attack maybe— And my God, I've got to tell Rosie—"

CHAPTER 9

Since yesterday, of course, they had had an A.P.B. out on Al Koonz who had loaned his old Colt to Ed Hobart for a heist job. He hadn' turned up yet; when he did he'd go right back to Quentin to finish : three-to-five for armed robbery—he was out on parole.

This morning there had been a teletype from Washington; the Fed knew Foster Sterry. He hailed from Tennessee originally, and he had : long string of minor charges in a dozen states, D.-and-D., petty theft attempted burglary, pimping. Nobody had picked him up again since h got out of jail in Alabama two years ago.

Coming back from lunch, Hackett and Higgins left the dispatching o this morning's paper work to Sergeant Lake, and went out to see Myrtl Boggs and Lilian Stafford again. Sometimes, after the initial shock wa past, a witness to violence would remember more detail.

Mendoza, hearing about the new one, went up to West Kensingto Avenue to see what Palliser had turned up.

"Well, not much yet," said Palliser. He looked a little tired; as usua when he was annoyed he'd been unconsciously rubbing his heavy eye brows, and they were untidily beetling. "The names. Rhoda Fleminç fifty-three, widow, worked at this gift shop in Hollywood. Marrie daughter Rose Scott, husband Gavin, he's a skilled workman of som kind at Lockheed. His day off today. Daughter usually talked to Mam several times a week on the phone—they live out in Sunland, don't ofte get in to see Mama—and she hasn't been able to raise her since Frida night, so not knowing any of the neighbors to call, she got her husban to come and look—they've got a new baby. Boom, he finds the apar ment door unlocked and Rhoda dead in the bathtub."

"Drowned?"

"No—I'd have a guess, strangled, but also beaten. Naked as a jaybird. And nobody knows anything."

"As usual. Interns have any guess about the time?"

"Vaguely. She's been dead at least two days and probably longer. I've talked to a couple of neighbors—" By now the squad car had gone, but the mobile lab truck was still there in front of the apartment house and little knots of curious residents were out along the block. Past the front lobby, where Mendoza had found Palliser, the manageress was up the hall talking excitedly to a couple of ground-floor tenants. "A Mrs. Faraday, who has the apartment next to Mrs. Fleming. She says she didn't hear anything from there the last few days, no disturbance or screams. So does the woman across the hall, Miss Binder. Mrs. Faraday doesn't work—Miss Binder is a stenographer downtown. She was out Saturday night, but both of 'em home every night since, and Friday. They say, and the manageress, a Mrs. Upjohn, says, that while most of the tenants here have been here awhile—Mrs. Fleming nearly four years —they don't, well, socialize. Know each other's names, that's about all."

"So. Fleming have any men friends? Go out with friends of either sex, and where?"

"I put that to Scott," said Palliser, scratching his handsomely straight nose, "and he looked horrified. I might have suggested that she went out hustling. She was over fifty, he said, and a respectable woman. Well—"

"*Así*," said Mendoza amusedly. "*Según y conforme*. It's funny how some people—puritans?—seem to think nobody over thirty-five should be at all interested in that old devil sex."

"Anyway, he said she didn't. Said she went to work and came home. Talked to daughter on the phone. Did her own laundry and cleaning. She had a couple of women friends here—Hollywood—I've got the addresses—but she certainly didn't go out in the evening often. But the door wasn't forced, and Scott said she always kept it locked."

"So, we go the long way round," said Mendoza. "And hope the lab picks up something useful."

Scarne and Duke came down the front stairs with their bags and Scarne said, "It's all yours, Lieutenant. They're just bringing the body."

The interns came down after them, slow on the narrow staircase, with the basket swinging between them, the body covered with a plastic sheet. Mendoza stepped forward.

"Let's have a look." Sometimes something about a corpse offered suggestions.

The interns set it down and unstrapped the fastenings at one end.

Mendoza turned the sheet back. Death was never pretty, minus the last-minute attentions of the mortician's art, but he looked at the upper half of Rhoda Fleming and made certain objective deductions.

She had still a good figure for a woman her age. Remnants of makeup and a curl in her hair; her hands had been manicured, nails enameled pale pink, before she'd struggled with somebody and torn a couple of them, one broken right off. She had taken care of herself. Well, she had been working, had to keep looking groomed, smart. He reached to push back the hair at one temple: hair kept in a short curly cut.

"What'd you find?" asked Palliser.

"Nothing. She kept her hair tinted," said Mendoza. The hand he had picked up, the right hand, bore a thin lighter mark on the ring finger. He stepped back. "O.K., boys, take her. Let's look at the apartment, John."

The apartment was on the second floor, a pleasant single unit—living room, kitchen with small dining area, bedroom and bath. These older places always had larger rooms, looked—and were—more substantial than the newer ones. *"Un día de estos,"* muttered Mendoza to himself, "one of these days—" Everybody saying so smugly that it proved the new high-rise buildings were safe, coming through the quake unharmed; the fact was, none of them had been anywhere near the line of the quake. Next time—

There were evidences of a struggle in the apartment. A scatter rug between living room and bedroom bunched up in a tangle: a chair over-turned in the bedroom: bloodstains on the made-up bed where the bed-spread was in disarray—bloodstains in the bathroom. And in the bed-room, a little heap of clothes untidily scattered on the floor. Aside from that, and the evidence of the lab men's activities, the apartment seemed to have been neat and clean. Mendoza looked at the little heap of clothes with his head cocked, and said, "Pulled off her in a struggle? I wonder if she was raped." He picked up the clothes piece by piece and put them on the bed. A white nylon brassiere, 36-B. White nylon pant-ies. Low-heeled white sandals. A nylon-jersey tailored pantsuit, bright coral color.

"What are we looking for?" asked Palliser ten minutes later. Men-doza had been prowling around the place opening drawers and closets and muttering to himself.

"Evidence of character. So often what a person was like points a small finger in the right direction. She was—mmh—up to date," said Mendoza. "Not dowdy or old-fashioned. She had several pantsuits in her wardrobe, slacks, a couple of worn but originally very good cocktail dresses. Sheer stockings. Medium heels for work, spikes for dress-up. She smoked. Chesterfields. In a holder. She took an occasional drink— there's a bottle of Scotch and a bottle of gin in the kitchen. She didn't take a newspaper—no old ones around."

"So?"

"No se. She just doesn't smell to me," said Mendoza, "like quite the dull workaday woman her son-in-law described to you. More I couldn't say at the moment. We'll see what turns up. I'll go down and chase Matt up here, you'd better talk to those friends of hers and the other tenants here."

"Sure."

Mendoza left him talking to a Mrs. Halpern who lived across the hall from the manageress downstairs, and went back to his office, which he found in a state of siege. The belligerent Murphys were there, Ron Dolan's grandmother, and two lawyers. Sergeant Lake, Piggott and Glasser were trying to calm them down enough to listen, and not having much success.

"—Never believed the stories about police, but by God I do now! When Eve told me how—arresting my son! My son in your dirty jail—"

"I *told* you, Jim, how those two came—I suppose *they're* out beating up some prisoners or something—" The lawyers, to their credit, were trying to calm them down too.

Mendoza's voice cut across Murphy's incisively. "Suppose you all calm down and be quiet. I said *quiet!* That's better. Come into my office." There, he gave them chairs; Sergeant Lake brought in more, silently. "Now, Mr. Murphy—"

"Who the hell are you?"

Mendoza sat back in his desk chair, lit a cigarette with a snap of the gold desk lighter, and introduced himself coldly. Murphy eyed his dapper tailoring, gold cuff links and tie-clasp suspiciously. "We really don't do things that way these days, you know," and Mendoza's tone was gentle. "You'll have been told the charges on your son, at the jail—"

"It's crazy! Just—"

"Mr. Murphy. We have not only some scientific evidence, but a full admission from one of the other boys—if you can call eighteen-year-olds boys—that they have been using narcotics for some time, and that last Friday afternoon, while under the influence of narcotics, they deliber- ately assaulted an LAPD officer in his own home. We don't know if he's going to live. He was very badly beaten—skull-fractures, broken bones, internal injuries, a severed artery. If he dies the charge will be murder in the second degree, which could carry a life sentence. We have evidence, Mr. Murphy. We don't arrest people without reason."

"I don't—believe— *Marty*," he said. "Marty." But the toughness had dropped from his voice. Suddenly his wife started to cry.

"But I don't understand what's happening," quavered Mrs. Dolan. "Ron's a good boy—I'm sure—"

Mendoza gave one look at Lake; the little show of authority had quieted the Murphys, who'd make no more trouble. But it was a while before Lake shepherded them out, and then Mendoza had to talk to the lawyers. He was feeling hot and irritated, and sent Lake down the hall for coffee, at three-thirty when Grace and Landers came in.

"And so what have you got?" he asked.

Landers sat down in the chair beside the desk and Grace strolled over to the glassless windows. "Stay *away* from there," said Landers. "Why, we've got a big fat mystery, that's what. Lightner didn't go to brooding over his fallen offspring, and decide Harlow was to blame. He told us he was a deacon of their church—little Southern Baptist church out on Main. And on Monday morning from ten to twelve-thirty he was at the church with the minister and two other deacons, discussing some repairs it needed."

"Oh, hell," said Mendoza.

"Just what we said," said Grace. "The minister and the deacons said so too—not oh hell, but that he was there. Sometimes these awful upright churchgoers make me feel a little anti-religious, you know?" He lit a cigarette and dropped the match out the window. Landers told him to come away from there.

"We even went to look for Kun Low Soo. Wasting time."

"He's got an alibi too?"

"He's not here," said Grace sadly. "He packed up his wife and ten worthless daughters and went back to Taiwan two months ago."

"Oh, hell," said Mendoza again. "Well, I never said they were likely leads, boys, but—where do we look now? Damn it, who *would* do a thing like—walk in and shoot up the whole office? Damn it—"

"Except little Celia Ann," said Grace dreamily.

"But where *do* we?" asked Landers.

Hackett and Higgins were drawing blanks too. Sometimes a witness remembered more clearly after thinking things over; but Myrtle Boggs and Lilian Stafford didn't. Of course Mrs. Boggs hadn't had a chance to see much, and Mrs. Stafford hadn't heard but a few words.

They took Myrtle Boggs down to the McLaren Building, stood her where she said she'd been in the second-floor corridor, and roped in the superintendent, Dr. Colcannon, short fat Dr. Blaise, and a few other men of various sizes from offices in the building, to play X fleeing. All that emerged from that exercise was that she very hesitantly indicated Dr. Blaise as being nearest in size to the man she had seen running, holding the gun.

"It was so *fast*," she said. "I didn't see him more'n five seconds, and he was down the stairs. I'm sorry, I'd sure like to help you—just a terrible thing—but that's all I can rightly say."

Mrs. Stafford was even more hesitant. "How do you describe a voice?" she asked helplessly. "I couldn't. In the first place, I was so surprised and—and startled, you know, by what he *said*. 'I'll kill you all,' or 'I'll shoot you all,' it was—and I simply ran back to our office to call the police. It was a man's voice, and that's all I can tell you. I can't say if it was deep or high or— Kind of, well, medium. And he didn't have an accent of any kind, it was just—just a man's voice, saying, 'I'll kill you all' —and I—"

It was discouraging, but they hadn't really hoped for anything better. They came back to the office and asked Mendoza if the lab had sent up a report yet. "You know the lab," said Mendoza. "We can try to jigger them up." He got Scarne on the phone.

"Listen, Lieutenant, you know how many latents we picked up there? Sure, a doctor's office, nice and clean, but the ordinary dusting doesn't remove latent prints. It'll take a month of Sundays to sort 'em out, and if you want a really thorough job we'd have to find and print all his patients. I think most of 'em belong to patients, because I don't think your gunman stopped to look at magazines or turn lamps on and off, or straighten pictures, before he started shooting—or wander around feeling of things in all the examining rooms. I don't know what we've got. I don't think we're going to give you much, I'm sorry. But we did say, from all you got, it looked as if it went pretty fast—he went in, threatened to shoot, shot and got out."

"Yes," said Mendoza. "Well—"

"It is a bastard," said Higgins. "Just nothing to get hold of."

They were still sitting there talking it over when Palliser came back. He said he'd left Piggott talking to tenants and come back to get the initial report out on Fleming. So Hackett and Higgins heard about that.

And Palliser had just finished the report, separated the triplicate sheets and signed them and put them in manila envelopes, when Sergeant Lake buzzed Mendoza. "Goldberg," he said tersely.

Mendoza picked up the inside phone. "Afternoon, Saul. Have you got your new windows in yet?"

"No, damn it. It's hot as hell in here," said Lieutenant Goldberg of Robbery. But he sounded a little amused for some reason. "I'll be taking the rest of your day, Luis. Sorry. And—" He sneezed, swore, and blew his nose. "Oh, yes, the allergies are fine, thanks. —And you'll bring one of your bright young minions with you who—whom—you can spare for a day or so. He'll be taking a little trip. We have a thing here—"

"What? What for? *Qué es esto?*"

"You'd better come down and hear about it," said Goldberg. "My God, but we do get them. Sometimes we do get them. A little trip up toward Bakersfield, escorting a prisoner. He says he thinks he knows where he left it, but he doesn't know that part of the country, he couldn't be just sure. If he could sort of see the place again maybe he could tell. And of course the sheriff up there will have jurisdiction, a heavier charge than we could bring, so we may as well kill two birds with one stone and take him back, so the sheriff can lock him up when we do find it. He and your minion and the sheriff. If he did leave it, and can find it again. In any case, if it's there we would like to find it, you know."

"Find what, for God's sake?"

"Oh, a body," said Goldberg.

Mendoza took Palliser with him down to Goldberg's office. Palliser, he reflected, had been looking a little tired lately, a little worried about something. Spat with his wife? Landers and Grace could take over what he'd been working, and maybe a couple of days away from the routine would cheer Palliser up.

—Whatever the hell Goldberg was talking about.

As they came into the Robbery Bureau, they passed a couple sitting in chairs under Sergeant Betts's eye, and the couple looked at them with dull forlorn eyes. The other half, thought Mendoza. The girl, not more than eighteen or so, had long tangled brown hair past her shoulders, no makeup, and she was chewing gum. She wouldn't have been bad-looking if she'd combed her hair, put on some lipstick. She had on a pair of black pants and a wildly multicolor tunic top, and sandals on bare feet. The man wasn't much older; he wasn't over-tall but very stocky and hairy, dark, and looking very sorry for himself; he had on dirty plaid shorts and a dirty T-shirt and sandals, and he needed a shave.

Mendoza and Palliser went on into Goldberg's office. "And have you got new windows in yet, friends?" asked Goldberg.

"When you say that, smile. What's up, Saul?"

Goldberg's sardonic, lined dark face was lit with amusement. "Oh, the things we run into. Sergeant Palliser, you are in for a day or so of adventure. Did you notice that pair out there?"

"We did. What about them?"

"She's Wilma Schultz. He's Tim Brodie. They come from Oregon— some little farm town up there. Ran away to get married because Wilma's father doesn't like Tim. Come to the big city and make their fortunes."

"And?"

"No fortune," said Goldberg. "Tim's got a little pedigree up there— I've talked to the chief in this one-horse burg—assault, attempted rape, D.-and-D., attempted burglary. I could deduce, the quick temper. They were picked up by Traffic detail a couple of hours ago, spotted smashing windows and rifling cars in a public lot."

"Yes," said Mendoza. "And what's that got to do with—"

"Piddling little pair, small-time," said Goldberg. "Betts talked to 'em —and came rushing in to me a few minutes later. Seems all of a sudden the girl said, 'Maybe we ought to tell them about that guy, Tim—didn't mean to kill him, it was just an accident, but sort of awful—' "

"¿Cómo?"

"Yeah. So I talked to 'em. They parted right away, no trouble. Maybe they figure if they say they're sorry we won't do anything to 'em for it. They've got an old beat-up Ford, Tim's. Drove straight through, and somewhere around Fresno, they think it was, they picked up a hitchhiker. All they know about him, his name's Steve. He was heading south too. So they got to somewhere around Bakersfield, they *think* it was—this was last Sunday, by the way—and Steve starts to get a little fresh with Wilma, so Tim hauls him out of the car and biffs him, they have a fight, and all of a sudden Steve doesn't get up and Tim finds he's dead."

"¡Caramba!" said Mendoza. Palliser just shut his eyes.

"He thinks maybe Steve broke his neck, or maybe landed on a rock— he wasn't sure. Dead, he was sure he was. So they pulled the body off the road behind some bushes and drove on south. To the big city. Only they never meant to do a thing like that, and they're sorry, and Tim thinks if he could go back there and look, he could find where they put the body."

"¡Porvida! We do run into things. My God."

"Well, you see the position, Luis. It is a homicide. And I really can't spare any men right now—"

"You think we're not busy too?"

"I *apologize*," said Goldberg. "There it is. The sheriff has jurisdiction in the homicide—if you find the body—and we'll then send Wilma up to join Tim. But somebody'll have to ferry him up there officially and hunt for the body."

"Yes, yes. Do you mind the job, John?"

"Would it matter if I said yes?" said Palliser. "For God's sake, the other half we can say. So when do we go?"

"I've laid on a car and driver for seven-thirty," said Goldberg. "You should be up there by ten or ten-thirty. I've talked to the sheriff—Roudebush his name is, seems like—" He sneezed explosively, swore and groped for Kleenex—"a very nice fellow. Stash Tim in jail for the night and get an early start tomorrow morning looking for the body."

"Why did I want to be a cop?" asked Palliser plaintively. "All right. I just ask you one favor, Lieutenant. It is now"—he looked at his watch— "half past five. Between now and seven-thirty will you please see that Tim is taken over to the jail and given a long hot shower and clean clothes? If I've got to ride next to him all the way up to Bakersfield—"

Goldberg laughed. "I'll do that."

"And you can hand your notes on Hauck and the new one over to Jase and Tom," said Mendoza.

Palliser had a word with Grace and Landers about the new case; Hauck they knew about. He went home to tell Roberta and pack an overnight case, after a hasty dinner. "Of *all* things," she said. "Just all casual, maybe they'd better tell—join the force and see life! The seamy side only. How long will you be gone?"

"I haven't any idea," said Palliser. "We may find the body by noon tomorrow, or never. Because it just could be that Tim was wrong, and after they'd driven off, Steve came to and got up and walked away somewhere."

"Heavens above," said his Robin. "You do run into— I won't say, have a good time, darling."

"I don't expect to," said Palliser. "And listen, don't you take advantage of my absence to decide to buy that fancy bedroom set you want—just because you can pay for it out of your earnings starting in September."

"Masculine pride," mocked Roberta. "It's silly, John—you know it'll help—"

"I'm just afraid it'll get to be a habit."

"Just until we get the furniture paid off—I promise. Let me know if you have to be gone long—and don't be, darling."

"Not more than I can help." He bent to kiss her. Well, they didn't have fights, but this working-wives bit he didn't approve of. . . .

Occasionally Mendoza brought the office home with him. He thought Alison and Máiri would appreciate Wilma and Tim. Hackett and Higgins, also on the way home, were doubtless thinking the same thing.

He was a little earlier than usual, and swore as he turned into the drive, and backed out again. The drive was cluttered with a small cement-mixing machine and bags of cement. He left the Ferrari in the street and walked up the drive, past the wide crack. The livestock was all in the back yard—four cats sitting in a row on the back porch, and Cedric the old English sheep dog barking furiously at *el pájaro,* who was shrieking raucously from the alder tree.

"*YAWK! YAWK! Yankee Doodle came to town!*" The mockingbird swooped down on Cedric, but Cedric's thick coat made him impervious to the savage pointed beak, and he just went on barking, his veil of face-hair flying up to show his one walleye. Mendoza went in the back door muttering—just how they'd come by them all was accidental, but there really was too much livestock for a city yard—to find Alison busy over dinner, the twins presumably having their baths after supper, with Máiri in charge.

"The cement man came," said Alison unnecessarily. "He couldn't actually start work—it was only an hour ago—but he left everything ready to do it tomorrow."

"So I see. Immobilizing the garage."

"Well, it'll only be a day or so. Anything new, *amado?*"

"Oh, wait till you hear." He got himself a drink; El Señor, hearing the bottle taken down, came through the cat door in a hurry demanding his share.

"Time they were in anyway." Alison went to shoo the cats in, locked the cat door and told Cedric to be quiet.

She duly appreciated Wilma and Tim. "The things you run into . . . but I have a surprise for you, *marido.* We really have quite intelligent offspring."

"*Naturalmente.*"

"They do say, children of elderly parents are more intelligent—"

"You will go on insulting me." Mendoza finished the rye.

"Come see."

Down the hall in the nursery, the twins were pinkly powdered and ready for bed, after the half hour of stories. "The lambs," said Mrs. MacTaggart benignly. Mendoza regarded the lambs warily; he had discovered in thirty-five months that a combination of McCann, Weir and Mendoza bloodlines could produce some lively characteristics.

"Now!" said Alison. "Johnny, remember what you learned today? The wolf. English."

"The wolf. English," said Johnny obediently. "*El lobo*. Spanish."

"Good. Two ways to say it."

"Two ways. *Sí.*"

"Terry," said Alison. "You remember? The witch. English."

"*Sí*. English. *La bruja,* Spanish. *La bruja* get all burned down in *la estufa!* Mamacita—"

"*¡El lobo! El lobo!*" Johnny seized the battered copy of Grimm and made one leap into Mendoza's lap. "Daddy read—read *el cuento* 'bout *la cabra* 'n' *los niños! El lobo* eat the little kids all down! *El lobo—*"

"Johnny!" said Alison. "Now remember—we practiced to show Daddy! The oven—*la estufa*. English—Spanish."

"The oven," said Johnny disinterestedly. "Daddy read about *la cabra!*"

"Want about Jingle!" said Terry. "*El cuento* 'bout Jingle!"

"Terry! We *practiced*. Come on, now. The little girl—*la niña*. English—"

"Jingle!" said Terry. "*La bruja* turn into *el gato!* I like *la bruja*—she put *la magia mala* to *la doncella*—"

"Oh, dear," said Alison. Mendoza was laughing. "She's taken quite a fancy to that one, Jorinda and Joringel—"

"*Sí*, Jingle! *La bruja* kill ever'body *con la magia mala,*" said Terry with immense satisfaction.

"No—no—*la cabra!*" shouted Johnny. "*El lobo* eat *los niños* all down!"

"Somehow I don't think you're making much impression, my love," said Mendoza.

"At least the driveway's getting repaired," said Alison resignedly.

And on Thursday morning about ten o'clock—just as Palliser, probably, was up there in the wilds hunting for a body with Tim Brodie and Sheriff Roudebush—Chris Hauck's Buick was spotted parked on Wabash Avenue in Boyle Heights. It was Palliser who had done most of the work on Hauck, though Landers had been in on the start of it; and as he'd said it was a very typical sordid little thing, and Hauck small loss. But things came up, and they were a team after all, taking the jobs as they came.

It looked as if there was just nowhere to go on the Harlow shooting; Mendoza was brooding over Harlow's records again, maybe hoping for a hunch to hit him. The four punks—Ken Burkhart, Jim Root, Marty Murphy and Ron Dolan—probably wouldn't be arraigned until Monday, now. They were all of age, and would be tried as adults; bail hadn't been granted yet, of course. Pat Logan was doing a little better, but was still unconscious.

Both Hackett and Higgins were off today. But they were both spending some thought on the Harlow thing: that shapeless, reasonless thing. Higgins mowed the lawn front and back; formerly Steve Dwyer's job, and the leg was nearly as good as new, after the hit-run, the brace and therapy, but he still favored it a little. Higgins still felt a little strange, Bert Dwyer's good kids his, Mary his, too, and now the new baby coming soon, in a couple of months.

Hackett had found a new diet and brooded over it rather gloomily, babysitting while Angel went to the market.

Landers and Piggott went to stake out Hauck's car, and at ten minutes to twelve a man walked up to it and unlocked the driver's door, so they went up in a hurry and nabbed him.

The man was Foster Sterry, by the I.D. on him. He looked at them and said dispiritedly, "Oh, hell. Fuzz. I s'pose you want us for rollin' that drunk. Only he wasn't drunk. That was the trouble."

"All right, Sterry," said Landers, "we have to inform you of your rights—" and he read that piece off to him. "Do you understand your rights as I have—"

"Sure, sure," said Sterry. He was a tall thin fellow with a lugubrious jowled face like a bloodhound, and he said, "I s'pose you want Linda too. She's at the hotel—we got a room there—on Soto. I just come out to find Danny, he owes me a sawbuck, but woulden you know, he's down on his luck too, he can't pay up. What a drag, and now you drop on us— Hey, I s'pose it was the car, hah? I tole Linda we oughta leave it somewheres, there'd be a record who owned it—"

They found Linda Schnell at the shabby old hotel. She was doing her nails, and she wouldn't come with them until her nail polish was dry. They were accommodating: maybe she'd open up and tell them all about it. The D.A. liked voluntary statements.

And Landers said later to Grace, "Pity John had to miss it."

"Oh, yes," said Grace. "Seeing he did most of the legwork. But on the other hand, Tom, kind of run of the mill. What we get. Not like Harlow—the offbeat one. Can we say?"

"Unfortunately, yes," said Landers. And he had a date with Phil tomorrow night; she'd be interested in Harlow. She was interested in the detective work, which policewomen didn't get to do, much. But it was so seldom they ran into anything remotely approaching the exotic plots in the paperback at the drugstore. The shapeless thing, like this Harlow thing, was just maddening to work.

And Linda looked at them, in the interrogation room that Thursday afternoon, and she looked like just what her pedigree said she was—raddled and tired with the hand-to-mouth living, picking up the johns, rolling the drunks, too many bottles and men and also, of course, the history of V.D. at the General Hospital. Her bleached blonde hair was lank, her skin flabby, and she looked ten years older than she was.

She said in a flat voice, "That guy. Foss said we shouldn't ought to keep the damn car. I guess that's how you dropped on us, huh? That guy—damn it, he wouldn't pass out, see? Never *saw* such a guy, I pick him up in a bar, he's riding a little high already, I think he's a good bet. He had a roll on him, I saw that. So I string him along, get him to a hotel, pretty soon he passes out and bingo, that's it. How it usually goes with a john. But damn it, he didn't pass out—just kept pourin' it down and pawin' at me—kept saying, come on, honey, have to love it up while you can—"

Hauck, who should have known better at his age.

"And so finally I get tired of it, see, and I go give Foss the sign. Sometimes the johns turn out hardheaded like that and you got to— So Foss comes in, he followed us to the hotel, been hangin' around, see, and goes to knock him out. They had a li'l fight but the guy's far enough gone then, it don't take much. So we got his roll, *and* spent it," said Linda reminiscently. "And now you damn cops—"

"Spoilsports," said Landers. "From way back, Linda. We don't like anybody to have a good time. You do know this all adds up to murder second?"

And she sat up abruptly and her voice went high and she said, "Murder? Murder? You don't tell me that guy's *dead?* Foss never meant—for God's sake—he's *dead?*"

CHAPTER 10

Landers typed up the last report on Chris Hauck, and as an after-thought, remembering what Palliser had said about the sister, hunted in Palliser's notes for the address and called Mrs. Roberts. . . . A funeral director had claimed Hauck's body on Tuesday and there had been a funeral yesterday. Mrs. Roberts thanked him; at least, she said, those people would be in prison awhile. "But I guess we've got to realize that if Chris hadn't been the kind—" She let that trail off, thanked him again. Landers signed the triplicate reports, separated them into envelopes and sat back and yawned.

He was supposed to be off tomorrow, but unless Palliser got back, and depending on what showed today, he'd probably be coming in.

The next thing was a call from the D.A.'s office; they were trying to speed up the court procedures, and now had Ed Hobart down for arraignment tomorrow morning. Which certainly meant that Landers would be in. Sergeant Lake went to tell Mendoza about that, and found him practicing the crooked deals, a cigarette in one corner of his mouth, talking to himself.

"I do not care, Jimmy," he said, "there was a reason on Harlow. A lunatic reason, but a reason of some kind. And all we can do is go over the same ground again and get nothing. *¡Condenación!* And damn it, a big building like that—people coming and going—it was just random luck, his luck, that nobody got a good look—that he got clean away— That Boggs woman— *¡Milrayos!*"

"Natural," said Lake. "That hour in the morning, a professional building like that—annoying, but natural, Lieutenant. Are you going out for lunch at all? It's one-thirty."

"Maybe. A wholesale slaughter—" Mendoza put the cards down; he might as well have some lunch. But as he yanked down his cuffs, straightened his tie, reached for his hat, Lake, back at the switchboard, put through an inside call.

"Fletcher, Traffic," he said. Mendoza swore and sat down again.

"Now we don't think this is anything for you yet, Luis," said Fletcher. "We hope to God it isn't. But I thought you'd better be alerted. There's two kids reported missing over on Elden Avenue. Single house. We don't know much yet, but I've got four cars over there now. First report is, the grandmother's babysitting them, missed them from the back yard about half an hour ago—"

"That's early for you to be agitating about it," said Mendoza inattentively, suddenly aware that he was starving. "Hardly the place for a snatch. And kids wander."

"They do," agreed Fletcher. "But the girl's sixteen months, the boy not three yet."

"Oh. Oh, my God, I see. But they could still—"

"We're looking. They couldn't have got far under their own steam. But it just could *be* something a little more serious. I'll let you know."

"Thanks so much." The kids had wandered down the block and were playing with other kids in a strange back yard. Or— But things did happen. Not nice things, sometimes. . . . And Harlow—Mendoza took up his hat and went out. He decided he was going through Dr. Harlow's records again, slow and careful. Hoping for the belated hunch. Because there was *some* answer on the Harlow shooting, and the irrational mind which had conceived the wholesale slaughter was not, could not be cunning enough—

But, thought Mendoza sardonically, pushing the button for the elevator, as an experienced cop he ought to know better than to go woolgathering like that. The real bastards to work and the cases that so frequently ended up in Pending were just the ones like the Harlow shooting. The shapeless ones with no handle to grasp, no lead pointing in any direction, nowhere to go to look for one. He hoped the Harlow shooting would not end up in Pending, but he wouldn't take any bets on it.

At one-fifty that Thursday afternoon, Patrick Henry Logan opened his eyes. He tried to turn his head, and the doctor beside the bed, holding his wrist, said quietly, "Speak to him, Mrs. Logan. His pulse is good—let's discontinue that I.V. for the moment, nurse."

"Pat? Pat darling—it's Sally, Pat, can you—"

Logan moved again weakly and got out her name on a little gasp. "Sally—"

"Oh, *Pat!*" She put down her head on the bed and began to cry.

"He'll do," said the doctor. "Keep him quiet. Please, Mrs. Logan—you're upsetting him—" Logan was trying to move, to lift his head; the nurse restrained him. Sally Logan sat up and wiped her eyes.

"I'm sorry, I'll— Pat darling, you're going to be all right—" And Royce was there, grinning down at him too. Logan's vague gaze wandered up to Royce's face and focused a little more clearly; and then, suddenly, it wasn't just a badly injured man lying in the hospital bed, but a cop—an LAPD officer.

"Royce," he said in a stronger voice. "Tell 'em—four kids—four young punks—never saw b'fore in my life—"

"We know, boy," said Royce gently. "We know. You relax and start getting well."

Landers and Piggott came back from their belated lunch at two-twenty, and found the picket drifting up Los Angeles Street just past the entrance to the parking lot.

"Children and fools," said Piggott. "Have you ever read any of Velikovsky? The *Worlds in Collision* fellow?"

"Yes, but I didn't think you would have, Matt."

"Oh, I may look dumb but sometimes I read more than *True Detective,* Tom. And you just can't prove that man's wrong, about all the catastrophes that have happened. We don't know how many times we've got to the top, with all the inventions and industries and airplanes and all, only using it for evil—so the Lord brings down the destruction. And isn't he right too when he says all those verses in the Bible were meant literally, about mountains overturning and the sea rising up and so on. We think we're so smart. We don't *know*."

"Yes, I think he's got something too. Plenty of geological evidence—" Landers put his hand on one of the double doors to the lobby, and the ground suddenly slid away under their feet and for ten seconds rolled uneasily under them. They felt the building move slightly.

"He did promise," said Piggott, "not to do it with a flood again. I don't know but what I'd prefer a flood."

They found the Homicide Bureau empty except for Lake. "Where's Jase? I haven't seen him since he fetched Linda and Sterry down to jail," said Landers.

Lake said he hadn't a clue. "The boss has vanished some place too." He was studying a paperback book, *The Doctor's Quick Weight-Loss Diet.*

"Goofing off," said Landers. "Nothing new gone down?"

"Not yet," said Lake.

There was no sign of any work crews replacing windows on this side of the building today; it was to be hoped they were on the other side, gradually working toward Homicide. Somebody had brought a thermometer into the detective office; it was on Palliser's desk, and right now it read ninety-seven. And whereas August was often a month of overcast gray skies and a little cooler air, preparing residents for the last hellish heat in September and October, this August of the earthquake was bright and sunny. The sun streamed through the glassless windows of Homicide cheerfully, and they could have done with less of it.

At three o'clock Lake buzzed them. "New one—call in from a doctor. Dr. Roger Stuyvesant. Direct to us, not Traffic—maybe he rode an ambulance awhile. He says he'll meet detectives there. It's Colyton Street over across the tracks."

They both went on it. They had a little hunt for it at that; it was a short street. It was one of the many narrow old streets down here on Central's beat, which was the oldest part of Los Angeles. The Los Angeles River meandered through part of that area, wandering into the city from the valley through a natural pass in the foothills. It was dry ten months of the year, but could be a menace in heavy rains, and the riverbed these days was encased in concrete walls forty feet high—an ugly trail through this part of town. Along the route of the riverbed ran the railroad tracks, converging on the great bare dirty expanse of the Southern Pacific yards, behind Union Station. Union Station was a handsome modern building, very clean-looking, very Californian, but away from Union Station with its tiled floors and mosaic walls there was the old and tired and shabby tangle of streets, the oldest in the city, the poorest now.

It was a street, when they found it, of little frame houses on narrow lots: houses older than the century, mostly. The one on the corner had been partly knocked down by the earthquake, and apparently abandoned. The one they wanted was in the middle of the block. No car stood before it; evidently Dr. Stuyvesant, whoever he might be, had farther to come.

It was a very shabby old house, very small, and it hadn't been painted for a long time, and what grass remained in the narrow front yard was brown. It had a narrow rickety front porch which shook under their feet, and an old-fashioned doorbell. The sagging front door was half open. Landers pushed the bell and it rang halfheartedly. He rapped on the door.

After a moment a faint quavery voice said, "Doctor—"

"Police officers, ma'am. Where—" The door opened direct on the living room, which was about ten by fourteen: a derelict sagging couch, a chair with torn upholstery, a thin strip of rug, a table with one lamp on it. There was a door opposite the front door, standing open; they went in there.

A bedroom, small and square and shabby: old brass bedstead, a straight chair, a chest of drawers, door to a tiny closet.

She was sitting in the chair beside the bed, an old woman, thin and bent, with white hair thin where pink scalp showed through. The sun streamed in a window curtained only with a torn dime-store shade.

"I called—the doctor," she said. "The doctor—at the hospital."

"He called us, ma'am. What's wrong here? You—" And then they both realized that the old man in the bed was dead. Landers went round to the other side and felt his neck; he was cold. He was a wizened, bald old man, and he wasn't wearing his false teeth, so his cheeks fell in like a death's-head. Landers looked around, saw on the makeshift bed table the old man's false teeth in a plastic dish, a used glass, a little paper box. He looked at that without touching it. It had a label: *Mrs. Mallory, 1 every 4 hours for pain.*

Behind them the door opened and footsteps sounded; they turned. "Police?" he said. "I'm Stuyvesant. In charge of the out-patient clinic at General—" He was a short, spare, competent-looking man in his fifties; right now he looked very shaken. He went across to the old woman and put his hand on her shoulder.

She had closed her eyes; at his touch she opened them and looked up at him. "Doctor," she said. "You do understand it, don't you? He was— so tired, poor Dan. The pain was so bad, Doctor. It was the last thing I could do for him, you see. The last thing. We'd been together for sixty-nine years, you see. Dan and I. I was seventeen when we were married and he was twenty."

"Mrs. Mallory—"

She reached up and laid her bony, distorted, shaking old hand over his square surgeon's hand on her shoulder. "A doctor should understand. That's a long time. I'm eighty-six, and Dan was eighty-nine, and I can remember—just as clear as anything could be—the day we were married. He had a good job on the railroad then. All his life he worked for the railroad. I don't know where the time went—I can recall so clear— but it passed by—and Dan was eighty-nine, and he was tired. You understand that, don't you?"

He freed his hand gently, came round the bed and bent over the body.

"Oh, he's gone, Doctor. I waited until I was sure. You doctors, you always fight so hard on the side of life—but there's no call be afraid of dying. Easier than living, it is, sometimes."

"He's been gone for hours," said Stuyvesant to Landers and Piggott. He picked up the glass and sniffed it.

"It's what you gave me for the pain," she said. "For the arthritis. There was a full box just yesterday, and I was almost sure it would—"

"Empirin Number Three," said Stuyvesant quietly to the Homicide men. "Codeine—not much, but enough for him, in an overdose. He had inoperable cancer—probably all through him."

"You see, Doctor, you've got to understand," she said. "Dan and I, we been helping each other for sixty-nine years—loving each other—we been together a long, long time. We hoped we'd have a family, but we never. Never any babies, and I didn't have any brothers or sisters, Dan had a brother but he died years back, and he hadn't any family either. There wasn't anybody. Just Dan and me. We were so proud when we finished paying for the house—that was thirty-nine years ago—twelve hundred dollars it cost and it took us a long time to save. But I was always a good manager. Dan earned steady—not much but steady. He always gave an honest day's work for an honest day's pay."

"Mrs. Mallory—you shouldn't stay—let me—"

"It's not much but it was ours. Only—things change. With the time going by." She looked at the dead man tenderly, smiling. "The pension wasn't much, but we made do. Dan went on the pension twenty-four years back. We made do. But since the arthritis got so bad, it's hard to do things, just get up a meal, wash the dishes. Dan helped me—we always helped each other, we never asked help from anybody else, never been on welfare. But it was hard. And Dan—was so—tired."

"Yes," he said steadily, gently. "I know he was."

"He begged me to help him. He said he was just so tired, and the pain so bad. Ellen, help me, he said. Help me to go. And it was the last thing I could do for him—I thought those pills would do it. I gave them all to him, and—I waited—until I was sure—before I called you, Doctor." She swayed a little.

"My God, my God," said the doctor. He turned to Landers. "We'll want an ambulance—there's no phone here, if you'd— My God. She's not fit to be alone, and"—he gestured helplessly—"to *prosecute* her—for— My good God."

And Piggott said softly, unexpectedly, *"For love is strong as death,* doesn't it say."

"I remember so clear," she said. "So clear. The minister said, *in sickness and in health. Cleaving only to one another*— And I just don't know how the time slipped by. But Dan—I'd always do whatever I could to help Dan, whatever he asked me to—and it was the last way I could help him. He was so tired—"

Landers didn't know where the nearest phone might be. He went out —have to go back to the office, or—and as luck had it, a black-and-white was just cruising past the corner up there; he shouted, and it came bucketing up. He had his badge in his hand, and reached in for the mike.

At about the same moment, John Palliser was standing by the side of a very empty road fifteen miles outside of Bakersfield, with Tim Brodie and burly, genial Sheriff Roudebush and a couple of deputies with the unlikely names of Forbear and Clearwater.

"Well, gee, it sort of looks like the place," said Brodie, "but I ain't just sure—"

"It's not," said Clearwater, and spat aside. "No body. Are you sure it *was* a body?"

"Oh, he was dead. He was dead, sure. That I do know, I was awful surprised—I didn't go to kill him, I was just mad because he'd been pawing at Wilma. I just hit him a couple times, and he hit me, and then I hit him and he fell down and— Oh, he was dead. I guess he hit his head on a rock when he fell down—it felt funny, all soft. He was dead. But this isn't the place, come to think, because there was a steeper shoulder on the road—I nearly slipped, gettin' him down it—"

Palliser and Roudebush looked at each other. They had been driving all around the roads outside of town since eight o'clock this morning, and this was the twentieth spot Brodie had said looked something like the place they had left Steve's body.

Roudebush, who somewhat resembled a large and amiable Saint Bernard, dropped his cigarette and stepped on it. "Now think, Tim," he said patiently. "You said it wasn't the main highway."

"No, on account of I got lost. We stopped at a place for hamburgers, and then I got lost—I don't know this part of the country, never been here before."

"All right. You don't remember any signs? Road signs? You don't remember the name of the place you stopped to eat?"

Tim thought. "It was just a little place along the road. It had a long counter, and stools. No booths. The hamburgers were fifty-five cents, and Wilma wanted a malt too, but we only had just forty dollars and I told her—"

Roudebush scratched his cheek. "No booths. Well, a lot of places like that—you drove through town first? Bakersfield?"

"Yessir, I see the sign—NOW ENTERING BAKERSFIELD. We were through town and there was just a couple real-estate places and billboards and then Wilma said she was hungry and pretty soon we come to this place, it said EATS on a big sign. Oh, and the waitress had red hair," said Tim. "I remember that."

Roudebush said to Palliser, "Marge Leatherhead at Barney's place. Possibly. We can go and ask if she remembers him."

They got into the car again. "I'm sorry," said Tim. "I never been in this part of the country before."

Palliser wondered how the boys were doing down at home, on what. If Hauck's car had turned up, and Linda and Sterry. If anything new had turned up. If they'd got any leads on Harlow. Well, that sort of shapeless thing so often did wind up in Pending. . . .

"Little change for you, Sergeant," said Roudebush as he shifted into high.

"Oh, that you can say, Sheriff. Out in the wilds, wandering around hunting a body. And if this was the place they stopped for hamburgers, does it help pinpoint the body at all?"

"How about it?" asked Forbear in the back seat with Clearwater and Brodie. "How long after the hamburgers did you have your fight with Steve?"

"Oh, gee, I don't know. A while. About half an hour, little longer maybe. See, I was driving, it wasn't till Wilma said, Make him stop doing that, I saw what he was up to—"

"We've got," said Roudebush to Palliser, "quite a lot of country up here to look at."

"I see you have. We've seen quite a lot of it already. I just wish," said Palliser, "we could be sure there is a body to find. Because—"

"Oh, he was dead, sir," said Brodie. "Listen, I used to help butcher— I'd know. He was dead. I was so surprised he was. Oh, I just remembered, there was some bushes around there—it wasn't farm land, just empty land, wild, you know, and there was these bushes with a lot of yellow flowers on them."

"About two feet high?" said Clearwater.

"Yeah, about—"

"Wild mustard," said Roudebush. "There's quite a lot of it around, wild on uncultivated land."

Palliser began to wonder when he'd see L.A. again. And Roberta.

Well, at least up here he wasn't feeling the aftershocks and wondering when the next big quake was coming.

He wondered if Homicide had got new windows installed yet.

Grace came into the office as Landers and Piggott arrived back from the General Hospital. "And where have you been?" asked Landers.

"None of your business," said Grace amiably. He was looking pleased with himself. "Anything new?"

Piggott said, "The lieutenant talking about love, the other day. A dangerous commodity, he said. Those two poor old souls—there but for the grace of God, do we say? I'll do the report, Tom. You look shook."

Landers was feeling that way. And he thought suddenly, he must tell Phil about this one, tomorrow night. A thing like that made you think. And just as suddenly he remembered another quote from Holy Writ— *man not meant to live alone.* . . .

"A thing, Jase," he said soberly. "One of the things we see that makes you think, that's all." Stuyvesant had taken charge, bundled the old lady off to the hospital, sent the body to the morgue; he said he'd be in to make the necessary statement. Stuyvesant had been shook too. Landers started to tell Grace about it, and Grace listened, brushing his moustache absently.

"And you can't feel the old lady'll come in for the Lord's displeasure, Tom," he said gently. "What do we do about it?"

"What the hell, Jase? I don't know. Ask the lieutenant. The D.A. The old lady living on borrowed time—the arthritis—do we charge her with murder second and trust she'll live to stand trial?" Landers made an angry gesture.

"I don't somehow think so, Tom. I kind of think," said Grace, still absently, "I'd like to call my wife. . . ." He went to his desk, swiveled around in the chair so his back was to them, and dialed. Piggott was busy over the report, and Landers didn't try to hear what Grace was saying in his soft voice.

"Well, they were a little surprised, but I was persistent, and—"

"Did they *say*—"

"Well, you know how cautious those people are, hon. All the red tape. The rules and regulations."

"But, Jase, did they *say* it might be?"

"Mostly the doubletalk. But I went on prodding at them, and by what I got, it's possible—if we keep right after it. I called Dad—he'd know something about how the rules work—and he's all for it. He said if he could help any way he will. What I gather, we might have an edge—after all I am a very upright fellow, Ginny, LAPD officer with a clean record—and when we can show, or rather they can prove, there aren't any—"

"Oh, Jase! Oh, if it does work out—" Virginia was excited.

"You hold your horses, it might take a while, all the red tape—"

"But if we *can!* Oh, Jase, it's got to work out! After the way you said, the guardian angel—"

"We'll have a hell of a good try, Ginny," said Grace. "We will."

Mrs. Candace Pine looked at Mendoza with a troubled expression. She wasn't a pretty woman, but kind-faced and friendly, a dark-brown woman with a round undistinguished face, a figure a little too plump, a warm deep voice. Her living room in the house beside the colonial house the Harlows had lived in was well furnished in early American, and Mrs. Pine was modestly clad in a long blue cotton housecoat.

She apologized again for not being dressed; she had been about to wash her hair. "I wish I could think of a thing to tell you, Lieutenant, but I just can't. Anything more. I see what you mean, about whoever did it having *some* sort of reason, just a crazy one but a reason. . . . It's just a thing you can't believe, somebody killing John and Ann and John's nurse—I'd never met her, of course—but I see that, when you say it. Only there couldn't be any reason—even for a crazy man!"

"It could be—probably was," said Mendoza, "something very trivial. Something nobody else thought twice about. Just think, Mrs. Pine. Anything, anything at all, Mrs. Harlow having an argument with someone—or Dr. Harlow—"

She was shaking her head. "They were a nice quiet couple. There wasn't anything like— And that poor baby! They'd just been in seventh heaven about that baby, Lieutenant—married so long, and not really hoping any more, and then the baby. And my husband and I—well, we talked about it, but we've got our own four and we just couldn't afford—we can hope, maybe some nice people—"

Mendoza offered her a cigarette and she said she didn't smoke. "But you go right ahead—I'll get you an ashtray—" Evidently the husband didn't smoke either; the ashtray was about two inches square, dime-store variety.

"Anything," he said. "Anything, however trivial, an argument about wrong change, about—"

And she started to shake her head again, and said, "Well, my goodness, I just thought of *that!* And it sounds just silly to tell you—but you saying— Well, they'd just, I mean Ann had just fired the gardener they had. Just last week."

"*Hagar sus apuntas,*" said Mendoza softly. "Stakes down and wait for the throw. . . . She had?"

"But a gardener—just silly. They just hired him to cut the lawn once a week, do the weeding—Ann did all the rest, she loved gardening, I told the other officer, always out fussing round her flowers. Feeding and mulching and all that— What? No, I don't know his name. My husband cuts our lawn on Sundays, and we haven't much planting to take care of, just the shrubs in front. Ann told me he turned up that day—he came on Tuesdays—drunk as a lord, and used, you know, offensive language— so she told him— Well, I think the Ashmans down the street hire him too. They might know—"

Jackpot? Mendoza wondered. It was very likely some slight motive behind the Harlow shooting, they'd thought that from the start, by experience.

He found Mrs. Ashman home and she told him they hadn't heard about Mrs. Harlow firing the gardener. They'd been terribly shocked by the Harlows' murder; hadn't known them except by name, but they'd seemed like nice people. Her husband was a physical therapist at the French Hospital. They'd employed the gardener—she thought he had several jobs right around here, coming once a week to cut lawns—ever since they'd lived here, seven years. His name—they paid him by check— was Sam Oliver, and she had his phone number, not his address. He had his own pickup truck, with his name and *Gardening Service* on it, so it was his regular job.

Heading back to the office at four-forty, Mendoza idly noted the headlines, stopped at a traffic light: *Aftershocks Number Hundreds, Greatest 4.3 on Richter Scale.*

He hoped to God they'd get new windows soon. And their air conditioning turned on.

In the Homicide Bureau he found Landers, Piggott and Grace exchanging small talk, and got on the phone to Information. Within ten minutes he got Sam Oliver's address—Bonsallo Avenue—and went across to the detective office.

"Goofing off," he said. "We've got a new lead on Harlow—a very small lead, but we never do know what might show up. Let's go and ask questions." He told them about the gardener.

"But my God, a little thing like that," said Landers. "And if he is a drunk, well, whoever shot up that office was shooting straight enough—"

"Even habitual drunks," said Mendoza, "are not drunk twenty-four hours a day. And in confined quarters such as Harlow's office, even the .22 can be lethal in amateur hands. As this one was, drunk or amateur or whatever."

"Oh, it's a lead," agreed Landers. He looked at his watch. Leave it for the night watch? The inside phone rang on Hackett's empty desk and Mendoza picked it up.

"Mendoza."

"Fletcher. I said I'd let you know. Now we know. Incredible as it is. The missing kids."

"Yes?" Fletcher's voice held some indefinable emotion.

"Gary Hildebrand, thirty-three months. Stella Hildebrand, sixteen months. Mother Alice works as a waitress, cafeteria downtown. They live with her mother—Alice is divorced, mother takes care of the kids. The kids went missing from the back yard about two-thirty, nearest we can pin it down."

"So?"

"So—" Fletcher uttered a little incredulous growl. "We've had patrolmen out looking. That area, no swimming pools, but empty garages and so on— But we just found them. And it's your baby, Luis."

"¿Cómo dice? You don't mean—"

"Behind a billboard in an empty lot about six blocks from the house. Both strangled. No evidence of sexual interference—just strangled, and left."

"¡Diez demonios desde el infierno!" said Mendoza.

CHAPTER 11

They all went out on that, and Mendoza called Hackett and Higgins in. Dr. Bainbridge came out to look at this one from the start, and the same thought was in the mind of every man there, looking at the two small bodies in the tangled growth of weeds behind the billboard. It wouldn't have taken much—the little pressure, the little strength put out —to snuff out those little lives. Lives hardly begun, so very fragile.

Bainbridge looked sick as he stood up. "Just strangled," he said, and then put their thoughts in words. "It wouldn't take much—and no evidence of any molestation—"

This was a thing to get on, and the kind of thing that made legwork. Mendoza, Hackett and Higgins went to the house on Elden Avenue to get some background. They knew approximately when the children were discovered missing, and what they'd been wearing; the rest of them started to ring doorbells and question neighbors.

At the Elden Avenue house they found that the grandmother, Mrs. Ella Pace, had broken down and been given a sedative; but the Traffic men had the gist of her statements earlier this afternoon. "Says she checked on them often, kids that young, but they were good about staying in the yard. Besides, it's fenced—" This was an old frame bungalow, but well enough kept up, trim newly painted; and there was a three-foot-high redwood fence completely enclosing the back yard. "And the latch is stiff, she doesn't think the boy could have unfastened it. Certainly the baby couldn't. She told us the longest time she left them without checking was just before she missed them—maybe half an hour between two and two-thirty. She was making a pie or something."

Now they knew the children had been taken away. The house was on a corner, the sandbox the children had been playing in at the end of the yard; it would have been relatively easy for anybody to call the children over, lift them over the fence. Why, and who?

"The nut," said Hackett angrily, unconsciously balling his fists. "The violent nut. But a *sixteen*-month-old, Luis, for God's sake—" Hackett's own Sheila wasn't much older. And Higgins said the same thing.

"It's early to say," said Mendoza. "I want some background."

They found the mother, Alice Hildebrand, perhaps still numb and not quite believing, queerly calm and readily answering questions. "I don't suppose I've taken it in yet," she told them. She was in her late twenties, a nice-looking young woman if not exactly pretty, with ash-brown hair and blue eyes; she wore glasses and kept pushing them up on her nose in habitual gesture. "I just can't realize—Mother's always good and careful with them—I have to work, you see, I work downtown —Mother's just got Dad's pension and of course the children—"

"Your husband, Mrs. Hildebrand?" asked Mendoza.

"He's—we're divorced. I didn't like to do that, I don't—don't approve of divorce, I put up with him a long time, but I couldn't—never holding a job long and drinking and all—I finally divorced him— What?" She turned unfocused eyes on Hackett.

"Do you think he could have anything to do with this?"

"Henry? Oh, of course not. He didn't—he hardly knew the children were *there*. He didn't care about them—any way. No, that's—"

"But does he live here in town?"

"I don't know where he is. I divorced him last May. I don't know if he's here. The judge said, child support, but he never—"

"I realize the children were young, too young maybe to recognize— but did the boy ever report some adult speaking to him over the fence, or—"

She shook her head blindly. "I don't know. He isn't three yet, he wouldn't—and it'd go right out of his head if anybody had, he wouldn't—"

"Can you think of anyone, Mrs. Hildebrand, anyone who might want to harm you or the children for any reason?"

She shook her head again. "That's silly—I'm sorry, but it is. Who would? I'm—an ordinary person, we're ordinary people. *Enemies*—silly. And to hurt the *children*—I go to work and back, I don't have trouble with people, get along with everybody all right—the biggest trouble I ever had my whole life was with Henry, and I've been upset about that yet—I didn't like to divorce him, but I could see it was no good going on. I never thought I'd be divorcing my own husband, but I guess, well, I just didn't know him good enough when I married him. How he was. He left me when he knew I was pregnant again, you know—he's never seen Stella at all. I been living here with Mother ever since, two years about."

"Do you have any men friends, Mrs. Hildebrand, who would know the children?" Mendoza was watching her.

She blew her nose. "Not to—no, not really. There's Frank Fosser where I work, he's the chef—a nice fellow, I guess, he's always been respectful, treated me like a lady—he's asked me to go out with him and I did once. And Burt Fowler, he lives up the block, I've known him years, and he's asked me to marry him. But I couldn't decide anything like that yet, I was still all upside-down in my mind like about divorcing Henry. I got to where I wasn't sleeping, the doctor gave me some pills—it just upset me so, I don't approve of divorce. I guess Burt's all right—I used to go with him some, we went to high school together, he's got a good job with the telephone company—but I been still so all which way about the divorce, I couldn't think of that. Anybody else. And besides, nobody we *know* would do such a thing—such an awful—" Suddenly she put her hands to her face and began to cry.

"The hunch hit you out of the blue?" asked Higgins on the sidewalk outside the house. "You asking about the husband, boy-friends? Ten to one it's the random pervert, Luis. Coming by, spotting the kids. We know that kind don't always go in for the sexual hijinks—sometimes the act of killing is enough."

"*Sé,*" said Mendoza, brushing his moustache back and forth. "In broad daylight, George, on a residential street? I don't know if it's a hunch, but I think—just as I've been saying on Harlow—the victims were picked *as* victims. Why—" He shrugged.

In any case, there was only one way to go at it. They started ringing doorbells. Had anybody seen the children that afternoon? With or without an adult? Had any stranger been seen in the neighborhood, acting peculiarly or not? All the indicated questions, and not only around the Elden Avenue neighborhood but six blocks away, around the empty lot where the children had been found. It was an area to cover; they wouldn't finish it tonight.

Higgins, ringing doorbells, was over on Magnolia, the next street behind Elden; he looked at his watch as he rang the doorbell of the house that backed up to Mrs. Pace's house. Mendoza had said, work it until ten; this was a working-class neighborhood and people waked from bed wouldn't feel cooperative toward cops. This would be his last call.

Their name was Fanchon, and like everybody else the Homicide men had talked to tonight, they were horrified about the children and eager to try to help. But they hadn't seen anything—both the younger Fanchons worked and Mrs. Fanchon's mother, who lived with them— "I wonder if she noticed anything, Bob. But I don't suppose—she left this afternoon, Sergeant, she's going to visit her sister in San Diego over the weekend. She was taking the Greyhound at three o'clock, from downtown—"

"Then she'd probably left before the children were missing. Well, thanks," said Higgins.

Schenke and Galeano had turned out too; and they all forgathered back at the office to sort out what they had. "Not a Goddamned thing!" said Hackett savagely. He looked rather sinister, the black eye just nicely developed. Both Higgins and Mendoza needed a shave, and Landers didn't look quite so boyish as usual, his eyes blistered and tired. Jason Grace was furiously brushing his moustache. "Nobody saw the kids—nobody noticed anything or anybody near the house—nobody—"

"There's the car," said Landers. "The car noticed parked—evidently not for long—in the street right by that lot. The retired postman noticed it, from the house the other side of the lot. Noticed it because it's illegal to park there, and it wasn't there long. A white car like a Dodge or a Buick."

"All *right*," said Higgins. "Absolutely nothing says it had one damned thing to do with— And how the hell do we look for it?"

"*Paciencia*," said Mendoza. "It's a first little something. Go home to bed, boys—we'll see what turns up tomorrow. Which is also a day." He got up wearily.

"Nothing," said Hackett. "Nothing will—it's another shapeless, handleless thing like Harlow—another lunatic—"

"*No sé*," said Mendoza. "Go home. There were people not home we didn't talk to. The witness may turn up yet. I'll see you in the morning."

He went home, and the garage and house lights were on for him, and the mockingbird produced a sleepy *Yankee Doodle came* before going back to sleep. In the kitchen, Mrs. MacTaggart inquired severely if he'd had dinner at all, and Alison came, hastily tying a robe.

"We heard it on the news, Luis—what an *awful*—you can't believe a thing like that. Did you find—"

"*Nada*," said Mendoza, kissing her. "I had a sandwich, Máiri. I'm O.K. Maybe tomorrow we'll get a lead." Cedric came up waggling his hind end in greeting.

"You'll be having a dram and another sandwich before you go to your bed," said Mrs. MacTaggart determinedly. And El Señor was officially retired with his mother and sisters at the foot of the king-size bed, but he could hear any word pertaining to whiskey through the walls, and appeared shortly demanding his share.

Mendoza said, "I won't say no to either," and stripped off his jacket.

Hackett went home and before answering Angel's questions went to look at Sheila, pinkly asleep in her crib. She was going to have a hint of red in her hair, like his mother, and a good thing she'd got Angel's eyes. . . . "Sixteen months!" he said to Angel. "What kind of a— And Luis's got a bee in his bonnet. The personal motive. I ask you—impossible enough to imagine even the random pervert, but—"

"He feels things," said Angel thoughtfully. She was sitting up in bed, the big smoke-silver Persian curled asleep on Hackett's side. "Does he think that? Queer—but he does feel things, Art. What's the family like? Those poor little things—and what the mother—"

Hackett told her all they knew while he undressed.

Higgins went home and found Mary reading a detective novel. "Did you find anything? That terrible— Well, it's a lot neater in books," she said wryly, putting the book down. "A lot less— But who would do such a—"

"Babies," said Higgins. "My God, just babies, Mary. And Luis had a damned senseless hunch. Something personal—somebody they know. With all the perverts around, we need to get as offbeat as that?"

"Did he? Well, he gets the hunches, you say," said Mary. "Wait to see, George." She sighed, and looking down at herself added, "Babies . . . I'm getting a little tired of this one where it is. And all my size-fourteen clothes gathering dust. . . . You're shook on account of the baby, George."

"This thing is enough to shake anybody," said Higgins.

On Friday morning there was more of the legwork to do on that, and other things as well. There was Rhoda Fleming; there was Hobart's arraignment; and an initial report had to be written on the Hildebrand case. Higgins stayed to do that, and pick up Hobart for his court appearance at ten o'clock. Piggott and Landers took over the Fleming case, and all the rest of them went out to finish up the legwork on the Hildebrand thing.

Landers had called Stuyvesant, who had yet to make a statement on the Mallory case yesterday; he could come by and dictate it to Lake. He told them that Mrs. Mallory had had a massive stroke in the ambulance and wasn't expected to live. They started out for Sunland in Piggott's Chevy feeling rather depressed about things in general.

"Of course it's just as well, poor old soul," said Piggott. And Landers, agreeing, didn't say anything else because he was feeling depressed. He'd been surprised that Piggott had read Velikovsky, and some other time he'd like to exchange more opinions with him; this morning, thinking about those kids, about the Mallorys, he felt a little gloomy and untalkative.

Nobody had yet talked to Rose Scott, Rhoda Fleming's daughter. They found the house, a modern split-level in the hills, and introduced themselves. "Oh—" she said, and began to cry. "Ab-about Mother—oh, I'm sorry, I'll try to—" She hiccuped, wiped her eyes, and added unnecessarily, "There's the baby—excuse me—sit down, I'll—"

They waited in the neat, conventionally furnished modern living room. They had both seen Palliser's notes incorporating Mendoza's little ideas on this. Piggott said, "She seems to be a nice girl."

"Um-hum," said Landers. "Everybody said Mama was too. But the lieutenant does see things, Matt."

"No denying."

She came back with the baby, quite a new baby, silent now, bald and pink in a blue blanket. "I'm sorry—I know there are questions you want to ask, Gavin said—" She sat down opposite them. "But I can't tell you anything. It must have been a burglar—breaking in and—"

"Well, the door wasn't forced, Mrs. Scott," said Landers.

"But nobody Mother *knew* would do such a thing!" She looked at them wildly, automatically jiggling the baby. She was a pretty dark girl, not more than twenty-three or -four, fresh complexion and big dark eyes, a nice figure in a bare-shouldered yellow sundress. "And—and she didn't know many people—she—"

"Just tell us about that, Mrs. Scott," said Piggott persuasively. "About, say, your mother's routine. She worked at this shop in Hollywood—"

"That's right. Daddy left her some stock, but not an awful lot to live on, the way prices—well, she could live on it but she was—she was still well and she liked to be busy, she liked the job— What? I don't know about Mrs. Elsberry, she owns the shop, Mother just said she was nice— I think she knew the other woman there better, Mrs. Weems."

"Weems?"

"Yes, it's a funny name, but she was about Mother's age and they

were friendly. Just casual, I guess. Well, Mother'd be at the shop nine
to five every day, and then she'd—well, go home. The apartment. I—we
didn't get in to see her often, I was sorry, but living up here—I didn't
think, I guess, when we moved up here. It's nearer for Gavin to drive to
work. But he gets some overtime, and on Sunday there's the yard to
take care of—and Mother didn't drive, you know. Ab-about once a
month or so we'd try to drive in, take her to dinner or—but with the
baby—" She blinked wetly at them. "Oh, I knew she was lonely—I
should have tried to make time, see her oftener—"

"It's easy to blame yourself after something like this happens, Mrs.
Scott," said Landers.

"But I should have! Daddy's been dead four years—they used to go
out a lot, you see. They liked the theater, and dancing sometimes, and
nice restaurants—of course there was more money then too, for things
like that. I didn't *think,* and I should have—how lonely it was for her,
with me married to Gavin and away up here— Of course there were
people, other couples, they'd known, but a woman alone doesn't get invited out much, and with her not driving—"

"Mrs. Scott, did your mother wear a ring on her right hand usually?"

"Why, yes. Her big diamond. Daddy gave it to her on their twentieth
anniversary. Describe— Well, it's got quite a big diamond in the middle,
a little over a carat, I think, and two smaller ones each side. It's yellow
gold, fourteen karat. I wouldn't know what it'd be worth, why, is it—
It's *gone?* Well, that's what I said—a burglar breaking in and—"

"Maybe and maybe not," said Landers.

There was also, of course, the gardener—Sam Oliver on Bonsallo Avenue. Fired by Mrs. Harlow last week. Things came along in a spate
sometimes; they'd get to Sam Oliver eventually.

Today they were looking for leads to the X who had strangled the
children. They didn't find any. Except for the very nebulous white car
parked briefly alongside that empty lot. Nobody they talked to had seen
anything to indicate a lead. It might have been a ghost who had taken
the Hildebrand children away and strangled them. But the Homicide
men didn't believe in that kind of ghost, and they went on asking their
questions doggedly.

They were, of course, a man short, because Palliser was still up there
in the wilds.

Marge Leatherhead at Barney's place didn't remember if Tim Brodie
had been in or not. "You don't notice faces unless they're people you

know," she said. Barney's place was on a secondary road about eighteen miles out of town, and most of the people coming in were locals
She couldn't say one way or the other about Tim.

He said he was sure this was the place, all right. He remembered her,
the redhaired waitress. He thought he'd started down this same road
after they'd had the hamburgers, but then he'd got lost. . . . "See, I was
lookin' for some sign, tell me where we was, reason I didn't wake up to
what Steve was up to right off—him and Wilma was in the back seat—til
Wilma yelled. I think I turned off somewhere, off that road, before—i
sort of curved and I thought it was the same road but awhile later it'
narrower and, you know, not a main drag, so—"

Palliser and Roudebush sighed. Unusual for August, it was overcas
and gray today, the sky even promising showers; once in a long while
Southern California got showers in August; up here, this much farthe
north, it wouldn't be as unusual. They were now driving slowly along a
narrow country blacktop road with wild land on one side and a fine
crop of sugar beets in the fields on the other, and Clearwater asked pa
tiently, "This look familiar?"

"Well, kinda," said Brodie, "but, gee, a lot of places around her
look the same. Just fields, and empty land, and trees and road. I
mighta been this road—but before I had the fight with Steve I'd turne
back on a better road, you know—a cement road."

"Right or left?"

Brodie thought and finally decided. "Left."

"Take the next cutoff toward Caliente," said Sheriff Roudebush
"We're showing you a lot of country, Sergeant."

"And I've got to agree with Tim," said Palliser. "It all looks an awfu
lot alike, Sheriff."

Before they got to the little town of Caliente it began to rain in
halfhearted sort of way. Roudebush parked on the one main street an
said, "Jim, you can drive awhile." He got into the back seat wit
Brodie. "You go through any towns after you left Bakersfield?"

"No, sir. No, I'm sure of that. I got off the main road some way,
was lookin' for some sign to say where I was, and then I found on
some better but still not a main drag—"

Roudebush grunted and opened the map, passing it over the seat t
Palliser. There were plenty of little towns around Bakersfield, some o
the main highway, some not; and enough secondary roads wanderin
around.

"Damn it, it's annoying, but you can't blame him," said Palliser, an
looking out at the dispirited gray landscape added, "A lot of the place

we've tried do look the hell of a lot alike—to anybody there just once."

"Granted," said Roudebush. "Jim, head southwest out of town and let's try that secondary road toward Arvin. There's a blacktop cuts into it somewhere, past the Youngblood ranch, I think."

With a martyred sigh Clearwater started the engine.

"But, gee, it all looks different in the rain," said Brodie. "It was a nice sunny day last Sunday—I wouldn't say I *would* know the place, all gray and foggy—"

"Now, Jim," said Roudebush, "that kind of language I don't like."

"That's a pity, Sheriff," said Palliser. "I could think of something even stronger."

The legwork, on a thing like the Hildebrand case, took time. Time and patience. They had to go back to find people not home the first time; they had to listen to a lot of irrelevant comment and speculation before they got answers. But by four o'clock on Friday Grace had covered his stint at that legwork, and ran out of doorbells to ring. He went back to thinking about the Harlow shooting.

He used the rest of the day to look at Sam Oliver, the gardener.

Sam Oliver he ran to earth at a gardening job in Hollywood, trudging back and forth behind a power mower. The pickup truck sat at the curb. He was a broad, very black man about thirty, and he eyed Grace belligerently and snarled at the badge.

"Fuzz!" he said, and spat. "What you want, pig?"

Grace, who had a well-developed sense of humor, reflected pleasedly on those enterprising cops in Inglewood—of course others elsewhere promoting it, it was spreading nationwide—who had had the inspiration to capitalize on that. It was, of course, the best way to neutralize the not-so-subtle attack, turn it into a joke. The T-shirts for off-duty wear, with the fat pink pig and *Pigs is Beautiful* legend; the cuff links with the handsome gold pig, the tie-clasps, and the watches with the pig in blue uniform, arms pointing the hour, and that very appropriate legend PRIDE INTEGRITY GUTS—Virginia had got him one for his birthday and he was, in fact, wearing it now. Make a joke of it, and more power to the inspired cops earning a little extra money on the side wholesaling all that. He touched the watch on his wrist, and he thought, *sticks and stones*— And that newer motto made even more sense, *pride integrity*—

"Now, Sam," he said gently, "just a few answers."

Oliver supplied them sullenly. Yeah, he had a lot of jobs like that, come once a week, cut the lawn, weed the beds—an hour or so each place, twenty bucks a month. Maybe six, eight places a day, it added up. So it did. To, Grace reflected, a lot of drinking money—only Oliver wouldn't hold the jobs long if he showed up drunk.

He was truculent about Mrs. Harlow. "She didn't have no call to fire me! I'd had a few, sure, O.K., I had, that day. It was—lessee—it was a week ago Tuesday, I'm due their place about two but I—" He looked at Grace from under heavy brows. "I, uh, been to a li'l party, thass all. Over lunch. See, this pal o' mine, Eddy Starr, he—his woman just had a kid, he's like celebratin'. Invite ever'body drop in, have a drink, like. So all right—I wasn't exactly *drunk,* she hadn't no call—look down her nose at me like she's a queen or somethin', sayin' *disgraceful*— Listen, she's black too, ain't she? She got no call do that—"

"So, let's hear about last Monday, Sam," said Grace. So convenient, he thought, if you could put people into slots like that. Unfortunately, human nature—both the good and the bad about it—didn't fit into the slots. Colorwise or any other way.

"Jeez sake, I don't hafta tell you—Goddamn pig! What about las' Monday—"

Grace persevered and got answers. He went out to check them; and at ten past six he caught Mendoza just leaving the office and presented his findings.

"*¿Cómo?*" said Mendoza. "Now that sounds interesting, Jase." He put down his hat and sat down again. "Details, *por favor.*"

"Some interesting details," said Grace. "Sam Oliver has a regular job cutting the lawn, weeding the flower beds, once a week on Mondays, at the Starks' house in Hollywood. Raeburn Way. He usually gets there about nine o'clock Monday mornings, is there about an hour. He then usually goes to the Petersens' house on Shadow Lawn Avenue, also Hollywood, from ten to eleven or so. Only last Monday he was late to the Petersens'. Didn't get there until around noon. Mrs. Petersen was sure, because it was the day he got paid, and she waited to give him his check—it delayed her shopping trip." Grace contemplated his cigarette.

"*¡Qué mono!*" said Mendoza. "Isn't that pretty."

"I kind of thought so. We might look at him a little closer, you think?"

"Such as does he have access to a Harrington and Richardson nine-shot .22? Yes. Yes, indeed," said Mendoza. "When you consider it, that is exactly the kind of irrational slight motive— On the other hand, there is the fact that it was Mrs. Harlow who fired him. The doctor wouldn't have been home."

"What?—oh," said Grace. "Oh."

"Whoever perpetrated the wholesale slaughter, it was at Harlow's office. The fact that Mrs. Harlow—and the baby—were there at the time was unplanned, fortuitous, and couldn't have been known to X beforehand. Sam Oliver, if he was nourishing a grudge, was doing so on Ann Harlow. If he got to feeling vengeful enough to go out with a gun, wouldn't it have been to the Harlow house, not the doctor's office?"

"I wonder," said Grace. "That kind—there is a kind of prejudice in reverse, can we call it. Resentment, on the part of the ones like Oliver, against the people like the Harlows—educated, successful people with the nice house and— I don't know. I just thought it was suggestive."

"In spades," said Mendoza. "I think we get a search warrant, just for fun, and look harder at Oliver. And this damned Hildebrand thing—just nothing showing. *Nada absolutamente.* You would think—in broad daylight—"

"So you would," said Grace. "And we've covered about every place in both neighborhoods."

"Tomorrow—"

But as they started for the door—Sergeant Lake already departed, this phone recirculated to the desk downstairs until the night watch came on —Landers and Piggott erupted through it, and Landers said, "Oh, you're still here—and you'll never *believe* this one, *I* don't believe it— but it came up, and we were interested enough to go look, and—"

"Satan converting whom he can," said Piggott. "The things we see. And that poor innocent daughter in for quite a shock."

They had been deflected off the Fleming case when they checked back with the office, by a hit-run out on Beverly, and then a call from a pigeon on that Al Koonz. The A.P.B. out on Koonz hadn't turned up a smell yet. The pigeon said he was at a pool hall on Third Street right now, so Piggott and Landers went to pick him up. He made a little trouble, and Landers was now sporting the beginning of a fine shiner. They'd brought him in and questioned him, and he had reluctantly agreed that he had loaned Eddy Hobart the gun—well, he knew he wasn't supposed to have a gun, on P.A., but this other pal of his had been holding it for him, and—

They had got his statement after lunch, and then taken him over to the jail on Alameda. He'd go right back to Quentin to finish out his sentence, but in the meantime of course there was that gun, the beat-up old Colt. So they had gone looking for Koonz's other pal, whose name also appeared in their records, and finally found him in the tenth bar they'd tried within a radius of his rented room. They had got the Colt. Landers had typed a report on all that; it was a minor charge, but a charge all the same and had to be followed up. And then they had gone back to the apartment building where Mrs. Fleming had lived.

"There were a few tenants who hadn't been questioned yet, you know," said Landers. (He'd enjoy telling Phil about this—he glanced at his watch—have to hurry, shower and shave again before picking her up; but she'd understand if he was late. A fellow officer—the endless human nature they ran into, she'd laugh over this one.) "We talked to this Mrs. McCloskey just an hour ago—I swear to God, *people!* The daughter gave us the clue, if we'd been bright enough to pick it up. Mama must have been lonely. But I swear, you'd think anybody would have better sense. The people where she worked, the gift shop, didn't know her well —said, ordinary nice woman, to work and home, the quiet life—"

"Until we came to Mrs. McCloskey," said Piggott. "And there'll be some more legwork tomorrow—"

"*¡Dios me libre!*" said Mendoza. "What showed?"

Mrs. McCloskey lived in the apartment across from the manageress, on the ground floor. She hadn't been home when detectives came before, questioning tenants. She apologized; she was a masseuse, taking private appointments, and her hours were irregular. She was a massive female with large square hands and a contralto voice and piercing dark eyes, and on her well-developed bosom hung a large gold cross and on her living-room wall a large religious painting.

"I didn't know her at all," she told Landers and Piggott.

"Even by sight?"

"Oh, by sight—I knew who she was, of course, that she lived upstairs."

"Did you ever see her with another person? Ever exchange any words with her, hello, nice day, like that?"

"Not at all," said Mrs. McCloskey regally. "Of course I don't like to say anything derogatory about anybody—I don't suppose she deserved to be *murdered*—and a murder, *here*—a nice quiet place, I've lived here for nineteen years and never the whisper of any scandal—and I would have thought that the manageress would be more particular whom she rented to, but I expect the woman put up a ladylike front—"

"What do you—Mrs. Fleming?" asked Landers.

"Oh, yes. She *drank,* you know. I had encountered her just a few

times when I had late appointments—coming in. Quite obviously—er—
under the influence. Just last week I came in about twelve-thirty and she
was in the lobby, positively *reeling,* and wearing pink trousers—I was intending to speak to the manageress—"

CHAPTER 12

"You don't mean it?" said Phil. "The respectable widow?"

"And what a shock it's going to be to her daughter," said Landers. "We only went to one place asking—Matt was going out on it again—but they knew her. We figured as she didn't drive, and wasn't going out *with* anybody apparently, it'd be the nearest bars up on Echo Park or Sunset, and the only one we tried, they knew her. We'd found some snapshots in the apartment, manageress pointed out one of her—"

"But why all of a sudden?" said Phil, wrinkling her freckled nose.

"She was lonely, we can have a guess," said Landers, swallowing Scotch and water. It wasn't beginning to cool off much, but it was nice out here on the terrace at Frascati's, Phil across from him at one of the patio tables. "Didn't drive, didn't get invited out much, it wasn't an interesting job. And we can guess too, a woman who didn't get much out of reading, out of watching TV. Liked people around—and probably found the few highballs cheered her up. You can read it. But—"

"Poor thing," said Phil, looking at the last of her martini. "But also stupid."

"Which is also human nature. But isn't it somewhere in the Bible, *man not meant to live alone—*"

Phil glanced sideways at him; his very darling—but intensely practical —Phil who worked the computer down in R. and I. and liked her job— and said, "You're hinting again, Tom."

"Well, damn it—"

She laughed. "Never mind. As I told you, you're passing tests. You don't use cologne, for one thing—I detest cologne on men. And you remember which jokes you've told me, which I think must be one of the more important attributes in a husband."

"You'll end up like Mrs. Fleming. Lonely spinster taking to drink because you were too damn particular." But looking at her neat blonde head and the spattering of freckles across her nose, he knew he wouldn't want Phil any other way: she was herself.

Piggott called Prudence and said he'd be a little late; but they hadn't been going out anywhere so it didn't matter. Prudence lived with her mother, whom Piggott liked, in Hollywood; and it was with the comfortable expectation of seeing them presently—his soon-to-be real family—that Piggott, that strict teetotaler, went into the Pink Pussycat Bar and Grill on Sunset Boulevard at eight-thirty.

"Have you ever seen this woman in here?" he asked the bartender, bringing out the badge and the snapshot at once. It was a good clear snapshot, showing Rhoda Fleming fullface, and seeing it at first Piggott had thought about Mendoza's deductions. The lieutenant did feel things. She hadn't looked her age, and she'd been a nice-looking woman, attractive. You could see that left alone, the daughter married, husband dead, she'd been lonely. And maybe, with the advent of the grandchild, resenting the implication that life was all over for her, any fun to life. But—

"Her?" The bartender looked at the snapshot, holding it to the light. "Yeah, I think I have, a couple times. No, I don't know her name, why? What? No, I couldn't say if she was with anybody, but I think I seen her here. You might ask Madge—" He beckoned the cocktail waitress over. "Cops. Askin' about this dame."

The waitress, a buxom blonde, looked at the snapshot and said, "Oh, her." She looked at Piggott. "You a cop? What's she done?"

"She's dead," said Piggott.

"Dead! Well, I'll be— She is? She looked healthy enough— Well, I'll be darned. She was one of the loners—I felt sorry for her, sort of. See, she wouldn't come in here"—this was the bar, dark and gloomy, redolent of whiskey and this early very quiet—"she came in the lounge." Through a door opposite the bar, and at right angles to it, was the neon sign, *Cocktail Lounge*. "It looks nicer for a woman alone, you can see."

"How often did she come in, Miss—"

"Mrs. Mrs. Martino—this big punk's my old man." She indicated the bartender, who looked sheepish and flattered at once; he'd be a good fifteen years older than she was. "Well, lately she'd been coming in almost every night. A loner like I say. The first times she came in—oh, about a year ago, I'd say—she'd order a club sandwich or something, like she really wanted a snack, but lately she didn't bother. She came in for the drinks and company. I'd have a guess maybe she'd been other places around, but she came here mostly because we've got a piano player, and customers—you know—sort of socialize. Get talking to each other, not just the ones they came with."

Which was just about how Landers had figured. But you'd have thought, thought Piggott, that the woman could have found some decent outlet for loneliness in joining a church, or doing charity work, or— But human nature was always in the picture. And the devil's busy hands.

"When was she in last?"

Madge reflected. "She hasn't been in the last few nights, I missed her —casual like the way you do. Her being pretty regular. It was either Saturday or—no, it was Sunday, I remember for sure because we had a nut in, I remember seeing her laughin' with some of the others when the nut raised the row. One of these squares—I'd never seen him before."

"A nut?" said Piggott, thinking about Rhoda Fleming beaten and probably strangled.

"Yeah. A creep. He made a big fuss on account of Jerry—he's the piano player—did a swing job on some old hymn, 'Rock of Ages,' something—the nut said it was sacrilegious, and on Sunday too, and he stamped out without payin'." She shrugged.

Piggott reminded himself that a good detective was supposed to remain objective. "Did she ever pick up anybody in here?"

"No," she said hurriedly. "Not like what you mean. Like I say, the customers get friendly, talking, sometimes. If they want to introduce themselves to each other, what's it matter? Their business. I can't say I ever saw her leave with anybody, no."

"Well, thanks," said Piggott. He had been to four other places within three blocks; this one seemed to have been her favorite hangout. "You have many regulars coming in? Most nights, a few nights a week?"

"Some," she said reluctantly. "You cops goin' to be hangin' round bothering customers? They couldn't tell you nothing—"

"Well, that we don't know until we ask, do we?" said Piggott mildly. Duty done, he set off for Hollywood and Prudence.

Mendoza had just sat down and opened Grimm, at seven o'clock, when everything loose in the house began rattling, the windowpanes clattered in their frames, the floor tilted and slithered uneasily, and the house shook convulsively. There was a low rumble, the furniture moved, and the floor seemed to rise in little rolling waves. Alison tottered to the doorway, obeying one of the few rules there are about earthquakes. Sixty seconds, and everything stopped and was solid again.

"*¡Caramba!*" said Mendoza. "That was nearly as big as the first one."

"About five on the scale, I'd say," said Alison, letting go of the doorpost. "Are you all right, Máiri? I wonder if we lost any china this time—"

"And I wouldna have set foot in a thousand miles o' the place did I know about the earthquakes—guidness to *mercy*—Janet bein' here or no, my own sister not having the guid sense, comin' to such a place—" Mrs. MacTaggart, accustomed to the uncompromising solidity of the Scottish Highlands, did not like earthquakes. Alison hurried to reassure her.

The twins, on the other hand, much appreciated the novelty. "Hooooo!" shouted Johnny, bouncing. "See-Saw Margery Daw! *¡Bueno!* Do again!"

Terry squealed, "*¡La magia* make everything go to *danzar!*"

"Do again!" demanded Johnny.

"You flatter me, *hijo*," said Mendoza. "I am not omniscient. If that's the word I want. I didn't do it."

Unfortunately he had no sooner said it than the walls shook and the floor rolled again in a milder aftershock. "See-Saw Margery Daw!" said the twins together, happily.

Alison came back and said, "What do you want to bet that ruined all our nice new cement in the drive? And you should see the china cabinet. Máiri's keening over it in Gaelic. We may lose her over this, Luis— her first one, and she doesn't like it at all."

"Heaven forbid."

"Do again!" said Johnny.

"Your father was not responsible," said Alison, and stopped, and added, "unless Detective Piggott is right and the Lord is warning of just destruction for past sins. You must have added considerably to the amount of sin piling up to earth's account, before you got domesticated."

"Insulting me in front of the offspring now—"

The picket with his sign warning of doom to come was leaning on a palm tree outside the entrance to the parking lot when Mendoza got to the office on Saturday morning. The desk sergeant said, "That was quite a shake last night."

"Did we lose any new windows? That'd be adding insult to injury."

"Not that I heard."

"Grateful for small favors," said Mendoza. Upstairs in Homicide Sergeant Farrell greeted him, sitting in for Lake, and asked him how he'd liked the shake last night. Quite something, Mendoza agreed, and went on into the detective office, where Hackett asked him the same thing.

"It enhanced my parental role," said Mendoza. "Johnny thinks I did it."

"Families," said Higgins. "You know, I think the kids actually enjoyed it—of course nothing got broken, but—and Mary saying, Fate."

But that earthquake was over and mercifully nobody could yet predict when another might occur, and there was business for Homicide to work. Mendoza phoned in a request for the search warrant on Sam Oliver's property, and listened to what Piggott had turned up at that bar. Landers, listening too, said, "Stake it out? Overtime? See if any of the regulars knew her, maybe saw her pick somebody up?"

"*Obvio*. Very possible you'll get a lead there. But I doubt very much whether it'd have been a pickup in the crude sense." Mendoza sat back and sent a stream of smoke ceilingward, reflectively. "She was a lady. It wasn't that old devil sex she was looking for so much as simple companionship—people around, friendly, talking to her. Unfortunately, of course, after she'd had a few drinks her judgment wouldn't be working so well, and it's possible she—mmh—accepted the offer of a ride home, something like that. Yes, stake it out and see what shows."

"And meanwhile, where do we go on Hildebrand?" asked Higgins. "As if I didn't know."

"Records," said Hackett. "We've done all the asking around both neighborhoods. Now we do some real legwork—collect all the known perverts in Records, go find them and lean on them."

"And I still think you'll be wasting your time," said Mendoza. "But it's the next thing to do. We have to go by the book."

Glasser phoned in just then to report sadly that the apartment garage had fallen on his car last night; he'd be late getting in. Earthquakes did unpredictable things. They offered commiseration to Glasser, who probably wouldn't collect insurance; earthquakes are regarded by insurance companies as Acts of God.

Hackett and Higgins, Landers and Piggott went off to start the routine on the perverts out of Records. Grace hung around waiting for that search warrant. Mendoza, after rumination, went down to the lot for the Ferrari and drove out to Elden Avenue to talk to the Hildebrand children's grandmother, Mrs. Pace. He hadn't seen her before.

He heard all over just what she'd told the Traffic men. She seemed to be a sensible, practical woman, grieved and incredulous now but in control of herself. When she said she'd checked on the children frequently he believed her. And he heard again how upset Alice had been over the divorce—"Not what she was brought up to, and I doubt she'll want to marry again, after such a bad experience with Henry—" But she couldn't think of anyone who would want to hurt Alice, the children— she looked at him in disbelief. Nobody but a *monster* would—

"*¿Para qué?*" said Mendoza to himself, getting back into the car. And he was the lieutenant—he was supposed to keep tabs on every piece of business, keep the strings separated. He went back to the office.

There, he found Jason Grace poring over Dr. Harlow's records. "Any hunches, Jase?"

"Nary a hunch. Ordinary patients—not a lunatic in the lot that shows." Grace put out his cigarette, getting up to drift aimlessly around the office, lighting another cigarette immediately. "Funny. We felt the big one, but nothing got broken. Last night, half the chinaware. Virginia was still moaning about it when I left."

"Mmh. So did we. And that damned crack in the drive—they just patched it up yesterday, and all the new cement came apart. My wife's— mmh—one-half Scots has come to the fore, and she's going to make the company do it over for free or else."

"Hot again. It's always hot when we get the quakes—" Grace's voice trailed off. After a little silence he said, "I might be asking you for a reference."

"*¿Qué ocurre?* Thinking of switching to an easier job?"

"Nope. We're sort of hoping we might get the Harlows' baby. Celia Ann. I've been prodding at the County Adoption people, and of course they'll look for blood relatives but what we heard of the Harlows' background— I don't think there'll be any trouble, we can show there aren't any. Keep your fingers crossed, anyhow."

"That'd be fine, Jase. Good luck on it. Only—it's a project to embark on. Hostages to fortune."

"They occur to a lot of people who don't really care one way or the other. I figure—"

"Oh, yes. That too. It suddenly occurs to me," said Mendoza, "that the time will inevitably come when my offspring will realize I'm not an all-powerful godlike personage causing earthquakes. A pity. However—"

"Here's that warrant you asked for, Lieutenant," said Farrell, looking in.

"Ah. So now we do some work, Jase."

Glasser trudged in as they were leaving and said dispiritedly the whole damn front end of his Ford had been demolished, he probably wouldn't get any insurance, and the agency said he'd better junk it. "Act of God!" he said. "What reason has God got to be mean to me? I try to live a reasonably useful life. At least it was paid for. But why should God go out of His way to wreck my Ford?"

"Take the larger view, Henry," said Grace. "Rain falling on the just and unjust. And there were all those bodies out in the valley—"

"Oh, my God, I know, it could have been a lot worse. But it's annoying. Have you got any jobs for me?"

"You can come along and help execute a search warrant."

Sam Oliver wasn't at home at the cheap rented house on Bonsallo Avenue. His wife, a silent, meek-looking woman, looked at the warrant, at cops on the doorstep, and said Sam wouldn't like it. But she let them in. She looked frightened to death, but she struck them all as a woman who'd be frightened of a lot of things, including cops—maybe of Sam Oliver too. There was a solemn brown little girl about three, with her hair in pigtails and red ribbons, and a baby about six months old.

The house was old, and it needed paint inside and out, and plumbing repairs, and one of the front windows was cracked, but it was clean enough if untidy. Not much furniture, and that old and shaky. Not many clothes in the bedroom closet. Not much food in the old refrigerator.

After a once-over-lightly, they asked her some questions. She was too frightened of Authority to try to lie; she answered in a faint voice. No, her husband didn't have no gun. She'd never seen him with a gun.

"He earns pretty good money, doesn't he?" asked Grace.

"I dunno," she said, "sir. I dunno how much, he don't tell me." They knew: he had somewhere around thirty jobs, gardening for people up in Hollywood, an hour or two once a week each place, and on the average he got twenty a month for each job, some of the jobs paying thirty or more. Grace told her that, and she was silent.

"He doesn't give you much of it to make do with?" She shook her head. "What does he do with it?" She shook her head again, and then she gave a little gasp and put a hand to her mouth.

"I dasn't—he knock me around, I complain any—but he gamble away ennathing he get his hands on—" And she shut up, looking terrified.

No gun in the house. She said he'd likely be home at noon, so Grace and Glasser came back then and found him there, and searched the pickup. No gun.

Oliver was furious and frightened. He started out blustering. "What call you got, come here look at all my stuff? You Goddamn pigs—"

"All right, Sam," said Grace. They sat him down in the bare living room. "Last Monday morning, you didn't show at the Petersens' when you usually did. Where were you between ten A.M. and noon last Monday?"

"Why I tell you that, big man?"

"Because I'm asking, Sam," said Grace coldly. "Have you ever owned a gun?"

"A g— No, I never. What for I need a gun? I don' go shootin' people like the damn fuzz do—"

Both the Homicide men thought rather tiredly of all the red tape, the formal hearing that had to be held every time an LAPD man fired off a gun on duty. The hearing to determine whether it had been justifiable to do so. But Sam Oliver wouldn't know about that. "Where were you?" asked Grace again.

"Why? Bust in here, you pigs, an' try to—"

"Because last Monday morning, Sam, three people were shot to death, and two of them were people you didn't like, and we've been wondering if it was you shot them," said Grace. "Was it you?"

"Me? Shoot— Who you talkin' about? What the hell you mean, people I—"

"Dr. Harlow and his wife—you don't look at the papers, Sam?"

Suddenly Oliver went gray with fright. "A *murder?* You think I done a *murder?* That guy, that dame that— Oh, man, you way off base—I wouldn't do no— What did you say, what time?"

"Ten A.M. to noon, Sam. Last Monday."

"Oh. Oh. I was—well, it was a hot day, I just—sorta knocked off after my first job, 'at day," said Oliver nervously. "I just—well, I just went down this place on Vermont, the Criss-Cross Club, see. Sat around 'n' had a few beers, is all. I guess the barkeep could say I was there O.K. Oh, man, you way off— Me, a murder—you go ask, he'll say I was there—"

And how much that was worth they'd guess after they'd checked the alibi. He could have got rid of the gun.

They went up to Federico's for lunch and met Mendoza and Hackett just going in. Hackett was complaining about the tedious routine: but it usually did get them where they wanted to go. Sometimes it didn't.

After lunch they checked back with the office, and a new call had come in: probable suicide, a rooming house over by the yards. Glasser went out on it and Grace roped Landers in. They drove up to the Criss-Cross Club on South Vermont. Landers was as pleased to get out of the other routine, hunting the perverts. Once the computer had efficiently ground out the list of perverts from their records, no excuse for a Homicide man to stay down there ogling little blonde Phil O'Neill, of course.

"Let's have a look before we ask questions," said Grace.

"Sure." They went in. It was an old building in a block of solid buildings, and a shabby place inside, smelling of whiskey and perspiration and dust. They weren't six feet inside the door when a slim white-aproned man stepped up to bar them. "I'm sorry, sir," he said softly, "we don't serve whites here."

Grace looked amused. "So I'll see you back at the car, Tom."

Landers went back to the car, reflecting on the peculiar notions some people had about the so-called racists. He'd smoked two cigarettes when Grace came up and slid behind the wheel. "You disadvantaged Caucasians," he said, and Landers laughed, and asked him what the setup looked like. "You want to have a bet?"

"I'm saving my money," said Landers, "hoping to get married."

"Well, I might make a little bet with you that there's the game going in the back room of that place. With the password to get let in. And maybe the pro gamblers holding the bank."

"Oh, really?" said Landers, surprised. "Oh, I see. Sam Oliver—"

"The gambling man. I think we'd better tell University division about it and see if they'd like to look into it."

"I think so too." They drove down to that precinct house and saw a Sergeant Adamski, who was mildly interested. "And what's Central's interest in a South Vermont bar for colored only?"

"We're trying," said Grace plaintively, "to check an alibi."

"Hope springs eternal," said Adamski.

"For a murder."

"Well, we'll let you know what transpires."

Even as Grace had guessed, University division broke up the illegal gambling in the back room of the Criss-Cross Club. The owner, the bartender, and four patrons swore in a body that Sam Oliver had been sitting in a crap game last Monday morning from about nine-forty to noon. The joker was that all of them had minor pedigrees and were friends of Sam's, more or less.

"On the other hand, Jase," said Mendoza, "they came out with the times voluntarily."

"So they did. We didn't have a tail on Oliver. He could have seen them before the raid."

"Being psychic and knowing which individuals the unexpected raid would nab? *Pues no*."

"Well, he could have told the barkeep, the owner."

"It could be. But I don't think we've got there yet, on the Harlows." Mendoza looked at Dr. Harlow's records, in their neat file boxes, stacked on one side of his desk, and sighed. "I had another small idea—"

This floor was still without windows, and it was still hot; the thermometer on Palliser's desk said it was ninety-eight today.

Palliser phoned Mendoza just before six o'clock. "This Goddamned thing is a waste of time," he said, "and you can pass that on to Goldberg. There isn't any body. Brodie dreamed it. We've driven hundreds of miles all round every road there is up here, and we haven't found a damned thing. Even the sheriff is getting annoyed, and the deputies are fit to be tied. I never saw so much wild land in my life, and I'm homesick for town—earthquakes and all. Hear you had another one, by the way."

"Oh, quite a respectable one," said Mendoza. "You're shutting down the hunt?"

"Well, damn it, Brodie sounds so positive," said Palliser. "He's had experience butchering, he says, and he knows the guy was dead. And I am bound to say that this wild country looks an awful lot alike, wherever you go—I can see where he'd be confused. The sheriff says, give it another day. It's stopped raining, at least."

"So you'll be home Monday? With Brodie for Goldberg to charge with petty theft?"

"I suppose. That's the program now, unless of course we do find a body."

"Always a possibility. A lot of inaccessible empty space up there where a body could lie for years."

"You can say it again," said Palliser. "Have we got our windows back yet?"

"No windows. I'd take no bets," said Mendoza, "that they get replaced and then we have another one to knock them all out again."

"Look," said Palliser, "I'm the one feeling pessimistic. And I'll put in a voucher for this call—official business—I'm running out of money. You might call Robin and tell her."

"I'll do that. Good luck—you may hit pay dirt yet."

"No bets," said Palliser grumpily.

Mendoza cocked his head at the phone. Palliser having a spat with his wife? Pity. Unusual for Palliser, that even-tempered man. Mendoza got up, took down his hat, and started home for Alison and their assorted livestock.

Landers and Piggott, doing the overtime, staked out the Pink Pussycat that night. Landers could order a highball and nurse it along indefinitely—places like this got about fifty highballs out of a fifth anyway; but Piggott the teetotaler sat over a cup of coffee.

They had asked Madge Martino to point out the regular patrons to them, and reluctantly she agreed. Her husband owned this place, and a liquor license cost in California.

On Saturday night, probably most of the regulars would be in. And most of the people, regulars or not, patronizing this place would be ordinary people, neighborhood people, who'd buy two or three drinks, listening to the piano player. Not drunks; not bums.

Madge pointed out a dozen people, mostly couples, a few men alone, and they talked to them, showing the badges, asking the questions, showing the snapshot of Rhoda Fleming. Most of the people remembered her vaguely. Recognized her as another regular in here. Some of them had talked with her casually—about the piano player, about the weather, about the headlines—last week, about the earthquake. But nobody remembered her being with any particular man, or picking up a man, until they came to Mr. and Mrs. Orlando Frazier, just as they'd been thinking of knocking off for the night, at ten-thirty.

Mr. and Mrs. Frazier operated a dry-cleaning shop a couple of blocks away, lived in an apartment over it. They were a self-satisfied, very ordinary couple in their thirties, lacking much imagination, but they were honest people willing to help out the cops, and they looked at the snapshot and said, Why, yes, they'd seen her here.

"Last Sunday night?" asked Landers. The autopsy report had come in this morning; Rhoda Fleming had been beaten and strangled, but— not raped. Time of death estimated to be between six A.M. last Sunday and six A.M. Monday. The length of time before the body was found, Dr. Bainbridge couldn't be more specific.

"Sunday—yeah, we were here Sunday. And Saturday. There was a little fuss when this nut—" They heard all about that, the piano player playing fast and loose with "Rock of Ages," and Landers asked if Mrs. Fleming had been here then.

"We didn't know her name. That woman. Yes, she was. With anybody? Well, about then—it was when that guy came in, wasn't it, May? That blond guy?"

"About then," she agreed. "He'd been in a couple of nights before too. But I guess it was that night—Sunday—this woman you're asking about, she sort of hung around with him."

"Picked him up?" asked Landers.

"Oh, well, I wouldn't like to say that," said plump blonde May uncomfortably. "I mean, this is a respectable place. But she was always alone, it looked like, and she'd talk to different people—well, I couldn't say about that, if she always bought her own drinks, I wouldn't know. We never saw her exactly *drunk*—just, you know, happy. But that night, she got talking with this fellow, and I know they were at the same table quite a while—"

Landers and Piggott exchanged glances. "Any idea who he is? A regular in here? Could you describe him for us?"

They looked at each other—nice honest rather dull citizens, willing to help but inarticulate. "No, I hadn't seen him in here before last week. He was, well, maybe about thirty," said Frazier. "Blond like I said. About, oh, five-ten or six feet, not fat but— Well, he had on slacks, a sports shirt, blue—" He looked at his wife.

"You could ask the piano player," she said brightly. "He knew him— he went up and talked to him between numbers, I mean like they were friends, not asking for a number or like that—"

They talked to the piano player after he'd finished a mean rendition of "Rhapsody in Blue." His name was Jerry Hoffman; he was about thirty, with an engaging pug-dog face and bright blue eyes and a crooked smile. "Cops?" he said, looking at the badges. "What'd I do?"

They asked him about the blond fellow. About Rhoda Fleming. He shrugged. "The female loners coming in—any place like this—I wouldn't know. I'm hired to play the box. Period. What? A blond— Last Sunday night?"

"And a couple of nights before," said Landers. "About five-ten, six feet, sports clothes, around thirty—"

"Hey," said Hoffman, "hey. You don't mean Howie?"

"I don't know. Who's Howie?"

"Howie Engel. He's a mean man on a horn—or used to be. Sax mostly. We played in a combo together once, a couple of years back. Howie's O.K., only—"

"What?" said Piggott as Hoffman paused.

"Well, he's got the little problem," said Hoffman with a grimace. "Me, I may not be so smart but I'm smarter than that. If you get me. To get hooked."

"On what? Just the Mary Jane?"

Hoffman shrugged. "I wouldn't know. To start, I guess. Maybe the hard stuff later. I hadn't seen him since he got fired off that job—goofing off, you know, not showing up. He came in here last week, first time I've seen him since. I greet him—a guy I knew—he's a good musician if he hadn't been damn fool enough to get the habit. He showed up a few nights, that's all. I didn't have much talk with him, why should I?"

"Last Sunday night," said Landers, "did you notice him with this woman?"

"Well, yeah, I did," said Hoffman. "That's right. I don't know if she made a play for him or the other way—but she's no chicken if she wasn't bad-looking, I'd guess it was her went after him. They were at the same table awhile. No, I got no idea where he's living, how should I? He never said about a job, no."

But that was a strong lead, of course.

"Has he been back here since Sunday?"

Hoffman said, "Sure. Tuesday and just last night, he was here. Over a couple drinks, about an hour. Sure, alone."

So, go on staking out the Pink Pussycat. Wait for Engel, hopefully, to show.

On Sunday they went on looking for the perverts out of Records, fetching them in when they could find them. Mendoza said, a waste of time.

"You saw a vision in your crystal ball," said Hackett.

"Just a feeling," said Mendoza obscurely. "Just a little feeling, Arturo."

And at five-fifty on Sunday afternoon, Palliser called. From the wilds. "We've found the damned body," he said. "We'll be busy on it awhile. Well, I don't know when I'll be back. But you can tell Goldberg to send the girl up. I may get back tomorrow—"

CHAPTER 13

They had found the body within half an hour of the time Palliser and the sheriff had decided to quit looking. When Tim Brodie suddenly exclaimed from the back seat, "Hey, this is it! That's the place right there—" They looked at him, and at each other. Forbear put his foot on the brake resignedly.

"We've been past this point several times, Brodie," said Sheriff Roudebush. "If this is it, why didn't you—"

"Well, this is all strange country to me, but just all of a sudden I reckanized that tree, the shape of it—it's right down the shoulder, behind some bushes—"

Surprisingly, it was. The week-old corpse of a young man in old and dirty clothes, a canvas flight bag beside it. "I didn't take his stuff," said Brodie. "I was just so *surprised,* find he's dead—"

They'd let the coroner decide how. Palliser rode back to town with the deputy and called Mendoza while they routed out the coroner and an ambulance. They couldn't do much out there. The coroner said, skull-fracture, and pointed out several rocks that could have been responsible, up on the road where Tim said they'd had the fight.

There was nothing in the flight bag or on the corpse to provide a name for him, and they coaxed Tim patiently to remember—had he said his last name, where he was from? They drew blank. He'd just said Steve—and he was heading for L.A., said Tim. They took his fingerprints for relaying to Washington.

Palliser hung around on Monday until an LAPD policewoman arrived with Wilma Schultz. A couple of reporters, looking for rural news, showed up and Wilma asked if this would be in the papers. "Gee, my dad don't know where we went, but if he sees about it in the papers and comes down here—he don't like Tim nohow—" It would penetrate her mind later that they'd be safe from Papa in jail.

The LAPD car which had ferried them up here was, of course, back in L.A. now. Palliser consulted a bus schedule and found he could get a bus at three-fifty which would get him into L.A. by eight-fifteen, with stops along the way. The sheriff thanked him, shaking hands, and Palliser said he didn't know what for. He felt he'd wasted the last three days.

He called Roberta to tell her when he'd be home. "Good," she said. "I've missed you, darling. And you won't have a chance for dinner— you'll be starving. I'll have something waiting. Oh, John—"

"Mmhm?"

"You'll be relieved to know you aren't going to have a working wife."

"What?"

"Well, no. A little joke on me. I'll have to call the principal and explain. The fact is," said Roberta, sounding amused and pleased and still a little surprised, "I'd been wondering, the day you left—and I saw the doctor, and he's just confirmed it this afternoon—I'm pregnant. So, no working wife—"

Palliser began to laugh. He laughed so hard he couldn't get out a word, and he hung up still laughing.

Monday morning, and the routine still going on. The routine often broke cases, but in a thing like the Hildebrand kill it was largely futile. The perverts were loners: haul them in out of Records, they could seldom produce an alibi, and that left it all still up in the air.

The Pink Pussycat was closed on Mondays, so Landers and Piggott would start staking it out, hoping Howie Engel would show, tomorrow night.

"And where the hell to go on Harlow?" said Hackett in exasperation. "Nothing solid on it in a week, and now no leads at all. A lunatic shooting three people—"

"But not quite at random," said Mendoza. "He knew who he was shooting at, Art."

"I'm not even sure of that now. It could have been very much at random for all we know. And don't say to me, he climbed the stairs. There he was on the second floor, just by chance, when the urge hit him—he goes in the nearest door and bang."

Mendoza said, "No. I know it can happen that way, but it didn't here. Those records—damn it, there's something trying to get through to me about those records—" He shook his head. "Wait for it."

They spent Monday morning looking up the known perverts. It was frustrating; they didn't find half of them, moved away or away from home, and those they found gave them nothing solid at all. And Mendoza, looking at a shot glass of rye at Federico's at a quarter to one, was still saying it was a waste of time.

"If he'd just suggest where else to look," said Hackett to Higgins, "he might be some use." The black eye had faded by now and he looked less sinister.

"I just have the feeling—impossible as it seems—" Mendoza swallowed rye and looked at Landers as he came up to join them. "What have you got?"

"Nothing!" said Landers. "What should I have? There was a hit-run called in just as we got back, Matt went out on it, said he'd pick up lunch later. Just the usual—a kid running into the street after a ball." Mendoza asked abstractly if there was any make on the car, and Landers just looked at him.

"It must be his age," said Hackett.

After lunch, Mendoza went back to the windowless office, where it was still very hot, and fidgeted around smoking too much. Lake, coming in with the autopsy report on the Hildebrand children, found him standing in front of a window and told him for God's sake to get away from there. "What with all these aftershocks—" The Lakes lived in the valley, but fortunately not in the area where the big one had hit; they'd lost part of a fence and a raised flower bed. But Lake, native Californian though he was, was nervous about earthquakes.

The autopsy report, of course, gave them nothing new. The lab report, arriving a little later, added up to nothing.

Hackett and Higgins had just come back with another known pervert out on P.A. when Sergeant Lake looked in and said, "Two agitated female citizens, with information. So they say. A Mrs. Fanchon and a Mrs. Burnett."

"So, shove them in," said Mendoza. "Information we can always use."

"Fanchon? I saw them," said Higgins. "They live in the house that backs up to Mrs. Pace's, on the next street. The back yards are right together. I wonder—"

Mendoza lit a cigarette. "So, sit in on it. So do I."

Both the women were excited. The younger one burst out, seeing Higgins, "Oh, I told you—you came to ask if we'd seen anything and we hadn't, but I told you about Mother leaving that day to visit Auntie in San Diego—excuse me, this is my mother, Mrs. Burnett, you said Sergeant—"

"Higgins. Lieutenant Mendoza. Sergeant Hackett."

"—And she did see something! She just got home an hour ago, and when I told her—and asked—so we came right away, because such an awful—"

"I haven't had my hat off," said Mrs. Burnett, who was a tall grenadier of a woman with a hawk's nose and shrewd eyes. "When Della told me—my heavens above, two babies like that—I couldn't believe it could be him, not that we know them but they've lived there years—they used to have a dog that wandered, he'd come looking for it—"

"Who?" asked Hackett and Higgins together.

"I didn't think anything about it at the time," said Mrs. Burnett, "because I know he knows Alice. We know the children, of course—often see them in the back yard. And I was just leaving to get the bus downtown, that afternoon, when I saw him with the Hildebrand children, walking down the street. Burton Fowler."

He worked for the telephone company as a lineman; but today was his day off. He lived with his mother on Elden Avenue a block or so up from the Pace house.

When they got there, they found Mrs. Pace standing on the front porch talking with fat, gray-haired Mrs. Fowler. "Oh," she said, looking at the two big men, the slender dapper Mendoza between them, "were you looking for me? Something else you wanted to— Alice is at work. They told us—I just came up to tell Mrs. Fowler, she's an old friend, you see—we can arrange for the—the funeral now. I—"

"Mrs. Fowler," said Mendoza, "is your son Burton at home?"

"Why, yes. It's his day off. Why? Are you *detectives?* What—"

"We'd like to talk to him," said Hackett easily. Ask him to come in for questioning, all polite. And didn't their Luis have the hunches indeed—but, thought Hackett, why? Why the hell? A neighborhood friend —a man who'd asked Alice Hildebrand to marry him. Just suddenly gone off his rocker in that direction? He didn't have any record at all; they had looked.

Both the women were staring at them. "Burt?" said Mrs. Fowler. "Why, what on earth do you think he could know about this terrible— Well, of course if you think he can tell you anything, I'll— He's just watching an old movie on TV—" She turned back into the house.

"Why do you think Burt knows anything about this monster?" asked

Mrs. Pace curiously. They didn't answer her. But monsters, thought Hackett, were in the mind; anybody might say, a monster, doing such a thing. And never thinking that the monster (maybe the primitive monster in most men, buried deep, but with most deep enough) lived next door to somebody, watched TV like other people, worked a job like other people . . . looking like the monster only after he was identified and caught.

He was, coming up to the screen door with his mother, not looking like a monster at all. He wasn't handsome, he wasn't ugly, he was—colorless. A neat sandy young man about Alice Hildebrand's age, clean-shaven, with pale-blue eyes. He came out to the porch, beside the detectives, and looked at them in silence as they looked at him. His ears stuck out a little; he looked more shy and awkward than anything else.

"Fowler—" began Mendoza, but Fowler opened his mouth at the same time.

"You're police officers," he said. "I—I guess you've found out about it, haven't you? Somehow. That—that was me. Did that. I don't guess I was sort of thinking straight—but—but that was me did it. I guess—"

"*Burt!*" gasped his mother, and tried to scream, and went over in a dead faint. Mrs. Pace began to scream hysterically.

"*You don't mean—*"

"Oh, hell," said Mendoza. "Get some females up here, Art—the phone—"

Both the women were taken down to Central Receiving in shock. Mendoza, finding Grace in the office when they towed Fowler in, said with relief, "Our sweet talker. Go talk to Alice Hildebrand, Jase. She'll be at work. Break the news—" He outlined the situation, and Grace looked at Fowler incredulously.

"I will be damned. All right—save the nicest jobs for me, don't you? But I'll be interested in what you get out of him."

They took Fowler into an interrogation room and read him the piece all about his rights. "Do you understand that, Fowler? Do you want to waive your right to remain silent?"

He blinked up at them. Higgins offered him a cigarette and he said he didn't smoke. "You mean, do I want to tell you about it? How it happened? I *want* to tell about it. Because ever since—ever since I did it, it's been in my mind it was the wrong way to think. I been all confused. It seemed so plain to me and then—and then—after, it wasn't."

"How do you mean, plain?" asked Hackett.

"Well, Alice was feeling so terrible about divorcing that guy. You got to understand, Alice and I went to high school together, I always wanted Alice to marry me, but she picked him instead. And then when she divorced him, well, ever since she came back to live here, she was feeling so bad about it—right down sick, she was doctoring for it, and *I* felt bad too because I still wanted her to marry me. I'd never treat Alice the way he—I just wanted to take care of her, so she wouldn't have to work, or get sick or be hurt— But she wouldn't marry me, and it was all on account of the bad time she had with that guy." He looked at them anxiously to see if they were following him.

"So?" said Hackett.

Fowler heaved a sigh. "It came into my mind," he said, "because it was just on account of the time she'd had with that guy, the time she was married to him, that she wouldn't marry me—and it came to me all of a sudden that if the kids—if the kids weren't there, it'd be like she never was married to him. To anybody. I thought with the kids gone, it'd be like it was before, her living down the block with her mother— and—I'd take her out on dates, like we did in high school—and—then maybe she'd marry me. You see how I figured? It seemed as plain as day right then. As plain as day. Without the kids, it'd be like it was— And—"

They looked at each other. "Go on, Fowler," said Higgins.

"Well, I—it was all that morning I was thinking about it. It seemed so plain—such a good idea. My car was in the garage, a lube job, and I parked the truck—I was out on the job, of course—round the corner, and got my car when it was ready and drove it back and parked on Twelfth, just round the corner from the house. And then I walked back to the truck, and I got sent on a job, repair a line over on Normandie, and I called in and said it'd take a while. It didn't really. I went back—I knew the kids of course, knew they'd be right in the back yard—and there wasn't any trouble, I just—took them. I—just—well, you know what I did. I took 'em in my car, I did it in the car before I put them— there, that place. It just seemed so plain to me, if they weren't there, it'd all be just like it was before Alice married that guy—and then she'd—"

Higgins had been taking it down in shorthand. When Fowler didn't say anything more, after a long silence Higgins asked, "Will you sign that as a statement, Fowler, if we get it typed up?"

"What? Sure. But you see—" He looked at them painfully, earnestly. "Ever since, I been feeling all confused about it. It seemed plain as could be, but it's been in my mind ever since it *wasn't* the way to do it— and nothing's like what it was before, and Alice isn't like what she used to—still feeling just terrible about things—and I been *confused*. Now, I just don't know—about anything. I just don't know."

"You just wait here for a little while, we'll have this statement for you to sign," said Higgins.

But when they had got him to sign it, and booked him in at the jail on Alameda, Hackett said, "My God, Luis, but he's nutty as a fruitcake. Schizo? Belatedly showing up? The D.A. won't even think about a trial—"

"So he won't," said Mendoza. "After what the head doctors will probably say. At least, be grateful for small favors, he'll get stashed away at Atascadero with the criminal insane. And anybody there who suddenly—according to the head doctors—regains his sanity, still has to stand trial for what he got there for. But—"

"But," said Higgins, "my God, what a thing. Those two babies—he thought if they weren't there— Christ. The things we see—"

"The dirt at the bottom of things, George. The mud we're paid to wallow in. I've stopped asking myself why I'm still down here when I don't have to be." Mendoza lit a cigarette and watched the smoke drift ceilingward; and the building moved like an uneasy sleeper and swayed a little; everything loose clattered.

"Damn aftershocks," muttered Higgins.

The outside phone shrilled on Mendoza's desk and he picked it up. "Mendoza, Central Homicide."

"Royce. Just thought you'd like to know that Pat's doing fine. The doctors say it'll be a little while, but eventually he'll be quite O.K. They let him sit up a few minutes today, and he passed on a message for you boys."

"That's good news—"

"Said to tell you he appreciates your getting right on it and catching up to those—"

"Now, Captain," said Mendoza. "He did not. He'd know we would get on it, whoever he was—and the old reliable LAPD usually does catch up."

Royce laughed. "I was being polite. What he said was, he'd never realized before—until those punks jumped him—how the citizen feels when something happens—never a cop around when you need one."

Mendoza laughed. "Well, give him our best wishes." And that was another thing—those four young punks were scheduled for arraignment tomorrow.

*   *   *

Dr. Stuyvesant came in hastily just before six, to make that statement. He apologized; nothing urgent about the statement, and he'd been kept busy. Piggott, coming in with Landers just then, asked about old Mrs. Mallory.

"She died. Never regained consciousness," said Stuyvesant shortly.

Palliser, arriving home at the forty-thousand-dollar house on Hillside Avenue, swung Roberta off her feet and kissed her soundly. "I've got dinner hot for you," she said breathlessly.

"Darling love, you aren't sorry, are you?"

"Of course not, idiot. I think I'm a little relieved." Roberta laughed. "Ever since I signed up, I've been thinking about dealing with the little monsters en masse again and getting cold feet. Do you care which it is?"

"Whatever you produce will be fine with me," said Palliser.

"And I've been thinking about names—well, we figure it should be around the last week of April," said Roberta. "Of course we've got plenty of time to decide, but I rather thought of your middle name— Andrew John for a boy—or possibly David for my father—"

"Right now I'm more interested in food," said Palliser. "We'll argue that one later, Robin."

They all went home and told their wives about Fowler, and Alison and Angel and Mary said much the same things. Occasionally the offbeat one did turn up: the thing the rational mind could hardly accept.

And Mendoza's subconscious mind was still trying to tell him something about Dr. Harlow's records. Leave it, he thought out of experience; stop trying to think what it was, it might emerge.

And the routine went on forever: they had now the Fleming thing still on hand, but other things would be turning up to work—maybe another puzzler, more likely the spate of routine violent death in the city, for any city is death-prone—the little things making more paper work, more legwork.

Palliser came back on Tuesday, to balance Grace being off, and told them all about the joke on his Robin, which was appreciated. "I never did like the idea of her going back to work, and now— Well, the doctor said about the last of April."

"And we can all keep fingers crossed for Jase," said Mendoza, grinning. "I take it he meant me to pass it on—they're hoping to adopt the Harlow baby."

"Good luck to that," said Hackett. "Cutest little thing I ever saw, that one—and we can guess, some pretty good genes there, judging by the parents. There'll be miles of red tape to unwind, that County Adoption Agency—"

"Yes, they know that. But in the end—" Sergeant Lake looked in and Mendoza sighed. "Here we go again, boys."

"Yeah, there's a new one gone down, but also—" A man in a tan jump suit came in past him, frowning at papers on a clipboard.

"Is this the Homicide place? Fourth on the list, this floor. You got, lessee, nine windows here some place. Three eight by four, vertical, six three by eight, horizontal. That right?"

"Welcome, friend!" said Hackett fervently. "We could kiss you. You've got our new windows?"

"This afternoon, we're scheduled to install 'em. Have to ask you to keep out of the way."

"That's all right." The interrogation rooms were minus windows—and if the window installers delayed a few reports getting typed up, it was worth it. Presumably once the windows were in, they'd get the refrigerated air conditioning turned back on.

"What's the new one, Jimmy?"

"Address over on San Marino—suicide," said Lake.

"I'll take it." Palliser got up.

It was just more paper work, of course, but—thinking of Robin, and the baby—he looked at it feeling a little angry. Which was senseless.

"He wasn't worth it," sobbed the live young woman. "A dirty bum he was—been in jail and all—she was a fool over him! I told her—time and again I told her—but Jeanie never would listen—over a bum like that—"

Palliser looked at the dead young woman, the note trembling in her sister's hand, and he felt angry because some people had so few guts. And he thought how senseless it was to feel that way—human nature—and unexpectedly he thought, *Men have died and worms have eaten them, but not for love.* . . .

"I'm sorry to have to bother you at a time like this," he said automatically, "but I'll have to ask you some questions—"

And the criminals, pro or amateur, were often stupid; but they couldn't count on that. It was entirely possible that Howie Engel wouldn't show at the Pink Pussycat again. On Saturday Landers and Piggott had found the Scotts at Rhoda Fleming's apartment, sorting through her belongings, and asked them to come in for a session with a police artist to give a description of that diamond ring so he could draw as accurate a picture of it as possible. Apparently it was a custom design.

They hadn't said anything to the Scotts about Rhoda's bar hopping. Time enough for them to get that shock later.

They'd sent copies of the drawing to all the local pawnbrokers and the press. Only the *Herald* had seen fit to run it. They thought the pawnbrokers were more likely to be seeing the ring itself than the citizenry, anyway.

On Tuesday night they sat at a table at the Pink Pussycat for three hours, Landers nursing a highball and Piggott bored over coffee. Howie Engel didn't show; the piano player had agreed to point him out if he did.

They had looked for him in Records. He wasn't in theirs, but he showed up twice as dropped on by the sheriff's boys: both times, possession of narcotics.

The new calls came in. The new windows got installed, and everybody heaved a sigh of relief when the air conditioning came back on. And Mendoza, sitting brooding at his desk, still felt there was something he should remember about Dr. Harlow's records—something very simple, and yet possibly significant—

On Wednesday night Piggott and Landers staked out the Pink Pussycat. Engel didn't show.

On Thursday morning, with Hackett and Higgins off, a couple of new calls had just got sent up by Traffic—an accident down at the Stack where all the freeways came together in a glorious jumble, one D.O.A., and another body in an alley over on the Row—when a neatly-tailored man came in and told Sergeant Lake the desk sergeant had said this was where he should come. "About this drawing," he said, and showed Lake the artist's sketch of Rhoda Fleming's diamond ring. "I have a pawnshop on Ninth Street, and—"

"Yes, sir. Tom—Matt! Hold it, you got something."

Landers and Piggott had just been leaving to look at the body on the Row. They let Glasser go instead and listened to Mr. Theodore Eisenstadt.

"This ring," he said. "A custom piece, I think. I know something about stones, of course. As soon as I see this sketch I realize, I got it. I took it in. I apologize, gentlemen, for the delay—I've just lost my older brother, he lived up in Carmel, I close the shop and go up for the funeral, naturally. I only got back to the city today, and of course I find this notice from the police, this drawing. And so—" He sighed. "I bring you the ring." He laid it on Landers' desk between them.

Rhoda Fleming's ring, all right, by the description and sketch. "When did you take it in, sir?" asked Landers. "Who pawned it?"

"Tuesday," said Eisenstadt. "No, no, I mean a week ago last Tuesday." Two days after Rhoda Fleming had died. "I have copied out the record from my books for you. His name was Harold Edwards." The old initials bit, thought Landers and Piggott. "I gave him three-fifty for it."

"What's it worth actually?"

Eisenstadt shrugged. "Fifteen hundred. Yes, he gave an address—Virgil Avenue. I write that down for you too. You think he's the one murdered this poor woman?"

"Could be. What did he look like?" asked Piggott. "You remember?"

"Oh, perhaps thirty—fair hair, six feet high, sports clothes—informal like you say."

Howie Engel. "Well, thank you very much," said Piggott.

"So what happens to my three-fifty? Stolen property," said Eisenstadt sadly. "I got to give it back. If you put out the notice sooner, I'd have spotted it then, made the excuse, call you and stall him. And I'd still have three-fifty I don't have now."

"We're very sorry," said Landers, "but we didn't hear about it until some time later, you see."

"Well, it's the way the cards go down," said Eisenstadt.

They went to the address on Virgil and it was an empty lot.

On Thursday night they staked out the Pink Pussycat again and at seven-forty the piano player caught Landers' eye and pointed to the bar. A tall blond fellow in navy slacks and blue shirt stood there, drinking a highball. Landers and Piggott went over and got him between them. "Mr. Engel?"

"Yeah, that's—" They showed him the badges and he looked nervous, tried to back away. "Hey, what you want with—"

"Just a few questions." Outside, they recited the piece about his rights to him and he said yeah, yeah, he understood that. They took him back to the office; it being a quiet night, both Schenke and Galeano sat in on the questioning.

He started out denying everything; never saw that dame, never had nothing to do with— "Then how did you happen to have her diamond ring?" asked Landers. "The daughter has identified it. The pawnbroker will identify you as the man who pawned it. For three hundred and fifty bucks. Where did you get it?"

"Oh, hell," said Engel unhappily. "Hell and damnation. All right. I got it off her. Off that dame."

"So, would you like to tell us about it? How you beat her and strangled her? Did you rape her too?"

"Who, me? Hell, no—I wouldn't do a— *That* dame? Listen, she was— Well, all right, I got to tell you how it happened, so you get it straight. You could say it was all her own damn fault, she was makin' up to me at that place that night. Makin' a play for me, yeah. I bought her a couple drinks, I think she's a neat enough little chick, and she asks me to take her home—so I—but, Jesus," said Engel, "we get there, I see her in good light, she's a bag!—an old bag, maybe forty-five, fifty, old enough be my— Well, I was kind of insulted, you get me, her thinkin' I'd— I laughed at her, what the hell an old bag like her expect, I'm interested lay a dame that old?—and she got mad, she hit me, and I— What? No, she wasn't drunk, she'd only had a couple before she got me to take her—" Of course that would have showed up in the autopsy. "And *I* got mad—what the hell, a beat-up old dame like— Well, you know that dim light in bars, it wasn't till I saw her plain— So then I, well, I guess I belted her—"

"You'd had a fix that day?" asked Piggott. "Are you on the hard stuff, Engel?"

"What the *hell?* How the hell you know— No. No. I'm not—" But then, of course, with the voluntary statement, they could search him. And in his jacket pocket they found a little pillbox with a screwed-up paper packet of heroin in it.

"All right," he said, goaded. "All right. I'd had a fix—that afternoon. I'm not on it regular. Just off and on. Not like I got to have it—"

"Not yet," said Landers. "So then you found she was dead. Why the bathtub, Howie?"

"Oh, hell. Well, damn it, I never meant her to be dead, my God, and I just thought—take her clothes off, put her in the bathtub, everybody think she fell and killed herself, see—I just—and it wasn't till then I spotted that ring, so I—"

Schenke was taking it down in shorthand. They got him to sign it, and booked him into the jail on Alameda.

"Satan," said Piggott, "going up and down."

Landers thought it was even simpler: human nature doing what comes naturally.

"Oh, yes," said Mendoza on Friday morning, hearing the account of that from Landers while Piggott typed the final report. Hackett and Higgins were back, there too because for the moment nothing new had come in. "Oh, yes. Maybe, just lately, Rhoda had been thinking about that old devil sex. Making up to Howie—asking him to take her home. And not drunk, even halfway. Mmh, yes." He laughed. "Can't we guess what the head doctors would say? Resentful of turning into a grandmother, the well-preserved, still female woman, wanting the reassurance that she's still attractive to the opposite sex— *¡Oye, no vale nada!*"

"I don't know, Luis," said Hackett. "A little something in that maybe."

Mendoza laughed cynically. "The head doctors sometimes sound like the puritans, Arturo. Nobody over fifty remotely interested— *¡Qué disparate!* It's the individual thing—some people yes, some people no. The individual human nature. Fatal for Rhoda Fleming."

Palliser had come in to hear that, and he said then, seriously, "That's funny. Your saying that. That suicide on Tuesday—a stupid thing, but most suicides are—I don't know what put it in my head—*Men have died and worms have eaten them, but—*"

"*Not for love,*" said Mendoza. "No, not for love. Self-love—he'll be sorry when I—oh, yes. *Pues sí.* Life—love, and death. And death." He put out his cigarette; his tone was vague. "*But not for love.* What the hell am I thinking—something trying to—Harlow—"

"Harlow?" Jason Grace came in. "That call on Figueroa just gives us more paper work. Looks like a coronary. Senior citizen, I.D. tags him as belonging to a rest home on Alvarado. Anybody's guess how he got so far downtown, or why."

"Yes," said Mendoza meaninglessly, his gaze unfocused.

"*Quieto,*" said Hackett interestedly. "He's having a hunch."

"Love, and death—" said Mendoza. Quite suddenly he sat up and said, "*Muerte?*" His eyes focused on Hackett. "A hunch? Well, Arturo, for what it's worth my subconscious just came through. And why it didn't come to me before—but what the hell it might be worth—love, and death—"

"You turning into a philosopher now?"

"*No hay tal*. You can come along if you like, and see what the hell it *is* worth. Probably just another wild-goose chase—"

"Your wild-goose chases are sometimes interesting," said Hackett.

CHAPTER 14

Mendoza said, "Give me five minutes to find out where we're going," and shut the office door on them. Sergeant Lake was on the phone, and held up a beckoning hand. Something new.

"So, have fun with the wild goose," said Grace; he and Palliser went over to Lake and on out. Three minutes later Mendoza came out of his office with his hat in hand and crooked a finger at his two senior sergeants.

Downstairs, they got into the Ferrari, Higgins squeezing into the jump seat behind, and Mendoza turned up to Grand and then to Wilshire. At the McLaren Building, the lot was not half full; they parked, and Mendoza led them up to the second floor.

"He's going to reenact the crime, just like the Paris *flics*," said Hackett.

"*Insolencia*." Mendoza led them down to the door still inscribed in gold *Dr. John Harlow, M.D.*, and opened it; they went into the waiting room. The glass window where the receptionist kept an eye on patients was open; lamps were on; there was someone here. The furniture was dusty, and past the open door to the hall they could see still a few faint marks where chalk had outlined the body of Harriet Jenkins. For a breath they all remembered the first time they'd seen this place, minutes after violent death had struck, and the screams and blood.

"I should think—" began Hackett, and steps sounded in the hall.

"Your husband told me you'd be here, Mrs. Short," said Mendoza.

"Oh, Lieutenant—you startled me." She was in an ordinary cotton dress, not nurse's uniform; her kind-eyed plump face wore a troubled look, and she looked down at the professional-man's bag she was carrying. "Yes, the lawyer asked if I'd do it, you see, as I'd be familiar with things. There's nobody else to see to things, and this has all got to be sorted out and cleared away. The office was on lease—the lawyer'll see to that, I suppose, whatever they do in a case like this. And some friends of the Harlows out where they lived, he said, they'd offered to see to the house, clean out the refrigerator and sort out clothes for the salvage people—they took all the baby's things down to wherever you people took her. That poor mite— You know, Lieutenant, I often think one of the worst things about people dying—for those left—is having to sort through all the odds and ends left."

"It can be. There'll be quite a lot to do here?"

She nodded. "It's a puzzle to me to know *what* to do with some of it —I'll ask the lawyer. The—"

"Who's the lawyer?"

"He gave me a card when he came to ask me—" She put down the bag and produced it from her purse; Mendoza copied the name and address. Grace would probably want to see the lawyer.

"I suppose some young doctor just starting out would be glad of his instruments, and the lawyer could advertise—all the equipment worth something, the sterilizers and examining tables and the new massager— but some of it's a downright puzzle. All the sample medicines, hundreds of boxes—and cotton and sterile bandage and tongue depressors and adhesive—I don't like to throw it away. I thought maybe some of the other doctors here could just take it. Use it. I asked Dr. Colcannon across the hall—" She shook her head. "All his regular patients, Dr. Harlow's I mean, are getting transferred to either Dr. Weaver or Dr. Tansey, they're both in this building and have all their own office equipment, they wouldn't be needing—and by the way, Lieutenant, we'll have to have his records back, I hope you—"

"Yes, of course, they're quite safe," said Mendoza. "I—"

"You don't realize what a place like this accumulates," said Mrs. Short. "All the odds and ends. And there's their house too— The lawyer said there was a will, but it just left everything to his wife. I didn't like to bother him, he's a busy man, but I wonder what will happen about that—"

Mendoza lit a cigarette. "A lot of red tape. In the end, everything going—after the lawyers have squabbled over it God knows how long—the property probably held in trust for the child, with an officer of the court as trustee. That is, if there's anything left after the lawyers are finished with it. Of course, if the child's adopted—"

"I do hope some nice people will take her, poor little thing. They were only paying for the house, of course. Well, it's a real headache to clear up this place, I've been at it for three days and it seems I've hardly

made a dent yet. There were some personal things in Harriet Jenkins'
desk and I couldn't locate her husband—" She sighed, and looked at
them with more attention, and said, "But here I am chattering on, and I
guess you'll have a reason for coming to see me, Lieutenant. Have you
found out who—"

"Not yet. Can we sit down?"

"Surely." They all sat down in the waiting room, which oddly still
had a professional feel to it. They felt that any minute a nurse might
look out the inner door to summon a patient.

"I brooded over those records," said Mendoza, "and this idea and
that came to me—nothing remotely plausible. But just lately, my subconscious has been nudging me—something about those records—but I
couldn't think what it was until—mmh—about half an hour ago somebody said something to me about death, and the bell rang. Loud and
clear. Those records, Mrs. Short—all those case histories of patients—"

"Yes, sir, what about them?"

"There were a lot of patients. And the records you handed me cover
the last three years or so. But there's not one recorded death in them."

"No, of course not—"

"Of course? I know he was in general practice, but surely any doctor
loses a patient now and then—"

"Of course. But when a patient died, his records would be transferred to the Deceased file. I don't know about other doctors, Dr.
Harlow was the only one I worked for privately, but he kept a Deceased
file for reference, like. For comparing, oh, new medications out for the
same thing the person had died of, and like that."

"I see. Did he lose many patients, on the average?"

"Well, general practitioners—no more than any doctor. Why?"

"Just offhand, before we have a look at that Deceased file," said
Mendoza, "how many in, say, the last six months?"

"Let me think back," said Mrs. Short. "Any doctor's apt to have a
few elderly patients and they're most likely to go, of course. There was
old Mr. Lord—that was around last February. He had rheumatoid
arthritis—it was an embolism took him off. A blood clot on the lung,
you know. It's more apt to hit sedentary, bedridden people. He was
seventy-four. His wife was still coming to the doctor—high blood pressure and colonic trouble. Let's see. Then there was Mrs. Snaith. She'd
already had two heart attacks. He'd ordered her into the hospital for
some tests, and she went all of a sudden with another one. She was in
her sixties. Oh, and one child—that was a tragic thing, but sometimes—
the little Bohlen boy. Leukemia. He was only six—"

"Parents seem to feel any—mmh—resentment against the doctor?"

She stared. "Why, no, of course not. They were just all broken up—he was an only child. And leukemia—well, everybody knows—"

"*Sí*. Any more come to you?"

"Mr. Lawrence," she said obediently. "He was a new patient—the doctor he'd been going to died, Dr. Wrather, and some of his patients were transferred to Dr. Harlow. Mr. Lawrence was only in his fifties, but he was an asthmatic—rheumatic fever as a child, and his heart wasn't strong. He'd been a semi-invalid for years—his wife used to come with him, he couldn't drive. What are you driving at, Lieutenant? When anybody dies, you don't blame the doctor, for goodness' sake. Any doctor's done all he can to stop people dying, but—"

"*Pues sí*. No rational person blames the doctor. Mr. Lawrence. And?"

"Well, for goodness' sake," she said thoughtfully. "But, Lieutenant—anybody like that, lunatic enough to think it had been the doctor's fault, wouldn't he have said so, and maybe made threats, right then—so we'd have known and I'd have told you—"

"Not necessarily. Lawrence. Carry on."

"Well, really—there was that Squires thing." Mrs. Short looked suddenly excited. "Oh, that could have—but thinking back, I don't really—Well, what happened, it was a patient of the doctor's, a Mrs. Squires, she brought her stepdaughter in. Her husband's first wife was dead, there was this girl, and she brought her to the doctor because she suspected the girl was using dope. Which it turned out she was—heroin—there was quite a scene in the office, I remember—the doctor called the police. And she was put in jail, or Juvenile Hall or somewhere, because they found some in her possession, but of course she got out on bail and ran away. She was only fifteen or sixteen. And some time later she was picked up dead—an overdose."

Mendoza looked interested. "Father resentful of stepmother—mmh—precipitating that?"

"I don't know. I don't think so—" She looked doubtful. "He was an educated man, a salesman of some kind, not the doctor's patient. But I know he came to see the doctor, with Mrs. Squires, and talked to him quite a time—like so many people he didn't really know much about narcotics."

"But—with the girl dead—" That one they could look up in their own records. Have a look around, how Squires might be feeling about that now—and about his wife—and about the doctor who, in the course of duty, had uncovered the girl's addiction and in a way precipitated her death.

"Well, I don't know. There was Mrs. Lessing. But heaven knows nobody could blame Dr. Harlow for that—her husband brought her in, last April it was—he was a regular patient—she didn't want to come, kept saying there wasn't anything wrong with her. But Mr. Lessing—" Mrs. Short chuckled, remembered where she was and sobered. "He was worried because she always seemed so dizzy and weak in the evenings when he got home—"

"Little too much *vino* inside?" grinned Mendoza.

"That's just what—only it was vodka. Mr. Lessing never suspected a thing. Well, the doctor suspected it, and even went to the trouble of dropping into the house unexpectedly to satisfy himself. But Mr. Lessing wouldn't believe it. He's an abstainer himself, and he thought she was. He—"

"Felt the doctor was insulting his wife?"

"Well, I guess he did, then. But the poor man had it proved to him a while later because she drank herself to death. Dr. Harlow knew the police surgeon who saw her, he told Dr. Harlow she must have killed a fifth of vodka, and naturally she passed right out."

"Mmh. Lessing could," said Mendoza, "have been brooding on that all right. But I don't see any way he could hold Harlow responsible—"

"I think this plot moves a little slow, Luis," said Hackett. "Your wild geese sound pretty tame to me."

"So, any more?" asked Mendoza, ignoring him.

"Well, let's see. It wasn't very often we did lose a patient, but sometimes the circumstances—there wouldn't be much he could do, you know. Did you ever read that old book about the Jukes and the Kallikaks? Genes—we had one new patient in just last month, he's in the General now, hereditary T.B. and syphilis, one lung collapsed, first stages of dementia praecox, and he had scurvy when he came in. Scurvy!—in this day and age—you could hardly believe it. But— Oh, I just remembered that."

"What?"

"Talking about genes reminded me. That poor young thing. I can't think of her last name, it'll come to me in a minute, her first name was Sue-Ellen. She was only twenty-three or so, and of course she hadn't any business getting pregnant in the first place. She wasn't, well, built for it at all, and besides that she had a congenital heart weakness and a history of pernicious anemia. When we took her history, it seemed her mother had died of dementia praecox, and her father was a complete invalid, premature senility and riddled with V.D.—he's in the General. Well, the doctor did what he could for her— What? Oh, yes, she was married, she was quite a nice young thing if not an educated girl—but the doctor said to me, a fifty-fifty chance if the baby did live it'd be a borderline idiot, physically defective, and if he had his way people with heredities like that 'd be sterilized. But he did what he could. Her blood count was way down, and she didn't respond to any treatment—he just couldn't get the red-corpuscle count up, at the last he was ordering a blood test every day—"

"She died?" asked Mendoza.

"Yes, she did. And the baby. The doctor said from the first it'd have to be a Caesarean, and when she was about at term, he did that. She was already in the hospital, for all the tests. But pernicious anemia— Well, the baby was dead when he took it, and she died on the table."

"Husband?" asked Mendoza lazily. Hackett shifted and sighed, bored.

"Oh, he carried on like a wild thing, the doctor said, weeping and wailing all over the place—I wasn't there, of course, the doctor told us about it. But there really wasn't anything the doctor could have—than he did. Freeman!" she said suddenly. "I knew it'd come to me. Sue-Ellen Freeman. And now I come to think, the doctor said her husband—"

"¿Qué demonio—? ¡Diez millones de demonios desde el infierno!" said Mendoza. He sat up with a jerk. "Freeman? Freeman? My God—"

"This says something to you?" asked Higgins.

"Because I've seen the reports." Mendoza got up. "Which you haven't. Come on. Mrs. Short, thanks very much. Art—George—¡vamos! We may just have got there."

In his cubbyhole of an office downstairs, the superintendent Enoch Shepard told them Dick Freeman didn't come in until one o'clock. Yes, he had his address, of course. Fifty-second Street.

But when they got there he wasn't home. It was one unit in a very ancient unkempt court, and just as they gave up ringing the doorbell the front door of the unit across the center walk opened and a woman came out. She was a rather handsome slatternly-looking female with a red turban wound around her head.

"You lookin' for Dick Freeman?"

"Do you know where he is?" asked Mendoza.

"You're fuzz. He in some kinda trouble? Thass a pity, but it don't supprise me none. Ever since his wife died, poor thing, he ain't been up

to much. Ain't been home much either. He took off from work a couple
weeks after, can't seem to get over it nohow."

"When did his wife die, Mrs.—?" They hadn't heard that.

"Thompson. She died, lessee, about a month ago, a bit less 'n that.
But—"

"Thanks so much," said Mendoza. So, they thought, the day Dr.
Harlow and his wife and receptionist had been shot was very likely the
first day Dick Freeman had returned to work at the McLaren Building,
after a couple of weeks off after losing his wife.

They went back there to talk to the superintendent again. He was
down in the basement—and it was in the basement that they found Dick
Freeman. He had made a little screened-off hiding place for himself in a
dark corner, with propped-up boards and an old cot, and they heard
him sobbing quietly to himself and went to look.

"He's acted sort of funny lately," said Shepard, "but I made allowances, knew he'd just lost his wife. She was a lot younger than him, and
he just thought the world of her." He was looking shocked, looking
down at Freeman on the cot. "But holing up here—I never suspected—"

And Freeman rolled over on the cot and said drearily, "I jus' couldn'
go back that house, Mr. Shepard—where Sue-Ellen 'n' I were happy—I
jus' kept seein' her there—"

"And thinking about the doctor, Freeman?" asked Mendoza. "The
doctor who didn't save her from dying?" Shepard had switched on a
main light in this part of the dingy basement, and Freeman blinked in
the sudden glare.

"Who're you?"

And Shepard said in a horrified tone, "Dr. *Harlow?* You saying
Dick—"

"How about it, Freeman?"

He raised a ravaged face to them. He was a stocky black man about
forty, with a big chest and a few pockmarks of some old skin disease.
His woolly hair was getting thin, and he had big square hands now fastened together tight in a kind of anguished silent gesture. "The doctor,
Freeman," said Mendoza. "The doctor who let Sue-Ellen die."

"He did! He did so—she *shouldn't've* died—my Sue-Ellen—"

"Oh, my God!" said Shepard. "But, my God, it was me told him to
take his wife there! It was me advised him—good doctor like—oh, my
God!"

"They know things, doctors—they got that great big hospital—needles
in her an' medicine an' her goin' see him all the time, an' he say—she
hafta tell me how he mean, some way take the baby before— She

shouldn't've gone 'n' died! That doctor—he could've stopped her dyin'! Only—only—he *wouldn't*. I heard him, I heard him my own self, I heard him one time I take Sue-Ellen there—he's talkin' to somebody, 'n' that window thing was open, I heard—my Sue-Ellen! Say, that doctor, how people with—I dunno how t' say it, but he meant like, sickness in the fambly like—hered-something—but Sue-Ellen tole me what it meant, how they ought not *have* babies— He *wanted* her to die, 'n' the baby too! All I ever had—my Sue-Ellen—"

"Oh, my God," said Shepard. He backed away.

"I thought about it—all the while I thought about it. After the funeral. Funeral—put my Sue-Ellen in the ground, an' the little baby too— we been so happy about the baby—I thought about *that doctor*. Look down his nose at people like us, ordinary folk—high 'n' mighty sayin'— I thought *good*. An' the Bible say, eye for eye, life for life. An' I took all I'd saved up—an' I went an' bought that gun—an' I—"

"Where's the gun now, Freeman?" asked Hackett gently.

And Freeman fumbled with the thin blanket spread on the cot and produced it meekly. Hackett took it and broke it; it was empty.

"I didn't have—no call for a gun—after that. I th'ew away the rest o' the bullets in the box. Mr. Shepard don't know—I been comin' here, know where the key is so I get 'nother one made, get in here. I was here —that day, before I— 'N' I don't care what you do to me," mumbled Freeman. "It don't matter. I teach *that doctor*—eye for an eye—"

They brought him in and booked him. "The vision in your crystal ball," said Hackett.

"Crystal ball hell, once my subconscious got through to me about there being no deaths listed—pure logical deduction," said Mendoza.

"Any bets on where he'll end up?" asked Higgins.

"He can't afford the tricky lawyer," said Mendoza cynically, "to claim temporary insanity, pull all the other dodges. He knew what he was doing." Freeman was just barely literate, and had signed a statement. "I'll guess life—and they'll keep him. Nobody's going to be that interested, to help him get parole when he's eligible." The joker was, of course, that in this state a lifer was eligible for parole after seven years. Of late, a few judges with some common sense had been handing down life terms with a rider, no possibility of parole; and seeing that Freeman had wantonly killed three people, he might get that rider.

At least they knew who, on the Harlow shooting. They sent the Harrington and Richardson nine-shot to Ballistics, just to get more evidence for the D.A.

Jason Grace took the name of Harlow's lawyer with thanks. "He may be persuaded to jump in on our side, who knows? Anyway, he'll know the right legal steps to take. Red tape—but she'd be worth it, you know." Grace grinned. "They finally let us see her yesterday, just for a minute."

"And good luck on it, Jase."

"Which I have the feeling we'll need. Adoption agencies—oh, well, never say die."

"I do hope they'll get her eventually," said Roberta. "You'd think even an adoption agency would have the sense to see it'd be a good home, and—"

"Yes, come to think it's a lot less trouble to produce your own," said Palliser. "My God, that Freeman—of course he's uneducated, ignorant, but essentially that couldn't matter less. When the incipient violence is in him— Well, at least he's stashed away. . . . Oh, and I forgot to tell you, Robin—"

Sheriff Roudebush had called the Homicide office on Saturday and asked for Palliser. "I just thought you'd be interested to know that we finally identified Steve. The Feds didn't know him, but they passed his prints to Interpol and they made him. He was a Canadian citizen, Steven Cockburn. Native of Vancouver. He had a little pedigree with the Vancouver police—petty theft, shoplifting, vagrancy, vandalism. Twenty-three. Raised in an orphanage there, so there's nobody to mourn him."

"And he doesn't sound like much loss to the world," said Palliser.

"I don't suppose," agreed the sheriff. "We'll probably try Brodie and the girl next month."

"Involuntary manslaughter, and Brodie'll get a year. Accessory to, the girl let off on probation."

"Oh, yes. We now have Papa Schultz," said the sheriff, "breathing fire at us. The girl's out on bail and wishing she was back in jail."

Palliser laughed. "Well, let them sort it out. The Tims and Wilmas usually in trouble of some sort."

"Any more earthquakes down there?"

"Not to speak of," said Palliser.

Landers took Phil O'Neill to dinner that night, and looking at her across the table, on the patio of Frascati's where it was just starting to cool off a little, he said, "You know, the things we see— Well, the lieutenant said the other day, it's a dangerous commodity."

"Your brilliant lieutenant with the crystal ball. What is?"

"Love," said Landers. "In"—he grinned at her—"the wrong hands, so to speak. Listen, how long are you going to play hard to get?"

"*Me?*" said Phil. She looked very delectable, his diminutive freckled Phil, in a narrow-strapped blue sundress and the high-heeled sandals that still brought her blonde head only up to his chest. "Me, playing— I told you, I'm only being sensible, Tom. We *haven't* known each other very long. And—"

"Don't con me," he said, reaching for her hand. "When you spent nearly your whole vacation chasing around playing detective to get me off the hook, back in June—well, you've got a sort of vested interest."

"And also some common sense. You got off the subject, you were telling me how your brilliant lieutenant came up with the X on the Harlow shooting. Go on. He wondered about deaths, so—?" She sipped her martini.

"It's my own fault for falling for a policewoman, I admit it. Too many brains," said Landers. "Which reminds me, what did your I.Q. test show, when you joined up?"

"What? Oh, a hundred and twenty."

"Well, by God, that settles it," said Landers pleasedly. "Soon or late, I'll overpower you, lady—you and your common sense. Mine came out a hundred and thirty-three."

"We'll hold some good thoughts for the Graces and that baby," said Angel Hackett, adding a dash of pepper to the pot she was stirring. "It'd be wonderful if they could have her."

"Jase can be persistent," said Hackett. "That Freeman—it makes you wonder."

"Genes," said Angel vaguely, tasting the contents of the pot. "Have you weighed today?"

"I'm down to two hundred and twelve," said Hackett with dignity. "And—" Mark, belatedly discovering that he was home, came shouting, and Sheila tottered up with arms upheld. Hackett picked one up in each arm, fondly. "So how are my two nuisances?" And, well, they were, at times, but love, thought Hackett suddenly and vaguely, was a funny thing. . . .

Higgins went home, and wanting to tell Mary about the Graces and their campaign to get Celia Ann Harlow, was pounced on by Steve and

Laura Dwyer. They had a library book all about earthquakes and what caused them and where they were likely to occur, and photographs of past destructions by earthquakes.

"There was one in nineteen thirty-three and it knocked down all the schools, George—it was just lucky there wasn't anybody in them when it happened—"

"And it says one can happen any time, just like the paper said—and wouldn't it be exciting if—"

Higgins didn't think it would be exactly exciting, if. Personally he could do without earthquakes. But of course he had all the seniority built up, in earthquake country.

Mary, exchanging a private grin with him, announced dinner. She was, these days, rather enormous around the middle—but she looked, thought Higgins, just fine.

Mendoza came home a little late that Saturday night. The driveway, as he turned in, was flat and smooth: the cement company had argued, and even mentioned Acts of God, but had proved no match for a redhaired Scots-Irish girl; they had repaired the drive the second time without charge.

It was getting dark, but the mockingbird in the alder tree, hearing the car, uttered a sleepy *YAWK* and a token *Yankee Doodle*. Mendoza went in the back door and found Mrs. MacTaggart just taking a pan of her special scones out of the oven. "You'll be wanting a dram," she told him. El Señor arrived posthaste as he heard the bottle taken down, and leaped to the counter top for his half ounce in a saucer.

"Ought to join A.A.," said Mendoza, and strolled down to the nursery. In the doorway he surveyed his various hostages to fortune, acquired in a somewhat helter-skelter manner over a period of time—the other cats, Bast, Sheba and Nefertite, would be having a dignified nap after dinner, elsewhere; but Cedric, their accidentally acquired shaggy dog, came to greet him amiably, shaking his face veil to show his wild walleye and offering a large paw. *"Bufón ridículo,"* said Mendoza, accepting it.

"Oh, *amado,* you're home," said Alison over the welcoming shouts of the offspring. "Now listen—I *am* getting somewhere, you know. Come on, Johnny, say it—the way we've been practicing. The wolf, English. *El lobo,* Spanish. Two ways to say it."

"Sí," said Johnny obligingly. "The wolf, English. *El lobo,* Spanish. Two ways. Daddy—Daddy—read *el cuento* 'bout *la cabra y los niños*—

the little kids, *el lobo* eat all down! An' they fill up *el lobo con* stones, an' *el lobo—*"

"Jingle!" said Terry. "Jingle! *La bruja* make *la magia—* I *like la bruja, I* like make *la magia*—like Daddy do, See-Saw Margery Daw—an' ever'thing go to *danzar!*"

Reminded of this interesting happenstance, Johnny instantly demanded, "Do again! Make all go to *danzar,* Daddy—"

Mendoza burst out laughing and Alison said crossly, "*¡Por Dios!* Just as I think I'm accomplishing— And it's a great help for you to find it amusing, I must say! If you'd try to *cooperate* a little—"

"A losing battle," said Mendoza. "As they mature, *enamorada,* they'll sort out the problem for themselves. I hope."

"And your father," said Alison to the twins, "may be the brilliant guiding light of LAPD Homicide, but he does not bring about earthquakes—"

It was, of course, unfortunate that just then there was a slight aftershock, and everything rattled and trembled for twenty seconds.

"Honestly!" said Alison. "I just can't win. Honestly!"

And of course, whatever cases they cleared away, filed final reports on, handed over to the D.A.'s office, the inevitable routine went on for Central Homicide. The new calls, the new bodies making more paper work, if seldom the mysteries posed in the paperbacks at the corner drugstore.

That Sunday, they had another body on the Row—probably natural death: the inevitable new suicide, and yesterday's traffic accident, one D.O.A., to finish the paper work on. Mendoza was reading the autopsy report on a body from two days back, without much interest, when Hackett looked into his office and said, "New one just gone down."

"*¿Qué?* Anything interesting?"

"Well, you might think so. Body just found up by the Dodger Stadium—I talked to the Traffic man. Young fellow, no immediate cause evident, no I.D., not a mark on him. And he's wearing a false beard and moustache."

"*¿Cómo? ¡Parece mentira!* What the hell— I think I'll come with you, take a look—"

"I thought you might," said Hackett. "A little offbeat, it sounds."

Downstairs, as they got into the Ferrari, there was no sign of the picket with his doom-predicting sign. "Maybe he's decided the doom isn't so imminent after all," said Mendoza. It was a warm sunny day, clear blue sky, and the aftershocks were gradually diminishing. But of course now they had to look forward to the worst of the summer heat in Southern California.

"Imminent hell, who knows?" said Hackett. "Another article in the *Herald* last night, we could have another big one any time, pressure building on the San Andreas—"

"Don't borrow trouble, Arturo," said Mendoza cheerfully. "Sufficient is the evil— And this new one looks a little interesting. . . ."

WITH
INTENT
TO
KILL

Mit der Dummheit kämpfen Götter selbst ver-gebens. Against stupidity the gods themselves struggle in vain.

—FRIEDRICH VON SCHILLER

Who sets his eyes on what is not his, loses also what is his.

—*The Talmud*

CHAPTER 1

Mendoza woke abruptly. It was pitch dark and out in the hall the phone was ringing, shrill and monotonous. He sat up, swearing. Beside him Alison stirred and muttered, and from the tangle of cats at the foot of the bed El Señor cursed at being disturbed.

The luminous face of the bedside clock informed Mendoza that it was two thirty-seven A.M. Swearing, he got out of bed and made for the phone in the hall. As he stumbled against the telephone table, the central light went on and Mrs. MacTaggart appeared at the end of the hall, looking like a woolly blue lamb in her fleece robe.

"Mendoza," he said through a yawn.

"Luis, it's me! Listen, I've got to—it's Mary, and I've got to take her —she says it might be pretty soon— Listen, you said—it's the kids, and I've got to—"

"Yes, George," said Mendoza. "Take a long breath and simmer down. I'll—"

"That's a hell of a lot of help!" said Sergeant Higgins wildly. "Mary says they're about twelve minutes apart now and— Listen, I know she's had experience at it but I haven't, damn it, and the kids—"

"You go on, Máiri'll be right over, George."

"But how the hell—we can't leave the house unlocked, for—"

"Now, you're not really taking Steve and Laura to the hospital with you, George."

"Oh!" said Higgins. "Oh, of— Well, all right, but I—Mary, don't you dare go down those steps al—" The phone crashed in Mendoza's ear.

"It's the Higgins' baby," he said through another yawn to Alison and Mrs. MacTaggart.

"But it's a good six weeks early, that'll be," said Mrs. MacTaggart interestedly. "They'll be wanting me to stay with the children, then. I'll be dressed and off in a jiffy—"

"You are not," said Mendoza, "going to drive clear across town alone at this hour of night, Máiri. I'll take you over."

She shook her silver curls at him. "And if you please, how am I to get on withoot my ain car? And who'd bother an old biddy like me at all?"

"I'll bring your car over in the morning," said Alison. "He's quite right. Isn't it funny how babies so often do start arriving in the middle of the night? But you said October, and it's only September fifteenth—"

"It'll be a lively one, anxious to get here," said Mrs. MacTaggart thoughtfully, and went back to her room to dress. Mendoza flung on shirt, trousers, jacket, and rummaged for car keys and cigarettes on the dresser.

"Well, now I'm up I think I'll have a glass of milk," said Alison, running fingers through her red hair. El Señor cursed again at the noise and lights. "I only hope we haven't waked up the twins."

The twins slumbered peacefully; but another member of the household had been disturbed too. As Mendoza came out to the hall again he nearly fell over Cedric, the shaggy Old English sheepdog, coming to look for burglars.

"George is in a dither," said Mendoza as he started the Ferrari's engine.

"And why wouldna he be, poor man? His first one, and him pushing forty, you said. Naturally he's all twittery over it," said Mrs. MacTaggart comfortably. "I warrant you the Dwyer children'll be in a state too."

That, they discovered at the old house on Silver Lake Boulevard, was an understatement. Higgins, the longtime bachelor, solemnly falling for Sergeant Bert Dwyer's widow, was fond of the Dwyer children too, and they of him. It was possible that twelve-year-old Steve and ten-year-old Laura Dwyer were more excited about the baby than Higgins was.

"Those kids won't get back to sleep tonight," Mendoza reported, laughing, when he came home. "They're wild to know which it is."

"Well, you'd better get back to sleep," said Alison, "or you'll be late at the office."

He was late to the office anyway; Alison let him oversleep. Finding her preoccupied with the twins' breakfast, he kissed her hastily and said he'd get something somewhere on the way; he stopped at a Mannings' coffee shop, and drifted into the office at half past nine, as usual immaculate in silver-gray Italian silk, snowy shirt, discreet tie.

Sergeant Lake was sitting at the switchboard in the anteroom, past the door labeled *Homicide*. "You're late," he commented. Mendoza agreed.

"Who's here? Anything new gone down?"

"You've got a new body," said Lake gloomily, and picked up his book again. The sedentary years had caught up with him of late, and the book was *How to Eat Well and Stay Slim*. Mendoza went into the sergeants' office. Its sole occupant was Sergeant Arthur Hackett, big and sandy, who was typing a report.

"You're late. So's George. Goofing off," said Hackett, and hit a wrong key and swore.

"George we may not see much of today," said Mendoza. "The baby started arriving about two thirty and he woke us all up dithering for Máiri to come stay with the kids. He'll probably call in, some time. What's—"

"It's early," said Hackett. "Well, I suppose they'll both be relieved to have it over. You taking a bet, boy or girl?"

"No bets. It won't matter to George," grinned Mendoza. "What's the new body?"

Hackett leaned back in his chair and it creaked under his weight. "I was saying to George just yesterday," he said sleepily, "most of what we see on this job can be summed up in two words. Stupidity and cupidity."

"That's quite an epigram, Arturo." Mendoza hoisted one hip onto John Palliser's desk and lit a cigarette.

"But I don't know which applies to the new body. Yet. John Hagan, forty-nine, worked for The Broadway department store as a bookkeeper. Lived in an apartment over on Virgil with his wife—one married daughter back in Florida. The Hagans have a dog. A Dachsie. Every night about ten o'clock Hagan took the dog for a walk round the block. Last night neither of 'em came home. A man named Fellows heard a shot about a quarter past ten—he lives just past the corner of Virgil and Fourth—went out and found Hagan. Shot in the body. D.O.A. The dog found its way home just about as Schenke got there to break the news to the widow."

"Hagan rolled?"

"It doesn't look as if he was," said Hackett. "Wife told Bob that he never carried any cash on him, out that late at night, and apparently nobody went through his pockets. He was still wearing a diamond ring worth about a hundred bucks, according to the wife."

"¿Qué es esto?" said Mendoza. "Funny. See what the lab gives us— ask around about quarrels and so on. Where's everybody else?"

"John went out on the Carroll thing—the heist. He'll probably fetch in a dozen witnesses to make statements, tie up the office the rest of the day. I don't know where Jase is, but I've been out on this thing—" And another two from the day watch were accounted for. It was Tom Landers' day off. And Matt Piggott's vacation had started last Monday, and he'd got married to his Prudence and gone off to Yosemite on a honeymoon; they wouldn't see Piggott until the end of the month.

And of course the deceased Mr. Hagan was just the latest thing Homicide had to work. There was also the heist job pulled on Wednesday night, at the little dairy store owned by Patrick Carroll, with several witnesses. He had evidently put up a fight and was still on the critical list at Central Receiving Hospital. There was the unidentified body of a woman, found in the street last Monday morning: no lead had turned up on that at all. There was the inevitable suicide with the paperwork still to do. There was the equally inevitable wino dead in an alley off Main Street, paperwork to do on that. Now, Mr. Hagan: and neither Mendoza nor Hackett would take any bets that a couple of more new things might show up, today or tomorrow or Sunday. The Homicide office of the L.A.P.D. was kept busy as a rule.

"I'll take a look at Hagan," said Mendoza.

"And welcome. I left Bob's report on your desk."

Mendoza went into his office, automatically straightened the desk-blotter, brushed a few ashes from the desk as he sat down, and lit a new cigarette, taking up Detective Bob Schenke's initial report on John Hagan. It didn't, on the one hand, look like a very interesting kill—few were—but on the other, it was just a little funny-peculiar. He read the terse phrases over twice, got up and took down his wide-brimmed homburg. "I'll go see the widow," he told Hackett. "Back in an hour or so."

It was an old apartment, the kind of place people like the Hagans lived; little people, you could say, living on modest incomes from the unglamorous jobs. The apartment was very neat, with a good deal of old furniture and flowered drapes and a fairly good amateur landscape in a gold frame over the imitation hearth. Mrs. Hagan, plump, tearful, still incredulous, told him, "Our daughter painted that, did you say Lieutenant? She's a very good artist, Annie is. But you asked—you said —and there's just *nothing*. No reason for anybody to— Why John? John never had a—an argument with anybody. He didn't like rows and upsets. I don't recall we ever had a quarrel all the twenty-six years we were married. I just can't take it in—"

"What about his job?' asked Mendoza. "The people he worked with?"

She had the little red Dachsie on her lap, stroking it automatically; she went on shaking her head. "There's nothing. He'd been there since we were married. Steady—John was always steady, you know? Everybody liked him, he always got on fine with everybody. There's just no—"

Well, see the people at The Broadway, thought Mendoza; they might have some different answers. Homicide was seldom very complex, and it had often been done for a very slight motive.

That thought reoccurred to him as he pushed open the door of the big headquarters building, Parker Center. Just ahead of him in the lobby was Jason Grace, half-turned lighting a cigarette, and he looked a little glum.

"Have you been goofing off again, as Art puts it? Over at the County Adoption Agency?"

Grace said, "So you finally showed up. Who's goofing off? Virginia's filling out more forms down there today." It had really been no motive at all, last month, which had orphaned three-month-old Celia Ann Harlow. And the Graces, disappointed in not producing their own family, were wading through all the red tape trying to acquire her legally. Grace brushed his narrow moustache in unconscious mimicry of Mendoza now, his regular-featured chocolate-brown face thoughtful. "Red tape," he said. "Well. No, I've been down to the morgue escorting another fearful husband. It isn't his runaway wife. Jane Doe still unidentified. I don't think we'll ever make her now, Lieutenant."

"Only four days. Oh, did—"

"And Higgins hasn't turned up, talking about goofing off."

Mendoza told him why. "It's getting on for eleven, he may be calling in."

They went up to the office. Hackett had apparently gone out and come back: he was taking a statement from an excited-looking middle-aged man who gestured violently as he talked. John Palliser was talking quietly to a scared-looking young woman in a tight green sheath.

"All the statements on that heist," sighed Grace.

"Any word from George, Jimmy?"

"Nope," said Lake, not looking up from his book.

Henry Glasser came in with an elderly woman. "It's just a matter of making a statement, Mrs. Ritter. Half an hour." She looked around the big room bewilderedly as he led her to his desk.

"There's something funny about this Hagan," said Mendoza meditatively.

"A hunch tells you. Who's Hagan?"

"I don't know that it's a hunch exactly—" Mendoza wandered into his own office. Hunches, he thought, maybe he didn't need: twenty-four years' experience on the job was what told him this and that. He hung up his hat and was just about to have a look at any other overnight reports when Sergeant Lake looked in and beckoned, with a resigned expression.

"*¿Qué?*" Mendoza came out, to find Assistant Police Chief Durward being hearty to a tall slim fellow in very British tailoring. Whenever Assistant Chief Durward sounded hearty, it was a sign that he was feeling annoyed. "Lieutenant Mendoza," he said now, punctiliously. "Assistant Commissioner Hayes-Worthington of Scotland Yard, Mendoza. Over here on business, and he'd like a look at our little operation here. Hope you don't mind our invading Homicide, Luis."

"Certainly not. How do you do," said Mendoza unenthusiastically.

Hayes-Worthington bared yellow false teeth at him and remarked in nearly understandable Oxfordese that he understood the Los Angeles police enjoyed a somewhat better reputation than most Amurrican forces, haw. Durward beamed at him steadily.

Mendoza bent a brilliant smile on him and said cordially, "We do like to think so, Commissioner, and it's always gratifying to have our own opinion backed up. I understand that your—mmh—well-known scientific laboratory has consulted ours for help on a number of occasions. We're always happy to be of service to baffled bobbies, you know."

Hayes-Worthington said, "Oh—haw—is that so indeed?"

"I'm sure," said Durward, looking remotely amused, "that a quick look around your facilities here—if you wouldn't mind— Now this is the sergeants' office, Commissioner—"

They were just rid of Durward and the Assistant Commissioner, and it was ten past twelve and Mendoza was thinking about lunch—the other boys could finish the paperwork later—when Higgins rushed in breathlessly and stood leaning on Sergeant Lake's desk. He was clad in the top half of blue pajamas and an old pair of slacks. He needed a shave, and with his dark hair on end he looked even more of a thug than usual.

"Luis—Art!" he croaked excitedly. "She's here, and it's a girl! It's Margaret Emily! Mary's fine! It's a girl, eight pounds even, even six weeks early! She's got a lot of black hair and fingernails! She—"

"Well, that's fine, George, just fine," said Hackett, coming out to pound his shoulder.

"And keep up the good work, *compadre*," added Mendoza. "But what about you?"

"Me? I'm just fine," said Higgins. "We thought it'd be sooner, but she didn't come till two minutes before eleven. And they wouldn't let me in right away—and then they let me—I phoned home to tell Steve and Laura, and then—"

"Yes, yes, all's well that ends well," said Mendoza, "but you're not exactly dressed for the office, you know, and when did you have anything to eat?"

"Eat?" said Higgins. "Oh, she's fine, she's just fine, boys! Wait till you— Now that you mention it, I'm starving. What the hell time is it? Well, I'll be damned!" He looked down at himself. "My God, I never thought—"

The rest of them were laughing. "We'll make an exception and let you tag along to Federico's," said Mendoza. "You've got an excuse, after all."

"Damn right," said Higgins. "Wait till you see her! She's got blue eyes but Mary said they all do at first, so maybe—but all that hair, a lot of babies don't have any, and she—"

"Judging from experience," said Hackett as they waited for the elevator, "we'll have to listen to all the rhapsodizing until the first few times he has to change her."

"If you ask me, boys," said Mendoza, "I'm keeping fingers crossed. Babies! We're hearing about nothing else these days. *¿Qué pasa aquí?* Here's John's wife expecting too—"

"Unexpectedly," said Palliser with a grin.

"And Jase using every spare minute to persuade the Adoption Agency they're fit parents—and now Margaret Emily. The fingers firmly crossed," said Mendoza. "Those twin monsters are quite enough to cope with!"

And when he got home, after an otherwise unprofitable day, he found Alison coping with the twin monsters, who were as full of energy as usual, and over their milk toast and apricot pudding demanding to be read to.

"*¡La bruja!*" nodded Teresa solemnly. "Make all the bad *magia*."

"*¡El lobo!*" shouted Johnny. "He eat *la abuela* all down!"

"The grandmother," said Alison absently. "English, Johnny. Hello, *amado*. Oh, damn." As both their parents were as apt to come out with Spanish as English, the twins at the official age of three had only the vaguest notion of any difference. The current campaign to correct the situation was not meeting with much success. The battered copy of Grimm, however, had been an instant hit.

"Burn up in *la estufa,*" said Johnny darkly now.

His sister contributed, "*La bruja* make ever'body dead *por la magia!*"

"Oh, dear," said Alison. "But isn't it *nice* about Margaret Emily? Máiri phoned—I'd just got back from taking her car over. Your offspring much enjoyed the ride in the cab, by the way. Quite a novelty. Johnny wants you to put a meter in the Ferrari—he likes the tick."

"He would," said Mendoza. "I suppose we'll be without Máiri for a week or so."

"At least. Anything exciting happen at the office? And I've got steaks and baked potatoes."

"*Muy lindo.* Nothing," said Mendoza, "but an Assistant Commissioner from Scotland Yard. And hasn't that breed of Homo sapiens brought the art to perfection."

"What art?"

"Oh, the simple arrogance."

"I told you it'd be a girl," said Angel. "The worst spoiled brat in the state, if Mary Higgins doesn't put her foot down. Bad as you."

"Me?" said Hackett. "Don't be silly." He'd been dutifully admiring four-year-old Mark's crayon sketches; now he squeezed his daughter and inquired fondly, "And how's Daddy's own Sheila?" At eighteen months she had suddenly developed a dimple, and her hair was definitely auburn.

"Men!" said Angel, casting her eyes to heaven.

"But I just can't hardly wait to see her, George!" Laura's big gray eyes, so like Mary's, were shining. "Our own little baby! I don't care a bit she's a girl—"

"I always said it'd be a girl," said Steve proudly. "I *knew* she was Margaret Emily all along, George! Gee, can't Mother come home with her till *next week?* Gee—"

"Oh, she's fine, just fine," said Higgins, beaming at them. "Wait till you see! And you know, I just remembered something—you know that old rhyme? She was born on a Friday—'loving and giving' she'll be—"

Mrs. MacTaggart, ladling out plates of rich stew, regarded the three of them benignly.

"Belatedly, I'm having qualms," said Roberta Palliser. "What you say about Sergeant Higgins. Heavens, you're thirty-five, and a first one—if it's a girl you'll spoil her rotten."

"Don't be ridiculous," said Palliser. "And it's not my fault we didn't start one right away."

"I rather wish we had now," said Roberta. "Oh, well, it can't be helped. Only—Margaret. It's one of my favorites, I'd almost settled on it if it is a girl."

"There's no law we can't use it too, Robin. Yes, I do like it."

"And David. Or possibly Andrew. And I really can't see you acting quite like that, dithering around, at that. You're much too reserved."

"Now really, Robin—"

The first news that greeted them on Saturday morning was that Pat Carroll was off the danger list and could be questioned, briefly.

Landers and Grace went over to Central Receiving to see him. Tom Landers was feeling annoyed at women, and said so. "Your level-headed blonde," nodded Grace.

"That Phil," said Landers. "Toss you for who drives?" He won; they climbed into Grace's little blue racer, the Elva. Landers had fallen for his blonde back in June—Phil O'Neill who was also an L.A.P.D. officer, down in R. and I., but Phillipa Rosemary O'Neill was a very common-sensible blonde and still saying they hadn't known each other long enough, and she was still making up her mind about him. . . . "I'll get her eventually," vowed Landers. "I'm smarter than she is, according to my I.Q. score."

At the hospital, they were allowed five minutes with Carroll. He'd taken a bullet in one lung, another in the stomach, and extensive surgery had been done; he was still very weak. But when he understood that they were police officers, he was anxious to talk: the nurse gently pressed him down as he tried to sit up.

"Two of 'em," he said. "Two. Big louts—but just kids—seventeen, eighteen. One—'bout six feet, long blond hair, dirty—both of 'em dirty, sloppy clothes—"

"Take it easy, Mr. Carroll," said Landers.

"Other one darker—not s' big." Carroll was a big man, an ex-Army sergeant who had kept in condition, but he wasn't a young man. They'd taken his false teeth out, which made it harder for him to talk. "Called th' other one Bernie. Bernie. Gun—maybe a .32, about—"

"Yes, sir." They knew about the gun. Ballistics had said, a Smith and Wesson .32 revolver, an old one and in poor condition. "Had you ever seen either of them before?"

He shook his head. "An' people in th' store—five, six customers. Crazy. Be about fifty, sixty bucks in the register. Just *louts*. Lazy sloppy dirty louts. An' high on somethin'. Dope, liquor, dunno. Don't think—drunk. High. Silly, laughin'—no reason. I went for my gun—"

"Your gun?" Both Landers and Grace snapped to attention; there'd been no gun found at the scene. Carroll was an old bachelor, no family around, so nobody had told them about his gun.

"Sure. Colt .38—under the counter. But the blond one—he had the gun—"

"I'm sorry, I think that's quite enough," said the nurse. Carroll sank back on the pillow, and Landers and Grace were firmly shepherded out.

"What the hell," said Landers, "so they took his gun. It'd be registered, Jase. Carroll's a very upright fellow."

"So it would. So we can chase down the serial number, put it out to the pawnbrokers. But Ballistics said the .32's in pretty bad shape. It could be the pair of louts were very pleased to pick up a gun in better shape, Tom."

"And how right you are," said Landers ruefully.

They went back to the office and communicated that to Mendoza, who just grunted at them. He was, dapper as usual, narrow moustache trimmed neat, swiveled around in the desk-chair contemplating the view of the Hollywood hills in the distance, very clear and sharp this bright day. It was very evidently going to be an early fall in Southern California. After the heat wave and the earthquake last month (they were still getting the aftershocks), suddenly mid-September had cooled off, and today there was a definite feel of autumn in the air. They could hope for some early rain: the mountains were tinder-dry and ripe for wildfire.

"But," said Mendoza, "there is something funny about Hagan. When X never even went through his pockets . . . Carroll, yes. The louts. Typical. *Conforme*. But Hagan—damn it, the insignificant little clerk type—and his hundred-buck diamond ring—"

"Well, these louts," said Landers firmly. All the men at Homicide had learned to be firm with the boss on occasion, when he sounded irrational. "We thought we'd ask Juvenile—and Robbery—passing on the descriptions. Which are no great shakes, but they might ring a bell in somebody's mind—"

"*Sí. Naturalmente*," said Mendoza. "You'd better do that. But this Hagan—why the hell is he in the morgue?"

He had gone to look at the corpse. A little man, in both senses. From what Mendoza had now heard from the people who had worked with him, the apartment neighbors, a good man: one of the do-right people, a respectable and reliable man, but insignificant. Unremarkable. A man set in a routine.

He had earned eight hundred a month. He hadn't any outstanding debts. He paid his rent on time. He'd attended the Central Christian Church most Sundays. He'd never been known to have an argument with anybody. He didn't drink or gamble. And when he took the little Dachsie for a walk every evening, he didn't carry any money on him.

Which a mugger would not have known. But a mugger would have pulled out Hagan's pockets, looking. A mugger would have taken that diamond ring.

There was something just a little offbeat about Hagan.

He agreed with Landers and Grace about the louts, on Carroll; they separated to ask questions in Juvenile and Robbery. He came out to the anteroom, wondering where else to go on Hagan, and Hackett and Palliser were just emerging from the other office.

"I swear to God," said Hackett, "George is in his second childhood over that baby—he'll be boring us for the next year with snapshots, I'll bet. Oh, Luis. We've got all the statements on Carroll, and they add up to two fairly worthless descriptions. Of—"

"The louts," said Mendoza. "Yes. It could be somebody'll recognize them—I wouldn't doubt they're in somebody's files somewhere—mmh, yes. But on Hagan—what was it you said, Art? Stupidity and cupidity—only which? And why? *¿Qué tal?* Such an ordinary little man, out walking the dog. And where else to go on it—"

"Hagan, oh, yes. Well, I did say—"

"Stupidity and cupidity, that's good," said Palliser appreciatively. "What we see, all right." On Saturdays Sergeant Lake was off, pursuing his latest diet at home, and Sergeant Rory Farrell was on the switchboard; he now gave them a sardonic grin and said he'd go along with that, it summed up 99 percent of the job. And the board buzzed at him, and he turned to it alertly.

"Hagan," said Palliser. "Something offbeat?"

"I don't—" said Mendoza, and Farrell swung round suddenly.

"Lieutenant—cycle man shot over on Olympic! Corner of Alvarado—ambulance on the way—"

They ran.

CHAPTER 2

At the normally busy intersection of Olympic Boulevard and Alvarado Street, the crowd had collected minutes ago, and stood on all four sides of the streets, talking, gesturing, watching. There were two black-and-whites there, four uniformed men; another car bucketed up and two more Traffic men got out of it just as Mendoza cut the siren and braked the Ferrari. The ambulance had just arrived.

Two of the patrolmen were out in the street, bent over the sprawled body of the uniformed man there. The L.A.P.D. motorcycle was overturned beside him, and grotesquely its radio was still going: "L70, come in, L70 . . . K80, a call, five four nine Atlantic, a 415 report—" The ambulance attendants come up and the patrolmen stood. Mendoza had brought out the badge automatically. "We're Homicide. What happened here?"

"McRea, sir—Gonzales. It's Mike Ahearn, sir—we haven't had a chance to hear much, but it seems he pulled a car over for a traffic violation and somebody shot him. A lot of these people claim to have seen it—"

"Claim is probably right," said Hackett; but he and Palliser split up and began asking questions among the crowd along this side of Olympic.

"He's still alive," said one of the attendants. "We'd better get him in fast." They got him onto a stretcher and into the ambulance. The motorcycle radio went on blaring, and Mendoza went over and shut it off. McRea looked very young and shaken; he turned to watch the ambulance drive away, and Mendoza asked, "Ahearn a friend of yours, McRea?"

"I guess you could say, sir. He lives—next door to us. He's the one got me to join the force, of course he's been in ten years, I'm still on probation. What? Yes, sir, he's married—two kids. Yes, sure I know his wife— Oh, my God, of course somebody's got to tell—and my mother'll want to help—"

Mendoza said to Gonzales, "Call in and tell them where McRea is. We'll probably take Mrs. Ahearn down to the hospital. You can help out my men here, sorting out witnesses."

Gonzales nodded shortly once, no word wasted. Mendoza led McRea over to the Ferrari. They didn't want Mrs. Ahearn to hear about it on some news bulletin: and it was queer that that well-known cynic Luis Rodolfo Vicente Mendoza of Central Homicide had never minded breaking the bad news to people until he'd acquired the hostages to fortune himself, belatedly. But it was his job: he started off to do it.

Hackett and Palliser and the squad-car men trying to sort out good from bad witnesses were feeling resigned as usual in that sort of situation. From a crowd, you got as many descriptions as there were people. Various people told them the car was a Ford, a Caddy, a Chrysler, a VW wagon, that it was blue, off-white, tan, green, and orange; and that it was towing a small U-Haul truck, a trailer, a four-wheeled camper. Most of the crowd was eager to tell what they'd seen, or thought they'd seen, and some of them worked along here in the many small stores lining the streets; they could be questioned later.

Hackett came, after about half an hour, to Hortense Brett, who impressed him at once as a good witness. She had, for one thing, waited patiently while he listened to a couple of other people, among them the voluble little butcher from the market up the block who at last admitted he hadn't really *seen* it, just dashed out when he heard the shots— "But I saw the car, it was an old Ford, it was tan, Officer, and it was pullin' a trailer some kind—"

"Yes, sir, thanks very much." Hackett eyed the woman who stepped forward dubiously.

"I saw the whole thing," she said calmly. "My name's Hortense Brett. I'd just come out of the office building there—I'd been to the dentist. I saw it all."

"Yes, Mrs. Brett?"

"Miss." She appraised his bulk interestedly; she was a little woman, far from young, plain and unmade up, in shabby clothes; but she spoke confidently. "I used to teach mathematics—sixth grade, Officer—"

"Sergeant Hackett."

"Oh, yes. So I suppose I've got a logical mind, and I don't lose my head, you see. The car—I'm sorry I can't tell you the exact make, but it was a medium-sized car, like a Dodge or a Buick, and at least six or seven years old. A sedan, four-door. It was light green, but very dusty and dirty. And it was pulling a small house-trailer."

"Two wheels—four?"

"Two, I think. Not very big anyway—one of those things that just have bunks inside, for camping, you know. The trailer was white."

"And what did you see happen?"

"I don't know what the driver did wrong—you see, I only looked up when I heard the siren—it just barely went on, and then stopped—and the car and trailer were just turned onto Olympic, the officer motioning the car over. The car stopped, about at that alley driveway—" The alley, created for delivery purposes, ran behind the office building on the corner. "And I suppose the officer was going to get off his motorcycle and walk up to the car. But he hadn't got off the machine, he was right up behind the trailer, when the door of the trailer opened—it had a door in the rear—and a man in the trailer shot at him. It was terrible—I couldn't believe it for a moment—and I couldn't see at all what the man looked like. The door just opened, and the shots came— And then the door shut again and the man in the trailer yelled something and slammed the door as I say, and the car drove off. Fast."

"What did he yell, could you hear?"

"I couldn't say. But I've got a very good memory and I'm sure of all I've told you, Sergeant. It was just terrible—"

"We'd like you to come down to headquarters and make a statement, if you will, Miss Brett."

"Whatever I can do to help, Sergeant. Is the poor man dead, do you know?"

The uniformed men had collected quite a few names for them—handed those over and got back on tour. Palliser had assembled three people to take in for formal statements by the time Hackett had selected Miss Brett—two men from the tailorshop down the block, and a young attorney who'd been on the way to his office. They sounded the most clear-headed witnesses, so Hackett and Palliser took them back to the office in a couple of squad cars and took down their statements with the help of Landers and Grace. They could come in to sign them later when they'd been formally typed. Meanwhile—

"How do they stack up?" asked Landers.

Hackett shuffled the shorthand pages thoughtfully. "Not too many discrepancies—good witnesses. They all say the car was an oldie, medium-sized, and they all say it was green except Connors, the lawyer. He says it was blue, but that's an easy mistake. All of 'em say it was a two-wheel trailer, white. Both car and trailer dirty and dusty. No vague descriptions of either man, no make on the plates, but that's enough to put out an A.P.B."

"Which you as the senior sergeant can go and do," said Palliser. "I'm starving to death."

Hackett put out the A.P.B. to four counties around, as a start, before he joined them for lunch.

Henry Glasser had come in late, and minus any breakfast; and that was entirely due to the earthquake last month. The second good shake had knocked down the apartment garage on his car; and what with his mother's recent surgery, and that new suit he shouldn't have indulged in, and a few other things, he hadn't any kind of down payment. Insurance companies regarded earthquakes as Acts of God—which technically he supposed they were, but it was all very damned awkward, and what God had had against his old Ford— He'd been driving his cousin's car: Fred was still in uniform, working out of Wilcox Street, and could hitch a ride to work; and he'd had a sworn-to-be-honest mechanic at a used-car lot looking for a bargain. The bargain had showed up yesterday, the mechanic had called him last night, and Glasser had foregone breakfast to make a quick deal. It was transportation merely: a seven-year-old Plymouth with seventy thousand on it, but vouched for as sound and reliable. Glasser had signed the papers, mentally groaning at the thought of even those modest monthly payments, and taken delivery. He thought about that insolent-nosed Italian hot rod Mendoza drove—of course it cost a fortune to run, a twelve-cylinder engine, and anyway not everybody had had a miserly grandfather who unexpectedly turned out to be a millionaire.

But in consequence, he'd gone out for an early lunch, and missed the alert about Ahearn. He came back about twelve and began to type up the statements taken yesterday on the Carroll heist; so he was the only one in the office when James Slater came in.

Sergeant Farrell sent him in; he stopped just inside the door and said, "I— Is this where I'm supposed to—?" He was a tallish thin man in his late thirties, well enough dressed, losing his hair.

Glasser got up. "What can we do for you, sir?"

"My name's James Slater. I didn't know if I ought to come, but my mother said—I've been away. On business. I have to travel some for the firm—wholesale jewelry. Just costume stuff, I mean. And Mother said there'd been something in the paper, and I ought to come."

"About what, sir?"

"That you found a—a body. Somewhere down here. A woman
About thirty-five, bleached blonde hair, it said, and—"

"Oh," said Glasser. "You think it's someone you know?"

"Mother said it could be Alma. My wife Alma. It could be." Slater
looked miserable.

"Do you want to see it, Mr. Slater?"

"I guess I'd better, now I'm here," said Slater thinly.

In the morgue, he looked down in silence at the cold tray, and finally
said, "Yes, it's her. It's Alma. My wife. She'd gone off before, you see—
while I was away from home—but she always turned up again in a
while. A month or so, when she ran out of money. This time—this time
it'd been nearly three months, and—" He shook his head.

He signed the papers. Out in the hall, Glasser said, "The—er—death
certificate, Mr. Slater—any funeral director will—"

"I guess I don't need to see the certificate," said Slater. "But I'd like
to know why, you know. Do you know why?"

The death certificate said, Acute alcoholism and advanced malnu-
trition. "Why, what?" asked Glasser.

"Just why, damn it! She had so much going for her—looks and
brains, she was a beautiful girl when we got married. Fifteen years
back. Why would she want to get on the stuff before she was thirty?
And she'd try to shake it—I got her to join A.A. once, even—but next
thing I knew, she'd gone, and maybe I'd get police calling, picked her
up D. and D. Just why? No *reason*. I make a good living, we've got a
nice house in the valley. And what do you suppose it's done to Norma,
my God? Our little girl Norma—she's twelve. Twelve. Seeing her mother
—and Alma going off leaving her alone— Just *why*?"

"I wouldn't know, sir," said Glasser. Act of God? he thought. If Matt
Piggott was here he'd be talking about the devil converting men's
hearts, and maybe he'd be right.

Slater just shook his head again, and turned away. But at least Jane
Doe had got identified.

Glasser went back to the office and heard about Ahearn for the first
time.

That afternoon Alison left the twins with that invaluable domestic
Bertha, put on her newest topaz shirtwaist dress, and went to the hospital to see Mary Higgins and admire the new arrival. She found Angel
before her.

"Thank heaven," said Mary, "we found an old-fashioned hospital
where they let baby stay with mama. And I can't tell you how relieved

am that she decided to come early—I was feeling like a dirigible. And she weighed eight pounds at that."

Miss Margaret looked to be, even at some thirty hours old, quite a personality. "All that hair," said Angel. "She's a darling."

"Her eyes are set like yours," said Alison.

"Don't say it!" said Mary. "Not that I'd like her to take after George —a girl, after all—but it's going to take all my time as it is. Between him and Steve, spoiling her—"

"Whatever age, they are difficult," sympathized Angel.

"Babies?"

"Men, darling."

Mendoza drifted into the office at four o'clock, and found Hackett, Palliser, Landers, Grace and Glasser all busy at their typewriters. "And where have you been?" asked Hackett. "Evidently George is taking the day off to celebrate."

"Has anybody called the hospital?"

"Just now," said Farrell from the door. "Ahearn's holding his own. They got the slugs out and sent 'em to Ballistics."

"And those boys'll take their own sweet time about a report," said Mendoza. "I deduce you're all typing up the statements from the best witnesses. What did they tell you?"

Hackett told him. "There's an A.P.B. out. Nothing so far."

"They probably got under cover as soon as they could. But it also occurs to me," said Mendoza, lighting a cigarette, "why shoot a cop rather than accept a traffic ticket? It seems rather drastic, if that's the word—"

"So, was there something in that car or trailer, such as a few pounds of H or a bunch of bombs or such? Yes indeedy," said Grace.

"Which leads me to wonder further if some other set of boys in blue might be interested in that car and trailer. I know we've got no description of the men, but we might just ask NCIC."

"Which I should have thought of," said Hackett ruefully, and took up the phone to pass that to Communications. The National Crime Information Center was proving a very useful clearinghouse, nationwide, for all forces everywhere. Geared to work with computers, it could produce answers within minutes. In this case it didn't, immediately.

"And what about the louts on Carroll, Tom?"

Landers abandoned his typewriter, sat back and lit a cigarette. "Goldberg didn't give us anything, but Juvenile was more likely anyway. The computers turned up three sets of pals for us—pairs known to operate together, who might match the descriptions. The usual punks—oldest nineteen, youngest sixteen—the usual pedigrees, petty theft, mugging, shoplifting."

"*Qué interesante.* You'll go looking."

"Sometime. We haven't had a lab report on it yet. Where have you been, by the way?"

"After I took Mrs. Ahearn to the hospital, and we got the first report —they're saying he'll make it but it's serious—I thought of that old adage about too many cooks, so I went nosing around at Hagan some more. *¡Condenación!*" said Mendoza. "I know the average homicide is damned unexotic and nothing like the paperbacks, but Hagan—why would anyone want to kill him? The original Caspar Milquetoast, I tell you. Nobody noticed him enough to care whether he lived or died—only his wife and the dog were interested in him. And I suppose the married daughter."

"So, no leads," said Glasser. "Oh, but I meant to tell you—we've got Jane Doe off the books," and he told Mendoza about that. "Hell of a thing. I felt sorry for Slater. It does make you wonder why, you know."

"*¿Quién sabe? ¡Sabe Dios!*" Mendoza shrugged. "Probably no loss. At least she's off our hands."

Just before six o'clock, a sergeant on the Santa Ana force called and said they'd picked up a pair driving a vehicle which corresponded to that A.P.B., and were holding them for L.A. Hackett swore, told Farrell to call his wife, and started for Orange County, stopping for a meal on the way. To hell with the diet for once, he had a hamburger plate, and arrived at the Santa Ana station feeling comfortably replete.

The two men being held were aggrieved and plaintive. Ben Walters and Alvah Negus, they readily gave their names and their I.D. checked out. They were both roofers, working for a big company in Whittier. "All this damn time wasted," lamented Walters. "We figured to be about up to Newhall by now! Why the hell couldn't the cops call like I said—call my wife, Al's wife, they can say who we are, I mean that we really are who we say— Just two ordinary guys, headin' for a fishin' trip up at Lake Hughes, we end up in jail! Or next thing to it. It's crazy—"

"They gave us permission to look over the car and trailer," said Sergeant Kleinert. "They're both clean." The car was a six-year-old Dodge, the trailer a humble two-wheeler containing two built-in bunks and miscellaneous camping gear. "I also got hold of their employer—"

"No guns, I suppose," said Hackett.

"Nary a gun. The employer vouched for 'em. I guess it's just a false alarm. Sorry to bring you all the way down here, Sergeant."

"All in the day's work. We're just glad to know you boys are on the ball. Whoever takes potshots at the uniform, we want to pick up fast."

"How's your man doing?"

"They say he'll make it, in time. He stopped one in the right chest and shoulder, and another slug creased his skull. All we know is, big slugs. But whoever fired them meant business."

"My God, just for a traffic ticket," said Kleinert.

"Maybe not just for a traffic ticket," said Hackett.

"Oh. Oh, I do see what you mean. Well, good luck on it. We'll continue to keep our eyes peeled."

Hackett waited until he got home to call Mendoza.

Mendoza came in the kitchen door. His entire household was gathered in the big kitchen: Alison inspecting something in the oven, the twins for once peacefully at their own small table eating their suppers: the four cats, Bast, Nefertite, Sheba and El Señor winding around table legs reminding humans that it was their usual dinner time: and the shaggy dog Cedric drooling hopefully at the twins, who giggled at him.

"*¡Santa María!*" said Mendoza. "How did I come by all this? Only one thing to be thankful for—that damned mockingbird is gone!" *El pájaro* had flittered away, after the latest family was out of the nest, and these days the back yard was more peaceful.

Cedric came politely to offer him a paw. Alison shut the oven door and kissed him hastily. "Only until January," she said. "He'll be back." The twins left their suppers and descended on him excitedly.

"Daddy, Daddy, read about Jingle! *El cuento* 'bout—"

"Rumple Rumple!" demanded Johnny.

"Now listen here, *niños*. All your bloodthirsty fairy tales are new to me too, and I'd like to read them all, not just one over and over. *¿Comprenden?* And besides, damn it," he added to Alison, "German fairy tales—it's unnatural. You ought to be telling them Irish ones, and I ought—"

"Damn it," said Johnny instantly. "Damn it. Rumple Rumple Rumple!"

"There, you see," said Alison. "Máiri said the same thing—about the fairy tales, I mean—"

"Damn it!" said Terry gleefully. "*El cuento* 'bout Jingle!"

"How in hell," said Mendoza, feeling harassed, "are you managing all this without Máiri, *amante?*"

Alison laughed. Her white skin was flushed from the oven and her red hair somewhat tousled; she brushed it back, laughing. "Up to the time I married you, Cophetua, I was an ordinary working girl, remember? And you're going to be reminded that there was a time you saved the half-smoked cigarettes and slivers of soap, and sold newspapers for three dollars a week—"

"Only until I got that Spanish Monte bank set up. I am?"

"You are. You're going to supervise your offspring's baths while I finish dinner."

Mendoza regarded the offspring with misgiving. He could only return thanks that they hadn't got her red hair. He said, "*¡Vaya por Dios!* I need a drink before that."

El Señor immediately forgot about dinner and floated up to the drainboard to demand his share of rye. Resignedly Mendoza poured him half an ounce in a saucer.

The baths were accomplished, Grimm duly read, the cats and Cedric fed, and the Mendozas were just finishing dinner when Hackett called to say that that pair in Santa Ana had been N.G.

"And tomorrow is also a day," said Mendoza.

Well, Higgins thought defensively, he had some sick leave saved up. He just somehow didn't feel like going into the office. It was Saturday, the kids home after the first week of school, and they were cross because the hospital wouldn't let children into the maternity ward. He didn't blame them. "I guess it's on account of measles and chicken pox and all that—you might be coming down with something, and babies—"

"That's silly! We've both had *shots!* I don't think it's fair we can't see Margaret till Mother comes home. When, George?"

"Maybe Tuesday, Laurie."

"Well, I just can't hardly wait," said Steve. "But anyway, Mrs. Mac-Taggart's an awful good cook, isn't she? And nice, if she does talk funny. Scotch, like."

"And it's good of her to be here, you know—she really works for the lieutenant and his wife."

"I'm going to ask her," said Steve dreamily, "to teach Mother how to make those things she calls scones."

"But I can't hardly wait," said Laura. "Tuesday!"

Some time in the afternoon Higgins went out and bought a camera. He'd never had a camera, and he didn't know much about them, but he thought they'd want some pictures of Margaret Emily. The clerk at the photographic shop had nearly sold him on one of those Polaroid things, until he discovered that the film-pack for it was astronomical in price, and he settled for an Instamatic.

"It's really foolproof, sir," said the clerk.

"Well, I guess it'll need to be," said Higgins.

He'd go back to the office tomorrow. After he'd seen Mary and the baby.

Bob Schenke and Nick Galeano, sharing the night watch in Homicide, found it a slow night. Usually, at this point in September, the temperature was still up and tempers flaring, passions easily aroused, in consequence. But this September giving evidence of an early fall and gratefully cool weather, business was a little slow. They didn't mind.

They'd heard about the Higgins baby from the day watch. "You know something, Bob?" said Galeano. "I kind of think Bert Dwyer'd be pleased about it. I mean, that somebody's taking care of them all—a guy he knew and liked, like George."

"I guess he would, Nick. Maybe he does know. Bert never was a fellow to be a dog in the manger, and he was proud as punch of those kids."

For just a minute they both thought about Bert Dwyer, dead on the marble floor of the bank with the heister's bullets spilling his blood in a pond. The next minute, the phone rang: the desk downstairs.

"Sniper report, vicinity Elks Hall on Sixth," said the desk impersonally. "Two cars on way—see the citizens at the Elks Hall."

"Be damned," said Galeano. "Here we go again."

They both went out on it. By the time they got there, there was a call in for an ambulance: a pedestrian wounded. He wasn't badly hurt, as far as they could see, a bullet in one arm. He gave them his name as Henry Prosser, a youngish man in a shabby business suit. He was indignant. "Just working late, favor to the boss," he told Schenke and Galeano. "And what a hell of a time of year to be taking inventory, but Mr. Ventnor, he died last month—he owned the store, see—and it's this damn probate thing. Got to take inventory, and Mr. Ventnor Junior he's a nice guy, I'm glad to oblige. Get off the last bus and start to walk home, some s.o.b. *shoots* me! For God's sake. For God's— Why anybody wants to shoot me, I'm a peaceable honest guy, no sense to it—"

There wasn't much. There had been a late gathering of Elks in the hall, and some late-leaving brethren had heard the shots, reported it and come out to find the inventory-taker on the sidewalk. The best Schenke and Galeano could guess was that the sniper had been sniping from somewhere across Sixth Street, very likely in the shadow of the building front there, as the trajectory appeared to be fairly straight. They called up two more cars and went over the whole block, but the sniper was long gone.

"Some punk tanked up, or high on something," said Schenke disgustedly.

"What it looks like," agreed Galeano.

But L.A.P.D. men, proud of the reputation of that top force anywhere, are thorough and careful. Galeano went over to Central Receiving and told the doctors in Emergency to send the slug from Prosser's arm to S.I.D., Ballistics. It just could be that a Ballistics make on that slug would match up with another one, out of an old or new case—sometime.

That report was on Mendoza's desk when he came in about nine on Sunday morning. He looked at it, listening to Hackett bring him up to date on the results of that A.P.B.—nil so far. He asked Lake to get him an outside line, and talked to the hospital: Ahearn was doing all right, had been conscious, and would be O.K. eventually, but of course it was a charge of assault with intent to kill, so it belonged to Homicide. He listened to Landers and Grace tell him about the punk j.d.'s Juvenile—and the computers—had turned up for them to look at, on Carroll. He looked back at Schenke's report. He looked up at his men, and the regular unremarkable features under the sharp widow's peak flashed into the unexpected charm as he smiled.

"A sniper. The senseless thing."

"Some punk riding high," said Hackett, and Higgins came in looking his usual self, the broken-nosed tough but neat in dark suit, white shirt. "So you're back—to normal?"

"You go to hell," said Higgins amiably.

"Some punk," said Mendoza. "*¿Pues qué?* The punks that shot Carroll—but there was also Hagan. I think we ask Ballistics some questions."

"But a straight heist job—and Hagan, that was at close range, wasn't it? Powder burns, if I remember the report—what connection are you—"

"Maybe, *nada*. I just think I'll have a word with Ballistics," said Mendoza.

CHAPTER 3

"I suppose," said the Ballistics man, "this is another of your hunches? What possible connection there could be—but you like them wild. You want us to run a comparison on the slug out of Hagan with the slugs out of Ahearn and the guy the sniper winged last night?"

"*Por favor, amigo.* Just for fun," said Mendoza.

"Wild," said the Ballistics man. "We're just here to cater to your imagination, Lieutenant. But we have got other jobs on hand, you know. I can't say just when we might get to it."

"Sometime today," said Mendoza, and put down the phone. "We'll get a report eventually, and now I think, it is a fairly long shot. Just no harm in being thorough."

Landers exchanged a glance with Hackett and said he and Jase would get on with the punks: they picked up Palliser just coming in. As they all started out, Sergeant Lake was taking a new call.

What the computers had turned up on the first try were three sets of names, known to run in pairs, all with the expectable j.d. pedigrees. Theodore Haberman and Ed Kiles; Bill Potts and Henry Widdemer; Chris Lanney and Tom Firmin. Each pair corresponded roughly with the descriptions Carroll and his customers had given of the heisters: one big and blond, the other shorter and darker. Carroll or the other witnesses might identify; but there was a little problem there. Of the six, only two were over eighteen, Widdemer and Lanney: and only Lanney had been dropped on for anything after he'd turned eighteen—rape charge, later dismissed—so Lanney was the only one they had a mug-shot on, and they hadn't really any reason to haul these j.d.'s up in a parade right now. This was just a place to start.

They had addresses: they split them up and went looking. Landers and Grace hit lucky their first cast: they found Haberman at the address they had for him. On Sunday morning, a nice sunny day, he was looking at the comic section of the *Times,* in the living room of an old two-story house on Powers Place, a cul-de-sac off Pico, very old and run-down. Haberman was a big kid, seventeen now, running to fat, with stupid little eyes and a case of acne; and they got the expected reaction to the interfering fuzz.

Thinking of his record, they looked at him, feeling tired. His pedigree went back to age eleven, malicious mischief. It went on like that, petty theft, shoplifting, vandalism, how many counts? Misdemeanors, and the courts couldn't do much. Sometimes the ones like this graduated to the big time.

"I ain't done nothin'," he said sullenly. "Why you guys after me now?"

"Just a couple of questions," said Landers. "To start with, where were you last Wednesday night?"

"Wednesday? What's with Wednesday? *Last* Wednesday? I don't know, I don't remember."

"Come on, try hard, Theodore," said Grace. "It's not so long ago."

"I was—maybe like out some place. With some guys. I dunno."

"With Ed Kiles, maybe?"

"I—I guess so," agreed Haberman. "With Ed and a couple girls. Why the hell, anyways?"

"Which girls?"

"I dunno, some Ed knew. We just—we went to a movie."

"Which movie?"

He was sullen and angry, not scared. If a pair of j.d.'s like these had suddenly gone big-time with a heist and a shooting, likely he'd be scared by now, cops nosing around. He said, "I don't remember which movie, damn it, who notices—why the hell you got to—"

"All right. We'll be talking to Ed too. You have a job, Haberman?" asked Grace.

"What's with a job? Who wants a job?"

"You look as if you like to eat," said Landers gently.

"So what's the problem? The old lady's on the welfare, rents out a coupla rooms." He shrugged. "She got enough for half a gallon o' *vino* ever' day, she don't notice what's left."

When they left him, he was just switching on the big color TV in the living room.

"I could make a little correction in Teddy's conclusions," said Grace, ducking into the Elva.

"And I might guess what. What's the problem indeed. How many of that kind on the backs of the idiots who're still working an eight-hour day? This can be a very depressing job, Jase."

"You picked it. You were worried enough about losing it back in June."

Landers grinned, thinking of his strange ordeal with Internal Affairs. "So I was. Let's go see if Eddy's home this nice Sunday."

The address they had was on Twelfth Street: it was a middle-aged apartment house, tan stucco. The door of Apartment Four opened to show them a big square man with curly gray hair, wrapped in an ancient bathrobe, who looked at the badges and said, "Eddy! My kid with a police record! You coulda knocked me down— *And* I didn't noways like doin' it, but I seen it was the only thing to do so I did. My kid—"

"What's that, sir? Are you Mr. Kiles?"

"I'm Kiles, Officer—"

"Detective Landers, Grace."

"How do. You look like a couple nice guys, come in, siddown," said Kiles. "Offer you a cuppa coffee?"

"No, thanks, Mr. Kiles. What about Ed?"

"Well, I figure it's on account I wasn't to home much, see. Bess, she did her best, but a woman, it ain't the same—a boy gets out from under her, see? See, all my life since I was seventeen, I been to sea—merchant marine. I'm a pretty good engineer if I haven't got all my papers, but I worked most jobs on a ship. Nearly twenty-five years I been at sea, it's my job, I don't never think o' doin' anything else. And then I come home on leave, 'bout a year and a half ago—I'd been gone then, call it mostly a year, we got stuck up in Reykjavik on that cargo deal, and then over to Taiwan and back—and I find my boy's got a police record! Bess felt just awful, but— So I figured what I'd best do."

"What's that, Mr. Kiles?"

He sighed heavily. "Went against the grain, gentlemen, it sure did— but a man's got responsibilities. I left the sea. Got a shore job. Not much of a damn job"—he shrugged—"drivin' a delivery truck for this department store. But at least I'm supportin' us, and I got Ed straightened out. By God I did. First I belted him and then I talked turkey to him. I don't care does he finish high school, I never did, but if he's outta school then he's old enough 'n' big enough to earn for himself. Like they say, Satan findin' work for idle hands."

"So where's Ed now?" asked Landers. The last time Juvenile had handled Ed Kiles had been last year, a charge of shoplifting.

"He's workin', o' course. Got a job at a gas station up on Santa Monica. He's off Fridays, gets a little overtime workin' Sundays. He's straightened out pretty good—I figure, it was just a couple bad apples he got in with at school, see."

"Theodore Haberman one of them?" asked Grace.

"Haberman—him. Fat bum. Ed don't see any o' those no more. He's—"

"Haberman claims he was out with Ed and some girls last Wednesday night."

Kiles swelled. "Well, that's a damn lie and I can prove it!"

"Yes, sir?"

"Yessir! Last Wednesday night? Ed was right here—his mother can say so too. There was this old movie on TV, we all wanted to watch it, an' we did. Starting seven thirty, I guess maybe to ten or so. An' not just us—Mr. 'n' Mrs. Wise that live acrost the hall, they just got a little old black-and-white set, they come 'n' watched it with us too."

"Well," said Landers downstairs in the Elva, "cross out Ed. But Haberman? Why'd he claim to've been with him?"

"He wasn't scared, Tom," said Grace slowly. "If you want a simple guess—knowing Haberman's type—he doesn't remember exactly where he was last Wednesday night and it was the easiest thing to say when we asked if he'd been with Ed Kiles."

"That could be. Let's forget them both for the time being and try to locate Bill Potts and Henry Widdemer."

They didn't, right away. The address they had for Potts was Diana Street; when they got there, it was an empty lot, and a man at the apartment next door told them "that old house" had been condemned and torn down six months ago. Nobody in the neighborhood remembered the Pottses. The address they had for Widdemer was New Hampshire Avenue; there, at an apartment house slightly newer and smarter than any on the downtown beat, the manageress told them the Widdemers had moved about four months ago, hadn't left any forwarding address with her. If they had left one with the Post Office, they couldn't find out until tomorrow.

It was just past noon. They headed back to the office.

Hackett had been derisive about Mendoza's far-out idea, and Higgins poured oil by talking about the baby. "You know anything about cameras, Art? I got one—we'll want some pictures of her—but—"

"I should think your wife could help you there, didn't she work in a—"

"Oh, she just did retouching, not the photography. But we'll want some pictures, right from the start, you know what I—"

Sergeant Lake looked in. "You've got a new one."

"Thank God," said Hackett, getting up. "If I have to listen to George much longer— Where?"

"You'll have to look it up in a County Guide, I never heard of it. Azusa Street. The black-and-white just called in."

Both Hackett and Higgins looked instinctively at Mendoza. "Azusa Street," he said; he was leaning back with his eyes shut. "Right on our doorstep, boys. Two blocks down and three blocks over. I'll come with you. That's a dreary little dead-end spot."

"Coronary or a suicide, and just the paperwork," said Hackett. "Want to bet?"

"Well, I haven't much else to do at the moment but wait for Ballistics' report on the comparison tests."

The paperwork was up to date on Carroll; they couldn't do anything more about Hagan or the sniper; and the rest of the boys were out looking for the punks. They all went over to Azusa Street in the Ferrari.

This was the oldest part of Los Angeles, and nowhere on Central's beat was there anything that could be described as a good residential neighborhood. There were many streets of shabby turn-of-the-century houses, some still wearing the gingerbread trim, few with any vestiges of lawns in front: and they ran between the city's main business streets, beset always with the noise of city traffic. Azusa Street was one like that, only shorter and a little farther away from a main drag. It dead-ended down toward the railroad tracks along the Wash, the cement cavern holding the Los Angeles River that wasn't a river at all ten months of the year.

There were no more than six or eight houses along Azusa Street, poor little ramshackle boxes of houses with narrow front yards. The one they were interested in was marked by the squad car in front. Mendoza slid the Ferrari up behind it, they got out and went up the cracked walk to the square porch. The door was open, and a correctly polite voice was asking, "Did you hear any unusual noises, maybe, Mrs. Moreno?" The accent was L.A.P.D. Police Academy, recent.

The accent that answered was thick and impassioned. "Noises, noises? Do I notice the noises, that good-fa-not'ing Gomez *familia* nex' door? Screeches, noises, such the noises! Not'ing else one to hear! I do not know not'ing about all this. Only I do not want a dead corpse nex' door, I ask *policia* take away. Is all."

Mendoza and his two senior sergeants came into a carpetless, narrow, barely furnished living room. Hackett said economically, "Homicide," and the two Traffic men looked relieved.

"Albertson, sir. Herman. We've preserved the scene for you best we could, sir—it's the back yard next door. The house is empty. This is Mrs. Moreno, she spotted the body when she went out back to—er—"

"Thiefs!" said the woman angrily. She was a thin, brown little woman about four-feet-ten, with graying hair pulled back to a meager knot on her neck; she wore a chenille housecoat of indeterminate color from many washings, and felt slippers, and what were probably dime-store spectacles, wire-framed. But the room was fairly clean and tidy, and a cheap religious picture hung on one wall. "Thiefs!" she exclaimed. "Is no disgrace to be poor! Poor all my life, me. *¡No es deshonra!* But these thiefs come, say got to pay, men take away all—all *la basura,* how comes in English—no money to pay! I am not dirty—clean, clean! I go to bury in yard, ever' morning I go to—"

"And she spotted the body next door," said Mendoza, looking faintly amused. "House empty. Recently?"

"I don't know, sir."

"Yes, well, we'll have a look at the body and then I'll talk to her." He turned to the old woman and told her that in Spanish; relief came into her eyes and she grasped at his immaculate Dacron sleeve.

"Yes, yes, I understand. Ah, thank God to have words to speak in a sensible tongue! I will tell you anything, only I know nothing, but you see how it is with me, sir, I am a poor old woman, I cannot afford the city truck to carry off the garbage and such, I am very careful to bury it well so there is no offense. You understand—"

"*Sí,*" he said. "*No hay porque afligirse, señora. El sol brill apara todos.* Come on, boys, let's see the corpse."

"You can get there easiest through the back," said Albertson.

There was a tiny kitchen, looking quite clean, with an old-fashioned black-iron stove. Past the rear door was a long narrow yard of packed dirt, the only signs of life a few geraniums in pots. The house next door, to the left, was of much the same vintage, a square box of a house long unpainted; like Mrs. Moreno's it sat high off the ground, and a flight of five or six wooden steps led up to the back door. The yard there, like this yard, was bare; a rickety picket fence ran between the two yards, about three feet high, but the end of both yards was unfenced. From here on Mrs. Moreno's equally elevated back steps, the corpse would be instantly visible to anyone. But these lots were unusually deep here, Azusa Street running in at an angle from San Pedro, with Third Street nearly a city block behind it, and a tangle of empty lots between.

"We didn't disturb it, sir," said Albertson.

"I should hope not," said Mendoza. He stepped over the fence and approached the body delicately; but the hardpacked earth wouldn't have retained any footprints.

The body was that of a young woman, and it was stark naked. She hadn't been a very big young woman: slight figure, fair skin, ash-blonde hair with, he estimated at one glance, a home rinse-job to brighten it. She was sprawled headfirst down the steps, and a second glance suggested how she had died: the ugly blue bruises on her throat. He stepped nearer and after a moment said, "Well, that should help in identifying her."

"What? Oh, yes," said Hackett. There was a scar on the girl's left arm, midway between elbow and wrist: a scar some six inches long, looking like the remnants of a bad burn. The only other mark visible on the body was an appendectomy scar.

"I think," said Mendoza, "that we want Bainbridge to look at this *in situ*. *¿Cómo no?* You go roust him out, Art. He'll kick, but he knows his job." Hackett started back to use the radio in the squad car. "And get a couple more cars over here, and a lab truck," Mendoza called after him. He stood up from where he'd stooped over the body. "She hasn't been here long. I don't think she's been dead long. Wait for Bainbridge. But meanwhile—" He looked around in all directions. *"Eso tiene gracia,"* he said to himself. "Funny. Meanwhile, we'll have a good look all around here. Albertson, you and Herman start working your way up toward Third. You'll come across a lot of flotsam and jetsam, but there just might be something that goes with the body. Anything that looks as if it hadn't been there long, give me a hail."

"Well, O.K., sir." The patrolmen shrugged at each other and started toward the rear of the yard. Hackett came back.

"Bainbridge cussed, but he's on the way. Also the lab truck."

"Bueno. Suppose you and George start bloodhounding toward the tracks. You take the street and George the back yards."

"What are we looking for?" asked Higgins.

"I don't know, damn it. Anything that might tie to the body. Anything not lying around long."

Two more cars came up within five minutes, and Mendoza set the four men hunting along Azusa Street, back and front yards, up toward San Pedro.

The lab truck arrived, with Duke and Scarne in it. "People do leave corpses in the damnedest places," said Duke. "What do you want?"

"Photographs, please. I don't think there's any scope for printing anything—" The place was bare as a desert: just the body, bare earth, the rickety fence—"but you might dust the steps, not that I think you'll get anything."

Dr. Bainbridge arrived, tubbier and dourer than ever, and surveyed the corpse. "What a hell of a place to leave the poor girl. What can I tell you here, Luis? She's dead." He was bent over the body. "Not very long dead. Tell you better after the autopsy, but at a guess twelve, fifteen hours. She was probably strangled. Manually. Put her twenty-two to twenty-six. Natural ash-blonde. Tell you one thing, I don't think she came from around here. You never know, but you can see she's taken care of herself—hands manicured, toenails—she looks clean." The fingernails had been recently painted with chaste pale platinum-frosted polish; the toenails the same. "Rigor's passed off, just. That figures, if she was killed some time last night. It's turned cooler, thank God, but not all that cold—rigor passed off naturally." He grunted and stood up. "I'll tell you more when I've looked inside. I suppose I can't have her till all your photographs are shot."

"Yes. I'd guessed all that," said Mendoza, and Bainbridge snorted.

"Why the hell I bothered to waste the time—"

Mendoza went back to the house to talk to Mrs. Moreno. She was voluble in her own tongue, but she couldn't tell him anything. She minded her own business. The Gomez family on the other side were all riffraff and probably criminals, but the other neighbors were decent people. She had heard nothing the night before—except from the Gomez house, a drunken party from the sound of it. She had gone out her back door to bury the garbage, she had seen the dead body, she was a law-abiding woman, she had called the police. She had no telephone, what use would such be to her, but she had gone to Mrs. Guerro two houses down, who had a telephone because her husband had a good job with the city. She had never seen the dead young woman before. And the house next door had been empty for a month, the people who had lived there had been frightened of the earthquake, and moved away. Mr. Lozano owned the house, but she did not know where he lived.

At this juncture Hackett came in and said, "We've turned something, I think." He led Mendoza out to the back again, across the yard next door and the one next to that. By this time one of the uniformed men was employed herding the various residents who had come out to goggle at the police, the body; but the ambulance was getting it ready to take away now. From this yard, a brief wilderness prevailed—probably owned by the Southern Pacific—to where the railroad passed beside the Wash. "George's standing guard. Maybe we'd better get photographs."

Mendoza followed him through a tangle of weeds and wild mustard to where Higgins stood. This little patch of emptiness was not likely to be invaded even by children playing—just a strip of unattractive ground with the railroad tracks ten feet away. *"Muy bello,"* said Mendoza.

It was a little pile of female clothing, stacked there in a patch of wild mustard with curious neatness. Mendoza waited until Duke had duly taken a couple of shots of it *in situ,* and then squatted on his heels over it. "Oh, very pretty indeed. It hasn't been here long, obviously—quite clean and, you know—I think— *Así, así,* let's take a look." He picked it up piece by piece carefully.

"This is very funny," said Higgins. "If he yanked her clothes off to rape her, Luis, I've never known a rapist to—"

"But he didn't," said Mendoza. "Oh, no. Here is one nylon and nylon lace brassiere, a good brand name but not expensive, almost new. Size 34-B. One pair of white nylon briefs, also a brand name but not expensive. Size 6. One white nylon tricot half-slip, ditto, also nearly new. One pair of nylon stockings, a brand sold only by Sears Roebuck, with built-in garters—"

"For a supposedly respectable married man, he's got a lot of specialized knowledge," said Hackett to Higgins.

"Quieto. Alison doesn't like garter-belts or girdles, she wears these too. Color, bare beige, very appropriate for September. One dress, which I'd classify as—mmh—afternoon-into-evening—size 12—subdued turquoise nylon jersey with lace insets—cap sleeves—scoop neck and the fashionable A-line skirt. One stole, and exactly the kind of thing a young lady might have taken along to wear with this dress on a coolish but not cold September evening—such as last night. A cream-colored hand-knitted stole minus any label at all. *Qué interesante.* And lastly, we have—" But he didn't touch those. They lay beside the little stack of clothes: a pair of shoes, black patent leather pumps with medium heels. One of them lay on its side and he twisted his head to read the label. "Leeds," he said sadly. "A big chain outfit. Size 5. So helpful. *But—*"

"If you were hoping for something offbeat, this is it—sort of," said Hackett. "Such a neat rapist. Tidily folding all the ripped-off clothes—"

"No, Arturo. As I said before. Nothing is torn at all. Everything quite intact," said Mendoza. "But where is her handbag?"

They looked at him. "She had one, *obvio.* Without much doubt at all, a handbag matching those shoes. Not, probably, a very big one— she'd dressed for a date, an evening out somewhere. Probably with somebody."

"Here we go," said Hackett. "The specific deductions from a handful of maybes."

"Not at all," said Mendoza. "She had taste—she hadn't much money but she knew how to dress. And she was a lady—that skirt was a modest length for her height. She was dressed to go out somewhere, and she'd have had a handbag. And of course it isn't here because any woman's handbag might contain some clue to her identity." He stood up and brushed down his trousers fastidiously.

"Yes, I see that," said Higgins. "But what it might say—"

"Well, one thing it says is that X doesn't want her identified. For whatever reason. We'll get all this up to the lab. I don't think they'll give us anything on it, but we have to go through the motions. Meanwhile, let's ask around the neighborhood if anybody knows where Mr. Lozano lives. ¿Qué? Well, he owns the house. I presume he'll be interested to know that a corpse was deposited on his property."

He left Hackett and Higgins there superintending removal of what physical evidence they'd turned, went back to headquarters and up to the Missing Persons Bureau. Pending Bainbridge's official description of the corpse, he handed Lieutenant Carey statistics: female Caucasian, five feet, blonde, blue, a hundred and ten, twenty-two to twenty-six, scar left arm, appendectomy scar.

Stocky snub-nosed Carey looked at that and said, "Carla Vroman."

"¿Cómo?" said Mendoza blankly.

"Carla Vroman," said Carey. "Could be. We've had her on the books a couple of weeks. I got the brother down to look at that latest Jane Doe—I see you made her—even if the ages didn't quite match, but N.G. But this does sound like her, all right. Where'd she turn up?"

"Two weeks? Well, I should very much doubt— What's the background on Vroman?"

"She's a stenographer, brokerage down on Spring. Shared an apartment with her brother Donald. He's a lawyer, just starting out practice, a big firm. All he gave us, she'd been acting evasive—that's his word, evasive—and disappeared from both job and apartment, lessee, first of the month. But that description fits—five foot nothing, blonde, blue eyes, scar left arm."

"Now you don't tell me," said Mendoza. "I don't think it is her, Carey, but we'd better make sure. Where do I find the brother?"

Carey told him. The body had by then been brought in to the morgue, pending autopsy, and Mendoza took a handsome and agitated young Mr. Vroman to look at it. Vroman looked, pressing a handkerchief to his mouth, and shook his head silently.

"You're sure, Mr. Vroman?" He nodded. "You mentioned a scar on her left arm—"

"That's not it," said Vroman unsteadily. "No. Carla's scar was—from a bad cut—she fell on a broken fence as a child. That's not it, hers is on the underside of her arm— And besides, that's not Carla. This woman's got a different mouth, and her eyebrows curve up different—"

Which, quite irrationally, made Mendoza feel better. The offbeat corpse intrigued him.

He came back to his own office to find Palliser and Glasser feeling annoyed. They had located, with some difficulty, both Chris Lanney and Tom Firmin, the punks; and both of them turned out to be solidly alibied, for last Wednesday night. One of those bleeding-heart social counselors had been with Lanney between eight and ten, trying to persuade him to take a trade-school course in carpentry ("Who wants to work that hard?" said Lanney). And Tom Firmin, when they finally traced him down, had been in the General Hospital since Wednesday afternoon when he'd piled a borrowed VW up on a freeway divider; he'd only regained consciousness yesterday.

Landers and Grace came in to compare notes with them. It looked as if the first possible leads they'd had on the Carroll case were N.G. It was annoying, but that was the way the routine went.

Lake had checked with the hospital. Ahearn was out of danger, but he'd be on the sick list awhile. And they'd still like to know who had pulled that trigger. The A.P.B. on that vehicle description had been widened to all counties in Southern California, with no results showing yet.

Mendoza came in just after they'd got back from lunch, and was telling them about the new corpse, when Hackett called in and said they'd located the owner of the house, for whatever it might be worth . . .

"But a corpse I would notice!" said Guido Lozano, with gestures. He lived three blocks away from Azusa Street, in a house much like those there: he was a fat little man, normally genial, with an immense handlebar moustache; he was bartender at a third-class restaurant uptown, and the house on Azusa Street, he said, had been left to him by his old auntie.

"A corpse!" he said. "A corpse in my house! *¡Santa María!* The house is for rent, yes—I am there on Saturday afternoon, a Mr. and Mrs. Lopez they want to see, maybe rent. They rent it. Pay thirty dollars, first month, advance. They gonna move in next week. But my God, we don't see no corpse there then— *¡Dios me libre!* It's maybe three, four o'clock Saturday—and no corpse, my God!"

Mendoza had just taken down the homburg, at ten past six, when the inside phone rang. "Mendoza."

"I know," said the Ballistics man, "that you're supposed to possess a crystal ball. Some day maybe we'll start to believe it and stop dragging our heels."

"So what have I done now?"

"These comparison tests. We found a little time to run them."

"And so?"

"The slugs out of Ahearn—and your heist job—no make. Just what we gave you, a beat-up .32. On Ahearn, a .45 Colt. But the slug out of your sniper victim last night is a match for the one out of Hagan. It's an S. and W. .38. The same damn gun."

"*¡Parece mentira!*" said Mendoza, gratified. "Thank you so much."

CHAPTER 4

"So the lab does sometimes hand us the answer," said Mendoza, passing that on at eight ten Monday morning.

"Big deal," said Landers. "So we know the X on Hagan is the sniper who shot Prosser—aiming for just anybody at random. That takes us not one step further toward putting a name to him or finding him—" Mendoza admitted it. "And meanwhile we go on working the damn routine on Carroll, about the longest way round there is to go, looking for the likely punks in Records, wandering around hunting them to question! So the computers are doing the locating, it's still the longest way round. And we haven't had a full scientific report from the lab on Carroll's place yet. I was just saying to John—"

"Blowing off steam," said Palliser, but his long dark face was thoughtful. " 'S a fact. Four days. Those scientific fellows up there playing around with their chemistry sets and forgetting us poor working stiffs trying to do the job."

"¡Por Dios!" said Mendoza. "We haven't? They always take their time, sure." He picked up the inside phone. "Jimmy, get me the lab . . . No, I grant you that, we aren't any nearer guessing who the sniper is, but at least we can assume it was also the random kill, on Hagan. Insignificant little Mr. Hagan— Duke? What the hell are you boys doing up there? You haven't sent us a full report on what you got on the Carroll case, and you've had four days."

"You're always in such a hurry," said Duke sadly. "Listen, Lieutenant, we've got jobs to do for other bureaus too, you know. Carroll? That heist—the dairy store. Oh, yes. Scarne said—listen, a public place like that, there were a million prints— Well, no, not many good ones, but some. Some of Carroll's, naturally, probably most of the liftable ones customers— Listen, are we going to print every damn bottle and can in the place, and check out everybody who ever bought a bottle of milk there? Just a second— Jim? It's Homicide—what were you telling me about that print? Oh, yeah . . . Lieutenant? If you'll remember the statements on it, and Carroll said so too, one of the heistmen started to put the bills into a paper bag, and then dropped it, just shoved them in his pocket. The bag was on the floor by the register. Well, Scarne's been using oblique-light and I don't know what all to raise any prints on it. That's why you haven't had a final report. He's working on it now, maybe he'll get something today."

"Well, make it as soon as you can," said Mendoza. He relayed that to Landers and Palliser.

"I suppose we wait for it," said Landers. "Meanwhile doing the old-fashioned routine."

"You're complaining about having to visit R. and I. where your lady love works the computers?" said Hackett.

"Computers," said Landers, "don't take long to work. They turned up six new names for us last night. At least we're not getting the usual September heat wave." What they were getting, of course, were the occasional aftershocks from last month's earthquake. "And that's another thing. We're getting names—Ed, Tom, Harry, Bill—and the one thing we do know from Carroll is that one of the punks is named Bernie."

"And the only Bernie in that age range R. and I. turned," said Palliser, "is in jail waiting trial for rape. Since ten days back."

"Frustrating," agreed Mendoza. "But there's the legwork to do. You may find a shortcut yet."

It was Glasser's day off. When Landers and Palliser trailed out, meeting Grace just coming in and collecting him to help out on routine, Mendoza sat back in his desk chair, lit a cigarette and said, "Any overnight deductions on Jane Doe?"

"Who was it said the more things change the more they stay the same?" contributed Higgins. "All that occurs to me is that other funny case—very simple once it came unraveled—another good-looking girl left in a dirty back alley down here. That one had on an evening dress—"

"Mmh," said Mendoza, "and lots of money. I don't think Jane Doe did. Leeds's shoes, middle-priced brands on her underwear— No. But I think she was a nice girl, George. Old-fashioned sense. I think she was— as I said yesterday—a lady. Those clothes—as smart as she could afford, but not flashy, you know. Quiet. Well-bred. And the frosted platinum nail polish—"

"Which takes us where?" asked Hackett.

"Well, for one thing, I don't think she was the kind of girl who'd hang around bars and let men pick her— *¡Vaya por Dios!*" said Mendoza suddenly. "But why the hell didn't I see that when— For God's sake. I wonder."

"What bit you?"

"Where's her jewelry?" asked Mendoza. "We said, some reason to take away her handbag, but why her jewelry? She'd have been wearing a little jewelry at least. She was dressed up. She'd almost certainly have had on earrings, a ring, maybe a bracelet, a pin. What happened to it?"

"You've got yourself in a corner there, boy," said Hackett. "Maybe she wasn't so poor. So the jewelry—whatever—was worth stealing. Maybe worth killing her."

"*Caray,* don't be obtuse, Art. When she was wearing eight-ninety-five shoes from Leeds, the bra selling for two-fifty, the slip for three bucks? No. But it could be"—he emitted a thoughtful stream of smoke—"that X thought it was. What was it you said the other day about stupidity?"

"And so that could still be the motive," said Higgins.

"I don't see it, George." Mendoza sat up. "She was a lady—she wouldn't be picked up, she wouldn't be going out with anyone she didn't know. And anybody stupid enough to mistake costume jewelry for the real thing, he'd hardly be smart enough to put up a front she'd believe, as a gent—"

"Look, you don't know one blessed thing about this girl," said Hackett patiently. "So she had nice taste in clothes. That doesn't say she had any common sense in her head. And these days, in the big city, anybody's apt to run into any type, all formally introduced."

"*Es verdad,* that I'll admit," said Mendoza. "And there's still legwork to do on it. George, suppose you check with Carey—he'll have it out to NCIC by now—and see if anything's come in. Art, you and I had better see the rest of the neighbors on Azusa Street. You can at least get around in Spanish."

And the people living on Azusa Street, most of them, were American-born and would use the English in their daily jobs, those who worked; but the stay-at-home housewives, some of the older people, would be more comfortable with the language they used among themselves.

There were three houses across the street from the Lozano house where they hadn't raised anybody yesterday: the riffraff criminal Gomezes had also been absent. Mendoza and Hackett separated to try the first two houses. Mendoza found a shy, pretty young woman, very pregnant, who told him they hadn't been home Saturday night; her husband had taken her to a movie. They'd got home about midnight, hadn't heard or seen anything unusual. Hackett, coming away from the house next door, had drawn blank too. *"Nada."* The third house on that side of the street had a rusty mailbox labeled *Morales* and a potted geranium on the porch; but there was nobody home.

"Let's call on the noisy Gomezes together," said Mendoza.

It was a larger house than most along here, long unpainted and cheerfully ramshackle. It had an old-fashioned doorbell, which brought to the door a stocky dark man in a gay Hawaiian shirt over bright blue pants. He had bushy black brows and a long thin bandit's moustache over a wide mouth; and he looked at their badges and uttered a gratified, "Aiiiii! *Policía!* About the dead lady! Mama! Carlos! Elisa! Paco! Padre! Come—the *policía!* Come in, sirs, come in!" He stepped back.

"If you would rather use the Spanish," began Mendoza in that language, and their host looked at him, interested, expansive.

"Aiiii! *¡El policía mejicano!* No, only the one of you! I am proud to welcome you to my poor home—" Various people had arrived in the living room at his peremptory summons by now: a boy about twelve, in pajamas and a sweater, another about eighteen, a pretty girl a year or so older, an elderly man in an ancient black suit, and Mama, fat and smiling in a flowered apron. "I am Francisco Gomez, sirs. Please to sit down. You will have a little glass wine, eh?"

"No, thank you, Mr. Gomez. Lieutenant Mendoza, Sergeant Hackett. What we want to—"

"Ah, Mendoza! That is an old name, an honored old name, sir. You are *criollo* maybe," and his expression was respectful. "Sit, sit, be comfortable—"

"I should doubt it," said Mendoza with a grin, sitting down in the chair insistently offered. "But about this corpse found in Mr. Lozano's back yard—"

"Terrible! A terrible, awful thing! It was said the poor lady had no clothes on at all! Outrageous! And on our street!"

Mama made a clucking sound and wiped her hands on her apron. The pretty girl said firmly, "Papa. So you said police would come and ask, so they come. They are busy men—don't waste their time."

"Aiiiii!" said Gomez, gesturing extravagantly. "I am about to say, the language it does not matter, I talk too much in both! Apologies, apologies—you are sure, just one little glass good wine? Elisa—"

"Now, Papa," said the older boy. "They want to know if we know anything about the body, and we don't. But what we did see—"

"My boy Paco!" said Gomez. "He goes to college, earns his own way

—smart boy! You're right absolutely, Paco, and I'll tell what we saw to anybody—"

"So tell it," said Mama.

"My manners! Forgive me! Papa—sirs, my father Jorge Gomez!" The elderly man bowed. "We all see it, all can say. My boy Carlos, you shouldn't think he don't go to school, but he's got the cold in the head, he stays in bed. My daughter Elisa, she studies at the beauty school, get good job pretty soon. Now I tell you!" Gomez planked himself down on the ancient couch across the room and lit a little brown *cigarillo*. "Last Saturday, it's the anniversary for Mama and me, when we are married. So we make a party—a fine party! Everybody comes—sisters, brothers, cousins, even old Grandma lives with my brother Tomás—Mama makes the big dinner, some bring guitars, we have four gallons good wine, maybe five, we sing all the old songs, have a fine party—"

Mendoza and Hackett wondered what imprecations Mrs. Moreno had called down on the party.

"Just a nice party, sirs, nobody drunk, just a fine time for everybody, and little kids there too. It's the twenty-third anniversary for Mama and me—"

"And you outta work again," she said good-humoredly. "Talk about *criollos!* I think there's too much lazy Indian in your blood." The old man chuckled.

"What's the job?" cried Gomez lightheartedly. "I get laid off, no fault my own, there is the twenty-six weeks' money from the state, then I get another job. Life, it shouldn't be all work and drudge and long faces, get up hurry to work in morning—we got to enjoy ourselves sometimes! So, we had this fine party like I tell you—"

"Papa, go on and *tell* them, or I will!" said the college student. "You've got to excuse him, he—"

"I tell it, I tell it! It's about half past twelve or maybe nearly one o'clock, Tomás is leaving the party—Grandma can't stay up so late, you see—and I go out with them to his car—so did Mama, others, door open here so maybe others saw it. This car, it was just backing out of the driveway to Mr. Lozano's house—up there. Sure I am sure. Only two houses up, isn't it? It was dark, but I saw the car—couldn't see the driver, too dark, but the car we all noticed. A big, big car—some dark color."

"It wasn't an old car either," said the older boy. "I saw it too—in the dark, sure, but it was long and low. I'd say a fairly new car. I wouldn't guess what—Caddy, Lincoln—" He shrugged.

"And where did it go?" asked Mendoza.

"Well, whoever drives it, he don't know the street, because he turns the wrong way—up there where the street stops. No way get out there, he turns around and comes back. Sure, past here. We are all out in yard, saying good-bye to Tomás and Clara and Grandma, when the car comes past. Going fast, too."

"And it just seemed like it could've been something to do with the dead lady," said Elisa. "It's not much, and Papa talking all round it like usual"—she smiled at him—"but anyway, that's what we saw."

"And very interesting," said Mendoza. "Thank you very much, Mr. Gomez. You couldn't have a guess at what kind of car—what shape?"

"Am I an expert? Me? I gotta 1949 Ford, only car I ever had, and she still goes—I got the money even look at cars in windows? I don't know. But it was big, big. Twice as big as the Ford. Dark. All I can tell you, I'm sorry. But, ¡Santa María y Jesús!—we hear about that dead lady, just down the street, and I say to Mama, that car it had something to do with—"

"Yes, yes, Papa, you don't need to tell them four times over. You think this helps you, gentlemen?" asked Mama.

"Possibly," said Mendoza. "Thank you very much, Mr. Gomez—" In a flood of social politenesses they escaped to the Ferrari up the block, which had collected the usual crowd of small boys.

"What was that he called you?" asked Hackett. "New one on me."

"Oh—" Mendoza laughed. "Pure Mejicano, snob value. It's slang for the aristocrats of pure Spanish blood, no trace of peasant. I have no false pride, Arturo—I'm afraid I don't qualify. What does that rigmarole tell us?"

"That maybe Jane Doe was deposited in Mr. Lozano's back yard between twelve and one A.M. Saturday night."

"In a big, big car. That's funny," said Mendoza. "The little scraps we've got on this, all contradictions. Her very modest, but tasteful, clothes. No money there. Unlikely she had on any valuable jewelry, but what she probably was wearing, costume stuff, was taken. But nobody with the money to drive a big, big car—just possibly a Caddy or Lincoln—would be likely to mistake costume jewelry for real."

"We still," said Hackett, "don't know anything about her for sure. And I'll go along that it looks as if this car could be something to do with it. But coincidences do occur—they foul us all up and send us on wild-goose chases sometimes—and it could also be that that was just somebody on his way home who took a wrong turn. Somebody who doesn't know this part of town. The freeway's only a couple of blocks off, and how many people get confused coming on or off freeways?"

"Don't drag your heels, Arturo. I like the big car. I rather like Mr. Gomez. Life to be enjoyed, and damn the job. The family seems fond of him." He started the engine. "You'd better get out a follow-up report on this."

But back at the office, they were reminded all over again that policemen's work, like women's, is never done: there is always some new job cropping up. Sergeant Lake pounced on them as they walked in and said, "Just in time. There's something going on, assault with intent or something, over on Twentieth. The desk's been calling in, there were three cars there five minutes ago—I tried R. and I. but none of our boys was there. You better get over and see what it is."

"Oh, hell," said Hackett. "Where did George go?"

"I don't know," said Lake, looking harassed. "I thought he was on the phone to M.P., but when I looked, he wasn't. This thing, whatever it is—"

Hackett took the address; they went downstairs again and Mendoza hit the siren on the way over to Twentieth Street. The block they wanted was off Orchard, and it was immediately evident that something was going on—the neighbors were out in their front yards in little bunches, there were three black-and-whites in the street, and a bullhorn blaring somewhere. The activity seemed to be behind one of the old houses lining this block: a few single houses, more duplexes and four-family units. This was one of the singles. There was a green telephone company truck in front of it.

Mendoza and Hackett went up the drive in a hurry.

There was a little crowd up there, at a closed chain-link gate in a stout chain-link fence round the back yard: four uniformed men, one with the bullhorn. They looked at Mendoza's badge and that one said, "I don't know what you can do any more than us, sir. It's a Mexican standoff. He's got a shotgun, and he swears if we try to come in he'll shoot us first and the other guy after."

"Shoot who?" asked Hackett.

"For God's sake," said the Traffic man. "It's a telephone lineman. I don't know what it's all about—we got this call, a prowler, possible burglar, we get here, and here's this old guy with a shotgun, threatening—"

"You hear what I said?" The voice was hoarse and loud, from somewhere around the back of the house. "You cops bust that fence and come try pertect him, I'll kill you all! He can't noways get out—I see him all right! I'm gonna get him! I told him I'd get him!"

"The telephone lineman!" said Hackett. "What the hell for?"

"I don't know! The lineman—I don't know if you can see him—he's holed up behind that big bush this side of the garage."

Mendoza peered and caught a little flash of dull green uniform.

"Sam and Joe are across the street talking to the neighbors." The Traffic man was tough and experienced, by appearance; he had the twenty-gauge shotgun out of the trunk of the squad car in his hands. "When we got here, about fifteen minutes ago, the lineman was just starting up the pole—" There was an ordinary telephone pole, that ugly necessity to modern culture, at the back of this lot. "And this old guy ranting away in the back yard at the lineman. The lineman came down, I guess he was going to explain what he was doing, and the old guy took a shot at him. He was just damn lucky not to get hit—when he saw the gun he took a dive, and—"

"I'm gonna get him!" came the hoarse voice. "I warned him! I warned him offa my private property!"

"Hey, Mac—" Another uniformed man came pounding up. The man with the twenty-gauge turned.

"Homicide dicks finally showed. Yeah, Bob?"

"We've been talking to some of the neighbors who know the old man, his name's Tugwell, Harry Tugwell—he's a nut on this house, they say, fanatic about it being his private property—"

The small front lawn, Mendoza noted, was green and lush from tender care, the flowering shrubs near the house and along the drive were clipped and neat; the narrow glimpse of the rear yard from here showed a strip of green lawn, an orderly row of rose bushes lining the house side of the separate single garage. Both the small frame house and the garage had recently been painted gleaming white with green trim.

"—And this last couple of weeks, there's been some trouble with the telephone lines, linemen sent out three or four times, and it upset Tugwell like hell, men coming in his yard—"

"Talk about nuts," said another uniformed man. "What do we do now? And where is he, in the house or—"

"Give him another hail," said Mendoza. "Tell him if he agrees not to fire, the lineman'll leave right away."

"But we can't take the chance—"

"With a nut?" Mendoza laughed sharply. "Keep him listening—say anything that comes into your head. Art, try the yard on the other side—"

"You think we didn't have that idea?" The Traffic man looked at him sardonically. "There's a thorn hedge eleven feet high and three thick all down that side of the lot. I guess Tugwell likes his privacy."

"¡Anda!" said Mendoza mildly. "Mr. Tugwell is keeping an eye, and very probably his shotgun, on the spot where he expects the intruder to show. Art?"

"Right behind you," said Hackett, unlimbering his gun. "And why I.A. doesn't come down on you for going unarmed—"

Mendoza walked down the drive and mounted the steps to the narrow front porch. "I don't like loud noises," he said. "I expect all the windows are locked."

"I expect so too. The citizenry—we never do know what we're going to run into," said Hackett. He pried the screenhook loose after a struggle, with his pocketknife, and lifted the screen down carefully. The window giving on the porch was locked.

"Count twenty," said Mendoza, and hared back up the drive. "Diversion, please," he told the Traffic men. "A few shots in the air when you've counted ten." They looked surprised, hauling out their guns. Mendoza trotted back to the front porch. Hackett had his jacket off, wrapped around one arm. As the shots went off, ear-shattering and unexpected, he drove his arm at the glass and it broke obligingly, a big hole just above the inside lock. Mendoza reached to unlock it as Hackett got out his gun again; they climbed through to an inhumanly neat dining room cluttered with golden-oak furniture. The kitchen was across a central hall, and the service porch and rear door beyond. Mendoza peered cautiously through the kitchen window.

Mr. Harry Tugwell was standing just underneath, back turned, shotgun leveled steadily at the corner of the garage. His back yard was a poem of plush lawn, neat flower-beds, a fancy line of colored stepping stones, a birdbath.

"I know where he is!" he bellowed. "One move and I'll get him! I warned him! Come on my property again, I told him—"

The rear door was, naturally, unlocked. Hackett pulled it open by the inch, but it was well-oiled and produced no creaks. Mendoza behind him, he went stealthily down the back steps and across the lawn directly behind Tugwell.

And it was, they all said afterward, all the lineman's own fault: of course he didn't know that Tugwell was all but disarmed. Two steps, and Hackett would have had him by both arms, got the gun away. Maybe the unexpected fire from several Police Positives had unnerved the lineman finally, or maybe just the minutes of crouching there hiding from threat. When Hackett was two strides from Tugwell, the lineman broke cover and ran desperately down the drive.

The shotgun went off like too-close thunder; and then Hackett had

Tugwell in a bear-grip, the shotgun fell and Mendoza dived after it, and the uniformed men poured into the back yard.

"I've got him," panted Hackett. "Give me a pair of cuffs—"

But it was a twelve-gauge shotgun, and Mr. Tugwell knew how to handle it. "Oh, my God," said one of the Traffic men, looking at the lineman. "My God, right in the body—"

"If he'd just hung on there another minute—"

But that was after the fact. And this would keep them busy most of what remained of the day, likely tomorrow. They called an ambulance. They called the telephone company. At least on this, no need for the elaborate lab work: it was all straightforward, in the legal sense. Mendoza called his office: Higgins had come back, and was summoned to help out. After lunch Palliser and Landers showed up and also got deflected onto this.

The telephone lineman had been one Richard Flaherty; thirty-two, with a wife and three kids.

They took nine neighbors of Tugwell's in to make formal statements, and what they heard from those people sent Hackett and Palliser hunting a Fuller Brush man, an Avon saleslady, and a couple of political-petition carriers, to make statements regarding Tugwell's views about invasion of privacy.

The paperwork on it was going to occupy quite some time; but most of the routine on one like this went to the D.A.'s office.

Mendoza being nominally the boss, he left the rest of them still typing statements and reports and went home at six thirty. The big Spanish house on Rayo Grande Avenue in the Hollywood hills was reasonably serene even without Mrs. MacTaggart—redhaired Alison busy over a salad, a succulent smell rising from the oven, the twins occupied with supper, the livestock ditto. Sheba and Nefertite had abandoned their own cat-sized dinners to sample Cedric's, and in the service porch, Cedric was sitting back watching them like a doting grandfather.

"*¡Bufón ridículo!*" said Mendoza, accepting his politely offered paw.

"You're late," said Alison. "Something interesting turn up?"

Mendoza kissed her rather meditatively. The twins erupted at him loudly.

"Nothing very much," he said. "Considering the nature of the job." He laughed. "*Mañana será otro día*—tomorrow is also a day. And the sad thing is, that fellow was standing for a principle of freedom—only he'd brooded on it too much and turned into a fanatic. The citizenry, as Art says— Yes, yes, *niños*, let me take a breath!"

"What fellow? What are you talking about?"

"Tell you over dinner. I need a drink."

El Señor left the rest of his chopped liver to Bast and leapt up to the drainboard requesting his share.

On Tuesday morning—with the paperwork on Tugwell still not finished, an inquest scheduled on the body of John Hagan at ten o'clock, and the A.P.B. on suspect vehicles turning up cars and trailers in Studio City, Whittier and Chatsworth—with Grace and Palliser supposed to be having the day off, and both of them coming in like the faithful public servants they were—

"But, Jase!" said Virginia. "We had an appointment at the Agency! And you've got to help me fill in this silly form. They want to know about all our ancestors back to Noah, and who does, for heaven's sake? There's a sort of family tradition that some great-great-grandmother was a Swahili witch-woman, but I can hardly put *that* down— And it's ridiculous, you'd think they could see— And we've just got to get her, such a darling, nearly five months now and just that impersonal hospital—"

"But, John," said Roberta, "I was counting on you to wash the kitchen windows—I'm not supposed to climb ladders. And the ones in the den—"

On Tuesday morning, there on Mendoza's desk was Dr. Bainbridge's autopsy report on Jane Doe.

Mendoza read it with interest, interrupted by Sergeant Lake. Somebody from the D.A.'s office wanted to talk to him about Tugwell's mental condition: psychiatric tests would be ordered, of course. "Tell him I don't think Tugwell's crazy—he just jumped the gun a little on all these bureaucrats invading everybody's privacy," said Mendoza, and went back to the autopsy. And ten minutes later, "No, I won't see any reporters—tell them to go annoy the D.A."

The autopsy was interesting, he told Hackett when he came in. This and that in it.

Their unceremoniously dumped Jane Doe had been just five feet, one hundred pounds, blonde and blue, the scars noted. Twenty-two to twenty-six. She had borne at least one child. She had died sometime between eight and midnight last Saturday night, by manual strangulation. She had not been raped, or had sexual intercourse recently. All organs had been sound and healthy; no alcohol or drugs ingested. She had, probably, been hungry when she died: her last meal had been a good way digested, and it had consisted of cheese, bread, potatoes, lettuce.

"Interesting!" said Hackett. "This is nothing—it gives us nothing at all."

"But it draws a picture," said Mendoza. "Or the vague outlines of a picture, Art. She hadn't eaten since lunch. Cheese sandwich, French fries, a salad. She was going out somewhere. Where she expected to have a meal, can we say? Yes. She was—at some point—in a big, big car. Being driven to have dinner some place—"

"Woolgathering!" said Hackett exasperatedly. "You don't know that for a fact."

"It fills in the picture," said Mendoza.

"And just how we're going to check all these men picked up on suspicion, that A.P.B. on vehicles— Look, they've had time to get rid of the gun, they'll look clean, what's to link them with Ahearn?"

"Why did they shoot Ahearn? They were carrying contraband, or they're on the run from another job, or— Yes, but they've got to be looked at. Questioned."

"And, for God's sake," said Hackett, "George is sitting there mooning over a book about how to take color photographs! And all these statements to type—"

Mendoza laughed.

"Even you didn't go overboard on pictures of the offspring," said Hackett. "Second childhood, I swear—"

The inside phone rang and Mendoza picked it up.

"Well, better late than never," said Duke, sounding pleased. "These things do take time, Lieutenant. I told you about that paper bag—"

"Yes. Have you got something?" The lab, taking its time.

"Oh, something very nice. Scarne finally raised some prints on it. Four nice prints. All made by twelve points, admissible evidence." Duke sounded proud.

"Yes?"

"Well, we've made them for you. I'll be sending the formal report up right away. They were in our files. A Roger Trissel—"

"And isn't that nice indeed. You do sometimes come through—eventually."

CHAPTER 5

The lab report came up a few minutes later, and Mendoza went over it with Palliser and Landers. The report just identified Trissel as having prints on file: Landers went down to R. and I. to get the package on him, and took the opportunity to make a date for dinner with Phil.

Roger Trissel was in L.A.'s records twice as a juvenile, once as an adult. The j.d. charges were petty theft and narco: the adult charge, two years ago, robbery from the person. They just grunted at the disposition: one year in the county jail, suspended, and probation. He was twenty-one now, and still on probation.

"At least there's a chance this is the right address," said Palliser. "He's got to see his probation officer once a month, and they're supposed to check."

Landers said he wouldn't take a bet on it; and as it turned out, the probation officer, with an overload of cases, hadn't seen Trissel in several months and hadn't had time to do anything about it. Landers said, "I'll go see Carroll—you can look at the address." He took the mug-shot of Trissel, mixed with a handful of other men's photographs, and started for the hospital.

Hackett had dragged Higgins away from his book and they were on the way to Studio City, where the Valley boys had picked up two men in an old Chevy, hauling a two-wheel trailer. Well, good luck to them: whoever had taken those shots at Ahearn, they'd like to pick up.

At the hospital, Landers found Pat Carroll sitting up, healthier color in his face and a stronger voice. "Remember you," he greeted Landers. "One of the cops—though you don't hardly look old enough, now I see you plain." And Landers was used to that too, though Phil said encouragingly that that funny business last June had aged him at least five years. "You caught that pair of louts yet?"

"We're working on it, Mr. Carroll. Like you to look at some photographs and see if you recognize any. Take your time at it." Landers handed over the little stack and Carroll began to go through them.

"Nope. Nope. Too old, I said they were— Hey, that's one of them! This one right here—the blond one. I'd swear it on a stack of Bibles. You got him?"

"We're looking for him now, sir. You can definitely identify that as one of the men who shot and robbed you?" It was, of course, Roger Trissel. And the scientific evidence was all very nice, when it showed up, but they couldn't rely on its showing up, and Landers thought of all the legwork they'd done, hunting for the punks, and felt tired. He thanked Carroll and drove back to the office. The Corvair needed a lube job; try to get it in on Friday when he was off, he thought.

When he got back, Glasser had gone out on a head-on collision down at the Stack: somebody else trying to enter a freeway on an exit ramp or vice versa. Grace was just going out with a pile of the paperwork, in manila envelopes, for the D.A.'s office.

"Well, Carroll made the shot. Very definite. Now if he's just here and we can get him to tell us who Bernie is—"

Ten minutes later Palliser called in. "What about Carroll, he make the shot?"

"Loud and clear," said Mendoza.

"Then maybe we're in business for a change. You'd better shoot Tom out to meet me here."

"Where?"

"Detroit Avenue in Hollywood. I'll be waiting."

Landers went off, and Mendoza reread the autopsy on Jane Doe. His instinct had been right: she hadn't been raped. Saturday night, he thought: that made it roughly fifty-six, sixty hours. If she had been living alone, not surprising that she hadn't yet been missed; on the other hand, there was "had borne at least one child." Oh, yes? So what had happened to it? And she hadn't had much money, had probably been working somewhere, at something. ¡Media vuelta! he said to himself on that. Only probably. She could have been living on alimony and child support. Maybe the child left with a baby-sitter, Mama off on a little vacation. In that case, eventually she'd be missed. But almost any situation could be imagined: almost, he thought. In spite of the lack of evidence, physical and otherwise, Mendoza felt obscurely that Jane Doe had been that rather rare thing these days, a nice girl. A lady.

And if anybody had pinned him down as to the exact why of that conviction—he muddled through to it slowly—he'd have to say, the length of her skirt. That had been a street-length dress: which could mean nearly anything, this year of grace. And she'd been a small girl, with a nice figure; but where females with all kinds of figures (and legs) were, these days, going around with hemlines practically to their thighs (without any apparent recognition of how ridiculous they looked) Jane Doe's skirt would have fallen a modest half-inch below the knee.

Palliser had driven out to the address in their files for Roger Trissel without much expectation of finding any trace of him. Trissel wasn't there, had once rented a room there; but the woman who owned the place, looking at his badge doubtfully, said that maybe Mr. Loose could tell him something, he'd known Mr. Trissel while he was here. Palliser said he hoped so. Mr. Loose?

"Upstairs front," she said.

Mr. Loose, whatever job he worked or any, was apparently night people; waked up suddenly, he was bleary-eyed, annoyed, and slow-minded. "Gah!" he said, forcing his eyes open on Palliser's badge. "Just what I needed—a cop." But after a trip to the bathroom down the hall, he appeared looking a little stronger and sat on the bed, yawning repeatedly, and talked readily enough. He was in his late twenties, an older man than Trissel, but he said he'd felt sorry for the kid. "Very handsome kid, you know—but so many that kind, they try to get by just on looks. I guess he's not what you'd call a strong character, know what I mean."

As to where Trissel might be living now—he wouldn't know, really. Palliser pressed him for anything Trissel might have said about other friends, any names, and after twenty minutes or so Loose, lighting his fifth cigarette, said suddenly, "Say, there is one thing I remember. Let's see if I got the name right, now. Some Swede name—Larson, Sorenson, Swenson, that was it. The kid said once—I forget how it came up—he said he always had one ace in the hole, he's real broke, some guy named Swenson, Detroit Avenue, he said—he lived there awhile, he said, and they were nice folks."

And that was that. Palliser called in, having looked in the appropriate telephone book, and waited for Landers sitting in his car opposite the address. It was a single house, a modest frame bungalow, on a residential street close in to the boulevard in Hollywood. A green lawn, house painted cream with cheerful yellow trim. When Landers pulled up across the street, he got out to join him, gave him a breakdown on how he'd got the address.

"Here we go round the mulberry bush," said Landers. They climbed steps to the porch, and Palliser pushed the doorbell; chimes sounded. Presently a woman came to the door; she was tall, deep-bosomed, with the red-gold hair that only fades a little with age, and she was crisply neat in a blue dress and pink apron.

They showed her their badges. "Mrs. Swenson?" The name was stenciled on the mailbox here.

"Yes—you are police?"

"Do you know Roger Trissel?"

"Oh, yes. You had best come in," she said, and held the door open. "Sergeant Palliser, Detective Landers." They followed her into a pleasant neat living room, with crocheted doilies under every lamp. There was a large marmalade cat asleep on the couch. Palliser sat down beside the cat and Landers in a nearby chair. The cat woke up and looked at them indignantly.

"You know Roger Trissel, Mrs. Swenson?" prompted Palliser.

"Yes, sir." She had the faintest trace of accent. "You are looking for him—is he in more trouble?"

"I'm afraid so."

"Ach! That boy!" she said. "We were sorry for him, that's how it was, but no more—he's a weak one, no backbone. I'll tell you how it was—"

"Excuse me, is he staying here?"

She raised her shoulder. "No—not now, and not again. Off and on he would come, ask to stay, he's got no money, ask a meal. I'll tell you, Sergeant, it was about three years ago we got to know Roger. My son Lars had just got out of the Navy, three hitches he served, and I think he'd have stayed in, but his father was gone then and I think he was feeling he should stay with me." She smiled. "He got out, and he was driving home from San Francisco that time, he picked Roger up hitchhiking."

Three years, they were thinking: in between the j.d. charges and the adult one, Trissel had been out of L.A. then. "Where?" asked Landers.

"Oh, up around Santa Barbara. They talked, and Lars was sorry for him—poor young fellow, only eighteen then, raised in an orphanage, no family—" and that was perfectly true, by Trissel's history as recorded in his pedigree. "He says he'll help him get a job here, and he can stay with us till he does. Well, he did. Lars got him a place where he went to work himself—a Dodge agency out on Santa Monica, he's a salesman there now, and he got Roger a job in the garage there. Roger's not trained for anything, it was just washing the cars, moving them, you know. He's such a handsome boy, and makes you feel he wants mothering. Or he used to. After a while we both saw he'll never change—he's weak, lazy. But you can't help liking the boy somehow."

"Do you know where he is now? If he's working?"

"I don't know if he's got a job anywhere. The agency fired him after a while, he's not doing the job right. He gets jobs off and on. I do know he came here last night and tried to borrow money from Lars. Well, Sergeant, as I said you can't help liking him, feeling sorry for him, but you've got to draw a line somewhere. Throwing money down a well, it would be. But—you're looking for him? Well, I do know he made friends with another young fellow works at the agency—Lars could tell you—and he might know."

At the big Dodge agency on Santa Monica Lars Swenson told them much the same thing, and eventually led them to a young fellow washing one of the cars on the used lot, Tony Gallio. He welcomed the excuse to knock off for a cigarette. "Roger?" he said. "Well, he doesn't like to work too hard." He grinned at them. "What? No, I don't know where he's at now, sorry. You looking for him—he's done something?"

"Let's just say we're looking for him," said Landers. "Have you seen him lately?"

"I run into him a few times since he got fired here," said Gallio. "Tell you—we got to help you fellows out, and he's no special pal of mine—tell you one place you might look. My old man's got a little restaurant, Italian you know, down on South La Brea. Roger sort of goes for the Italian stuff, and he drops in there sometimes. Dad knows him, account of he came there with me first few times, see."

It was a place to look. "You like Italian cuisine?" asked Palliser. "We might as well have lunch there."

Hackett called in from the Valley Station at twelve thirty to report that so far as any fallible human agency could guess, the suspects picked up on the A.P.B. for the vehicles were respectable citizens and had had nothing to do with shooting Patrolman Ahearn. The car—an old green Chevy—and the trailer conformed to the description, all right, but the owner of both had plenty of I.D. He was Jerry Whetmore, and he was a technician of some sort—film-cutter or whatever—at Disney Studios. The man with him also offered identification: he was Whetmore's brother-in-law, Dick Jasper, connected with a firm of stockbrokers in Hollywood. Both men were in their thirties, looking like responsible citizens; they were on their way to a camping trip up in Angeles Forest, both on vacation and, they said cheerfully, their wives only too happy to have them out from underfoot. No guns had been found.

"And we are now going on to Chatsworth," said Hackett. "I'm not going out to Whittier. I talked to a sergeant on the phone. That car was a blue Buick, the trailer had four wheels, and the men numbered four—you needn't bother with names—all of 'em Southern Pacific superintendents, all with solid I.D., bound for a camping trip on the desert."

"*¡Porvida!*" said Mendoza. "Every man to his own poison. It can be a frustrating job, I know. You'll be back some time today, I suppose?"

"I hope so," said Hackett.

At the little Italian restaurant on La Brea, Palliser and Landers talked to Gallio Senior. "That one, I know the one you mean, this Roger," he said. Yes, he came in sometimes, not regular, but fairly often. Sometimes alone, sometimes with another fellow or two.

They pressed him for any names; he was very willing to help the cops, but kept shaking his head: "How would I know names? He's just a fellow drops in, I know him because Tony brought him here, but any young fellows with him that he knows, how would I— But, now, wait a minute, wait a minute, it just comes to me, there's one of them I see with Roger I do know his name. Now wait a minute." He pressed his temples, eyes shut, thinking. "Bud Stern," he said. "Sure. I know him because he used to work at the Shell station up on the corner, drop in here for lunch. I don't know how Roger knew him unless it was from in here, but I remember a couple times, they're here together, lunch, middle of the afternoon, like that. Yeah, yeah, last week—week before."

"The mulberry bush," muttered Landers. They went up to the Shell station, showed their badges again and asked. Again, the manager was anxious to be helpful, but all he could tell them was Bud Stern's home address; Stern had quit here last month, he said, because the hours didn't fit with his part-time classes at L.A. City College.

The address was Edgemont Avenue. They drove up there; it was an old-fashioned court, duplex units on both sides of a double front walk. The woman who answered the door was thin and worried-looking, and she looked more worried at sight of the badges. "Bud?" she said. "Police? Asking for— What do you think he's done? You can't—"

"Nothing like that, ma'am," said Landers hastily. "We think he might have some information for us, that's all."

"Oh!" she said. "Oh. Well, of course he's at school now. That is, college. He's taking three classes this semester, business administration—"

They got up to L.A.C.C. on Vermont just as classes were changing at two o'clock. They wasted a little time waiting to see the registrar: this was a big campus for a city college. When they explained, asked for Bud Stern's location at the moment, they were told severely that it was against the rules to disrupt a class. "Police business," said Palliser, annoyed, and reluctantly she told them which classroom.

But at that, it was after two thirty when they finally isolated Bud Stern in the corridor outside the classroom, and started to ask him questions. He was a thin young man with lank brown hair and an abrupt manner. "Roger?" he said. "Roger Trissel? You're looking for him? Why?"

"Just say, we'd like to talk to him," said Palliser. "You've been seen with him recently, we're told. Do you know where he's living?"

"And if I did, why should I tell you?"

"Why not?" said Landers.

"Well, I don't want to sound unreasonable," said Stern. "But from what I hear from Roger, you're always shoving him around some. I mean, look, I know you've got a job to do, but just because a guy like Rog has been in a little piddling trouble with you—nothing big—you're always coming down on him, checking up."

"Is that a fact?" said Landers. "According to Rog."

"That's right. Always giving him trouble, just because—"

"Not a big-timer, no," said Palliser. "Until last Wednesday night, Bud. That night he moved into the big time. He's wanted now for attempted murder."

"Att— You've got to be kidding! Murder! Roger?"

"That's a fact, Bud. Now, do you know where we can find him?"

"Well, I'll be damned!" said Stern. "Sure. Sure, I'll tell you what I know, but—boy!" He shook his head. "I don't know where's he's hanging out, now. I run into him now and then at this Italian place on—"

"We know about that."

"Oh. And I like to bowl, I'm on a team that meets Saturday mornings, this bowling alley down the street. I ran into Rog there last Saturday, I don't know what he was doing there, he isn't a bowler far as I know, but anyway there he was, and we talked some, and he said he had a room in a place just a block away. And that's all I can tell you. But—I can't believe it—murder! Rog?"

They called in for help on that one, a bastard to work. As Landers said, it was a case of so near and yet so far. Grace came up to help on the legwork. They found the bowling alley down on Vermont; it was in the middle of a block, and "just a block away" might mean any of four or five streets around, all residential streets of old houses new when Hollywood was young and many of them now turned into rooming houses. Grace had waited for copies of Trissel's mug-shots to bring with him, and they split and began to go door-to-door along the first block up from the bowling alley on that side of Vermont. They drew blank on that block, and tried the next one down.

It was four thirty before Landers rang a doorbell at the end of that block and asked the woman who opened the door, "Do you recognize this man, ma'am?" to have her stare at the mug-shot and nod reluctantly. He showed her the badge, introduced himself, and summoned Palliser and Grace with sweeping gestures.

"Oh, dear," said the woman. "Police—oh, dear. What do you think he's done? Such a nice young man—and so handsome! He hasn't done anything, has he?"

"He rents a room here, Mrs.—"

"Kane. Mrs. Kane. Yes, sir, that's right. Just since last month. But—oh, dear," as the other two men came up. "What do you think he's done?"

"Is he here now, Mrs. Kane?"

"I don't know. You could go see, I suppose. He's got the last room on the left, upstairs."

They went up quietly and along the hall, the woman pattering fearfully after them. Palliser tapped on the door. "Yeah, what is it?" responded a voice. Palliser rapped again. "Oh, hell—just a second." Footsteps approached; the door opened. He knew them for what they were at a glance, and stepped back uncertainly. But there was a gun in plain sight on the bed, an old revolver, and he was moving in that direction. They all hauled out their guns.

"That's handy," said Landers. It was, because any move, or even tentative move, on the part of the arrestee to resist arrest, gave them legal leeway for a once-over-lightly of the premises. Palliser said, "You're Roger Trissel?"

"Yeah, yeah, but I'm clean, you can't tie me up to anything, fuzz. I haven't done a thing, I'm clean."

He wasn't, very. The woman stood at the open door, fearful and puzzled; and her nose wrinkled slightly. Palliser read out the monotonous rigmarole about his rights to Trissel, who just said, "Yeah, I know the bit. You takin' me *in*? What the hell for? You got nothin' on me!"

And Palliser could understand, seeing Trissel, the slightly contradictory reports they'd heard. Carroll: dirty, sloppy lout. And high. Mrs. Swenson: felt sorry for him. Mrs. Kane: such a nice young man. Trissel was a good-looker, all right: wavy blond hair, almost girlish regular features, a handsome mobile mouth. Dressed up, clean, putting on some manners, he'd look fine. But Landers was saying pleasedly, "Well, well, what have we here?" and turning from the old white-painted chiffonier with a little plastic bag.

"Mary Jane?" said Grace.

"That's just what. You holding anything else, Roger?"

"No!" he snarled.

But they went on looking, and found a handful of capsules—Methedrine, bennies, Nembutal.

And that explained a few other things, thought Palliser. Once you got in the habit of hitting a high every so often on anything like that, after a while you just didn't remember to take baths or keep yourself neat or—Trissel needed a shave; his blond beard didn't show much, but he hadn't shaved in several days, or taken a bath. But at least he wasn't high now.

They took him in—by then the warrant had come through—and stashed him in an interrogation room. It was getting on for five thirty then, and the sooner he was questioned the better, of course.

"Listen, I've got a date," said Landers.

"So run along. Wives have to put up with it," said Palliser resignedly. "Girls, not so necessarily."

Landers went, thankfully. He went home and showered and shaved again, thinking absently that it must be handy to be blond and not need a second shave if you were going out. He went to call for Phil O'Neill, and took her to the Tail o' the Cock for a change, out on La Cienega. And damn it, they'd known each other nearly five months now, and Phil still saying, *sensible*. His darling Phil, her flax-blonde curls just up to his chest, and he'd never known a girl with navy-blue eyes—

It would all come right eventually—it had to. He smiled at her across the table, over preliminary drinks, and she took a swallow of her martini and said, "So what's new at Homicide? Have you located those punks you were hunting?"

"Look, I'd nearly forgotten the job for an hour. Shop talk I can do without, lady."

"Then you shouldn't date a lady cop, Tom. You know I'm interested in the detective side of it. It gets you, somehow—"

"It gets you," agreed Landers. "Frustrated, annoyed, wasting time, meeting all the lowest elements of the population, and probably, in the end, ulcers."

"Oh, don't be a fool," said Phil. "Have you got any leads to that Jane Doe?"

Higgins had had the foresight to drive his own car out to Studio City, and he didn't go on to Chatsworth with Hackett. "I've got a private life too, you know," he said. "The hospital's releasing Mary this afternoon. I've got to—"

"Oh, hell, I'd forgotten that. Well, I suppose you've got to—"

And on the way back to Hollywood, Higgins suddenly thought that it wasn't his own car. Or hadn't been. Registered to him now, but it had been Bert's car, the two-year-old Pontiac Bert had been driving when— Higgins had taken it because it was newer, and Mary had his Dodge . . . They were all ready for him, Mary's little overnight case packed, and Margaret Emily. It was a thing he didn't quite believe even now, that Mary was his—and now, Margaret Emily.

Against Mary's protests, the nurse took her out to the car in a wheelchair. "Silly—I'm just fine."

"You'll have enough work to do, starting very shortly," said the nurse cheerfully. "Better take all the spoiling you can get, Mrs. Higgins."

All of a sudden that sounded very strange to Higgins; and it had been sixteen months now, since he'd got up his nerve—but it sounded strange; and he didn't start the engine right away. He looked down at Mary, with Margaret Emily in her arms, and he said in a low voice, "Do—do you think Bert would mind, Mary?"

She looked up at him steadily, her clear eyes suddenly a little wet, and she said, "I think he'd be glad to know you're taking care of us, George. That's all."

And Higgins turned the ignition key without saying anything. Without saying, Bert was a good friend of mine. Because even now, it wasn't a good thing for either of them to think about Bert, dead on the bank floor at thirty-seven. Especially now, it wouldn't do. So he said, "The kids are just wild to see her, you know. And Luis' Mrs. MacTaggart is just fine. A nice woman. She says she'll stay to the end of the week, you won't feel like getting meals yet."

He got her home half an hour before Steve and Laura were due home from school, and Mrs. MacTaggart made a little fuss over her and got her settled on the couch in her warm housecoat, and Margaret Emily in her new bassinet was sound asleep. "My, but she'll be a forward one, won't she, coming with all that bonnie black hair!"

The little Scottie Brucie hopped into Mary's lap in an ecstasy of affection, and Mrs. MacTaggart had what she called a posset all ready— " 'Tis strengthening for you, and guidness knows you'll be needing tha and all, this family to take care of. That's a fine boy you have, and Laura so clever at the piano—"

And before Higgins could think, at the mention of Steve, how much he looked like Bert, the kids were home. Banging the front screen— "Mother! Are you *here?* Where *is* she?" "Mother, I just can't *wait to see*—"

"All right, Roger, let's take it from the top," said Palliser. "Who is Bernie?"

"I dunno any Bernie," said Trissel.

"Come on, come on," and Grace's soft voice was gentle. "We've tied you into this one, Roger. But good. That dairy store heist—and what a stupid place to pick to knock over! You might've known there wouldn't be a C in the till. But you were both high on something, weren't you, and neither of you very bright in the first place—"

"I dunno what you're talkin' about," said Trissel.

"Oh, for the love of God!" said Palliser. "Shall we spell it out for him again? Words of one syllable, Roger—"

It was seven forty-five. They had called their wives to say they'd be late, and both of them supposed to be off today too, but that was the way the ball rolled sometimes. The paperwork on Tugwell had occupied all hands while other things piled up. They had snatched a couple of sandwiches, and come back to tackle Trissel in an interrogation room at the jail on Alameda, where he'd been booked in now.

"There are fingerprints, Roger," said Grace. "You know about fingerprints? At that dairy store, you grabbed up a paper bag to put the loot in, and then you dropped it and put the loot in your pocket. You left some nice prints on the bag, Roger. We made them. We know that was you."

"You coulden get any prints off paper. Don't kid me."

"Shall we take him up to S.I.D. and show him how the boys do it?" said Palliser. "Some very smart, scientific angles we've got these days, Roger. We've got your prints. From the paper bag. You pulled that job —you took a couple of shots at Carroll. Where's the .38 Colt you stole from him?"

"Who's Bernie?" asked Grace.

Trissel sat up suddenly and put his arms on the little bare table. "Is that straight? Honest? You can get prints off paper?"

"Off a lot of things, Roger. The boys use different kinds of powder. Prints show up almost anywhere."

"To—get used in court, like?"

"Admissible evidence? Sure," said Grace. "Your prints tie you in here tight as a drum, Roger. You're going up for attempted homicide, whether it gets sorted out as one or two. Maybe you wouldn't like to think Bernie'd be running around loose when that happens."

"Yeah," said Trissel thoughtfully. "Yeah. Bernie Schultz, he lives over on Gleason. It was sort of his idea to knock over that place, see, and it was his gun."

"Oh, is that so? Address on Gleason?" Palliser wrote it down. "Then how come you've got it now?" By then, they'd sent the old .32 found in Trissel's room to Ballistics, with a request for a hurry-up make, and Ballistics had just told them it was the gun which had fired the slugs into Carroll.

"I—uh—well, see, Bernie he took the other one. It was newer."

"The Colt .38 you got from Carroll."

"Yeah, that's right."

"All right, that's all right now, Roger." They came out, told the guard he could take Trissel back to his cell. "You taking any bets, Jase?"

Grace smoothed his neat moustache. "That he'll sign that, when it gets typed up tomorrow, and at the hearing say the brutal cops beat it out of him? Uh-uh. We'll have too much physical evidence. And the evening's ruined already, you want to go find Bernie?"

"You're just a glutton for punishment," said Palliser. "Bucking for sergeant, of course."

"I don't think so," said Grace seriously. "Not yet, anyway. Likely I'd get reassigned to Forgery or somewhere, and I like working Homicide. With the boss with his crystal ball. I wonder if he'll come up with a hunch on Jane Doe. That is a sort of handleless thing."

They took Palliser's Rambler and drove over to Gleason Street in Boyle Heights. The address was a run-down old apartment house on a narrow dark street. The door labeled 4-B finally opened to them, to reveal a girl in her twenties, very barely mini-skirted, about twenty pounds overweight, wearing a patent silver wig and false eyelashes. She was blowing on one hand to dry a coat of hot-pink nail polish. "Yeah?"

They had the badges out. "We're looking for Bernie Schultz," began Palliser. "Is he—"

"You fuzz!" said the girl. "Always have to keep bothering a guy. Leaning on him. He's not here. Bernie. He's my brother. I got a job, I pay the rent, he don't and I get tired of it. I don't say he's a saint but he can't get a job here account of that little record he's got with you. Fuzz.

So he's gone down to Dago, try to get a job there. Here, he isn't." The door shut.

"Well," said Palliser. "We go back to the office and send a teletype to the San Diego boys. Please locate if in your territory."

"And we'd better tell them," said Grace, "about Mr. Carroll's .38 Colt."

And after that they went home.

"I don't say," said Mendoza, "that it's funny she hasn't been missed, because we don't know what circumstances she was living in. In spite of that having borne at least one child bit . . . Is the offspring better?"

"Asleep, I hope," said Alison, who had just come back. "Poor darling. It's the first time they've missed Máiri really." Terry had developed an earache an hour ago, and been fretful; and her mournful wails for Máiri—"Want *bonnie doon!* Want *Afton!*" had roused Johnny to similar demands. "The olive oil seemed to do the trick. I think they're settled now."

Mendoza had taken off jacket and tie and was stretched out on the sectional with Bast asleep on his stomach and El Señor crouched on his chest. Cedric was imitating a Crusader's dog at Alison's feet, the other two cats tangled together asleep in the other big armchair. "She may have been living alone. She might not have had a job. So nobody's noticed she's gone. But I've got a feeling about her, *cara*—what? *Eso no quiere decir nada*—it means nothing, but I get the feeling she was a good girl. And out of the blue, she ran into—" He was silent, and laughed sharply. *"El mundo malo,"* he said.

"The evil ones? What on earth do you—"

"Dressed up," said Mendoza. "She'd dressed up for something, you know. I didn't tell you all the details of that first lab report on the clothes. She'd taken care, dressing—I'd like to know, damn it, what happened to her costume jewelry, and that would have been in good taste too, and not too much of it—she'd taken pains. Probably the best and newest dress she had. The newest underwear and stockings. The handbag had to match those black patent leather pumps, you think?"

"Naturalmente."

"Did I tell you the FBI kickback came through? They don't know her—nobody knows her prints." A lot of respectable citizens as well as criminals had prints in the Feds' files, but not everybody, of course. "And she'd put on cologne," said Mendoza somnolently, reaching up to stroke El Señor's blond Siamese-in-reverse mask. "No trace of any other cologne on the clothes. By inference, the only cologne she ever used."

"What was it?" asked Alison interestedly.

"Blue Carnation. Roger and Gallet."

"*¡Una sorpresa!*" Alison laughed. "And you didn't spot it without a lab report?" It was the only cologne and perfume she ever used.

"Maybe what set my subconscious working, *mi corazón.*"

"Well! That could be read this way or that way, Luis. It's an old firm, not a firm that goes in for the glamorous advertising, the full page ads in *Glamour* and *Vogue*. It's relatively inexpensive, that cologne— three dollars the bottle, and a yearly sale where you get a spray-bottle thrown in. On the other hand, I started using it because it's one of the few colognes that stays on me with any permanence—it's something to do with chemical reactions of the individual, I think. Some of the most expensive French ones, I might as well put on tap water. So—"

"So, *obbio,* some women well able to afford the expensive advertised colognes will use a cheaper one because it's more—mmh—effective on them personally. Which Blue Carnation certainly is, my love. On you. And other women will buy them because they're not as expensive. But—"

"But, the two can go together. She couldn't afford Chanel Number Five or Tuvaché, but of a variety of inexpensive colognes she used Blue Carnation because it stayed on, it suited her."

"*Exacto,*" said Mendoza. "All of which says nothing at all. As to how she came to be in the big, big car on Azusa Street. Or where she— thought she was going."

"Art's quite right there. You don't *know*. The car mightn't have one thing to do with her."

"*Conforme*. But I think it did."

"Oh, so do I," said Alison. "Luis."

"*¿Enamorada?*"

"I think it was something important," said Alison. "That she got dressed up for. Something important to her."

Mendoza sat up slowly, bringing El Señor to drape over his shoulder, and looked at her.

"Not that I claim," said Alison, "to have a crystal ball . . . There's Terry again—" She got up hastily.

On Wednesday morning, with still no lead at all on the X's on Ahearn, who was doing a little better in the hospital—with the word out to the San Diego force on Bernie Schultz—with Jane Doe still unidentified—but the entire Homicide crew on the job, if thinking now and then of Piggott on his vacation-honeymoon—Hackett came into Mendoza's office at eight ten and said, "You haven't seen this. Or you'd be— I don't know. God, this job. Me being all clever, stupidity and cupidity. I just showed it to George—"

Higgins came in, looking the complete tough as usual. "Just as I was relaxing last night, over the evening paper," said Hackett, "I spot this."

"¿Pues qué?"

"The question is," said Higgins, "what do we do about it, Luis?"

"I didn't sleep too well, wondering that myself," said Hackett.

Mendoza took the paper from him. The first section of the *Herald,* folded back to the second-to-last page. Hackett's blunt forefinger stabbed the smallish head:

Wife of Candy-Maker
Alfred Carmichael Dies
In Home Accident

CHAPTER 6

"*¡Diez millones de demonios desde el infierno!*" said Mendoza, looking at that.

"Do about what?" asked Landers. He came in with Palliser and Grace trailing him.

"Didn't I say it then?" said Hackett savagely. "He'll try it again. He'd got away with it twice, and now it looks as if he's got away with it a third time round. And damn whatever evidence there is or isn't, he should damn well get caught up with, Luis!"

"I wouldn't have believed he'd dare," said Higgins. "Talk about nerve. Talk about—"

"What are you talking about?" asked Palliser.

Mendoza sat back, lit a new cigarette, and read the casual report of a sad accident, tucked away in the last pages of the newspaper.

"Mrs. Florence Carmichael, fifty-one, drowned accidentally in the bathtub of the Carmichaels' West Hollywood home yesterday. Mr. Carmichael, returning in late afternoon and alarmed at receiving no response to his calls, was forced to break in the bathroom door, to find his wife facedown in the water. Prompt aid was summoned and resuscitation attempted, but it proved useless. It was surmised either that Mrs. Carmichael had suffered some sort of attack, or possibly had struck her head in some manner and thus been incapacitated sufficiently long to drown. There is no family, and funeral arrangements are pending."

"Funeral arrangements— Now I like that touch," said Mendoza. "Of all the nerve indeed. Something ought to be done about it all right, but just what the hell?"

"Who's Carmichael?" asked Grace, picking up the paper curiously where Mendoza had flung it down. Hackett began to tell him absently.

"This isn't on our beat," said Mendoza. "The other two were—God, how the time goes! Ten years ago—" Of the men now in Homicide, only he and Hackett and Higgins had been working out of this office then; and other men, since shifted or retired or dead. . . .

And the first one had looked, even to the canny and thorough detectives in Homicide, quite straightforward. The tragic kind of blunder that does happen, and can't be blamed on anyone.

Ten years ago, and a hot summer night, Mendoza remembered. The crime rate up, as always in summer, nothing like what it was now, but up. And there were all sorts of businesses in the city you never knew were there: when he first saw it, Mendoza recognized the building, he'd been past it before, but he'd never known what business it housed. Golden Maid Candies, Inc.—a biggish outfit manufacturing a middle-priced brand of everything from fancy boxed chocolates to bubble gum. It was a tall, middle-aged building of eight or nine stories, out on Soto Street, which was on the Central beat. And that summer, Golden Maid Candies had had a couple of burglaries—probably j.d.'s hunting anything portable and remotely pawnable—and a little senseless vandalism. That wasn't too classy a part of town; manufacturers of anything seldom occupy fancy sections of any town.

Ten years ago Alfred Carmichael, Junior, had been third man on the totem pole at Golden Maid. His father Alfred Senior had owned the company outright. It was very much a family enterprise, no stock outstanding and Alfred Junior's older brother Robert was the junior partner, Alfred the manager. It came out that all three of them having an interest in the business, it wasn't unusual for one, or two, or all three of them to be there after hours, in their own offices. And on that particular night, Alfred Junior had thought—so he testified later—that he was alone in the building, about nine P.M. There was a night watchman, but he didn't come on the job until eleven. And, hearing stealthy sounds and footsteps somewhere in the building, Alfred—thinking of those burglars—had seized the .32 automatic from his desk drawer and gone looking for intruders. The building was dark, he explained later, the only light from his office door; he should have waited to be sure, he should have—he shouldn't have— But the fact remained that he had spotted a dark figure at the end of the hall, challenged it to stop, and fired. He said he'd fired wide, just to scare the fellow, but admitted he wasn't at all used to guns. And the burglar had turned out to be Alfred Carmichael Senior, just leaving his own office. He hadn't been killed outright, but he wasn't a young man, the bullet had punctured a lung and eventually he contracted pneumonia and slipped off.

There had been a hearing: Alfred had been eloquent, a tragic figure of Fate. The judge ruled it Involuntary Manslaughter, suspended sentence of one year. And that was just what it had looked like.

So far as everybody except Homicide was concerned, and one or two suspicious souls in the D.A.'s office, that was still what it looked like. But about four years after that, there had been a second tragic accident at Golden Maid Candies. The two brothers were then in partnership in the business—Robert and Alfred. Evidently they had maintained their hard-working, out-of-hours devotion to the business, for it seemed that Robert had been alone in his office that night, when he turned off the lights and started downstairs, on his way home. The night watchman had found him, coming on the job three hours later. He'd been killed outright, apparently by the fall downstairs. The inquest verdict said, Accident. The flooring there was tough vinyl laid directly on cement.

But that one Homicide had looked at very carefully. Coincidences happened, but the second one was such a convenient coincidence for Alfred . . . However, his wife and their maid told the Homicide officers that he had been home since six o'clock, had never stirred out, and there was no useful physical evidence at the scene.

"Gall," said Hackett. "My God, the gall, Luis! He got the partnership the first time, the business outright the second time. Now maybe he was a little tired of Florence, not so young and pretty any more, so—"

"Prove it!" said Mendoza sardonically. "Prove it, Art! We haven't got jurisdiction in this one. If those were contrived accidents—"

"And I'd bet my pension on it," said Higgins.

"There's not one solitary piece of evidence to show it."

"But right under our noses—"

"Not ours this time," said Mendoza. "But while we like to flatter ourselves we're the star force, there are just a few more around nearly as good. The hell with protocol, we're going to bring this into the open, at least—"

"Hand it to the press?" said Hackett, alarmed. "That's not such a hot idea, Luis. They could have a field day if they really took the bait, so even in the unlikely event that a charge was made, there'd be the yell that the case was tried in the papers—"

"I wasn't thinking of the press," said Mendoza. "*A su tiempo maduran las uvas*. We'll have accumulated some records in ten years—even in the last six—but you chase down to R. and I., Art, and turn up the package on Carmichael. It'll be on microfilm by now, but still there. Get it. What's the Carmichaels' address?"

"It just says West Hollywood."

"County territory," said Mendoza. He told Lake to get him an outside line, while he flipped over pages in the phone-list on the desk. "It's Olympia 2-3525, Jimmy. Tell 'em who I am."

"You're going to hand our records to the sheriff's boys," said Higgins.

"And you and Art were both on the—mmh—accidents. You'll come with me."

An hour later three of them sat in the office of Sheriff's Captain Fred Webb, at the West Hollywood Sheriff's station on San Vincente Boulevard, and listened to what Webb and a couple of deputies had to say. Quite a lot of it was incredulous and the rest profane.

"You're telling me this cute joker has pulled this kind of thing twice before, on your beat?" Webb, who was as massive-shouldered as Higgins, gave the same effect of his clothes being too small for him as a pro boxer dressed. He flung himself back in the desk chair. "This—"

"That's slander, Captain," said Mendoza. "Nothing, absolutely nothing, says he knew that was his father and not a burglar. That kind of accident has happened before, all aboveboard, when people are nervous and not used to guns. The judge cleared him—that's a closed book."

"*But,* for God's sake—three so-called accidents happening around the same man? All so profitable for him? He couldn't—"

"But he has," Hackett pointed out. "Got away with it. Not the same kinds of accident, Captain. Anybody can fall downstairs. If he lands just right, on a hard surface, he can kill himself. There's no evidence at all that Robert Carmichael wasn't alone when he fell downstairs."

"You will notice," said Mendoza, "among all those reports, what our surgeon said about Robert. Bainbridge is no man's fool. What Robert actually died of was a depressed skull fracture, and of course that was the second time round on Alfred for us so we went into it very thoroughly. Bainbridge said then, after a detailed examination of the body, that it was possible the man had only been stunned by the fall. If somebody else had been there, he could have heaved the man up and slammed his head down on that hard floor with sufficient force to cause the fracture."

"A strong man, I take it," said Deputy Wooster dryly. "What size was Robert?"

"Five seven, a hundred and forty," said Mendoza, flicking his lighter. "Alfred's bigger—call it my height, ten pounds heavier."

"Five ten, a hundred and seventy. Heaved him up by the shoulders, slammed his head down—and left bruise marks on the shoulders," said Webb with a small snarl. "So he didn't do it like that—"

Mendoza grinned. "See the medical report. Bainbridge spotted a small bruise at the back of the left shoulder, high up. Nothing inconsistent—Robert could have got it in the fall. Could have got it stumbling against something that afternoon. And three thicknesses of clothes—he had on jacket, shirt, undershirt. Bainbridge said to me then, if the D.A. lost his marbles and brought it to court, he'd have to testify that it was quite consistent with the evidence that all injuries were sustained in the fall."

"Son of a bitch!" said Webb. "And two people swearing Alfred was peaceably at home!"

"That's it," said Hackett.

"Are you telling me"—Webb seemed to swell—"are you boys telling me that a murder's been committed in my territory and I can't do a damned thing about it?"

"I don't know," said Mendoza. "I haven't seen the evidence on this one. I don't know where Alfred says he was when Florence was supposedly taking a bath. Maybe he got a little careless on this one and you'll find something to say so. I just think you ought to look."

"And so by God do I!" said Webb. He looked at Mendoza, slim and dapper in Italian silk, his dark cap of hair growing to the widow's point and his moustache trimmed to a precise line: he looked as if he couldn't quite credit Mendoza to be a fellow cop, thought Hackett amusedly. "Evidence!" said Webb. "We all know what that can say—or not say. But you think Alfred did it. Three times."

"I'm damn well sure he did it," said Mendoza.

"How?"

"Papa was no problem. Alfred knew he was in his office, he just said he didn't. So, prove it. On Robert, I admit I don't know how he did it. It's possible his wife gave him an alibi for love and the maid gave him one for money. He'd have the money, all right."

"I was going to ask what kind of profits that business makes."

"We even went into that, on Robert. It's an old established firm, they don't do much advertising—don't have to. All the machines for actually making the candy, cutting the overhead on employees. At the time Robert died, he was taking an easy hundred grand a year out of it as senior partner, and the gross has probably gone up since then. And after that, Alfred had it all—call it a hundred and seventy-five grand net per year."

"My good Christ!" said Webb.

"You're welcome to borrow the package on him," said Mendoza. "We just thought we ought to pass all this on."

"And of all the damn headaches to hand me— But the gall of him, pulling a thing like that, *three*—no, I see that, different accidents."

"And accidents will happen," said Hackett. "Prove they weren't. We can only wish you luck, but I doubt if you'll nail him."

"My good sweet *Christ!*" said Webb. When they left he was staring down at the parcel of microfilmed records, one fist unconsciously balled.

Palliser, Landers and Grace had spent a while kicking the Carmichael thing around—a new one to them, and intriguing. They agreed nobody could ever build a legal case against Alfred, a waste of time to try; but maybe the sheriff's boys, knowing his background, could scare him a little.

Two more citizens came in to look at Jane Doe, and Landers took them down to the morgue; but she wasn't the vanished wife or the mentally retarded sister.

About ten fifteen Sergeant Lake announced that he had a sergeant in San Diego on the line. "I'll take it," said Palliser, and picked up his phone. "Sergeant Palliser, Central Homicide."

"Sergeant Tinker," said a bland voice a hundred and fifty miles away. "You boys put out a call for a Bernard Schultz, wanted in connection with a homicide—"

"Just attempted," said Palliser. "Have you picked him up?"

"Well, we put out the word to the pigeons," said Tinker, "but so far as we know Schultz is new on our beat, and we've got a fairly varied sort of, er, underworld here, what with being a port and all the smuggling—"

"You tell me nothing," said Palliser. The early city fathers, unwilling that that immense seaport should bear the name of any of the towns actually on the coast, had cannily retained a mile-wide strip right down to the sea, in order to christen the harbor Los Angeles too. As one result, the L.A.P.D. operates a Harbor division which pursues its job largely in boats. "Have you got him?"

"Yes, we've got him," said Tinker. "He, er, turned up in the drunk tank this morning."

"In other words, more luck than good management," said Palliser, laughing. "Well, hang onto him. Somebody'll be down with a warrant to pick him up."

"Glad to oblige you," said Tinker.

Palliser put the phone down and asked if the warrant had come through on Schultz. It had. "Jimmy, when's the next plane to San Diego?"

"I should think you'd get one out of Burbank quicker—I'll check." Five minutes later Lake reported, "Southwest Airlines' got a plane leaving for Mexico at eleven-oh-five. Lands in San Diego at eleven forty."

Palliser ran. This time of day, the freeway was relatively empty. He made it out to the Hollywood-Burbank airport with fifteen minutes to spare.

Mendoza came back after lunch, with his two senior sergeants, feeling annoyed at the general frustrations accumulating on the job. He sat down at his desk, got out the deck of cards and began shuffling it, muttering to himself. He didn't often get to sit in on a game of draw these days, domesticities having prevailed; but he always thought better with the cards in his hands.

He heard about Schultz. "If John can pick up an early flight back, he should be fetching Bernie in by three or so."

"If," said Mendoza. He heard about the two abortive visits to Jane Doe.

"We'll never find out anything more about it if we can't identify her," said Landers.

"Which was the object of the whole exercise," said Mendoza.

"A hunch tells you that?" asked Hackett.

"¡Seguramente que sí! That's obvious," said Mendoza. He began to deal hands around, having set up the deck for a crooked deal, and was slightly gratified to find his ability to stack a deck was still operating. "Comes the crash," he muttered, "I can always earn the eating money— At least, nothing new showing up to work." And guiltily he remembered, speaking of domesticities, his hostages to fortune; he put the cards down, dialed the house on Rayo Grande Avenue.

"How's the offspring, cara?" Alison had been up half the night with Terry.

"Better," she said through a yawn. "I got her down to the doctor's office early, and he slipped her in before his first appointment. He says just a little infection, he gave her a shot and she's feeling fine now. Only it's reminded both of them how they're missing Máiri. Well, thank heaven she'll be home on Friday night."

As he put the phone down, Sergeant Lake was taking a call. He swung round from the switchboard to see who was in. "Just another accident," he said. "On the Hollywood—"

"Don't say that word!" said Higgins.

* * *

A couple of new calls came in almost at once after that, and when another came in at five minutes to three Mendoza was the only one in the office. It was the lab reporting in: Scarne.

"On your Jane Doe. I don't know how much good this is going to do you, but we've got a dandy set of prints."

"¿Cómo no? Where from, for God's sake? I know you're good, but I didn't think you were getting latents off nylon yet."

"Well, it's funny how you overlook the obvious sometimes. It was her shoes. That patent leather takes prints just fine, you know. These are beautiful, beautiful. When we finally got round to looking. You'll like where they were, too. Four fingers, pointing upward, on the right side of the right shoe's heel—the outside surface, that is. Thumb, pointing upward, on the inside of the heel, underside I mean—"

"Mmh, yes. Muy significante. Exactly where anybody would take hold of a shoe to pull it off somebody else's foot. Now for the really significant point—"

"No," said Scarne sadly. "Not in our records. I sent 'em to Washington."

"So, wait and see," said Mendoza. The Feds had a lot of prints.

And it was no use at all to speculate about Jane Doe unless and until some solid facts showed up: until they knew who she was. But Mendoza, for good or ill, had an active imagination, and he found it impossible not to do so.

The nice girl. Carefully dressed in her modest (in both senses) best clothes, expecting to go out to dinner somewhere. Ending up in the big, big car (already dead?) and being deposited so gracelessly in Mr. Lozano's back yard. Why exactly there, by the way? Or had it been just at random? Come to think, reflected Mendoza, X must have known that that house was empty. Because one really would hesitate to stop in the driveway of an occupied house, carry a corpse even a little way down the drive, and calmly drive off. Too many chances of being noticed and challenged, even in Azusa Street. Especially in Azusa Street, he amended—narrow lots, and in a lot of those streets down there the neighbors were friendly, running in and out of each other's houses.

Had Mr. Lozano advertised his house for rent? After some difficulty with the Classified personnel at the Times, Mendoza tracked it down. The ad had run all last week: the address on Azusa Street had been given, and Mr. Lozano's phone number.

So there it was. But why? Who had wanted her dead and unidentified?

*   *   *

Landers had just come back and said laconically, "Paperwork. Coronary—old woman in a rooming house on Gary," and was beginning to type the report—Mendoza could see him in the sergeants' room across there, cussing when he hit a wrong key—when Sergeant Lake called, "Lieutenant! That sniper again—MacArthur Park, the boat-keeper called—two cars on the way—"

"Didn't I say, wait for him to get the urge! But, *Dios,* broad daylight —Tom!" Mendoza yanked open the top drawer of his desk, took out the .38 and a box of ammo, reached for his hat. Landers behind him, he dove for the door.

Downstairs, he hit the siren as he started the engine, and the Ferrari snarled to life, parting the traffic like a bow-wave up Los Angeles Street. He braked once for the turn onto Wilshire and roared up under the freeways stacked midway toward the pleasant little park in the middle of the city, with its lake and boats. As he braked the Ferrari in a red zone they saw a black-and-white drawing up on Seventh just ahead.

There wasn't a big crowd; this park didn't attract crowds on weekdays; but there was a scattering of people down by the boat-landing, two uniformed men, one man pointing.

Mendoza and Landers were halfway down there when they heard the shots. The patrolmen, starting up this way, converged with two more out of a second car. Mendoza flashed his badge.

"He's up here somewhere—in those trees, sir." Three more shots, and water splashed as the slugs hit the lake, too close to the little knot of people, who shouted and dispersed, running. "God's sake, he must be crazy—in broad daylight—"

There wasn't much cover in MacArthur Park: the sniper had taken what was offered. A thin cluster of young trees and tall planting partly masked the little stucco building up there: the double rest rooms. "He's round the back," panted one of the Traffic men: and then there were more shots, sounding more muffled, and screams from a different direction. "He's firing into the street, for God's—"

"Get back to your unit and call up some more help," said Mendoza. "You"—he turned to a second man—"get out there and see if anyone's hurt, on the street. He's—"

"That's a rifle," said another man suddenly. "Not a handgun. Sounds like a high-powered job—"

It spoke again. And as they came under the first trees, spaced out to cover both sides of the little building, they all had their own guns out. Another black-and-white came screaming up Seventh. The crowd was collecting in earnest out on the street, along Wilshire, now—damn fools, packing together to gawk—

Mendoza and one Traffic man went right-hand around the building, Landers and the other man the other way. They met, past the discreetly labeled doors. No cover in back of the building, no sign of—

A fusillade of shots. "By God, he's on the roof!" shouted Landers simultaneously with a patrolman. "How did—" But they all spotted it at once: a young oak, beginning to spread its branches, right against the building: and the roof wasn't more than ten feet high.

"For God's sake, be *caref*—" said the patrolman with Landers, and staggered back as a slug took him in one arm. Another siren came nearer.

Landers was in the tree, head low. He came part way down. "He's lying flat on the roof, he's got a rifle, and he swiveled and shot this way in about half a second—I don't know how we're going to get near enough to—"

"Draw his fire," said Mendoza. "He hasn't got an unlimited amount of ammo up there with his high-powered rifle." He glanced over the terrain, beckoning the patrolmen—another pair running up now. "How bad is that?"

"Not bad," said the man examining the wound. "Slug through the upper arm, you're O.K. Len—better get back to the unit, you're losing a little blood." He completed a makeshift bandage with two handkerchiefs. "What do you want, sir?"

"All of you—and whoever else shows up," said Mendoza rapidly, "over there the other side of the trees—" No other tree was within reach of the building, but there was some cover. There wasn't time or room here to think about danger, about possible death. There was a wild man, berserk, crazy, or whatever, with a dangerous weapon, running loose: and they had to get him fast and however they could, at whatever risk. It was one hell of a terrain for such an operation. "Get up high enough to aim at him, but don't aim to kill—just keep his fire headed your way—" And that was the hell of an order to give any man. But it was the kind of risk a man took on with the uniform. "Tom, come down from there!"

"But with any luck I can—"

"Come down! *¡Ven acá!* Damn you, get down out of there!"

"But I—" Reluctantly Landers came down. "What's your idea? Draw his fire, for God's sake, get some of those men killed— He's aiming that damn gun right down on the street, and if he's the one killed Hagan— But he's got a rifle, not—"

"*¡Paso!*" said Mendoza. "Out of the way. You stay here and pick up the pieces if this goes wrong." He swung himself to the first crotch of the oak and raised the .38.

"Lieutenant—for God's sake, get yourself *killed*— No!" The fire started from over there to the left. "Let me—"

"Don't be foolish," said Mendoza. The shots stopped as the uniformed branch reloaded; he sounded testy. "We can't spare you youngsters." The fire started again, and the rifle spoke above, in a different direction. Mendoza went up another five feet, balanced himself carefully, took aim and fired twice.

All of a sudden the rifle came sliding down the slant of the roof and fell to the ground.

Mendoza came down out of the tree. "Playing Tarzan. I never claimed to be a marksman." He brushed down his trousers. The Traffic men poured over here. "You may need a ladder, I got him in the shoulder."

"You all *right?*" asked Landers shakily. "My God—I could have just as well—"

"You O.K., sir? I've put in a call for an ambulance— No, nobody else hit—"

A shout from the oak tree. "I can pull him over this way, a couple of you stand by to bring him down!"

"My God," said Landers numbly. "I—"

Mendoza gave him his sudden one-sided grin. "Cheating you," he said. "I never thought of that. By God, I should have let you take him— he'd likely have winged you in the arm or somewhere unimportant, and you'd have got all the glory and your stubborn lady love would have wept all over you. That's what you get for being junior to Mendoza. Everybody knows I'm an egotist."

"So long as you're all right—"

Mendoza looked at his .38. "Art would never let me forget it if he knew."

"Knew what?"

"I aimed for his shooting arm. I got him in the left shoulder."

The sniper, when they got him down off the roof, looked impossibly young and innocent, laid out awaiting the ambulance: a willowy youth with long blond hair, no hint of a beard. He came to as they loaded him into the ambulance, and it was pretty clear by the incoherences he came out with that he was high as a kite on something.

They couldn't question him for some time, probably.

The rifle was a fine new Enfield. He'd had a hundred rounds of ammo for it in a carton on the roof.

But there was identification on him: a driver's license. His name was William Pratt, an address on Vancouver Avenue in east L.A.

By the time they had everything cleaned up at the scene, it was after five. Mendoza and Landers went back to the office. "You can do the report tomorrow," said Mendoza. He was starving, and wondered what Alison was planning for dinner.

Grace had been in when they got back, and was now on his way to the Vancouver Avenue address to learn something more about William Pratt, if possible.

Mendoza thought about Jane Doe. If she never got identified—which could happen—finis. They'd never know any more about it. And Alfred Carmichael was now a headache for the sheriff's boys, and they were welcome to him.

He was sitting at his desk finishing a cigarette when Hackett and Higgins came in. "You Goddamned idiot!" said Hackett. "Could've got yourself killed—Tom was just—"

Mendoza opened his eyes and said mildly, "Hogging all the glory— that's me."

"Don't tell me!" said Hackett. "Let me guess. Because he's just turned thirty-one and—"

"*¡Insubordinación!* You needn't remind me of my age, *amigo*. For my sins, twenty-four years on this thankless job—"

"Listen," said Hackett, "I kind of like that redhaired wife of yours, and so does my wife. For whatever idiotic reason, your wife might miss you a little. Even with the nice will in her favor."

"Preserve calm," said Mendoza. "I am still alive, Arturo."

"Which surprises me," said Hackett, "the kind of sloppy score you usually shoot."

"For God's sake, no postmortems," said Mendoza. "I'm going home."

But as he passed the desk and switchboard, fumbling for his keys, Sergeant Lake hailed him.

"This just came in from Communications, Lieutenant. A new bulletin from NCIC. It looks like maybe business for us."

"*¿Cómo?*"

"It's an A.P.B. to all points west of Council Bluffs. From Garrison, Iowa. This pair wanted—two men, no make on names or descriptions, wanted suspicion of homicide. But they're driving, as of the eighteenth, a seven-year-old Dodge—here's the plate-number—and hauling a two-wheel trailer. Possibly in possession of a Savage-Stevens twenty-gauge shotgun and a Colt .45 revolver. No serial numbers available."

"¡Ca!" said Mendoza. "How very helpful! So we'd better add that plate-number to our own A.P.B.— And who's checked lately on how Ahearn's doing?"

CHAPTER 7

By the time Mendoza got home, he was thinking chiefly of food, and kissed Alison abstractedly. "Dinner?" she said. "Heavens, I thought you must be early—is it after six? That daughter of yours—she's been driving me distracted. No, she's perfectly all right, she's just fretting for Máiri and acting like a spoiled child—which I didn't think she was—"

In the nursery, Terry was face down on her bed, sobbing monotonously, "Want Máiri! Want *bonnie doon!* Want *Lomond!*" Johnny scowled at her darkly. "Now, please, Terry," pleaded Alison. "See, Daddy's home, he'll read to you if you sit up and be a good girl—"

Terry went on sobbing. "Want *bonnie!*"

Obviously strong measures were called for. In the kitchen, the four cats and Cedric were lined up in the last stages of starvation; and Mendoza felt rather like that himself.

"*¡Vamos!*" he said to Alison. "Go get dinner, woman—I'll handle this."

"Now that I'd like to see," said Alison.

Mendoza went over to Terry's bed. "*¡Silencio!*" he shouted. Johnny jumped, and so unaccustomed was either of them to hear his voice raised, Terry hiccuped once and sat up wide-eyed. "Now, silly little girls don't deserve any bedtime stories, but I'll tell you one, *hijo.*" He sat down on Johnny's bed with his back to Terry. "All these tame European fairy tales! I'll tell you a story my grandmother used to tell me when I was *un muchacho muy pequeño.*"

This novel idea struck Johnny as exquisitely humorous. "You ver' little boy? When?"

"A long time ago, *chico*," said Mendoza with a grin. "Now this story's about a beautiful Aztec princess, and her name was Cihuacoatl.

She turned into a goddess later on, but this was before that." Terry had got off her bed and was slowly approaching.

"What's Aztec?" asked Johnny.

"The Aztecs, you little ignoramus, were some of your ancestors, and they were very proud, fierce people. Now this princess—"

At any rate Terry had stopped crying. Alison started for the kitchen, but not before she heard the next question: "Where they come from?"

"Atlantis probably, but that's another story," said Mendoza absently. And what Máiri was going to say to that when she got back, heaven knew, thought Alison, hastening to feed the starving livestock.

"The damn fool!" said Hackett to Angel. "Taking the risk instead of Tom, just because— Oh, don't I know it! He'd never admit it, of course, make some wisecrack about saving promising youngsters—"

"More truth than poetry," said Angel, tasting the salad dressing. "Mark of a good officer, isn't it, never order a man to do a thing he wouldn't do himself."

"That's our Luis," said Hackett. "It wouldn't worry me so much if he'd keep up to snuff on the practice range. But Tom's a better shot than he is any day."

He went off to corral the children, playing in the back yard, for dinner. "Have you weighed today, Art?" she called after him.

"I am up to two eighteen and I couldn't care less," said Hackett.

Higgins wasn't thinking about the sniper at all, much less his spectacular capture. If anything dangerous had to be done, it was natural for the senior officer to take it on. It was just something of a miracle that nobody had been killed, and it was over with.

He did vaguely wonder what had happened to John; they hadn't had a word from him since he caught that plane south.

Higgins was investigating the intricacies of photography. He wasn't being helped at all by Steve and Laura Dwyer, who hung entranced over the baby and the camera alternately, begging to be allowed to take just one picture, please, George, and take one of her with me, George. Brucie bounced around getting in everybody's way, and exactly what got down on the film they wouldn't know until Saturday, if Higgins dropped the negatives off at the drugstore tomorrow. Through all the commotion Margaret Emily lay dreamily on her back or waved fingers and toes like starfish, perfectly undisturbed.

"Born on a Friday, loving and giving," said Mrs. MacTaggart. "She's a sweet temper, I will say."

"She'll need to have," said Mary, "in this family!"

*　*　*

Palliser had had an uneventful flight down to San Diego, taken a cab to the police station downtown, and introduced himself to Sergeant Tinker. There was a bunch of nice fellows there, and they took him to lunch before he took delivery of Bernie Schultz. There was a Southwest Air passenger on its way back to L.A. from Mexico City, landing briefly at San Diego at two thirty. Palliser, with Bernie cuffed to his left wrist, caught it.

But five minutes after takeoff, the plane developed engine trouble, and landed precipitately at Escondido. They sat there for two hours while a crew was sent out from the city to effect repairs, and didn't take off again until after five o'clock.

By then Palliser had had all he wanted of Bernie, who was a cocksure brash young fellow, not at all despondent at getting dropped on again. "Whaddaya bet, Sergeant?" he kept saying. "I get a two-to-five 'n' serve maybe one, I'm out. P.A. No sweat—"

"Not on attempted homicide, Bernie."

"Whaddaya bet? It was Rog had the gun. He's the one pulled the trigger. And the guy dint die, I seen in the papers."

"By the way, where is that gun, Bernie?" The San Diego boys had searched the cheap hotel room he'd had: no gun.

"I dunno—I thought Rog still had it."

"He says you took it."

"Well, I never—but I won't get much outta this, out in a year, whaddaya bet?"

Palliser handed him over to the Alameda jail at six thirty, thankfully, and went home.

"Usual routine day, I suppose," said Roberta. "You look tired, darling—a lot of legwork?"

"I could say, vice versa," said Palliser.

Overnight, Communications had supplied NCIC with the news that the L.A.P.D. might have some follow-up information on the car and trailer wanted in connection with that homicide in Iowa; when Mendoza came into the office on Thursday morning NCIC had passed that on to one Sheriff Lord McCauley, who had promptly teletyped the story straight through. Mendoza read through the yellow sheets, grunting, and looking up to find his henchmen arriving, passed them on to Palliser to share with Landers and Grace.

A John Murray had owned a large farm outside Garrison, lived there with his wife and, until recently, a crew of harvest-hands temporarily hired. But the harvest was over in August, and the last time the Murrays had been seen alive was on the ninth of September, when a neighbor had stopped by. Murray had said that he had hired a couple of strangers passing through, to do some odd jobs around the place. On the twelfth, the two strangers had been seen driving Murray's old Dodge with the trailer hitched to it. On the fourteenth somebody had stopped by the Murray farm and discovered the bodies—both shot, dead several days. An immediate A.P.B. had been put out on the car, but all that netted was a sighting across the line in Nebraska. It was assumed they were heading west. It was also assumed that they had in their possession the two guns missing from the farmhouse: a Colt .45 revolver and a twelve-gauge shotgun. Murray was known to have kept cash in the house. There was no make on the men at all: nobody had seen them close or heard names mentioned.

"The same old story," said Mendoza. "At least, if they're still here, we should pick up the car by the plate-number."

"It's been on the hot list since last night," said Landers.

"Meanwhile, enough chores for us to do. This Pratt—what'd you get on him, Jase?"

Grace hoisted a hip on the corner of the desk. His chocolate-colored face with the lean regular features was grave. "If Matt was here he'd be talking about Satan. Another old story. Poor damn creep of a female, waits on tables at a fourth-class restaurant for the grocery money, the rent. She's been worried about William, but she didn't know what to do —he's been acting funny, but he got so cross if she asked questions— we've all heard it too many times. He's seventeen, a dropout, and the father's in Atascadero. I haven't looked to see what for." That was the asylum for the criminal insane.

"Nice," said Mendoza, took up the phone and asked for an outside line. "Search warrant for the house—apartment?"

"Apartment. It should be here by now."

"*Bueno.*" Mendoza got Central Receiving, asked if Pratt could be questioned. He could: the slug hadn't done much damage, and the dope was out of him now. Mendoza stood up. "Eeny-meeny-miny-mo—"

"Why, Lootenant, suh," said Grace, "you nasty old racist you, quoting that one! All right, I'm It, I'll go with you . . . Did you hear about that bunch of silly people agitating at the library to take *Little Black Sambo* out of the juvenile section? Fact. Just how ridiculous can you get?"

"I've come to the conclusion," said Mendoza as they went out, "that the first requirement for becoming all liberal and progressive and problem-conscious is to lose any sense of humor you've got. It seems to be a mark of the breed."

"Oh, aren't you right," said Grace. "Would you like a ride in a poor man's racer for once?"

"I would not."

At Central Receiving they saw the doctor first, a steady-eyed middle-aged man who saw a lot of trouble and grief and somehow stayed wryly sane in dealing with it. He shrugged at them. "Seventeen," he said sadly. "And I'd have a guess the damage is done, Lieutenant. The permanent brain damage. He admits having been on the acid for at least two years, since he was fifteen. He's rational in spots, as it were. He was on Methedrine yesterday, that I can say definitely, and he says he hasn't had any LSD in about a month, for what that's worth."

"The father's in Atascadero," said Mendoza.

"Really? Interesting—it could be there's some hereditary factor then. It's just a guess, though I've seen a lot of these people, but I'd say he wouldn't have tested above dull-normal even before he got hooked."

"Well, the main thing I want to know," said Mendoza, "is whether it was Pratt who shot Hagan, and if we tie the right gun to him that'll do it, but will we? With that pretty rifle yesterday, he could have ditched any other guns."

"You're welcome to ask him about it," said the doctor.

They saw William Pratt in the little lounge at the end of the corridor: this was the security wing of the hospital. He'd be transferred to the Alameda jail sometime today. His shoulder was bandaged, and he was wearing jail-issue clothes already, tan chino pants and shirt. He looked young and unhealthy, and at first he just looked from under his brows at Mendoza and Grace, sullenly silent.

"Where'd you get the guns, William?" asked Mendoza.

After a long dragging moment Pratt said, "Pawnshop."

"Buy them?" He shook his head. "Break in?"

"I like guns."

"You've got a little habit to support, haven't you?" said Grace. "Where've you been getting the money?"

After another silence, "The guns. It was easy. It was easy. Guys out late—ladies sometimes. Sometimes I wouldn't get much, was all."

"All right," said Grace in his gentle voice, "how about shooting at people, William? Yesterday and before? Did you shoot at people before? Shoot a man in the street?"

Pratt licked his lips. "The guns," he said. "It was just on account of getting the money with the guns, I got the idea. I just got to wondering. You know how you get to wondering."

"Wondering about what, William?"

"Well, well, you see, it was easy. With the guns. The other littler gun
I got. Just show it, and the people hand over the money. Easy. Funny
but easy. I—never—shot—that gun atall, see. I had bullets for it, and I
got a book at the liberry showed all about puttin' 'em in—for the other
one too, the big one. That's how I knew. But I never had to shoot it. To
get the money. And I got to wondering—just how it'd feel—to shoot
somebody. I just got to wondering."

"And when did you shoot the gun the first time?"

"I dunno," he said. Suddenly he giggled, high and thin. "But that was
funny too. It was in some street after dark, I needed money for a fix—I
needed a fix bad. Bad. I was gonna show the gun, this guy coming
along, but he—he wasn't—afraid o' the gun. He said he dint have no
money—he had a little dog on a string—and I sort of forgot the money
just then, I just wondered—how—it'd—feel and I shot it off then. The
gun. But that big one shoots faster, only—" He lapsed into silence and
then said, "Could I have a chocolate bar? With nuts in it?"

"We'll ask the doctor, William." In the corridor, Grace said, "Betting
on where he ends up?"

"*Pues no.* Upstate with Daddy. But that was Hagan, wasn't it?"

"Has to be. Now we go looking for that other gun to prove it."

When they got back to headquarters the search warrant had come
through and Grace and Landers went to execute that. Mendoza went
downstairs to Robbery.

"Keeping you busy, Saul?"

Lieutenant Goldberg looked up from a report. "You kidding? At
least, praise heaven for small favors, we're going to have an early fall.
My sinuses settle down some as soon as it turns cool, thank God. And
what can I do for Homicide?"

"Other way round. You had a pawnshop break-in, I don't know exactly when—"

"Which one? We've had seven in the last three months."

"Oh. Well, among, probably, other things stolen from this one was
an almost new Enfield rifle and a .38 Colt revolver. Ring a bell?"

"Old man Vincent on Wabash. Couple of months ago. The gun
showed on something of yours?"

"The Enfield, so far. Tell you later about the Colt. That sniper yesterday. You've also had some holdups on the street—pedestrians."

"When haven't we? Which ones?"

"I haven't got any idea which ones," said Mendoza. "But some of
them at least were this sniper. William Pratt. He's a hophead, probably
legally nuts as well. He's tied to one kill, if we find that Colt in his pos-

session, but we'll never send him for trial. I just thought you'd like to know."

"That one—I heard something about it." This big busy building had a built-in grapevine, of course. Goldberg looked at Mendoza sardonically. "Climbing trees at your age, yet. Giving your loyal minions heart failure —everybody knows any average rookie could outshoot you."

"A man in my rank is supposedly paid to think," said Mendoza.

"That's just what I say," said Goldberg. "Leave the energetic work to the younger generation. You ought to start growing old gracefully, I always say."

"Speak for yourself," grinned Mendoza, getting up.

"Now, Luis. Just a little kind advice." Goldberg sneezed and reached for Kleenex.

"I thought you said the allergies were better."

"Only comparatively," said Goldberg in a muffled voice. "At least we can clear one off the books—thanks very much."

Mendoza went up to Federico's on North Broadway for lunch, and ran into Grace, Palliser and Landers just going in. The big table at the front of the room had been more crowded, sometimes, when all or most of them knocked off at once; today both Hackett and Higgins were off.

"Some more paperwork turned up after you left," said Palliser. "Suicide. Messy. Young married couple had a fight and she cut her wrists in the bathtub after he left for work."

"For real?" asked Landers. Landers had once spotted a murder camouflaged as suicide, and been inclined to examine all suicides narrowly ever since.

"Doors all locked on the inside." Palliser lit a cigarette and added that he thought he deserved a drink before lunch.

"Yes, sir, bourbon and water," said the waiter. Grace passed; Landers ordered a Scotch and soda, and without being told the waiter brought a cup of black coffee to Mendoza.

Who said, "And that's another thing, damn it. Wasting time. The damn puritanical rules. There'll be a hearing—"

"Oh, that," said Palliser. "Nuisance, sure." Whenever an L.A.P.D. officer had cause to fire his gun away from the range, there had to be a solemn hearing by Internal Affairs to determine if he had just cause. Probably on this one, seeing all the ammo expended by the uniformed branch, it would be a joint hearing. Wasting a little time, for the inevitable conclusion that the shooting had been justified by the circumstances.

"Bathtubs." Mendoza swallowed hot coffee. "I do wonder what Captain Webb is doing on Alfred."

"That's a queer one," said Grace. "Only thing he can hope to do, scare him off ever trying it again."

"I wonder. But that's academic. What did you turn at the Pratt apartment?"

"Quite a lot of stuff." Landers answered first. "That Pratt woman—dumb enough to tuck away, you ask me. Didn't like to meddle with William's things, he got cross. She'd been afraid he was taking this terrible dope—wringing her hands, you know? There was ten caps of H and some pills—average representation, bennies and Nembutal and so on, and a bag of Mary Jane—"

"And the gun? The other gun?"

"Oh, that—yes, that was there, and a hundred rounds of ammo for it."

"Speaking of .38's," said Palliser, taking a long swallow of his drink, "before the suicide came in—"

"Who found her?" asked Landers. "The suicide?"

"Who—oh, her mother. Knew she was home, they'd been going shopping together, so she broke a window and—it really was a suicide, Tom."

"What about .38's?" asked Mendoza.

"Before the suicide turned up, I spent a while talking to Bernie Schultz. You remember we didn't find that gun on him. Well, it is the one stolen from Carroll and if the D.A.'s going to build any kind of case he'll need it, to back up the ballistics report."

"So where do we look?"

"Bernie said yesterday he never had it. Today he admits he had it. He pawned it down in San Diego for drinking money. Doesn't remember where, and he hasn't got the ticket."

"Oh, fine," said Mendoza. "San Diego being a Navy town, there must be twice as many pawnshops as in the average city."

"I haven't had a chance to call Tinker yet," said Palliser.

Back at his desk, Mendoza had just picked up Landers' latest report when Lake put through a call from Missing Persons.

"I've got another citizen who wants to look at Jane Doe," said Carey. "Thinks it might be her niece. But I swear to God, Mendoza, a man may not get rich at this job but he sees the damnedest things. You know what we just had? A car agency calling in to report one of their salesmen vanished right off the floor. Well, he's probably gone home with a headache—adult, supposedly in his right mind, we can't move on it. But

I ask you. Well, of course you never know *what* people will do. I'll bring this woman—"

"I'll meet you at the morgue," said Mendoza.

"Well, O.K."

And at the morgue, a stout, wheezing Mrs. MacAlister looked fearfully at the body in the cold tray and said with a gasp, "Oh, no, thank God that's not Marion—"

Carey shrugged and turned away. "Did you ever locate that Carla Vroman?" asked Mendoza absently.

"Oh, her. Yes, she turned up yesterday—she'd eloped to Vegas with a boyfriend her brother doesn't like." Carey shepherded Mrs. MacAlister out, and the attendant started to roll the tray back; Mendoza stopped him with a gesture.

He was feeling unreasonably worried about Jane Doe, if that was the word. This was Thursday; she'd been killed on Saturday night. She should have been missed by somebody in five days, but that could happen plausibly, that she hadn't been. If everybody who knew her thought she was on vacation—or, if she'd been living alone, not holding a job. That wasn't what worried him. It was the shapelessness of it: just the body, so crudely killed and left: and the curiously tidy parcel of clothes stashed some distance away. It was a funny mixture of rudimentary planning (the ad in the paper, to say the house was empty) and the carelessness (anyone with common sense might figure the police would search the area, and the clothes had been only about a hundred feet away).

He looked at Jane Doe. He had said, a lady. Somehow the small, pretty features looked ladylike. A pert straight nose, a mouth a little too wide but well-shaped; rather high cheekbones, a small chin: and her eyes, he remembered the autopsy had said, were blue. She hadn't had money for beauty salons: the home rinse-job to brighten the natural blonde hair. The lab report had been detailed, down to her cosmetics: the brand of lipstick, face powder—all modestly priced brands. Apricot coral lipstick. A trace of blue eye-shadow. Brown mascara. And the Blue Carnation cologne.

That hand-knitted stole minus a label. Had she knitted it herself, in some cheaply-rented room or apartment, evening by evening?

Eventually she must get identified, unless all the odds were against them. If she hadn't been holding a job, she'd been getting money to live on from some source—unemployment compensation, insurance, welfare, alimony, name it: such a source would show eventually. It could be a while. Few people were so alone that there was nobody at all to write letters to, chat with on the phone. Even if those who knew her thought she was placed, on vacation or wherever, sometime they'd begin to wonder.

Jane Doe—he had a picture of her dressing so carefully that night, expecting to go to dinner somewhere— Costume jewelry? Yes, there'd have been some— Swinging that stole round her shoulders, hurrying to meet—*el mundo malo*. The evil ones to steal her life and leave her graceless in death.

Twenty-two to twenty-six. If she'd been as old as twenty-six, she'd have been two years old when a young and maybe too cocksure Luis Mendoza had applied to wear the L.A.P.D. uniform.

He shook his head at her. A cop with that many years behind him of seeing the sordid, the stupid, the wanton and occasionally the evil things that happened in this imperfect world, had no business getting emotional and imaginative about just one more corpse.

When he got back to his office, the lab had called and left a message. The FBI kickback had come in, on that dandy set of prints on Jane Doe's right shoe. The Feds didn't know the prints. That said for about 99 percent sure, X had no criminal record. Well, there had to be a first time, for anybody.

The report went on to say that the set of prints had been forwarded to Interpol, as per request. "Request?" said Mendoza.

"*¿Cuándo ocurrió eso?* Who in hell requested— Jimmy, get me the lab!"

"Interpol?" said Duke. "Oh, yes, I noticed that. I don't know why they did that, I didn't— Well, you see it says something about regulations, maybe it's a new rule or something, they do it automatically. I wouldn't think—"

"We don't know much about the corpse," said Mendoza, irritated, "but I should very strongly doubt that any Parisian jewel-thief or British bandit had anything to do with the murder."

"I shouldn't think so," agreed Duke. "But those European countries, you know, they collect a lot of prints from ordinary citizens. More—er—regimentation, like. The Feds have got a lot of those too but we don't have the requirements, the—"

"Regimentation. Yet."

"Well, no. And Interpol—"

Interpol, of course, was not a police force: just a gentleman's agreement, among all the regular police forces of the western European nations, to cooperate and share information.

"I still doubt very much," said Mendoza, "that the X on Jane Doe is known to any section of Interpol. *¡Ca!* What an idea. The Feds getting a little zealous these days."

"Well, don't blame me," said Duke.

Mendoza put the phone down. And Sergeant Lake said, "New one just gone down. Want to go look? Tom's just leaving."

"*Condenación,* I might as well."

And irrelevantly, as he took up his hat and joined Landers, he was trying to dredge up from old memory some of those stories the old lady had told him, all those years ago—the stories to amuse a child, the garbled legends that had been half pagan religion . . . The Aztec princess had been appreciated. Maybe there'd be something at the library, collections of mythology.

He laughed suddenly and Landers looked at him inquiringly as they got into the Ferrari. At least, he thought, the offspring were acquiring a varied background. Máiri with her stories of the saints and Scottish bogles, and Grimm, and Alison vowing to look up some Gaelic fairy tales—

"It's Hunter Street," said Landers.

That was an unsavory district of Boyle Heights. There were two black-and-whites there already. With one glance at the new one, Mendoza dispatched one of the uniformed men to call for a lab truck.

And he'd wish the science boys joy of this place. The hippie pad—was that still the word? The hype talk changed fast. It was an ancient apartment building, and what had been a family apartment twenty years ago —living room, two bedrooms, bath between, kitchen and dinette—had become a chaotic commune.

No furniture but an old phonograph: the records lying around were expectable, all the propagandizing rock groups, the loud combos with the sanity-challenging fast beat. Mattresses on the floor. A couple of the psychedelic lamps to throw weird shadows at night. Scant food in the kitchen: no liquor. And the filth.

In the kitchen, a pot of soup overrun with ants, black and scurrying. Dust and dirt everywhere. Here and there, dirty clothes flung down. In the bathroom, a scum of old dirt over all the fixtures, the floor; the toilet stopped-up some time ago.

And three bodies, in what had been the living room. Two girls and a man, the girls not over eighteen by looks, the man not much older. The girls were both brunettes, dressed respectively in dirty jeans and shirt, a sleazy mini-skirted dress. The man—in name only, thought Mendoza—

was naked except for red shorts. He had straggly brown hair past his shoulders and a full beard. All three had apparently been beaten to death. No weapon immediately visible, but considering all the disorder—

"My God!" said Landers disgustedly. "But typical, of course. We can guess all of 'em were high, didn't put up any defense."

"We can guess," said Mendoza. "The commune. All brothers and sisters together, universal peace and love. But even without the fatal addition of the acid and the H and the speed and so on, it's depressing how human human nature remains, Tom."

It was the rent collector who had called in. He was a scruffy little man looking frightened. "Listen," he said, "I don't know nothing about it, I just collect the rents. This building, a coupla others—big comp'ny owns 'em, hires a coupla us collect the dough. It's sixty bucks a month, this pad, and a guy named Acey usual paid me in cash, 's all the name I know. These hippies— Naw, that ain't him in there, I see that one here too but it was the other guy usual paid me—"

CHAPTER 8

"I don't know any of these characters, I just collect the rents." He'd said it four times; Landers was patient. The collector worked for a company that handled a lot of property like that, residential and business, collecting rents, superintending leases, servicing the buildings. But nobody had serviced this one in some time. It was just another of the old places down here that had been taken over by the flower children.

"I couldn't tell you nothin', just, the door was open, I look in, so I yell for cops—"

"But you've been collecting rents here how long?"

"This building, five-six months. These Goddamn crazy kids, they don't use names. In that place with the bodies, I heard one o' the girls called Marge. I dunno which. The guy Acey, he usual paid—"

"He lived in that apartment?"

"I guess. Usual there, I come."

"What's he look like?"

"Uh—big, sort of fat, long brown hair, the works—hair all over, y' know. About twenty-five maybe."

The lab men were in the apartment; the ambulance had arrived, and Grace and Palliser been summoned to help out. They got the usual reception in a place like this, and few answers. Little knots of crowds on the street, watching; in the building, the other nominal tenants were vague and unhelpful. It wasn't so much that they didn't like the fuzz; they really didn't know much. Every other apartment in the building was drearily like the one with the bodies in it: the mattresses, phonograph or stereo, the general dirt and clutter—and the people all the same, the flower kids if that wasn't an obsolete term by now too.

It was hard to tell them apart: the girls with wire granny glasses if they wore them, jeans or mini-skirts, the boys with as much hair as they could grow, jeans and love-beads; and most of them looking dirty and sloppy and unkempt.

In the unit next to the murder apartment they had found a couple freaked out on something, and took them in. Downstairs Landers talked to an indolent teen-age girl who gave her name as Sally. "Sally what, miss?" asked Landers.

"Names have no meaning," she said. "That place upstairs—Marge lived there. I knew her, to say hello and all like that. One of the fellows there's Dogie. No, I don't know why they call him that. Names— We're free spirits, man, we don't interfere with each other. We believe in individuality, we don't conform."

Landers nearly laughed at her. She said it solemnly, and she was tricked out exactly like any other female he'd seen in this place, the jeans, the long straight dirty hair, the granny glasses. Behind her, the dirty mattresses on the floor, the clutter.

He passed the names on to Mendoza, who was leaning on the hood of the Ferrari smoking a cigarette. "What the hell's going to happen to these mixed-up kids when they get a little older?"

"Fortunately," said Mendoza, "a good many of them never will— pass out early from the dope. The names—ten to one we'll find at least one of them by prints." These love communes weren't supported by air: most of the kids got money for groceries, for narco buys, by petty theft and shoplifting.

Grace came out towing an amiable-looking black boy about fifteen. He was in a torn shirt and jeans, and staggering a little as Grace held his arm. "As you see, this is one we take in," said Grace. "He's under the influence—don't ask me what. But I thought you'd like to hear what he told me. You know Acey, Pearlie?"

"Pearlie, 'at's muh name. Acey, sho I know—said so—Acey gi' me s'me stuff f'r free oncet—Dogie 'n' Marge 'n' Jennie—they all dead, s'mebody said— Prolly it was him did it." He nodded dolefully; his accent was so thick he was barely understandable. "Owed him a lotta bread, f'r the stuff—Dogie said. Prolly th' s'pplier killed 'em. Gotta have bread, man—"

Grace towed him to the nearest squad car and came back looking disgusted. "But that makes some sense, I suppose. The supplier. If they owed and couldn't pay up—"

"Oh, yes. And the hell of that is," said Mendoza, "that probably a number of other people in this building and along the street could tell us his name and where to find him."

"How in hell can people *live* like this?" said Landers. "I need a bath just walking through it."

"When you've been high enough, enough times, Tom, things like dirt and ants in the kitchen and stopped-up toilets don't have much reality. But we have to poke round, try to find this X—and identify the bodies he left behind—even though they're not much loss. Let's leave the lab to it. I feel like you—I need a bath."

They got back to the office at five forty, and Landers volunteered to type the initial statement. His day off was coming up, and it wouldn't mean much overtime: there wasn't much yet to go in a report.

"What gets me," Grace was saying, "is the runaways from decent homes that end up in spots like that. All right, the dope. But before they get so far down that they don't give a damn, you'd think there'd be a point they'd *realize* things—the dirt, the smells, the rotten food. All in the name of—"

"Outside call, Lieutenant," said Lake from the open door. Mendoza picked up the phone.

"—Love," said Landers. "Yeah. Brotherly love."

"Mendoza, Central Homicide."

"This is Sergeant McArdle, Santa Monica. You've had an A.P.B. out, a Dodge sedan and trailer, plate-number—"

"Have you got it?"

"Oh, yes. Half an hour ago. Two men, they give their names as Marvin Hooper and Fred Walsh, but they haven't any I.D. We're holding them here. It was just a fluke we picked them up," McArdle added apologetically. "We had a complaint from Parks and Recreation, these two have been living in the trailer along the beach—parked on the road, you know—since about last Monday. It's illegal, of course, but the Traffic man spotted the plate-number when—"

"Good. Somebody'll be down for them, thanks very much." Mendoza relayed that. "Any volunteers?"

"You're looking at me," said Palliser suspiciously.

"Well, the two senior sergeants aren't here." Mendoza took up the phone again and dialed . . . "¿Cara? How are the recalcitrant offspring?"

"All serene," said Alison. "Everything's fine. You know that calico female down the street, the people who don't know much about cats and let her run at night and probably don't feed her properly— Well, it seems she made a nest under our garage and had some kittens. She just brought them out for their first airing this afternoon—their eyes are just open. The offspring are fascinated. Four kittens—"

"*¡Dios me libre!*" said Mendoza hollowly. "And you're going to say we've got to find good homes for them."

"Don't be silly, Luis. We contribute enough to the Pet Pride people. We'll just hand them over when they're weaned, and let Pet Pride find the homes. Those people down the street needn't know a thing—"

"And hand the calico over too?"

"Well, they don't take any sort of care of her, Luis—"

"I refuse to be involved. As a law enforcement officer, I'm supposed to protect private property."

"Well, there you are being silly. Nobody owns a cat. And you called to say you'd be late."

"That's right. I'll be home sometime. I suppose you fed the calico?"

"Well, Luis, she's nursing those kittens—"

The two men picked up with the Dodge and trailer were not exactly prepossessing specimens. Both were in their mid-thirties, with several days' growth of beard and general dirt. Marvin Hooper had a dish nose and a scar on one side of his face; Fred Walsh had suffered a broken nose and was missing a front tooth; otherwise they were similar, and the minute Mendoza and Palliser clapped eyes on them they recognized the general type.

The Santa Monica officers had welcomed them cordially, Sergeant McArdle and Lieutenant Neal. They had Hooper and Walsh fetched up from the jail; Mendoza looked them over out there in the corridor and went back to Neal's office.

"Ex-cons," he said briefly. "It's all over them."

"Sure. We spotted that," said McArdle. "By a great piece of good fortune, gentlemen"—he went over to the corner— "Hooper put up a little fight, so we had just cause to look around a little." He produced the guns: a revolver and a shotgun.

"Oh, my, how nice," said Palliser.

"What d'you want 'em for?" asked Neal.

"For a start, we want them for taking those shots at Officer Ahearn the other day. Iowa wants them for a double homicide. At least, if these are the two who've been driving that Dodge for the last ten days or so."

"You don't say." McArdle rubbed his jaw. "First off, they claimed they'd just bought it for cash, from some fellow along the beach. But no papers, no receipt, and it's registered—as is the trailer—to a John Murray, some place in Iowa, all right. And the P. and R. man gave us a couple of witnesses who could swear they'd been living in the trailer—

people with a beach house right above, who'd been keeping an eye on them because—"

"Of their general unsavory appearance," said Mendoza. "Well, we'll take them off your hands, thanks very much—and the Dodge and trailer. Iowa will have priority on them, but just for fun we'll run their prints through NCIC and find out what their real names are. Tomorrow, O.K.? Come on, John—nothing we can do here tonight."

"How's that fellow they shot?"

"Going to be fine—hospital will probably let him go home this weekend."

On Friday morning, with Hackett and Higgins back and brought up to date on the new one, Palliser went down to Santa Monica in a squad car and ferried Hooper and Walsh up to the Alameda jail. There, their prints were taken and a set fired off to NCIC as well as Sheriff McCauley in Iowa. Mendoza dictated a teletype to the sheriff. The guns went over to S.I.D., Ballistics.

At nine thirty the lab sent over an interim report. Two of the corpses from the hippie pad yesterday had got identified by prints. The man was in records: two charges of petty theft, a mugging as a j.d.—that time they couldn't print him, but it was on his record. Ray Tucker, twenty-two, known narco user; the first time he'd been picked up, some five years ago, he'd given his home address as Fresno. Grace took down the address and got on the phone. One of the girls was Margaret Berry, and the only reason her prints were on file was that her mother, reporting her as a runaway two years ago, had had a set of prints to hand to Missing Persons and Juvenile: at the private school the Berry girl had attended they kept a fingerprint record. She'd been seventeen then, and the mother's address was given as Bel-Air.

Mendoza made that call; after a little silence, when he'd told her the facts, Mrs. Berry said, "May I—may I see her?"

"Well, Mrs. Berry, we can't release the body, there'll be a mandatory autopsy, when it's homicide—"

"I understand that, Lieutenant. I'd just like to—see her, if I may." She sounded controlled and steady, and he agreed cautiously.

"Tucker's father's coming down from Fresno," said Grace. "Not so much grief-stricken as mad."

"Which is understandable," nodded Mendoza. "In the old days, a black sheep had chosen his own way, at least it was all his own doing. These immature, ignorant kids get sold the propaganda deliberately, and not always by pushers—"

"Some professors, too," said Grace dryly. "Isn't it the sad truth."

Just before Mrs. Berry arrived, Communications was on the line: NCIC, with all its computers, had come up with a make on those prints. Marvin Hooper was Francis William Hausman, wanted for P.A. violation in New Jersey; he was on parole from a third felony conviction, armed robbery. Fred Walsh was Edgar Raynor Beeman, three months out of Folsom from a second felony conviction, armed robbery. How the two had got together, probably they'd never know; but like calling to like, they had joined forces.

Aware that probably nothing would come of it, Palliser and Grace went down to the jail to inform them that they'd been identified, and ask a few questions. "What were you doing in Iowa?" asked Palliser curiously.

"Oh, hell," said Hausman, "new territory, hey? Some place—" He looked at the floor.

"Where your ugly mugs weren't known?" said Grace. "Broke, and actually offering to do some work for pay. For that farmer."

"Oh, we seen he had a roll—" Beeman shut up suddenly; but that told the story. The stupid story, often told. The trusting citizen who went around loaded with cash, and the pro hoods always on the make.

The sheriff teletyped back: extradition papers were being prepared. Eventually the red tape would get unwound and somebody from Iowa would arrive to escort the two hoods back there for trial on homicide charges. L.A. would never get them back to try for taking the shots at Ahearn.

"And when you come to think of it, why the hell did they?" said Palliser. "They weren't known here. Ahearn—oh."

"Yes indeedy," said Grace. "It's a funny thing, John, but the one thing cops know is pro hoods, and the one thing pro hoods know is cops. The minute Ahearn looked at that pair, he was going to spot them as a pair of tough pros, ex-cons at the very least. And what's the next thing he would have done?"

"Run a make on the plate-number."

"That's right. And Hausman and Beeman didn't know those bodies had gone unfound for a few days—they might have expected that plate-number to be listed as hot."

"But then why in hell stick with it? Living in the trailer, for God's sake, along the beach. On the shoulder of the road, with that plate-number—"

"Because," said Grace, "they're stupid. Just how stupid, only a cop can know. Maybe they forgot about it once the cop was disposed of. Maybe they liked the ocean view—"

"Just the way Art said," said Palliser. "Stupidity and cupidity." Of the unknown amount of cash the two hoods had taken from Farmer Murray, they'd had exactly four-seventy-five left.

About all the lab men had turned up in the car and trailer was full and empty liquor bottles and a stale loaf of bread.

Marilyn Berry turned blindly away from the cold tray, and Mendoza put a hand on her arm. "I warned you, Mrs. Berry. You really shouldn't have—"

"But—to do that to her—beaten, she was beaten, wasn't she?" He guided her out to the corridor. "After two years, to find her—I don't understand it. I just don't understand it." She sat down on the bench. She was a nice-looking woman, not fighting middle age: obviously there was money for the beauty salons, the cosmetics, the clothes. (Fleetingly he thought of Jane Doe.) She wasn't crying; maybe she'd done all that a while ago. "It's just as well her father is dead," she said. "He was—so proud of her. Why, Lieutenant? Why did it happen?"

"I don't know, Mrs. Berry." Matt would say, Satan. *The evil ones* . . . A nice girl, Jane Doe—unwitting that she had fallen among the evil ones . . .

"Not as if we spoiled her—not as if—" She made a gesture of futility; she got up. "I shouldn't have come. She was a very pretty girl, you know—when she—went away. When can I—have the—"

"We'll let you know. Are you all right, to get home alone?"

"What? Oh, yes, thank you. I—think I gave up any hope—a long time ago. Thank you, I'm all right."

And what was the answer? Mendoza thought about it, but his mind slid away, back to the anonymous, pretty, ladylike-looking girl in another cold tray.

It was unfortunate, of course, that it should have been Higgins who took the call that came in from a squad car about eleven o'clock. There had been another pile-up on a freeway entry ramp, and Hackett was out on that. The inevitable body over on Skid Row had turned up, and Glasser was typing a report on that. When Lake relayed the new call, Higgins got up automatically.

The address was Westmoreland Avenue, just this side of Beverly, and it turned out to be a four-family apartment house, elderly as were most buildings along here, but reasonably well maintained: the kind of apartment housing middle-class working people. Most of the people in the street, attracted by the black-and-white, the ambulance, were women: most male residents along a block like this would be at work. Higgins parked behind the ambulance and excused his way through the little collection of housewives.

"That's a cop!" came one overloud mutter. "Wrote all over his face, he's a cop!"

As he climbed the steps to the front door, Higgins absently passed a hand over his face. The various ridges and valleys in it certainly, he thought—as he had thought before—added up as if he'd had COP emblazoned on his forehead. Well, after nineteen years on the job— But he hoped to God that Margaret Emily was going to look like Mary, not him. Of course his nose hadn't been exactly straight even before it got broken; and at least, knock on wood, he didn't seem disposed to take on weight like Art—two hundred on the nose regular. Still, with the baby weighing eight pounds even six weeks early—

Another small crowd in the foyer, one woman crying. Whatever it was, it was upstairs. He climbed, thinking that Mary was only five-four, a very snug one hundred and fifteen: and Margaret would have her genes too. He only hoped—

"Oh, my God, oh, my God, Jesus, no! She can't be dead she can't be she can't—it was only a minute, it *wasn't* a minute—oh, Jesus—"

Higgins came to the second floor and an open apartment door, to that panting hoarse voice loud with pain. Two uniformed men in the hall; he got out the badge. "I'm Homicide. What's happened here?"

One of the Traffic men turned; but Higgins had already taken it in. The ambulance attendants, there in the living room of the apartment, were silently stowing away all the emergency resuscitation equipment, the oxygen, the respirator. And the young man in the middle of the room was bent crouching, anguish in every line, above the small bundle on the floor.

"She can't be she can't be—she's only three months—oh, Jesus, I was careful, I was *careful*—not a minute, it wasn't—she can't be she can't be —she's too little—just the talcum, I forgot the—oh, Jesus, no, she can't—"

"His wife's in the hospital," said the Traffic man tersely in a low voice. "Strep throat. It's only the second time he'd given the baby a bath."

"She can't, oh, Jesus, no, don't tell me, she isn't—"

"Oh, my God," said Higgins. The Traffic man suddenly turned and put a hand on his arm.

"You O.K., sir? You're white as—"

"I'm O.K. I just— Ours is just a week today."

"Oh. They better give him a shot, don't you think?"

Higgins did. He felt as if he could stand a good stiff drink himself.

Mendoza had just come back from a late lunch when Sergeant Lake put through a call from Lieutenant Carey.

"Say—this is going to make you cuss," said Carey. "And when I think how I laughed about it— Well, you remember I told you yesterday about that car agency reporting a salesman missing?"

"What about it?"

"Well, what would I tell them? It was the manager called. Said Mr. Bayne was a very steady man, wouldn't just walk out because he had a headache. But an adult, right mind and all, I—"

"Yes. Why are you telling me all over again?"

"Well, I will be damned but his body just turned up," said Carey. "Oh, you are going to cuss about this one, Lieutenant. He was found in the parking lot at Pasadena City College a couple of hours ago, and the Pasadena boys tagged it as a natural death, so they hauled him off to their morgue without, I gather, bothering to photograph the scene—and then a doctor noticed a bullet-hole in him—"

"¿Cómo dice?" yelped Mendoza. "Pasadena— ¡Dios!—they just scooped up the body and took it to the morgue? Are you saying the corpse belongs to us? That—"

"I've just been talking to a Captain Pole over there. I don't think they can be quite as unscientific as all that, but I gather he looked like the ordinary drunk passed out from a coronary or something—anyway, a natural death. And a public parking lot—one of the students spotted him when he, the student, that is, came out for an early lunch. Well, it looks like your baby, Mendoza, he vanished from this beat—the agency's over on Wilshire. But you'll have to sort it out with Pasadena."

"Thank you so very much!" said Mendoza. "My God, everything happens to me!" He got up and went into the sergeants' office. "Art—"

"What's up?" Hackett looked up from his typewriter.

"All hell," said Mendoza succinctly. "But, porvida, a car salesman? Disappearing from the agency in the middle of the morning? How, for God's sake? And why? And Pasadena—I thought they had some reasonably intelligent men on that force. I'll tell you on the way. Where's George?"

"Out buying aspirin. He came in a while ago looking as if he'd had a shock, said he didn't want any lunch, he had a headache. What's with Pasadena?"

"They've got a body belonging to us," said Mendoza. "And I have a hunch it's going to pose a little problem to unravel. Want to bet?"

"No thanks," said Hackett. He was to think later he should have taken Luis up on that. The hunches didn't always work out. That one didn't. The little problem of Mr. Brian Bayne turned out to be painfully simple.

Palliser had called the lab to ask about that third corpse, the other girl in the hippie pad. They had one name for her: Jennie. That wasn't going to be much help in identifying her. The lab had run her prints through R. and I. without result: she had no record with L.A. The prints had been sent to Washington, with no reply as yet.

"May never make her," said Grace. "These kids—they're flying the coop younger every day, John. How many under-eighteens get printed, by the school or whatever, to be on record somewhere? They don't. It could be she's listed and described in some Missing Persons bureau, take your choice, New York to Portland to Miami. And what did we say about conformity? You try to describe one of these females, the only difference is dark or blonde hair. She'd taken a beating around the head, that one, but what you could see of her face—ordinary, John. Not pretty, not ugly. Not one to notice in a crowd."

"All too true," said Palliser. "Hand a description to NCIC and the name Jennie. And?"

"And hear about thirty or forty from all points of the compass." Grace sounded sadly amused.

But Palliser suddenly scowled. Time, he thought: it went by so fast. The baby due in April. The unexpected baby, just fine with him, stopping Robin from turning into a working wife, which he'd always disapproved. They made out all right on his salary, even with the house payments and the necessary new refrigerator and washer . . . But, Time. Before they knew it, the baby—whichever—a teen-ager. And if all these damnable propagandists and pornographers and agents of Satan were still around—

It made you think, as parent or prospective parent. Try their damnedest to instill the morality and integrity and some sense— But it made you think.

"John—"

He looked up. "This is Mr. Tucker," said Sergeant Lake expressionlessly. And suddenly Palliser remembered that Jimmy had kids too, and would be thinking along the same line. Three kids: and the oldest one, a girl, into her teens now. He stood up.

"How do," said Tucker. He was a thick stocky man about fifty, obviously not a city man: his dark suit and white shirt sat awkwardly on him. "About my boy. Ray."

"Yes sir," said Palliser.

"I'd like to see him," said Tucker.

Palliser took him down to the morgue.

Tucker looked at the body for a long minute, and then looked at Palliser. "You got any kids, Sergeant?"

"We're expecting—in April—"

"Oh," said Tucker. He sighed. "It shakes me," he said. "It does for a fact. Like things wasn't—steady no more, like two and two don't add up to four. You think, you bring 'em up right, you love 'em, you teach 'em the right way to act—know what I mean, Ten Commandments and all the rest of it—you think they'll be all right. Bound to grow up all right. You set an example—try to set an example, live right. You punish 'em when they do wrong, and you try to pass along some common sense— well as you can to youngsters. I guess common sense is a thing you learn by living. With any luck. But you try—naturally, you try, with your kids."

"Yes, sir," said Palliser.

Tucker looked at the body again: the beatnik hairy body, misused so young and wanton, and he said softly, "That's nobody I know, Sergeant. Nobody I loved and tried to do right by. Let him go. Four others that turned out just fine. And I don't know why he didn't. I just don't know." He reached into his breast pocket. "Five years ago, he was my son." And silently he showed a snapshot. A black-and-white snapshot of a boy, fifteen or sixteen. The boy was laughing into the camera, the sun full on him. He was a nice-looking boy, not exactly handsome, but happy and healthy-looking, freckled, a good American kid with everything ahead of him.

"Yes, sir," said Palliser meaninglessly.

Tucker turned away. "I'll pay for the funeral," he said. "I wouldn't let my wife come down—she wanted to. But I can't feel—that that's anybody of mine."

On second thought, before sorting out whatever there was to sort out with the Pasadena Police Department, Mendoza and Hackett had gone over to Kenister Motors on Wilshire Boulevard.

Kenister Motors dealt exclusively in imported automobiles. The badge brought them Mr. Victor Kenister himself, agitated and gabbling. "I really could not believe—Mr. Bayne! Brian! One of our top salesmen, and such a reliable man, so responsible—I could not understand that police officer, when Mr. Gill informed me what had happened yesterday morning, I called the police at once, but the officer—a Lieutenant Garry, Ferry?—all but told me I was imagining things. Talking about adults, and being in his right mind—Brian!" Mr. Kenister was a tall cadaverous fellow with very white false teeth and correct tailoring

"Mr. Kenister, if you could just—a few questions—" Hackett got a word in. "Mr. Bayne was a regular salesman here, working full time?"

"Was!" said Kenister. "Was! My God, it seems impossible—murdered! It isn't, it simply isn't, a thing that could happen. My God—he was only thirty-three, and who's to tell his wife—the other police only called half an hour ago, and such a shock I never—" He mopped his forehead and was suddenly human, appalled and uncertain. "A good salesman, a steady man."

"He was here yesterday morning?" asked Hackett.

"Yes, certainly, just as usual. At ten o'clock. You understand, hours are indefinite in this business, a good deal of selling is done in the evenings. But we have people dropping in at all hours, and— Oh, I see, you haven't heard exactly what did happen. You'd better talk to Mr. Loveless—oh, Guy! Would you ask Loveless to come over here, these are police officers, about Brian— Mr. Loveless, ah, Lieutenant—"

"Mendoza. Sergeant Hackett."

"How do you do." Mr. Loveless was also impeccably tailored, in sports clothes. "Police?" he said, eager and horrified. "Brian—well, this is just impossible, that's all, I couldn't believe—"

"But you'd better tell them," said Kenister. "I wasn't here, but you and Guy saw the man—"

"That's right," said Loveless. "It was that Facel-Vega sportster. Bright yellow, the only one of that model we had in. This customer came in, wanted a run in her, and Brian checked it out. I was in the office when he checked it out. For a trial—"

"He took the customer for a trial run," said Mendoza, "and you mean to tell me—"

"He never came back," said Loveless baldly. "That's right. Or the Facel-Vega."

CHAPTER 9

"We hadn't put everything together when I called the police yesterday," Kenister was going on. "The other men realized that Brian had been gone for some time, but it wasn't until we added up everything and found he hadn't been to the garage or anywhere, that we realized he'd never come back."

"That's definite," said Loveless. "We went into it thoroughly, checked with the men in the garage. Nobody ever saw him again after he took that fellow out for the trial run. You can see the book where he checked it out, he put down the time, ten past eleven."

"But—the customer!" said Kenister. "I can hardly believe—and why?"

"Can you describe the customer?" asked Mendoza.

"Sure—Guy and Eric and I all saw him, Brian just got to him first," said Loveless. "But it's impossible, that's all. The customer murdering him—well, for God's sake, why? Sure, I can describe the customer to you, so can Guy and Eric. He was a young fellow, not more than twenty-five, and dressed sharp—sports clothes, all brown and tan. He had dark hair, a lot of it—not long, I mean, but thick, and curly. He had a sort of high voice. And Brian didn't have to give him any pitch—he came in off the street and made a beeline for that Facel-Vega, said right off he was interested in that."

"Did you hear him give Bayne any name?"

Loveless shook his head. Another immaculate-looking salesman-type had come up, was introduced as Guy Lane. "We were right over here," said Loveless, pointing, "at the table there, you can see we had a good look at the guy. He'd stand out in a crowd, he was good-looking. He looked like money all right. It looked like a definite sale, for no fast talk either. But you think that's the one—killed Brian? It doesn't seem—"

"I don't know," said Mendoza. "But the car's still missing?"

"It certainly is," said Kenister grimly.

"You'll have the engine number and so on, but was it wearing plates?"

"It certainly was not," said Kenister. "It's a brand-new car, we only got it in last week, part of the new shipment. Temporary plates don't go on until a car is sold."

"Yes, I know. Let's have a description of it, please."

"It's a Facel-Vega Sportster," said Loveless. "New model. Hardtop two-door with a sun-roof. It's bright metallic yellow with black rally stripes. All power, radio, air, the works."

"Seventy-two ninety-five," said Kenister with a small groan.

Hackett asked for a phone and called that in; an A.P.B. would go out on it at once. A car without any plates, and this unusual a car, shouldn't be hard to pick up. But of course there was no telling where it was by now.

They asked more questions. There hadn't been any other customers or shoppers in at the time, and the other two salesmen in the showroom, slightly envious of Bayne's picking up such an easy sale, had observed the customer. They all gave the same description. They all said positively that he'd never looked at or touched another car, went straight to the Facel-Vega. So it'd be no good bringing a Prints man up. The Facel-Vega had had to be driven out through the garage; it was the only one of that new model they had in, and the customer had insisted that that was the only one he was interested in. In fact, the garage had half-filled its tank; it had had barely half a gallon in it.

"And who is to tell his wife—"

"But when he didn't come home last night—" said Hackett.

"Oh, she's staying with her sister this week," said Loveless. "Sister just had a baby. I don't know the address, but I suppose it'd be at their house, Bayne's I mean, it's somewhere in Hollywood."

That was what the agency had to say, and they'd all have said it four times over. On the way to Pasadena, Hackett said, "But if it was the customer, Luis, what an idiotic thing to pull! He must know the car'd be spotted once we started to look for it—stand out like a sore thumb, that color and no plates. And to kill Bayne—it's crazy! He must have noticed those other men there, to see him and remember him—"

"You said it yourself, *chico*. They do come pretty stupid sometimes. But this is one for the books, all right."

At the Pasadena police station, a Captain Pole came to greet them apologetically. "Look," he said, "we all commit the human errors, no?

I've been talking to your Lieutenant Carey. What can I tell you? I've got the two patrolmen for you to talk to. They got a routine call, man down, possible 390—drunk. At that parking lot. They get there, spot the body—it was in plain sight, they say, only off at one end of the lot—and find out it is a body. Not a mark on him, no blood, what do they think? And it's getting on for noon, most of the student-body's going to be coming out, a lot of 'em to their cars—"

"All right," said Mendoza resignedly. "Not a mark on him?"

"Nary a thing—you'll have to see him, hear the doctor."

"So let's do that first."

At the morgue, Dr. Armoudjian was waiting when they arrived. He showed them the body silently. "When your office called, I assumed you'd want the body sent down to L.A.—"

"How right you are," said Mendoza. "No offense, doctor, but our own surgeon I know."

"No offense. I haven't touched him except to make a superficial examination."

Brian Bayne had been a nice-looking fellow, square-jawed, clean-shaven, with brown hair and a dark tan as if he spent all his spare time at the beach. He was dressed in gray slacks, a tailored Western sports shirt, gray-blue, with a leather *bolo* tie and a sterling clasp on that. Pole said, "You notice he's still wearing a ring—Air Force insignia, I think—and we did go through his pockets, that's how we identified him, of course." The doctor showed them a little heap of miscellany on a table nearby; Mendoza poked one long forefinger into it, turning items over.

A clean handkerchief. A small pile of loose change. A billfold, with bills still in it, and various pieces of I.D. in the plastic slots—driver's license, Social Security card, library card, a gasoline credit card. A silver pocketknife. A leather case with business cards in it—*Mr. Brian Bayne, Kenister Motors*. A folding pocket comb. A folded receipt from a boat rental outfit on a Newport Beach pier. A brochure from a newly-opened sports shop advertising surfing equipment.

"He wasn't robbed," said Pole unnecessarily.

"Carey said something about his being shot," said Hackett, looking at the body.

"If you'll look here—" The doctor turned the corpse's head. "I spotted the blood when he was brought in, but then I'm trained to notice details." He gave them a quick smile. "It's not surprising the patrolmen didn't spot it. And it must have been a fluke shot, is all I can say—unless the man was asleep or drunk, and I don't think he was. It's a small caliber, of course, and it entered his head straight through the ear-hole. There's very little blood. There'll be more inside."

"I will be damned," said Mendoza mildly.

"How long has he been dead?" asked Hackett.

The doctor looked at his watch. "Call it twenty-four to thirty hours."

"My God, Luis," said Hackett, "he must have been shot less than an hour after he left with the customer. Which says for almost certain it was the customer—"

"But listen," said Pole worriedly, "I don't know how much you know about this already, but one thing we do know, because the patrolmen talked to the boy who reported the body. He'd come out to get his car, he has an early lunch break. And he said the body definitely wasn't there when he parked at eight A.M."

"*¡Qué demonio!*" said Mendoza.

"He shot him and then carried him around in that car for twenty-four hours before dumping him?" said Hackett incredulously. "And at such a place—why wasn't he seen?"

"You'd better talk to the patrolmen—and have a look at the campus," said Pole. "After nine A.M., most of the students would be in class, nobody'd be in the lot—and it's not overlooked, there's a row of trees between—"

"But it's right on the street!" said Hackett, who had had his first year of college at Pasadena. "A side street, but still—"

"Piling madness on madness," said Mendoza. "Just blind luck no-body did see him, Art. I'd like to talk to the patrolmen, and the student who reported the body."

"What can he tell us?" asked Hackett.

"Well—that description of the customer. It could fit one of the nice clean-cut college kids—the few left around. And they do say, who hides can find."

But Mark West, who had spotted the body, didn't fit the description of the customer; he was dark and stocky and obviously honest. He did say that the body definitely hadn't been there at eight A.M. Having seen the terrain, they agreed that he'd have noticed it; there wasn't any cover in the parking lot.

"This is the damnedest," said Hackett. "He's got to be a nut, Luis—or he can't think two minutes ahead."

"And how many of that kind come our way, Arturo? One thing, Traffic shouldn't be long in spotting that Facel-Vega."

"I think I should have made that bet. One like this, we'll have no trouble dropping on him."

"And what leads you to that conclusion?"

"Well, if he was crazy enough about that overpriced hot rod to kill the salesman for it, he'll still be in it," said Hackett with conviction.

Mendoza himself was feeling a little incredulous about the stupidity of this one when he turned into the drive and braked abruptly. It was still light, daylight saving being in force, and what looked like most of his household was clustered at the top of the drive. Alison's green Facel-Vega was parked in front of the house in the circular drive.

He got out of the Ferrari and walked up the drive. "And what is going on here?" he demanded. The four cats, out of sight until he rounded the back of the house, were sitting in a dignified row on the back steps, El Señor with his back turned for emphasis. Cedric barked and offered a paw, and the twins fell on Mendoza.

"Daddy, *la gata hermosa* she has the babies out—an' scratch Cedric's nose all *sangre*—"

"Mama make a nice *cama caliente* for the kitties, an' she say— Daddy, come see *los gatillos!* Pretty—"

"Now, for heaven's sake, I told you, Johnny, Terry, leave her *alone!* She wants to be alone with the pretty kittens, she's afraid they'll be hurt— Hello, *amante.*" Cedric pawed at Mendoza's trousers until he accepted the polite handshake.

"Have you taken in that cat?"

"Well, these kittens—I told you last night, she's got to be fed, Luis. As a matter of fact I walked down the block to that place and made an excuse—luckily the woman was out in the yard—to ask about their cat, and she said—honestly, people!—she guessed it had run away. So they don't care a bit, they weren't looking after her at all, and she's just a youngster herself, and the kittens are adorable—"

"So you said. All kittens are, as a rule. But you can see how our four aristocrats feel about it—"

"Yes, they're pretending she isn't here. Or the kittens. Cedric tried to make friends with her and got his nose scratched—"

"All *sangre*," said Johnny. "*Pobre* Cedric!"

"I've got a bed fixed in the garage, and I think she's decided to accept it. She's got the kittens there anyway. When she's fed up a little she'll be a beauty."

"Want to see *los gatillos* again!" said Terry.

"No, Terry. Not tonight. We're all going in to have supper now, and Máiri'll be home soon, remember?"

Los gatillos forgotten suddenly, Terry began to cry. "Want *Afton!* Want Máiri! *Bonnie doon!*"

"Oh, Lord," said Alison. "Would you like to try for another gold ring, *marido mío?*"

"Come on," said Mendoza, picking them both up. "Máiri's coming home, *niña,* and if you don't stop crying I won't read about Jingle, Terry."

"I'll tell you one thing," said Higgins seriously, fondly watching Mary as she powdered Margaret Emily and reached for the fresh diaper. "I'm damn glad you've had prior experience at this."

"And what prompts that?" Mary laughed.

Higgins sighed. "Just something I came across today. I don't know— sometimes I wonder about Fate. Things being predestined. I'll hold her for a while, she isn't sleepy yet."

"It's a wonder," said Mary, smiling at him, "that she ever gets any sleep at all, the three of you wanting to cuddle her all the time."

"She's very nice to cuddle," said Higgins. "I hope some of those snapshots turn out."

On Saturday morning, with Sergeant Farrell sitting in for Lake, there was an overnight report from Schenke on Mendoza's desk. He was just reading it when Farrell put through an outside call.

"Mendoza, Homicide."

"Listen," said Captain Webb aggrievedly, "you drop this damn Carmichael thing into my lap and walk away. We've been round and round on it, and I—"

"This one's not on my beat. All your own baby. I just handed you the background."

"Are you telling me!" said Webb. "Listen, he's guilty as hell. I even know—or I think I know—how he did it, but I haven't got a chance in a million of proving it."

"I've been there, *gracias,*" said Mendoza. "I thought I knew how he did for Robert, too, and I still think I was right. But evidence? *¡Nada absolutamente!* How did he work it with Florence?"

"Among us we've seen every female she knew," said Webb. "She was pretty social, Florence was. Out a lot—shopping with her girlfriends, concerts and teas—she wasn't a bridge fiend, but she liked to be on the go. She also liked clothes and jewelry, nothing but the best—probably quite an expense to him."

"Mmh, yes, and he had others. Has he still got the same girlfriend, or a new one?"

"Oh, the same lady he was keeping six years ago when you were trying to pin him for Robert. One Tamaris Holt, apartment on Cherokee."

"I'm surprised at his faithfulness. But go on about Florence."

"Well, by everything everybody said about her—and I've worked it very discreet, no police questioning, a couple of our girls out of uniform getting into casual conversation and like that—Florence was a little vague about time. She never wore a watch. But she did love to fritter away time getting ready to go out—you know a lot of females do that, the leisurely bath with plenty of bath salts, the works. And it seems—the maid they've got now backs this up—if she was going out in the evening, dinner or something, she'd be taking a bath about five o'clock, with all the appurtenances, bubble bath and talcum and—"

"Oh," said Mendoza. "I begin to see, yes, how very simple."

"All he had to know was that she'd be getting ready to go out by five. He could arrange that himself, say they were going out to dinner. It was the maid's day off, logical they should. And then before he left the house he set all the clocks forward by the best part of an hour."

"*Me gusta,*" said Mendoza appreciatively. "*Muy astuto.* He'd take care to have an alibi, in public, up to five forty or so by real time. Get home about five of six, to find her already in the hot bath. And George Joseph Smith showed the way there. Catch hold of her heels and send her under—"

"She was overweight and never took any exercise."

"*Sí.* Three minutes, the job's done. He sets the clocks back—"

"There are only four in the place."

"You have done your homework. And he says he spent a while trying to revive her before calling for help—"

"But I ask you, how can I nail him on it legally?"

"You can't," said Mendoza, lighting a cigarette one-handed. "All you can hope to do is scare him some. So he'll think twice before trying another one."

"And that is no news to me," said Webb. "I don't like to ask you—I know you're busy too, damn it—but I think we could scare him better together."

"Now that is a thought, *amigo.* He'll remember me from Papa and Robert. When?"

"I've had three sessions with him. Ostensibly clearing up details on the sad accident. He's a cool one—not a hair turned, and he'll know what we're thinking. I know quite a lot about Alfred, what sizes his girlfriend wears, where he goes for lunch, what he pays for his suits—and I've got nothing solid at all. He's been asked to come in again at ten o'clock."

"I'll be there," said Mendoza pleasedly.

It was getting on for nine then; he looked to see who was in, and beckoned Hackett and Higgins into his office. "John and Jase are back at the hippies," said Hackett. "That other girl's going to get buried by the city as Jane Doe, you know that—that Jennie. We'll never find out who she was. Don't tell me we've got something new?"

"That's just what, but it doesn't look very complicated. The same old triangle—just people to see, statements to get and a fellow to arrest after you've got him to admit he done it." He handed over Schenke's report.

"Where are you bound for?"

"Up to West Hollywood to help Captain Webb scare Alfred Carmichael."

The new one didn't look like anything much: more routine. It had erupted at five minutes past midnight, at a bar on Beverly Boulevard. There had been shots fired; the bartender had called in, and the black-and-white got there three minutes later to find a body on the sidewalk and some voluble witnesses.

"Witnesses Marcia Coleman, Jack Galvin (bartender), Peter Squires, Richard Coleman, identified victim as Linda Karpis, twenty-five. Karpis, boyfriend and Colemans regulars at bar," ran Schenke's report succinctly. "Karpis succession boyfriends but for about three months had been steady with Leo Fratelli, insurance salesman Western-National Co. Fratelli out of town business past two weeks, Karpis took up with Squires, everybody expected row when Fratelli came back, which he did last night. Karpis with Squires and Colemans at bar app. 8:30 on. Fratelli came in about 9:00, sat over a couple of beers an hour, eye on Karpis and party, and left. When Karpis came out with Squires, about midnight, sniper fire from across street, Karpis D.O.A., at least three slugs. All witnesses definite must have been Fratelli, Colemans leaving app. same time, witnessed fire, but nobody can swear saw him to identify. Approximate spot killer stood, by trajectory, sidewalk clean, no evidence at scene. App. in front of tailor shop catercorner from door to bar."

A list of names and addresses was appended. "Well, that's a simple one," said Hackett. "I suppose the slugs out of the body have got up to Ballistics by now."

"In an hour or so? Don't be optimistic," but Higgins tried the lab.

"Oh, those," said Scarne. "They came up from the morgue just now. New corpse, hah? You do get kept busy. So do we. Nobody's looked at them yet, what did you expect?"

"Well, just take a quick glance and guess what caliber," said Higgins.

"All right, all right . . . For ninety-nine percent sure a .32," said Scarne a minute later. "Revolver. We'll run a make on them sometime, tell you the brand. When we get round to it."

"So, the legwork," said Hackett. "We want statements on this from all these people."

"And even more urgent, we'd like to talk to Fratelli. Let's go look."

Just as they were leaving the office, Farrell beckoned them back, handed the phone to Hackett.

"Central Homicide, Sergeant Hackett."

"This is Tinker, San Diego. I thought you'd like to know we've found that gun for you—the .38 Schultz pawned. Lucky you had the serial number. We picked it up half an hour ago, pawnshop on the waterfront. We'll send it right up."

"Oh, thanks so much," said Hackett. At least, the Carroll case was now all wrapped up, clear legal sailing for the D.A.

They went out to look for Fratelli, and failing him, to bring in the witnesses to make formal statements.

At about the same time that Mendoza was reading the report on Linda Karpis, a girl named Betty Collier was talking to Mrs. Wilma Yelverton.

"You mean she hasn't been here all week? But that's funny—did she say anything about moving, or—"

"Not to me. Last time I seen her was, lessee, week ago today—leavin' for work she was, about ten thirty. Like always. I don't always see her come and go, but what I noticed, her car's been here all the time. Right in her carport out back."

"But she might be *sick!* She might be—"

"Well, I got to admit that crossed my mind, young woman alone, and a nice girl she is—nice quiet tenant. I went up and looked, with my key, you see, miss. She's not there, and everything's all neat and clean, just like she walked out an hour ago."

"But that's—" Betty Collier frowned. "Look, I don't know her except at the restaurant, the only reason I came by now, she promised to lend me that dress pattern—I've been off on vacation this week, I just thought— But I know her good enough to say she's reliable, she wouldn't just walk off a good job like that. If she has walked off. It's funny."

"She'd always speak to me, if she was goin' away a couple days—like on vacation. She's lived here three years."

"But it *is* funny. I wonder— Well, I'm on my way to work right now, and maybe Mr. Schilling'll know something about it."

"Come in, Mr. Carmichael," said Captain Webb cordially.

"I really fail to see why you want to go over all these details *again,*" said Alfred Carmichael, sounding annoyed. "I have cooperated fully with the police, I have no wish to—" He stopped suddenly, spotting Mendoza, who was leaning back in an armchair in the corner of the office, smoking lazily, dapper as usual in silver-gray Italian silk. Recognition and a momentary flash of some indefinable emotion showed in Carmichael's eyes, and then he said stiffly, "Well, it's Lieutenant—I'll remember your name in a moment, I just—"

"Oh, you remember me, Alfred," said Mendoza genially. "We had quite a few little talks six years ago, didn't we, when my office was looking into that—mmh—tragic accident your brother had."

"I remember well enough that you came near committing slander," said Carmichael. "Am I to understand that Captain Webb brought you here today to try to frighten me? Me?" He laughed contemptuously. "I don't know what you think you're doing, either of you." He was a big florid man, these days carrying too much weight round the middle; he was carefully and conservatively dressed in a dark suit, white shirt, black tie. Mourning? wondered Mendoza sardonically.

"I'll tell you in words of one syllable," said Webb, leaning forward across his desk. "I—"

"Be careful, Captain. If you admit you are trying to prove that I've committed murder, I will certainly sue you for slander, with every expectation of—"

"You said the word first. We're always very careful, Mr. Carmichael," said Webb grimly. "And we do have to know the law. If Lieutenant Mendoza and I did happen to be convinced that you have committed three murders, we should have to admit that we could never convict you—on the second one, Mr. Carmichael. Your brother Robert. That case has already been judged and a verdict recorded. But there's no statute of limitations on murder one, Mr. Carmichael."

"Outright slander—"

"I said if," said Webb gently.

"And if you did a little more planning just recently to get rid of your wife, Alfred," said Mendoza, "it was a rather neat idea, if—mmh—rudimentary. The clocks. And a really efficient method of murder needn't be anything new—George Smith found it quite effective too."

"What the hell do you—I don't have to put up with this!" Carmichael got up from his stiff pose in the chair beside the desk. "Just because I happen to have suffered three tragic accidents in my family—and some years apart, I'd remind you—you dumb cops think I'm some sort of— Well, you're out of your minds, that's all! And with my wife just dead, too—I should think some respect—"

"Oh, are you missing her?" asked Mendoza politely. "I should have thought Miss Holt was sufficient comfort to you, Alfred."

"What the hell do you know ab— Have you people been following me? What the hell has Miss Holt to do with anything?" Carmichael had flushed, but his voice was steady and still contemptuous. "I don't suppose I'm the only man in Los Angeles to have something on the side. That, for God's sake, doesn't say anything."

"No, it doesn't. I'd advise you to be careful, Alfred," said Mendoza, putting out his cigarette. "You look to me as if your blood pressure's up. Had it checked lately?"

"You can go to hell," said Carmichael. "This is quite enough! If I'm called down here again I'll lodge a charge of police harassment. My lawyer—"

"I'd remind you," said Webb, "that there hasn't been a formal inquest on your wife yet. You might not hear the verdict you expect."

"And what other verdict could there be except accidental death?" Carmichael was a canny one; they hadn't rattled him. "She was alone in the house—she was dead when I came in. That's just a fact, and you can't get round it."

Mendoza, who had shut his eyes, opened them. "*Vaya,* and how triumphantly you said it, Alfred. Giving yourself away."

"If you're trying to shake me into saying something silly, you haven't got a hope in hell," said Carmichael.

"I didn't hope to shake you, Alfred," said Mendoza. "I intended to scare you. If, Alfred—just if—you have committed three planned murders—two for gain and one for reasons we might guess—if, Alfred—then as the reasonably smart cops Captain Webb and I are, we'd suspect that. For one hundred percent sure. Unfortunately, the law sometimes gets in the way of justice, and that I needn't spell out. But cops don't like killers, Alfred. Known killers. And whatever we can or can't stick on you all legal, we'll have an eye on you, Alfred. From here on in. And if you should ever be tempted to build another cute little accident, for somebody in your way to have happen to him, we'll be on it before you know what hit you."

"Just before our friend came in," said Webb, "you had a little idea."

"So I did," said Mendoza. He grinned at Carmichael. "As a wealthy man, you move in some nice social circles, Alfred. Among the elite. ¿Cómo no? There's at least one newspaper in this town that loves juicy gossip and knows just how to stop short of libel. We all know its name. Suppose one of its reporters got handed the salient facts on Papa, and Robert, and Florence? Quite a coincidence, three sad accidents in the family, two of them swelling your bank account, and the other getting rid of a wife—who might just have known this and that about the other two— And then there's Miss Holt."

Carmichael stared at him, and there was a white line of anger round his mouth. "And who pays any attention to that rag?"

Webb laughed. "That's what I said when he mentioned it. I said, Good God, everybody who knows him must have suspected the truth. Florence was just the topping on the cake. I said—"

"I think we'd better let him go home," said Mendoza, "before he has a stroke in your office, Webb."

But when Carmichael had gone, wordless and tight-lipped, he asked Webb ruefully, "How'd we do, compadre?"

"I wouldn't make a guess," said Webb gloomily. "He knows we've got no evidence at all, and that's the one important fact. Hell and damnation! He's got away with three murders—premeditated killings, murder one—and by God we can't even charge him with—with a traffic violation!"

"That's right," said Marcia Coleman. "It must've been Leo Fratelli. There wasn't anybody else with any reason to shoot Linda! Oh, it was just terrible—just as we all came outta the bar, that Reno Bar and Grill, it's a nice quiet place, family place sort of, with a piano player and all— Those shots, and Linda— Not that I didn't warn her she was asking for trouble—"

"Is that so?" said Hackett. They'd split up to locate these people; Marcia Coleman worked at a drugstore on Third Street, and talked to him readily over the cosmetic counter.

"Sure. And look, like this statement thing you said, I get off at one, I'm on a split shift, so I could come in then, if that's O.K.? Well, O.K. Look, I don't want to say anything against Linda, she was a good kid, but she sort of played the field, had to have a man around, and I guess— well, you get me, it didn't much matter who. Well, live and let live, she

vas fun to be with and we can't all be alike. Me and Dick been married
a couple years, he suits me fine and I guess I him, but Linda—well, out
of sight out of mind. She'd been married a couple of times, and divorced. But that Fratelli—well, when she took up with Pete Squires
when Leo was out of town, I said to Dick—"

"Excuse me, did Miss Karpis have a job?"

"Why, sure," she said, surprised. She was an ordinary type, call it
that: about twenty-five, dark, mini-skirted (a good pair of legs, he had
noted academically when she crossed the aisle from stationery and sun-
dries), middling pretty, too pale lipstick and overlong fingernails probably glued on. "She was a market checker, at a Safeway out on Melrose
in Hollywood. What? She had an apartment on Bronson. We got to
know her last year, she was going around with a friend of Dick's, Jerry
Fielding, he got married since. But I said to Dick, that Fratelli wasn't
going to like it, her taking up with Pete—"

"Excuse me, Mrs. Coleman, would you know whether that amounted
to anything more than ordinary dates? Were either of them her lovers?"

She flushed. "Her business," she said. "We can't all be alike. I
wouldn't know." But she could guess, Hackett surmised. Well, just as it
had looked, the sordid triangle.

"But you can't definitely say you saw Fratelli fire the shots?"

She shook her head. "It must've been him all right—he came in the
bar, you know, and the way he *stared* at her—well, Italians got hot
tempers, don't they? But when we came out, it was dark, you couldn't
see anything that far off, across the street like he was. Hear, that's
different."

"You heard something? When?"

"Right after those shots, mister. About half a minute after. I heard—
and so did Dick and Pete—a car take off like a bat out o' hell, tires
screaming, motor wide open. That Italian—who else had it in for Linda?
told her—"

Mendoza came past the door marked *Homicide* at a quarter to
twelve, and asked Farrell, "Who's in?"

"Nobody. Art and George are out on the new one, John and Jase are
chasing down the flower children, and Henry went out on another case
of L.A.'s new invention for homicide dicks."

"*¿Cómo?*"

"You know, the rocks tossed off freeways. This one went through the
sun-roof of a VW and killed the driver."

"*¡Dios!* Anybody important?" asked Mendoza.

"A civil service man. Driving a Federally licensed car. I.R.S."

"Well, that's one way to get rid of the leeches."

"Somebody waiting to see you. Carey sent him up about five minute ago. Name of Johann Schilling."

"Oh?" Mendoza swung round. On the bench up toward the ser geants' office sat a man smoking a cigarette; seeing Mendoza start to ward him, he rose and sketched a continental bow.

"Sir. Johann Schilling. You are in charge here—an officer? I have nat urally gone to this Persons Missing office, the officer sends me here. I—

"Yes, Mr. Schilling? What can we do for you?"

"I do not know." He was a short thin fellow, dark, with a moustach twin to Mendoza's; his dark suit was of good quality. He looke worried. "I do not know why that officer tells me to come here, on th door it says— That is murder. You see, Betty tells me, and it is nc right, all week I have thought there is something not right, but we ar busy like always. It is not like the little Rebecca to go off and say notl ing. So when Betty tells me just now, I think somebody must do some thing. And that officer sends me here."

"Rebecca? This is someone missing?"

"Yes, sir. Rebecca Dantry. I tell the other officer how she looks—fiv metres, excuse, the five foot high, small, blonde hair, a nice girl, a goo waitress, reliable, blue eyes, and I—"

"¡Don de Dios!" said Mendoza. "Come to Papa, friend!" Th sounded most remarkably like Jane Doe.

CHAPTER 10

Johann Schilling looked down at the body in the cold tray, and his face was pinched and sorrowful. "It is her," he said. "It's Rebecca. This is a dreadful, a sad thing—to see her like this. Why? Is it a madman murders her? No one could have a reason—"

"We don't know, Mr. Schilling. We didn't know who she was." Mendoza steered him gently. "We'd like to know all you can tell us about her."

"Yes, of course. Of course," said Schilling mechanically. "You will want to see the other girls too, the other waitresses. But it must be a crazy man has done it. The quiet little Rebecca—"

In Mendoza's office, Mendoza settled him in a chair, told Farrell whoever showed up to shoot him in—they'd want several hands on this to start with. He offered Schilling a cigarette, asked a few questions to get him started.

"I am the maître d', sir, at the Golden Bowl—you will know it, of course, finest European cuisine, the owner insists upon quality—the very quiet, dignified atmosphere, and the girls are all well trained, the modest uniforms— But it is Rebecca you wish to hear about—"

Rebecca Dantry had been one of the waitresses at the Golden Bowl for more than three years—"One of our best girls, reliable, efficient, polite." She was a widow, said Schilling, her husband had been in one of the services, but that was all he knew of it. The other girls might know more. She had been a good girl, a hard-working girl. He was obviously distressed at her death, but impersonally.

"Betty comes to me, she has been off work on vacation, and she told about Rebecca—her car there at her apartment, and of course she had not come to work. It had surprised me very much, all of us, Rebecca's reliable, but no phone call, nothing. We had to hire a temporary—not a girl of the class we like. One of the girls, and then I, we try to phone Rebecca, the cashier too tries, but no answer. And we're busy—I think it is strange, I worry a little, but not until Betty comes this morning—"

"When did you last see her, Mr. Schilling? Mrs. Dantry?"

"She worked Saturday, a week ago today. Usually she had a split shift Saturday—we get a heavy dinner crowd then. We open eleven A.M., and she'd be on eleven to three, then again six to nine for the dinner crowd. But she asked me, special favor, to get off that night. I let her. She didn't do that ever before, she's reliable as I say. She—"

Mendoza thought of Alison saying she had dressed up for something important to her, that night. "Did she give a reason, Mr. Schilling?"

"No reason exactly, no. She's a quiet one, reserved like they say. She told me—she said, she would not ask but it was important, she was to meet—no, she said she had an appointment to be introduced. I don't know to who. She went off at three, and that's the last time— She was supposed to be in Sunday, her regular day off's Monday, but she—did not come back. She—was murdered that night?"

"So the doctor says." And what a curious way to put it: an appointment to be introduced. Mendoza asked if those had been her exact words; yes, as far as Schilling could remember, they were. In a restaurant everything was a rush, and he had not thought much about that.

Mendoza wondered. Was she ambitious toward a show-business career? An introduction to a producer, a director? Was that why she'd dressed so carefully? He put that to Schilling, who looked surprised.

"Oh, I would not think that, sir. Rebecca liked her job, I do not think she ever thought of the stage. A quiet girl, as I said—"

Hackett looked in and said, "What's up?"

"We've got an I.D. on her, Art." Mendoza introduced him to Schilling. "We do certainly want to talk to the other waitresses. I realize it may interfere a little with your service, I'm sorry, but you understand we want to find out as much as possible—"

"I understand," said Schilling unhappily. "Rebecca, murdered—it is some madman, it must be. And I must get back—it is my working hours —if you will ask for me, I will see you have a quiet table to talk to the girls."

"Do you know where she lived, Mr. Schilling?"

"It will be in her records; I will look for you." He went out quietly, a dignified, sorrowful little man.

"A waitress," said Hackett. "You said not much money. See if any of these other girls knew her better. A widow? Boyfriends then, maybe."

"Maybe. What'd you get on the Karpis girl?"

"She wasn't like our Rebecca," said Hackett. "A fun girl, had to have a man in tow. Not particular. George is chasing down Fratelli, who's probably X. I brought Marcia Coleman in to make a statement."

"Let Rory take it," said Mendoza. "Let's see what the other girls can tell us about Rebecca."

Disappointingly, the other waitresses at the Golden Bowl couldn't tell them much. It was a large lavish place, with crystal chandeliers and a good deal of red velvet around; the two principal dining salons were Parisian and Viennese respectively, and Rebecca had been assigned to the Parisian Room with six other waitresses. Only one of them, Betty Collier, had been there longer than Rebecca. All of them told Mendoza and Hackett that Rebecca had been a nice girl, but quiet and reserved. "All I know about her," said Betty earnestly, over the quiet table at the far side of the room, "it came out a little bit here and there. You know the way. Well, nobody pushes your life story at everybody, I guess it was natural. We used to take the same dinner time—the girls get dinner here, see. And we'd be talking, nothing important, something'd come up and—well, like I can tell you she was born in a little town named La Porte, upstate. She came down here about four years ago when her husband joined the Marines, I think they'd only been married a little while then. And she'd had a baby, but it only lived a few days, I don't know what was wrong—she just mentioned it. And her husband was killed in an accident at Camp Pendleton. But she still wore her rings—engagement ring and wedding—she said it helped to keep off the wolves. Not that we get that here. This is a class place."

"Can you describe the rings?"

"Sure. Little diamond solitaire in yellow gold, and a plain gold band, not very wide. Gee, I don't know as I'd recognize them, off her finger. Did he steal them?" Betty looked as distressed as Mr. Schilling; her round freckled face was drawn. "Doesn't seem possible she's—she was an awfully nice girl, you know. I guess you'd say a cut above most of the rest of us, Lieutenant. I mean, a lot of girls take a job like this—even in a fancy big place like this, it's just waiting on table—because we haven't the education for anything else. But Rebecca, she could've done anything—she talked nice, she was a lady. But she said once, she never had any urge to be a secretary or like that, this job gave you the chance to see a lot of interesting people, and no overtime, your spare time was all your own."

"Did she have any relatives?"

"Her mother and father, and a sister older than her. But they didn't live in that little town any more. I wouldn't know, but once we were talking over dinner, and she said she sort of missed a small town, and then she said Lilian—there, I just remembered that, that's her sister's name—said she did too, by her letters, and so did Mother and Dad. So they'd moved somewhere else. And besides, you know, Dantry was her married name."

They talked to all the other waitresses, and again to Schilling. What emerged was discouraging. Rebecca had never mentioned a boyfriend, or dating anyone; and no one had ever met her at the restaurant after work, male or female. She hadn't talked much about herself to anyone: more to Betty Collier than anyone else. A couple of the girls said they'd thought she must be lonely. All the waitresses had small lockers in the employees' room at the back of the kitchen; Rebecca's was unlocked, and in it they found a pair of black flat-heeled slippers and a paperback book, a Gothic novel.

"¡Ca!" said Mendoza. "Talk about anonymous—but there'll be more to see at her apartment." The place a person lived would always say this and that about the person.

Betty and Schilling had both supplied the address: Cole Place in Hollywood. It was a sixteen-unit place, newish, ugly and square; the manageress, Mrs. Yelverton, was horrified by the murder and cooperative. "Such a nice quiet girl," she kept saying, like an incantation. "I knew there was something wrong, her just going off without a word—her car here all week—"

The car, in the carport at the rear, was a six-year-old VW with over a hundred thousand miles on it.

Mrs. Yelverton let them into the apartment. "But who'd have a reason to murder Mrs. Dantry? A lady, a real nice girl, always polite spoken and the rent right on time—"

The apartment told them things about Rebecca Dantry. It said she'd been a neat, clean housekeeper. After a week, the film of dust here and there, but the order and lack of clutter said she'd normally kept things dusted. No dirty dishes in the kitchen; only the electric can-opener, an electric blender, standing out on the drainboard. An ordinary supply of groceries on hand: in the refrigerator, a carton of milk, eggs, bacon, a couple of lamb chops, lettuce, the usual odds and ends. No liquor anywhere.

Hackett went into the bathroom when Mendoza wandered into the bedroom. In the medicine cabinet, aspirin, and that was all in the drug department. Everything clean. She'd just started a new tube of toothpaste. Bottle of blonde rinse. One of those gadgets, hanging from the shower rod, to dry stockings and underwear on overnight.

Mendoza was roaming around the bedroom. A double bed, the blue chenille spread neat and unwrinkled; the bed made up neatly. On the bedside table, an ashtray—so she smoked—lamp, another paperback, one of Mary Stewart's novels. The matching table at the other side had a carton of cigarettes—Benson and Hedges—in its single drawer, a box of book matches half empty.

The dressing table— "So the lab told us what brand of face powder she used," said Mendoza. There was the Blue Carnation cologne, a half-empty bottle, an unopened bottle. There was the frosted platinum nail polish, tidily in the second drawer with other manicure implements. There was also a good-sized box covered with brown leatherette. "I said so," said Mendoza. "For the costume jewelry." He lifted the lid.

On top of a miscellany of costume jewelry lay a single folded piece of paper. *"Vaya,* don't tell me, a clue?" He used his pen to manipulate it off to the dressing table; Hackett holding down one end with his pen, the paper was pushed open from its single fold. They contemplated it interestedly.

Just to the eye, the paper was very thick and expensive bond. A few lines of heavy black writing in ink covered the center. "The boyfriend," said Hackett.

"Dearest," ran the black scrawl in a backhand, slanted slightly upward, "I will not let you say no to me. I know I can make you happy, we will get over the difficulties somehow, my darling, and you know I wish to stay here, not there any more. It will be all right! Love, Johnny."

"Johnny," said Hackett in satisfaction. "I knew—"

"No boyfriend showed anywhere," said Mendoza. "Mrs. Yelverton just told us she never knew Rebecca to go out on a date, have any men here—"

"Mrs. Yelverton lives in Apartment Four at the back. She wouldn't be noticing who came or went from Apartment Fourteen upstairs. She also told us she didn't often see Rebecca coming or going, just when her car was in, the carport being in sight of her front window."

"De veras. All right, she was quiet and reserved, she wasn't all that reserved. She talked about her husband, her family—and natural enough that none of the girls could give us an exact place. When something comes up and you say, Oh, that reminds me of what my sister said, you don't add, who lives on Smith Street in Eugene, Oregon. Why didn't she ever mention Johnny to anybody?"

"It didn't come up. The subject of boyfriends."

"Those are all young women—not one over thirty. It's a subject that quite frequently does come up with young women," said Mendoza dryly.

"I'll give you that. I don't know why. More important, who is Johnny and how do we find him?"

"I wonder if this came by mail. Wastebaskets—" But Mendoza made no move toward looking. "We want a lab team here." Hackett went down to Mrs. Yelverton's apartment to call in, and Mendoza went back to the living room. There was a narrow bookcase, filled mostly with paperbacks. Probably that was one of the items she'd brought into the place, not standard furniture. Other little touches—softening and brightening the deadly conformist face of furnished apartment *per se:* a reproduction Renoir on one wall here, a Degas in the bedroom; a small early-American hooked rug between the two rooms; on the coffee table here, a pretty piece of Danish ceramic, a fat spring robin fluffing out his chest-feathers. She'd had taste, an eye for the good line, the nice things. He went over to the bookcase. Mary Stewart, a few Gothic novels, detective novels, and Mary Roberts Rinehart— There was a small desk; he pulled the top drawer open and discovered an address book. It was the nearly square kind that opened out flat; he turned pages with his pen, and didn't find any addresses out of L.A. County.

"Naturalmente," he said to himself. Addresses you knew by heart, addresses of family, you didn't bother to write down.

Now they knew her name, what kind of girl she'd been: but at first glance the knowledge hadn't turned up any leads as to why or how she'd ended up strangled in Mr. Lozano's back yard.

And—those rings—better get them on the pawnbrokers' list. Doubtful if anyone could identify them positively, when and if they turned up.

Mendoza stood in the middle of the living room and swore. His nice girl, the lady fallen among thieves, was still anonymous.

Palliser and Grace had gone back, expecting frustration, to Boyle Heights. They were aware that almost anyone they talked to might know which supplier had sold narcotics to the communal pad where the bodies had been found. They didn't really expect to get anything on that; if they could learn a little more about Acey, whoever he was, they might at least identify the third body.

And wandering through the dirty, smelly old buildings where this kind of tenant had all but forsaken any semblance of civilized living, they felt dirty themselves, seeing all the far-out types so curiously conforming to type, as it were.

"I tell you, it makes you think, Tom," said Palliser. "I mean, we laughed at Higgins, but—" He shook his head. "The baby due in April, and they grow up before you know it. If this kind of thing's still going on fifteen years from now—"

"God forbid," said Landers seriously. "I see what you mean." They went up the steep stucco steps of another building; there was a long crack down the front, from the earthquake last month. Once one of the communes moved into a unit in one of these places, very shortly the other tenants moved out, and eventually the flower children took over the whole place. These hadn't been fancy apartments, but the people who'd lived in them had higher standards of sanitation than the new residents.

"I'll say something else. You know up in Haight-Ashbury the hepatitis was an epidemic. Not to mention V.D. I just hope to God none of us catches anything wandering around here. What number did that girl say?" In the last place they'd tried, a fat girl in a granny dress and bare feet grimed with weeks of dirt had said they might find Acey somewhere here, "Only some people call him Bob, I guess."

"Four." The corridor was dark; as they peered and Landers got out a match, there was a scurry ahead of them on the bare boards. "Augh!" said Landers. "That was a rat, damn it. My God, why doesn't the Fire Department get after these damn places?"

"They couldn't keep up with it—look at this whole block." Palliser rapped on the door. After a minute it opened and he showed the badge. "We're looking for a fellow called Acey. You know him?"

The bearded longhair at the door wore a sort of yellow toga and love-beads. "Fuzz," he said. "All the time got to come leaning on people. Shoving and leaning. No, I don't know him."

"We think you do," said Landers. "Spoilsports, that's us all right. Where is he?" He wondered just what it was about, this cult of hair: Neanderthal man could beat these primitives at that any day. Of course, on looks it took them right back to Neanderthal, at that.

"Come on," said Palliser patiently.

"Police?" It was another voice, plaintive and scared. She appeared at the door suddenly, peering up at them from the side, trying to insinuate her thin self between the toga-ed one and the door. She looked very young; she had on a sleazy green cotton dress and her long blonde hair hung lank and she said timidly, "Police?"

"She don't know either, man. Blow!" said the longhair, and tried to shut the door, but Palliser was leaning on the jamb.

"You know this Acey, miss?" She shook her head. Inside, the glimpse they had through the quarter-open door, the expectable room, the mattresses, another couple sitting on one of them, unkempt but clothed after a fashion. The other girl, dark and thin, got up and came to the door.

"Come on, honey, they can't do nothing to us," and she took the younger girl's arm. The last look they had, she cast them an imploring glance. The man shoved Palliser roughly back and slammed the door.

Palliser looked at it thoughtfully. "Do you think we've got something there, Tom?"

"Could be," said Landers. "Could just be. She looked damn young. I wouldn't say more than fifteen."

"Un-hum," said Palliser. "She had something to say to us?"

"Well, she said police. Few of the people we've been talking to are that polite."

"Reason to suppose she's being held against her will?"

"Maybe just reason," said Landers. "She's a minor, at least. One thing I'll say. If we had legal reason to ask for a search warrant on all these places, I'd lay odds we'd find something in nine out of ten, from Mary Jane to the acid."

"No bets. How do we play it? The safe way. Go call Juvenile."

Landers walked a block up to a public phone. He got Juvenile Division and explained the situation. A Sergeant Kurtz said, "Could be tricky, if it turns out they're clean—in the legal sense only, of course. We'd better fetch along a couple of the girls too. Hang on, somebody'll be with you in ten minutes." As he walked back, Landers thought about his darling Phil, who'd like to get into the detective side of the job—well, she'd had some practice unraveling that funny deal he'd had landed on him last June. He'd get her to marry him sooner or later. Yes, and then start worrying about the kids, he thought . . .

Juvenile came through with two men and two uniformed police-women, who arrived in an unmarked car ten minutes later. "This had better be good," said Sergeant Kurtz, blond and stocky. "We look crosswise at one of these wild-eyed nonconformists and we get the bleeding hearts down on us."

"Nonconformists—bunch of ignorant damn-fool sheep," said the other man. They went in and Landers pointed out the door. Knocks got no response. Kurtz said loudly, "Police officers—open up!"

There was a little scuffle just inside the door, and all of a sudden it opened. "Goddamn you—why'd you let her loose? Damn little chick, why the hell'd she land here if—" The hairy one came charging out, and Kurtz intercepted him deftly; he struggled and hit out, and the other man came up with cuffs.

The girl had come plunging out, awkward as a frightened colt; she blundered into Palliser and he caught her shoulder, steadied her. "Are you all right, miss?"

"You're policemen?" She looked up at him, at nearly handsome Palliser with his long dark face, black bars of brows, sensitive mouth; she looked at the rest of them there, the neat policewomen in navy uniform, the men in reassuringly conventional male attire, clean-shaven and tidy and washed; and she burst into tears and wailed, "I want to go home! I want my mother!" One of the policewomen put her arm around her and took her out. The hairy one mouthed obscenities at the fuzz.

"Just for that, we can have a little look around here," said Kurtz pleasedly.

"You got nothing on me! You got no charge—"

"Well, let's see if we can find one," said Kurtz.

Palliser and Landers left them to it and went out to the car at the curb where the girl was just hiccuping and breathing hard after sobs. She looked at them forlornly. "I never knew how it'd be," she said. "The kids talk, they say about do your own thing, just gr-great, no rules and all—and I was m-mad at my mom, she said I c-couldn't go to the junior-class dance with Tommy—and I—and I—but I didn't know how it *was!* Meet a lot of new friends, they said— *Them!* Those awful— Oh, it was just awful, they m-made me take those pills—I never felt so awful in my *life!* And—" She started to cry again. "I want to go *home!*"

"You'll be going home, dear. Tell us your name." The policewoman patted her heaving shoulders reassuringly. "How old are you?"

"F-fourteen. I'm F-F-Frederica Hawkins and I live in Bakersfield and *I want my mother!*"

Palliser and Landers hit the office again at five forty, to pass on that news to Mendoza, and heard about Jane Doe getting identified. Hackett was typing a report and Mendoza was playing with the cards on his desk, muttering.

"And when they looked," said Landers, continuing with their own story, "there was about a quarter pound of H in the stereo cabinet, so we called Narco and Lieutenant Callaghan came down himself. My God, that gorilla's bigger than you."

"And what do you know, the one with the love-beads had *Acey* tattooed on one arm. He's booked," said Palliser, yawning, "and we'll talk to him in the morning. I'm bushed."

"Well, something accomplished, something done," said Hackett. "Congratulations. And at least your juvenile seems to have learned her lesson, if the hard way. As Luis says, tomorrow is also a day . . . what bugs me is, we identify that girl, and no solid leads show on her at all. That scar on her arm—Betty told us about that. Accidental burn when Rebecca was in high school. Just nothing—except Johnny, of course. Well, see what the lab turns at her apartment—"

Mendoza had come back, muttering about nice quiet girls, and let Hackett get on with the report. *Love, Johnny*. Who was Johnny and how could they locate him, if nobody she knew knew him? Well, names in her address book, see all those people, ask. And if they drew a blank?

Two things occurred to him. Johnny might not show in her life because he was new there. Or because for some reason she was keeping him covered up. Of the two, Mendoza liked the first. Rebecca had been the lady he deduced she was, the nice girl. She wouldn't have taken up with a bum. He could wish she had been less reserved.

That Karpis woman. Just the opposite, Art said. They hadn't looked at her apartment. Why? For 99 percent sure, Fratelli was the one who killed her.

Brian Bayne. That Facel-Vega hadn't been spotted yet, and it should have been.

Carmichael he had cynically dismissed from his mind. Just hope they'd scared him a little.

The outside phone rang on his desk; it was Webb. "I thought you'd like to know," he said, "that I just got the autopsy report on Florence. The surgeon was thorough. And it's a handful of nothing. No bruises, no marks, nothing—"

"Inconsistent with accident," said Mendoza sarcastically. "I could have bet on it."

"Goddamn that bastard!" said Webb. "I'll have an eye on him from now on!"

Mendoza started out, ran into Palliser and Landers and heard about the hippies and Frederica. At least the one lost sheep saved. And then Higgins came in.

"Luis. I was hoping you'd still be here. I found that Fratelli—"

"*Bueno*. Fetch him in on suspicion to be leaned on?"

"I did not," said Higgins.

He had found Leo Fratelli on a second try at his apartment, an hour ago, after listening to a couple of other witnesses and taking their formal statements. The apartment was a nice modern one on Las Palmas in Hollywood; he didn't expect any answer this time either—he was half thinking Fratelli had run—and was taken by surprise when the door opened. "Mr. Fratelli?" He got out the badge.

"That's me." The man looked at the badge, looked at Higgins, and smiled. "You don't need to carry that, do you? Anybody'd know."

"So I've been told," said Higgins. "Sergeant Higgins."

"Come in. I've been expecting you," said Fratelli abruptly. "Excuse the place—I've been away, just got back last night." He was a big man, nearly as tall as Higgins, but slenderer, very dark, with sleek black hair and a rugged face that just missed being handsome. "Come in here," he said, leading the way to the bedroom. "I'm not all unpacked yet." A half-empty suitcase lay on the bed; Fratelli started taking shirts and underwear out of it. "About Linda. I heard it on the late news. What a hell of a thing. And I suppose, by what everybody at Reno's told you people, you've fingered me for it."

"We wondered," said Higgins noncommittally.

"Sure you would." He finished taking clothes out of the suitcase, shoving them carelessly in bureau drawers. But left in the bottom of the suitcase—

"Have you got a permit for that, Mr. Fratelli?"

"What—oh, sure. I sometimes make collections for the firm, I got a permit to carry it. You want to see it?" He handed the gun to Higgins. It was a Smith and Wesson .32 revolver.

"Come and sit down, Sergeant," said Fratelli, "and I'll tell you what you want to know." He flung himself into a chair in the living room and lit a cigarette. "Did I date Linda kind of hot and heavy? I did. Did I make love to her? That's my own business and I don't brag about all my conquests—especially the easy ones. Did I get jealous when she took up with somebody else and shoot her? I did not, Sergeant." He sighed gustily. "To tell you the truth, poor little Linda sort of opened my eyes. I suppose you'd refuse a drink."

"That's right," said Higgins. He sat down on the couch, holding the gun. "How do you mean?"

"Well, as you've heard, I've been away—company business, and then one of those damned dreary conventions, down in Kansas City. I landed back here about eight last night, and I was tired. I went down to Reno's —it's a nice little place, no jukebox, and the pianist's not loud—for dinner and a couple of beers. And there was Linda with this guy and the

Colemans, who are ordinary people, not very interesting. And the first thing I know Galvin—the bartender—is telling me I'll be damn mad at Linda, her taking up with a new fellow. As if he expected me to—to swagger up to the guy and—I don't even know his name—and challenge him to a duel or something. At least beat him up. In fact, I gathered that all the regulars who knew Linda were hoping for some excitement."

"Is that so?" said Higgins.

Fratelli let out a long stream of smoke. "I tell you, Sergeant, I sat over my innocent beer and I looked at Linda there, that little empty-headed female—eyeing me while pretending not to and by God expecting I'd feel like beating up her new boyfriend—and I thought, what the hell was I doing, pick up a cheap piece like that? And what the hell did these people think, what kind of principles have they got, to think one like that was worth a black eye—or a bullet?" He made an angry gesture. "I'm thirty-two years old, Sergeant. Some sense about women I've got. We play around, don't we, take it where we can get it, but—call it basic morality if we've absorbed any or blind instinct, none of us is going to feel the hell of a lot serious for any female we can lay at the drop of ten bucks for a cheap date. If not my ten bucks, yours. No?"

"It's a point," said Higgins.

"Oh, hell, I just suddenly saw, what's the point? My mother always after me, settle down with a nice girl, start a nice family." Fratelli laughed. "I just might do that one of these days. I think I've sort of outgrown the Lindas. But"—he grinned at Higgins—"I didn't shoot her, I assure you. And I've got no idea who did. Who thought she was—important enough to shoot. Don't tell me it was a gun like mine?"

"It was a .32," said Higgins.

"Oh, well, your scientific boys can tell you it wasn't mine," said Fratelli. "Take it along. They'll tell you."

"So I brought in the gun," said Higgins. "I dropped it off at S.I.D. He doesn't smell right for it, Luis."

"I'll trust your nose," said Mendoza absently. "Damn it, if there was any handle to get hold of— You'd think once we'd identified her, there'd be something to point in some direction, but— The nice quiet girl. The lady. Put those rings on the pawnbrokers' list, but— And that beautiful set of prints from her shoe, nobody knows them . . . That Facel-Vega should have been spotted by now, minus any plates—"

"Luis, go home," said Hackett.

To, thought Mendoza, the cats ostentatiously boycotting them in silent protest of that innocent calico and her kittens in the garage. To Alison's spectacularly unsuccessful campaign to get Spanish and English untangled in the twins' limited vocabulary. He felt frustrated.

Higgins, half an hour later, felt excited and triumphant. Foolproof, the clerk had said; well, some of the finished snapshots, picked up at the drugstore on his way home, were blurred, but a dozen of them were pretty good, considering he'd never taken any before, and in color too. Of Mary with the baby, and Laura with the baby, and Steve with the baby, Margaret Emily alone on the blue blanket on the living room floor, and one where Brucie the Scottie had got into it, and Mary had taken one of him holding the baby—

He'd only asked for one copy of each, until he saw what they looked like.

And they were passed from hand to hand excitedly.

"Oh, George, they're *wonderful*—I want some to show at school—please, George! Miss Prescott was int'rested, she said something funny about siblings, and I want to show—"

"I want the one of me holding her!" Steve proud and masculine. "Our own little baby—"

And Mary, unexpectedly, "George, that's a marvelous one I got of you—I want an enlargement of it."

It was indeed practically a foolproof camera.

CHAPTER 11

Sergeant Lake had just come in, on Sunday morning, and opened the switchboard, when Higgins came in with the envelope of snapshots in his breast pocket. Lake had been feeling rather grouchy, what with black coffee for breakfast and the scales still showing he'd only dropped ten pounds so far; but Higgins' fond exhibition of his snapshots cheered him up—and she was a cute baby.

"For the first pictures I ever took, I think they're damn good, don't you, Jimmy?"

And as the men trailed in, they all had to admire the snapshots. "The kids want to take some to school, but I brought them all in to show you—" And Palliser frowned a little at them; Higgins bristled.

"It's just all these damn-fool kids we're seeing," said Palliser. "You can't help worrying—"

"Oh, you bring them up right," said Higgins, "they won't go off the rails."

"Yes, that's what Mr. Tucker thought," said Palliser.

Mendoza, slim and dapper and tidy in his favorite silver-gray, exchanged an amused glance with Hackett over the snapshots; but they duly admired them and agreed that for a first effort—both with the snapshots and Margaret Emily—he'd done just fine.

"But we do have work to do," Mendoza reminded him. Higgins admitted it. And on Mendoza's desk was the autopsy report on the three flower children; he called the rest of them in to hear any salient new facts from that.

There weren't any. All three of them had been full of Methedrine when they died, probably incapable of putting up much defense. Dr. Bainbridge suggested something like a wrench or a claw hammer as the weapon.

"Well, so we go lean on Acey," said Landers with a sigh. "He's up on a kind of charge, if the D.A. can make it stick—contributing to delinquency. And he'll know the supplier of course, but I don't think he'll come across for the asking."

"You know, Tom"—Grace cocked his head—"I did have a simple little idea about that—"

"You and your simple mind," said Palliser. They drifted out, bound for the day's legwork, and Mendoza shoved the autopsy report aside and opened Rebecca Dantry's address book.

"She must have known some people better than those other waitresses. She must have had friends who knew more about her, know her family or at least of them. So let's try to turn some, boys." There weren't many names in the book, and among them was a doctor's office address and a dentist's, which probably said they weren't personal friends. Mendoza skipped those, divided the rest among the three of them, and got up. "Nice quiet sunny Sunday. Let's hope they aren't all at the beach or on picnics. ¡Vamos!"

"That Karpis thing," said Higgins. "I don't like Fratelli for it worth a damn, Luis, but he's got no alibi—he says he went home and wrote a business report and went to bed at one A.M."

"I don't think it's likely," said Mendoza, "that whoever was mad enough at Linda to shoot her, would bother to use another gun if he already had one to hand. If Ballistics says it wasn't Fratelli's gun, take it from there."

"Where?"

"Sufficient is the evil," said Mendoza briskly. "Right now I'm more interested in Rebecca. Let's see if we can find somebody who knew Johnny. I'll meet you at Federico's at one o'clock."

For his own first cast he tried a Mrs. Jim Davids at an address on Delongpre toward West Hollywood. He found her home, just finishing breakfast: a nice-looking brownhaired young woman, in her mid-twenties, a little plump. It was a modest frame house, and in the side yard a toddler played in a sandbox.

Saving him time, the news of the identification had been on the late news last night and she had seen it. "I couldn't believe it," she told Mendoza, and horror was in her eyes; but at least he didn't have to wait while she assimilated the fact of death. "I'll tell you whatever I can, you said Lieutenant—but there's nothing, no reason for anyone to—Rebecca! Do you know who—"

"No, not yet. Did you know Mrs. Dantry well?"

"You could say so. You see—" She was voluble; she had been genuinely fond of Rebecca, and told him several times over what a nice girl she'd been. They'd met four years ago when both their husbands were in boot camp at Pendleton. "Jim's still in, of course, he's overseas now— And then that terrible explosion, Dan was killed. Rebecca's husband. They were terribly close, an ideal marriage, and it knocked her right out. She was months getting over it—if you ever really do. And losing the baby just before— But she had a lot of sense, she pulled herself together, and—" There was more along the same line. No, they hadn't actually seen each other, got together, very often, Sylvia Davids had the baby, they were both busy, but they'd chatted over the phone, oh, maybe once a week.

"So you'd probably know if she'd been dating any man?"

Sylvia looked surprised. "Had she been? Well, I don't know, Lieutenant. She said to me once, she'd like to be married again, have her own home, but she'd have to be awfully sure about the man. After Dan, you see—they were so close, so much alike. I don't think she went out with men often at all. I know, last year she began dating some fellow she met at the restaurant, but she only mentioned it to me after she'd turned him down. She said he was all right, a nice enough fellow, but she just couldn't see marrying him. Yes, he asked her. I don't remember his name."

"Had she mentioned a Johnny to you recently?"

No, she hadn't. "I don't think she was lonely at all—people thought she was, but she wasn't. Poor Rebecca. She liked her job, and she liked to read, she kept busy—"

"Do you know where her family is living? We understand there's an older sister and her parents—"

"Yes, that's right, they live in— Oh, it's right on the tip of my tongue!" she said, annoyed. "Wait a minute. The parents went to live with her sister Lilian—I can't get it, I know I know it—not a city but a good-sized town upstate—it wasn't Oroville, but—Marysville? No—I'm sorry, I just can't—"

Mendoza asked her to call in if it came to her—the relatives really ought to be notified—and left her a card. He proceeded to the address of Mr. and Mrs. Martin McFall in Santa Monica. He got no answer to the doorbell; a paunchy middle-aged man pushing a power mower in the yard next door shut it off and volunteered information: the McFalls had gone to early Mass. Mendoza asked questions, which were answered promptly. The McFalls were nice folks, good neighbors, no kids yet, he was a salesman of some kind, he'd been in the Marines—

Which was probably the connection. "Say," said the paunchy man, "you selling insurance or something?" And considering what he'd got from Sylvia, Rebecca hadn't been the type to gush on about a newly-acquired boyfriend. It was quite likely she wouldn't mention a boyfriend at all until she'd made up her mind about him, as per the fellow last year. With her background, the good marriage ended by death, Rebecca the sensible reserved young woman, that was natural. It was also hampering to a detective trying to find out who had killed her and why.

He found three more young women to talk to up to twelve thirty, and they were all much the same type, nice respectable young women, two married and one single, and they all told him much the same things about Rebecca Dantry. One of them dated from Marine days too, her husband now out of service and working here; the other two had met Rebecca originally through proximity: one at the local library, one while working at the Golden Bowl.

None of them had ever heard her mention anybody named Johnny.

"¡Fuera!" said Mendoza, sitting in the Ferrari. "Round and round and where do we go?" There was, of course, Marian Greenbaum: Sylvia and the other Marine wife had told him that Marian had been about Rebecca's closest friend. Hackett had that address.

Feeling that if he'd wasted the morning, he had a slightly clearer picture of Rebecca, he drove back down North Broadway, parked in the lot and went into Federico's. Neither Hackett nor Higgins was there yet; he sat down at the big table in front and told Adam to bring him a drink.

"Yessir, straight rye."

Hackett came in with Higgins behind him, the two big men threading their way among tables, as Mendoza took the first swallow of rye. Hackett stood looming over him and eyed the glass. "You'd better finish that," he said. "You'll need it." He wore a peculiar smile.

"¿Qué ocurre?"

"Oh, boy," said Hackett. He sat down on one side of Mendoza, Higgins on the other. "I think we both need drinks too, Adam. We don't very often get mysteries on this job, but when we do, they can be lulus. You're not going to believe this."

"I don't believe it," said Higgins querulously. "Somebody's goofed, that's all. It makes no sense at all."

"What?" asked Mendoza suspiciously.

"Oh, brother. We went back to the office just now to see if anything urgent had gone down, and there was Duke. He was looking sort of bewildered, and I can't say I blame him. He said this had just come in from the FBI, and did it mean anything to us."

"What, for God's sake?"

Hackett lit a cigarette and handed the yellow sheet over in silence. The drinks arrived and both he and Higgins picked them up gratefully.

"¿Qué es esto?" said Mendoza loudly. "What the holy hell—"

The FBI kickback on that set of beautiful latent prints from Rebecca Dantry's right shoe. Interpol, cooperating generously, had spread copies around; and quite a few city police forces in Europe now had the computers too. The prints had been identified by the scientific laboratory of the Rotterdam police. They were the prints of one Pieter Schoonhorn. Schoonhorn had no criminal record at all; his prints were on file from his army service in 1939–40. He had been born in Deventer, The Netherlands, and he was now forty-nine. If any further information was—

"¿Qué sé yo? What the hell is this?" Mendoza upset the remaining half of his rye. "Born in—a Dutchman? Schoonhorn—of all damned silly names—what the hell is a Dutchman doing in the middle of this? His prints on Rebecca's— Oh, God give me strength!" Adam came up to clear away the spilled rye and Mendoza demanded a refill. "A damned Dutchman—a middle-aged Dutchman—killed Rebecca? I don't believe it. What the hell is he doing here?"

"Echo answers why," said Hackett enjoyably. "It sort of complicates the mystery, doesn't it?"

"I tell you, it's just a mistake," said Higgins. "How could a quiet respectable girl like this Dantry, a waitress in L.A., have any connection with this Schoonhorn? Or vice versa?"

Mendoza swallowed rye. "They must have print experts over there, George. Duke said they were nearly a perfect set. But what the *hell*— Well, I'm going to know more about this before I'm much older! Any further information, hell! If prints don't lie, Schoonhorn is in this country, or was a week ago yesterday. So he must be traveling on a Dutch passport—how the hell do we find out about passports, anyway? Obviously, cable the Rotterdam police for everything they can get on Schoonhorn, and when he left the country, where he was headed here and why, if they can get at it. For God's sake, he must have come through customs somewhere, there'd be a record of the passport and— Unless, of course—"

"Unless he's entered illegally," said Hackett. "Yes."

"But what the hell he had to do with Rebecca—!" Mendoza swallowed rye. "This is *ocura, amigos*. The wild card with a vengeance. And what bureau of the government meddlers does the passport office come under, do either of you know?"

Hackett leaned back and contemplated the ceiling. "The State Department."

"*¡Diez millones de demonios desde el infierno!*" said Mendoza violently.

Palliser, Grace and Landers had got nothing useful out of Acey at all; he was sullen and surly. Possibly he was still sulking because the jailers had made him take a bath. He wasn't answering questions, about the supplier or Frederica Hawkins or anything else: but he did, gratuitously, give them the name of the third victim.

"She was a friend o' Marge's," he said. "Her last name was Hitchens or Kitchens or something." And that was the extent of what they got out of Acey, alias Bob. But by all the needle marks on him, said the guard cheerfully, he was hooked all right and maybe the next time he needed a fix he'd come out with something more.

They came out and stood on the steps of the new jail. "You know, the continued legwork in that neighborhood is going to give us exercise and that's all," said Palliser. Landers agreed gloomily.

"Well, I did say I had a little idea," said Grace. "Having the simple mind, you know—"

"And what was—" Landers stopped and said, "Oh."

"All of these users, hooked or part time, have a sort of vested interest in protecting the supplier. But our one rescued lamb—"

"So we overlooked the obvious and it takes Jase to point it out." Palliser dropped his cigarette. "We'll meet you at Juvenile Hall in five minutes."

A call had been made to the Hawkinses in Bakersfield, the policematron told them; but they were off on a lead the police there had turned up—they were in San Francisco. It was the baby-sitter who had taken the call, staying with the two younger girls; and she burst into tears at the news that Frederica was found and safe. She had the Hawkins' phone number; she'd call right away. Probably the parents would land here sometime today or tomorrow to take delivery of the remorseful runaway.

She'd been given a clean jail-issue dress, and she'd had a bath and washed her hair, and she looked a good deal happier than she had yesterday. The matron had said, "Believe it or not, she wasn't raped, thank God."

And she was, now, quite willing to talk about it, answer any questions. She'd got to know this girl Cora on the bus to L.A.—she'd had some money saved up, to run away on—and Cora knew L.A. and took her to this place first, she didn't know where—and there was another girl, maybe eighteen, named Sally. They'd been to several different places— "They slept just anywhere, it was funny, like it didn't matter—" And she'd finally ended up in the pad where they'd found her sometime last week. The man named Bob had taken all the rest of her money, nearly thirty dollars, and that had been after they made her take the pills and she'd felt so awful. She'd passed out and been sick later, but everybody said she'd get to like it after a while—

"I never would!" she said, shuddering. "It wasn't a bit like what all the kids said it'd be, just no rules and doing whatever you wanted—it was *awful!* I—why, you know, that one place, there wasn't even any— any bathroom, I mean the toilet was all dirty and didn't work— And there wasn't anything to eat half the time, or it was all stale or dirty. And I wanted to get out of that place, it was the day after we'd gone there and I'd said I was hungry and that Bob said we'd get some hamburgers, I thought once I was out in the street, you know—if I could just find a policeman, he'd help me, Daddy always says you go to the police, if you're in trouble. And I saw this police car up by the corner, I ran, and I was nearly up to it when that Bob caught me—he hurt my arm, he jerked me around so fast—"

"You're all right now, dear," said the matron.

The men from Homicide exchanged glances. If they'd wondered why Acey and the rest in that pad—they were all lodged here now, on various charges—had bothered to hang on to Frederica, that was the answer. The cynical sophisticates, they'd thought she was going to blow the whistle on them to the cops.

Grace smiled at her. "Do you remember anyone else who came to see this Bob and the others while you were there?" She nodded. "Could you tell us about them?"

"Well, there isn't much to tell—all of them were sort of alike, you know, the same kind of clothes and all. There was a Sue, and a Norma, and oh, just ordinary names. And some other fellows—and they kept playing this music on the phonograph, I used to think it was groovy but it sort of gets on your nerves when it's on all the while. And they tried to make me let one fellow use a hypo thing on me, but I *bit* him—after those pills—"

"Good for you. You remember anybody having an argument with Bob? Asking for money?"

She looked at him curiously. "You mean that man Bob called the Coke Blower? Sure. He had a fight with Bob—only the people called Bob Acey at that place, it was before we went to the place you found me, with Sue. That man kept yelling about Bob and them owed him five C's—I don't know what that meant. He was a big black man, all wild and dressed funny, and I was afraid—"

"That's a big help, Frederica," said Grace. "Thanks very much."

She smiled at him uncertainly. "Of course I wasn't afraid of him because he was a black man. He was just so—all wild and mad, and his hair all bushy—"

She smiled back at all of them as the matron led her out.

"So what do we do with that?" asked Landers. "What I'm thinking?"

"It's an age of specialists," said Palliser amusedly.

They drove back to Parker Center and rode up in the elevator to the floor where Narco lived. Past the door labeled *Narcotics Bureau* they paused at a desk in the anteroom and Palliser said, "Don't know if you remember me, Sergeant—we met over that funny business of Lieutenant Mendoza's, that nurse—"

"Palliser," said the plump balding fellow, getting up.

"Right. This is Grace, Landers. Sergeant Benedittino, correct?"

"And what can we do for Homicide?"

"Mutual cooperation," said Grace. "Does the name of the Coke Blower ring any bells in your head, Sergeant? Described as a big black fellow with bushy hair?"

"Oh-oh," said Benedittino, and went across to a door at the end of the room. "Pat? Something."

Lieutenant Patrick Callaghan, emerging from his office, dwarfed the space containing him; he was bigger than Hackett, and his hair flamered. "Hello, Palliser. I ran into you the other day—you're Homicide too," he added to Landers. "What's up, Steve?"

"Something on Rufus Lee. The Coke Blower."

"That thug," said Callaghan. "Where and how did he show—something of yours?"

"How," said Palliser, "would you like to see the D.A. hang a homicide rap on him, Lieutenant?"

"With the greatest Goddamned pleasure," said Callaghan. "Don't tell me? Come in and sit down—what's the story?"

Palliser outlined it and Callaghan sat thoughtfully massaging the red stubble on his jaw. "I like it," he said. "It's a wonder the bastard hasn't killed somebody before. Rap sheet as long as my arm, and he's been blowing coke for years."

"That's sort of unusual these days, isn't it?" asked Landers.

"Cocaine? There are always users around. Lee's been a pusher, a buyer, a seller, off and on for years—between stretches for possession, a little burglary here and there, muggings. You know what kind of stretches. But his name came up in connection with something last month—that big wholesale pharmacy robbery, Goldberg was on that too —and we had the word that just lately the users are getting a little leery of friend Lee, he's taken to acting violent when they can't pay up. This fits him like a glove. You say it's a juvenile identified him?" He heard about Frederica in silence. "Well, other ways to tie him in, whatever a judge might think of her. Could very possibly be, users of anything not using their brains just so efficiently, that we'll find that wrench or hammer or whatever in his car or his pad. Come on." He towered.

"You know where he lives?"

"I wouldn't know how Luis Mendoza runs his office," said Callaghan, "but, boys, anybody with anything to do with Narco business, I make it my business to know where he is and if possible what doing. Lee had a pad over on Cornwell up to last week. Let's see if he's still there. Steve, go tell Joe to put in a hurry-up request, search warrant. You just heard the just cause."

"Will do. With you in three minutes."

"I hope this is a true word, boys," said Callaghan. "A nice homicide rap—even murder two—would get Rufus Lee out of our hair for a satisfactory stretch."

Mendoza heard about that from Palliser at two fifteen, back at the office. They hadn't found Lee, but the woman at the place had admitted he was living there; they were still waiting for the search warrant, had the word out on the street they wanted Lee. Mendoza said absently that was fine, good luck on it. Waste of time, of course: the flower children no loss.

He was still fulminating about impossibilities, over Schoonhorn. "A Dutchman!" he said again to Hackett. "A fat middle-aged Dutch burgher, writing love-letters to Rebecca? I do not believe—" But he fired off a long cable to the Chief of Police in Rotterdam, demanding a number of answers about Pieter Schoonhorn, so unexpectedly turning up in Rebecca's life. Or, at least, death. "And this Greenbaum woman— Rebecca's closest friend, according to—"

"She's not home," said Hackett. "I've had another idea. Come on." Still muttering, Mendoza followed him up to the lab, where Hackett asked if that note signed Johnny had been printed. It had. There was one good print belonging to Rebecca on it, and a lot of smudges. Mendoza swore.

"Gimme," and Hackett took it and went out. He went across the hall to the door marked *Questioned Documents*. In the miniature lab inside, Sergeant Kurt Musak was examining an envelope under a microscope. He looked at the note Hackett handed him.

"What do you want to know about it?"

"Anything you can tell us," said Hackett.

Musak put it under the scope, flattening it out with blunt spatulate fingers, and examined it with interest. After a long minute Hackett asked, "Well?"

"Well." Musak looked up. "I can't tell you much. This was written by a man, a man who was probably educated in Europe—western Europe. If I had to make a guess, I'd say either Austria or Germany, but I could be wrong. He's a young man, in good health, with plenty of physical energy—"

"*¡El brujo!*" said Mendoza. "Don't con me, you're not a gypsy fortune-teller—"

Musak grinned. "Matter of the slant of the writing, firmness of pressure. And that's about all I can tell you about it."

"Could it," asked Hackett, "have been written by a man of forty-nine?"

"I should very much doubt it," said Musak.

Mendoza snarled.

Higgins, drifting up to the lab after the other two, had stayed. He found Scarne and asked him whether he'd had a look at that S. and W. .32 yet.

"Oh, that. No, I haven't. I'll *get* to it," said Scarne. "You're always in such a hurry. What did you want on it?"

"Comparison test on the slugs out of Linda Karpis," said Higgins. Luis was right, of course: if you were the kind who'd lose your cool enough to take a shot at a girl, just for that reason, and you already had a gun to do it with, you wouldn't borrow, buy or steal another one.

"Karpis? That chick gunned down outside the bar Friday night?"

"That's right."

"I've seen those slugs. Wait a minute." Scarne went away and came back with the .32 Fratelli had handed Higgins. "You want to know if this gun could have fired those slugs?"

"It could be. It belongs to the former boyfriend."

"No way, Sergeant," said Scarne. "No way."

"What do you mean?"

"I mean this is a Smith and Wesson revolver. It has a clockwise twist—it leaves clockwise marks on the slugs, get me?"

"So?"

"So, I have seen the slugs out of Karpis. Counterclockwise twist marked those. She was shot with a Colt .32, Sergeant. This gun here couldn't have fired those slugs. You'd better start doing your homework all over again."

"I'll be damned," said Higgins. But he wasn't surprised.

When Mendoza started home at six fifteen he was feeling as exasperated and puzzled by a case as he ever remembered. The unexpected intrusion of an unlikely Pieter Schoonhorn into what had been a homicide frustrating enough to work—his nice quiet ladylike Rebecca had been just too much so, and they were even farther, he thought, from finding out how she had come to fall among the evil ones than they had been. If she had only been a trifle more confiding—

And the devil of that was, it was in the cards she had been, to her mother, her sister. Somethingville, upstate? And nobody they had talked to had known her before her marriage, they couldn't say what her maiden name had been. And he wouldn't like to guess how many Somethingvilles there were in California.

Marian Greenbaum, they had finally learned from a neighbor, worked at Bullocks' Wilshire, but she was currently on her summer vacation, somewhere up at Big Bear or Crystal Lake or Arrowhead, "one of them resorts up there."

There was also the frustration on other things. So Fratelli hadn't shot Linda Karpis. Who had? And on the flower children, Callaghan's search warrant hadn't come through yet and they'd been stymied on that. More rocks off the Harbor Freeway had hailed the other boys out; regrettably, the D.O.A. hadn't been an I.R.S. employee this time, but a schoolteacher.

Sometime this week Trissel and Schultz would be up for arraignment. God knew when the psychiatrists would be finished with Tugwell.

"¡Condenación!" said Mendoza, catching the light at Hollywood and Highland. He reached out and snapped the radio on. He'd had the highband radio installed at the same time as the siren, and though he seldom put it on, once or twice it had brought him useful news on something. Right now, take his mind off this damned rigmarole—

"2194," it said, crackling, "a 415 heavy, Code 3, 1155 Sunset . . . 4K72, code seven cleared. . . . 4K72, thanks."

A damned Dutchman—and Rebecca, just turned twenty-five, as they knew now? That note. Johnny? A young man, said the handwriting expert, educated in—

"2L96," said the radio, "a 390W, Santa Monica and Edgemont, Code 2 . . . 2L96, Roger."

The Karpis thing—well, George had a nose for unlikelihoods, like any experienced man . . . Just go looking deeper . . . Those snapshots. Mendoza grinned, looking forward to telling Alison about that; and she was a cute baby.

"All units vicinity Hollywood and La Brea," said the radio suddenly, "4K79 is in pursuit, A.P.B. want yellow Facel-Vega sport coupe minus plates, repeat, no plates on car, going west on Hollywood from La Brea —4K79 is in pursuit, Code 3—"

"Hell!" said Mendoza. He heard the sirens a block ahead; he switched on the Ferrari's siren in one motion and gunned the engine. The Ferrari roared, traffic skittered away to all sides and he was past La Brea, looking ahead, the speedometer needle arching right.

He saw the black-and-white just ahead, expertly handled, making time up the boulevard—and a flash of bright yellow ahead of that, in the still-bright sunlight. Another siren behind him, another black-and-white pulling up on his left, and a uniformed man with an angry expression leaning out this side, and then registering sudden confusion as he realized the siren on the Ferrari was competing with their own. Mendoza waved him ahead in this lane.

The Ferrari's speedometer was touching ninety. Briefly he thought of that night he had passed this way cursing and praying, after Alison and that rapist killer, following another siren.

Gardner, Spaulding, Genesee, Fairfax— ¡Dios!—the flash of yellow ahead made the wrenching turn, hardly letting up speed, tires screaming unheard below the sirens, onto Fairfax, and the radio said, "4K79, he's turned onto Fairfax, going south on Fairfax . . . 4K79 in pursuit, the vehicle has turned south on Fairfax . . . 4K94 is in pursuit with 4K79."

The traffic was heavy at this hour; it got out of the way as best it could, but Fairfax was only two lanes each way. There were a few breathtaking moments, and the flash of yellow drew farther ahead—the two black-and-whites dodged in and out of lanes, and there was a big semi-trailer truck blocking both at one point, cars in the north lane backing frantically—

That damn Facel-Vega. The eager interested customer, and Brian Bayne with a bullet in his head. Two days, for God's sake—of course, only twenty-four hours since the A.P.B. was out, a little more—but it should have been spotted before if he'd been driving it around at all. Hackett said—

Colgate, Maryland, Lindenhurst, Sixth— Ridden a squad car along this beat, he had, too many years ago. The squad cars ahead catching up, he could see the yellow gleam struck by the westering sun, half a block ahead, and whoever was driving it would have piled it up on something miles back if it hadn't been for the sirens—

San Vicente cutting in diagonal, the light against them, traffic frozen— Olympic—Edgewood—Packard—

"¡Dios!" he said involuntarily, stepping on the brake. Above the sirens this time came the screech of tires as both squad cars were flung around right—

"4K79 in pursuit," said the radio, "with 4K94, vehicle now going west on Pico from Fairfax—all units stand by—"

They swept past La Cienega and the red light and stationary homegoing traffic at ninety-eight m.p.h.

That Facel-Vega was quite a car—Mendoza had driven one himself awhile. The squad cars, of course, were tuned-up, but still even a tuned-up Ford or Chevy—

Robertson Boulevard. Were they gaining on it at all?

And was the driver of the Facel-Vega the eager customer who had (for God's sake) shot Brian Bayne?

Durango, Oakhurst, Rexford, Reeves, Beverwil—traffic obediently stopped, while the imperative sirens screamed by, led by the yellow gleam— And up there, off to the left, was a great rolling expanse of green, mounds and hollows and little flags—

The Hillcrest Country Club: the golf course. The entrance-gates were on Motor Avenue, and now they had a clear view—the bright yellow Facel-Vega was sailing around to the left and into the narrow avenue leading up toward the clubhouse. But it made the turn too sharp, it swung out too far left, hit the shallow curb and was thrown up onto the green, still traveling at nearly ninety. It lunged up a hundred yards, slowing, and hit the sand trap there by the tenth hole, and lurched over once, and landed on its side at the bottom.

The two squad cars braked violently, still in the narrow road. Mendoza braked the Ferrari just behind, shut off siren and radio, and trotted up to the cars ahead.

"And who the hell are you?" said the driver of the second car. "Got a permit for that siren? Why?" He looked at the badge. "Oh, excuse me, sir—"

"No importa. Let's see what we've got here." They ran up across the green turf to the sand trap. The two men out of the first squad car were bending over a limp body laid out on the green.

"Looks like he was thrown clear—no blood on him, and no broken bones as far as I can tell. These Goddamn fool drivers—but there's no liquor smell on him. Better call an ambulance just in— Who in hell are you?"

"I put out the A.P.B.," said Mendoza. He looked into the sand trap at the defunct Facel-Vega. Very defunct, if he was any judge. "Mr. Kenister will not be pleased."

CHAPTER 12

By the time Mendoza called home Alison had half decided to worry.
"Where on earth have you been? You always call if you're going to be
late—"

"I know—sorry, *cara*," and he explained. "I'm still at Central Receiving. You should see that car, and I'll be damned but he's got a sprained
ankle and that's all. They say I can talk to him presently—I'm hailing
Art down. I'll pick up something before I come home."

"You do run into things, don't you? One of your wanted X's showing
up practically on your doorstep—"

"Not so surprising. His home address in Poinsettia Place in Hollywood. And the mechanics are always telling me I ought to drive this
thing at high speed occasionally to work out the engine. I'll be home
sometime, *amada*."

"Cops!" said Alison.

Mendoza grinned as he dialed Hackett's number. Hackett swore, said
at least they had him if he was the one they wanted, and he'd be down
in twenty minutes. He, of course, had just finished dinner. Mendoza
wondered if the hospital cafeteria would serve him, and called Kenister
Motors.

"Oh, heavens," said Mr. Kenister. "Oh, my dear Lord. Is it—do you
think it's in shape to drive, Lieutenant?"

"You had better," said Mendoza, "bring along a tow truck. When I
left the scene, the club secretary was rather upset about his sand trap.
Your Facel-Vega just fills it quite nicely, in several pieces."

"Oh, my God," said Kenister. "But when I think about Brian—my
God!"

Mendoza and Hackett were both thinking about Brian Bayne twenty
minutes later when they faced the young man on the hospital bed. The

hospital would keep him overnight for observation, but there wasn't much wrong with him but the sprained ankle. His name was Charles Thomsen and he was twenty-five years old. He lived, he said in a thin high voice, with his parents in Hollywood, and he had a job as a window-dresser at a department store on Wilshire.

"It's not *p-s-o-n*," he said, "it's *T-h-o-m-s-e-n*."

"All right, Mr. Thomsen," said Mendoza. He had read him the piece about his rights. "Along Wilshire. Is that how you came to go into Kenister Motors, it's near where you work?"

Thomsen conformed to the description of the customer all right; he had a lot of curly dark hair and he was good-looking, a fresh boyish complexion; but he had a small girlish chin and too-light eyes that moved restlessly. "I never meant to do such a thing," he said, and suddenly looked as if he might burst into tears. "I don't know how it *happened*. I never meant—it just, one thing led to another, if you— You see, I always wanted a car like that. A fine high-powered car—something really sporty. Like that one. I saw it there in the window, every day the week before, when I walked past there on my way to work. It was a beautiful thing—and—I thought, no harm to just ask for a ride in it. As if I—well, it worked just fine." He looked at them deprecatingly. "We get a discount on things at the store, and I got pretty nice clothes. That salesman thought— And he got it out in the street, and he let me drive it. Oh, it was a beautiful job."

"The salesman," said Mendoza; and he brought out a small something from his pocket. "They found this in your jacket when they undressed you. There's one bullet gone."

"That's a pretty thing too," said Thomsen unexpectedly. "It—I don't know—it surprised me so when it went off. Like I'd forgotten it was a real gun." That might be easy to do: it was a little replica derringer, scarcely four inches long; but it took .22-short ammo. "I got that last year, after a big lout of a kid tried to rob me on the street. This place up the street from the store, it was in the window and it sort of took my eye. I'd—forgotten it was there, you know—in my pocket. It was—a sort of joke, about the car I mean—I never meant what happened—"

"What did happen, Thomsen?" asked Hackett.

"Well, I—after I'd driven around some, he kept saying wasn't it a beauty to drive and so on, I figured—well, I said it sure was and I wished I could buy her, but I didn't have even twenty bucks for a down payment. He was surprised and sort of mad. He looked at me funny and said kind of short, I'd better take it back to the agency. But I didn't want—I drove up into this parking lot, a big one by a row of stores, there wasn't anybody else around, just cars. I was going to turn around in there. But I guess he thought—anyway, he said to let him drive and he tried to pull me out from under the wheel, and he tore my jacket pocket. He needn't have started a fight, I was going to do like he said! Anyway, that—fell out on the seat, and I—it was mine, I picked it up, I said all right, he could drive, and he was just starting to get out on his side—when it went off. I never meant it to! I wasn't aiming it or—I was just *surprised*—and he—he sort of fell back in the seat and there—there I was."

"Go on," said Mendoza.

Thomsen gestured uncertainly. "Well, he was dead. I didn't believe it —a little thing like this, and I couldn't see any blood on him or anything, but he was dead! It was just a kind of loud pop, and— Well, I didn't know what to do. First I thought, I better get out of there, so I did. I didn't know what to *do*," and he was nearly wringing his hands. "I drove around awhile, and then I stopped in a little dead-end street, all empty, and I got him out and shoved the right front seat down and put him in the back, under the jump seat. And I—I guess after that, for a while, I forgot all about him. It was such a beautiful thing to drive!" He looked dreamy, thinking back. "You know, I never went to work all that day or the next. I just—drove around. In that beautiful thing."

"And when did you remember Bayne?" asked Hackett.

"Oh, was that his name? It was the next day. I parked it up the block from our house and locked it, overnight. I started out early next day, and I was still trying to think what to do, but it was such a lovely thing to drive—and I could see people staring at it, you know, it makes you feel good, just driving a car like that. I got the tank filled three times, I was just driving around. And then, all of a sudden, I remembered him— back there. I got nervous—I thought, better put him somewhere, and I looked around where I was then, and there was this parking lot pretty full of cars. I just drove up to one end of it, I didn't even stop the motor, and pulled him out."

"And went on driving around," said Hackett.

"That's right. I guess I always knew you'd find me and I'd have to tell about it sometime, but it was all kind of like a dream—" Thomsen sighed. "I'm sorry. I'm awfully sorry about that man. I never meant to do such a thing, it just sort of happened."

In the corridor, Hackett asked, "Do you think the head doctors'll get him off?"

"Well, you could call him irresponsible, but there are a lot like him walking around," said Mendoza. He looked at the tiny derringer. "If this thing didn't have such a light pull— *¿Quién sabe?* Let the D.A. figure out what to call it."

And on Monday morning Hackett had the last report on that to type. Mendoza had seen the parents last night, ordinary people bewildered and horrified to be suddenly part of police business.

There was no new information in from the Rotterdam police. Mendoza swore about that and Hackett reminded him of the time differences. Palliser, Landers and Grace had just come in when there was a call from Callaghan's office—the search warrant for Rufus Lee's pad had just come through. They went off on that again, Callaghan after a cache of the foolish powder and the Homicide men hopefully after evidence of that kill on Rufus Lee.

At nine thirty a new body got called in, and Hackett went to look at it—Higgins was out somewhere, probably on Karpis again.

The new body was that of a woman, elderly and shabbily if strangely dressed, and she'd fallen over the mezzanine railing at the Ambassador Hotel and broken her neck landing in the lobby. She didn't seem to have been drunk; and there was no identification on her and no handbag to be found. It looked like a plain accident, so Hackett let the ambulance take her and began asking around the hotel. The desk clerk denied that she was registered there. A couple of bellhops had seen her sitting in the lobby, in the mezzanine. In the coffee shop he found two waitresses who remembered her by her clothes—a bright pink chiffon dress, a man's old black sweater, canvas shoes.

"She came in here yesterday afternoon and had a cup of coffee. Yeah, she paid for it O.K. But she acted funny," said one of the girls, and was backed up by another. "She was talking to herself all the time." But that was all they'd seen of her.

Hackett came back to write an initial report on that, and found Mendoza restlessly practicing crooked deals at his desk. "What the hell are these damned Dutch police doing? They have the effrontery to—to hand me this damned Schoonhorn, who is simply impossible to connect with Rebecca Dantry, and then they don't tell me another damned thing! So all right, time differences, but it's been twelve hours, near as—"

"Patience, patience," said Hackett.

"And the damned Passport Agency—the request had to go through Washington, damn it, how do we know where he entered the country? And those damned bureaucrats—"

"Eventually something will come through," said Hackett. "I'm curious too." He was halfway through the report when Higgins came in.

"We just got a flash from Chicago," he said absently. "One Don Bell, P.A. violation. He was in on a ten-year stretch for attempted murder, and just now they go looking for him and find he bought a plane-ticket for L.A. last Thursday. They want him back if we can pick him up . . . I've been back over Karpis, and I can't turn a damn thing, Luis."

"She wasn't much loss, by what we've heard."

"If Matt was here he'd say equal in God's sight," said Hackett, and swore and X-ed out a word.

Higgins had called Fratelli and told him he could have his gun back any time, it was clean. "I told you," said Fratelli. "I'll be by to pick it up. But I wonder who did kill her, Sergeant. Thought she was worth killing?"

Higgins had no idea. He talked with Marcia Coleman again. "You mean it wasn't him? Leo Fratelli? We sure all thought—"

"Well, he seems to feel she wasn't important enough to him to shoot," said Higgins diplomatically.

She thought. "I guess I can see that," she said. "I don't like to say anything against Linda, she was fun on a party, like. She—sort of enjoyed life. But I've got to say, I guess she maybe wasn't particular, if you know what I mean. But you know, at least she wasn't *mean*. D'you know, she used to send a little money to her first husband sometimes, he got down on his luck. It sounds funny, but she did. She didn't, you know, hold grudges."

Which colored the picture of Linda, but it wasn't any help in getting a lead on who might have pulled the trigger of that Colt .32. Higgins went and saw the bartender, John Galvin, again, and then Peter Squires; both were surprised to hear that Fratelli was in the clear. Both admitted that Linda had had other boyfriends from time to time; Galvin gave him a name, a Walter Eilers, and Higgins found him at a Gulf station two blocks from the bar. Since Walter Eilers had stopped dating Linda he'd got married and said he hadn't seen her for six months.

It was all up in the air, and Higgins wasn't really much interested in Linda Karpis or who had taken her off. He stopped at a drugstore a block down from the headquarters building for coffee, and found Lieutenant Goldberg sitting on one of the stools sneezing into Kleenex. He greeted Higgins genially. "How's the world treating you these days?"

"Oh, just fine," said Higgins, beaming. "Here, I've got some snapshots to—first ones I ever took, and they're not bad at all—see, here she is with my wife, and me—the kids took the rest to school, they're just wild about her, and you can see—"

"Oh, my God," said Goldberg, "and I'd heard about the new baby too, I had to invite—" But he grinned at Higgins and admired the snapshots dutifully.

Mendoza finally left the office to go to lunch, and came back at one thirty to begin swearing all over again at the absence of any cable from Rotterdam. "Listen," said Hackett, "you cussed out the FBI for being so zealous as to pass those prints to Interpol. Now it turns up a lead, you're cussing again. Be thankful the prints got identified."

"Schoonhorn!" said Mendoza. "My God, a fat Dutchman named Schoonhorn! Just what the hell he had to do with Rebecca—and that's another thing, damn it. Somethingville, California, I ask you. She said she'd try to remember—Sylvia Davids—where Rebecca's family lives. And damn it, if she remembers, we don't even know what her maiden name was— And probably the family will know something about Johnny."

"Preserve patience," said Hackett again. "I suppose I'd better ask Carey if he's got this new corpse in his files. It doesn't seem as if anybody'd miss her, by the description." She'd been old, thin and undernourished, gray hair and false teeth, and extremely dirty under the peculiar clothes. "I wonder—"

Sergeant Lake came in and shut the door behind him. "You've got a caller, Lieutenant. Asking if this is where she should come to discuss some murders. Asking for you by name. I think you'll be interested." His expression was half amused and half avid. "Keep your fingers crossed."

Mendoza sat back, putting out his cigarette, and asked, "Who?"

Lake opened the door and stood back, and a woman came in. Mendoza stood up, looking at her. "I should know you—"

She was a tall woman, looking to be in her late thirties and maybe older. She was groomed and smartly dressed in black and white: her obviously tinted hair was reddish-gold and she had rather hard blue eyes above a mouth delicately widened with coral lipstick. She stopped, facing the desk.

"That's right," she said. "I remembered your name. I'm Tamaris Holt."

Mendoza's eyebrows shot up. "Sit down, Miss Holt."

She sat gracefully in the chair Hackett held for her, glancing up over her shoulder, and he introduced himself.

"You told Sergeant Lake you had something to tell us, Miss Holt?" asked Mendoza.

"That's right," she said. "And in case you think I'm being vindictive, Lieutenant, you are absolutely right. Alfred Carmichael's been keeping me for twelve years, I've given him the best years of my life, years a woman can't get back. I've slaved over taking care of myself, to hold him—a woman's got to. And he's grown into a fat slob who thinks he can wave good-bye with five G's and Nice to've known you. He's got a little bitch on the make, a little snit of a blonde chippy with her eyes on that bank account, and him conned she goes for the older men." Tamaris Holt smiled thinly. "So all right, he made me mad. Twelve years, and he pats me on the back and waves good-bye, takes up with this cheap piece."

"But?" said Mendoza. He got up to light her cigarette.

"But. I don't want you to think I haven't some conscience. I didn't like it six years ago and I don't like it any better now, and if Alfred and I are going to call it quits, I've got another card to play, Lieutenant. You see—he told me all about it. After Robert. He told me just how he'd played it, with his father and Robert too. I tried to stop him, I didn't want to hear—my God, not that I hadn't wondered—but he just had to confide in somebody, I suppose, boast how clever he was. This interest you?"

"*¡Cómo no!*" said Mendoza. "*Conque esas tenemos.* You interest us both very much, Miss Holt. But—"

"So, seeing he was bound to tell me all about it—well, I listened." She shrugged elegant shoulders. "I can't say I enjoyed hearing it. But—"

"But if you're thinking your statement on this can get him charged with homicide, I'm afraid you're wrong. Legally speaking it's only hearsay, and that isn't admissible—"

She smiled slowly at him. "Little Tamaris learned how to protect herself a long time back, Lieutenant. I've got a tape of it. Of him telling all about it."

Mendoza stared at her and then yelped delightedly, "*¡Es hermoso sin pero! ¡Ay, que risa!* Talk about beautiful—" He jerked open the door. "Jimmy, get me Webb on the line!"

"I've never played it back," she said a little grimly. "But I've kept it safe—and I brought it along to hand over." She took it out of her bag and laid it on the desk: a round little tin of dynamite.

The outside phone rang. "Here's Webb," said Lake.

"Mendoza? What the hell do you want? I'm—"

"You. Here. Now. We've got Alfred, I think," said Mendoza.

"Goddamn! I'm leaving now!" said Webb.

*   *   *

There would, of course, be long discussions at the D.A.'s office. The finicky ways of the law could be frustrating; it might be some while before the red tape was unwound and it was decided what charge they could bring on Alfred, if they decided to bring any. But it was going to get some publicity.

Mendoza was still at the D.A.'s office at three o'clock when Palliser, Landers and Grace came in, looking triumphant.

"It's all tied up," said Palliser. "My God, the places we've been seeing lately—how can people live in such filth—"

"Actually I understand they're quite clean animals," said Hackett. "You nail this Lee?"

"On the button. We found a claw hammer, bloodstains still on it, in the kitchen of that place—and a nice cache of everything you can name for the Narco boys. No, he wasn't there but the word was out we wanted him, and by what Callaghan said he wasn't very well liked, you could put it—we'd just got all the evidence in to the lab when somebody tagged him and a black-and-white picked him up. There were—accounts, I suppose you'd call 'em," said Palliser. "Primitive accounts, who'd bought what and who owed him, and we managed to pin him down by those, he'd had dealings with those four in that pad—"

"Anyway, it doesn't matter if he won't talk," said Grace. "There's all the nice solid evidence. Yes, he's booked in."

"And all the legwork and risking the hepatitis and God knows what," said Landers, "just for those no-goodniks. Why the hell did I ever pick this job?"

The cable from Rotterdam arrived just as Mendoza came back at five minutes to five. He seized it eagerly, read it with growing gloom and handed it to Hackett.

"¡Santa María! Now will you tell me, will you just tell me, Arturo, what possible connection—and what damned possible use this—this handful of nothing is!" He paced the office, trailing smoke behind him angrily.

The cable said: "Pieter Schoonhorn native Deventer, son local farmer, nothing known against family. Schoonhorn educated to fourth grade level local school. Army service 1939-40 known member Dutch underground during war, given good character as patriot several well-known men. Has been employed various cities in The Netherlands laborer, cook, manservant, chauffeur, and holds an international driving license. Unmarried. Schoonhorn applied passport first time last May.

Brother Wentz farmer Deventer states Schoonhorn most recent employed Bernhard Van Kuypers banker estate near Venlo. Enquiries passed to authorities Eindhoven in re Schoonhorn's local record. Physical description five feet eleven blond hair blue eyes one hundred ninety. Repeat no criminal record what is Los Angeles interest in." It was signed by Chief of Police Willem Van Eyckers.

"*¡Diez millones de demonios!*" said Mendoza. "Now what the hell does that tell us?"

"Not much, for a fact," said Hackett. "But this is the hell of a funny thing, Luis, you know that? Here's this fellow, no record of his ever having done anything against the law, never been out of The Netherlands before, menial employment but he must have at least a normal I.Q., and all of a sudden he applies for a passport, arrives here by whatever route, and we turn him up stripping the clothes off a murdered body—"

"Her shoe. Her right—"

"Be reasonable, *amigo*. If he took her shoes off, it was him took everything else off her. It's crazy, Luis. This—"

"I said so, I said so!" Mendoza took back the cable and read it again. He said, "I can't make head or tail of this—how the hell did Rebecca run across him? Wait a minute—wait a minute—the big, big car. Schoonhorn has worked as a chauffeur and—"

"He not only suddenly decides to come to California, he brings his employer's limousine along?"

"His empl—now *wait* for it," said Mendoza. "But no, damn it, that won't fit. This says 'most recently employed,' not that he's employed there now. That sounds to me as if Schoonhorn was out of work."

"At the age of nearly fifty he decides to try his luck in the New World," said Hackett.

"How the hell should I know?" Mendoza tossed the cable on the desk and went out to the anteroom. "Jimmy, cable back to Chief Van Eyckers." He lit a new cigarette, and dictated rapidly. "Evidence here ties Schoonhorn into homicide would appreciate info on where when left country for what destination if possible and alone or with others. Is he employed now where. Has he acquaintances U.S. or any former connection. Prints definitely connect with murder. Will appreciate earliest info."

"That should make them sit up—their known good patriot," said Hackett. "But the more I think of it the crazier it is—"

*   *   *

Mendoza drove over to the Golden Bowl and asked for Schilling. When he came, he exclaimed, "Ah, the Lieutenant! Have you found out who is the madman has murdered Rebecca?"

"Not yet, Mr. Schilling. I just want you to listen to a description, and tell me if you've ever noticed such a man in here, or talking to Mrs. Dantry." He read out the description of Schoonhorn, and for good measure the data on his background.

Schilling was shaking his head slowly. "No, sir," he said. "Dutch—one knows the type. That one, he'd be what you call here lower middle class—not much education, a simple type. Not the kind of man to go traveling abroad, have such money for that—or want to travel. As for his looks, that would describe many men, Lieutenant."

Mendoza acknowledged it. "But we know he's here, and that he—mmh—had something to do with Mrs. Dantry. Now you told me that this restaurant specializes in European food. And it's a fact that these days more people are traveling around, visiting other countries, than ever before. Do you get—"

"The visiting travelers from Europe here? Assuredly," said Schilling. "But a type like this you describe—no! That kind of Hollander I know—a bowl of potato soup with leeks and fried herring what he would call a meal! Here, we serve both Parisian and Viennese specialties, the finest of all these fine dishes, and nothing but imported wines. When we have visitors from anywhere in Europe coming here, they are people of the highest class, the people who know what is fine cuisine, whether they have much money these days or no." He shrugged.

"And you never saw anyone like this man talking to Mrs. Dantry?"

"Never!" said Schilling. "I will ask the girls, but I am sure no one ever saw such a fellow here. Why? What has this clumsy dumb Dutchman to do with it?"

"¡Porvida!" said Mendoza. "I wish to God I knew!"

He went home and blew off steam at Alison, who was trying to placate the cats with fresh catnip. She was on her knees over a sheet of newspaper in the living room, and listened inattentively to the saga of the cables and the European cuisine. "Yes, very funny," she said. "Such a nice woman from Pet Pride came by this afternoon, a Mrs. O'Hanlon, and saw the kittens. She says if we can keep them until the kittens are weaned, they'll come and take them then. They're getting cuter every day—" El Señor hissed at her. "Now don't be silly, Señor, we're not going to keep them. It's just a little while and they'll be gone—" Bast and Sheba had their ears back stiffly, ignoring the catnip.

"And just what in the name of God this rigmarole is all about—I need a drink!" said Mendoza. "You haven't heard a word I said—"

"Yes, I have. A Dutchman. And they'll take the calico too, find a good home—"

Mendoza started for the kitchen. El Señor was boycotting humans as hard as his mother and sisters, until those strange and lowly cats in the garage were turned out with the garbage, but the lure of rye was too strong; he galloped after Mendoza demanding his share. Grumbling, Mendoza poured him half an ounce.

Cedric came up and nudged him until he accepted a paw. "At least you're still speaking to me, *bufón* . . . If there was any glimmer of a possible connection, but how the hell could there be? I simply do not—"

The twins, fresh out of their baths, had discovered he was home; they arrived at full gallop with Mrs. MacTaggart panting after them.

"Daddy, *los gatillos,* the lady's goin' take away! Don' let! The nice *gatillos* all *muy lindos!*"

"Now, Terry, you know our own nice cats don't like them—" Mrs. MacTaggart was firm. "They'll have fine new homes—"

Johnny was uninterested in *los gatillos.* He presented Mendoza with Grimm, its cover nearly off now, and said loudly, "Read Rumple. Don' listen to Terry—*la niña tonta!*"

Mendoza swallowed rye and suddenly laughed. "All right, *hijo.* Terry, *los gatillos lindos* will be fine and happy— *¡Bastante!* I needn't give myself ulcers—"

Higgins came home to the house on Silver Lake Boulevard to be pounced on by Steve and Laura Dwyer.

"George, Miss Prescott looked at the pictures and said she's a darling! And she laughed when I told how Mother let me help give Margaret her bath, and said it was good practice— And it is, George, I'm going to have at least six babies when I get married and I've got them all named—three boys and three girls—"

"And I knocked Harry Woods down and gave him a black eye," said Steve proudly.

"Hey," said Higgins. "Why'd you do that? You shouldn't—"

"Because he said it was sissy for me to like Margaret and want to hold her," said Steve darkly. "And I told Mr. Simms why too, when I got sent to his office, and I showed him the picture of me holding her, and—"

Mary was laughing helplessly.

"Well?" said Higgins apprehensively. "The principal, you mean? What did he do?"

"He showed me a lot of snapshots of his new grandson," said Steve. "Only he's just an ordinary baby, not like Margaret—"

Tuesday morning, and Palliser and Grace off. The Graces had another appointment at the County Adoption Agency, and the supervisor who talked to them—for, as Virginia said cxasperatedly, the twentieth time—all but admitted they were bound to be given Celia Ann in time. "When there aren't any relatives," she said vaguely. "But there's always a certain amount of red tape, you know."

By now, they knew.

Palliser was set to washing those windows for Roberta. There was more to this home-owning business than met the eye, he reflected; he'd never had to wash windows in the apartment. At least they had those hippies cleared off the list; and to replace them, the funny old biddy who'd broken her neck at the Ambassador. And also, of course, the Dantry woman the lieutenant was fussing over. A queer one all right. He wondered if anything new would show up on it today.

The urgent query for information on Schoonhorn, to the Passport Agency in Washington, had brought in nothing by Tuesday morning. There was nothing new from the Rotterdam police. Mendoza was swearing again, and Hackett again reminded him of time differences and legwork.

"You might," said Higgins, "turn your crystal ball on Linda Karpis, Luis. If we hadn't already dropped on that random sniper, I'd be inclined to say it was a thing like that. I've been all round again, everybody who knew her, and nothing shows. Ordinary apartment—she was a sloppy housekeeper—but nothing there to suggest any leads. Nobody can think of anybody who had a reason to kill her. It'll get stashed in Pending. Or could we have another sniper around?"

"Unlikely," said Mendoza.

"And this female at the Ambassador," said Hackett, "it's just a blank. Evidently, by what Tom got yesterday after they'd tied up that Lee, the woman had been seen around the lobby for a day or so, but not registered, and nobody knew hcr. It's nothing to spend much time on—accidental death—"

The outside phone rang. "Mendoza, Central Homicide . . . Oh, hell. Yes, all right, tell him I'll be there."

"What's up?"

"The D.A. wants a discussion—me and Webb and the usual deputy attorneys—on Carmichael. That tape—well, he came over very loud and clear, as I told you, and it was just about as we'd figured too, if he only covered Papa and Robert. But the D.A.'s pussyfooting on it—and the way the Court's been acting, no wonder. I did have a thought there, which I'll pass on. The Voiceprinter."

"That's my boy," said Hackett. "They can't get round that, it's been ruled admissible evidence." And that newish little gadget, marking the individual voice as clearly as fingerprints, was being useful to them.

"But listen, if a cable comes in you call me!"

A new body turned up—nothing much, said Landers, coming back to type the report; looked like a natural death, an elderly woman in a third-class hotel on Grand.

A teletype came in from Sheriff McCauley in Iowa: the extradition papers were getting expedited, on those two hoods sitting in the Alameda jail.

No cable came in from Rotterdam.

There was another head-on collision on the off-ramp of the Pasadena freeway, one D.O.A. One of the drivers was drunk.

Another body was reported in a flophouse on Skid Row: probable coronary. But it all made the paperwork.

At half past two, Hackett, as curious about Rebecca Dantry as Mendoza, was a good deal annoyed by the receipt of a teletype from the Passport Agency, Department of State, Washington, D.C., which said: "Your request info unclear detail and rechannel." "Bureaucrats!" snorted Hackett. "Rechannel! The typical doubletalk—" He didn't waste time sending the bureaucrats another teletype; he fired off a request to an office where efficiency prevails, the FBI, asking the Feds to cut the red tape and put a burr under the tail of the bureaucrats at the Passport Agency.

He had been out for lunch. Another one went down, with Higgins and Landers out on it—a hit-run along Alvarado, with the usual contradictory witnesses. And then unexpectedly the D.A.'s office called to say that the psychiatric tests on Harry Tugwell had been concluded and the arraignment would be set some time this week. That thing—the telephone lineman.

They really couldn't expect anything more from the Rotterdam police this soon. Probably Charles Thomsen would come up for arraignment some time this week too. Hackett wondered who had broken the news to Bayne's wife. And in this job they saw life in what was sometimes called the raw, and sometimes it was tragic, but other times it was just silly. Unsensible. If you counted out Fate.

There was no sign of Mendoza. Hackett was sitting there listening to Landers type a report at three o'clock when Lake routed a call at him. "Central Homicide, Sergeant Hackett."

"Central Receiving," said a cool practiced voice. "By what the Traffic officers say, I think we may have someone here to interest you, Sergeant."

"Oh?" said Hackett.

"The patrolmen say there's a—er—want out on him. A Donald Bell. He appears to be under the influence of some drug, and there was a gun found on him. The patrolmen—"

"Oh, really," said Hackett. Bell? It didn't mean anything to him: a want? "All right, thanks, somebody'll be over. George!"

CHAPTER 13

When Higgins got over to Central Receiving Hospital he found the two Traffic men waiting for him at the main desk. "Homicide?" said one of them when Higgins introduced himself. "Is he wanted for homicide?"

"Well, the desk called us, I don't know why—what's the name again?"

"Bell, sir. We got this call, a 390, only when we picked him up it looked more as if he was high on dope. Along Alvarado. We started to bring him in, and I searched him for any I.D. and found this." He handed Higgins a crumpled piece of paper, with carbon smudging it here and there. "You can see it's a P.A. release—I guess most places do it the same way, when a prisoner gets out on P.A. he has to sign this, agree to report to his officer and so on. Only this is from the Illinois pen, and we figured if the guy's on P.A. back there he's got no business walking around loose in California, so I called in to see if there was a want on him, and there was."

"Bell," said Higgins. "Oh, yes. He was in for attempted homicide, I guess that's why—" The want on Bell would have gone automatically to all the precincts, every division. "I'll take care of it, thanks."

"He had a gun on him," and the other man handed over a revolver.

"O.K.," said Higgins. He saw the doctor, who said Bell was just high on the Mary Jane. He'd be tucked away in the security wing until called for. Higgins went back to the office and teletyped Chicago that they had him.

Mendoza came back from the D.A.'s office, annoyed at that gentleman's caution; but it had been decided to bring a charge, and a statement had gone to the press which should bear fruit in headlines tomorrow.

The autopsy on Bayne came in: dead wood.

About five o'clock Carey called. "I just got back and saw the description of your new corpse," he told Hackett. "The elderly party with the funny clothes."

"Have you got her listed?"

"Maybe—I think I have. Anyway, I've got—along with every other Missing Persons bureau in the state—this Maybel Slick, longtime resident of Camarillo. She wandered away about three weeks ago, evidently she's not dangerous and given the run of the grounds. The description fits, of course she wasn't wearing those clothes when she wandered off. I called Camarillo and there'll be somebody down tomorrow to say if it's her. Don't tell me somebody murdered her?"

"As you know very well," said Hackett, "homicide is not a synonym for murder. Looks like a plain accident. But we'd like to get her identified, thanks."

"I'll be in touch," said Carey.

Mendoza was still fuming over the silence from the Rotterdam police. "And damn it, she's been dead for ten days and we can't locate the relatives to notify! If only somebody here had known her before she was married—" But they did know, of course, that Rebecca had married Dan Dantry somewhere else—her home town?—and come down here when he was in training at Camp Pendleton. "Damnation, I wonder if it'd be any use to ask the Marine Corps for his personal data, Art. If they were both from the same town."

"Nothing says they were. It's a long chance—we might try it, I suppose."

Mendoza phoned Sylvia Davids. "I know it's stupid of me," she said. "But as far as I remember Rebecca only mentioned the name once—otherwise it'd be, she'd had a letter from her mother, from Lilian, naturally she wouldn't say— Well, I'm almost sure it was something ending in *ville,* but I—"

"And the funny thing is," said Mendoza after he'd commented on that, "I'd have expected Rebecca, sensible as she was, to have one of those little cards in her billfold, notify in case of. But she didn't. Her regular handbag—you saw it—was right there in the apartment. As I'd expected it to be."

"So you said, and I never asked you why."

"She was going out. On a date, or somewhere. She wouldn't carry all the everyday things. And damn it, Marian Greenbaum—"

"I called the apartment manageress. She said Marian would be back this weekend, her vacation's up."

"Helpful."

But they were stymied on that in all directions right now. Eventually, they all went home. Higgins, stopping to buy more film for the camera, suddenly remembered that Thursday was Mary's birthday, and wondered what to get her. Something extra-special, he thought, on account of Margaret Emily . . . Hackett, getting caught in a jam on the freeway, was thinking about that new diet Jimmy had found. It was supposedly guaranteed . . . And Landers, remembering that this was Phil O'Neill's day off, called and offered to take her to dinner if she wouldn't make him shave again. "We've cleaned up that hippie thing—I thought you'd like to hear about it."

"I'd love to," said Phil.

"I feel," said Alison, "as if we're living in a state of siege, with the cats spitting and looking daggers at us. I called Mrs. O'Hanlon and asked if they won't please come and get that poor family of felines as soon as possible, kittens weaned or not."

"*Bueno,*" said Mendoza sleepily. Dinner was over, the offspring tucked away, and the living room was passably peaceful, with Bast, Nefertite and Sheba asleep in a tangle on the sectional and only El Señor, green eyes remote, staring balefully from the credenza. "But it's like toothache," he added half to himself. "Nagging. Rebecca—the nice quiet girl—what the hell is the connection? A Dutchman—"

"I suppose you'll be finding out about that sometime," said Mrs. MacTaggart, coming in to pick up her knitting bag left in an armchair, "but what sticks in my mind is that Carmichael fellow you were telling about. D'ye think they'll try him for it?"

"Anybody's guess what he'd get, Máiri—the courts these days—but at least it's going to be obvious to everybody that he's guilty as hell, whether he ever serves any time or not."

"Well, I suppose that's something."

"Tamaris Holt," said Alison somnolently, wrinkling her admirably straight nose. "I'll agree with Máiri, at least it'll all come out in the papers and everybody'll know about Alfred—"

"Fred Webb is chortling happily over it."

"But that's not a very nice woman, Luis."

"And whoever said she was?"

There was an inquest scheduled on Brian Bayne at ten o'clock on Wednesday morning. Hackett would cover it: no need to offer all the evidence there. Higgins came in just as Mendoza was sitting down at his desk and said, "I move we stash Karpis in Pending. We'll never get any more on it."

Mendoza agreed absently. There was nothing in from Rotterdam, or Washington either, for that matter. "What the hell are they doing? Our own bureaucrats I know, but you said you sicked the Feds onto them— They must have some record of foreigners entering the country—"

"I can ask the Feds to try again," said Hackett gloomily.

But about then a new call came in, a collision at the S.P. yards, a laborer killed. Train wrecks fell to Homicide whether anybody was killed or not, and Glasser went out on that with Palliser.

When Carey called at nine fifteen, Hackett said he'd meet them at the morgue. There, Carey introduced him to a Mrs. Dundon, tall, brisk and cheerful. Anybody, thought Hackett, would spot her as a trained nurse, in uniform or not: she was invisibly branded with her profession as clearly as George Higgins.

She didn't turn a hair at the corpse. "Oh, dear, yes," she said, "that's our Miss Slick. Poor creature, what happened to her?" Hackett told her, and she nodded. "She was terribly nearsighted, and we couldn't trust her with glasses. The poor thing, in a way it's a happy release—she'd been committed for nearly thirty years. Manic depressive. Well, I'll see that the family's informed, and someone will be claiming the body—I know you like to be sure the funeral gets paid for," and she gave them a brisk smile.

Hackett went back to the office to start typing the final report on that before he covered the inquest. Jason Grace was sitting on one hip on the corner of Higgins' desk. Landers beckoned Hackett silently, grinning, and indicated the pair of them. They were, Hackett discovered, carrying on a kind of dual monologue, both of them apparently convinced the other was listening.

"And that supervisor said, just the red tape— Not usual for a baby to be born with all that hair— Went to see her again, and Virginia says she's a very intelligent— And the kids just crazy about her, took some of the pictures to school— After all her real parents, that doctor and his wife, both educated people— And I want to get a better one of her with Mary— Five months now, and about the cutest— She's gained a quarter of a pound already and the doctor said— Sugar 'n' spice 'n' everything n—"

Hackett burst out laughing and they both turned to stare at him. "Now you've spoiled it," said Landers. "They've been going on like that for five minutes. I swear it's enough to make a man scared to get married."

"Going on like what?" said Grace. "I was telling you about Celia and the Adoption—"

The phone shrilled on Higgins' desk and he picked it up. "Scarne," it said. "Say, you're getting more on the ball now, Sergeant. This is the right gun."

"Which is the right gun, on what?" asked Higgins.

"This Colt you sent up yesterday. I've just been looking at it—fired some slugs for comparison—and this is the baby, all right. Not a new gun, but it's been taken care of—"

"What are you talking about?" asked Higgins. "I never sent you a gun yesterday."

"Well, your office did. And you hit the jackpot."

"On what, for God's sake?"

"Karpis, you dumb cop. This Colt's the gun that killed her. I told you it was a Colt."

Higgins stared at the telephone. "Just a minute," he said. "Jimmy?"

"What's up?" Sergeant Lake looked in.

"The lab says we sent a gun up there yesterday, a Colt .32. You know anything about it?"

Lake looked surprised. "That's right. You brought it back after you went out on that call to Central Receiving. You left it on my desk and I assumed you wanted it sent to the lab, I sent it up. Why?"

"Well, for God's sake!" said Higgins in astonishment. "*That*— Well, I will be Goddamned! That Bell? On P.A. back east? But what's the sense in— My God!"

Landers went with him on that. Bell was still in the hospital awaiting transfer to jail and eventually the extradition to Illinois. The doctor said the dope was out of him.

They found him sitting in bed, in the clean jail-issue clothes here in the guarded wing, leafing through a magazine. He looked up as they came in. "More cops. So all right, you pick me up, I get a free trip back to Chi. Who're you? I got nothing to say to any more fuzz."

"Whether you say anything or not, I don't think you're going back to Chi," said Higgins conversationally, hands in pockets. "Where'd you get that Colt we found on you?"

"None of your damn business. I know I don't get it back." He gave them an insolent grin.

"No, you don't. It'll be Exhibit A in a homicide trial, Bell. Why'd you want to shoot Linda Karpis?"

The grin vanished and he sat up with a jerk. "How the hell did you know—" He shut up abruptly. He looked wary.

"Oh, you stupid idiot," said Landers, "nobody would have known, but you had to get high on the Mary Jane and got tagged as a public nuisance. Naturally we had a look at the gun on you. And the nice lab evidence says it's the equalizer that took off Linda. Why did you, Bell?"

"Oh, Jesus' sake, that puts the damn lid on!" He went on swearing, monotonous and unimaginative, until Higgins told him to shut up. "Damn it to hell! She ran out on me, that little bitch, I was gonna get even if I had to wait twenty years—I nearly got her once, with another gun, and she got me sent up for it—"

"When did she run out on you? She'd been out here for three or four y—"

"Five," he said sullenly. "We was only married six months, after she divorced that other guy—she ran out on me, cleaned out the bank account and every dime I had on me, and runs out. I got a notice she's got a divorce in Nevada. That little bitch, takin' every man she can con—I swore I'd get even with her—"

"Out on P.A., you get hold of the gun and—where'd you get the money for that and the plane ticket?"

"Heist job," he said unwillingly.

"And how'd you know where she was?" asked Higgins.

"Oh, hell," said Bell, "I know a girl back in Chi still wrote letters back 'n' forth with her. All I had to do was follow her, once I—I rented a car—"

And Landers said to Higgins, "My God, we forgot to give him his rights!"

They were still talking about that, and Higgins was typing the final report, when Palliser came in with nine witnesses on the railroad collision. Mendoza came out to see what the commotion was about, and stayed to help get the statements down. Two of the witnesses spoke only rudimentary English and he took their statements, trying to stem the tide of repetition and dramatics.

That took them up to noon, and by the time they'd got all the statements typed and the scrawled signatures down, it was past one when the witnesses straggled out. "Someday," said Mendoza, stretching, "we're all going to drown in a sea of paper, boys. Let's go have some lunch. At least all that took my mind off those damn Dutch police—and the bureaucrats, damn them."

When they came back from Federico's at two twenty a new one had gone down—body in a flophouse on the Row. Resignedly Palliser and Landers trailed out on that; Higgins hadn't finished the report on Bell. Hackett was back then, and got on the teletype to Chicago to break the news that they couldn't have Bell back: a homicide charge, and murder one at that, took priority.

Mendoza, looking at the clock every five minutes, was practicing stacking a deck and muttering about Dutchmen and bureaucrats.

At three twenty Sergeant Lake looked in and said, "The desk wants you. You'll be interested."

Mendoza raised his eyebrows and picked up the phone. Thirty seconds later he barked, "I'll be there *pronto!*" He dropped the phone and ran. Hackett went after him curiously.

At the desk in the main lobby downstairs, the duty sergeant was nursing a female handbag on the desk. He nodded at Mendoza and Hackett, and tilted his head in a gesture beyond them. "I heard about your little mystery on the grapevine, Lieutenant, and when I saw the initials on this I thought it might interest you. This is Mrs. Valencia and Juanita."

Mendoza and Hackett turned.

Sitting on the bench along the wall was a pretty young woman staring fearfully at them. Her dark hair was neatly combed to a huge round knot on top of her head, and she was obviously wearing her best clothes —a very much starched pink cotton dress and white sandals. Sitting beside her was an equally solemn and fearful little girl about six, in a stiff white cotton dress and black leather strap shoes over long white stockings. They sat there expectantly, silently, and watched the men with twin pairs of big dark eyes. They were out of earshot of the desk here, but they watched.

"*¿Qué?*" Mendoza looked at the bag. "*¡Carape! ¿Qué mono?*" The bag was a medium-sized envelope of black patent leather, looking new; and on its flap it bore two gold metal initials. R.D. "Oh, isn't that nice." He looked at the two on the bench, smiling; he went over there. "Mrs. Valencia?"

"*Sí.* Please, sir, my Juanita did not mean nothing wrong. Is only a child—six year. Please, we are honest people, we don't steal, we don't have nothing to do with—"

"You'd rather speak the Spanish," said Mendoza in that tongue, and she flushed prettily.

"You are Mejicano! Yes, I thank you, sir. My husband Carlos, he is American, he says I must learn to speak the English better, and I try.

Because now we are all Americans. Since I married Carlos and come here as his wife, it is seven years. I am of Durango, sir—"

"Yes. And you brought this in?"

She swallowed nervously. "It is Juanita, sir. I do not like her to play near the railroad track, I have said she is not to do this. But you know how children are—and it is this reason, when she finds this little bag, she does not tell me or show it. Only today did I see it, and I asked her—she is only a child, sir, she can say only that she found it beside the railroad, and took it for the pretty things in it—she did not mean wrong, sir, and I have spoken to her very severely, she tells me she has taken nothing that was in it, but put all back—"

"No hope of prints, Luis." Hackett handed him the bag and smiled at Juanita, who did not smile back.

"Mamacita, do the policemen put me in prison?" she asked in Spanish, a thread of whisper.

Hackett squatted down in front of her. "Little girls as pretty as you," he said in his accented Spanish, "don't go to prison. But you're an American, as your mother says, you must practice the English."

"Yes, sir. Papa says, too." Her eyes were still solemn.

"But don't you go mixing them up. You see the Lieutenant there?"

"Mejicano p'liceman."

"Well, he's got a pair of twins about half as old as you and they don't know the difference at all, you know that?" Mrs. Valencia laughed and he smiled at her. "It's a fact. Talk half and half all the time, and it's sort of confusing."

"One would certainly think so! You see, Nita, the policemen are very nice and nothing bad will happen. But you must never do such a thing again."

Mendoza said, "You'll like a ride home in one of our cars. Where do you live, Mrs. Valencia? Wood Court? Mmh, just a short block from Azusa—"

"You are very kind, sir."

When he'd seen them off Mendoza carried the bag up to the office and contemplated it pleasedly there on his desk. "A very pretty thing. I said it matched her shoes, didn't I? Almost a new bag, in excellent taste. Let's see what's in it."

What was most obviously in it was the jewelry. A big costume leaf pin, gold metal; a pair of gold button earrings; her plain little set of wedding ring and engagement solitaire, and an old-fashioned garnet and pearl ring. "That's fourteen karat. Probably a grandmother's or aunt's."

There was a clean handkerchief, a dollar bill tucked in a side pocket, a green enameled compact filled with loose powder, a clean powder puff, a lipstick labeled apricot coral, a comb, a tiny pillbox with four white tablets in it— "Aspirin," said Mendoza—and a keyring with several keys on it. There was a full pack of Benson and Hedges cigarettes in a leather case that took a whole pack, and one of those disposable lighters, nearly full. Mendoza said happily, "Isn't that nice?"

"I can't see that it takes us any further," said Hackett.

"It confirms our deductions, Arturo. She was going out somewhere, with somebody. She—"

"Schoonhorn?"

"That is the silliest damned— No, of course not, *imbécil*. She was being driven, so she didn't need her driver's license, all the workaday appurtenances in her billfold, credit cards and so on. She took a modest amount of mad money, enough for a bus fare if she should get stuck somewhere. She took a good supply of cigarettes, and her makeup, and naturally her keys. And that was all."

"She was being driven, I suppose, in the big, big car."

"At some time she probably was. It's possible she was killed in it," said Mendoza.

"At least we know she was killed. Take it from there. I suppose Juanita couldn't show us exactly where along the railroad tracks she found that."

"No, and it doesn't matter. The clothes weren't far from the tracks. As I said before, it's a funny mixture of cunning and simplicity. He took off the clothes and her jewelry to delay or prevent identification—though neither could have helped us much, at that. Either he saw that most of the jewelry was worthless or he wasn't interested in robbing her. He wouldn't get much on the good pieces—that diamond is about fifteen points—call it fifty bucks from a pawnbroker. So he drops the jewelry into the purse, drops it a little farther along the tracks from the clothes, and goes back to the big car. We know he isn't familiar with the streets down there, you remember he turned the wrong way on Azusa, hit the dead end and had to turn and come back. And we can have a guess that sometime early the next morning, before Mrs. Moreno went into her back yard to bury her garbage, Juanita came wandering along and found the bag. Didn't notice the clothes, admiring the pretty things in the bag."

"I'm with you so far."

"But that's as far as we go." Mendoza put everything back into the bag and frowned into space. "Where this damn Schoonhorn comes in— and nothing from the Dutch police yet, my God—"

"Well, they said they were pursuing inquiries," said Hackett. "At some place called—that struck me funny. They said Schoonhorn had worked lately at some place called Venlo. Why—"

"Eindhoven is apparently the nearest large town, I looked it up on a map," said Mendoza. "But why the hell it's taking them so long—"

He arrived home, however, to a peaceful house. The all-but-homeless calico and her four kittens had been removed by the Pet Pride people to one of their excellent shelters, and it was guaranteed that the best of homes would be found for them. The Mendoza cats had prowled and sniffed suspiciously over every inch of the garage before being assured that the low-bred strangers were indeed gone. They had all come in, eaten enormous meals, and were now heavily asleep in various places in the living room.

"What a relief!" said Alison. "I've been feeling like a pariah, the way El Señor was looking at us—" The twins came shouting down the hall.

"Daddy, Mama bring us *cuentos nuevos!* See, the big *Guerrero* with a *espada muy grande!*" Johnny displayed a big green book insistently. "Read *los cuentos!*"

"I got it at the library," said Alison. "You and Máiri both saying—"

Mendoza took the book, *"Gaelic Tales from Myth and Legend."* Well, well. I said, they ought to be given a well-rounded background, to complement their—mmh—unusual collection of genes. All right, *niños,* I'm game, come on."

With the twins settled expectantly in bed and Mrs. MacTaggart folding away clean laundry in dresser drawers, he opened the book and looked at the title page. "Who's *el Guerrero* with *la espada?*" demanded Johnny.

"I don't know yet, *hijo.*" Mendoza looked with some dismay at the subtitle and made a gallant stab at it. "Stories of Fionn mac Cumnhaill and Cuchulain of Emain Macha." Mrs. MacTaggart made a slight moaning sound. "Now," he said, turning pages. "Here's the story of Cuchulain and Conchabar the Ard-Righ—"

Mrs. MacTaggart said firmly, "No. I realize ye're not conversant with the Gaelic, but that's no the way to pronounce it."

"It's the way it's spelled—"

"No. 'Tis Kuk-hoo-lin, and Connor the Ard-Ree, that is the High King—there are letters inside the word ye don't pronounce."

"Then what are they doing there?" Mendoza looked down the page, aghast. He said, "What the hell? Briccrui? Aoife? Cathbad? Eoghan mac Turacht? What is this, Chinese?"

"Och, now—" Máiri looked pained. "The Gaelic has just a few peculiarities, as you might put it—that'll be the Irish for Eve, and merely Owen MacDura—"

"Tain Bó Cualnge?" said Mendoza in horror. "How am I supposed to read this mishmash?"

"Quelgny," said Máiri firmly.

"*Quelgny?* What kind of language is—"

"Well, it will have a few peculiarities, as I said." Mrs. MacTaggart came and removed the book from him gently. "I'm thinking the twins are just a bit young for those old tales about Cuchulain, him and his young women and all—and you'd best be letting me read about them if need be." In fact the twins, uninterested in grown-up colloquy, were squabbling happily over a stuffed cat.

"I think so too. My God, I never saw such stuff," said Mendoza. He stalked out to find Alison rocking with laughter in the hall. "Well, it's gibberish," he said. "Complete—"

"It only s-struck me," said Alison weakly, "that you didn't have any trouble the other night, with Cihuacoatl and Mictlantecutli and Quetzalcoatl—"

"Well, damn it, I know how to pronounce them!" said Mendoza. "I thought Irish names were Murphy and O'Brien and Patrick—"

She leaned on the wall gasping. "And Tezcatlipoca—"

"I think I need a drink," said Mendoza.

On Thursday morning, with Hackett and Higgins off—Higgins probably practicing on the camera—the first call came in at eight thirty. Palliser and Landers went out on it; and Landers had made the joke about Higgins and Grace, yesterday, but parent or not, that kind of thing reached you. They looked at it sickly, incredulously; the job sometimes showed them the very worst muck at the bottom.

The dead baby, wizened and blue and starved, left in the cheap rented room in an old house on Alcazar Street.

"They was only here a couple weeks," said the landlady vaguely. "Gave the name o' Benson. Left last Tuesday. I didn't get round to comin' up here to clean the room till today."

There were things to do on it. They called an ambulance, got a mobile lab truck over. There wouldn't be much hope of prints here, but they had to try. Landers said, "Just as well Higgins doesn't have to look at this."

* * *

Higgins had indeed taken some more snapshots; but then he went out to buy Mary a birthday present. He thought, something special. He drove up to Robinson's Department Store in Westwood, and looked at houserobes. He remembered once hearing her say, while she was still working, before they were married, what heaven it was to come home and get into a robe.

The one he bought for her was starry-night blue, long, slinky nylon jersey with a gold tassel on the front zipper, and it cost more money than he should have spent, what with the hospital bill. He had it gift-wrapped and gave it to her when he came home for lunch.

"George!" she said. "Robinson's! How much—"

"Well, it's only money," said Higgins.

Mendoza was listening to what Palliser had to tell him about the new one—one thing this job taught them, depressingly, was that Homo sapiens hadn't progressed very far upward in quality—when, at twelve ten and at long last, there arrived a cable from Rotterdam.

It said: "Info obtained authorities Eindhoven Schoonhorn still in employ Van Kuypers as chauffeur police Eindhoven state excellent local record Van Kuypers one of oldest aristocratic families in country wife daughter Baron Van Renselaet Van Kuypers said to be traveling abroad with son Schoonhorn accompanied as servant chauffeur. Detail evidence linking homicide prior background obviously nullifies."

"Obviously nullifies!" said Mendoza wrathfully. "The beautiful set of latent prints! And Goddamn the Passport Agency! This is *nada absolutamente*— Wait a minute. These aristocratic Van Kuypers, he's with them—him and his international driver's license. All right. Is it logical to say they landed in New York? Airport or harbor? Damn the customs or the Passport Agency, ask there—"

"No," said Palliser, "it's not necessarily logical. That just says, 'traveling abroad.' They could have gone to the Orient first—or the Caribbean—and entered anywhere, San Francisco to Miami."

"You are so right," said Mendoza savagely, lighting a new cigarette from the stub of the last one. "But—they're here now. That we know, don't we? Or were here, a week ago Saturday, because Schoonhorn was here." He took up the phone and told Lake to get him an outside line, that Golden Bowl Restaurant. "The high-class European travelers," he said. "Mr. Schilling, please . . . Mr. Schilling? Lieutenant Mendoza. Will you do something for me, please? Will you look back in the reservations made there for—oh, six weeks or two months back? You're looking for a Bernhard Van Kuypers and party. That's right. Let me know if you come across the name."

"But," said Palliser, "so what? If these high-class Europeans did go to dinner there? They wouldn't invite the waitress to dinner later on."

"I know, I know. We just have to look where we can—"

And he was just back from lunch, with Grace supplying the only cheerful conversation, both Palliser and Landers feeling fairly grim about that baby, when Lake put through an outside call.

"It's Mrs. Yelverton. Sounds agitated."

"The manageress at Rebecca's— Yes, Mrs. Yelverton? Mendoza here."

"I thought you ought to know," she said. "The phone's been ringing like anything in there—Mrs. Dantry's apartment. Ordinarily I wouldn't hear it, of course, but I've been busy in Fifteen right next door, they just moved and I've been checking over what needs doing. I hire the heavy work done, but— Well, anyway, that phone's been going off every half hour, yesterday and today, ringing and ringing—"

"*Vaya*," said Mendoza thoughtfully. "Thanks very much for telling us. I am interested, yes." He put the phone down. "It's ten—twelve days. Since Rebecca Dantry died. If she was in the habit of corresponding often with the family, they'll be getting worried by now, *de veras*. I wonder—that could be Mama or sister Lilian trying to get in touch. And it might give us a shortcut."

"How do you mean?" asked Palliser, who had just come in with the initial report on the baby.

"I'll bet you against any odds," said Mendoza, "that she told Mama and/or Lilian all about Johnny. Damn, I should have asked Mrs.— what's her phone number? Never mind—" He dialed four-one-one and got the phone number of the Dantry apartment. He got the supervisor. "This is police business—Lieutenant Mendoza, Central Homicide. A call has been put through to this number," he read it off, "repeatedly in the last two days. Possibly a long-distance call. I'd like to know the origin of—"

"I'm sorry, sir, you'll have to clear such an inquiry with the regional supervisor. If I may have your number—"

"Hell!" said Mendoza. "Red tape!"

CHAPTER 14

After a little argument with the supervisor, Mendoza got her to accept Rebecca Dantry's phone number. Ten minutes later she rang back. "I'm sorry, sir, it is impossible to trace an uncompleted call. If a long-distance call was dialed direct there would be no record immediately av—"

"Hell," said Mendoza; and he should have figured that out for himself. "Well, damn it, we know these people were here at least up to a week ago Saturday. Jimmy, get a hotel check started. You can start with the obvious ones—there's money—the Century Plaza, Sheraton West, Hilton—and go on from there. Damn it, if there was some—" He stopped in the act of flicking the desk lighter and said, "*¡Santa María! ¿Sabes una cosa?* I'm an imbecile—a cretin—I've got no business sitting at this desk. My God, the Post Office! Why didn't we—"

"Oh," said Palliser. "Oh, my God, yes, the mailman—"

Mendoza was reaching for his hat.

The Post Office which would sort and deliver mail to Rebecca Dantry's address was the central Hollywood Station on Cole Street. The badge got Mendoza in to see the postmaster, who agreed with him calmly. "You said she'd lived at this address for three years? Well, the regular carrier would probably notice this and that. It's a while since I walked a route, but you do. If this woman corresponded with anyone frequently, probably the carrier could tell you what city she got regular mail from."

That would narrow it down, at least. Mendoza waited impatiently while the postmaster went away to look at schedules. When he came back fifteen minutes later he said, "Afraid you're out of luck, Lieutenant—at least temporarily. The regular carrier on that route is Henry Danton, and he's on vacation. They've gone back east to visit his parents."

"Hell!" said Mendoza, but not so violently as he might have thirty seconds before; he was again telling himself he was an idiot. The most obvious thing—why hadn't it occurred to any of them? He thanked the postmaster and drove up to Cole Place. Mrs. Yelverton answered his impatient ring and stared at his question.

"Why, yes, there's been mail. So many of these catalogues and all, these days, and letters too—it began to pile up, I finally took it in."

He pawed through the stack looking for personal letters, for postmarks. There wasn't much but, as the manageress said, unsolicited ads and catalogues. She'd been killed the night of the sixteenth, and this was the twenty-eighth. Very likely the family wouldn't have been alarmed at not hearing from her for a week or so: but when had they heard from her last?

The first postcard was dated the twentieth: last Wednesday, that was a week ago yesterday. And the date was all he could make out: the cancellation was right across the stamp and the postmark was a black smudge. The card bore just a line: "Are you all right? Haven't heard from you in nearly two weeks, please write. Lilian."

The second card was a little more useful; and the two constituted the only personal mail in the pile. Its date was illegible; the message was in a different hand. "Dear, do write, we've been worried at not hearing from you, is everything all right? Mother." But—he peered at the postmark. It was smudged and smeared, but he held it under a strong light and said, "Can you make anything out of this? The *ville* I can just make out, and about four letters ahead of it—"

She agreed, peering. "It looks something like a V at the start of it, I think—"

"Vacaville!" exclaimed Mendoza. "Vacaville—it's got to be, Somethingville upstate—"

And why the hell he hadn't thought of the Post Office before—

And of course it only narrowed it down. But he looked up Vacaville in the atlas and found its population listed as thirteen thousand and something: not a city. Even when they didn't have a name, it should be possible to trace the family of Rebecca Dantry there. He fired off a teletype to the Chief of Police there. Probably he wouldn't get an answer until tomorrow.

The answer was waiting on Friday morning: a laconic promise to check it out.

The Van Kuypers had not showed up as registered at any of the better hotels here for two months back.

"All right," said Hackett, "there are the hell of a lot of hotels, take in the whole area, Luis. Don't be insular. You think, Los Angeles, the Century Plaza and so on. But there's that classy big one in Pasadena, even classier ones in Beverly Hills, Santa Monica. And if they're driving —which it looks like they are, with a chauffeur along—some of these new big motels—"

That widened list would take a while to check. And Marian Greenbaum should be home this weekend, and with any luck Marian Greenbaum, said to be Rebecca's closest friend, knew something about Johnny. But about Schoonhorn?

"¡Condenación!" said Mendoza. "So we wait some more. Have we got anything new to work? I haven't been reading reports since I got the brainstorm about the Post Office."

"That baby," said Hackett with a sigh. "John and Jase are trying to trace the parents—if they were the parents. I think the autopsy report just came in."

Mendoza found it and grimaced, reading it. The baby, a girl, had been around six months old, Bainbridge estimated, and had weighed only twelve pounds. She had died of starvation.

"Another one just called in. George went out to look at it, but he's got to cover that Slick inquest at ten."

The new body was just more routine, though Higgins felt tired looking at it. A kid about eighteen, flat on his back in an alley off Temple, eyes wide; there wasn't anything on him at all but a shirt, pants, and the needle marks in arms and thighs. Higgins let the ambulance take him and went back to the office to type the report before covering that inquest.

The press had been running headlines about Alfred Carmichael, rehashing the old and new tragic accidents, and Tamaris Holt had come in for some publicity too, and Alfred's new piece, a sharp-faced blonde. That was water under the bridge, thought Mendoza. Give the media something like Alfred, the dramatics and salacious gossip, they built the headlines: they weren't interested in Rebecca Dantry, that nice girl who had somehow fallen into the clutches of the evil ones. There had been only two stories in any newspaper: one about the discovery of the body, one when she got identified. Neither had been on the front page.

It was Friday afternoon before Johann Schilling called Mendoza. "I am sorry. I have looked back at all the reservations for the past month, the record isn't kept longer. This Van Kuypers name, it is not there."

"It was just an idea," said Mendoza. But the lead to Vacaville had to turn up the family.

They had been stymied on this one at every turn, it seemed: even the couple of leads they'd turned up seemed to be meaningless.

Nothing came in from Vacaville on Friday. The Passport Agency in Washington was unforthcoming. They were to have a polite letter from the Passport Agency nearly three weeks later, asking them to detail the particulars of what they wanted to know. Bureaucrats were all alike. But at eight forty Friday night, when Mendoza sat over a collection of MacKinlay Kantor stories doing more brooding than reading, the phone rang. "Say," said Schenke, "this police chief from Vacaville just called, wanting you. Chief Romero. I gave him your number . . . Quiet night so far, no new bodies."

Mendoza put the phone down and five seconds later it rang. "Romero?"

"That's right. What gave you the idea this Dantry woman's family lived up here?"

"Hell, was I wrong about that damn postmark? It was an educated guess, but—"

"*Nada*," said Romero. "We don't have many new people coming in, and I've been chief here ten years, I know most of the old-timers. I didn't know the name myself—Dantry, I mean, and I likely would have if she belonged here. But we checked—even farms around. Nobody knows her. Sorry."

"Hell and damnation!" said Mendoza.

But at noon on Saturday, with Farrell sitting in for Lake, the thing finally started to break. Mendoza was on his way to lunch when Farrell stopped him with a gesture and pointed to the phone. He fled back to his office and picked it up.

"—The officer in charge of the case, miss. Lieutenant Mendoza," Farrell was saying.

"Mendoza here."

"I don't know if you know my name, Lieutenant—Marian Greenbaum." Even over the miles between, it was a clear contralto voice, sensible, steady, and yet still holding overtones of shock and sorrow. "I—"

"At last," said Mendoza. "Yes, Miss Greenbaum. I take it you've heard about Rebecca Dantry. How? We understood—"

"Yes," she said. "Yes. It's Mrs. I'm a widow too, it was one—sort of bond— I simply can't imagine who—I've been up here at Arrowhead for two weeks, and you know you don't bother about newspapers, on vacation—but just th-this morning I was in the lobby when the man was bringing in a pile of old ones—for the fire, and I—the name just jumped at me, and it was Rebecca's address—I couldn't believe it, but— Do you know *who*—"

"No, we don't, Mrs. Greenbaum. We're hoping you can give us some answers."

"Me? I don't know anything— There's nobody would have a reason to hurt Rebecca! Nobody—and— But I don't understand, Lieutenant, why you—I called the family, I didn't have any idea they didn't *know!* The paper was *days* old—I'm afraid it was a dreadful shock to her mother, they'd been worried because she always wrote at least once a week, and they hadn't heard a thing— They were going to go right down. Scott has his own plane and he can fly them d—"

"Scott."

"Lilian's husband, Scott Carson. But, Lieutenant, I don't understand —they were angry and I don't blame them—when you found out who she w-was, why didn't you notify—"

"We didn't know who or where," said Mendoza. "The other people here who knew her all date from her married days or right here, and none of them knew her maiden name or where the family lived."

"It was Constable. Oh, my God, I see—of course—"

"And you were out of town."

"I still am—I'm at the Arrowhead Inn. I'm leaving to drive down now. But who would do such a terrible—"

"Mrs. Greenbaum, can you tell me—had Mrs. Dantry recently met a man named Schoonhorn?"

"*Schoonhorn?* Why, no, not that she mentioned to me. Oh, dear heaven, when I think, I left to come up here the very day she must have been killed. It doesn't seem possible—when she hadn't had any more out of life—" She gave one harsh sob. "I'm s-sorry. I just thought you—the police—should know that her family is coming—"

"From where?"

"What?" she said, and then, "Oh, Roseville. It's just north of Sacramento—"

"¡Ca!" said Mendoza. He'd been right about the number of letters, anyway. "We'll be very glad to see you, Mrs. Greenbaum. But meanwhile, can you tell me anything about a Johnny who seems to have been interested in Mrs. Dantry?"

She breathed into the phone for ten seconds and then said forcefully, "Has *he* got something to do with—? Oh, my God, I *told* her no good would come of— Oh, my God!" The receiver crashed in his ear and she was gone.

There was no telling when any of them might show up. Sometime later today, with luck.

And Jason Grace and Palliser were still out trying to get some lead on the people, if you could call them that, who had left the baby behind. They had traced Mr. and Mrs. Benson to a bar down the street from the rooming house, where the bartender said reflectively that that female had known how to pour it down, all right; but that was as far as the trail led. Higgins had got that teen-ager identified; it had been, of course, an overdose of heroin. Aside from another accident on the freeway, two D.O.A.'s, nothing much had turned up to occupy their time, and they were all in the office at three forty when Marian Greenbaum appeared, and on her heels the family, or most of it. Mrs. Constable had been ordered into the hospital by her doctor; she had a heart condition. Rebecca Dantry's father, Lilian and her husband had flown down from Roseville.

Constable was inclined to be truculent; just why hadn't they been informed—

Mendoza explained. They looked taken aback. Constable was obviously much shaken, his face drawn with grief. Rebecca had, Mendoza thought, looked like her sister: Lilian was little and blonde too, and she had been crying; she clung to the hand of the tall fair young man who was Scott Carson, and he looked angry.

"And listen, Lilian—Mr. Constable!—" Marian Greenbaum was a tall, dark, vital-looking girl, just now her face ravaged with shock and grief. "They think it was something to do with that Johnny—isn't that what you meant?" She swung on Mendoza.

"We don't know. I'd like to know anything you can tell me about him," said Mendoza. Hackett and Higgins had come in silently, and he introduced them. "Who is he?"

"But that can't be," said Lilian. "Rebecca said he's the kindest soul— not that he'd be the right husband for her. But he was persistent, and she—"

"Who is he?" asked Mendoza. They all started to tell him at once, and he stopped them, got up and lit Marian's cigarette for her. "You knew about him?"

"Yes—what Rebecca told me. It was just a silly little thing at first, and then— But she didn't really think seriously about it for ten minutes. Marrying him, I mean. Well," she sighed, "we can't deny that money—it does enter in. But not at the—the expense of other things. But you don't think *he*—"

"Tell me about him, *por favor*," said Mendoza patiently.

"Well, but— Oh, well. These people went to dinner at the restaurant, Rebecca waited on them, and he seems to have fallen in love with her at first sight. He was waiting when she left work that night—she was late, she said, nobody around, and she was frightened for a minute when he came up and then she saw he was—oh, quite the gentleman. He introduced himself, begged her for a date. She turned him down, of course. But he found out her address, followed her she supposed, and he kept turning up and writing her notes and— Well, she was flattered. Any girl would— I never laid eyes on him, but the way she described him he's good-looking—"

"What she wrote home"—Lilian emerged from her handkerchief— "when she got to know him, she liked him, but not to marry. He was just a nice boy, she said—an enthusiastic boy. A—"

"Enthusiastic about Rebecca," said Hackett, getting out a cigarette, and about to ask if Johnny had been jealous.

"Oh, but— You see, that was another reason she was sympathetic to him—until he got so terribly persistent about begging her to marry him—" Marian put out her cigarette and at once got another one from the pack, turning it round and round in her fingers. "He was so in love with America. He wants to stay and be a citizen. He'd met some American students at the college he went to, and he'd been crazy to come here ever since. He was—she said—just mad about America, knows all sorts of American history and things you'd never expect a foreigner to know—"

"A foreigner," said Mendoza. "Where—"

"He wanted everybody to call him Johnny, because it's an American name—she wrote that," nodded Lilian. "The l-last letter we had—it was dated the ninth—she said she was afraid she'd have to be pretty plain with him, that she didn't want to marry him, because he was being so— well, taking it for granted."

Marian nodded. "That's right. And she was so thankful—that was the last time I talked with her on the phone—he was going off on some trip with these college friends, he'd be gone a couple of weeks, and she'd be rid of him. I mean, she felt sympathetic, but—"

"Do you know his n—"

"But how could he have anything to do with—what happened? She didn't want to marry him but he's a nice young man, kind and—he wouldn't—"

"His name?" asked Mendoza rather loudly.

"Why, certainly," said Lilian. "Jan Van Kuypers. He's Dutch, and the family has scads and scads of money—which was the only reason she even thought about it for ten minutes. But after the really happy marriage, she said to me, you don't settle for less. She and Dan—you don't often get an ideal marriage like that. She'd kept all their things, you know, wedding presents and all they had together—left it all with Mother and Dad, her marriage license and— But she said, with this Jan it'd be more like being a nursemaid than—"

"Do you know where we can find him—and his parents, I understand they're here too?"

Marian stared at him. "But what could they possibly have to do— Well, they're staying with some people here. In fact, we were all quite impressed—" She laughed unsteadily, a hand to her cheek. "Rebecca attracting— It's a big producer, that Len Diamond, his son was one of the Americans this Johnny met at—I think it's somewhere in Bel-Air—"

"¡Cómo!" said Mendoza. "And how very simple once we know! And, damn it, a big producer won't be listed in the phone book. How do we get there?"

"Pressure on the studio," said Hackett briefly. "Urgent police business." He got up. "It's Ace-Star Productions, I think."

They left Palliser and Grace taking the formal statements. They'd get Rebecca's letters sent down for photostating later. And Hackett was saying, "But it's still a rigmarole, Luis. This impulsive young fellow being persistent with the nice girl—quite the gentleman—what the hell? He wouldn't—"

"Schoonhorn," said Mendoza, stepping on the accelerator and making an intersection on the amber. "Where the Van Kuypers are, Schoonhorn will be. Or close by. And it is Schoonhorn—"

It was a big Mediterranean house, set in a quarter acre of landscaped ground; it had a circular drive, and parked in front of the house was a new and gleaming black Lincoln Continental.

"The big, big car the Gomezes saw?" said Higgins.

A neatly uniformed maid answered the door. "Mr. Diamond, please," said Mendoza. She stared at the three badges and vanished without a word, leaving them to look in at a generous square tiled entry hall with a few expensive pieces of Spanish furniture. Two minutes later a man came to them from a door to the right. He was short, slightly plump, with strongly-marked Semitic features, and he looked at the badges and said, "What did I do?" He was wearing expensive sports clothes.

"Nothing as far as we know," said Mendoza. "We're interested in your house guests. The Van Kuypers."

Diamond uttered a heartfelt moan, and reached to shut the door into the inner room. "This is the absolute last straw!" he said. "That these—these—*people* would bring police on me! Enough is enough! Look, you like to be friendly, nice to people, no? Polite? My God, I'm polite! Look, fellows, a long time ago my father says to me, Lenny, don't you ever do anything so any man can say, a Jew did that to me. I'm an honest man, I like to think I'm a good citizen, but enough is enough! What'd they do, go shoplifting or something?"

"Or something, we think. How do they happen to be here?"

"Because I'm polite," said Diamond angrily. "My boy Milton, he wanted to go to Europe to college, a year or so, be interesting, he says. I got the money, he goes. This is four-five years back. To Leyden University he goes, and he meets this Johnny. Now Johnny's all right, a nice boy, you understand. A little young for his age maybe. I like Johnny—he's crazy about America, wanted to come here all his life. So now the whole family comes, see the whole country—I don't know where they've been, toured round the East before they landed here. And me, I have to be polite, ask Milt's friends to stay while they're here. Fellows, you don't know what I put up with! Milt says maybe they'll stay a week, two weeks. Two months yet! And all they talk about, this pair of—these *people,* is what grand ancestors they got, nothing but barons and counts, and how much money, and all Americans low-class peasants—living on me all the while, and they've got good appetites, not to mention that dumb Dutch driver—and if they'd realized Johnny's friend was a Jew—not to me they don't say that, but to each other. So what the hell kind of name they think Diamond is? And so much I take, but—"

"Are they all here now, Mr. Diamond?"

"All four of them," said Diamond, scowling. "My wife's fit to be tied. She says if I like getting insulted at my own table I can put up with it, but she won't. She's gone to visit her sister in Brooklyn. Johnny—I don't say anything against Johnny—he just came back today, he and Milt and a couple of Milt's friends went on a camping trip up in the Sierras."

"We'd like to see them," said Mendoza. Diamond looked at them and shrewd speculation was in his dark eyes.

"Something's up, no?" He nodded once, and opened the door to the next room. "Papa and Mama are in there guzzling canapés and my liquor before dinner. Do you want that dumb driver too? He'll be in the kitchen eating already, and my houseman threatening to leave if he has to listen to him snore another night."

"Get him," said Mendoza, "please." Diamond gave him a half-salute and went away down the hall.

Mendoza went into the enormous living room, his two senior sergeants behind him. The Van Kuypers were there. Bernhard Van Kuypers was a big man with a round red face and little greedy eyes. His wife was thin and angular, platinum-gray hair in a complex coiffure, and she had an arrogant long nose that cleaved the air like a ship's prow.

"And who may you be?" said Van Kuypers in a thick accent.

Before Mendoza could show him the badge, a clear young voice came from the hall. "Papa, you will tell Mr. Diamond I don't stay for dinner—I must see my Rebecca, tell her all about—"

"Jan Van Kuypers?" Mendoza swung to him as he came in.

"I am, yes, sir." He stared at the badge in Mendoza's hand. He was a big, boyish-looking young man, in his early twenties but with the same look about him that Landers had, the fresh complexion making him look younger than his years. He was nearly handsome; and he was dressed almost aggressively in American clothes, sports shirt, slacks, jacket, a leather *bolo* tie.

Mendoza turned and showed the badge to the elder man. "Police, if you aren't familiar with—"

"I can English read. What do police do here? The Jew robs somebody, eh?"

"Our business is with you, I think."

Van Kuypers swallowed the last canapé from the handful he'd been gobbling and turned a contemptuous shoulder. His wife looked down her long nose.

"So you're going to see Rebecca Dantry?" said Mendoza to Jan.

"She is my—we are to be married. What is it police—"

"I'm afraid not," said Mendoza gently. "She's been in a cold tray at the morgue for two weeks. She was strangled and stripped and left naked in what you'd probably call a slum. And she wasn't going to marry you anyway."

Naked shock and disbelief convulsed the boy's face. "Rebecca—you are saying—Rebecca is dead—is—" He went paper-white and swayed a little.

"Here he is," said Diamond from the door.

They turned to look at Schoonhorn.

He'd taken on a little weight since that description had been written. He was growing a paunch, and he had lost most of the blond hair. He was wearing the lower half of a navy-blue uniform, his shirt collar open, and he'd been eating, was still wiping his mouth.

"Pieter Schoonhorn," said Mendoza pleasedly. "Do you understand English? You do. Then you'd better listen to this," and he read off the bit about his rights. "Do you understand that?" Schoonhorn looked puzzled; he had dull china-blue eyes without much intelligence showing. "Would you care to tell us why you murdered Rebecca Dantry two weeks ago tonight? Strangled her, stripped her and left her—"

"Oh, my God!" said Diamond. "My God—"

Schoonhorn took a step forward and said something in Dutch to his employer. And young Van Kuypers uttered an anguished, wordless roar and lunged forward to seize him by the throat. Hackett and Higgins pulled him off. He struggled and then went limp in their hands, and he looked at his father and the hate and incredulity and fury were live things in his eyes. And he screamed at Schoonhorn, nearly spitting the words, "Say it in English, the policemen understand! Say it, say it, what you say just now—you murdering pig, you filth—"

Schoonhorn stepped back from him; he looked vaguely frightened. He licked his thick lips. He said, looking at the older man, "But the Mynheer said no one would ever know. The Mynheer said it was safe—"

Jan Van Kuypers began to cry; he sank down in an armchair and wept. "My Rebecca—my darling—she would marry me, she would—and to stay here in beautiful America, all my life—"

"My God in heaven," said Diamond.

They took them all in. Young Van Kuypers was taken over to Central Receiving in shock. After listening to the other Van Kuypers' opinions about police, America, and American customs, and the importance of the Van Kuypers wealth and ancestry, Mendoza took some pleasure in saying, "They'll keep. Overnight. In jail." Mrs. Van Kuypers was trying to work up to hysterics when he left.

In the end, they got statements. They got one from Schoonhorn with no trouble at all; he was anxious to explain just how it had been.

"The Mynheer is a very important man," he told them. "Lots of money. Big house, servants. He thinks Jan is crazy, want to come here. But Jan is always talk, talk, talk about America. So the Mynheer says they will all come, so Jan does not make the foolishness with bad American girls or be fooled by robbers." They were to find out that

Van Kuypers, expectably, kept the purse strings tight and controlled all the money. "All the time he is saying what a terrible place, people all low-born ignorants. I like all right—plenty good food! But we come here, Jan he meets this girl, right away says he's going to marry. The Mynheer, he is very angry—so is Jan's mama. They say, this low-class American, ignorant, waiting on tables like servant—and she's been married once yet, these Americans always divorcing, immoral—"

"Yes," said Mendoza, making a steeple of his long hands. "So?"

Schoonhorn shrugged a massive shrug. "The Mynheer says, she makes fool of Jan, just for money. He pays her much money, she goes away, but he don't mean to waste money like this. She is nothing, she's nobody important at all. When Jan goes away with these others, the Mynheer says, we get rid of—*kaput,* no trouble. The Mynheer talks with the telephone at this woman, invites to dinner, says Jan's mama and papa like to meet, he will send me—the driver—to bring her."

Hackett let out a long breath. "I see," said Mendoza. And he thought of Alison saying, she dressed for something important. So she had. A rather difficult little interview, from Rebecca's viewpoint. She would have known that the parents disapproved of Jan's projected marriage; Johnny had, of course, led them to think it was all arranged. She'd had no remote idea of the strength of their prejudice; but the vagaries of prejudice are unlimited, and she'd have realized, ruefully, that the news that she wasn't at all interested in Johnny as marriage material would perhaps have annoyed them even more. Their important heir with all the aristocratic genes—and the money to come. Mendoza looked at his cigarette. The nice girl had fallen into evil hands all right, but it was the evil of stupidity.

"You called for her at her apartment," he said. "When and where did you kill her?"

The man blinked. "Waste time drive off with?" he said. "I open the door for her get in, take her throat behind." He flexed big hands. "I have killed people. In the war, we killed many, silent, from behind, like so."

"And you'd looked in the paper, found that empty house—"

He looked bewildered. "Paper? I don't the English read good. The Mynheer tells me, drive this place, bad, dirty part of city. Be sure nothing with name, label on. Nobody will ever know. Nobody will care about her, she is nobody." He looked at them, a little pained. "How do you find out?"

*　　*　　*

They got nothing from Mathilda Van Kuypers. They couldn't prove she'd known anything about it.

From Bernhard Van Kuypers they got contempt. "She was nothing— what is the family? Poor nobodies, no money. It is Pieter who has made her dead. What crazy story he tells you, I don't know about. Maybe he is in love with her, eh?" He chuckled soundlessly. "Make up all this. This crazy boy Jan, he finds out about his fine America—money, it does not go to jail in any country. We take him home, he's maybe cured of his craziness."

"I think you may find out," said Mendoza meditatively, "that it's not so easy as all that to bribe even an American judge and jury. Even these degenerate days."

"You talk insolent," and red flooded into Van Kuypers' fat face. "You *verdammt Lateinischer—*"

Mendoza sat up straight and gave him a wolfish smile. "And some other blood too, with more iron in it than you soft Northerners ever had, if we're talking about genes."

Aristocrats! Alone in the office, he started to laugh.

But it wasn't, of course, funny at all.

Not to Rebecca Dantry, or the people who mourned her.

"You don't mean—just because they thought she was on the make—" Angel stared at Hackett indignantly. "Boasting of being aristocrats, and she was—"

"Just a low-class American. I wonder if they'll nail Van Kuypers too. The courts—"

"But of *all the impertinent—*the *gall—*the impossible arrogance—I never *heard* of such a—"

"Look out," said Hackett, "that pot's boiling over. Too." Angel flounced around to turn down the burner, and Sheila tottered over holding up her arms. He picked her up.

"How's Daddy's own Sheila? Oh, George had another batch of snapshots today. And she is a cute one all right, but not as sweet as my Sheila—"

Angel didn't say, *Men.* She was resolving to put out the flag every day, not just on holidays.

"But that's *wanton,*" said Roberta. "Just—get rid of her, the low-class American. And she wasn't going to marry him at all, didn't want to. John—you know—" she looked at him dangerously. *"That makes me mad!"*

"Oh, yes," said Palliser. "Yes, doesn't it. I wonder if the D.A. thinks there's enough to charge Van Kuypers too."

"I certainly hope so," said Roberta vindictively. And got up suddenly from the breakfast table and said, "Oh, damn—this *baby*—" and fled. She had just developed morning sickness.

"It's wicked," said Mary. "Will they get him for it too, George? Van Kuypers?"

"Up to the D.A. I hope so. Luis thinks so." Higgins wound the film up to where it said One. "A hell of a thing all right."

But it was just another piece of muck at the bottom they saw on this job. The aristocratic arrogance be damned; that, in essential analysis, was just more of the stupidity.

Higgins smiled fondly down at Margaret Emily, squirming and cooing after her bath, and the Van Kuypers went out of his mind.

Released from the hospital on the day his father and Schoonhorn were arraigned on a charge of murder one, Jan Van Kuypers took out the rented Lincoln Continental and ran it and himself over the palisades cliff in Santa Monica. It made quite a mess.

"And you can say he was foolish, and weak, and even silly," said Alison, "but it all seems so—unnecessary and tragic. Fate?"

"Human nature," said Mendoza. He was stretched out on the sectional, shoes and tie off. The cats were back to normal after the invasion of the low-bred strangers, and at the moment the offspring were asleep. Cedric drowsed at Alison's feet.

"That man," said Alison, "saying such things about America! I think we ought to fly the flag every day, not just—"

"The really comic thing," said Mendoza sleepily, "about people like Van Kuypers is that the only thing they've got to boast about is ancestors—who are all dead. Tragic? Human nature, my love—the tragedy and joy and comic together. Especially the comic."

But the comedy didn't often come the way of Central Homicide, L.A.P.D.

The phone rang down the hall. Alison was still muttering. Mendoza removed El Señor from his stomach, stepped into his shoes, and went into the hall.

"Mendoza."

"We've got a funny one showed up," said Schenke, "I thought you might like to come look at it from the start. It looks just a little offbeat, and Nick said—"

Mendoza reached to button his collar, yawning. "I'm on my way," he said.

NO
HOLIDAY
FOR
CRIME

But human bodies are sic fools
For a' their colleges and schools,
That when nae real ills perplex them
They make enow themselves to vex them.
—Robert Burns

Let a bear robbed of her whelps meet a man,
rather than a fool in his folly.
—Proverbs 17:12

CHAPTER 1

"I can just hear the whole force laughing at me," said Lieutenant Goldberg, formerly of Central Robbery and Theft LAPD. He squinted up dolorously from the hospital bed.

"Don't be such an egotist," said Lieutenant Mendoza, formerly of Central Homicide. "We're too busy to think about you, and you're nearly over it anyway."

Lieutenant Goldberg's last investigation for Robbery and Theft had been a case involving stolen goods smuggled across the Mexican border. The stolen goods had been a dozen cagefuls of exotic tropical parrots, and Goldberg and one of the San Diego detectives had subsequently succumbed to parrot fever.

"It's a judgment on me," he said gloomily, "for laughing at you when you caught the measles from the twins. Have you caught up to that burglar yet?"

Mendoza's grin gave way to a scowl. He stabbed his cigarette out in the ashtray on the bedside table. "Set me chasing burglars—I might as well be riding a black-and-white again," he said. "No, we haven't."

"They say it's a sign of age," said Goldberg, "when a man can't adjust to change." He sneezed and reached for Kleenex.

"¡Vaya al diablo!" said Mendoza amiably. "I'm not the old dog learning new tricks—that'll be you, and I wish you joy of working under Pat."

"Don't be petty, Luis," said Goldberg. "The Jews and the Irish always get on fine. So what about that houseman—has he pulled any more jobs?"

Mendoza stood up and yanked his cuffs down automatically, straightened his tie. As usual he was dapper in gray Italian silk, snowy shirt, discreet tie, his hairline moustache neat. "That nurse said ten minutes. Well, if it's the same boy, yes, he has, but I'm not sure of that, and we've got no leads at all. Don't remind me. And don't offer any suggestions—it's not your job any longer."

"Oh, well," said Goldberg philosophically, "you can't win 'em all. At least I'm getting out of this damned place tomorrow. Thanks for dropping in, Luis—say hello to the gang, hah?"

"You'll be adjusting to change in no time," said Mendoza. "Merry Christmas, Saul."

"And a happy Hanukkah to you, Luis."

Waiting for the elevator, Mendoza thought about the burglar and frowned. Change be damned, he thought. Doubtless they'd settle down to it, but to be dealing with housebreakers like any team in a squad car— *"¡Por mi vida!"* he muttered.

Change had come to Central Headquarters LAPD in the name of greater efficiency after the powers that be had discussed and decided. Los Angeles might boast the top force anywhere, but it was also the smallest police force any city of size possessed. Keeping it at top performance, the changes sometimes came. Robbery and Theft had been dissolved as a separate department, last month, and the new bureau of Robbery-Homicide created; that was the major change, but there'd been a few others. Captain Medina had got shot up by a hood a couple of months back, and retired a year early, so Pat Callaghan had got his step in rank and Goldberg was transferred up to an expanded Narco bureau, with most of the men from his old office. Mendoza had inherited Robbery's policewoman, Wanda Larsen—he couldn't imagine why, there wasn't much for her to do—and a couple of men, Detectives Rich Conway and Emil Shogart. With that small addition to staff, Robbery-Homicide now covered all theft and death on the Central beat, and these days that could be quite a job; as usual, they were busy.

Getting into the big black Ferrari downstairs, Mendoza glanced at his watch. Two-fifteen; he'd stopped to see Goldberg after lunch. In another six hours it would be officially Christmas Eve: a mild, clear December Sunday: one time, like a few others in the year, when police officers got reminded that the hoods and crooks didn't take holidays off. Alone of all the men in the office, Sergeant John Palliser would be off tomorrow: to the others it would be just another day, hopefully a quiet one. But there were always cases to work; Mendoza reviewed what they had on hand at the moment, heading back toward Parker Center.

The hijacker. Inside information there?—not necessarily. In the last three weeks three trucks ferrying expensive cargoes of liquor from warehouses to retail stores had been hijacked. It was a job difficult to get leads on: there were a lot of restaurants and bars in L.A. whose owners might jump at getting a few cases of liquor at a cut rate.

The burglar and/or burglars. That case—if it was a single case—had got underway back in November before the departmental changes. It looked (said Goldberg's records) like the same M.O., in a vague sort of way. Six hits, four apartments and two single houses, entry made through windows, and the places picked clean of all possible loot: at one place he'd even taken an obsolete set of encyclopedias, at another a cheap cigarette-making machine. Otherwise, a run-of-the-mill burglar, working evenings, and no lead on him at all.

The latest teen-age body full of the acid, found in an alley along Main, not yet identified.

The hit-run along Wilshire four days ago: a vague make on the car, the first two letters of the plate-number. The victim had been an elderly pensioner on the way home from a Christmas shopping trip.

A couple of service station heists, no leads on those either. The rate on that kind of thing always rose in December, people needing money for Christmas shopping. He could only return thanks that the hordes of shoplifters were dealt with on a lower level as a rule.

And, of course, the new one just reported this morning . . . Parking the Ferrari, Mendoza grinned to himself. That one ought to belong to Bunco—the victims having only themselves to blame.

Upstairs, he found Sergeant Lake studying a new paperback on dieting. At least the powers that be hadn't asked them to move: they'd given Robbery-Homicide another corridor of interrogation rooms and a second communal detectives' office across the hall: four more desks and typewriters. The new sign pointed the way just beyond the elevators.

"Anything new, Jimmy?"

"Nope," said Lake. "Not much. Art found that Elphick, where Dakin said he'd be, at work. He's talking to him now. John and George are out on that gas station heist, and Jase just came back from somewhere—"

As if conjured up by his name, Detective Jason Grace rushed out of the old sergeants' office. "Hey," he said excitedly, "hey, we did it! We've got her! Ginny just called—the agency just called her to—we can have her right now, today! Oh, by God, but that's the best Christmas present we'll ever—" His chocolate-colored face wore a broad grin. Matt Piggott and Henry Glasser, just coming in, heard that and they all beamed back at him.

"That's great news, Jase—congratulations," said Lake, swiveling around from the switchboard. The Graces had been sorting through the red tape with the County Adoption Agency since August, trying to get little Celia Ann Harlow, so unexpectedly orphaned by that wanton killer.

"Say, look—if I can take off now—Ginny says they say we can *take* her right now, this afternoon—just some more papers to sign, and—" Grace was excited.

"Go, go," said Mendoza. "Merry Christmas, Jase."

"It surely will be!" said Grace, and vanished precipitately toward the elevators. They looked after him, smiling.

"And for the baby too," said Piggott, his long dark face serious. "Cute little thing. At least some good news to brighten the day. Listen, I'm not sure it's the same boy pulling all these break-ins now. The one on Friday night, he didn't find some cash this Moon had stashed away, and everywhere else, the place was picked but clean."

"*¿Qué?*" said Mendoza absently. "Well, as Saul reminds me, we can't win 'em all." He went across the hall to the new office, where Sergeant Hackett sat at his desk talking to a nervous citizen.

"Mr. Elphick," he said to Mendoza. "Lieutenant Mendoza." He shifted his bulk in the desk chair and sighed. A recent bout with flu had, happily, reduced him by thirteen pounds and he was trying to stay there by skipping lunch.

"Listen, I dunno why Al hadda go and tell you guys about that. He dint have no call," said Elphick aggrievedly. "Look, it was only about four bucks, and hell, you guys make me go in court, evidence, that bit, my wife'll give me hell—listen, can't we forget it, huh?" Mr. Elphick was about forty, shabbily dressed, and needed a shave.

"Not necessarily court, Mr. Elphick," said Hackett. "We'd just like a description to add to Mr. Dakin's. Come on, just tell us what happened and where."

"Oh, hell," said Elphick unwillingly. "It was only about four bucks, I let it go—I wasn't hurt any. I make good money, you know construction pays good now—and my wife—Al dint have no call drag me in on it—he was just tellin' me what happened to him and I said I bet was the same lousy pair conned me, and when—"

"Yes, yes," said Hackett. "From the beginning, please."

"Well, hell," said Elphick. "My wife— Well, I know Al just casual, see, we worked on a couple jobs together, and we both drop into this place sometimes, see, this Irish Bar. He was tellin' me about it yesterday, this dame give him the eye and he, well, like makes a deal with her, and she leads him down this alley, says it's a way to her back door, and this guy strongarms him and picks him clean. He was mad—"

Al Dakin had been mad enough, on thinking it over, to come in this morning and tell his story to cops. Al Dakin, however, was a bachelor.

"So, let's hear a description," said Hackett.

"My wife'd go straight up in the air," muttered Elphick. "Oh, hell. Well—well—the dame was kind of medium, not tall or short—she's got a lot of black hair, and one o' these little real short skirts—I never got a look at the guy, he jumped me from behind, I guess he was hidin' behind a trash-can or some place—he's kind of big, all I could say— And look, if you expect me to go in court, just forget it, I'm not about to—"

"All right," said Hackett. "Any guess at the woman's age?"

"How'd I know that? She's young, I guess—looks maybe twenny-five—" He shrugged. "Dames, all the makeup and all, I wouldn't say—"

"Any further on?" said Mendoza when they'd let Elphick go. "And any guess how many victims haven't reported it?"

"Oh, don't be silly," said Hackett. "A Mrs. Stone came in a while back and wanted to look at that body, said it might be her nephew by the description of his clothes. Shogart took her down to the morgue—"

"And is now," said Mendoza, "bringing her back, I would guess." A wailing female voice came nearer up the corridor.

"But why did it have to be Johnny? Why—all this awful dope—those fiends who make the kids use this awful—" A burst of sobs, and Shogart's deep phlegmatic voice.

"If you'll just sit down, Mrs. Stone, and try to—I know you're upset—"

Policewoman Larsen hurriedly crossed the hall from her desk. This was the kind of thing Policewoman Larsen was there for, presumably, but it didn't happen often.

"Merry Christmas," said Hackett tiredly.

"Nothing new, Arturo. *Se comprende.* Anything more on the hijacker?"

"*Nada.* I had that last driver down looking at mug shots, but what can he tell us? The fellow had a ski-mask on, same as the other jobs. People!" said Hackett. "And we haven't even got the tree up yet, with this damn flu going through the whole family—"

"*¡Tenga paciencia!*" said Mendoza cheerfully. "We could be busier. And you haven't heard about Jase—" Hearing about that, Hackett looked a little happier; Palliser and Higgins came in to hear that, and smiled.

"Good news, all right. Say, Luis, come to think I haven't had a

chance to show you the latest snapshots—" Inevitably Higgins reached
for his breast pocket and Hackett uttered a mock groan.

"Dangers of late marriages—at least I will say, Luis, you never
foisted all the snapshots on us—"

But Higgins was busy passing them out, his craggy face fond. "Isn't
she a doll? And smart as they come too—even at just three months
she—"

They grinned covertly at Higgins, looking at the latest snapshots of
Margaret Emily. Higgins the longtime bachelor, so unexpectedly falling
for Bert Dwyer's widow, had been pleased enough with his secondhand
family, Bert's kids Steve and Laura; now he was still a little incredulous
that he and Mary had a firsthand daughter. Well, she was a cute baby.

"You just wait till April," said Palliser. "We'll outproduce you,
George." And he was still feeling amused at the joke Fate had played
on his Robin, starting a baby when she'd planned to be a working wife.
"It's a handful of nothing on that heist, by the way. Stanton couldn't
give us any description."

"Helpful," said Mendoza. "Burglars and heist-men—¡condenación!"
But he had had to admit that the change had been, in a way, a logical
one; on a beat like Central's, the robbery and homicide were so often
connected.

"It was just one man, and that ties it in loosely with that one last
week," Palliser went on. "But even that isn't sure, because—"

"Lieutenant—" Lake poked his head in the doorway, looking resigned. "A new body. Of all places, over by the museum in Exposition
Park. One of the maintenance crew just found it and called in."

"¿Y cómo no?" said Mendoza. "All right, Jimmy. Come on and do
some legwork, Art."

Higgins went along too, while Palliser started a follow-up report on
the heist of last night.

Exposition Park was a complex of buildings out on Exposition Boulevard, a generous tract squared by Figueroa Street, Santa Barbara Avenue, and Vermont. There were the famous every-variety-known rose
gardens: the Armory, the great Coliseum, the Sports Arena, the L.A.
County Museum of Natural History, and in a separate building, the Science and Industry Museum. Turning in the narrow avenue from Figueroa, the Ferrari nosed up past the Science Museum where a little
knot of men gathered. The ambulance hadn't come yet.

They showed their badges. "One of you called?" asked Hackett.

"Yessir, I did—I spotted it first. Ben Bates is my name, Officer, I'm

1ead o' the maintenance crew here, and one thing I tell you right off, she can't've been here long, not more'n a few minutes. We been cleanin' floors today—look, Sunday, usual we'd be open, but day before Christmas, a holiday, it ain't. Open, I mean. We been doin' the floors, this building and over in the other museum—and I only got over here about half an hour ago, figured start on the top floor anyways before we knock off for dinner—I come in the front way with my key, right up here, and she wasn't there then—" He was a big stocky man, excited and upset.

Mendoza and Higgins had parted the little crowd and were looking at the corpse.

"And then about twenty minutes later, I come back out to go help Bill fetch over that heavy polisher—and there she was! And I figured—"

It wasn't a very big corpse: a slight girl with blonde hair, sprawled limp just at the curb where the walk led to the building steps. Mendoza squatted over it.

"No handbag," said Higgins, fingering his prominent jaw. There was no cover for twenty feet around: just pavement. "Poor girl. Seems—well, I don't know. Christmas Eve." She was lying on one side, and from what they could see she'd been middling pretty: small pert features, fair skin. The short well-shaped nails of the hand outflung from the body were carefully manicured, painted pale peach. "Not raped?"

Mendoza shook his head. "*No sé,* but it doesn't look like it. Strangled at a guess." There were marks on the girl's throat. He picked up the hand. "Did she fight him at all? Her nails are too short to have a guess. She's still warm, she can't be an hour dead."

"But right here in broad daylight—" Bates was still shaken. "Poor young lady—who coulda done such a— Not half an hour ago I come right by here and she wasn't— It was when I come out after I'd unlocked the other door for—"

The ambulance came purring up, and the attendants came to look. You want photographs, Lieutenant, or shall we take her?"

Mendoza stood up and lit a cigarette. "What for? There's just the corpse. I don't need a crystal ball to guess what happened. She was moved out of a car, already dead. But let's have a good look all through the grounds for her handbag." He surveyed the scene. "He couldn't turn around here, not even if he was driving a Honda. He'd have to go up to the Coliseum before he'd have space to turn. None of you heard a car?"

"Heard a car? In the grounds like? With all that traffic out there a block off?" Bates shook his head. "How'd anybody notice the difference? No, I didn't see a car nowhere in the grounds, all day, except our own cars over there behind the other building." It developed that the other five men had been occupied with the floors at the Natural History Museum during the short time the corpse could have arrived on the scene.

"All right," said Mendoza. "Let's try up by the Coliseum first." Hackett and Higgins started up there in silence, each taking one side of the narrow drive, peering at the ground. "You can take her," said Mendoza. And everybody knew that Luis Rodolfo Vicente Mendoza was a cynic from the word go, but as the ambulance men lifted the small body to a stretcher, he thought, Christmas Eve. She couldn't be older than the early twenties. Her clothes were good, a brown tailored suit, lemon-colored blouse, rumpled now; he noticed that the skirt was a modest length for these days, just covering her knees. One low-heeled brown shoe had come off. "I'll want her jewelry." There was a ring on one hand, a necklace.

The ambulance left, and he drove the Ferrari up to the Coliseum gates. "Any luck?"

"Not so far, and there's not much cover. You think he just drove in the handiest spot empty of people and dumped her?"

"That's what it looks like. So he may have dumped her handbag too." There wasn't much cover here, or back there where the corpse had been: what shrubbery there was, formal and low-growing. Hackett was pacing up to the left where a walk led around the Coliseum to the various gates, Higgins up to the right. "I don't think," said Mendoza, "if he did dump it here, he'd have got out of the car—it probably wouldn't be—" But Hackett had suddenly pounced.

"He didn't bother to turn around, Luis. He came round the Coliseum and drove out on Hoover. Dumping the handbag as he went." Mendoza and Higgins had hurried up.

"And just the shapeless kind of thing that's a real bastard to work," said Higgins.

It was almost certainly the corpse's handbag; it matched her suit, a capacious dark brown leather bag with several compartments. Hackett lifted it delicately by thrusting his pen under the double straps. "Any bets on prints?"

That, of course, was the first thing to look for. Mendoza used the phone in the Ferrari to call up a mobile lab truck, and when it arrived Scarne dusted the entire outside of the bag. Latent prints always offered them a shortcut, but only if there were any liftable ones present. This time, as so often happened, there weren't.

"Smudges," said Scarne sadly. "Sorry."

"Way the cards fall," said Higgins. "It's still going to help." Then they could open the bag. They took it back to the office, to look at the contents; as usual with any female handbag, there were quite a few. They spread them out methodically on Mendoza's desk.

A blue billfold with a change pocket; there was forty-seven dollars and fifty-eight cents in it. In the plastic slots for cards and photos, an I.D. card: Lila May Askell, an address in Santa Barbara. In case of accident notify Mr. Edward Askell, an address in Salt Lake City. Snapshots of, probably, family groups: a couple of girls in their late teens or early twenties, an older couple, a young man. A library card for the Santa Barbara public library. A California driver's license good for another two years. A gasoline credit card.

One used and two clean handkerchiefs. A large gold compact full of loose powder. A clean powder puff. Three lipsticks, two nearly new: Coral Glow, Peach Glow, and Cherry Frost: different brands. A bunch of keys on a ring. A paperback novel, *Neither Five nor Three* by Helen MacInnes, with a paperclip probably marking her place about midway through. A small bottle of aspirin. A two-page letter signed *Mother*. A small unopened package of Kleenex. A ballpoint pen.

And in the zippered center compartment, they found a Greyhound Bus line ticket from Santa Barbara to Salt Lake City, with changes indicated at Los Angeles and Las Vegas.

"She was on her way home for Christmas," said Hackett. "We'll ask, but she probably had a layover for her bus here."

"Let's go and see," said Higgins. There was still part of a working day left: it was five-fifteen. The night watch would come on at six—right now, Tom Landers, Rich Conway, Bob Schenke and Nick Galeano, an expanded night watch as their job had been expanded. Any indicated legwork that could be accomplished they could take over: not much, tonight.

And now somebody had to call Mr. Edward Askell of Salt Lake City, to tell him that without much doubt his daughter was dead here. Murdered here. Why and how? Echo answers, thought Mendoza; he pulled the phone toward him, lighting a new cigarette, and told Lake to get him headquarters at Salt Lake.

A captain of Homicide there took what information Mendoza could give him, said they'd be in touch with Askell. "You'll want an identification, I suppose. Soon as possible. Shame, on Christmas. Well, I'll take care of it. You might give me your office number—he'll probably want to call."

Outside, the sudden dark of tropical places had descended. It was officially Christmas Eve. Mendoza went out and across the hall. "I understand you got that teen-ager identified," he said to Shogart.

Shogart looked up from his typewriter. He had been a fixture in Goldberg's office for years, and phlegmatically accepted the change to a new superior: a heavy-shouldered dark man in his forties, another plodder like Piggott. He detested his Christian name and was known by his initials to anybody he called friend. "Poor damned female," he said. "Just another fool of a kid getting hooked on the dope. By the time the aunt found out, too late to do anything. Boy's parents are dead, she'd raised him. Seemed like a reasonably respectable female—widow. Shame she had to find out on Christmas Eve. Though any time—" He shrugged and went back to the typewriter.

Mendoza scratched and yawned. "Unions," he said.

"So what about them?"

"Not for cops any more than the pros. No holidays—just the routine going on forever."

Shogart grinned. "We need our heads examined, all right."

"But I am now going home," said Mendoza.

He went home, to the big Spanish house on Rayo Grande Avenue in Hollywood, to his late-acquired hostages to fortune. Redhaired Alison was supervising the twins' supper while their jewel, Mrs. MacTaggart, put the finishing touches to dinner. Alison, hearing him come in the back door, flew to greet him.

"Thank heaven you weren't late—we'll get them to bed early and start on the tree, I've smuggled everything into the hall closet—"

The twins erupted at him. "Daddy, *Mamacíta* reads a new *cuento* all about *La Navidad—y San Nicolás—*"

"—With *el ciervo* that come when it rains—*la lluvia,* an'—"

Mendoza burst out laughing. This was going to be the first Christmas that the twins, three in August, would really take deep interest in; but Alison's attempts to impress them with traditional Yule stories had evidently met an obstacle in that the twins were still oblivious to any difference between Spanish and English.

"No, Johnny—*El Reno,* I told you," said Alison. "Go and finish your supper now, *querido*—your father'll read to you later—"

"Johnny is silly," said Miss Teresa solemnly. "*I* know 'bout *El Reno. El santo* come in a *trineo*—Mama says—"

"Now, my lambs," said Mrs. MacTaggart briskly, "you come and finish your nice suppers." Their accidentally-come-by sheepdog Cedric ambled up to offer Mendoza a polite paw; the four cats, Bast, Sheba, Nefertite and El Señor, had hardly looked up from their plates in the service porch. "Let your father catch his breath now. You'll be wanting a dram before dinner—" El Señor understood English and abandoned his haddock to demand his share of rye whiskey. But Mendoza shook his head.

"*Nada*, Máiri. It seems I'll be too busy." He kissed Alison again and she cocked her head at him.

"Tough day, *amante?*"

"The usual. I must be getting sentimental in my old age." Luis Mendoza, for his sins, had put in twenty-four years as an LAPD officer. "*Feliz Navidad, mi corazón*. I'm just feeling sorry for Lila Askell, who didn't make it home for Christmas—and I wonder why. I think I'll have that drink after all, Máiri."

El Señor floated up to the drainboard and received his half-ounce in a saucer.

"Oh, and the Graces have got the Harlow baby—the County relented finally this afternoon."

"How wonderful—the nicest Christmas present anybody could—Luis, you haven't brought the office home with you?"

"Not really," said Mendoza. "We'll get the tree up after—"

"Shh! It's going to be a surprise, they were too little last year—"

Hackett found Angel in their bedroom frantically wrapping Christmas presents. "That damned flu—I got all behind, and I meant to get these fruitcakes ready weeks ago—"

"The County gave Jase a Christmas present," said Hackett. "They've got the Harlow baby."

"Oh, Art, how wonderful! I'm so glad—yes, the baby's fine, all cured, thank goodness, and— For heaven's sake," said Angel suddenly, "get *out* of here, I've got all your presents to wrap—"

And four-year-old Mark and twenty-month-old Sheila came shouting about Santa Claus; Hackett laughed and went to pick one up in each arm.

Matt Piggott and his Prudence had just been married in September; they had an apartment on Rosewood Avenue, but Prudence was house-hunting. Prices now—but a police officer was reckoned a good risk, and that, reflected Piggott, was just plain crazy. As the devout fundamentalist Christian he was, he thought the craziness was just more of the devil's handiwork.

But as he drove home he looked forward to telling Prudence that the Graces had at last got the Harlow baby. As a kind of unexpected Christmas present.

And when Higgins came home, to the house on Silver Lake Boulevard, Steve Dwyer had a new set of snapshots to show him, just picked up at the drugstore. Steve had definitely decided to be a professional photographer since Higgins had got the Instamatic to take pictures of the baby.

Mary said resignedly, "Between you and Steve, George, it's going to take all my time to keep her from being a well-spoiled brat, you know that."

"Now, Mary." Higgins picked Margaret Emily up from her crib.

"And she *was* asleep—"

"I think she's awful photogenic, George," said Steve seriously.

"Let me hold her, George," pleaded Laura.

Margaret Emily, awakened, began emitting regular loud bellows. "Honestly, George! I'd just got her settled down—"

"Oh, the Graces got the Harlow baby. The County called this afternoon—"

"Wonderful," said Mary, necessarily raising her voice over the bellows.

The tree had been up, shiningly decorated, for a week, and a multitude of wrapped presents waited under it.

"The County just called this afternoon," said Palliser, "and Jase took off—never saw a happier man—"

"What a nice Christmas present." Roberta smiled at him. "I'm fine, don't fuss, John—since I got past the morning sickness, I'm fine."

There was a tree up at the Pallisers' too, in the living room of the forty-thousand-dollar house on Hillside Avenue, and presents under it in gay foil. Of all the men of Robbery-Homicide, Palliser would spend Christmas Day at home.

Theoretically, the boss could too; but he probably wouldn't.

Tom Landers came into the office a little late, on night watch, and found Rich Conway there alone reading a paperback. He and Conway had taken to each other at once; they were the same age and shared interests. Landers was still in pursuit of Policewoman Phil O'Neill down in R. and I., and Conway had recently been dating one of their girls too, Margot Swain who was stationed at Wilcox Street in Hollywood.

They'd set up a double date for a week from next Tuesday; they were both off on Tuesdays.

"Bob and Nick went out on a head-on, down by the Stack. More routine. Shame, Christmas Eve—two D.O.A.'s." Conway put his book down. He was a wiry dark fellow, lacking Landers' slim height; he had a long straight nose and a mobile wide mouth and the most cynical gray eyes Landers had ever seen. "Day watch didn't leave any loose ends, except this new body. Nothing to do on it, but Jimmy left a note—we might get a call from Salt Lake."

They did, about an hour later: a shocked and saddened citizen asking questions, where, how, why. They didn't know too much about the corpse; Landers explained about the need for identification. Edward Askell said, in fading tones, that he would come over at once, and hung up suddenly.

"Pity. Christmas," said Conway. Landers echoed him. It would be nice to be home for Christmas—up in Fresno with the family—but to cops, Christmas was just another day. He had a date to take Phil to Christmas dinner tomorrow; she hadn't any family here either.

Nothing showed to give them any work; they sat talking desultorily, until ten past nine when a couple of calls came in at once. Schenke and Galeano had come back by then, and finished a report on the head-on collision. The first call was from a citizen over on Alcazar Street, something about an assault, by what Landers could gather. The other was a body in a parking lot on Wilshire.

Landers and Conway drove over to Alcazar Street in Landers' Corvair.

"I don't know what it's all about," said the citizen, one Alfredo Ramirez. "The lady's all upset, looks like somebody's beat her up, I don't know, she comes ringing the doorbell, says please call cops—my wife tries to help her, she's bleeding— Look, lady, here are the cops, so you tell what happened—"

She was crouched on the sagging couch in the living room of this old frame house; she looked up at Landers and Conway slowly, and ordinarily she'd have been a nice-looking middle-aged woman, still a good figure, neat clothes, well-dressed; she was clutching an expensive mink stole, and her torn black lace dress looked expensive too, and her now-ravaged face had been made up. Incongruously, her quantity of mousy brown hair straggled about her face wildly, a stout hair-net still attached by one pin; and she raised a hand to her head and said suddenly, "My—my wig—my best wig—oh, I must look— But *Stanley,* what's happened to—"

Landers had his badge out. "If you'll just tell us what this is all about, ma'am."

There was a Christmas tree here, a small green tree on a table in front of a window, brave with gold tinsel and lights; and a few presents waiting under it.

"Oh, yes," she gasped. "Yes—he held us up—I fought him, I tried to— but he pulled me into the car—*our* car—there was a shot, and Stanley— my husband—we'd gone out for dinner, Roberti's on Wilshire—we'd just come out—"

Landers and Conway exchanged a glance. The state of her clothes, probably an examination for rape was in order. "Can you tell us your name, ma'am?"

"I'm Mrs. Stanley Macauley," she said mechanically. "Christmas Eve —we're having all the family for dinner tomorrow, it was easier to go out tonight—we'd just come back to the car, and this man—he had a gun —*Stanley*—"

"Did he attack you, Mrs. Macauley?" asked Conway gently.

She began to cry. "Yes—in the back of the car—I tried to fight him, but—when he let me out I just—the first house I saw—"

They called an ambulance. The doctor at Central Receiving said she'd been raped and mauled. She'd also been robbed; there had been about seven dollars in her purse.

When they got back to the office they heard from Schenke and Galeano about the other one: part of the same thing. A Stanley Macauley, plenty of I.D. on him, shot dead in the parking lot behind Roberti's restaurant on Wilshire.

"It looked like a small caliber," said Schenke.

Landers looked at the clock; it was eight minutes to midnight. "Merry Christmas," he said with a crooked smile.

CHAPTER 2

Christmas Day was sunnier than the day before, one of the mild blue-and-gold days southern California can produce in midwinter. The family men on day watch drifted into Parker Center late—just another day or not, it was necessary to watch the kids, big and little, open presents under the tree. Mendoza came in at a few minutes past nine and met Hackett and Higgins in the lobby. Upstairs, Shogart hadn't come in yet, but he had a long family ranging from a baby to a teen-ager; Piggott was in, reading a report, and Glasser was on the phone.

There wouldn't be much they could accomplish today anyway, except for reports and the most urgent witnesses; they couldn't chase down statements from witnesses or do any legwork today. Mendoza had told Wanda to stay home. They wouldn't need her. He wondered again why she'd been assigned to them.

Jason Grace came in in a hurry. "I'm late, sorry—we were pretty sure we would get her, but at that we didn't have everything—the crib, and enough blankets, and—we were out shopping to the last minute—we're having a party tonight— Say, what's that camera you got?" he asked Higgins. "I don't know much about it but we'll want pictures—"

Mendoza sat down at Palliser's empty desk and lit a cigarette, a report signed by Landers in his hand. "These Macauleys. Jimmy, get me Bainbridge's office."

Bainbridge wasn't in, but one of his bright young men, Dr. Amherst, had had a look at both bodies. "What about the girl?" asked Mendoza.

"Not raped, for ninety-nine percent sure—no interference. Knocked around and manually strangled, best I can do pending autopsy. Have you got her identified?"

"Yes, Doctor. We'll probably get identification on both the latest ones today—"

"Both?" said Amherst sardonically. "There are a couple more here, well mangled, and what looks like a wino from the Strip."

Mendoza hadn't got to the report of the head-on at the Stack. "Well, this Macauley."

"Never knew what hit him," said Amherst. "He looks like a healthy specimen, around fifty. All his own teeth and hair. The bullet got him square over the heart, and my guess is that's where we'll find it. There's no exit wound so it's still inside somewhere. Small caliber, but I'll tell you better after autopsy."

"You'll let us know about that? . . . Yes, Doctor, thanks very much." Mendoza asked for Central Receiving and asked about Mrs. Macauley.

"You want to talk to her, of course," said the doctor there. "Not yet, I'm afraid, Lieutenant. She's only just awake—she was rather heavily sedated. Say about one o'clock, she'll be able to talk to you. The family's rallied around, I understand—with her now. What happened to her husband? We just heard her story."

"He was shot dead," said Mendoza. "One o'clock, Doctor, thanks . . . That restaurant. Roberti's. Where is it, Art?"

Hackett picked up Schenke's report. "Just past the Ambassador Hotel. String of restaurants along there—"

"Not the kind of restaurants, *obvio,*" said Mendoza, "that have uniformed attendants in their parking lots."

"No. Or we'd have at least another witness. Seems funny to be writing reports on burglars, doesn't it?"

"Saul tells me it shows you're aging when you can't adjust to change. *Como sí.* Here's a note from Tom"—he'd just found it—"that Askell should be here sometime today. Anything else new in, Jimmy?"

"Not so far. There will be," said Lake prophetically. "On a holiday, with all the liquor flowing."

Mendoza looked round to hear Piggott say something about the devil. "Where'd Matt vanish to?"

"Somebody else's Christmas spoiled," said Lake. "Bob left a note on it—that head-on on the freeway. A fellow just came in to identify the bodies, Matt took him down." Glasser had wandered down the hall after coffee.

"Seems funny, writing reports on burglars," he said, sipping.

"The resistance to change around here—" said Mendoza.

"Now, Mrs. Macauley, do you feel well enough to answer some questions?" Mendoza sat down in the plastic chair facing her. She looked at him for a moment in silence. She'd be a nice-looking woman at a different time and place: now she'd been crying and her eyes were red and puffy and she hadn't any makeup on and looked her full age.

"At a time like this, I don't see why the police have to—" Young Mrs. Linda Swift looked at him angrily.

"Now, honey," said her young husband, Bill Swift. The rallying-around family consisted of the Macauley's married daughter, and Florence Macauley's sister and brother-in-law, a Mr. and Mrs. Hendry. "They want a description of this guy if she can give one, and as soon as possible—you can see that."

"Oh," said Linda.

"I'm all right," Florence Macauley said to Mendoza tiredly. "I see that, Bill. Of course. I just don't understand—why he had to shoot Stanley. He'd given him all his money. I don't understand why he had to kill him—just for no reason. No *reason*. Stanley saw the gun, he didn't try to put up a fight and maybe get us both—hurt. He gave him the money—"

"Just a minute, Mrs. Macauley. We'd like to have it from the beginning, just what happened. We've got the doctor's report, it doesn't matter about that part. When you came out of the restaurant—"

"I'm all right. Linda and Bill are going to take me home in a little while, the doctor said—" They were in one of the patients' lounges at the end of this corridor, a neat sterile place of plastic furniture and metal tables and few ashtrays. Mrs. Macauley was dressed; probably her daughter had brought her fresh clothes, for the ones she'd been wearing had been sent to the lab by now. She sat on a plastic couch and looked at Mendoza and Hackett wearily, and her daughter sat beside her and looked at them a little doubtfully.

"What time did you get to the restaurant?" asked Mendoza, to start her off.

"About eight, a little before, I think. Maybe a quarter to. We'd expected it to be crowded—we were late, but I'd been—getting things ready for—for today. The family dinner, you know." She swallowed and suddenly Linda sobbed once, and pressed a handkerchief to her mouth. "The tree's been up for a week, all the decorations, but all the last-minute things—I'd got the gelatin salad all made and the turkey ready for the stuff—I'm all *right*, Linda. I must tell them—all I can, so they can —try to find the man. Well, we'd expected a crowd there, but there wasn't. Not at all. But then Christmas Eve's—a sort of family time as well as Christmas Day, isn't it? So we were waited on right away, and Stanley had a drink—bourbon and soda—and he said I should too because I'd been working so—I had a martini—and then we had dinner. I don't know what time we came out to go home—" They knew by then that the Macauleys owned their own home up in Hollywood, had driven down to Roberti's because they both liked it, it was a nice place with good food. "It wasn't late, we didn't sit over dinner—maybe ten to nine."

"Yes. The parking lot's at the side and behind the restaurant." Mendoza had been there to look. "Now think about the lighting—where your car was." There was an A.P.B. out on the car, a four-year-old Buick sedan. "There are just a few arc-lights in the lot, it's not altogether dark. Did you—"

"He came from behind the cars," she said. "Stanley'd parked in the first line, nearest the building. He—he came out from behind the cars, there were about ten or twelve other cars there but nobody else—just Stanley and I—"

"You mean he'd been in front of the cars?" asked Hackett. "They were parked facing in?"

"Yes, of course. That's what I meant. It all happened so fast, I—I hadn't time to be frightened until— We both saw the gun in his hand right away. What? I don't know anything about guns. I don't think it was very big. He said to give him all our money—no, he said that to Stanley—and Stanley did. He gave him his billfold, and—"

"Can you describe the man at all, Mrs. Macauley?"

"I'll try. He was a Negro, but I don't think very black. Shabby clothes—dirty old clothes, like overalls. He was taller than Stanley— Stanley's five-foot-nine—and awfully thin. What? Oh, he was young—I'd say in the twenties, that's the best I—"

"Any accent?"

She shook her head. "Just, he spoke—you know, awfully rough, and he swore. Stanley gave him his billfold and I was frightened then, I tried to give him my handbag, but he threw it into the car and took hold of my arm and pulled me into the car with him—or started to, and Stanley said something like, what was he doing, and there was a shot, and he just—shoved me down across the seat and the next thing I knew we were driving away—"

"All right, Mrs. Macauley," said Mendoza. "That's all we'll ask you right now—"

"Oh," she said suddenly. "And he smelled—I just remembered that— he smelled like a—a gas station. All oily, you know, his clothes and— when he, I mean later when he—"

"Mmh," said Mendoza. "All right, thanks very much. If you think of anything to add to that description—" She was blinking away tears. Mendoza caught Hendry's eye and moved away to the window. "You understand, Mr. Hendry, we have to get a formal identification of the body. Could you do that for us now?"

Hendry's lips tightened; he was a big stocky man, nearly as dapper-neat as Mendoza if a good deal fatter. "I see. Yes, sure, I can do that. The kids can take Florence home."

They took him down to the morgue and he made the formal identification. "Poor devil," he said above the corpse. "Stanley—the best fellow you'd want to meet. Only fifty. Just for—he wouldn't have had more than twenty-five dollars on him. And an animal like that—where the hell do they come from, Lieutenant? And damn what color they are —there was that gang over in West Hollywood beating that pensioner the other day—just *animals*—"

"I wouldn't dignify them by the word, Mr. Hendry," said Mendoza. "Even wild animals never kill wantonly. Only by necessity. Do you think your sister-in-law might be up to looking at some photographs in a day or two?"

"Mug shots," said Hendry, nodding. "In case you've got him on file. I think so. I'll ask her. She's a pretty level-headed woman, and after she's over the first shock—I expect she will be."

"We'd appreciate it very much."

Landers, in his newest suit and a tie even Mendoza would have approved, picked up Phil O'Neill at her apartment at four o'clock. "The captain said I could take off early, I did some overtime last night," she told him, shutting the door after them. Landers looked at her pleasedly. Everything was just right about Phil, that was all. Phillipa Rosemary— only not, as she said, for a lady cop. If she just wasn't so damned sensible about not having known each other long enough—

"You promised to be good," she reminded him.

"Oh, I am—I am," said Landers. "You just look good enough to eat." Her flaxen curls just reached his chest, despite her medium-high heels; she had on a plain navy dress with a big gold pin on one shoul-der, and a bright crimson wool stole: it was really very mild for Christ-mas Day.

"Where are we going?"

"New place—new to us, anyway. Is it too early for dinner?"

"You get all out of routine on a holiday. Can't be, anyway—you go on watch at six. I'll be ready for food when we get there, I skipped lunch."

"I won't get the axe if I'm half an hour late," said Landers comfortably.

Inexplicably, their favorite restaurants, all the six Frascatis', had closed. It was rumored that they'd been merged with a big chain. The new place was out in the valley, high in the hills above Burbank; it was called The Castaways. In a quiet and nearly empty dining room, they sat beside an enormous picture window that gave them a view right across Hollywood, the ocean-range of foothills, into the beach towns, on this clear a day. The light was rapidly fading in the sky.

"And on a really clear day you could see the ocean," said Phil, sipping her drink. And a moment later, "Oh, Tom, watch! It's just like jewels!" The sudden dark of midwinter was coming down almost within seconds, and all across that range of city and hill spread before them, the lights were flashing on, diamond-winking and colored.

"That's pretty good." Landers was fascinated too. They watched in silence until nearly total dark had fallen and the panorama of the city's sprawl of lights was complete. "It's clear enough now, on a night just after it'd rained that would be something."

"I hope to goodness," said Phil, sitting back, "it stays clear for New Year's. And as warm as this. Those poor girls on the floats—some years it's a wonder they don't all get pneumonia."

"Hey, don't remind me of that," said Landers in alarm. "The list won't be posted until tomorrow."

"Oh—" said Phil. "Have you ever got picked out of the hat?"

"Once—when I was a rookie. Just hold kind thoughts it doesn't happen again."

Phil's navy-blue eyes smiled. "I've heard rumors that the special rest rooms have meters that take a quarter."

"That's only one damn thing about it," said Landers, and turned to the waiter.

To the rest of the nation, New Year's Day may mean this or that; to L.A. County it means the Rose Parade and the big game in the Rose Bowl. An average New Year will attract the out-of-state visitors and bravest local residents to make a crowd of half a million for the parade; and for the hotelkeepers and merchants it means gratifying profit, but to the police only a large headache. It had been the practice for some time now that long lists of names from the Pasadena force, the LAPD, and the sheriff's department, were fed into a mechanized lottery-like machine to turn out a temporary force of men to police the parade and game. The unlucky ones whose names were chosen started the day at 2 A.M. at Pasadena headquarters for briefing; the plainclothesmen had to don uniform again, and they'd be lucky to stagger home by mid-evening. To complicate the traffic problems, there are only two main roads leading in or out of Pasadena.

"I'm just keeping my fingers crossed," said Landers.

"I'll hold the good thoughts." But Phil was entranced again by the view. "Tom, let's come here for that double date next week. Am I going to like this Conway—and the girl?"

"Conway is no business of yours," said Landers. "Not having met the girl, I couldn't say."

About five o'clock a fattish man of middle age came slowly out of the elevator and looked at the sign that said *Robbery-Homicide*. He stopped at Lake's desk. "Lieutenant Mendoza? I was told to ask—"

"Yes, sir." Lake buzzed Mendoza.

"I'm Edward Askell," said the man.

Taken into Mendoza's office and given a chair, offered a cigarette, he said, "Thank you, I don't smoke. I don't understand it. At all. It's a hard thing to say, God's will, and try to believe it. I can't. I can't understand how it could happen."

"We don't know much about it either, Mr. Askell. If you'd answer some questions about your daughter—we'll try to find out. But—you know I have to ask you to identify her body."

"So the captain said—a Captain Shearling—he came to tell us. All right. She was our oldest, you know. Three girls and a boy—and Lila was our first. She was a good girl—bright, quick, we raised her—the right way. In the church—"

Mendoza listened to more of that on the way to the morgue, with half an ear. Families didn't always know everything about pretty young girls.

Askell, it seemed, was a construction engineer; it wasn't a poor family background in any sense. And he identified the body without breaking down. He just kept asking, "Why? How could anything like this have happened to Lila?"

Mendoza would like to know too, for his own satisfaction. He took Askell back to his office. "If you don't mind some questions—"

"Anything," said Askell. "Anything I can do to help you. Her mother's—" He shook his head. "It's a hard thing to think, God's will. She was twenty-three, Lieutenant. I can't understand how a thing like this could happen to Lila. Some girls—wild, not brought up right—but Lila—" Dully, without being asked, he told Mendoza about Lila: Hackett came in, with Higgins behind him, to listen in silence. And it all sounded depressingly, from their viewpoint, as if Lila had been the nice modest Christian young woman he claimed.

The family belonged to the LDS Church, attended services regularly. Lila had never had a steady boyfriend, in high school or later. She'd gone out with several young men, but she'd never been serious about anybody, except for—but that was a while ago. She'd taken a course in therapy at a local hospital, she was an accredited hospital therapist, and that's what she'd been doing in Santa Barbara, working at a hospital there. She and another girl, a girl she'd known in school who'd taken the course too—Monica Fletcher—they'd seen the ad in some hospital newspaper, the job in Santa Barbara, and they'd thought it might be interesting, California and all. They'd been rooming together in Santa Barbara, Monica could tell them all about Lila and what she'd been doing recently, who she'd known. But so could the Askells, because she wrote home every week. She hadn't had a regular boyfriend here either, she'd been working hard at the hospital. She'd been homesick. She liked the job all right, she liked the money, but she didn't like being so far from the family.

"She'd just decided, you see," said Askell. "She called us on the twenty-third, in the morning. She said she'd decided to come home, it was the idea of being away from home at Christmas made her decide. She'd given up the job, it meant losing a week's salary but— She was all excited, and bound to get home for Christmas if she could." He stopped a moment, collecting himself. "She told us—she'd sent all our presents by mail already—they'd already been delivered—and she'd send most of her things on by United Parcel, so she wouldn't have much to carry with her. She said the first bus she could get was the morning of the twenty-fourth, it'd get her into Los Angeles about noon and she'd have to wait over a bit for the next bus to Las Vegas, but if she couldn't make it home for Christmas Day it'd surely be the day after." He stopped again.

"Was Miss Fletcher coming with her?"

"No. She said Monica liked Santa Barbara fine, but I guess—well, maybe her family isn't so, what they call close, as ours is. Lila was homesick."

"Do you think—" Mendoza wondered what to ask him. "She wouldn't have—mmh—picked up with any—"

"Of course not!" said Askell, not so much indignant as bewildered. "Lila was particular—choosy her mother calls it—about people. She was a—a serious girl, she took her job and her religion all serious. You mean, would she have walked off with some fly-by-night—well, of course not. What do you think happened?"

"Well, all we know is," said Hackett, "by what it looks like, she was thrown out of a car after she'd been strangled. But—"

"Lila'd never get into a car with some man she didn't know," said Askell. "That's just plain silly. It couldn't happen."

They exchanged glances. "Maybe it was somebody she thought she knew," said Hackett. "After all, it was broad daylight, Luis."

"She wouldn't have," insisted Askell. He looked at them anxiously. "Are the papers going to say that? Her mother—her sisters—"

"We don't give everything we know to the press," said Mendoza absently. "We'll do some poking around and see what turns up. You understand there has to be an autopsy?"

Askell nodded dumbly. "We don't hold with—but if it's the law, I suppose— When—when could I have her?"

"Probably tomorrow or next day."

"Well, I'll stay over. I'd best call home. I'll take her back with me, of course. But I just don't understand how it could have happened."

Even knowing that she had got here by Greyhound Bus, they hadn't been able to do any legwork on that yet. There had been only three buses due to arrive or leave from the station at Sixth and Spring today; the single ticket-seller on holiday duty was not the regular one. Tomorrow, try to find the driver of that bus, ask around the station. The Salt Lake City captain was on the ball; he had suggested to Askell that the LAPD might want a good photograph of Lila, and Askell had brought one with him: "She still wears her hair that way. Wore, I mean." Get some copies, ask all around that area.

And quite possibly, of course, they never would find out anything more about what had happened to Lila Askell. That nice modest moral girl.

"It's about time that burglar hit again," said Hackett, standing up and stretching.

Mendoza yawned. "I'm going home," he said.

But as usual, the little mystery, the slightly offbeat thing he couldn't see through, worried him. Essentially, he thought, his egotism: the notion that Mendoza couldn't figure a thing out bothered him. Lila bothered him. A nice modest religious girl, who wouldn't have got into a stranger's car: so she ended up getting strangled and dumped out of a stranger's car. Askell said she hadn't known a soul in L.A.

A stranger?

His mind slid back to those child rape-murders. He had said it then, the familiar stranger. Somebody placed, somebody known, but still a stranger. Even these days, the essentially honest citizen had a terrible trust in life, in his fellow citizens: that they would not suddenly strip off masks to be revealed as—the animals, he thought, and grimaced. Not the word. Animals lived by rules and did not kill without reason. To distract his mind from Lila he snapped on the police-frequency radio, halted for a light at Sunset and Vine.

"—A 211, in progress now, code three," it said suddenly. "K492, see the man at Woodman and Spencer, a 240PC." Robbery and assault of the person, Mendoza translated automatically. The radio was silent for a block and then spoke again. "K541, see the resident, 3120 Manning, a 390–415." A drunk disturbing the peace . . . "K943, at corner Hollywood and Highland, a 390W." A drunken female, probably also disturbing the peace. "K980, the drugstore corner Sunset and Fairfax, a 484." Purse snatching. As the Ferrari turned on to Rayo Grande Avenue, the radio crackled again. "K411, see the woman northeast corner Hollywood and Vermont, a 311." How nice, thought Mendoza. Indecent exposure.

And it was full dark of another Christmas Day, the electric lights making day again of the city: the city where, whatever its name or place, crime never paused for holidays. As he turned up the drive he muttered to himself, "Progress? *Claro que esto es según se mire*—it all depends how you look at it."

He went in the back door to be greeted solely by Cedric the Old English sheepdog, who offered a paw and shook his hairy face-veil to show his walleye. "Well, *bufón,* where is everybody?" Sounds of revelry led him to the living room, where the twins were still engaged with Christmas presents, Johnny getting the hang of a new tricycle with triumphant yells and Terry attempting to fit a doll's hat to an indignant Bast. Alison turned from rescuing Bast to exclaim, "Good Lord, are you home already? I'm sorry, Luis, but where time went today—"

"A very wifely welcome." He bent to kiss her. "But what are you doing here, Máiri? It's supposed to be a day for family joy, and you've got your sister—"

"Ach," said Mrs. MacTaggart, "we're not so much for the Christmas at home, it's Hogmanay is the great day—that is, the New Year—and this pair enough to wear out their puir mother. I'll get you a dram. There's a roast of beef near done, and I'll be getting the twins' supper."

"Luis," said Alison.

"*¿Querida?*"

"We don't spoil them, do we? Give them too much?"

Mendoza laughed. "I don't suppose a happy childhood can do anybody any harm, *cara*." Thinking of his own somewhat less than happy one, he added absently, "Progress. Yes, indeed." The twins suddenly discovered he was home and made a beeline for him, shouting. The cats fled to take shelter.

"Oh, well," said Alison, starting for the kitchen after Mrs. MacTaggart, "I suppose it's all right if they're *disciplined*—" All the money: the money the miserly old man had concealed all those years, and Luis running the slum streets. She shouldn't feel guilty about spending the money, but she supposed they both always would, having grown up without any . . .

"At least," said Mendoza as he sat down to carve the roast beef, "you seem to have got them away from all the bloody horrors of Grimm. The new fairy tales—I like this fellow—"

"Andersen," nodded Alison. "A special edition, and nice illustrations. You're worried about something."

"*Un poco*," said Mendoza. "The state of the world, *cara*. As well as Lila."

But after dinner, with the twins asleep and Alison busy over letters, he sat at his desk in the den and absently handled the cards, practicing the crooked deals. He thought better with the cards in his hands, though the domesticities had ruined his poker game.

It was funny about Lila. . . .

"You don't usually bring the office home," said Mary. "Something offbeat?"

"In a sort of way," said Higgins. "After listening to that Askell, I just wonder what could have happened." He buttoned his pajama jacket slowly. The house was very quiet; the family, first- and secondhand, was asleep; and Mary looked very fetching in a new blue nylon gown, sitting up in bed over a book, her gray eyes smiling at him. "What Art was saying back a while, you know—what we mostly see, the stupidity and cupidity. But once in a while you get a thing that—doesn't fit. The pattern, I guess I mean. This Askell girl—"

"So I'll be a good listener," said Mary.

"Well, that wasn't quite what I had in mind."

"—Always providing the baby doesn't wake up and start howling—"

Hackett was wondering about Lila too, but sensibly he reflected, wait and see what showed with a little legwork on it.

Grace wasn't thinking about anything except the baby. Their very own baby, at last, legally theirs.

Landers was wishing that Phil O'Neill wasn't quite such a sensible woman.

The Pallisers were discussing names. Roberta had settled on David Andrew or Elizabeth Margaret. Palliser objected to the latter. "It gets nicknamed," he said, "Liz. And Betty. And—"

"I rather like Betsy."

"It's too cute, damn it. The other way round, I'm agreeable. But—" They bent over the Dictionary of Common Christian Names, arguing amiably.

At eleven-twenty the night watch had a call: another burglary.

"We just got home, we went to the movies," said Dan Purdy angrily. "Locked up same as always—I been tellin' the manager here, these old apartments aren't safe! My God, Officer, near ever'thing we got— ever'thing we *had*—all our clothes and the radio and the little old TV, just a black and white, I work for a livin' honest, those bums on Welfare all got color TV but we don't—didn't—and Millie's garnet ring and necklace belonged to her ma—and my dad's old watch, the case was solid gold, he was a railroad man—"

Landers wrote up the report, yawning and thinking about Phil O'Neill.

CHAPTER 3

When Mendoza came into the office, late, on Tuesday morning, Hackett was sitting in his desk-chair reading Landers' report on the burglary. "Here's our boy again, Luis. He sort of stands out. I mean, we inherited a lot of break-ins, we've had more since we took over, but this bird is just a little different. I've been thinking of a word for him. Diffident."

"Maravilloso," said Mendoza, hanging up the perennial black homburg. "Get out of my chair. Why?"

"The M.O.—all the same. Private residences, mostly apartments. And I've been looking at addresses—it's roughly the same territory. He's never hit west of Virgil, east of Alvarado, above Third or below Olympic."

Mendoza considered that, taking the report. They had indeed inherited this and that from Goldberg's unfinished business. The hijacking. On Central's beat, there was hardly a night went by without a mugging, but that too was anonymous: and not all of them got reported. The break-in at a big pharmacy out on Third had been earmarked for Pending when Mendoza's team took over. The two gas station heists from ten days and a week ago scarcely tied up to the burglar.

"The loot," said Hackett, "not big. I wondered if maybe he hasn't got access to a car?"

"Now that is a far-out idea, Arturo," said Mendoza. "And I'd remind you we've got other things to think about than that burglar. You and George, or somebody, will do some solid legwork around the Greyhound station." He went across the hall to see who was in. It was Grace's day off; they were probably out buying more equipment for the baby. Piggott and Glasser were both typing reports: they'd been following up a couple of cases due to be tossed in Pending. Palliser wandered up with a paper cup of coffee, and Shogart sidestepped him, coming out.

"Where are you off to?" asked Mendoza.

"Got a witness coming in to look at some mug shots, that mugging in MacArthur Park last week."

"And so what job do I get?" asked Palliser.

Before Mendoza could tell him, Higgins marched in with a long sheet of mimeographed paper dangling from one hand. "Here's the bad news, boys. I stopped off at Communications to see if they had copies yet. Parkinson said he didn't think any ranking officers out of Central got on it, but I want to check."

"Oh-oh," said Hackett. "It isn't *likely*, but you never do know." Higgins thumbtacked the sheet onto the bulletin board: the list of unlucky ones, fingered at random to police the Pasadena streets and the Rose Bowl, on New Year's Day. They scrutinized it in silence for several minutes, automatically following the alphabet down from C to G to H to L to M to P and S. Nobody from this office had been fingered. "Small mercies," said Higgins. A copy of this list would be up in every precinct house and every sheriff's station, and the chosen ones cussing their luck. It was another of the thankless jobs reserved for cops, a thing that had to be done.

And Sergeant Lake was answering a call. "Seventy-seventh," he said tersely to Mendoza. "They've got the Macauley car."

"So have it towed in. Where?"

"Rammed into a service station pump out on Manchester. They say, inoperable."

"Fancy words. Have it towed in, and I'll see it when it arrives. Art, the—"

"Greyhound Bus station, all right. But somebody ought to look at that burglary, it does belong to us."

"John can take a lab truck and poke around. A waste of time, but we have to go through the motions."

"I've got Callaghan now," said Sergeant Lake. "He wants to see you."

"Well, he knows where my office is."

"He says it's about a hired dropper supposed to be in town—"

"*¡Dios me libre!*" said Mendoza.

Palliser went to look at the scene of the burglary. The Purdys, a couple in middle age and not looking exactly prosperous, were still furious. They'd been asked not to clear up after the burglar; they said they hadn't, and Duke started dusting all possible surfaces for latents while the Purdys unburdened themselves to Palliser.

"Just out to the movies, come home and find this—the few little pieces of good jewelry I had, my mother's ring and—the radio and the TV—it's not right—"

"It's not that we blame you, did you say Sergeant?" Dan Purdy was a smallish man with false teeth that clicked. He was a salesclerk in the men's department at Robinsons'. "You guys do a good job when you're let, the damn judges letting these thieves out as soon as you catch 'em. And you can't be everywhere at once. If I told that damn Morrison once I been at him a hundred times, the locks on this place are no damn good at all! All he says is, he's just the manager, don't own the place, it isn't up to him install new locks—some big company owns this place, and the rents like they are you'd think they'd give you something for it, but catch them! I don't say we got much, Sergeant, but what we've got we'd like to keep if you get me. I went so far to get a locksmith up here, ask how much to put good locks on, and he tells me seventy bucks, windows and all. Now who's got that kind of money loose, I ask you! I just ask you!"

Purdy had, thought Palliser, a valid complaint. It was a middle-aged apartment, about twenty units on three floors, and the Purdys' apartment was on the ground floor at the back. It would have been easy enough for anyone to come through the front door, whose lock lacked a deadbolt; the burglar had just as easily pried up the bedroom window, an old double-hung one with a rusty bolt offering little resistance.

"And Morrison says, we don't like it, we can move. You know what it costs to move these days? Even the little stuff we got? Even six or eight blocks? I don't make the biggest salary in the world, Sergeant. What do they expect us to do, anyways?"

Palliser couldn't tell him. Duke said presently that he'd come up with nothing but partial latents, all useless. He went away in the lab truck, and Palliser went to see Morrison, the building manager, who lived in a third-floor apartment. Morrison growled at his diplomatic suggestions. "Look, I don't own the place. If the owner don't want to lay out for new locks, it's not up to me." Mr. Morrison, however, Palliser noticed, had a stout chain on his front door and a lock with a deadbolt.

He went back to the office to get a report out, and like Hackett, read over the back reports on the burglar with some interest. In the welter of muggings and heist jobs over the past couple of months, the rather modest burglar stood out curiously. An amateur? Picking places easy to break in? Palliser read lists and added estimates. There was nothing reported stolen valuable enough, or identifiable enough, to go on the hot list to pawnbrokers. The average loot from one of those jobs might yield twenty, thirty dollars. It really added to petty theft. Anonymous loot: grandmother's garnet ring, the transistor radio, the old tape recorder. The burglar needn't even know a fence.

It was just a little offbeat. And it seemed funny to be chasing a burglar.

"All I know is," said newly promoted Captain Patrick Callaghan, "I get the short end of the stick." He looked at Mendoza querulously: in the absence of Hackett and Higgins he dwarfed the office, wide-shouldered and looming, with a crest of hair redder than Alison's. "So, the big shake-up, greater efficiency, and what happens to me? Half my men get transferred away from me because Seventy-seventh and Harbor need beefing up—damn it, I know that, but Central isn't exactly about to shut down for lack of business, Luis. So they hand me a whole office of plainclothes dicks who've been dealing with these nice genteel burglars and heist-men for years and wouldn't know a deck of H from headache powders—"

"Oh, I wouldn't say that. A lot of heist-men on the job to support a habit these—"

"And the new lieutenant they give me hasn't reported in yet, for God's—"

"Now, Saul was pretty sick, Pat. Psittacosis can be—"

"All right, all right. Ten-dollar words. Parrot fever, for God's sweet sake! He's supposed to be in after New Year's. Oh, Goldberg's a good man, but all these burglar chasers of his— Ah, I blow off steam, it's just that we've got quite a little business on hand. And now this thing. This Harry Singer."

"So what about him?"

Callaghan lit a cigarette and sighed. "Convictions the D.A.'s office has to sweat for, with the damn judges and courts. But we've got this one nailed but good—a supplier, a big supplier, with a pusher ready and willing to sing loud and clear on him, dates and facts and names and all. The pusher, if you'll believe me, never was hooked on the stuff himself —in business strictly for profit—and, if you'll believe me further, he's now got religion."

"¡Qué mono!" said Mendoza. "What's it got to do with me?"

"If we nail this one," said Callaghan seriously, "we'll put a lot of pushers out of business, Luis—at least temporarily. Anyway, dry up one big supply. We'll get him. But I've got a lot of dope from a couple of pigeons that there's a dropper in town hired to get my pusher so he can't sing. This Harry Singer. He's done time back east, I got a package on him from the Feds. I just thought you'd better know he's around. He's wanted for P.A. violation from Leavenworth."

"Thanks so much. Who is your pious canary and where to be found?"

"Oh, you don't need to worry about him," said Callaghan. "I was feeling a little nervous about him anyway, and I've got him in protective custody. Nice private cell of his own, all the Bibles and hymnbooks he wants. I just thought you'd better hear about Harry. If you should come across him—here's the package on him."

"I'll bear it in mind," said Mendoza.

The ticket agent at the Greyhound Bus station was cooperative, but not very helpful. Yes, he'd been here on the twenty-fourth. "But I wouldn't be noticing the passengers off a bus unless somebody asked me about something or—" He looked at the photograph of Lila Askell; copies had been made up by the S.I.D. overnight. He shook his head. He was an alert-looking man in his forties with friendly eyes. "Nope, doesn't ring a bell, sorry."

But he could tell them about buses. There'd been a bus in from Santa Barbara at 11:50 A.M. that day. A bus out for San Francisco at twelve noon. A bus in from San Diego at—

"How about one heading for Vegas?" asked Hackett. "On the way to Utah?"

He had the schedule out to show them. "Yes, Sergeant. Due to leave for Vegas at three-fifteen that day."

"She had a three-hour wait," said Higgins. They didn't ask because they knew that no records were kept of passengers' names; the tickets just handed over as they boarded the bus. The baggage would be carried on the same bus; Lila's, tagged properly at Santa Barbara, had probably reached the station in Salt Lake by now. "She wouldn't have stayed here." The station was bare and not very big: a pair of rest rooms, a few dusty benches, a cigarette-machine. The agent didn't remember her, but— "Do you remember if that bus was very crowded?"

"Well—day before Christmas. It was pretty full, yes. I do recall there were four or five servicemen, they'd be on Christmas leave, maybe near enough to go home for Christmas."

"Army, Marines?"

He shook his head. "I didn't notice—uniforms much the same now. Just uniforms, I noticed. They all got off the bus, the passengers, out in back there, and came through the station. I don't recall that anybody hung around—maybe a couple used the rest rooms. Sorry I can't tell you any more. This girl—er—missing or something?"

"Or something," said Higgins. They went to the door and looked out into the street. "A three-hour layover, Art. Where would she go, not knowing anybody here? She'd have time to get some way off and still make it back by three-fifteen."

She had got some way off, Hackett pointed out. "It was noon. She'd been on that bus for a couple of hours or more—call it a hundred miles from Santa Barbara. I think she'd have wanted some lunch."

Sixth and Spring streets was not the best area of Los Angeles, and Lila Askell, according to her father, hadn't known the city at all, only passed through it once before. But to the east down Sixth, she would have seen the tall shabby buildings, no greenery, while in the other direction she'd have caught a glimpse of the greenery of Pershing Square, the cleaner-looking red brick of the Biltmore Hotel up there. She might have guessed that better streets lay that way—with, presumably, more attractive coffee shops and restaurants.

They started up Sixth. Just past Broadway there was a big cafeteria on this side of the street; from outside it looked clean if rather bare. "It would be a cafeteria," said Hackett: but they went in and asked. Yes, the same cashier had been on duty on the twenty-fourth. No, she couldn't say she remembered this girl coming in. She couldn't say she hadn't; they had a lot of people coming in, some regulars and some just casuals.

They went on to the drugstore on the next corner; it had no fountain. The next square block, of course, was taken up by Pershing Square with the tri-level parking lot under it; and on all sides of that, there were drugstores, two small coffee shops, another cafeteria: but most prominent, across on the corner of Olive, was a big chain-name restaurant under a flashing neon sign. They waited for the light and crossed to it.

"This is a waste of time," said Hackett. "We've skipped a dozen places. We ought to split up and cover every place where you can buy a sandwich, four blocks around the station."

"We might get lucky."

Palliser had got switched onto the Macauley case when he got back to the office; the Buick had just been towed in to the headquarters garage, and he went down with Mendoza to look at it. Scarne and Fisher from the lab had been alerted and met them there.

"What a mess," said Scarne. The Buick—Mrs. Macauley, called and

NO HOLIDAY FOR CRIME

asked, had said there hadn't been a dent in it anywhere, Stanley was very careful with a car, a careful driver—was a wreck. Its nose was stove in, the right fender crumpled, all four tires flat. They peered inside without touching it; the driver's window was down all the way.

"What the hell's that?" asked Fisher. "An animal of some—"

Mendoza said interestedly, "Mrs. Macauley's best wig. Well, well. Pulled off in the struggle. And I think her handbag. Well, you boys can start dusting, and hope you come up with something useful."

"Just an educated guess," said the man from Seventy-seventh Street precinct who'd brought it in. "It could've been drag-raced, you know these wild punk kids. Or the driver could've been drunk, of course. Anyway, the tank's nearly dry. Its front end got rammed in when it was left in that gas station, just rammed up against one of the pumps."

"Mmh," said Mendoza. He had sent Wanda Larsen down to R. and I. with the description Mrs. Macauley had given them: the computers should turn up a few names and faces to match it, and then they could haul those men in for questioning, for Florence Macauley to look at. If the lab turned some latents to match one of the names and faces, that would be a useful shortcut. They watched them work for a while without picking up anything, and Mendoza said, "Well, let us know."

Macauley's body had been found, and reported, by another couple coming out of the restaurant. They hadn't seen or heard anything before coming on the body, very likely within a very short time since it had become a body; but a small-caliber handgun doesn't make much noise. They had nothing else to offer: useless to ask them any questions.

Upstairs, Wanda was back, neat and blonde and efficient. "Six turned up in Records, sir. The computer—I got the packages for you."

"A starting-point," said Mendoza. "Could be he's right here." Records, the inevitable routine and piled-up filed-away case histories, did quite often clear up the new ones coming along.

The six men turned up by the computer, fed information by Phil O'Neill, were not the most respectable of citizens. All were Negro; they ranged from light to medium dark. They varied from five-ten to six-one, a hundred and thirty to a hundred and seventy, nineteen to twenty-seven. Five had previous convictions of rape, one of attempted rape. Three had records of armed robbery, two records of assault, one count of manslaughter. Mendoza sighed at the dispositions of these cases. One-to-three, three-to-five and P.A. after a year, probation, Sheriff's Farm one year, one-to-three and P.A. after six months—

Lo que no se puede remediár, se ha de aguantar—what can't be cured," he muttered, "but I sometimes wonder why we work so hard catching up to them. So we go look for these louts to start with, ask for alibis and so on, and most of them won't be able to prove where they were when and it'll stay up in the air." He looked at his watch. "I wondered why I was hungry—after lunch, John."

Mike Donlevy was the fifth truck driver to have his cargo hijacked; that had been a week ago. What with the fractured skull, he hadn't made a statement at the time; they hadn't been able to question him at all.

He turned up at headquarters at eleven o'clock, just as Hackett got back. "You're not the guy talked to my wife before. A middleweight like, she said, and talking about the devil bein' behind it. You ever do any pro fighting?" He glanced Hackett over professionally.

"Only in the course of the job," said Hackett. "I hope you're feeling all right now, Mr. Donlevy. Come in and sit down." They were alone in the sergeants' office.

"Sure. I'm O.K., only I'm still Goddamn mad," said Donlevy. "You didn't? You got the build, I just wondered. I was in the ring twelve years, see. Which is one reason I'm still Goddamn mad."

"Is that so?"

"I am telling you, it is so," said Donlevy. He raised a fist the size of a ham and contemplated it. "Me," he said. "Me! Basher Donlevy! I never been knocked right out all the time I'm in the ring. I won a few, so I did. I had a right cross nobody could see comin', Sergeant. Acourse I been out of training, I got to admit that. But *me,* jumped and laid out without I put a finger on him! Whoever it was. I was mad then and by God I'm still mad. Me, with a fractured skull! I hit the canvas a few times but I never took no kind of real hurt, even from that Spanish guy outweighed me twenty pounds." Mr. Donlevy was looking belligerent and dangerous. He exactly matched Hackett's six-three-and-a-half and weighed in perhaps at two thirty. Some of it would be beer and starch and apple pie, but not all of it by any means, thought Hackett.

"Well, I can see that," he said, grinning. "The doctor said there was a weapon used, something like a lead pipe. He got you from behind, we figured. Just like—"

"Even *so!*" said Donlevy. He had a large flat bulldog face, very bright blue eyes, large ears, and tightly curling black hair. His wife had given his age to the doctor as forty; he didn't look that.

"Well, the M.O. was the same on all of them. He waited in the back of the truck for the driver to come back—none of you expecting it, even after the first couple of times it happened and got into the papers."

There were a lot of trucks driving around everywhere in the city, making routine deliveries of liquor to retail liquor stores, markets, restaurants. The hijackings had been fairly crude. They had wondered after the first couple about inside information, but the subsequent ones showed a pattern. The trucks, all leaving from central warehouses down here, had been hijacked after making only one or two deliveries. Quite naturally the drivers would make deliveries to the nearest consignees first, which was why all the hijackings so far had occurred on Central's beat. In the two cases where the hijacker had waited for a second delivery to be made, the first deliveries had been to places minus any parking lot off the street. Canny, thought Hackett: a truck parked on the street, it was more likely that someone would see the driver attacked, and he'd be found much sooner. In every case, the driver had been left unconcious in the parking lot, not to be found for five or ten minutes.

And there were all too many owners of restaurants and bars who would jump at the cut-rate stuff. There'd be nothing about it to say it hadn't come from a legitimate source; by the time it was loaded by cases onto warehouse trucks, it was all labeled and sealed.

The trucks, of course, had been abandoned later in places which offered no clue at all as to where they'd been. Boyle Heights, Monebello, Rancho Park, Alhambra—even one down is Santa Monica. Park a truck on the street, walk away, who would remember?

"I can't give you any kind of description," said Donlevy regretfully. "That's what I can't get over, Sergeant. Back I come to the rig—I been driving for Smart and Final since I left the ring, ten years back—back I come, climb up to the seat, and bang! That's it."

"Even if you'd seen him you probably couldn't give a description. The two drivers who got a glimpse at him said he was wearing a ski-mask."

"Well, I'm no help to you," said Donlevy. "I'm sorry. The wife said they told her I should come make a statement when I could, so I come. But that's all I can tell you. When I think what these damn bastards are getting away with! I'd only made one delivery, a couple o' cases o' beer to a joint on Spring doesn't even have a hard-liquor license. There must've been ten thousand bucks' worth of stuff in that rig. Bourbon, scotch, vodka, gin—by God! And Smart and Final standin' the loss. It in't right, Sergeant."

"Well, I'm sorry you can't help us," said Hackett.

"So am I," said Donlevy. "I'm damn *mad* I can't help you, Sergeant. But I'll tell you this, Sergeant." He looked at his balled right fist. "These bastards, whoever, I just hope to God they'll pick my rig to knock over again. Because if they do, I'll be ready for 'em. Me, knocked clean out before I even made a fist! I tell you, from now on—Goddamn lead pipe or whatever—they want to play dirty, Mike Donlevy can play just as dirty any day! Every time I come back to the rig from now on, I'm gonna be wearing a set of brass knuckles, and I'm climbin' in the rig face first, you can bet. With both eyes peeled, Sergeant."

"And I'll wish you luck. But they say lightning never—"

"Don't take any bets," said Donlevy. "I'll be ready for 'em if they do."

The afternoon papers had made minor headlines of the Macauley killing; he had been a prominent realtor, a former city councilman.

Palliser, Piggott and Glasser had gone out looking for the six men out of Records. They hadn't found any of them by three-thirty.

At three-forty Higgins came to an Orange Julius bar just past the corner of Hill on Seventh Street. Doing the tedious routine, he had started back at the bus station and hit every place that dispensed food of any variety between there and here. At one o'clock he had taken twenty minutes for lunch at the chain-name restaurant. He was wondering now what use it might be to find a waitress who could say, yes, that girl was here, she had a sandwich and left a quarter tip. Who could not say, she went on up Broadway, or wherever.

But the routine had to be done.

The Orange Julius bar was a hole-in-the-wall, like all of them. It offered the standard hot dogs, hamburgers, malts, besides its famous fizzy orange froth. At this hour, even along a busy block, there wasn't a customer in the little place: he counted six empty stools before the clean white counter. There was a girl, slim in a white uniform-dress, a dark-brown girl with straightened black hair piled on her head in a topknot, very neat. Higgins got out the photograph of Lila, and his badge.

"Oh!" she said to the badge. She smiled at Higgins, and said respectfully, "Sergeant. You'll be out of the detective office. My brother's just a rookie yet."

"That so?" Higgins smiled at her.

"Out of Seventy-seventh," she said. "Can I help you, Sergeant? You like something—"

"No thanks. This girl—have you ever seen her in here?" And what a hope that was.

She studied the photograph. "She's pretty. You know, I did, Sergeant. I surely did."

"What?" Higgins was startled. "Are you sure?"

"I'm sure. I've got a good memory for faces, but I had a reason, too." She raised suddenly troubled dark eyes to him. "I should've done something. I don't know what I could've done, but I— But, you know, it was getting toward Christmas Eve, and I was off at two—I was watching the time—and I still had Mama's biggest present to pick up, and—I let it go. I let it be." She looked at the picture.

"Tell me about it," said Higgins gently. "If you're sure it was this girl."

"It was this one." She spoke in a low voice. "They came in about twelve-thirty. Like I say I was going off at two—"

"On Sunday?"

"That's right. Getting to Christmas Eve. She was dressed nice, kind of plain. A brown suit and a yellow blouse. And they had hamburgers— he had an orange and she had a vanilla malt to go with them."

"A man. Can you describe him? I'd better have your name, Miss—"

"Louise Chaffee, Sergeant. Yes, a young man, and—I don't know if I can make it plain to you, how it was. Why I noticed particular. She was —she was nervous with him. I could tell. Like—well, like that time I let Maggie set up a blind date—not *knowing* a fellow, you're nervous, kind of. Not knowing what he's like. It was like that. It wasn't anything I heard her or him say exactly, he laughed a lot, but— Oh, a woman'd know what I mean! Just, she was shy of him, sort of. I had some other customers in too, but I noticed. They were only here about twenty min-utes."

"The man? Young? I think we'll want a statement from you—"

"Well, there wasn't anything—anything really, I could suspect any-thing wrong about it—you know? I couldn't have done anything, no reason. It was just a *feeling*. I hadn't thought about it again till you showed me the picture. Well, he was just a fellow. I don't know I could describe him—I guess he had sort of light hair. He laughed a lot. He had on a gray jacket, and no tie. Did—did something happen to her, Ser-geant?"

"Yes," said Higgins. "We'll want you to make a statement. If you're sure."

"I had a feeling about it," she said wretchedly. "She was—shy of him. I—but it was Christmas Eve, I had Mama's present to—and it was broad daylight, Sergeant. Patrolman Kaplan right at the corner out there. If she was that leery of him she could just go off— And I'd clean forgot about it till you showed me the picture. But whatever I can do to help—"

*   *   *

Palliser came back to the office at five o'clock, after an abortive hunt for one Thomas Waffer, still on P.A. for armed robbery, and was handed a new complaint: attempted break-in. He went out to see what it looked like, feeling sour and tired. They hadn't anything to show for a long day's work; but that was nothing new.

It was an address out on Third Street, and turned out to be a market wearing a well-known chain name. The manager, Raymond Osney, apologized to him.

"Bring you out here for nothing, Sergeant. I'm sorry, just thought I ought to report it. I didn't notice it until just a while ago when I was out in the stockroom, when the Smart and Final truck came in. We've been held up six times in the last two years and had four break-ins and four attempts the last year, you know? My God, the crime rate." He showed Palliser the jimmy-marks on the door of the big stockroom behind the market. "Obviously, they didn't get in. Probably Christmas Eve—possibly last night, we were closed yesterday, of course. I've wondered about dogs, you know."

"Dogs?" said Palliser.

"The guard dogs. Why the company doesn't use them. Very efficient, by all I've heard. And the losses from burglaries alone—let alone the holdups. This market alone, the holdup men got away with over ten grand all told, but the burglaries are worse. It's the liquor and cigarettes they're after, mostly, and you'd think the company would invest in some adequate protection. Our burglar-alarm system here, in my opinion, is useless. An old installation, and the last time I tested it, it wasn't working properly. I called the head office, but—"

It would be a waste of time to turn out a lab man on those prymarks, thought Palliser.

"Considering the crime rate, especially in this area, I suggested the dogs. To the head office. I understand you can rent them. From places specializing in the trained guard-dogs, that is. Well, I suppose I've wasted your time, but I thought I ought to report it—"

Higgins had just finished briefing Mendoza on Louise Chaffee, who would be off duty at five o'clock and come in to make a statement, when a uniformed man brought in a manila folder.

"Autopsy reports," said Mendoza. "Now let's see what showed. Stomach contents should tell us if Louise's girl was Lila Askell, at any rate." But he hadn't slit the flap when Sergeant Lake looked in.

"I've got a call from Central Receiving, Emergency. They've just had a man brought in, beaten up, possible skull fracture, says he was attacked by a man and a woman posing as a prostitute—"

"¡Condenación!" said Mendoza. "That pair of cons—I said we'd hear about them again." And just how to mount a hunt for them—and for all the good it would do to catch up to them, human nature being what it was— But it was another job to work.

CHAPTER 4

Shogart was in: all of Goldberg's old files had been brought up here, and as the only man familiar with them Shogart was weeding out the dead wood. Mendoza chased him over to Central Receiving to get that story, and came back to find Higgins telling Hackett about Louise.

"So she did pick up with a stranger after all. Funny," said Hackett thoughtfully.

"No," said Mendoza. "Or, the familiar stranger. I've got a little idea there— Well, let's see what the autopsy says."

The autopsy report confirmed that Lila Askell was the girl Louise Chaffee had noticed. Contents of stomach, ingredients of a hamburger—bread, cheese, mayonnaise, tomato, mustard, ground beef—milk, ice cream, french fries. Digestion just started, estimated time of death a scant hour after eating. "One-thirty," said Mendoza. She had died a virgin. Healthy young woman, no indicated diseases, no vestiges of alcohol or narcotics. She had been beaten, not severely—a precise list of contusions, right eye, mouth, left cheekbone, various places on the body—and manually strangled. "Yes," said Mendoza, passing it on to Hackett, "and that doesn't take long. Somebody in a temper, maybe because she was going to walk out on him—"

"But when did she pick him up and who was he?"

"She didn't. I had a little idea there. She wouldn't, by her past history, have picked up anybody. But she'd been on that bus for two hours or more, and we heard it was crowded. Any bets she didn't have a seatmate?"

"My God, of course," said Hackett. "That feels right, Luis, for what this Louise says."

"And just maybe," said Higgins, "it was one of our fine upstanding young servicemen on Christmas leave."

"*Pues sí.* Or said he was. Not in uniform, Louise would have noticed that." Mendoza was swiveled around looking out the high window at the line of Hollywood hills on the horizon. "Mmh, mitigating circumstances can we say? It was Christmas, and if the fellow was polite, friendly, she wouldn't want to be rude to a fine upstanding young serviceman—or anyone else. He says, let's go to lunch together, what can she say? Not that it was much of a lunch, and a funny place to go—"

"But he paid. Louise was definite on that."

"Mmh," said Mendoza again. "You can see how it might have happened. After all, it was—"

"To take the words out of your mouth, broad daylight," said Hackett. "If he started to get fresh, threw a pass, she could just walk off. Or yell for cops. Why—"

"We don't know where they were when and if that happened, Arturo. He wouldn't throw a pass on the street."

"But she wouldn't have gone anywhere—private—with him."

"We're arguing ahead of evidence," said Mendoza. "The lab's got her clothes, they may turn up something." He was still frowning as he took up the other autopsy report.

Stanley Macauley had probably never felt the bullet that killed him; he had died instantly. The bullet had been lodged in his heart. Bainbridge estimated it was a .22, had sent it to S.I.D. Macauley had been a healthy specimen for his age, only slight indications of beginning arteriosclerosis. Stomach contents, with digestion barely started, small amount of alcohol, salad greens, salad dressing, beefsteak, potato, cream pie. "Condemned man ate a hearty meal," said Mendoza to himself, passing the report on to Higgins. The only way to work that one was by the routine, look for and then at the men in Records conforming to the description with an appropriate background for that kind of assault: that was a place to start. Unless Mrs. Macauley could pick a face out of the mug shots. And she might pick one, and be wrong.

Sergeant Lake looked in. "There's a Miss Chaffee here."

Mendoza was waiting for the elevator, hat in hand, when Shogart emerged from the next one. "So the report can wait till morning," he said. "To brief you, it sounds like the same pair. Woman with black hair, medium-sized, medium good figure, the same old routine—alley a shortcut to her back door, bingo, the guy jumped from behind, wallet gone. He wasn't seriously hurt. Lost about fifteen bucks. He's feeling like a damned fool, which he is."

"Yes," said Mendoza, "and that's a shapeless sort of thing too, E.M. How do we go looking? Are they worth setting up a decoy?"

"Well, they could end up killing somebody," said Shogart. "All accidental like. I'll do the report in the morning."

When Hackett got home, coming in the back door, he found Angel frosting a cake. "Nice," he said, bending to kiss her, and as she dropped the spatula in the dishwater, rescued it in midair to lick it off. "Mmh, almond. Very nice."

"Not for you," said Angel. "Calories." But her mountain-pool eyes smiled at him. "Have you found out any more about that poor Mormon girl? It seemed so odd—"

"Well, I'll try this on you for size, see what a female thinks of it," and he outlined Mendoza's idea about the fellow bus passenger.

"Y—es," said Angel. "Yes, I can see that, Art. She wouldn't want to be rude, and there'd be no reason to, well, be afraid of him. In broad daylight. If they'd been talking on the bus, sitting together—people do, and on a holiday too, the day before Christmas. I can see her going to lunch with him—and what a funny place—but I can't see her going anywhere private, where he might have the chance to throw a pass. And besides"—she set the cakeplate on the drainboard—"you said she'd been thrown out of a car. If it was another passenger on the bus, just passing through, where'd he get a car?"

Hackett stared at her. "My God, I never thought of—my God, yes! Only—"

Mark came shouting, discovering that Daddy was home, and the great silver Persian shot past fleeing a pursuing Sheila, these days less tottery on her fat legs. "Mustn't chase the kitty," and Hackett bent hastily to pick her up. "You know, Angel, that is a thought. Luis just talking off the top of his mind—"

"Belatedly I'm improving my education," said Mendoza, coming into the living-room at seven-thirty. "All the fairy tales I never had read to me. I like this Andersen fellow." He looked around at this part of his household, all serene: the cats settled in a pile on the sectional, Cedric dutifully at Alison's feet. Alison was wearing a favorite topaz hostess gown, and her copper hair caught gleams from the shining ornaments on the great Christmas tree across the room.

"Um. The Ugly Duckling," she said vaguely, looking up from her book. "Which reminds me, you know if it stays as sunny and warm as this for long, that mockingbird's going to be back to nest early."

"*¡Dios me libre!* Our little feathered friends—"

"Luis, I've been thinking about that girl." She put down her book. "You're woolgathering, you know. The nice story about the other bus passenger. But she was thrown out of a car. In Exposition Park, of all places. So where did the other passenger acquire a car all of a sudden?"

"*¡Vaya!*" said Mendoza, struck. "My God, I didn't—" he stopped. "My God, you're right. My maundering wits—"

"And I know it sounds farfetched," said Alison meditatively, "but they do say Los Angeles is getting to be quite a crossroads. Like that place in Egypt. What I thought was—it *is* farfetched, but I wondered if she ran into somebody she knew? From Santa Barbara? Well, look, it's only a hundred miles up the coast. How long had she been working there?"

"Since last February. But—"

"Well, there you are. She'd have met all sorts of people in eleven months. And she was working at a hospital," said Alison, suddenly further inspired. "A patient—"

"If you're going to say a mental patient, I don't think it was that kind of hospital," said Mendoza. "That's reaching, *cara.*"

"Well, it was just an idea. With just what you've got on her now, I don't see that you've got any leads to work at all. The Louise girl said she couldn't be sure she'd recognize the man—even if he is in your records, and nothing says he is."

"Let me relax in peace, woman. Put some more brains on it tomorrow. Of course it's possible the other passenger's destination was L.A. because he lives here, so he'd have a car—"

"Talk about reaching," said Alison.

When Mendoza came into the office on Wednesday morning Grace was there—"He was waiting for me when I got here," said Lake—with a sheaf of snapshots. Oh, of course, Celia Ann. "We took these at the party last night—" He began passing them around eagerly. "Isn't she a doll?"

"How'd you get snapshots so quick?" asked Higgins, coming in on the heels of Palliser and Hackett. "Let's see. She surely is cute, Jase. Of course she'd older than Margaret—I've got some new shots in the camera now, finish up the film tonight if Steve doesn't get hold of it first—"

"Oh, I got one of these Polaroid outfits, you get the picture right away, you know. Here's one I got of her eating ice cream—get those big eyes—"

"Say, the film-pack for that really costs," said Higgins. "You'll be sorry about that. I looked at it too, the camera isn't bad, it's the up-keep—"

"Well, when you get the pictures right off it's worth it. Here she is with Dad—and in this little pink dress Ginny got—"

They looked at the snapshots, smiling at his eager pride, and they thought back, inevitably, to that day last August, the quiet professional office, with the shocking, bloody corpses, and the sudden discovery of three-month-old Celia Ann, brown and plump and smiling, hidden in the shower where her mother had left her before the wanton bullets were fired. At least Celia Ann was one orphan who'd found a good home—shoe on the other foot at that maybe, the way the Graces had been moving heaven and earth to get her legally adopted.

"She is a honey, Jase," said Hackett, handing back the snapshots. "Don't let George be a wet blanket."

"I just say, you take many pictures, that thing'll keep you broke buying film," said Higgins. "You wait and see. Did I show you the ones I got of Margaret in the bath—"

"Yes," said everybody. Grace put the pictures away reluctantly. He'd be having more to show tomorrow, all too likely. But little Celia Ann was special to the Graces.

"By the way," said Hackett, following Mendoza into his office, "Angel's a smarter detective than you are. I tried the other passenger on her, and she said so where'd he get a car? I—"

"Yes, so did Alison. Me maundering away ahead of any solid evidence—the car we're sure about. Nobody could have brought her there on foot."

"So where do we go on that now?"

Mendoza shook his head, looking frustrated. "A forlorn hope—get the press to run a story, please will any passenger on that bus trip come and see us? Over a holiday? With the bus full? Who might have noticed anything? Or would see the story in the paper?"

"Likely those passengers are scattered to the winds now," agreed Higgins.

"The lab may come up with something on her clothes," said Mendoza.

"And they may not too. There's no solid lead at all."

"I think I'd like to talk to that girl she's been living with," said Mendoza. "Once in a while my Scots-Irish wife uses a little ESP. Just once in a while. Meanwhile—" He put out his cigarette in the brass tray. As usual he was smartly dressed, the gray Italian silk, a dark tie with a severely plain gold tie-bar. "What we do have is a lead on Macauley. I'm going to get Mrs. Macauley down here sometime today to look at some faces. But we've got these names out of Records to look at, so let's get with it. I take no bets we don't get handed something new today. The holiday's over—nice quiet Christmas."

"Nice and quiet," said Hackett. There'd been another body last night, a natural death, just an old fellow slipping away in his sleep, but there'd be paperwork on it. The paper this morning had spoken of sudden death on the freeways and surface streets, the expectable drunk drivers. There were, as always in this week of the year, many out-of-staters around town, many with cars, crowding the hotels and motels, attracted by the parade and game. A lot of them were unfamiliar with California traffic laws. Every cop in the county would heave a sigh of relief next Tuesday, with a new year officially underway and traffic getting back to normal.

Lake thrust his head in. "There's been another hijacking. Retail liquor store out on Wilshire."

"Not Mr. Donlevy," said Hackett regretfully. "I hope sometime they do try him again. I'll go."

The driver wasn't much hurt, only banged on the head and shaken up. His name was Herman Keller, and he kept saying, "I was so surprised, and I seen the stories in the papers too, but you just never think it can happen to you—I was so surprised—" It had been his first delivery of the day, and the liquor store had its own small parking lot at one side. He'd only had one case to take in, and when he came back, the waiting hijacker knocked him over the head from behind, pushed him out of the cab, and made off with the truck within thirty seconds. The keys had been in it—"You don't bother, every stop—it's not like a private car, God's sake, I'm only gone three-four minutes—" And by the time Keller came to and got back to the store to phone, the truck was long gone.

The hijackings fairly crude. The trucks carrying the liquor practically always bore advertising to mark them, not like the ones ferrying ordinary groceries to markets.

Hackett called the warehouse—not Smart and Final this time—and got the plate-number of the truck, and after some delay, some idea of the manifest. Looking at his hasty notes, he groaned mentally. At today's prices, ten G's easily, all the cases of liquor; and also, doubtless intended for some of the fancy liquor stores in the suburbs, a good deal of gourmet foods, teas, imported candies, choice olives.

He went back to the office and put out an A.P.B. on the truck. They were on it early; but they'd been on a couple of others early too without picking up the truck before it was abandoned.

Grace, Higgins and Palliser were out hunting the men Records had turned. Mendoza reported Mrs. Macauley to be on her way down to look at mug shots. "That's another little something, Art. She said he smelled oily, 'like a gas station.' Well, it's a job men like that can get—not much education needed."

"What are we doing about these hijackings, anyway?" asked Hackett. "Writing up reports, for God's sake. Wait for the next one."

Mendoza was reading a report; he shrugged. "*¿Qué?*" he said. "It's nothing new in crime, but it's only lately there's been a rash of it again all over the country. With good reason—inflation, black markets, barter. Almost any kind of hood, damn what his record says, might go off on that kick. Where do we look? The drivers ought to be alerted by now."

"That's not a very constructive attitude."

"If you have any suggestions—"

"I've brought in one of these boys," said Palliser from the door. "Thomas Waffer. Anybody like to sit in?"

"I've got this damn report to write," said Hackett. "Isn't there anybody else in?"

"Sure. Just asking," said Palliser amiably. He passed Sergeant Lake in the doorway.

"Mrs. Macauley's here. Mr. Hendry's with her."

Mendoza got up.

It was Piggott who escorted them down to one of the little private cubbyholes in R. and I., and got a couple of books of mug shots to start Mrs. Macauley off. Phil O'Neill brought them in, her flaxen curls shining, her uniform crisp. Mrs. Macauley looked at her with faint interest.

"Say," said Piggott, "is Tom minding his manners, Miss O'Neill?"

She smiled at him. "You can trust me for that. These do to start?"

"Fine. Now, Mrs. Macauley, if you'll just take your time and look at the photographs carefully. I know it's hard to be sure sometimes, and if the fellow who attacked you is in here, the picture won't look exactly like he did when you saw him. But if you find one that might be, just speak up." He'd stay here awhile to get her settled down; if was confusing to anybody, set down before a book of hundreds of photographs. Hendry beside her was looking curious and interested.

"There are such a lot," she said doubtfully. "Well, I'll try." She was in black, but not dowdy; pearl earrings and pin. Outside of crisis, a sensible woman; and she'd want this X found and punished.

Well, they might find him, thought Piggott.

"Interesting plant you've got here," said Hendry. "All the latest scientific gadgets, eh?"

"Well, sir, we need every bit of help we can get to keep on top of it nowadays. The devil getting around pretty fast and furious."

Hendry looked surprised. "Well, I guess some of the things you fellows run into seem pretty satanic all right. This thing right here—just no reason—"

"No reason except the devil's prodding," said Piggott, still thinking about the judges and courts. "The smartest thing the devil ever did, Mr. Hendry, was to convince people he doesn't exist." However, it was Wednesday: choir-practice tonight. Both he and Prudence were in the choir, and they were rehearsing some of the good old rousing ones that had a swing to them, "When the Roll is Called," and "Onward Christian Soldiers"— "You just take your time," he said, "and if you think you spot the right man, you tell Miss O'Neill out there."

Thomas Waffer had a rap sheet of some length, but the most serious listing on it was for armed robbery, five years back. The rest read, possession of narcotics, petty theft, attempted assault, D. and D., auto theft. He was a native of Los Angeles, a dropout from sixth grade, probably illiterate. He didn't like cops, and he eyed Palliser and Glasser sullenly.

"I ain't done nothin'. Why you bring me in? I ain't—"

It always started like that with this kind; it got tiresome, but it was part of the job. They prodded at him patiently. Where had he been last Sunday night, the twenty-fourth, at nine o'clock? Was he with anybody who could back him up?

"Sund'y," he said. "Las' Sund'y? At night? Whyfor you guys wanta know? None o' your business—I'm clean, I ain't—" They went on prodding, and he finally said, "Well, I was just home. Sure, I was home—say, that was Christmas Eve, so sure I remember—I was home with my wife, an' she—"

"Which one?" asked Glasser. By his record, he had lived with several women on and off. There was no record of a formal marriage.

"Which—why, Gloria, acourse. My wife. Well, it's a name I don't recollect, the Welfare lady said, somethin' law—"

"What's the address, Waffer?" asked Palliser. "Where?"

He gave them an address on Forty-second; it wasn't in his recent records, but he was off P.A. and that didn't matter. "You have a job?" asked Glasser.

"What? Nosir, I ain't workin' reg'lar right now, but I been lookin' for a job—"

"Has Gloria got a job? What are you living on?" A fool question, Palliser thought.

"Well, she get the Welfare for the young 'uns, see—gonna get 'nother seventy, eighty, time she have the baby nex' month. But I ain't been doin' nothin', we get along, you got no call to—"

"Will you tell me why we waste time like this?" said Glasser outside in the corridor. "So we go see Gloria, was he there, and she says, oh, yessir, he was. So what do we have? An alibi?"

"I suppose," said Palliser, scratching his handsome straight nose, "that we get too cynical, Henry. There must be a few people living on Welfare who really need it, handicapped people, and old people, and so on, who'd starve without it."

"Damn few," said Glasser.

Just after noon, Phil O'Neill called from R. and I. "Your witness has turned up two shots she likes. I suppose you want her back with the packages on both."

"I suppose we do," said Sergeant Lake, who was feeling slightly bilious after an unappetizing lunch of celery sticks and raw carrot. He caught Mendoza just leaving for what would be a more substantial meal —Mendoza's metabolism did not threaten the extra poundage.

When Mrs. Macauley came in, Mendoza took the manila folders from Lake and without looking at them asked, "How sure are you of these? Any preference?"

She looked at Hendry. Her eyes were red again, because she'd been crying yesterday and then this morning used them hard on pages and pages of not-very-big photographs. "I—after a while they all look alike. I thought I could be absolutely sure—I'd never forget that man's face—it was dark but there was some light, you know. But—I tried to be careful. I found that one first, he looked *almost* like—I was *almost* sure—and I looked at some more and went back to that one, his name's Hibbs—and then I found the other one, and I could be almost sure about him too. They're alike, I know. I—if I had to say, I'd say the second one's more like him. What I remember."

"Mmh." Mendoza sat down again and offered cigarettes; she declined, and Hendry got out a cigar. Mendoza opened the folders.

Jasper Hibbs. An interesting record. Petty theft, auto theft, shoplifting, D. and D., armed robbery three counts, statutory rape. Suspended sentences, probation, thirty days in the County jail, one-to-three, three-to-five. He was twenty-eight now and had served exactly two years and eight months inside. He was Negro, light-medium, five-eleven, a hundred and fifty, knife scar on one arm. He was on P.A. now from the latest armed robbery count; the address was Sixtieth Place.

The second one was the same general type, but the face was tougher, even stupider-looking. A mean one in drink, Mendoza could guess. The rap sheet was longer too: j.d. counts of assault, weapons possession, narco possession, mugging; as an adult, attempted rape, rape, armed robbery. He had done a little more time. He was Chester Gosling, Negro, medium, twenty-seven, five-ten, one-forty, a user when he could get anything—Mary Jane, bennies, speed, H.

"Thanks very much, Mrs. Macauley. We'll see if we can turn these two up. We appreciate your taking the time—"

"And then what?" asked Hendry. "I mean, so you find 'em. What then?"

"We'd like to arrange a show-up. That is, if Mrs. Macauley will come in and look at them, in a line of other men, and see if she can positively identify one of them."

"I see. And suppose she can't? To be positive."

Mendoza shrugged. "We like a positive identification. Barring any more solid evidence. The lab is still going over the car, and if they come across any latents—fingerprints—that can be tied to either of these men, that'd be nice solid evidence. But we can't arrest people on suspicion."

"I suppose not," said Hendry. He was eyeing Mendoza's beautifully-tailored Italian silk with a mixture of surprise, small hostility and curiosity. By his own tailoring, he would guess accurately at its price tag; and honest cops weren't supposed to make that kind of money. Mendoza supposed that in the interests of upholding the integrity of the LAPD, he ought to explain about the miserly grandfather; he let it go.

"What—what about our car?" she asked hesitantly. "We heard you found it—"

"Rather a total loss," said Mendoza, "I'm afraid. You'd better get your insurance firm on it. We'll let you know when S.I.—when the lab's finished with it."

"Well, I see. Thanks," said Hendry. "I don't know what for."

"We try to do the job, Mr. Hendry."

"Now, Walter. We've got to help them any way we can. With Stanley —Stanley dead for just no reason at all."

Mendoza sat down at his desk again and brought out the cards to practice crooked deals. He thought about Lila Askell. An Orange Julius bar, for God's sake. Funny place to take a girl to lunch. How long had they been around? Forty years. At first, just the sweet orange froth—advertisement for the Golden State, tourist attraction, everybody who drank orange juice lived to be a hundred. These days, the sandwiches, the snacks. And Broadway—Seventh Street—those crowded busy streets, even more hectic than usual the day before Christmas, crowds at the last-minute shopping—who'd have noticed that anonymous couple?

Where, in fact, to look, to find out just what had happened to Lila Askell? Who the young man was—more fair than dark, a man who laughed a lot?

"Are you going out to lunch at all?" asked Lake.

Hackett had just come back to the office at two-fifteen, to check in; he and Palliser and Grace were still running down names from Records. Lake gave him the two new ones, the ones Mrs. Macauley had fingered, and those would take priority now. But before he started out on that, a call came in from a sheriff's station out in Belvedere. They'd just found the hijacked truck.

All according to pattern, thought Hackett; and Luis might say what he liked, they ought to try to do something constructive about it. Almost anybody might go in for that, so all right, the pigeons had the word and were supposed to be looking around—but that was a slow way to do it.

He went out to look at the truck. They had always been turned up the same day: the hijackers knew the plate-numbers would be out on the air very soon. Take it somewhere private, a big commercial garage would be ideal, and strip it, drive it off and leave it.

This one had been left parked along a main drag, Mednik Avenue. It was a busy street; nobody had noticed when it had been left or by whom. Just, there it was.

As if in contempt, all the fancy gourmet foods had been left in it; only the liquor was gone. The cases and cases of bourbon, Scotch, rye, vodka, gin—

"I suppose you'll tow it in and go over it," said the sheriff's detective. "Never left any latents yet, I understand, but we have to go by the book."

"That is a fact," said Hackett. "As if we hadn't enough else to do." As plain Homicide: and now, all the stealing to deal with too. Well, supposedly the computers made it easier. As if anything to do with human nature was ever easy, or uncomplex.

He called the lab to come and tow the truck in. It was five to three. He went back to the Central beat and started looking for Jasper Hibbs.

*   *   *

There was another incident of what Higgins called L.A.'s own invention in slaughter: the rocks thrown off freeway overpasses. This one produced a D.O.A. There was, in the middle of the afternoon, a heist-job at a small market over on Virgil. A good deal of new construction was going on in L.A. now, the new high-rise buildings on Wilshire and all over—"Everybody," said Piggott, "rejoicing because they didn't fall down in the quake, hah! It didn't hit anywhere near—just wait for the next one!"—and an accident at a site on Beverly Boulevard came along a little later, an earthslide with two men suffocated. So at four-fifteen Mendoza was alone in the Robbery-Homicide office, practicing the crooked deals and thinking about Lila Askell, when Lake buzzed him.

"Call from Traffic. Assault with intent, sounds like, at the Biltmore Hotel."

"¿Y depués?" said Mendoza. "Woman's work, Jimmy." He reached for his hat.

At the Biltmore, the badge brought him a twittering manager, concerned for the hotel's reputation but also humanly shaken. "A nice old fellow," he told Mendoza in the express elevator. "The ambulance just came, thank God, I hope he'll be all right. A nice fellow, old Mr. Pound. I like him—we all like him. I shouldn't say mister. A terrible thing—here in October, you know, a vacation he said, and then he decided to move to California—he'd been living in Chicago—it's down here, seven-fourteen—" He led the way. "The men from the squad car were very good, they—"

Two men with a stretcher passed them, moving fast. One attendant recognized Mendoza and said, "We've got to get him in fast, he's lost a lot of blood—he's past talking now anyway."

"Oh, dear, oh, dear," said the manager. "Old Mr.—I shouldn't say that—decided to move out here, he said, no family at all, he's a widower, and he came back just before Christmas, but he hadn't—"

The room was the ordinary Biltmore Hotel room, well and quietly appointed, a double bed made up, white-tiled bath off to one side, closet the other. There had been a struggle of some kind here: the desk was lying on its side, inkwell spilled in a dark splotch on the beige carpet, Gideon Bible upside down beyond, a pen, a notebook scattered. Two water glasses lay nearby, apparently empty. There were other, darker stains nearer the door, one great puddle with clusters of clots visible.

"We think it happened a while ago," said one of the uniformed men. "The ambulance men said—"

"He didn't come to the dining room," gabbled the manager. "For his Christmas dinner. Yesterday. He said—you see, he hadn't decided exactly where to settle down—he liked Santa Monica—he'd rented a car, you see—but he liked the valley too—and when the maitre d' came and told me—Gustav noticed he hadn't come down—not a young man, and I thought I ought to investigate—"

Mendoza raised his brows at the Traffic men. "He found him and called in. Looked like assault all right, he was beat up but good. Poor old fellow. Looks as if the room's been ransacked too."

"All alone in the world—" The manager passed a handkerchief across a wet brow— "Such a nice old man. Retired Army officer, did I tell you that? Lieutenant colonel, a career Army man, and he was only staying here till he decided—"

"It looked," said the other Traffic man thoughtfully, "touch and go, whether he makes it."

CHAPTER 5

Mendoza sent the Traffic men back on tour and called the office; Higgins was in, and would get the lab on it. Waiting for that, Mendoza heard more from the manager, Carlos Di Silva. Lieutenant Colonel (ret.) Archer Pound had been at the hotel since the twentieth, this last time; he came and went every day, an active man, but had always had dinner in the hotel dining room; Di Silva did recall him saying that he hadn't any friends in Los Angeles, adding cheerfully that doubtless he'd soon make some. "He's such a nice old fellow," said the manager agitatedly. "I'd been afraid—a heart attack or—but this! Whatever could have happened—"

The men from the lab, Duke and Fisher, arrived with Higgins behind them; they looked around the room, Di Silva hovering in the background. The closet door was open. "Not many clothes," pointed out Higgins. "Only one suitcase." It was aged scuffed brown leather.

Di Silva said, "Excuse me, but the lieutenant colonel has several suits. Good suits. And three suitcases when he came. He has a light gray suit, I know, and I've seen him in a navy—"

Mendoza inspected the dresser top. "Wallet, empty—don't yelp at me, Duke, it'd never take prints, it's new deerskin, and"—he looked—"not much in the rest of it." In the little plastic slots, an Illinois driver's license, membership card for a veterans' organization, a library card for the Chicago Public Library. "Do you know if he used any credit cards?"

Di Silva shook his head. "I don't know, he paid the hotel in travelers' checks, sir, but a lot of people—"

"Well, if he had any, they're gone. And," added Mendoza, "I don't see a watch. Check with the hospital, see what was on him—"

"He always wears a ring," volunteered Di Silva, "I noticed that, it's a West Point class ring, and he's got a gold wristwatch—I told you he rented a car from—"

"So we'd better check that too," said Higgins. Duke had just dusted the phone and pronounced it clean. The garage said the rented car was still there. With the keys in it: a Plymouth Valiant. Pound had left it there—they had a record—at 5 P.M. on the twenty-fourth, hadn't been back since.

"*Así, así*," said Mendoza. "So what do we deduce? The good officer made the wrong kind of new friend?"

"What it looks like," said Higgins. Fisher beckoned from the bathroom and they went to look. A bottle of bourbon, half empty, sat on the back of the toilet, with a dispenser soda bottle beside it. "Um. They were having a friendly drink, witness the glasses out there, when—what? They got to arguing politics, or the new friend turned out to be a fag and propositioned him—"

"Oh, I'm sure the lieutenant colonel—quite the gentleman, and—"

Mendoza went back to the office and called Central Receiving Hospital. The night watch was just coming on; he flipped a hand at Landers and Conway passing his open door.

"Oh, the assault," said the intern he finally got. "Well, he's in serious condition. Lost a good deal of blood. I take it he'd been in a fight? On the elderly side for that, but his knuckles are skinned raw and he's got a broken thumb, as well as the usual contusions—possible skull fracture, but the most serious thing is a stab wound just under the heart. He was damn lucky it wasn't a fraction of an inch deeper, he'd be dead hours ago. As it was, it nicked a vein, and he's been slowly bleeding internally— What?"

"Any idea when it might have happened?"

"That's why I said he was lucky. That it just barely nicked that vein. I'd estimate that he got these wounds at least twenty-four hours ago. Why on earth wasn't he found sooner? Well, obviously I can't tell you whether he'll make it. He seems to have a very sound constitution for a man of his age, but—"

Mendoza thanked him and picked up his hat. He started home through heavy traffic; nearly rammed into a Buick wearing New Jersey plates which made an illegal left turn in front of him, and was nearly rammed by a Cadillac wearing Illinois plates which tried to change lanes too fast. He got to Rayo Grande Avenue, possibly with the help of guardian angels, and was told he was late.

"And you look fagged to death, man—I'll pour you a dram," said Mrs. MacTaggart. El Señor heard the bottle taken down and came floating up to the drainboard like a fat black bird, his smudged face with its blonde Siamese-in-reverse markings expectant.

"Alcoholic cats," said Mendoza, kissing Alison and reaching for the shot-glass. "It's a wonder to me—¡Válgame Dios!—that there aren't even more accidents than we usually get, this one damned week of the year. Are the monsters in bed, amante?"

"All ready to be read to."

"¡Ay de mí! Why did I ever get domesticated?"

"Well, it took you a while," said Alison.

Hackett, Higgins and Shogart were off on Thursdays. When Mendoza came into the office Grace and Piggott were just coming in. He gave them a rundown on Pound.

"We've also got these two Mrs. Macauley fingered—Hibbs and Gosling. I've put out an A.P.B. on both of them, but that kind can fade into the woodwork and some kind pigeons will probably let them know they're hot. But go looking—we've got an address for Hibbs at least. And the Askell thing—¡Caray! Of course if Pound does come to he can tell us who attacked him." Sergeant Lake was unaccountably late; Mendoza, who had experienced most phases of police work, manipulated the switchboard and got an outside line, then the hospital.

"Well, he's holding his own," said the intern. "We've been pumping blood into him and he's rallied slightly. No, not conscious yet—I doubt whether he will be today, but we'll let you know."

"So we can't question him yet. If he does come through he can tell us all about it, so don't break your necks at it today, with all the rest we've got on hand. Ask around the hotel, was he seen with anybody, who did he talk to. He was robbed of money and clothes at least. But, priority on Hibbs and Gosling—¡Vamos!"

"Aye, aye, sir," said Grace. They passed Sergeant Lake coming in; he said apologetically that they'd been up most of the night with the eight-year-old.

"Gastric upset. Caroline said, just too much rich food and candy over Christmas."

Mendoza went into his office, and found Policewoman Wanda Larsen efficiently polishing his desk. The blotter was neatly aligned and the ashtray spanking clean. One use for a policewoman; he said genially, "I always thought we needed a housekeeper around here."

"There doesn't seem to be any work for me, everything rearranged, Lieutenant." She smiled at him uneasily. "I'm so used to Lieutenant

Goldberg's way—well, it made work, taking the men's reports for typing up and I always—"

"*¡Caramba!*" Mendoza looked at her in awe. "Taking reports— Do you mean to tell me those lazy louts of—of thief-takers dictated reports to you? For typing? Your typing? Well, I will be damned! For two weeks I've been wondering just what jobs I'm supposed to give you. They dictated— *¡Dios!*"

"Why, don't—didn't you have a girl to do that, sir? In Homicide? I thought—"

Mendoza sat down and lit a cigarette. "*Esto no me huele bien*—if you ask me, something fishy about this. A private secretary, those privileged sons dictating reports! Well, I will say," and he smiled slowly, "they won't be doing that up in Pat's office, which is gratifying to contemplate."

"I did wonder," said Wanda. "There hasn't been anything for me to do, really—I kept waiting and none of the men asked me—I thought you, well, maybe were sorry I was left—"

"*¡Santa María!* Just wait till the boys find out they've got a private secretary! And a housekeeper! All of a sudden, I appove our shaking up and rearrangements." He grinned at her. "But I'd like to know how in hell Saul rated such a thing all this time—Homicide never got offered any secretaries—"

"Well, it was on the schedule, at least one policewoman attached to Robbery, on account of searching female witnesses sometimes, I think," said Wanda. Suddenly she laughed. "Oh, my goodness, Lieutenant—you not knowing! Any of you! Here I've been hanging around this place, nobody giving me any jobs, and thinking you didn't *want* me—didn't like me being here—"

Mendoza burst out laughing. "And I've been eyeing you nervously wondering what in God's name I was supposed to do with you! Comedy of errors—but wait till the boys find out! *¡Gracias a Dios!* They'll be all over you, young woman—"

"Well, that isn't part of the job, Lieutenant," she said demurely.

"I can't get over it, a private secretary—"

"And I speak Spanish too."

"Talk about dark horses," said Mendoza. "That Saul, never saying a word—"

"Well, it never occurred to me either. I thought maybe your policewoman had got transferred too, maybe up to Narco—and you didn't like having me instead." She laughed.

"*¡Pobre hija!* Now I know what you're here for, you'll be kept busy!

My God, all my years out of uniform I never heard of such a thing—I've worked the wrong departments."

"I'll try to do everything just the way you want, Lieutenant." She looked at his neat clean desk. "But, oh, dear—"

"¿Como?"

"It looks," she said, "so *empty* without all the boxes of Kleenex."

Mendoza was still laughing when Sergeant Lake came in.

"Mr. Askell's here. Says he doesn't want to bother you, but—"

"Let him in." Mendoza looked at Wanda. "You're going to be like Old Man Kangaroo, my girl. As per Mr. Kipling. Very truly sought after. Most popular female at Headquarters." She grinned a little self-consciously back at him as she went out.

"I know you're busy, Lieutenant," said Edward Askell apologetically. "But—have you found out anything yet?"

Mendoza wondered what further questions to ask him. And would he know the answers to some of the questions? Lila Askell had been away from home for nearly a year: but, her father said, she wrote home. . . . "Not much, I'm afraid. Did your daughter write home about any of the men she dated?"

"Once in a while. She didn't go out much, to put it like that, dated. Lila was a—a serious girl. She was interested in her work. She never dated much even when she was in high school and later on at college—it was a two-year course she had to take in this therapy, operating machines and so on. So many new things they have now. She was—a quiet girl. The only fellow she went out with a good deal—that was when she was in college, eighteen months, two years back—was Paul Mencken. Oh, they weren't engaged, but Lila went steady with Paul for six months or so, and that was—"

"Do you know where Mencken is now?"

Askell nodded, looking at the floor. "He joined the Army. He was killed in Vietnam last year. That was one reason, I think, that Lila took this job over here. She—minded about Paul, she wanted to get away from—from places they'd been together."

Mendoza was feeling frustrated again. "What about men she dated in Santa Barbara?"

"She didn't, much. She used to write about patients sometimes, people the therapy helped—I don't recall she ever said about going out on dates, except two or three times Monica asked her to go on a double date— Oh, there was one of the interns at the hospital asked her to go out with him, but she wasn't interested. His name was—let me think—

Wormser. Henry or something. But, Lieutenant—it didn't happen up in Santa Barbara. It happened here—Lila getting killed that way—and I can't understand it. She didn't know anybody in Los Angeles, and—I hope you'll believe me, I know my own daughter—she'd never have let a stranger—pick her up, or—"

The familiar stranger? thought Mendoza. But there she had been, at the Orange Julius bar, with the stranger. The fair young man who laughed a lot. And if he told Edward Askell about that, Askell would just say that Louise Chaffee was wrong, that couldn't have been Lila.

The driver of that bus was due back in town today. Any good to talk to him? Put out a plea in the press, anybody riding that bus on that trip, please come forward? Again he wondered, vaguely, if she had been on that bus. She had said she would be: they knew now from Salt Lake that her baggage had been checked straight through. And she'd been seen at the Orange Julius bar within forty minutes of the bus's arrival. But—

"I'm taking her home," said Askell. "They told me last night I could have her—her body today. I've got all the arrangements made—" His face worked a little. Mendoza said the indicated things mechanically. "Well, thank you, I know—I hope you'll find out who—did this terrible thing. That is—well, we know vengeance belongs to the Lord, but—and when someone did that to Lila, some other girl—"

"Yes. You know we'll work it—we want to find out too, Mr. Askell."

Askell got up. "You've been very—" he said, and stopped, and said, "kind." And then he said, after silence, to nobody in particular, "She was only twenty-three." He went out quietly.

Steve Dwyer, who at twelve years old had a more agile and sponge-like mind that Higgins', and could now quote amply from the *Guide for Beginning Photographers* about f-stops and filters and light-meter readings, had got hold of the camera before Higgins got home last night, and finished the film.

"I got a good one of Margaret with Brucie, I know it's good," he boasted. "I took the roll in, George, but it was after four and so it won't go out till today, and we can't get the prints back till *Tuesday* on account of Monday being a holiday—" He patted Brucie the Scottie mournfully. "But I got another twelve-exposure, I hadn't enough left out of my allowance for a twenty—"

Higgins felt a little annoyed about the intervening holiday too. He'd got a few shots on that film he was anxious to see—one of Mary with the baby, and one of Steve and Laura with the baby. "Say, Steve," he said.

"I wonder if we could learn to do the developing and all. It'd save some money, and it might be interesting—"

When Mary came to ask if he needed cigarettes or razor blades, she was just off to the market, oblivious to Laura's piano practicing he and Steve were absorbed in the illustrations of developing tanks and enlargers in the *Camera Guide*.

The lab called and reported that the hijacked truck had yielded no latents at all except a number belonging to its legitimate driver. Mendoza asked if they'd turned up anything useful from the Askell girl's clothes. "I think Scarne's on that," said Fisher. "I suppose you'll hear sometime."

Frustrated, Mendoza took down his hat and went out to look for the driver of that bus. He was now, the Greyhound station informed him, off for two days before making the same run again, up to San Francisco, back down the coast and over to Vegas. He lived in South Pasadena. Mendoza called, explained, and drove over to talk to him. He was an amiable middle-aged man named Soames, and he told Mendoza that he had his back to the passengers mostly.

"If somebody comes to ask me something, or there's a disturbance any kind, is the only times I notice the passengers. You drive a bus, the passengers"—he shrugged—"they get to have no faces. Just people in the bus. You get a drunk once in a while, or the yelling baby, it's a nuisance, other people complaining, but otherwise I got no call and no time to notice passengers." He looked at the photograph of Lila Askell and shook his head. "She could've rode in my bus that day—I couldn't say. Usually by the time I get on to start the haul, the passengers are all in. I drive the bus, that's all."

What with the holiday traffic, it took a little time to get there and back. And what other result had he expected?

He stepped out of the elevator, almost under the new sign, *Robbery-Homicide,* and came in past Lake and the switchboard. It was five minutes to eleven by the white-faced wall-clock. Wanda Larsen's desk was just inside the original sergeants' office, facing the open door; she looked up and smiled at him, and he laughed.

"I just thought, to get everybody straightened out—"

"*¡Seguramente que sí!*" said Mendoza. She had lettered a large sign on mimeograph paper and propped it on her desk facing outwards. *Private Secretary for Typing Reports,* it said. "Oh, brother. Wait until the boys—and I cannot get over Saul. And I can just hear what Pat said, if they expected to find your duplicate waiting their commands up in

Narco—" He went on into his office and got out the cards, thinking about Lila Askell.

Ten minutes later he jumped as an inarticulate shout sounded past the open door. He went out in anticipation. Detectives Jason Grace and Matthew Piggott were staring at Wanda Larsen incredulously.

"You mean *that's* what you're *here* for?" asked Grace. "Type *our* reports? Instead of us? By God, Matt—"

Piggott was looking almost reverent. "A private secretary? Now to tell you the gospel truth, Miss Larsen, we didn't know just what job you were supposed to be here for—we didn't like to—"

"Wanda," she said, smiling at them. "Just a sort of misunderstanding. The lieutenant was surprised too. I thought you didn't like me, not giving me any work."

"Didn't *like*—" said Grace. "Oh, lady! I did take touch typing in high school but it's not a job I take to."

"Is that what you did in Goldberg's office?" asked Piggott. "For all the Robbery boys? All their reports? Well, I will be—" Piggott was not a swearing man, but they saw words trembling on his lips.

"I just now decided," said Grace, "I approve of all the changes around here."

"I thought you'd all like it," said Mendoza. "You'll make it up to the poor girl, thinking she wasn't wanted, all of us ignoring her and wondering why the powers that be attached her to us."

"I'm pretty fast at dictation. Er—Mr. Grace, *I* didn't get to see those snapshots of your new baby."

Grace pulled them out, beaming. "Oh, by the way," he said to Mendoza, "we found that Hibbs. He's parked in the first interrogation room to the left."

Hibbs was annoyed at being picked up, and said he was real clean. He was only just off P.A. last month, and his parole officer had said he'd been a good boy the whole eighteen months. Now he was off P.A., very possibly he'd be less careful: that was a pattern too. But if there was any consciousness of guilt in him, it didn't show; they were necessarily experts at assessing that.

They asked him about last Sunday night, and he said he'd been at work. "Mr. Taddo can say. I come at four, business was slow but Mr. Taddo can say I'm here till we shut at nine."

He had a job at a bowling alley on Wilshire, minding the automatic setting-up mechanism, cleaning up, checking equipment. Grace went out to find Taddo, who managed the bowling alley. He came back at twelve-fifty to find Palliser and Glasser standing transfixed before Wanda Larsen's desk.

"Are you telling me," said Palliser, "that all this while those—those—never had to type their own reports? Dictating— Well, I will be damned! We wondered why you were assigned to—I mean, we never had a policewoman before, no real job—I will be *damned!*"

"I don't believe it," said Glasser. "So now we know. I wasn't sure I liked all this changing around, but now I do. In spades."

"Nice to be pampered, isn't it?" said Grace, and found Mendoza on the phone.

"Do you think he'll make it? . . . Doubletalk! . . . So he's slightly improved, *bueno*. You'll let us know if he does come to? Thanks so much."

"The alibi checks," said Grace. "Taddo says Hibbs was there all right, four to nine. He's a good type. I'd say that definitely clears Hibbs. Whatever he might get up to next week or next month."

"*¿Qué más?*" said Mendoza. He brushed his moustache the wrong way and back again, which meant he was annoyed. "So let him loose."

"I think so. And then lunch."

Sometimes they all foregathered at the big table at Federico's, happening to knock off from the office at once; sometimes only a couple of them. Today, with their two senior sergeants off, the newest bureau of the LAPD occupied the big table. Mendoza was brooding. The tall Jamaican waiter brought him a shot-glass of rye without being told.

"Gosling has a likelier record for Macauley," said Grace. "What are you fussing over, Henry?" Glasser had a ball-point pen, figuring on the back of an envelope.

"Damn car payments. Act of God, hell. What God had against my car—" Glasser's Ford had been demolished by the quake last August.

"And there was that article by the Chief," said Mendoza, "in that true-detective magazine last month. And isn't he right. The miniskirts and hot pants—mindless silly females and most of them respectable too, just following fashion—but inviting the assault, the rape. Looking like easy females, asking to be taken for such."

"And isn't that the truth," said Piggott. "Prudence says she can't buy a ready-made dress with the skirt a decent length."

"But not," said Mendoza, "Lila. No. Her skirt covered her knees." He finished his rye.

"Which says?" Palliser swallowed Scotch-and-water and looked at the steak sandwich set before him.

"*No sé*," said Mendoza. "But everything doesn't always get into letters written home." He took up his knife and fork, looking at the small steak (very well done). "Even if she was a nice moral Mormon girl. I wonder—"

There was a little silence while food was consumed. "I think," said Mendoza, "you'd better take an airplane ride, John."

"What? Where?"

"Santa Barbara. To talk to Monica Fletcher. I think I'd like to hear what Monica has to tell us about Lila—and any double dates—and that intern Askell mentioned—and any other men Lila knew there—"

"Well," said Palliser, slightly surprised, "all right. But whatever happened to her, it happened here—"

"It's only," said Mendoza, "a hundred miles up the coast."

The formal lab report on the bullet out of Macauley had come in. A Colt .22, could be any of several models, old or new. Mendoza was inclined to agree, of the two men Mrs. Macauley had picked, Gosling had the likelier record. Piggott and Glasser were out looking for him.

Lieutenant Colonel Pound was still unconscious. Grace had gone over to the Biltmore to ask questions on that.

Wanda Larsen was happily transcribing Grace's notes on Hibbs into a formal report.

There would be an inquest on Lila Askell tomorrow morning; an inquest on Stanley Macauley tomorrow afternoon. Other inquests: those construction workers, the D.O.A.'s from the freeway accidents.

The inside phone burred at him and he picked it up. "Mendoza, Hom —Robbery-Homicide."

"Well, it's just a funny thing," said Scarne. "I'll be sending up a report, but I thought you'd like to know right off. These clothes—the Askell girl. Wool-nylon suit, cotton blouse, nylon underpants and bra, garter-belt and stockings. I've been going over 'em. The underwear's just ordinary stuff, looks as if she put 'em on clean that day. But—"

"Well?"

"On both the skirt and jacket of the suit, there are traces of grass and dead leaves—not enough to analyze for type. On one shoe, the sole that is, bird-droppings, a very small amount, embedded in cotoneaster leaves—"

"*¿Cómo?*" said Mendoza. "What the hell—"
"I'll send up a formal report."
Cotoneaster leaves? Grass? At Broadway and Seventh?
"*Diez millones de demonios desde el infierno!*" said Mendoza.

CHAPTER 6

They had had an address for Chester Gosling from his recent P.A. officer—a housing project on Fifty-second down in Vernon. Palliser and Piggott had started there that morning with no luck: no answer to knocking, and a neighbor across the hall told them Gosling had moved out a couple of weeks ago. Mrs. Gosling was still there; she might know something about him, so they'd try there again.

He had had a job at a service station on Florence Avenue. That was their next stop. The owner, a paunchy oil-stained fellow named Cutts, said, "I like to oblige Mr. Talmadge—" that was the P.A. officer—"but I don't think I'd take another ex-con. It's always the same story, see, they stay and do the job O.K. so long as they're on parole—then the day they're off, that's it, they goof off so you have to fire 'em. Most of 'em just lazy bums can't be bothered to work, easier to steal." Gosling had been fired two weeks ago.

Now, with Palliser deflected elsewhere, Piggott and Glasser went back to the housing project to see if the wife was home.

"A gas station," said Piggott. "And Mrs. Macauley said—"

"Yeah, I think he's hot for it. Wonder if the lab came up with anything on the Macauley car."

In the narrow dirty hall of the apartment building, which offered ample evidence of the habits of the residents, they knocked on the door and waited. After a moment a woman opened to them, stared at the badges, and said, "That snotty li'l Sonny Weaver tole me you was after Chester again. He ain't here."

"Would you have any idea where he's living, Mrs. Gosling? You are—"

"Yeah, that's me. What you want him for?" She was a tall, deep-bosomed woman with a defiant slatternly air: her pink cotton slacks were wrinkled and stained, the tentlike white T-shirt dirty.

"Just to ask him a few questions."

"Huh!" she said, and cackled with laughter. "I hope you get him 'n' work him over real good! Bassard run out on me an' take up with that high-yaller girl— You ain't heard about her, huh? Well, I tell you, he's prolly hidin' out her place, time he hear you after him."

"And would you know where that is?" asked Piggott.

"Name o' Ruby Jewel she call herself—got a job dancin' nekkid, some bar down Slauson. You fin' her, you likely fin' that bassard, or she know where he is. An' you work him over good!" She stared at them a moment and shut the door with a bang.

"Well, a lead of sorts," said Glasser, as they walked back down the odorous hall. "There are a lot of bars featuring topless dancers on Slauson Avenue, Matt."

"What with Sodom and Gomorrah getting rejuvenated," agreed Piggott. "But it just occurs to me, Henry, that Ruby Jewel might be in our records."

"And you might have something there. Let's go look."

They went back to Parker Center, down to R. and I., and asked. The computer turned up Jewel, Ruby, as an alias of one Ruthene Lincoln, who had a modest rap-sheet for shoplifting, petty theft, prostitution. She'd been picked up last for soliciting a couple of months ago, and at that time her address was listed as Denker Avenue.

They drove down there; it was a shabby side-street off Florence, lined with tired old apartment buildings. A fat brown woman was in the front yard of the one they wanted, watering a bed of rose bushes against the building. They walked up and Piggott showed her the badge. "Do you live here, ma'am?"

"Yes, that's right. I own this place, that is, my husband and me. You're policemen? Can I help you some way? I'm Mis' Towner."

"We're looking for a Miss Ruthene Lincoln—sometimes she calls her-self Ruby J—"

"*Her!*" said Mrs. Towner. "A bad lot that one is, all right. She wasn't here long, Officers. Less 'n three months. I suspicioned what she was, but I didn't have no proof till you arrested her that time. We tole her to get out—we don't want no trash like that in our place, we got decent people livin' here."

"I see. I don't suppose you know where she moved?"

"Nor I don't care. Trash like that—it's hard enough to keep up the place, look halfway nice, ever'thing so high nowadays—"

"Do you know where she was working then, if she was?"

"Yessir, at least I know where she *say* when she move in. Said she was a waitress at a place down on Slauson, place named the Cool Cat or such-like. Waitress!" Mrs. Towner snorted. "I can guess what she's doin' in a place like that! You're after her again, huh? Well, I wish you fellows luck, find her. But that's all I could tell you."

They thanked her and went back to Piggott's Chevy. "Nearest public phone," said Glasser. They found one three blocks up; Piggott pulled into a red zone and Glasser got out to consult the Central book. "Just this side of Figueroa," he said, getting back in.

It was the kind of tedious routine that they were used to doing; but it occupied time. When they got to the Cool Cat Bar it was four-thirty. Los Angeles sprawls far out; they had put more than fifty miles on the odometer, through city traffic, always heaviest this one week of the year.

The Cool Cat was open for business: a sign proclaimed that it was open twenty-four hours a day, and also promised topless dancers, three shows nightly, a hot piano-player and a combo on weekends.

They went into near darkness, only a few wall lights burning, a brighter light down by a center platform that formed an impromptu stage. There was a rich effluvium of old dirt, perspiration, whiskey, beer, cheap perfume and an elusive hint of marijuana. Past the narrow entrance they felt the room widen out, but it was too dark to see corners. A bulky something came up to them; as their eyes adjusted to the little light, it resolved itself into a large, very black man in dark pants and a light shirt. "We don't serve whites here," he said abruptly in a grating voice.

Glasser flicked his cigarette lighter with one hand and displayed the badge in the other. "We're looking for Ruby Jewel."

The man swore, expressively if not elegantly. "That girl in more trouble? Bring the pigs down—"

"We're not after her, just her address. We want one of her boyfriends," said Glasser.

The man relaxed. "Man, you pick him up, she never gonna know he's gone from the crowd!" He laughed, with a gleam of white teeth. "Thass a load off my mind. I don' want no trouble here. Ruby, she's got a pad over on Nadeau Street—" He added the house number and Glasser took it down.

When they came out to the street again, dark had shut down; the light fading for the last twenty minutes, and now gone entirely. Street lights were on, and the neon flashing.

"This Gosling, Matt. If he is there, he's big and mean. We don't want to lose him. Go back to base and see if Jase is there to come along?"

"There's less than an hour of the day left," Piggott pointed out. "I'm tired of driving in traffic, Henry. Another ten miles and then down here again? Come on, let's go see if he's there."

It was another aged apartment building. There was, in this one, a row of locked mailboxes in the slit of a lobby, and *Jewel* was listed as Apartment Fourteen, upstairs. They trudged up in silence, Glasser reaching to loosen the Police Positive .38 in its shoulder holster. Piggott pushed the bell.

"Hey, man, you early— Oh!" She faced them, disconcerted by strange white faces. She was something, all right; a smooth light tan all over, a spectacular figure in pink and gold hostess pajamas just barely there, not-very-opaque nylon, midriff bare, and gold mules on bare feet. She had a wild mop of black hair, frosted purple lipstick, and a heady aura of perfume surrounded her. "Now who the hell are you and what do you want?" she demanded.

Glasser brought out the badge. "Is Chester Gosling here?"

"Chester?" She looked them over thoroughly, thoughtfully. "You want him? I thought he was clean these days."

"Just for some questions," said Piggott. It had been a long day, and it was going to be good to get home to Prudence.

"Oh," she said. She leaned one elbow on the door, displaying a long-fingered hand tipped with purple-frost nail polish. "Well, he's been here, sure. He oughta be back just a few minutes, he went out for cigarettes. You can come in and wait, you want." She stepped back, and they went in to a gaudy overfurnished room with an expensive stereo in one corner, too many pictures, and a heavy pall of incense. There was marijuana under the incense.

"You fellows like a li'l drink while you wait?" She smiled slowly at them, and they both stepped back a little, farther into the room, as she came forward.

Glasser started to say, "No, thanks," but she had them away from the door now, and shouted Gosling's name. The inner bedroom door burst open and he came out in one lunge, running for the open front door. Glasser went for his gun as he saw the gun in Gosling's hand, and he and Piggott dived flat as shots spurted. The girl screamed. Glasser tripped over her, making for the door. In the hall, they heard Gosling's feet clatter on the stairs, and plunged after him.

"Gosling—stop! Gosling!" Glasser fired once over his head as they burst into the street, Gosling twenty feet ahead. It was dark in the street, but they heard as they ran the slam of a car door, an engine gunned. The car came bucketing past them, a small dark shape with no lights, and Glasser fired at it. "Goddamn the luck to hell!" he said bitterly. "Goddamn that—"

"Why, that Goddamn bastard!" said Ruby Jewel from the top of the apartment steps. "That ever-lovin' bastard's gone off with my car! I never said he could take my car—now how in hell am I gonna get to work?"

"Well, the luck runs that way sometimes," said Grace. But Mendoza was not so complacent. He said this and that.

"I said we ought to pick up Jase or somebody to help take him," said Glasser. "And damn it, now I'll have to sit through another board hearing, did I have a legit excuse to fire the gun! Of all the damned luck—"

"Now, Henry," said Piggott. "Temporary setback, like they say. She was mad enough at his taking her car, she gave us the plate-number right off—she wants it back. It's a dark-blue VW, I told Jimmy to get the number on the air."

"Grateful for small favors," grumbled Mendoza.

He got up resignedly, massaging the back of his neck. "Maybe I'm feeling my years, boys. But tomorrow is also a day. Better brief the night men on Gosling, and hope that VW gets spotted."

"It's just an idea," said Piggott. "I think one of those bullets hit the wall in Ruby's pad. We might dig it out and see if the lab can match it up to the one out of Macauley."

"I am getting old. I'd have thought of it thirty seconds from now," said Mendoza. "First little job for the night watch. And I wonder what John's getting up there . . ."

None of the regular commercial flights of the big airlines deigned to land at Santa Barbara that day. Palliser had called Burbank Airport and been referred to a local company, Intercoastal Flights, which said they could drop him off there from a scheduled flight to San Luis, leaving at three o'clock. He drove home to tell Robin, put a second shirt and a razor in a briefcase in case he had to stay over.

"I'll probably be back tonight, depends what turns up."

"You'll call if you won't be? Don't fuss, John, I know enough to lock doors, after all. But I have been thinking, now we have the house, nice to have a dog."

"Well," said Palliser.

"After the baby's here, so the dog won't get jealous. A Sheltie or something."

"We'll think about it, Robin."

The plane dropped him at Santa Barbara Airport at three-forty. The hospital where Lila Askell had worked was across town, a small private hospital very Spanish-colonial, with a red tile roof. He was received with curiosity, exclamations and questions; evidently Monica had spread the news about Lila far better than the local press. Just an awful thing, you could hardly believe it, the crime rate these days—and inevitably, he was told what a nice girl Lila had been.

Monica Fletcher appeared in the bare little waiting room in five minutes. She was a tall thin dark girl with prominent light-brown eyes and a rather foolish slack mouth outlined in pale pink lipstick. She was quite willing to answer questions, after all the exclamations— "Her poor family! She was so happy about getting home—I couldn't believe it when I heard—" But she didn't understand what he wanted from her, and Palliser wasn't too sure himself. Mendoza seemed to have some idea that Lila, away from home, had unbuckled her rigid morality, so he started asking about boyfriends.

"Oh, she didn't have any, Mr. Palliser, excuse me, you said Sergeant. She didn't date hardly any at all. Really. She was awfully serious, she went to church and all. She was more interested in the job than anything else. But nothing happened to her *here*. And she wouldn't *know* anybody like whoever it was did that to her—I just can't stand thinking about it!" She blew her nose dolefully. She was in the plain white uniform-dress of a nurse, white flat-soled shoes, but he suspected that when she was dressed in her own choice, it would include ruffles, dangly bracelets and spike heels.

"But she did go out with men?"

"Well, only a few times. I used to sort of worry about it—it wasn't natural, her not wanting to go out—she liked to *read*," said Monica. "Just sit and read books. Well, a girl ought to go out sometimes. I know Dr. Wormser'd asked her for a date, he's sort of pompous and stiff, you know, but—but Lila wasn't interested. My boyfriend got her dates a couple of times, we double-dated—"

"Who's that, Miss Fletcher?"

"Ronald Stettin, he's a teacher at the college, his first year. We went—"

"All right, who did Lila go out with?"

"It was only about four times. There was Gene Stover, he was a friend of Ron's and I think he really liked Lila, but she only went out with him twice, on a date with Ron and me. There's a nice place outside town, a roadhouse, with a good combo and dancing, but Lila just didn't go for it. Or this Gene. He called her a few times, but she turned him down. But why're you asking about that? I don't see—"

"Well, we have to ask all sorts of questions," said Palliser vaguely.

"Oh, I suppose so, I just—"

"Did she go out with anyone else?"

"Well, Ron set up another one, one of the postgrad students, Bill Saxon. He was nice, but Lila said he was a smart-aleck, he made fun of her going to church and she didn't like that. And then the next time Ron suggested—well, it was me really—she said she wasn't interested. She was already thinking about going home, you know. I like it here but Lila didn't. Except the job, and she said she could get one at the hospital back home and it's a lot bigger and had more equipment and all. Oh, it's just terrible to think—one of those dope-fiends or something, when Mr. Askell called I—"

"So far as you know, she'd only dated these two men here, Gene Stover and Bill Saxon?"

"And Dr. Wormser had asked her to go out, but she—"

"All right. Did either of them seem—oh, angry when she turned them down for dates?"

"Well, I don't think so. It wasn't anything—anything big, you know. I guess she was just another girl to them. What? Well, sure we got along O.K., sharing the apartment, except she was a lot fussier than I am, at housekeeping and all—" Monica uttered a little half sob. "I've been sorry, think about the little spats we had about my not hanging things up, and the dishes— A person's made the way they're made, you know."

"Yes. This Saxon still at the college? And Mr. Stettin?"

She nodded. "Do you want to see them? But I don't see why—"

"What about Stover?"

Monica blew her nose again. "Oh, Ron said he moved down to Los Angeles a while back."

Schenke and Galeano had gone to dig the bullet out of Ruby Jewel's apartment wall, and delivered it to S.I.D. They sat around waiting for the first call of the evening, and they didn't wait long; at eight-ten there was a call, a break-in out on Third. Landers and Conway went out on it.

It was a chain market. The manager was waiting for them; the Traffic men had wanted to call an ambulance, but he said he was all right. His name was Raymond Osney, and he said balefully, "I just hope the district manager will listen to me now! And I'll just bet it was the same punks who tried to break in the other night! I had one of you fellows out here looking at the marks—a Sergeant Palliser, very nice fellow. Six holdups and four break-ins we've had, the last— And the burglar alarm system no damn good. *I* keep saying about the dogs. Trained guard dogs. You can rent them, you know. I just hope the district manager—"

"Well, what happened here, sir?"

"The crime rate— Well, I stayed late. I'm usually the last one out, we close at seven-thirty on Thursdays. Everybody else was gone, the butcher'd just driven off, I know his car, needs a lube-job—and I'd locked up and started out the back door, when they jumped me. Knocked me out and tied me up with all this damned adhesive tape, where they learned that one—all the crime on TV—and when I came to, they were busy as packrats carting stuff out—cigarettes and liquor, of course—"

"Did you get a look at them? How many?"

"Three. Three big louts with the long hair and sideburns and boots— Mex," said Osney. "Not that it signifies. You get all sorts. They didn't know I'd come to. I got a pretty good look, they'd put on the stockroom lights so as to see what they were doing. I can give you descriptions, all right. I think I'd seen one of them in here before—probably casing the joint."

"Do you feel up to that now, sir? Could you come in tomorrow to look at some mug shots?"

"You're damn right," said Osney. "I will. I'll do that. Now if we'd had a trained guard dog here—" he sounded wistful. "I've seen articles. Much more efficient than burglar alarms—"

They got back to the office at nine-fifty, and Landers had just sat down and lit a cigarette when a new call came in, from a Traffic unit. Robbery, possible rape, possible shooting, meet the Traffic men at Central Receiving.

"What the hell?" said Galeano. "Business picking up." He and Schenke started out on that. Five minutes later the phone rang on Schenke's desk; Landers picked it up.

"Who's this? Oh, Tom. I'm stuck up here," said Palliser, "overnight. Something showed, and I've got to see this Stettin but of course the college is closed for vacation and he's out on a date, nobody knows where. I'll catch him in the morning. I've called Robin, but you might tell the boss."

"Will do. Something showed on Askell?"

"Just maybe. I'll just pass on a name. Gene Stover. Said to be male,

Caucasian, very general description could fit the fellow at the Orange Julius bar. Nothing solid. You might look for him in the phone-book."

"What's he got to do with Lila?"

"I don't know," said Palliser. "It's just the first faint smell of a lead we've had. I'll probably be back sometime tomorrow."

"O.K.," said Landers. He put the phone down and turned to face Bill Moss and his rookie partner, with a large prosperous-looking male citizen wearing a broad red welt on one temple and an indignant expression.

"Mr. Joseph Lambert," said Moss. "This is Detective Landers, Detective Conway. Mr. Lambert wants to lay a complaint." He was grinning.

Lambert came up to Landers' desk and sat down with a thump in the chair beside it. The Traffic men went out; Landers and Conway stared after them. Lambert was about fifty, bald as an egg, a big heavy man with china-blue eyes and a petulant mouth. He was wearing what had been an impeccably tailored suit, Oxford gray Dacron, white shirt and a gaudy tie; but the suit was smeared with dirt and oil all down one side and the tie was torn.

"Say, what kind of burg is this anyway?" he demanded aggrievedly.

"Are you all right, sir? Your head—"

"I'm all right. Bang on the head. But what kind of burg—I've never been here before. Came to our convention—Association of Rural Employers of America. We're at that big hotel—Ambassador. What the hell, I'm away from home, not that I'm married, not me, boys—I slip a sawbuck to the bellhop, fetch a dame, and he looks at me like a damn deacon! Says it's against the law! My God, any city I ever been in—any hotel—"

"We tend to be kind of puritanical here," said Landers gravely. He exchanged a glance with Conway. L.A. tried to be: they weren't about to tell Lambert all the trouble and mess the Vice Bureau was in, trying to close up all those massage parlors.

"You don't look old enough to be a cop," Lambert informed him. "My God! So I go out, find a friendly bartender or something, I know the ropes, any city—and I run into this dame. Looks good—sounds good, she leads me out and next thing I know I'm coming to in a back alley some place, stripped clean—"

"Could you describe the woman, sir?" Conway's lips twitched.

"Damn right. Good-lookin' dame, medium-size, swell figure, one o' these little tiny skirts, good legs—she had black hair. By damn!" said

Lambert thickly. "This is the damndest burg I ever struck, even the dames for sale shortchange a guy—"

After they'd called a cab to take him back to the hotel, they started to laugh. "General description, but could be that pair going around luring the marks," said Conway. "Little windfall for them. Did he say three hundred bucks and a diamond ring?"

"That's just what. We're in the wrong job," said Landers.

At Central Receiving Hospital, Schenke and Galeano met the two uniformed men in Emergency. "What's up?"

The older man shrugged. "She flagged us down along Eighth—screaming, hysterical, clothes all torn. Assault of some kind. She was pretty upset, we brought her right over here. The doctor's got her in there."

"O.K., you get back on tour. If we need any more from you we'll let you know." They waited five minutes before a doctor came out to them.

"You can see her now—she wants to talk to you. I've given her a sedative. She's calmed down now—just hysteria and shock, she's not hurt much."

"Raped?"

"Assaulted, I gather. No, she hasn't been raped. She said she got away from him before— She's a Mrs. Sidney."

She was sitting in a low plastic chair in one of the examining rooms, her head on one hand, moaning a little still as the doctor's sedative quieted her heart. "Mrs. Sidney?" said Galeano gently. "Can you tell us—"

"Oh, are you police? Please, are you— It's my husband!" she said urgently. "It's Ken—please find out what happened! I thought there was a shot—I tried to fight him, he dragged me into the car, I tried to scream and I couldn't—oh, please—"

"Where was this, Mrs. Sidney? Your husband was with you?"

"*Yes,* of course—oh, why won't you understand?" she burst out passionately. "Ken—we'd just come back to the car—in the parking lot behind the restaurant—when this terrible man—he had a gun, a big Negro man, and he robbed Ken and dragged me— Oh, please find out what's happened to Ken!" She began to sob, and the doctor came up efficiently.

They looked at each other. "Are you thinking what I'm thinking?" said Schenke.

"*Camerato,*" said Galeano, "we all make mistakes. It looks as if Mrs. Macauley made one picking this Gosling. And he's running because he doesn't like our company, period. It's not very likely, if he was the X on that one, he'd stop running to do it again." There was a public phone halfway down the hall; he fished out a dime and called the office, and got Landers. "Have you by any chance had a call to a new body?"

"Are you psychic? We're just rolling on it. Man, said to be shot."

"Where?"

"Parking lot of a restaurant on Wilshire—Il Trovatore. Why?"

"Oh, brother," said Galeano. "I can just hear what the lieutenant'll say tomorrow morning."

"What?" said Hackett and Higgins together. They were staring at Wanda Larsen.

"You mean, you're here to do our *reports? Type* our reports? I will be damned!" said Hackett. "We wondered why you were—well, I mean—"

"She thought we didn't like her," said Grace, grinning. "It's what she did for Goldberg's boys. A private secretary. Did you ever hear of such a thing?"

"Well, for God's sake," said Shogart, surprised. "You didn't know? I couldn't figure it—didn't like to stick my neck out and ask why you were giving Wanda the cold shoulder. We've all got our own ways of doing things, I said when Wanda asked me about it. Thought maybe you didn't trust her, or missed your own girl— You didn't know? You mean you didn't have a girl in your old office? Be damned."

"We're used to doing it the hard way," said Higgins.

"The lieutenant laughed like anything and said it was a comedy of errors," said Wanda. "Lieutenant Goldberg was always satisfied, and I'll try to do my best—you don't even have to dictate to me, just give me your notes—"

"Oh, Wanda's a whiz," said Shogart casually. "I haven't typed a report in four years, since she got assigned to us." Hackett and Higgins were dumb.

"Very truly sought after and wonderfully popular," said Mendoza sardonically from the doorway. "Same like Old Man Kangaroo. We now have complications setting in. Whoever pulled the Macauley assault, it doesn't seem to have been Gosling. He did it again last night."

"You don't say," said Hackett.

"But the way he ran—" said Piggott. "And took a shot at us—" It was Glasser's day off, supposedly; in reality he'd be attending that board hearing up in I.A., because he'd fired the gun last night. Rules and regulations—

"All right, Gosling's got a rap sheet as long as my arm. Cops come after him, he runs. An involuntary reaction, if that's the term I want." They had followed him into his office: Hackett, Higgins, Shogart, Piggott and Grace. "We still want Gosling, to try to clear him out of the way. I doubt very strongly that, knowing we're on him, knowing we'll likely have the plate-number on his girlfriend's car, he'd succumb to temptation again last night. But it looks as if we start over again on that. *¡Condenación!*" Mendoza brushed his moustache back and forth. "And what the hell John's come across up there, on Lila—"

Sergeant Lake looked in. "A Dr. Locke at Central Receiving."

"*Bueno.*" Mendoza picked up the phone.

"You asked to be kept informed about Mr. Pound. He has regained consciousness—he's still very weak, but we think he'll pull through now. If you want to talk to him, very briefly, Lieutenant—"

"Thanks so much. Someone'll be over. . . . Pound. We can talk to him, very briefly, so says the doctor. Matt, you go and do that. Now we've got this new break-in, a Mr. Osney coming in to look at some mug shots—Jase, you can take him down—"

"What about Macauley, do we start all over?" Hackett looked annoyed, Higgins just resigned. The citizenry, however well-meaning, was frequently muddleheaded and mistaken.

Mendoza put out his cigarette and immediately got out another, turning it round in his fingers. "*Palabra suelta no tiene vuelta,*" he said. "Careless talk—she was upset, she'd just seen her husband killed, and photographs can be confusing. We can't blame her for an honest mistake. What we can deduce, she was right about the general type—"

"Which is very damn general," said Grace.

"*De veras.* Feed the general description into the computer for some more names out of records. The long way round we usually go. And I do wonder what John's come up with. It was only on a vague hunch I sent him up there—"

"Your crystal ball," said Hackett sardonically.

"But," said Piggott, and was silent, and said, "Oh, well, they are spooky, the ones like Gosling—that's so. Even if he's clean, take off like a jackrabbit when he knows we're after him."

And Sergeant Lake was back. "New body," he said tersely. "Out at the Medical Center. One of the maintenance crew just called in."

"*¡Válgame Dios!* Come on, Art. We'll go see what that is. Talk about women's work!" But as Mendoza got up to follow Hackett out, Lake back at the switchboard put up a hand.

"Here's John."

"You go on, I'll meet you there." Mendoza took the phone. "John? What have you turned up?"

"I don't know, could be nothing at all. I'm starting back in half an hour. I just thought I'd pass it on, so you can follow it up. This Gene Stover. He's supposed to be working for a brokerage—Stone, Fox and Meyer—on Spring."

"What's he got to do with Lila?"

"I don't know that he's anything to do with the murder. Just, you might ask him about it."

CHAPTER 7

Mendoza was delayed five minutes by the arrival of a packet from the lab: Lila Askell's jewelry. He'd asked for it, he remembered; he wondered why. There were four modest items: a high-school class ring in ten-karat gold, a necklace and a pair of earrings. Those were just costume jewelry, but the necklace was rather unusual, large daisy-faces, flat polished goldplate, strung together by a chain.

There was a note from Scarne: "We got two good latents off the necklace. Not in our files, sent to Feds."

"Well, how gratifying," said Mendoza. But if they weren't in the FBI's files either, not much help.

When he got out to the U.S.C. Medical Center, he spotted Hackett's scarlet Barracuda parked in front of the first building on Zonal Avenue, and turned up beside it. It was a big four-story building, and over the tall front entrance the graven letters read *U. S. C. School of Medicine*. There were voices beyond the double doors.

In a large square lobby Hackett and Higgins were talking to a little crowd of men, all in rough work-clothes, all looking shocked and shaken. "Luis," said Hackett, turning to him, "another funny thing. It's upstairs—third floor. We left it for the ambulance and lab men. There's a truck on the way. One of the maintenance crew, a Joe Daly—"

"We aren't a maintenance crew," said one man. He stood out from the other four nondescripts, two white, two Negro. He was a stocky man about fifty with a shock of gray-brown hair, and he said, "You another detective? We aren't nothing to do with the college. Superior Cleaners, office on Sunset Boulevard. We go all over, we got contracts, buildings, offices, public and private—houses too. But who in hell would want to hurt Joe?"

"Nobody had no call," said one of the colored men. "He was a good guy, never had no trouble with anybody. Just had their first grand-baby last week, and Joe was proud as punch. It don't seem possible, Joe up there all cut—"

"All right," said Hackett. "We haven't done much more than look at the body, Luis. Now, you'll be the foreman of this crew, Mr.—"

"Hansen. Chris Hansen. Well, we just lay out the work like it falls. Listen, he musta never gone away last night. Jim—"

"Yeah, that just came to me now too. We see he's cold. But how in hell—"

"One at a time," said Hackett. "You were here last night? Cleaning?"

Hansen nodded. He got out a cigarette slowly and lit it: a methodical man, slow of thought. "I don't know what coulda happened or why. Or how. Joe! Joe's been working for Superior fifteen years, steady quiet guy. Never any trouble with anybody—a good worker. I don't know what coulda— Well, see, general speakin' we clean this place at night. Like a lot of public places. Once a week, floors and windows, it's one of the steady jobs. A contract on it. College's shut for vacation now, so it don't matter when we come in, but we was here last night, about five to eight I guess, doin' the first two floors. This is a big place, can't finish it all in one night." A little murmur from the other men. "So, we get the first two floors done, I'd thought maybe we could get to the third, but then I look at the time—"

"I and Dick was already startin' up there," spoke up one of the white men. "It comes to me, could be Joe'd already gone up, Chris. I don't recall seein' him after about then. You said leave it, on accounta that job that got wrote off for this mornin', we could finish up here today, and we all took off."

"That's right. I said as long as the college's shut, we finish off the top floors this mornin', we got a empty office building to do this afternoon. I didn't recall about Joe—I guess we all figgered he left when the rest of us did—"

"This was about eight o'clock?"

"A bit after. About. We come on about"—he looked at his watch—"forty minutes ago— I oughta say, I drive the truck with all the heavy cleanin' equipment, the other boys drive their own cars. And here's Joe's old Dodge right in the lot, he's early on the job I think, but he isn't nowhere, so we go looking—"

Scarne and Fisher came in with a couple of lab kits, and the ambulance attendants after them. Mendoza drifted up the stairs after them. The first couple of floors, open doors gave on obvious classrooms, blackboards and desks. Elsewhere would be autopsy rooms, laboratories—whatever they did have at a medical school. Their steps echoed in the emptiness of the big building.

At the top of the third flight of stairs he stopped and cocked his head. "Scarne."

"What's up?" Scarne turned, came to look. "Well, well. Hey, Pete." It was lying there on the second step down, almost against the outside wall. A pair of desk scissors, the blades about eight inches long, half-open, and dark-stained. Scarne squatted, opened his case, found a plastic bag and delicately edged the scissors into it.

They went down to the middle of the wide corridor. The rooms up here all seemed to be small offices: Mendoza glanced at the little plaques on the doors. Dr. William E. Danielson. Dr. Paul Friedman. Dr.—

"At a guess," said one of the ambulance men, "about twelve hours, Lieutenant."

"Mmh," said Mendoza. He pulled up his trousers and squatted over the body, which was sprawled face up just outside a half-open door. Joe Daly had been a middle-aged Negro, his skin curiously sallow-saffron in death, his scant tight-curled hair graying, and his face wore an odd serenity. He wore striped overalls and a blue shirt, and there were dark stains along his left side. The flaccid wrist was cold and limp. Mendoza stood up and looked at the open door. Dr. Frederick Loose. *"Extraño,"* said Mendoza. Vacation, the college closed, who would have any reason to be here last night but the cleaning crew? "I want the works," he told the men from S.I.D. "Photographs and a careful look around here."

He left them starting to work and went back downstairs. The men were talking to each other, and Hackett and Higgins comparing notes. "Well, you heard the gist of it," said Hackett. "Short and sweet. They thought he'd left last night. He hadn't. What did he run into up there on the third floor? The two who started up didn't go all the way, but nobody heard a thing."

"What he ran into was a pair of desk scissors," said Mendoza. "Let's hope X left some prints. So that looks like the very impulsive thing."

"All they say about him, a very ordinary guy," said Higgins. "Respectable hard worker. Went to the Baptist church. Wife and family. Reliable, quiet, no arguments."

"Mmh," said Mendoza. "I think you can count out the crew, George. Those scissors came out of an office up there, very likely Dr. Frederick Loose's office. *¿Porqué?* Who knows?"

"So now we go break the news to the widow," said Higgins. "Wonder why she didn't miss him last night? Talk about shapeless things—"

"You might find out who Dr. Loose is, and who might have had occasion to be invading his office with him out of it," said Mendoza.

The hospital had released Mrs. Sidney; she hadn't been hurt much. It was a house on Milner Road in the hills above Hollywood, a section of older homes on narrow curving streets, not particularly fashionable. When she opened the door to him and looked at the badge, stood back to let him in, he saw she was alone.

"I know you've got to ask me things," she said. "I'll—I'll try to help you however—I haven't met you before. Lieutenant? They—they told me I couldn't make any—arrangements right away—"

"You haven't any family, Mrs. Sidney?"

She shook her head, a handkerchief to her eyes. "They said—the other man, he had an Italian name, I don't—he said something about identifying—K-Ken. That if there was some relative, or—but there isn't. We were both only children, and—"

"Where did your husband work?" Mendoza offered her a cigarette, and she blew her nose, sat up and took it.

"Thank you." She bent to his lighter. "He was a C.P.A. with a big firm on the boulevard—" She named it. One of the men there could probably make the formal identification. Mendoza let her take her time; this one, he suspected, was a little flighty, not as sensible as Mrs. Macauley, and he didn't want her fingering another wrong X. "Oh!" she said, and burst into tears and put down the cigarette in a big fancy ceramic ashtray on the coffee table. "But that just r-reminds me, it was all my fault! That we were *there* at all—last night! I tried, you know, I tried to keep expenses down and save and—but everything's so high now, he made good money but everything— And I'm not *used* to thinking about all that—and he was awfully patient but we did have sp-spats and —oh, oh, oh! We'd just m-made up and he said he was sorry and he'd take me out to dinner—"

Mendoza didn't press her. After a minute she sat up and said chokingly, "Oh, I'm sorry, I didn't mean to say all that—only you can see how I'd—I know you want to ask questions." She blew her nose again, forlornly, and looked at him.

"We won't press you too hard right now, Mrs. Sidney. Do you think you'd recognize the man who attacked you?"

"I don't know. I'm not sure. It all happened so fast—and of course it was dark. He was big, and a Negro, sort of medium dark I think, and— oh, it was awful! We'd just got back to the car—"

It was, she had told Galeano last night, a Dodge four-door, two years old. They had the plate-number from the D.M.V., and there was a call out on it.

"—When he just *lunged* out of the dark, I don't know where he came from, and we saw the gun, and he said, Give me your money or something like that, and Ken— And then he grabbed *me* and I tried to scream, but he got me in the car, I think he must have grabbed the keys from Ken—"

Definitely flighty, another proposition than the down-to-earth Mrs. Macauley. Mendoza wouldn't lay a dime on her chances of being right, picking a mug shot. She was a pretty woman, not looking her probably forty-plus years: a nice figure, her golden-brown hair exquisitely tinted and waved (or was it a wig, he wondered), and her fair complexion delicately made-up; her eyes were faded blue, a little sunken now. Her hostess robe was in excellent taste, dusty rose fleece. She had beautiful hands, small and long-fingered, and her engagement solitaire was a fair size; on the other hand she wore an oval opal set round with baguette emeralds.

"You can't describe him definitely? Height, clothes?"

She thought, "Well, he—he swore at us. Dreadfully. And Ken didn't try to put up a fight when he had that gun. I don't know anything about guns, I couldn't say what kind it was. But I heard the shot, and then he had hold of me and I tried to struggle with him, he tore my dress—in the car—and I think he must've thought he'd knocked me unconscious, because he let go of me and the car wasn't moving very fast then, we'd just turned a corner I think, and I managed to get the door open and I fell out—I hardly noticed that then, falling I mean—I just got up and *ran* —as fast as I could, toward the lights—and it was Wilshire and when I saw the police car—"

"Do you think you could identify him if you saw him again?"

"Why, have you arrested somebody?" she asked excitedly. "For Ken —oh, that other man too! I saw it in the paper. He did that before—and it didn't *say* he, you know, raped that woman but I thought probably— Well, I don't know," she said. "It was dark, and I was so frightened—"

The citizenry, thought Mendoza in the Ferrari. But they came all sorts, and you couldn't expect careful, sensible witnesses in every case. You could make allowances for Stella Sidney: she was rather a silly woman to start with. He started back to the office to see what else might have turned up.

The man in the hospital bed looked weak and gray; but the bright blue eyes were alert on Piggott. "You—p'lice?"

"That's right, sir." The nurse stood by watchfully. "Now don't tire yourself, but can you tell us anything about who did this to you? You were attacked and robbed, we—"

The head inclined slightly. Lieutenant Colonel Pound had been a handsome man in his prime and in old age might be called distinguished, dressed and upright. He had straight features, a strong mouth, his plentiful hair was curly and gray, and he had his own teeth. He said, "Damn—son o' bitch, con me—thought at first—"

"Just take it easy, sir."

"Got tell you," said Pound. "Must be—senile, old age. Said—officer back—Vietnam. Seemed—nice young fella. The men's store—new tie. 'Cross from—hotel. Fox. Fox, said. Carl—Fox, Lieutenant."

The nurse had her hand on his wrist. "Now don't strain yourself, sir," said Piggott. "I'm getting it."

"'Vited—room for drink. But—not—so easy—fool ol' warhorse. *Not* officer—wrong—" He sank back with a long sigh.

"I think that's enough," said the nurse firmly. But the blue eyes opened again and glared at her.

"You—mind your business, bossy. I got tell—Goddamn common thief —call 'self Army Off'cer—son o' bitch," said Lieutenant Colonel Pound. "Fox. Carl—Fox."

"All right, sir, we'll try to pick him up." You had to admire the old boy, thought Piggott, chuckling to himself. Still plenty of fight left in him.

He went back to the office, automatically intending to write up the report on that interview, and it wasn't until he came past Wanda Larsen's desk that he remembered what she'd said. "You mean it? You can type up reports from notes?"

"Surely, Mr. Piggott." She extended her hand, "Oh, your writing's not nearly as bad as E.M.'s! So the old man gave you something. Good for him. I'll have this ready this afternoon, I've got one of E.M.'s to do and then one for Sergeant Hackett. *That's* a funny thing, that man stabbed to death at the medical college. No rhyme or reason, he said."

Piggott realized all of a sudden what a boon Wanda Larsen was going to be to Robbery-Homicide. Now he could go right back to the legwork, the tiresome typing off his mind. Doubtless the paperwork would pile up on occasion, but with Wanda doing all that (as long as the reports came along eventually, administration would be satisfied) it should make for a much more efficient use of the men's time.

"You," he said, "are going to save us a lot of work around here. Pity we didn't find out about it sooner."

Grace came in with, inevitably, a sheaf of Polaroid shots in one hand, just displayed to Sergeant Lake. "I've got Mr. Osney settled down looking at mug shots. Any new jobs?"

"You can come help me on a pretty wild goose chase," said Piggott. "Show me the snapshots first."

Grace laughed. "Bore you all to death, Matt. It's just, we've been married five years and Ginny so anxious—I suppose we're a little nuts over Celia."

"But she is a cute one, Jase."

There was a men's clothing store catercorner to the Biltmore Hotel on Olive Street, and another about a block up. They drew blank at the first one—none of the clerks or the manager reacted to a description of Lieutenant Colonel Pound. At the second one, a boyish-looking clerk very nattily outfitted in the latest mod style said, "I think I remember him. I noticed his West Point ring. Tall old fellow, about seventy maybe, but looked like somebody."

"That's the one. Do you remember him talking to anybody in here? He was only here once?" All of a sudden Piggott thought, but that couldn't have been Christmas Day when the old boy was assaulted, the store would have been closed. He'd taken it for granted that Pound had meant he'd asked this Fox up to his room right then, but—

"Yeah, that's right. It was the day before Christmas. Along in late afternoon. I couldn't say if he talked to anybody. We had a lot of customers all that day—women buying ties and belts and wallets, you know. He could have, I wouldn't notice. He'd been here, looking around like, awhile before I waited on him."

"Well, so where do we go from there?" asked Piggott in the street.

Grace scratched one ear. "I," he said, "have got a simple mind."

"We all know that, Jase."

"The old fellow said this Fox told him he was an ex-Army officer. Then for some reason—by implication, after Fox took up the invitation and came to see him—Pound spotted he wasn't."

"I took it that—"

"Well, it occurs to me," said Grace, "that the fellow must have known enough about the Army to fool the old boy even awhile. So let's ask Uncle Sam if the Army knows the name. I think the lab picked up some latents there."

"It's a good thing you've got a simple mind," said Piggott. "Let's."

Mendoza had just sat down at a single table at Federico's, for an early lunch, when Palliser came up and sat down across from him.

"Head winds. And the flight was delayed. I only got into Burbank an hour ago. Jimmy said you were here. Has anybody found Gene Stover?"

"We've been a little busy. Elucidate. The small steak, Adam."

"Same for me. Well, it's the only link with L.A. that showed. She was a serious girl, not interested much in dating. Stover is a sort of pal of Monica's boyfriend, Ron Stettin—new teacher at the college. And—" Palliser filled him in on that. "It sounds like nothing, but the mention of L.A.—"

"*Pues sí*. Why a sort of pal?"

Palliser was silent; he'd cut himself shaving, and unconsciously fingered the nick in his long jaw. "Stettin," he said, "isn't going steady with Monica, who would pall on anybody—almost anybody. Nice enough girl, a little silly. He was out with somebody else last night, I don't know who. I got him on the phone about eleven. Introduced myself, and he said he'd be busy all day today. I pressed him, and he said oh, well, he was usually up early, I could come round about seven-thirty. He teaches political science—"

"*¡Ay de mí!*" said Mendoza.

"—And looks about as you might expect. Van Dyke beard—I suspect he dyes it, it's darker than his hair—and a bushy moustache. He said he and Stover went to college together down here—UCLA—and he hadn't seen him in at least three years until he ran into him up there about eight months ago, in a record shop. They both collect folk music." Mendoza uttered another groan. "Well, I can't help it. Anyway, Stettin says it was all very casual, those few dates with Lila, mostly Monica pressuring him to get her dates, and Stover obliged. It wasn't, he said, anything important. In fact, just what Monica told me, and it doesn't seem to have been. But Stover is said to be in L.A."

"And not interested in Lila or she in him. What was he doing up there?"

"Working in another brokerage. Stettin said he told him—Stover, that is—that he thought he might do better in a smaller town, but he didn't, and finally he came back here. To the brokerage he'd been with here before."

"And how would Stover have known—if he would have cared—that Lila'd be here for three hours only that day?"

"I don't know. It was the only link with L.A.," repeated Palliser. "But—"

"But?" said Mendoza. Palliser was not as diffident as he had been once, one of the youngest sergeants on the force; but he still had moments of self-doubt. "I've got the priority on hunches around here, John, but as I've told you before, never ignore your feelings."

"Yes," said Palliser uneasily. "He was nervous about something. Stettin. And he hadn't any reason to be. He told me about nine times what a lovely girl Lila was and how terrible it is she's murdered. And by everything Monica said, and everything else he said, as far as he was concerned she'd just been a dog he'd had to dredge up dates for."

"There's a saying about not speaking ill—"

"Oh, he could have been—just observing the amenities. Sure," said Palliser. "But he was nervous."

"Which might be interesting," said Mendoza.

Shogart had covered the Askell inquest: pure formality, the open verdict. The Macauley inquest this afternoon would be more of the same. This afternoon somebody had better chase up to that C.P.A. firm in Hollywood and ask one of Ken Sidney's coworkers to make the formal identification of his body.

As Mendoza and Palliser came into the office, a tallish gray-haired man was just coming out. He stopped. "Sergeant Palliser—nice to see you again."

"Oh—Mr. Osney. Don't tell me—"

"Yep, a break-in. Bet it was the same ones tried it that time. But I just made one of the bastards for you, out of your picture books." Osney smiled. "Guy named Biretta. I had 'em spotted as Mex, but turns out this one's Italiano. Well, people come all sorts. One thing, it convinced the district manager. I've been at him, like I told you."

"About what?"

"The dogs," said Osney. "A lot of our other stores have got hit too—crime-rate like it is. And he calls me last night, he'd been reckoning up how much it'd come to, got some estimates and all. Turns out it'd be cheaper to rent the trained guard dogs than put in a new burglar alarm system. He's got it set up, with one of these kennels hires 'em out."

"That's good."

"You bet. Dobermans, they are. Anybody think twice, try a break-in with something like that waiting the other side of the door," said Osney with satisfaction.

Hackett and Higgins had spent a tedious and largely unproductive morning. The reason Mrs. Daly hadn't missed her husband last night was that she was staying with her daughter helping with the new baby. They seemed to be a close family: everybody upset and crying and saying why did it happen to Joe. No trouble on the job, he never had fights with anybody—

They had got names of the faculty and where they could be reached. Hackett didn't think much of Luis' idea that this Dr. Loose had something to do with it, but sometimes Luis' ideas led somewhere; he'd see the man, anyway.

Belatedly he realized what a blessing their policewoman was going to be, handing over his notes to be transformed into a report. "You're going to make quite a difference around here, lady," he told Wanda.

He was still trying to skip lunch. The flu, going through the family, had been a virulent type: he'd been down to two-oh-six, and even with skipping lunch he was now up to two-ten. It was, he decided with dismal humor, a losing battle. George would be settled somewhere now consuming a steak sandwich or a hamburger with everything on it, and he never gained a pound. It wasn't fair, of course, but nothing said life had to be.

Thinking about hamburgers and french fries, he called the morgue. Bainbridge as usual said, "I've only just seen the damn body. Give me time."

"Well, you can say something, Doctor. We found a pair of scissors on the scene—desk type, about an eight-inch blade. Blood all over 'em."

"So what more do you want?" asked Bainbridge. "That's probably the weapon. It's the ragged kind of wound scissors would make, what I've seen so far. I can't do the autopsy until you've got a formal identification."

"Coming up," said Hackett. Daly's son-in-law had offered to do that.

He got up and started for Mendoza's office to bring him up to date on all that, but Lake stopped him at the switchboard. "Mr. Purdy. That latest burglary."

"Oh," said Hackett. That. The amateur burglar, and nowhere to go on it at all: no latents, no leads. He took the phone. "Sergeant Hackett."

"Now I tell you," said Dan Purdy. "I don't care which of you comes, but some detective just better come and ask this guy questions. See? Because there they are as big as life, I see 'em with my own eyes and the Lord knows both Millie and I ought to *know*. There they are, where this damn thief sold 'em—the man won't answer any of our questions, you he says he'll talk to, and you just better—"

"What, Mr. Purdy? What are you—"

"Why, Millie's garnet ring and pin that belonged to her ma! That's what I'm talking about! Plain as day in the window of this pawnshop on Grand Avenue, and it's only accident I noticed 'em. I happened to be up that way just now to a secondhand place, looking for a cheap radio—can't afford to buy another TV, even secondhand—and I come past, look all casual at the window, and there by God they were. Right in the window, for sale! So I come home and get Millie to look, see—I was on my lunch hour and I never thought to tell the boss, but what the hell—and she says they are too, so you better—"

"All right," said Hackett soothingly, his stomach rumbling. "I'll come right away. Where?" He jotted down the address. The burglar, taking the petty loot—if all the loot available: maybe now a lead of sorts. He went downstairs to the scarlet Barracuda in the lot and drove up to Grand Avenue.

Indubitably, there was a garnet ring and brooch, old-fashioned-looking, in the pawnshop window. He supposed the Purdys would know their own property.

"Damn right," grunted Purdy; they had been waiting for him. "So you just tell the sergeant where you came by them, huh?" He looked fiercely at the pawnbroker.

The pawnbroker looked at the badge uneasily. He was an undersized, scrawny man with a pug nose. "They weren't on the hot list, Sergeant. Are they stolen property? I couldn't know—when they weren't on the list. These people said—but how should I—"

"So, where'd you get them?" Hackett looked at the two humble pieces as they were fetched out and laid on the counter.

"Well—he said he didn't want a ticket on them, wanted to sell. I gave him ten bucks apiece."

"*Ten*—" said Mrs. Purdy faintly. "Why, my mother set such store by—"

"Who?" asked Hackett.

"I never saw him before," said the pawnbroker. "I don't know. Describe—well, he was just a guy. A—an elderly guy. Ordinary. I got him to sign a receipt, of course." He started to scrabble through an ancient filing case behind the counter. "I always— Here it is." He handed it to Hackett gingerly.

Hackett took one look at it and began to laugh. He leaned on the counter laughing helplessly. They stared at him, indignant and surprised, and he bent double, guffawing.

In neat half-printing, across the bottom of the sleazy paper form, was the signature: *O. N. A. Fixedincome.*

It was too good a joke not to share; he took it back to Mendoza's office. "This burglar, Luis. I like him. I like him the hell of a lot. A sense of humor he's got. Purdy spotted some of the loot they—Luis?"

"*¿Qué?*" said Mendoza, looking up from a report. "But that's funny —an automatic— Some of the loot, yes?"

Hackett told him, produced the slip. Mendoza dropped his cigarette and laughed, began to cough, rescued the cigarette and gasped, "*¡Dineross son calidad!* More truth than poetry, Arturo. Oh, by God, that's priceless—" and they both dissolved in mirth at the word.

"If we ever catch him, I'll hate to arrest him," said Hackett.

Mendoza sat back and groped for a new cigarette; his dark eyes were alive and alight with laughter. "*¡Qué hombre!* And why the pawnbroker didn't spot— But that's another thing, of course. We see—what we expect to see," and he looked back at the papers on his desk without touching them.

"Meaning?"

"Well, I read it—Tom's report—and it was just another fact. Now—"

"What?"

"*No sé.* The wild ones can be—inconsistent. Traffic spotted Ruby Jewel's VW, by the way. Left down on Manchester. No smell of Gosling."

"Well, we're pretty sure he's out of the running now, aren't we?"

"*No sé,*" said Mendoza again. "Let me see that thing again, I like it. More truth than poetry—" He laughed.

He sat, at seven-thirty, before the belated hostages to fortune, the twin monsters who, combining the unlikely genes of McCann, Weir and Mendoza, were unpredictable. Who were, of course, only three. And, speak of small mercies, hadn't inherited Alison's red hair. Two pairs of eyes regarded him solemnly—Johnny's his mother's hazel-green below his father's widow's peak, Terry's her father's dark-brown under his sharp-arched brows—and he said, "So, *hijítos.* More stories in the nice new book. About an emperor—"

"*No comprendo,*" said Johnny uninterestedly. "*Mamacíta* say, maybe *el pájaro* come back, makes nice nest for *los niños*—"

"And this emperor was very fond of fine clothes—"

"Whoooo!" contributed Terry. "*El pájaro* fly down an' bite Bast 'n' Sheba!"

Mendoza persisted, "And one day there were two very clever thieves —listen, *niños—dos ladrones muy hábiles*—came to the—" He stopped and looked at the twins resignedly. He had persisted with Andersen because he liked the stories—nobody had ever read Andersen's fairy stories to Mendoza, forty years back; but reluctantly he realized that Andersen's subtleties were a little sophisticated for the twins, just turned three. Alison would have to be convinced that Andersen could wait. It was a pity, but the emperor's new clothes were a bit beyond—

After the simple bloodthirsty joys of Grimm.

Terry suddenly dissolved in tears. "Never no more 'bout *El rinoceronte*—or *El Jaguar*—"

And Johnny, suddenly reminded of past joys, shouted exuberantly, "*El Gato* all by himself! *Sí, El Gato*—"

Well, the Just-So Stories more suited to their age. Mendoza put Andersen down. And nobody ever any better than Mr. Kipling, at storytelling—but he rather liked Andersen.

The Emperor's New Clothes—

CHAPTER 8

The signature on the pawnbroker's receipt had tickled the whole office. Wanda Larsen, arriving early on Saturday morning, thus had the privilege of telling Sergeant Farrell, who sat in for Lake on Lake's day off. Farrell was still chuckling when Mendoza came in, natty in silver gray, with the others straggling in within five minutes.

There were reports centered on Mendoza's desk; he scanned them rapidly. The Sidneys' Dodge had been spotted by Traffic just after the watch changed last night, parked on Leeward Avenue. It had been towed in for examination. A fairly quiet night, last night had been, for this office: a couple of accidents with D.O.A.'s, a mugging down on Fourth, another gas station held up.

"This Loose," began Hackett.

"About that Fox," said Grace. Mendoza lifted a hand as the phone buzzed at him.

"Scarne."

"Hold it a minute," said Mendoza, and asked, "did anybody arrange for identification of Sidney's body?"

"I did, yesterday afternoon," said Piggott. "You said to try the place he'd worked. Fellow named Dombey said he'd be glad to oblige, he'll be in this morning. Shall I hang around to take him down?"

"I'll see him . . . Scarne? What have you got?"

"This and that. First of all, that hotel room. A lot of latents there, we covered the personal stuff first. And one of those glasses was wiped clean. But we picked up four pretty good prints off the other—"

"Belonging to Lieutenant Colonel Pound."

"Funnily enough, no. In fact, it looks as if in the heat of the moment your X wiped off the wrong glass. If they didn't make mistakes we wouldn't catch 'em. They're not in our records, I sent 'em to the FBI."

"All correct. That's a step on. Anything else?"

"Something," said Scarne, "I sweated blood over. That hijacked ruck. I had to get the legit driver's prints for comparison, and he said omething about the gear-lever being stiff. Truck was due in for an overhaul. Well, I just had a hunch—you know they haven't left even a mudge on any of those trucks, and we figured they were wearing gloves -but you can't get as good a grip with gloves on. I went over the whole lamn gear lever practically with a magnifying glass, after I'd dusted it— t'd've been easier if I could have dismantled it first, but I didn't dare— nd I picked up two pretty good prints, on the backside of the shaft. She vas sticking, and he jerked off one glove to get a grip. I sent 'em to R. nd I. before I left last night, and the answer was waiting when I got ere just now."

"Don't tell me—"

"I do. In our records, one Kurt Kramer. I'll send up the details."

"*Por favor.* How very nice." Mendoza put the phone down and assed that on.

"Well, so maybe we catch up to Fox without the Army's help," said Grace. "I don't suppose we'll hear from them today. The FBI, possibly -they're on the ball."

"I've located Loose," said Hackett. "He's meeting George and me out at the college in twenty minutes. But what you've got in your head bout Loose—there can't be any connection, Luis—"

"Go and find out. The computer, I see, ground out some new names o look for." Fed the general description which fitted Chester Gosling— ut also a number of other men—the computer had obliged with a dozen ther names out of their records. "No, I don't suppose anything on your ake Army lieutenant will turn up today," and he handed over the list to 'iggott.

"More legwork. And you know it'll stay up in the air," said Shogart hlegmatically. "Prove an alibi? Most of these fellows are drifters, ometimes drunks—couldn't say where they were yesterday afternoon, et alone five days ago."

"We've got a bullet," Mendoza reminded him. "That .22 slug can be atched to a gun, when and if we find—" he paused and added to him- elf, "*¡Ca!* There was that . . . Off you go. Rory, get me the lab."

This time he got Duke. "On the Sidney kill. Tom Landers sent down shell-casing they found somewhere around the body in that parking t. Anything on it?"

"In the way of prints, no. It's an ejected shell case out of some kind f automatic—domestic for a guess."

"Well, the pros can always get hold of any kind they want," said Mendoza. "Thanks. Rory, let me know when a Mr. Dombey shows up." He sat down at his desk and lit a cigarette, and for some reason he was thinking about the emperor's new clothes.

"I can't get over it, a murder here," said Dr. Frederick Loose. "One of the cleaning crew? I will be damned. I don't think any of us would know any of them—and I'm sometimes here when they're working, at night, but I don't think I ever exchanged a word—" They were climbing stairs in the big modern building. "But what do you want with me? Any way I can help you, as I said on the phone, but I haven't been here for a week—nobody's been here—we're closed for the Christmas vacation. Until Tuesday."

"Yes, sir, but the man was found, and probably killed, right outside your office. When were you here last?" asked Hackett.

"My office? Well, I'm damned. It was a week ago Friday. The last day of classes before vacation. I left, let me see, about five that afternoon—" They came to the third floor and started down the hall. "We were going out to dinner that evening and I—but, here!" He stopped, and then moved forward quickly. "What the hell is my office doing open? I locked my door then, it shouldn't be open now. Did you find it like this, when you—"

"That's right," said Higgins, a little surprised. "It was locked?" He and Hackett both looked at the door at once, examined the lock, without touching it. "No deadbolt. Easy enough to get in with a piece of stiff plastic. Doctor, you'd better check to see if anything is missing. Art, I wonder if it'd be any use to get a lab man out to dust the door."

"But I don't see— What about it, Doctor?"

Loose was already at the big desk, opening drawers, riffling through manila folders. He straightened up presently and looked at them perplexedly; he was a man in his sixties, but still erect and alert; with steady dark eyes in a clerkly face. "Well, there wouldn't be anything of value here, if you're thinking of a burglary. There's never any money or—" He got out a pack of cigarettes slowly and looked down at the stacks of folders neatly piled on the desk. "Dear me," he said. He lit a cigarette. "Dear me."

"What's struck you?" asked Higgins.

"Well, the fact is, when I say anything of value—why anyone might want to break into my office—there is just one thing here I can think of, which someone might have a—a motive to get at."

"And what's that?"

"The examinations," said Loose. "Dear me, I don't like to think that of any of the students. The end-of-semester examination questions for all my classes—exams get under way the second week of January, you see. Conceivably—though as I say I don't like the thought—some student might have wanted to get a look at those. Did you say this isn't a safe ock? I thought—"

"No deadbolt," said Higgins. "But, for God's sake, what's that got to lo with Daly?"

"Nothing," said Hackett, "obviously. If that's what happened, which s the likeliest thing, it could have happened any time since a week ago yesterday afternoon."

"But Daly was killed right here, Art. Suppose he came up here and heard—"

"Oh, now, really," said Loose. "Really. Between snatching a look at examination questions and murder—"

"Farfetched," said Hackett.

"Is it? Don't drag your heels," said Higgins. "And trust your Uncle Luis' hunches. Here's two unusual things happened right here. I don't care how irrelevant they sound—to each other, as it were—doesn't the place sort of tie them up?"

Hackett passed a hand across his jaw. "Well, when you put it like that—but—"

"And what about the scissors? Dr. Loose, do you keep a pair of scissors on your desk? Are they there?"

It seemed they were missing.

"There you are," said Higgins. "You can read it. Purely an impulse kill. Whoever got into the doctor's office, for whatever reason—"

"When the building was filled with cleaners tramping around— But, by God! Of course—"

"When else could anybody get in the building? It was closed for vacation—and I'll bet that front door has a better lock on it than this one," said Higgins.

Ray Dombey showed up at headquarters at a quarter past nine, asking uncertainly if this was where he was supposed to come. He thawed quickly at Mendoza's overtures, accepted a cigarette and a cup of coffee from the machine down the hall— "Unless you're in a hurry, Mr. Dombey."

"Not to see Ken dead, I'm not," said Dombey. "Poor devil. Who'd have thought a quiet guy like Ken Sidney'd end up shot by a pro hood? Damndest thing. These days, I guess anything can happen to anybody, but you never think the—the violence can happen to you or anybody you know. How's his wife?"

"She wasn't as badly hurt as the other woman—she got away from him."

"That's good. I sort of gathered the first woman was raped. A terrible thing. Poor Ken. We've both been at Scott-Burnham a good many years—nearly twenty for me, getting on for twenty-five for Ken. It just shows you," said Dombey suddenly. He was a nondescript fellow in his late fifties, conventionally dressed, with a big Masonic ring on his right hand.

"Shows you?" Mendoza leaned back smoking lazily.

"How it's no use to worry. You know? Ken was a worrier. He worried about money—well, he made good money, but what I gathered, his wife could spend it as fast as he made it. He worried about her—she's a good deal younger, you know, they'd only been married about six years, he lost his first wife matter of ten years back—he worried about what'd happen to her if he had a heart attack or a stroke or something and couldn't work. Or if he dropped dead—he worried about keeping up his insurance. It just shows you, Lieutenant—like they say, the things we worry about never happen. Imagine him going like this— *shot.* Like the other one. It looks as if it was the same one killed Ken?"

"That's right. We've got a description of him," said Mendoza. "And we don't want to waste your time, Mr. Dombey. If you don't mind—"

"No, no, not that I'll enjoy it, but you can't ask his wife, I see that. Poor woman. He just doted on her, Ken—wanted her to have anything she wanted, and then worried because it cost money. Well—"

In the cold room at the morgue, he looked in silence at the body in the tray. Mendoza was a little surprised at the body, for no reason; Dombey had just told him that Sidney was older than his wife. And death wrought changes. But the body was that of an elderly man, sharp-nosed and sunken-eyed: a man in his sixties at least, possibly seventy. A thin old man with pinched cheeks, a few straggly gray hairs on his flat naked chest.

The bullet wound was in the right temple, and there was no exit wound. So they'd have another slug for comparison, unless it was damaged.

"Yes, that's Ken," said Dombey soberly. "I knew him twenty years. Do I have to sign something?"

Palliser was feeling annoyed. He was annoyed at Ron Stettin for setting him off on what was probably a wild goose chase, and at himself because he knew logically he was wasting time but something he couldn't get hold of made him persist.

Yesterday afternoon, on the straightforward legwork, he had gone to the downtown office of Stone, Fox and Meyer and asked for Gene Stover. Nobody by that name was currently employed there. He asked for the office manager, who told him with circumlocutions that Mr. Stover had severed connections with the firm some time ago.

"Was he fired?" asked Palliser bluntly.

"Well, let us say we didn't suit each other," said the manager.

"Look, this is official business. Was he fired for dishonesty or office politics or what?"

The manager hedged. "Well, quite frankly, we suspected that he had been—er—making up to a couple of our more elderly—er—clients. Er— female clients. In a personal— You understand, he was merely a sales-man and—" The manager looked unhappy. "He was working under Mr. Gordon, one of our top advisers—naturally a young fellow like Stover not a qualified expert on investments, but he had been—"

Passing himself off as, Palliser deduced, to the possibly gullible (and wealthy?) elderly clients. "Did he ever ask for a reference from you?" No, he hadn't.

Palliser had taken an hour to ask for Stover at seven other broker-ages along Spring, and drew blank. So this morning he had got hold of Stettin on the phone, and again Stettin made him feel uneasy. For abso-lutely no reason.

"Well, I'm afraid I can't help you," said Stettin fretfully. "All I can say is, when he went back to L.A. he hoped to get taken back by that company."

"You don't know his home address here?"

"No, I'm afraid not. It was a very casual friendship, if you can call it that at all. He was just a fellow I'd known in college."

"Does he have any family here?"

"Really I couldn't say," said Stettin. "It never—ah—came up. What we mostly discussed—that is, on the very few occasions when I saw him—was, ah, intellectual subjects. I don't know—"

"Such as."

"Oh, well—politics and the various protest groups on campus and—ah —I did tell you we're both interested in country western music—"

"You can't have talked exclusively about that."

"Well, no. But I really know very little about him and I—"

"You knew him well enough to have arranged dates for him."

"I won't be harassed like this," said Stettin. "That was Monica's doing, damn it. Must arrange a date for her roommate, and it wasn't the easiest thing to do. Gene was just—obliging, I don't see why—"

"You said Lila was a very nice girl."

"She was, she was! Don't get me wrong, Sergeant," and Stettin was placating. "But what *is* all this, anyway? It wasn't anything important, those couple of dates. And I expect Gene couldn't get another job down there and—ah—went on somewhere else. I wouldn't know. Really, I won't be—"

"Harassed," said Palliser. "Well, thank you, Mr. Stettin." He looked at the dead phone with dissatisfaction. It wasn't anything important, of course.

Coincidences—Mendoza's first answer was probably the right one. The other passenger on the bus, somebody who lived here. Who just happened to be on that bus heading home. Who got talking with Lila. Went with her to that Orange Julius bar—and having a car here, maybe offered to drive her around the city a little before her bus was due to leave. It had been broad daylight, people all around. She wouldn't have hesitated—

Damn Stettin and his political science classes and his beard; it was just nothing. He had wasted the morning on this. He had even taken the time to check all five phone books: Stover wasn't listed. Which didn't say he wasn't here, with or without a phone; some people had unlisted numbers. Or he might be sharing an apartment, the phone under another name.

Palliser decided that his imagination had been working overtime. He was still sitting there over a paper cup of coffee, wondering about Lila Askell, when Farrell had a call.

"Accident of some kind, Traffic unit's on it so it must be a D.O.A. when they route it to us. Public school playground on Ninth just past Hoover."

Palliser went out to see what it was.

Hackett, after some more argument, had called up a lab truck and ordered a thorough coverage of Loose's office, including the door. Loose said miserably that he couldn't be sure the papers had been disturbed, his examination questions for five classes. The door, of course, yielded a fine crop of smudges and partials, and the best pair of liftable latents turned out to belong to Loose.

The desk yielded a lot more; it would be a job to sort them out.

There were no dormitories here: the students all lived off campus.

The college could produce a list, of course. There were about five hundred of them, but not all of those would be in Loose's classes.

"I still say it's up in the air," said Hackett.

"Well, I don't. I think we follow it up," said Higgins.

They got back to the office at noon, Hackett's stomach rumbling, and found Farrell sitting with a switchboard jack in his hand looking undecided. He brightened at sight of them. "Whatever you had in mind, forget it. Not another soul here, and I just had a call from one of our pigeons. Chester Gosling is sitting in a bar on the Row right now, so he says. The Aztec Room."

"Oh, for God's sake!" said Hackett, who had just decided to start having lunch again. "There's no reason—"

"He's been fingered and there's a warrant out for him," said Farrell.

"All right, all right. I suppose the boss is out to lunch?"

"I've got no idea where he is. He went out about ten, after that Dombey came in to make the identification on Sidney."

"Come on," said Higgins.

They took Higgins' Pontiac instead of the Barracuda, thinking of transporting the prisoner. Skid Row in broad daylight was old and tired-looking, the aged buildings, the dirty streets, the cheap little stores and noisy bars. The Aztec Room hardly lived up to its elegant name: it was a hole in the wall past a cracked narrow sidewalk, and the lettering on the one window was so old that it was illegible. Higgins parked the Pontiac in the red zone at the corner and they walked back. Neither of them was much looking forward to going into the place, not so much because it was dangerous—which it wasn't—as because it would be smelly and unpleasant and dirty; and as it turned out they didn't have to. As they came past the empty store next to the bar, the door opened and a man came out, a tallish, thinnish Negro in dark pants and blue shirt: Chester Gosling.

"All right, Gosling, hold it!" snapped Hackett, bringing out the gun. Gosling's head jerked round and then he ran, desperately, the other way down Main. They pounded after him and what with the crowds impeding all of them, didn't gain on him much down that block. But he made the strategic error of cutting across an empty lot at the corner of Third, and with no obstacles in the way picked up speed. Higgins, carrying twelve or fourteen less pounds than Hackett, caught up and tackled him from behind and brought him down, flailing wildly.

"Take it easy," he panted, and as Hackett caught up Gosling bucked under Higgins like a spooked steer, and there was a knife in his hand.

"Goddamn!" said Higgins, and then Hackett had Gosling up, both arms behind him in a tight grip, and the knife dropped.

"Did he get you?"

"Scratch, I think," grunted Higgins, and twisted his head to look at his left arm. It was bleeding freely, and his jacket sleeve ripped six inches. "Goddamn it, this was nearly a new suit!"

"Come on, we'd better get you back to First Aid," said Hackett. His stomach was rumbling like Mount Vesuvius.

The package on Kurt Kramer, linked by two latent prints to the hijacking jobs, came up from R. and I. at eight-fifty. He had the expectable rap sheet, heists, muggings, break-ins. He was now off P.A. from the latest little stretch he'd done, but they could try that address first. Piggott and Glasser went out on that, and Grace and Shogart started out with a couple of the new possibles out of records on Macauley-Sidney.

"This job can be a drag," said Shogart, yawning. "Sometimes you wonder why you picked it."

"It can get boring," agreed Grace. "But on the other hand, there are compensations. The things we run into—like that burglar."

"Oh, him," said Shogart, and began to laugh again.

They didn't find either of the first two on the list, so they went looking for the next.

Piggott and Glasser were disappointed too. At the address listed on Kramer's P.A. record, they found an ancient four-family apartment. Kramer's father still lived there. He was on Welfare; he didn't like the cops; and he told them they just liked to come bothering people who'd been in a little trouble. Kurt wasn't there any more, and he didn't know where he was living and if he did know he wasn't about to tell the cops.

"I suppose there'll be a warrant out on him sometime today," said Glasser. "We could probably get one to search the old man's place in case there's something to show where Kramer is."

"I suppose," agreed Piggott. "Let's go back and see if the boss wants to play it that way."

But Mendoza had already gone out.

Mendoza parked the Ferrari in a public lot on Van Ness up from Wilshire and walked back to Wilshire. He wasn't sure what was in his mind exactly—when what Hackett called his *daemon* was starting to operate, he frequently wasn't.

He knew this city like the lines on his hand. . . . That fortune-teller he'd once picked up for operating in city limits had told him he had the Mystic Cross in his palm, and pointed it out. The Cross of Intuition. He didn't know why he was here.

He walked across Wilshire with the light and on down Wilton Place. These side streets would be fairly dark at night. Wilton was more of a main drag than others, but still not as bright as Wilshire up there. He came to a cross street: Ingraham Avenue. Off the main drag here, humble single houses, small apartment buildings. It would be zoned for multiple residence.

Mrs. Macauley, escaping—after struggle and rape—had run to the nearest house for help.

He came to another cross street: Seventh Place.

It was, after how many years of very tough so-called gun-control laws in New York, very easy for any pro there to come by a gun. Any kind of gun. And the pros were not too particular, except of course for the droppers, the hirelings who would kill for money, and they preferred the big guns, the .45's and the big magnums.

Quite suddenly he remembered that hired dropper Pat had mentioned, Harry Singer. There was a warrant out on him. And Pat's reformed pusher ready to tell all sitting safe in protective custody.

He ought to call Goldberg, ask how he was coming on. Back to the new job next week, and he and Pat would grumble at each other and exchange insults and pull in harness just fine. But it was going to be, reflected Mendoza, a little shock to Saul to find that not every LAPD bureau was supplied with a smart policewoman to type reports for the men.

"Una verdadera sorpresa," he said to himself. To be hoped Saul had appreciated what he'd had. And all the men from the old Robbery office screaming their heads off, having to type their own reports.

He came to another cross street: Leeward. He turned down it at random. He didn't know why he was here. He walked down to Norton Avenue and turned up toward Wilshire again.

He felt, he decided, uneasy. No more. And about what he wasn't quite sure. The sure cold finger up his spine, the hunch that said, Look there, or Ask about that, was not present.

He knew this city—had ridden a squad car, not on this beat, but he'd had to know the city like a map memorized.

And he was wasting time, for no rhyme or reason. It was eleven o'clock. Always things to do—at the office, on the street, the routine coming along—

A faint lead to the hijackers. Anybody's guess how many in on that; the profits were high enough to stand splitting several ways.

The burglar . . . standing on the corner of Wilshire and Norton, he laughed. More truth than poetry; but they ought to put him out of business. Stash him where whatever income didn't matter.

And what the hell he was doing here—Mendoza pulled himself together. *Daemons* be damned. He collected the Ferrari, got stuck in a jam on the freeway where a head-on piled up traffic, and when he got back downtown it was twelve-thirty and he was starving. He went straight up to Federico's and consumed a shot of rye, four rolls, french fries and the luncheon steak.

When he got back to his office Hackett and Higgins had just come in. Hackett was savage with hunger, and Higgins bitter about his suitjacket. In First Aid, the nurse had taken three stitches in his arm. "And what the hell *use* it is to pick up Gosling—I know there's a warrant on him, damn it, but we can have an educated guess now that Mrs. Macauley was wrong. It's a very damn general description." Higgins' arm hurt and he was querulous.

"Did he have a gun on him?" asked Mendoza.

"No. Just the knife," said Higgins bitterly.

"Mmh. We had a request in for a search warrant on the Gosling apartment and Ruby Jewel's. Are they in?"

"Why, for God's sake?" said Hackett.

Mendoza, replete, was shuffling the cards rapidly, a cigarette in one corner of his mouth; he dealt hands around, the deck neatly stacked, and surveyed the results with satisfaction. "The fixed income," he muttered. "Providing for the hostages to fortune—in case it all blows up— *Como sí.*"

"*Well?*" Hackett was exasperated.

Mendoza looked up at them vaguely. "There are all these new possibles to look for. We'd better question Gosling. You can have the jacket mended, George. Tailors. The Emperor's New Clothes—"

"For God's sake!" said Hackett. "He's no more use than a halfwit like this!"

"—And so we spent the rest of the day looking for the new names out of records," said Hackett disgustedly. "Gosling just clammed up and wouldn't tell us so much as his middle name. After he was reminded of his rights, of course. Talk about hamstringing us—inform him all polite he doesn't have to say a word, and then try questioning—"

"Yes, darling, very annoying," soothed Angel. "You sound hungry. Go round up Mark, will you? Dinner in five minutes—"

And it smelled very appetizing. Feeling somewhat mollified, Hackett went to find Mark watching a cartoon on TV, and Sheila for once patting the cat in civilized fashion. "How's my Sheila girl?"

"That sleeve's ruined," said Mary. "What a nuisance, George—"

"Does it hurt, George?" Laura's big gray eyes were sympathetic.

"But you got him," said Steve. "You mostly do. Say, George, I've got the new *Photography* magazine and there's a neat enlarger for only sixty-five bucks—"

"I suppose one of these invisible menders—" said Mary.

Feeling a little better for sympathy in the bosom of his family, Higgins grinned at Steve. "So let's look at it."

"—And when I mentioned taking the tree down," said Alison, "you should have heard the yells. Well, it's the first one they'll really remember much, the darlings. But once Christmas is over, it seems weeks ago—and the tree's dropping all over the carpet. I—"

Sheba leaped for Mendoza from behind and dug all claws into his shoulder. "*Monstruoso,*" he said mechanically, and hauled her down to his arms.

His household was serene, Alison snug in one of the big armchairs, Bast coiled on her lap: Nefertite and El Señor curled together in the other chair: their hairy sheepdog Cedric snoring at Alison's feet. The twins had been settled down with Just-So stories and dinner had included Alison's special souffle and Máiri MacTaggart's scones.

Mendoza put Sheba down on top of El Señor and Nefertite. She spat at him amiably and began to wash El Señor's ears.

"You," said Alison amusedly, "are either experiencing a first-class hunch, or trying to. You haven't heard a word I've said since dinner."

"Yes," said Mendoza absently. "And tomorrow's New Year's Eve, and neither of us has even suggested going out on the town. I must be feeling my age—"

"When have we ever, *imbécil?* Neither of us enjoys that kind of thing —and besides, the one big night in the year to a Highland Scot is Hogmanay, and Máiri deserts us tomorrow for sister Janet. They may even hail in the New Year with a few wee drams of whiskey." Alison laughed. "We're stuck with the offspring . . . Luis? You don't really want to go out carousing?"

"Carousing. I think," he said, "I could do with a little dram, now you mention it." He wandered out to the kitchen, where Mrs. MacTaggart was just whisking open the oven on an appetizing smell.

"Your New Year's dinner, and all you've to do is hot it up," she informed him. "For I'll not be back till New Year's morn. A grand beef pie with dumplings. And there's a new bottle of rye if that's what you're after."

"*Bueno.*"

"I'll just set the oven to the automatic timing— Ach, that cat!"

El Señor had heard the bottle taken down, and arrived posthaste for his share. Mendoza laughed and poured him half an ounce in a saucer, filled a shot-glass.

"If I didn't know better," said Mrs. MacTaggart, "I'd say ye'd had more than enough as it is, man."

He carried the glass back to the living room. "I wish," said Alison, "it would dawn on you. Whatever it is. You're *muy difícil* in the throes, as it were. Would it be helpful if I asked questions? I don't know all the cases you're working, you've just mentioned that Mormon girl, and the hijackers, and of course Mrs. Macauley—and that burglar. That is really priceless, the pawnbroker's receipt—"

"*No sé,*" said Mendoza, swallowing rye. He turned and looked at her, and his gaze focused. She was smiling slightly, her one-sided provocative smile that took ten years from her age. His redheaded Alison, who had at long last domesticated—if halfway—Luis Mendoza: and given him the hostages to fortune.

"*Vaya, mi corazón,* don't be foolish," and he finished the rye. "I can think of other occupations—" And she squealed as his arms closed round her, lifting her from the chair.

CHAPTER 9

It was Saturday night, and the last night but one of the old year: the night watch, sitting snug in the sergeants' office with the desk downstairs relaying calls, could only imagine what Traffic detail was handling on the streets: the drunk drivers, the accidents, the pile-ups on the freeways. It might be a busy night for them too, or not; they'd be finding out.

"Did you hear about that pawnbroker's receipt?" asked Galeano. They all had. "Sometimes I think Mendoza attracts the offbeat ones."

Conway opened a new pack of cigarettes. "I'll be just as glad to get off night tour. I've heard this and that about him, he should be interesting to work under."

"Too much so sometimes," said Landers. "Hackett says he jumps. No logical deduction from A to B to C, way we're trained. His mind jumps, like A to L. He says his poker game's ruined, but I don't know I'd like to sit in a hand with him. He's an artist with the cards."

"I heard he's a gambler. Also quite a chaser."

"Was," said Galeano sadly, "was. He got caught up to belatedly by a redhaired Irish girl. God, what a combination—I'll bet those twins are terrors."

They were called out around nine-thirty; there was a collision on the freeway with two D.O.A.'s, later a mugging up on Olive, but it was a quieter night than they might have expected. At eleven-fifty the desk relayed a phone call.

"H—Robbery-Homicide, Detective Galeano."

"I want Robbery-Homicide, the Robbery-Homicide office, he said that was—"

"Yes, sir, can I help you? Detective Galeano speaking."

"I want Sergeant Palliser—" It was an uncertain male voice.

"I'm sorry, Sergeant Palliser is on day watch, not here now. Can I—"

"When will he be there?"

"Any time after eight, sir. Who is this sp—" But the phone was dead at the other end. "That's funny," said Galeano.

Mendoza was supposed to be off Sundays; sometimes he was. When he drifted into the office that Sunday morning, he walked in on an argument between his two senior sergeants.

"Listen, it's wild," said Hackett. "There's no evidence at all—"

"I don't say there is, Art, I just say there might be. If we look. I know I don't usually get these spells, making like Luis, but on this one I just *saw* it—"

"Jumped," said Hackett. "As if Luis wasn't enough to cope with! And as for looking at it, my God, George, that doctor said somewhere between sixty and seventy students—and another thing that strikes me, they won't be an average lot. Medical students, solid academic records and older than the usual college kids, not very likely to be the type—"

"What is the type? I just saw—"

"Break it up," said Mendoza. They swung to face him, the pair of them looming over him.

"I'd just like your opinion," began Higgins, and Hackett swore.

"You just want him to back up your starting to have hunches. Look, Luis—"

"No," said Mendoza. "For the moment, forget about Dr. Loose and his students." He went into his office, sat down at his desk (polished and neat courtesy of their policewoman, who *was* off on Sunday) and lit a cigarette. "Overnight," he said, intently eyeing the desk-lighter, "my subconscious came through and revealed a hunch which has burgeoned out into beautiful flower. *Pues sí.* A very pretty thing indeed. Now what went down last night and what's on hand to work? I—"

"Oh, you're here," said Palliser, coming in. "Here's something funny. Somebody called asking for me about midnight. I was curious enough to put a tracer on it, and it was out of this area code. They're checking some more. What I'd like an opinion on is, where do we go on the Askell case now?"

"Askell," said Mendoza as if he'd never heard the name.

"Matt and Henry are starting to look for Kramer again," said Palliser, "and there's about ten more possibles on Macauley-Sidney to haul in. At least the burglar hasn't struck again. The woman who got mugged last night says she left her teeth-marks on his arm, so if we pick up anybody with—"

"And what are we supposed to do with Gosling?" demanded Hackett. "Now we've got him?"

"Find out if he had a gun," said Mendoza. "We had an application in for search warrants, his wife's apartment and Ruby Jewel's. Are they here?"

Lake had been listening, at the switchboard outside the open door. "I've got 'em, Lieutenant."

"*Bien*. John, you and these two—mmh—detectives go and execute them. Now. *¡Vamos!*"

"*What?*" said Hackett. "Search the—"

"That's right," said Mendoza. "Go, go, and have a good look. Jimmy, get me the lab . . . and close the door when you leave," he added to Palliser.

Temporarily speechless, they went out.

"Now what the hell is in his mind?" wondered Higgins. "I don't know why we kept Gosling at all."

Palliser was wondering about the phone call. From out of the area. Asking for him personally.

They took the Barracuda. They all thought this was a complete waste of time.

Mrs. Gosling was shrill and angry at cops invading her private place, but authority in the form of the warrant turned her sullen. They were trained to search thoroughly; they did. Beyond the fact that Mrs. Gosling was a very indifferent housekeeper they didn't turn up anything.

They went on to Ruby Jewel's place. They were unwelcome anywhere, this morning: she and an erstwhile boyfriend were just up and nursing hangovers; neither of them had the energy to cuss much, but they let the detectives know their feelings.

"Talk about silly," said Hackett. "What the hell he's got in his head now—and even if by some long chance we came across anything remotely incriminating, this isn't Gosling's place and there'd be no proof that he—"

"Well, I will be damned!" said Palliser. "I will be Goddamned!" He swung around from the old-fashioned chiffonier, and there was a gun in his hand. "Under her stockings." It was a .22 Colt.

They had left the bedroom door open, and Ruby came on uncertain legs to complain more about invading cops. "You got no call treat me like a— Hey!" she said. "Hey, you leave that alone! Chester give me that—for pertection, said isn't safe for a girl, I better—that's mine!"

"After it was Chester's?" said Higgins. He looked a little happier. "Any comments, Art?"

Hackett shook his head as if trying to clear it. "I still don't see what he's aiming at, George. All right, Gosling's got the right rap sheet for Macauley-Sidney, but it's way out of character, when he knew we were after him—"

"Give the lady a receipt, and let's go. I'm sort of curious," said Higgins, "to hear how the rest of the lyrics go."

They got back to the office at eleven-fifty and dropped the Colt at S.I.D. "He'll be on the phone to you," said Higgins, and Duke said he didn't doubt.

"He already has been. What the hell is he playing at now?"

"What did he want?" asked Palliser.

"I'll let him surprise you."

Upstairs, they found Mendoza on the phone. "You can send up a formal report when you get round to it, Doctor. Just the gist, please. What showed up? . . . Mmh. Slug in any condition for examination? *Bueno*. You sent it to the lab, I trust . . . That's interesting . . . Oh? . . . Now you don't tell me." Suddenly he laughed. "*Hoy por ti, mañana por mí*. Thanks, Doctor." He put the phone down, contemplated the extraneous object lying across the desk and picked it up.

"And what the hell do you want with that?" What he'd asked Duke for, they could deduce.

"The miracles of science do give us useful tools. . . . Mr. Kenneth Sidney," said Mendoza, "was killed dead by a slug in the right temple. The slug is in good condition and can probably be matched to a gun. But it was—mmh—a redundant kill. He wouldn't have had long to live. His heart was a good deal enlarged and he had started to grow a brain tumor. At a guess, says Bainbridge, he'd have been dead in three to six months."

"Not like the healthy Mr. Macauley, so what?" said Hackett.

"Did you come across anything?" Mendoza hefted the long length of metal and squinted down it absentmindedly.

"A Colt .22," said Palliser interestedly. "Ruby says Chester gave it to her for protection."

"Oh, I like that," said Mendoza. "I do like that, John. You left it at the lab." He picked up the phone and got Scarne. "Priority, please. That Colt .22 you were just handed. Test fire, please, and run a comparison with the slug out of Macauley."

"I was just going to lunch," said Scarne.

"How long will it take you, half an hour? Forget your stomach."

"While you go to lunch."

"No. While I study a map. *Por favor*." He made a long arm and reached for the County Guide. "You can go snatch some lunch, but don't sit over it. We've got work to do." He opened the big book.

"You're skipping lunch now?" said Hackett.

"I'll get Jimmy to send in a sandwich. See you back here in forty minutes."

There was, as always, enough work for them to do. Piggott and Glasser had brought in two men to question on the hijacking, picked out of records as longtime pals of Kurt Kramer. Shogart was out looking for Kramer.

As Palliser passed the switchboard he asked, "Any calls for me, Jimmy?"

"Nope. Looks as if your midnight caller has changed his mind. Funny."

Funny wasn't the word.

Hackett, Higgins and Palliser went on out, and a moment later Mendoza came out of his office and said, "Have the canteen send down a sandwich, Jimmy. Doesn't matter what." He went into the sergeants' office and began to look into drawers in Wanda Larsen's desk.

When Hackett, Higgins and Palliser came back to the office, he was just putting the phone down, looking pleased with himself. Hackett looked at him shrewdly.

"A real kingsize hunch, huh, Luis?"

"The subconscious," said Mendoza, "is a peculiar thing, Arturo. Logic is all very well, but on this job what's even more important is human nature. In the end, damn the facts, it's human nature we're dealing with."

"Like I say, stupidity and cupidity," said Hackett.

"And quite often both. A thorough and cynical understanding of human nature is more valuable to a detective than every scientific tool down in S.I.D.," said Mendoza seriously. "Though—mmh—S.I.D. is useful to prove what we already knew."

"What do we already know?" asked Higgins.

"Yes, and that comes in too—seeing what we expect to see." Mendoza stood up, yanked down his cuffs where heavy gold links nestled, settled his Sulka tie, and reached for his hat with one hand and his requisition from the lab with the other.

Hackett looked at that. "Are we going treasure hunting? In the middle of L.A.?"

"That is just what," said Mendoza. "We'll take your car, John."

In the Rambler, they went up Wilshire Boulevard to Van Ness, and left the car in a public lot. Mendoza led them across Wilshire down Wilton Place to Leeward three blocks down, and stopped, and looked up to the right.

"The black-and-white was just past Manhattan Place on Wilshire. So useful, the private secretary filing away precise facts. Mmh, yes. And it was dark. But without any doubt at all, there'd have been a dry run on it by daylight. *Como sí*. Because there wouldn't be much time at all." He looked up Leeward, and added, "A psychological strength there to bolster a rather weak point. Mmh, yes. Well, let's get on with our treasure hunt."

The others just exchanged exasperated glances. He led them down Leeward half a block, stopped, and said to himself, "Right here. But no possible place to be seen. No. And nothing on Wilton, so—" He went on to Norton and turned up that, toward Wilshire again. Up to Seventh. At the corner he paused. There was a small apartment building on one corner, single houses on the other three, small frame houses with cars parked in front of them. "No," said Mendoza. He went up Seventh, looking from side to side. Nearly at the corner where Wilton crossed, he stopped before an empty house. The blind windows were minus curtains and a sign was propped on the lawn: *For Rent by Owner*.

"*Es posible*," said Mendoza, and went briskly up the front walk. "Now how the hell does this thing work? I read the directions, but—"

Hackett took the long metal-detector from him. "Where do we look?"

"Try the flower beds all round the front."

Fifteen minutes later, Higgins and Palliser showed him the collected loot: an old dog-collar with a rusty name plate, half a keychain, a blackened nickel, and several strands of wire.

"First cast," said Mendoza. He went on down to Wilton and turned up that; they almost saw his nose twitching, a hound casting for any wayward scent. Up Wilton to the next cross street, Ingraham, and he turned right on that. It was a block of old frame houses, mostly, with a couple of new apartment buildings, stark and square and ugly. Nearly up to the next corner, Mendoza stopped and looked across the narrow street, and his long nose did twitch once.

"The ideal place," he said. "But absolutely. What a beautiful place. Because just up there is Manhattan Place. And the foundation is already dug up, there might not be anybody digging around there for quite some time."

The house across the street had been readied for moving: its foundation had been cleared, and the house moved onto blocks all ready for the big dollies which would trundle it away to some new lot. It was a big stucco house painted dirty tan.

Mendoza crossed the street at a trot. "All right," he said to Hackett, "let's see what treasure we can turn up here."

Hackett trudged back and forth in front of the house several times, moving gradually toward it. The metal detector was silent. Presently it registered faintly and Higgins came resignedly to dig up a rusty bent spoon. "You should have had the foresight to borrow a spade too, Luis."

"All right, try over to the side," said Mendoza. "Along the hedge, Art." There was a scraggly juniper hedge between this lot and the next.

Three minutes later Hackett stopped. The detector was registering strongly. Higgins squatted and probed with the longest blade on his pocket knife. It touched hard metal; he dug the dirt away, and it came loose easily. They hadn't had rain in six weeks and normally the clay-heavy soil would be packed firm; but this had been loosened before, not long ago. Higgins grunted as he felt something heaved up under the blade. He dropped the knife and picked it up, getting slowly to his feet.

"And I knew it had to be there," said Mendoza with a long sigh. "Somewhere . . . Scarne called just before you got back. That .22 is the gun that killed Macauley."

They didn't exclaim. They were looking at the thing in Higgins' big hand.

Mendoza dropped his cigarette and stepped on it. *"Es hermoso sin pero.* That Hi-Standard Supermatic, brand sold by Sears Roebuck. It takes .22 long ammo. It hasn't been there long. And I would lay my current bank account, boys, that S.I.D. is going to tell us it is the automatic that killed Kenneth Sidney."

After a long mute moment Hackett said, "And haven't I said it before. A couple of hundred years back, *compadre,* you'd have burned for a warlock."

And Palliser said incredulously, *"Gosling—do you mean—"*

"That's just what I mean, John," said Mendoza pleasedly.

She opened the door to them, looking a little bewildered at four men on her doorstep, two of them looming. "Why, Lieutenant Mendoza—"

"And Sergeants Hackett, Higgins, Palliser. May we come in?"

She stepped back at once. She was dressed today, and well-dressed. Her good figure showed to advantage in a beige silk sheath, tastefully embellished with one large gold brooch where diamonds glistened; her golden brown hair was beautifully arranged. "They—they told me I can probably make arrangements—for the funeral—by Tuesday," she told Mendoza. "Have you arrested anyone yet? I'm sorry I couldn't be more helpful to you, but—"

"Mrs. Sidney," said Mendoza enjoyably, "Sergeant Palliser is about to tell you something, and I'd like you to listen to it very carefully. Give the lady her rights, John."

Palliser suppressed a grin at him as he stood there, hands in pockets, rocking slightly heel to toe, watching her. He said gravely, "Mrs. Sidney, you have the right to remain silent, and the right to the presence of an attorney before any questioning, and—" he recited the rest of the little ritual. "Do you understand these rights, Mrs. Sidney?"

"Why—" She stared at them uncertainly, and a first faint alarm showed in her blue eyes. "What do you m—"

"Do you understand your rights, Mrs. Sidney?" asked Mendoza. "As Sergeant Palliser just explained them to you?"

"Yes, I—understand what he said. But—"

Mendoza gave her a rather wolfish smile. He brought one hand out of his pocket and showed her the .22 automatic. Traces of dirt still clung to the grip.

She stared at it for a long moment, and then slowly she began to back away from them. "Nobody," she said, "nobody could—"

"You read the story in the papers about the Macauleys," said Mendoza conversationally. "Last Monday. Christmas Day. The Macauleys accosted in the restaurant parking lot by a Negro, who robbed them and abducted and raped Mrs. Macauley after shooting her husband. We all know that violent crime is on the increase. You thought about it, didn't you? If a criminal did a thing like that once, nobody would be very surprised if he did it again, would they? And it would be a chance to take, but with luck and nerve you could bring it off."

"But nobody," she said, "could have—"

"You wanted to be rid of him, didn't you? Your elderly and perhaps difficult husband, always complaining about your extravagance—the husband you'd married only a few years ago, possibly thinking he had more money than he had. You knew he carried some sizable life insurance. And this gave you an idea how you might be rid of him, and nobody the wiser. Copy the Macauley crime and you'd be quite safe— another bereaved widow. I think you read the newspaper stories about the Macauleys very carefully."

She came up against the built-in bookshelves across the room. She was slowly shaking her head.

"But the papers don't always get all the details, you know. They told you that Macauley was shot, but not by what gun. They told you that Mrs. Macauley said it was a Negro, but not her description of him—you had to play that by ear, and it was a very nice act. The flighty female, too frightened to remember exactly what he looked like. And the papers told you that the Macauley car had been found abandoned, but not where, or that it had been wrecked. The car was a little problem, and I must say I admire the way you solved it."

"But how—did you—"

"You had to leave the car somewhere, and get rid of the gun, and you wouldn't have much time. It was rather strongly implied in the papers that Mrs. Macauley had been raped. And unless, presumably, you got away from your attacker rather shortly, he'd have raped you too, and that you couldn't fake, to a doctor. It took nerve," said Mendoza, regarding her with objective admiration. "You shot your husband, probably, as he was unlocking the driver's door. You got the keys from him, and you simply drove out of the lot. You knew where you were going—straight down Wilshire to Wilton Place, and down to Leeward. You parked the car and left the keys in it—and you'd remembered to wear gloves so your prints wouldn't show up as the latest driver. You had, of course, chosen the terrain by daylight. Spotted that house to be moved. That was a very convenient place to get rid of the gun. Because you really had very little time. And—mmh—talk about a double play," said Mendoza, "you could gamble that we wouldn't be too surprised at finding the car so near to where you turned up crying murder, robbery and abduction—when you'd got away from him, conceivably he'd be nervous about keeping the car, and abandon it at once. I like that."

Her eyes fixed on his, blind with desolate fury now. "Damn you," she said tiredly. "Damn you. You devil, *how did you know?*"

"Well, we had a suspect on the Macauleys, you see. And while a man of his type can acquire a gun very easily, it isn't often that he has the money or desire to acquire two. And your husband was shot with an automatic—we found the ejected shell-casing near his body. You don't know much about guns, do you? You intended, of course, after getting rid of it, to run up toward Wilshire all hysterical, stop someone on the street—the squad car was an unexpected bonus. Yes. The automatic belonged to your husband, didn't it?"

"Goddamn you to hell. Yes. He—showed me how to fire it—once. In case of burglars. That's funny. That's really funny."

"Oh, I can tell you something funnier than that," said Mendoza. His deep voice was sardonic, and genuinely amused. "He only had a few months to live. I just heard the results of the autopsy. You really needn't have gone to so much trouble."

"Oh—my—God," she whispered.

"He can be damned annoying," said Hackett to Higgins, "but I confess I always get a kick out of him like that—all lit up like a Christmas tree, one of his hunches working out just like a diagram. But what a hell of a thing—"

"And why anybody ever thought about it— She could have got away with it, you know. When we tied Gosling to Macauley by that Colt. The different guns looked a little funny, but the ones like Gosling, a pro hood—and he probably wouldn't have had any alibi to stand up."

Mendoza had booked Stella Sidney into jail himself, set up the machinery on the warrant. Palliser and Grace had Chester Gosling down the hall in an interrogation room trying for some admittal on the Macauleys. But in spite of the obstacles presented now by judges and courts, they thought they had Stella Sidney tied up tight for the D.A.'s office. And, with the lab evidence on the gun linked to Gosling, him too.

"So, Happy New Year," said Hackett.

And Joe Daly was waiting autopsy down in the cold room, and Higgins had had the unprecedented hunch on that, listening to Dr. Loose talk about examination questions. Hackett was still dragging his heels on that, but less reluctantly.

They would probably write tomorrow off as far as routine went. New Year's Day—even the citizens who wouldn't be celebrating its arrival with too deep libations would be watching the parade and the several big games, and resent interruption.

Dr. Loose had promised them a list of all the students in his classes by five this afternoon; Higgins started for the Looses' big house in West Hollywood to get that, and Hackett, reflecting on what a thing *that* would be to work—even if George's hunch was right, question every one of those bright medical students—wandered into Mendoza's office at four-fifty and found him swiveled around in his chair looking at the line of the Hollywood hills clear and cold against the horizon.

"What does the D.A. think about the case on Stella?"

"I haven't talked to him. He's not in his office. It's New Year's Eve," said Mendoza. "And Lila never got home for Christmas."

"You're back to that. I don't think we'll ever know what happened there."

"Dead grass," said Mendoza. "Cotoneaster leaves. *Caray.*"

"What?"

"The lab report on her clothes. I wonder. I'd like to know," said Mendoza. "By what John heard, I think she was rather a dull girl, Art. Serious and respectable and hard-working. No sense of humor and not much interest in the opposite sex. The earnest Christian, maybe looking down her nose a little at less puritanical females. But she wanted to go home for Christmas, and I'd like to know who stopped her."

"When you put it like that—"

"Without robbing or raping her."

"Yes, that is funny. But where to look—"

The phone buzzed and Mendoza picked it up. "Hom— Robbery-Homicide, Mendoza."

"Happy New Year, Luis," said Goldberg, and sneezed.

"Well, and to you, Saul. How are you doing?"

"Fine, just fine. Back on the job Tuesday. The new job. Say, I've been getting blasts from all my boys—"

Mendoza laughed. "Having to type all their own reports. No obliging private secretary attached to Narco. You never appreciated how good you had it, *hermano*. And thanks very much for Wanda. So well trained, and she's appreciating my nice polite boys after your roughhouse crew."

"Ah, you go to hell," said Goldberg. "I just hope you do appreciate her, Luis. A nice girl."

Mendoza put the phone down, laughing, and relayed that. "You know, Luis," said Hackett, "I've got a kind of suspicion that Glasser has his eye on that girl. Just a look about him—"

"Well, good luck to that—what am I saying? Get her married off and we'll lose our private secretary." Mendoza stood up. "I'm going home. Tomorrow will be wasted time. Nothing moving."

"Except maybe a couple of new ones to work."

"*¡Dios me libre!*"

Jason Grace took home a bottle of Cold Duck to chill. It was a very special New Year's Eve to the Graces. "Here's to us," he said, an arm around Virginia. Celia Ann was sound asleep in her new crib, under the padded coverlet embroidered with lambs and angels in pink for a little girl. "We made it, Ginny. We've got a family."

Virginia chuckled, sipping wine. "I didn't tell you what your father said. I mean, he should know—" Grace's father was chief of Gynecology at the General Hospital.

"What?"

"Well, he said it happens so often, right after the baby's adopted, the wife finally gets pregnant. Wouldn't it be funny, Jase—"

"The more the merrier," said Grace largely.

"Happy New Year, darling," said Angel, "and damn the calories for once." She'd had a bottle of champagne waiting. "Don't look so gloomy, you're only up to two hundred and fourteen."

"I was thinking," sighed Hackett, "about all those poor damned souls picked to police Pasadena. Happy New Year, my Angel."

"Don't be such a pessimist, Matt," said Prudence severely. Their first New Year's Eve in their own place, and her mother was there for dinner; Piggott liked Mrs. Russell. They were going to church after dinner, for the special service. "It *can be* a happy new year, however unlikely it looks. You got to have faith."

"Sodom and Gomorrah," said Piggott. But of course, a man in his job, dealing with human nature in the raw, was not conditioned to automatic optimism. "It does say, man He made a little lower than the angels."

Landers snatched five minutes to call Phil and wish her Happy New Year. "I can't tie up the phone. Listen, about Tuesday night—you wear that blue thing, and the perfume like roses."

"Six dollars the bottle. Six-thirty, yes. That Castaways place, Tom. Because of the view."

"I told Rich. He's never been there. See you then, Phil. Oh-oh, there's a call on the other phone—"

There would be, on New Year's Eve, a lot of hard work for the LAPD, chiefly for Traffic.

Roberta had a bottle of champagne chilled. "To us, darling. And David Andrew—or Elizabeth Margaret—"

"Margaret Elizabeth," said Palliser. "Or what do you think about Martha? I like old-fashioned names—"

"Well, I'll think about that one," said Roberta, wrinkling her nose.

"I'll get her settled down," said Higgins. He patted Margaret Emily's small rump fondly.

"Well, if you can, George. I've got a bottle of champagne in the refrigerator—it *is* New Year's Eve—and you should have heard the wails when I said we ought to take the tree down—but Christmas seems years ago, and—"

"Oh, Mother! We don't have to take it down *yet*—"

"Can I have some champagne, George? I'm twelve now and— Just a sip, to see what it's like—"

It was Higgins' second New Year with a real live family of his own, and it was just as nice as he'd always thought it would be.

Alison offered him a glass of champagne. Mendoza was not a wine-drinker, but accepted the ritual resignedly, touching her glass with his.

The twins were settled down with Just-So Stories, and of course neither of the Mendozas was much given to carousing in nightclubs; they spent a domestic evening at home, Alison busy over letters and Mendoza uneasily prowling the living room; his mind was back on their other mystery now.

Later on, as he slid into the kingsize bed beside the familiar carnation scent that said *Alison,* he decided a little sleepily that he didn't mind being domesticated. Ten minutes ago, the whistles and rockets had signaled the official end of the old year; ten minutes later, as he was drifting to sleep, they died down.

Ten minutes after that, he suddenly sat up in bed.

Outside the bedroom windows, there sounded a Voice. A sleepy, low voice, but unmistakable. The crooning note of the mourning dove, *coroo-coroo, coroo-coroo.* A muffled *AWK. Tu-whoo.* And then, on a low note, but quite clear, *Yankee Doodle came to*—

"*¡Diez millónes de demonios desde el infierno!*" said Mendoza. That damned mockingbird was back.

CHAPTER 10

"At least," said Alison sleepily, pouring his coffee, "it can't stay this warm, Luis—it's bound to turn cool again, and we're due more rain. The creature won't be nesting."

"I wouldn't put anything past *el pájaro*," said Mendoza darkly. The livestock was all out in the back yard, Cedric barking and the twins shouting. The mockingbird was up in the alder tree, cooing to himself.

"Have a good day," said Alison, yawning. As he backed the Ferrari down to the curve of the circular drive, with due care for cats, Mendoza reflected from experience that it would be either a feast or a famine. Holidays—

The streets, the freeways, were oddly empty, deserted. The Ferrari was the only vehicle to be seen on the Hollywood freeway for a mile, until he got closer in downtown. This one morning of the year, a large proportion of the citizens stayed home. And those who didn't—

Over in Pasadena, those specially-chosen ones (some of them with difficulty squeezed back into uniforms unworn since a few years and inches had been added) had seen the first of the coming crowds begin to straggle in at 3 A.M., finding parking places, finding their seats in the tiers of wooden seats that had lined Colorado Boulevard for a month, or just finding curbside spots to stake out folding chairs and blankets. Steadily, the crowds had been swelling ever since, to fill the street-sides. About five-thirty the television crews would have appeared, to set up cameras and platforms for their guest M.C.'s. The telecast would be getting under way about now—it was eight-fifteen—and for two hours the great gaudy parade, with its elaborate floats and marching bands headed by baton-tossing drum majorettes, and prancing equestrian groups, and local and national personalities on horses and in sports cars, would slowly stream in all its bright garishness down the long boulevard,

watched by that tightly packed huge mob of people. This morning they
wouldn't need the lap-robes and blankets and heavy coats, and the girls
on the floats, mostly in diaphanous costumes, wouldn't be in danger of
catching pneumonia. At last the great parade would turn off the boulevard, to disband a few blocks down, and the flower-covered floats
would be trundled to Central Park to remain on public display the next
few days. And the crowd—which would already have kept the uniformed men busy enough, with people fainting, being taken ill, losing
children, losing mothers and fathers, losing dogs off leashes to get lost
in the parade, quarreling with each other over curbside rights, and scattering food containers all over, and a hundred other difficulties—would
begin to disperse, milling in the streets, losing more children, forgetting
where cars were parked, raising rows over parking fees, filling every restaurant and coffee shop along Colorado and the side streets, and eventually most of it would be leaving Pasadena.

A lot of that crowd would be tourists from out of state, cramming
every motel and hotel around and in Pasadena. The two roads leading
away from the city would be one massive traffic jam to keep moving.
And just about as it was all moved out, on its way home or to motels,
the second crowd would be starting to arrive, again jamming the freeways and the roads into town: the great crowd bound for the Rose
Bowl to watch the biggest football game of the year. Well, it was a nice
day for football. . . . The game usually ended between four and four-
fifteen, and then that second crowd would straggle out—having strewn
the great stadium with litter, lost children, lost friends, forgotten where
cars were parked—and make another traffic jam to be herded out of the
city in an orderly manner.

Those special duty cops would be lucky to get home by the middle of
the evening, after an eighteen-hour stretch. Mendoza returned devout
thanks that with his rank and age he wasn't likely ever to get tagged
again for New Year's duty in Pasadena. He had been caught twice in
twenty-four years, and that was twice too much.

At the office, everybody else was in.

There was an FBI kickback from the query about those prints: the
latents on Lila Askell's necklace. Mendoza looked at it hopefully, but it
was N.G.—the Feds didn't know the prints.

Hackett and Higgins now had a list of Dr. Loose's students. "And
you know what use it would be to start on that today," said Hackett.
"Have you heard the details on this, Luis, and if so, is George going senile?"

"It's a fairly wild one, if he isn't," said Mendoza. "I don't know, there's a weird sort of logic in it. Two unusual things happening in the same place—it could say they're linked. Anyway, you've got a reason to go asking—Loose's office was broken into. But as you say, you won't find many of those home today, or if you did half of them will be nursing hangovers—"

"What, those hardworking medical students? More likely half of them are at the Bowl."

Sergeant Lake had brought a portable TV with him—"My oldest daughter's," he said—and was watching the parade, with Piggott, Glasser, Grace and Shogart looking over his shoulder.

A light flashed on the switchboard and Lake reached to turn the volume down, plugged in. After two weeks he had nearly trained himself; he said at once, "Robbery-Homicide, Lake."

"I want—Sergeant Palliser," said a hesitant voice sounding a distance off.

"I'm sorry, he's not here, can I—"

"They said he'd be there—after eight."

"It's his day off," said Lake. "Can I help you, sir?"

After a little silence, "Can you give me his phone number?"

"I'm sorry, sir, against regulations. If you'd like to give me a number, I'll be glad to relay it to him."

Another silence. "Will he be there—tomorrow?"

"Yes, sir, but can't I—"

The phone clicked at the other end. "That's funny," said Lake. "I thought at first it was one of our pigeons, but they're not usually quite so shy as— My God, I wonder if it was John's midnight caller?" He retailed all that to Mendoza, who hadn't yet got as far as his office.

"*Extraño*. Put a tracer on the call, just for fun, Jimmy. And get hold of John."

Most of the population of L.A. and environs who didn't have hangovers and didn't have to go to work today were watching the parade on TV. Palliser had probably been among them. But he listened to Lake and said, "Now who the hell could it be? What did he sound like, Jimmy?"

Lake considered. "Male, high tenor, no special accent, and he hisses. His *s*'s."

"I'll be damned," said Palliser. "Who does that—that Stettin! Ron Stettin. Now what the hell—"

"I put a tracer on the call."

"Well, let me know if it was from Santa Barbara."

"Will do."

Just then a uniformed messenger came in from Communications; Mendoza took the manila envelope and a moment later said, "Oh, Jase -Matt. Here's your kickback on Fox. Only he isn't."

"Isn't what?" Grace took the teletype; he and Piggott read it interstedly.

It was from the Department of the Army. It identified the fingerprints ent from Scientific Investigation, LAPD, as belonging to one Carl Wilam Fawkes, description appended, who was AWOL from Fort Ord. awkes was twenty-seven, five-eleven, a hundred and seventy, brown nd blue, tattoo on right forearm of a hula dancer, a heavy drinker and compulsive gambler. He was unmarried, had attained private first-lass rank; he had been AWOL for three months.

"Well, it's nice to have him spotted," said Piggott. "I wonder if he's till here. I think I'll go and wish the lieutenant colonel Happy New ear."

Lieutenant Colonel Pound was sitting up in the hospital bed, looking great deal better. "I remember you," he said to Piggott. "Police fficer."

"That's right, sir. I'm glad to see you're looking better."

"I'm fine, just fine. Constitution of a horse—always had. But what a ell of a way to spend the holidays, eh? Hell of a thing. Have you aught that son of a bitch yet?"

"No, sir, but we know who he is. He left his prints on one of the lasses." Piggott showed him the information from the Army, and he rowled over it.

"Stupid as well as crooked, eh? To think he fooled me for a minute! ut he was pretty smooth. And he didn't claim to be a career man, y' now. Damn it, I *liked* the fellow—just talked to him a few minutes in at store, day before Christmas it was. Said I'd be here another couple f weeks, drop up to have a drink with me—fella all alone here, he said, nd Christmas—" Pound snorted. "And when he did—"

"That was Christmas Day."

" 'S right. About three in the afternoon. Well, talking with him, it idn't take me long to spot he was no officer. Let him see it. Here, I aid, who d'you think you're kidding anyway—on account of this and at he'd said, y' know—and that's when he knocked me down. I gave im a fight," said Pound reminiscently, "but age does tell, I suppose. ut I think I surprised him, fight I put up, or he wouldn't have grabbed y knife—it was on the table. But life in the old dog yet, eh? You think ou'll catch him?"

"Have a look for him," said Piggott. That waiter at the hotel had just been mistaken about seeing Pound then. "There'll be a warrant out. Now we haven't any idea what he got from you, sir. Could you tell me roughly how much money? Do you carry any credit cards?"

"Fellow got my West Point class ring, damn him, and my watch. Aside from that, four dollars and seventy-eight cents cash, and I understand from Mr. Di Silva, who very kindly came to see me, my four best suits. Damned thief," said Pound. "I'm an old campaigner, Mr. Piggott, and my checkbook and travelers' checks were in the hotel safe. Credit cards? Don't use 'em. Don't like bein' in debt."

"And I wish there were more like you," said Piggott. "Well, I hope this hasn't soured you on California, sir."

"By God, no, sir. As soon as I'm out of here I'm looking for a nice little apartment in Santa Monica. Good luck on catching up to that son of a bitch."

"We'll have a look, but the devil," said Piggott, "is good at taking care of his own."

"And isn't that the truth," said Pound. *"I've* had some encounters with the devil in seventy years myself—"

Lake got Palliser again at nine-twenty. "That call was from Santa Barbara."

"Be damned," said Palliser. "You know, I think I'll come in. I'd like to hear what the boss thinks about this."

What Mendoza thought was not immediately apparent. He was shuffling the deck smoothly, and listened to Palliser absently.

"You think it was Stettin. Why?"

"That's what I'd like to know. Why the hell should Stettin be phoning me? What about? I don't know anybody in Santa Barbara, and from Jimmy's description it was Stettin's voice. But when I was there—and when I talked to him on the phone—he was very damned upstage. And all he and Monica gave me was Stover, and that's N.G. I said a link to L.A. but when I thought about it, it isn't, really. He just obliged Stettin —and Monica—and double dated with Lila a couple of times. She wasn't interested in him, and vice versa. How would he have known she'd be here, for just three hours that day?"

Mendoza squared the deck carefully and cut it once: to the ace of spades. "On the face of it—" He cut the remaining deck again and looked at the ace of diamonds. "No, he couldn't, could he?" He cut the remaining half of the deck, to the ace of clubs. *"Donde menos se piensa salta la liebre*—sometimes an answer shows up from way out in left field." He cut the deck again and looked at the ace of hearts. "And I get the feeling, John, that your Mr. Stettin—"

"He's not mine. I don't like him worth a damn."

"—Is blowing hot and cold. He calls you here at midnight on Saturday—but not again. Until today. Why?"

"That's what I'd like to know. I'll try to call him back—"

"No," said Mendoza. "From what you say of Mr. Stettin, and what we've just deduced, he's jittery about something. It's too easy to hang up a phone. I think"—he shuffled the deck together and put it down—"you'd better go see him again. Drop by headquarters and take a local officer along. Impress Mr. Stettin with your importance, and see what you get."

"Up there again?"

"It's only a hundred miles up the coast. And if by some incredible chance Mr. Stettin knows something to give us a lead on Lila, I'd like to know what it is."

"And this was supposed to be my day off."

"Well, you came in under your own steam."

For want of anything else to do, Hackett and Higgins went down to the jail on Alameda and pressured Chester Gosling some more. This time, they finally got it into his head that he was tied tight to the Macauley job by the scientific evidence on the gun. The actual lab work he didn't understand, but he knew that that was solid evidence. He glowered up at them and said, "I didden know what I was doin'. I wasn't in my right mind."

"Is that so?" said Hackett. "Were you drunk?" Mrs. Macauley hadn't reported any smell of liquor.

"I'd had a shot of the stuff. That afternoon."

"Heroin?"

"Yeah, yeah. The horse. I wasn't in my right mind."

"But you did hold up the Macauleys and then—"

"I don't remember nothin' else about that. I wasn't in my right mind."

That was something, of course. They went back to the office and handed notes to Wanda for a further report on that.

Palliser had got a flight up to Santa Barbara at eleven-fifteen.

The warrant came through on Stella Sidney. The D.A. would try for murder one on that. Gosling would be luckier: probably a charge of voluntary manslaughter.

* * *

Hackett had just got back from lunch—if you could, he thought, call cottage cheese and low-calorie peaches lunch—when Lake, plugged in to a call, started to laugh. "Oh, that's a good one. Just a minute, I'll get you— Oh, Art! Like to take this? It's Sergeant Barth up at Wilcox Street."

Hackett took the phone. "So what've you got for Central?"

"Maybe a nice solid lead to your hijackers," said Barth. He sounded amused. "There are a few honest men left among us, Sergeant, and one of this bunch made the tactical error of approaching him on a deal. The honest citizen grabbed him for us. I've got 'em both here. I didn't need to think twice to guess it probably ties in with your hijackings."

"Oh, isn't that nice," said Hackett. "I'm on my way!" He took Grace with him, and looked at last night's Polaroid shots on the way.

"But I'm beginning to think Higgins is right about that camera," said Grace thoughtfully.

At Wilcox Street in Hollywood, they found Sergeant Barth waiting for them. "You'd better hear the honest citizen first. He'll tie it in for you. You've got a warrant out on the other one."

"Who?"

"Kurt Kramer."

"Oh, very nice," said Hackett. Barth took them up to a little office on the second floor of this ancient precinct house and introduced them to Mr. Andrew Post. Mr. Post was a large, broad man in late middle age, dressed in very expensive sportswear. He had a bald head and bulging shoulders, and a diamond ring on his right hand. "You the men from headquarters like he said? Please to meet you. I wasn't born yesterday, see, and when this joker starts talkin' about—"

"From the beginning, please, Mr. Post," said Hackett. He sat down and offered cigarettes.

"O.K., O.K. I've got a restaurant out on La Cienega. The Blue Bull." They looked at him in surprise: it was a very well-known place, with a high-class reputation and prices to match. "I've been in the restaurant business all my life, and my father before me. And everything strictly aboveboard, see? So O.K., a liquor license costs in this state, the liquor costs too, but that's how things are. I make a good profit, I don't cheat anybody—my customers *or* the state, whatever I think about taxes. You get me."

"We get you."

"So my maitre d', he says there's this guy around asking to see me. Won't say what about. This was, oh, couple of days last week. I'm in and out, I got fingers in a few other pies, and my employees I can trust, run the place smooth. So am I interested in what this jerk might want? Anybody wants to see me can say what his business is plain out. But I happen to be there—this is about an hour ago—when he drops in again. And I'm curious enough, give him five minutes. And he's got the nerve, offer me a deal on the hot liquor for a cut price! No sweat, he says, all sealed and kosher—nobody'd know. And high-class brands. Do I need to be an Einstein to know it's this hijacked stuff? What else? And you don't need telling, all the stolen property, damn what it is, just ups the prices to you and me and Joe Doakes. So I grabbed him. I called up a couple of waiters to hold him and I yelled for the cops. I got him," and he nodded at Barth, "and he said it was your beat was on it."

"And thanks so much," said Hackett. "It's nice to meet an honest man, Mr. Post. We had this one tied to the hijackings, and there's a warrant on him."

"Say, is that so? Well, glad to do you a favor," said Post. "Hope you pick up the rest of the gang."

Kurt Kramer was about what they'd expected; and he wasn't saying anything at all. They took him back downtown and booked him.

"Now look, Mr. Stettin," said Palliser patiently, "we'll ask you to stop insulting our intelligence." He wondered if Ron Stettin, in acquiring his degree in political science, had ever been required to study logic, and decided it was unlikely.

Stettin looked at them with a curious blend of emotions passing over his expression: nervousness, fear, attempted dignity, incredulity, horror. "I mean," he said. "I mean—" and he stopped. He had, in the last half hour, got himself boxed in a corner, and he didn't know where to go from here. He wanted out, and there was only one way to get out and he didn't want to go that way.

He had been surprised to see Palliser and the local man Palliser had picked up: a big wide-shouldered sergeant named Delaney. Palliser had asked him why he'd been calling Robbery-Homicide and Stettin said, showing the whites of his eyes, he hadn't. Palliser said the calls had been traced. Stettin hesitated and then said he'd just wanted to know if they'd arrested anybody for Lila's murder yet. Monica had asked him to call, he added. Palliser asked him why he had wanted to talk to him and nobody else. Stettin said, well, he was the man he'd talked to before. Why had he called at midnight? Well, he'd just thought of it, didn't realize the hour—

Palliser asked him what he was afraid of and he said nothing. He shouldn't, he added hurriedly, have said anything about Gene Stover to them, or any of those dates. It wasn't important at all, and Stover had been just one of several men he'd known he'd got to date Lila. "So you said before," said Palliser, and asked him if he'd had any contact with Stover recently. No, no, said Stettin, he hadn't seen him for a couple of months. "I didn't ask you that. Have you been in contact with him?"

It was purely Palliser's instinct that kept him on the right line; that, and Stettin's essential stupidity. Palliser had been here before, on Mendoza's vague hunch, and he hadn't thought anything Stettin or Monica told him was important; the equally vague link to L.A. didn't, on examination, look like much of a link. But here was Stettin for some reason very jittery, and the mention of Stover's name seemed to make him more so, so naturally Palliser followed it up. "Well?"

"I—" said Stettin. He kept casting nervous glances between them. "I don't see what reason you have—it's no business of yours—"

"Why did you want to talk to me at midnight last Saturday?" And as he said it, sudden light dawned on Palliser and showed him a little way ahead. He'd been asking for Stover at that brokerage, and others, on Friday. Stover quite possibly had a pal or so still working there, who might have passed the word that a cop was asking for him. "He called you, didn't he?" said Palliser. "Some time on Saturday. You and Monica were the only ones who could have told us about his knowing Lila. He didn't like it, did he? You bringing cops down. What did he say?" A pang of doubt struck him even as he asked. It was so vague, so up in the air. Nobody could have known that it was the Askell case brought a cop asking for Stover there. And—

Stettin looked ready to cry. "That's an unwarranted assumption! I never knew the man very well, and it's quite absurd to think he could have had anything—anything to do with *that*. And I have a reputation to keep up as an instructor, I—"

"What's that got to do with it?" asked Delaney. Stettin opened and shut his mouth.

"I don't want anything to do with it," he said. "I'm not involved—in *that*. It's nothing to do with me. Monica asked me to call you—to see if anybody'd been arrested. That's all."

"What about Stover?"

"*Nothing* about Stover! I don't *know* anything about him—I shouldn't have—those dates weren't important. Not at all. Stover didn't care anything about that girl. She was a dead bore and a—a bundle of repressions and *nobody* could have cared a damn about her—"

"Did Stover call you? Write you? On Saturday? What about?"

"It doesn't matter," said Stettin. His hands were shaking and he gave up trying to fill the manly collegiate pipe. His little dark beard waggled as he talked, absurdly. "He wasn't—none of us was involved with *that*. People like us wouldn't—"

"Like who?" asked Delaney. "College people?"

"No, no, Gene's not attached—I mean, well, I mean *intellectual* people, Gene's very—"

"Did he contact you on Saturday, Mr. Stettin?"

"Who? He's—he's got nothing to do with it, he said so! I don't know why I thought for a minute—I haven't got anything else to say to you."

That was where Palliser told him to stop insulting their intelligence. "You seem very nervous, Mr. Stettin, and every time I mention Gene Stover's name you get a little more so. Why?" Why indeed, he wondered. What the hell this rigmarole was about—

"Just like Monica," gabbled Stettin rapidly, "a *bundle* of repressions —so unhealthy—these days, we are *aware* of the need for full expression of the natural emotional impulses—in time I'll make Monica understand that—but of course the other girl was hopeless—I said to—"

"Now what are you talking about?" asked Palliser.

Delaney shifted stance. "If I translate the double talk, Sergeant, they were both nice decent girls who had moral scruples about sleeping around."

"And what's that got to do with Stover?"

"I—I—" Stettin looked around wildly. "I *will not* be involved in this! Oh, my God—why did I ever—but he couldn't possibly have—a thing like *that*—and besides he said he didn't! He said he wasn't—and I hadn't any reason— Oh, my God, but if—"

"You'd better pull yourself together and tell us all about it," said Palliser. "Never mind who's involved. What are you talking about?"

Stettin shied like a spooked horse at the steel in his tone. "Oh, my God," he said wretchedly. "I—he was mad as hell about it, about the police—and about the other too—I thought it was funny—he's not *used* to a girl turning him down—and I—and I—it was a joke, damn it, she was such a dog, a nothing—I knew from Monica and I dropped him a note, she'd be there, L.A., so he could make another play for— It was a joke! And—then—he—phoned me—and said—and said—he hadn't seen her, didn't know anything about—but he sounded—but I—"

"My good God," said Palliser disgustedly.

"Of course he couldn't have—*that*. People like us— But I won't be involved," said Stettin desperately. "It wasn't anything to do with *me*—"

* * *

They'd towed in the car Kurt Kramer was driving: a beat-up Dodge. There wasn't anything significant in it.

Lake, Glasser and Shogart were watching the big game at the Rose Bowl.

Hackett and Grace thought it might be just worthwhile to take a look at the place where Kramer had been living. The address had been on a checkbook on him. When they got there they were gratified to find that it was a rooming house, not an apartment. Technically, no search warrant necessary if the owner granted them permission to search.

The owner of the old three-story house on Donaldson Street was a big spare old man, Hector MacFarlane. He was surprised about Kramer, stared at their badges curiously. "Said he was a salesman, dressed sharp enough, looked like a nice young fellow. He was never here much. But these days, you don't know t'other from which, good or bad. Can't judge a book by its cover, like they say. He was obligin'—polite. Got me a case of right good whiskey for wholesale cost, three weeks back."

"Is that so?" said Grace in his soft voice.

"I ran into him just comin' in that day—and not that I'm a man to tie one on, I like a little nip o' good whiskey now and then, and these days the price is just sinful. Sinful. I'd just bought a bottle, I said about prices, and he said—there was a fellow with him, friend of his I suppose—he said he could get me a good deal, if I'd take a case. I still got eleven bottles of it." That was interesting, and Mr. MacFarlane would be livid to have it impounded as evidence. "The fellow with him—Tiger he called him, what kind of a name, but nicknames—he said, plenty more any time I— So he's a crook, hey? You got him in jail?"

"We'd like to look at his room, if you don't mind."

"Oh, I got no objection. Have to help the cops. Law 'n' order."

And Grace said, half an hour later, "How anybody can live like this—" The sordid single room, untidy and squalid: the flamboyant sports clothes in the cardboard wardrobe, the bottle in the dresser drawer. The ones like Kramer lived like this, uncaring about their private surroundings: he wouldn't have been here much. When the money was flowing in from some caper, it got spent elsewhere, on the cheap women and liquor and ephemeral entertainment. But they found, in the breast pocket of the one suit, a list of addresses. "So very stupid," sighed Hackett. A list of customers, could be—the less-than-honest men who were only too happy to make the under-the-counter deals for the cut rate liquor.

"Very helpful," said Mendoza, hearing that.

"Tiger," said Hackett thoughtfully to himself. "Tiger."

"Quoting William Blake?" asked Mendoza.

"It just seems to say something to me," said Hackett. "It's a funny kind of nickname. Not exactly like a nickname—"

"In this corner," said Grace lazily, "weighing in at." He lit a cigarette.

"My God, yes," said Hackett. "My God. I wonder—" He brought out his notebook, went into the sergeants' office.

It was a Hollywood west exchange. Truck drivers made money these days. "I hope I didn't disturb you, Mr. Donlevy."

"Just sittin' here watching the game, Sergeant. Can I do something for you?"

"Well, I just wondered," said Hackett. "You have been in the ring—if you keep up with it any these days?"

"Sure. I work out regular, help out some at Pete's Gym, my time off. Keep an eye on some of the young guys comin' along. Why?"

"Well. Fighters pick up names—nicknames, you know. Is there one around they call Tiger?"

Donlevy laughed. "Tiger Faley. Why're you interested in him? Tiger, my God. More like Canvasback, Sergeant."

CHAPTER 11

"So there you have Stettin," said Palliser. "Did you say, blowing hot and cold? We took him back to the station and got a statement from him, here it is—but what it's worth is anybody's guess." He lit a cigarette moodily. He had had a rather busy day off. It was five-twenty and he'd just got back.

Mendoza regarded the typed statement without picking it up. "*¿Quién sabe?*" he said. "There's this and that, John. Stettin was nervous enough—at the notion that Stover could be X—to try calling you twice. That much of a—mmh—civic conscience. Getting cold feet each time, because it couldn't possibly be—and he didn't want to be mixed in. I wouldn't rely on Stettin's character reading, but—"

"Oh, I think we want to talk to Stover all right. The one hard fact that emerges is that Stover knew Lila would be here. Stettin gave me his address. I'll look him up tomorrow."

"Yes. It's the only excuse for a lead we've got—and those cotoneaster leaves, in the middle of town—*caray.*" Mendoza looked up as Hackett and Higgins came in, and passed on the gist of that.

"You had a full day off," said Hackett to Palliser. "Look, Luis, have you any useful ideas about how to use this damn list of Loose's students? There are seventy-one in five classes, and while I dragged my heels on George's brainwave I can just see there might be something there, but—"

"It'd take every man in the office and two weeks to question them separately," said Higgins. "And it's not worth the time—just *as* an idea."

"*De veras,*" said Mendoza. He sat back in his desk chair and folded his long hands together, making a little steeple. "*Tomaremos otro rumbo*—more than one way to skin a cat, as they say." He looked at his two senior sergeants and grinned. "Make a good act out of it, boys—you both look so formidable and muscular. One of you, say, at Loose's first class, the other after lunch. The same act. It's often useful to let your quarry think you know the hell of a lot more than you do. Be sinister at them. Hint. Starting with the break-in of Loose's office—"

"He's worried enough about it, he's making up different exams."

"Very good. Mention that. It's obvious that that was the motive for the break-in. Let them think our miracle-producing scientific lab has turned up evidence—as budding young scientists they'll believe anything along that line. Experience convinces me that it's easier to con the intellectual scientific mind than any other kind."

"I believe you," said Palliser.

"And then what?"

"Stir up the animals," said Mendoza. "It's like any other school—there'll be talk. Gossip. And human nature always enters in. I'll take a bet that something will show up as a result."

"Well," said Hackett doubtfully, "it's a way to play it. George?"

"All right with me. Human nature—" He looked at Mendoza. "There's always a busybody somewhere, you mean. The rumors."

"*Exacto*. Wait for it." They shrugged at him, went out arguing amiably about ways and means.

Mendoza slid down in his chair and lit a cigarette. "You know, that burglar," he said meditatively. "We've dismissed him sort of airily, him and his fixed income—no lead on him. Art said, an amateur. *De veras*. So how is it he's so slick about getting in and out?"

"Most of the places in this area are old—useless locks," said Palliser.

"But how does he know it's safe to go sailing in? That the place is empty? Most people leave a light on when they'll be coming home after dark, even people without much money. It's not all that expensive, and a simple safeguard against burglars. I just suddenly wondered—"

Palliser yawned. "Those poor devils over in Pasadena will just about be shepherding the last of the traffic jam out. What a way to spend a holiday. Oh, well, I'm going home."

Mendoza went home, to find their Máiri MacTaggart back, supervising a ham baking in the oven and various pots and pans on the stove. Alison was mixing salad dressing. "You're early," she said as he bent to kiss her. "If you want to be helpful, you can settle the offspring—"

The offspring, audible in the distance as he came in, became more so by the moment. They were racing the course round the house, bedrooms to front hall to living room to kitchen, on the new tricycles, shouting at the tops of their voices. Alison dropped the spoon and raised her own voice as they appeared. "Johnny! Terry! *¡Bastante ya!* *Not* the tricycles on the carpets! I told you—for heaven's sake, quiet down!"

They stopped, and abandoned the tricycles, only to plunge at Mendoza. "Daddy, read *los cuentos!* Read about *el lobo* again!"

"*El Jaguar!*" shrieked Terry. "*El Jaguar* in *el bosque* all painted!"

"Yes, yes, *niños*—I'll take them off your hands, *amante*— Did you have a good New Year, Máiri? Here, *hijítos,* don't strangle me—"

"Ach, good enough—not like at home. Just me and Janet together talkin' over the old years past. At home now, there'd be the visiting house to house, and the men going out first-footing—"

He took the offspring down to the nursery, nearly tripping over Cedric in the doorway. The cats would be napping elsewhere.

When Palliser got home, he found Roberta just finishing the task of dismantling the Christmas tree. "Now why didn't you wait till I could help you, idiot? Climbing that ladder—"

"I didn't mind. I only had to use it for the top branches and the star. And besides, if you helped me I wouldn't know where half the decorations had been put, the hall closet or wherever. But I'm glad we got an artificial one, John. They're so realistic looking, and don't drop—and I always simply hate to put a Christmas tree out for the refuse truck. It's almost sacrilegious."

"Sentimental!"

"Well, I am. You can take it all apart and put it back in the box for next year."

He kissed her again. "And next year we'll have a real honest-to-goodness family."

"Um-hum," said Roberta. "You know what occurs to me? You'd better get a camera and start practicing with it. To get back at Sergeant Higgins and Jason Grace."

"Well, now, that is a thought," said Palliser. "It is indeed."

Tom Landers' Corvair had just had a complete tune-up and was purring along smoothly. He wasn't thinking about the job, heading downtown at five-thirty; mostly he was thinking about the date with Phil tomorrow night. He got off the Hollywood freeway on the off-ramp which led him to Grand, and as he did so he clapped a hand to his jacket pocket and said, "Damn." He'd forgotten to get out a new pack of cigarettes, and the half-empty one was in the slacks he'd worn all day.

Well, he had time to stop. Instead of turning left on Grand, he went up right towards Sunset Boulevard, which had its unlikely beginning eight blocks away at the old Plaza. This wasn't exactly a classy section of L.A., and a holiday, with most places closed—but there ought to be a drugstore up on Sunset open, where he could get cigarettes.

He turned left on Sunset—in the other direction were the outskirts of Skid Row—and two blocks up spotted an open drugstore on the corner. There were other places open along that block, two bars and a dimly lit small restaurant labeled *La Cita,* which looked deserted but displayed an *Open* sign. Landers found a parking slot half a block away, and walked back to the drugstore, bought a couple of packs of cigarettes. Neatly stripping one open, he came out to the street and started back to the car. He'd been vaguely aware of a figure in the entrance of the second bar as he passed it—echoes of jukebox drifting out, mutter of voices —but now it moved out to the street, and a woman's voice accosted him. "Hullo, dear!"

One of these damned street girls, Vice ought to do something about it, thought Landers, and shook off the hand on his arm.

"Ah, don't be like that, dear. You look like a nice guy, and my place's just up the block—I show you a real good time, honey—"

Landers lengthened his stride, and she stepped around in front of him, almost directly under a street light. "Five bucks," she said in a seductive voice; and Landers stopped. About twenty-five, a mop of black hair to her shoulders, good figure in a very miniskirted outfit, not at all bad-looking, if the makeup was a little heavy. That con pair, he thought. Could it be?

"That's right, lover," she said, and linked her arm in his. "You just come home with me, we have a real good time—"

He was going to feel like a damn fool if she wasn't that girl, thought Landers; but a minute later he was sure. She led him up past the Corvair to where a narrow alley cut through between buildings. "Shortcut to my pad, lover—you just—"

She had him, luckily, by the left arm. Landers peered ahead cautiously—the man would be somewhere ahead ready to jump him. Faint light drifted into the alley from the street lights at either end, and he made out, about twenty feet ahead, a pile of crates of some sort stacked man-high. He hoped that was where the man waited.

"Come on, cat got your tongue, dear? My name's Sue, what's—"

He judged it as best he could in the semi-dark. They came alongside the crates, he sensed a movement there, and felt her arm slacken in his. He jerked out the gun and snapped, "All right, come out with your hands up! You, you stay where you—"

"Jesus, it's a heist!" she yelled, and started to run. Landers lunged and grabbed her with his left hand. A man came plunging from behind the crates, took one look, and bolted.

"Stop! There's a gun on you—" the girl was screaming, and apparently that was what stopped the man. He halted in his tracks.

"Don't hurt Sue, mister—we ain't got much, but you can have—but don't hurt—" Landers got hold of him then, one arm behind him, and headed him back for the street. He only had two hands; he'd had to let go of the girl, but she was yelling now not to hurt Barney, and circling him like a gadfly.

"March!" he said. And just how the hell he was going to take them both in—there must be a call-box somewhere around. He could see himself going into either of those bars and telling the bartender to call cops —but the clerk at the drugstore had looked respectable enough. Take them up there and—

The girl suddenly said, "My God, Barney, it's a cop! My God—" and she started banging Landers with her handbag. "We didn't do anything! You let him go!" She kicked him and connected painfully with his shin.

"Aw, Sue, he's got a gun—"

She hit Landers in the face with the handbag, which was large and heavy. He staggered back, hanging onto Barney desperately. They were at the mouth of the alley, nearly under the street light. He shoved Barney onto the sidewalk, and the girl ran around and hit him in the face again, screaming. In the confusion of the moment, he thought, if the customers in that bar came out—likely none of them liked cops very much—

"Damn it, shut up," he said, dodging her and wishing he had a pair of cuffs on him; better, two pairs.

"You let him go—we didn't do anything!" This time she remembered one of the oldest tricks—she snatched off one spike-heeled pump and aimed it at his eyes. He jerked his head to the side and it connected with his left cheekbone. He renewed his grip on Barney, and then quite suddenly a blinding searchlight caught them all in its glare and a reassuringly hard young voice said, "All right, break it up—"

Like Mrs. Sidney, Landers was pleased to see the black-and-white, even when one of the Traffic men in it pulled him away from Barney and tried to take his gun. He said, "Well, the Marines to the rescue. Thanks very much." The other man had Sue and Barney up against the wall.

"So what's going on here? Have you got a permit to carry—"

"I don't need one." Landers reached for the badge. "Robbery-

Homicide. I'm on my way to work, I'm on night watch. It was just a fluke I spotted the girl, we've been hearing stories about this pair—" And about then he realized that the Traffic man was Bill Moss. "Say, you brought in one of the—"

"My God, Landers—I didn't recognize you in the tangle—you're bleeding, you know? We'll take 'em in, and you'd better stop at First Aid—"

Landers finally got up to the office at seven-fifteen. When he walked into the sergeants' office three voices enquired sarcastically, "And where have you—" before they took him in. "My God," said Conway, "what did you tangle with, a she wildcat?"

"Reasonable facsimile thereof," said Landers. It was the shoe had done most of the damage, though the handbag hadn't done much less. In the handbag had been, among other things, a pint flask full of cheap gin, a large compact, and a goodsized switchblade knife nine inches long even when closed. Whichever of those it had been, Landers had the beginning of what would be a fine black eye, and a couple of savage three-inch cuts on his left cheek from the shoe-heel. He told them about it, feeling the cuts: the nurse at First Aid had painted them and put a bandage on.

"It was just a fluke she picked me—I suppose, looking back, she hadn't found any likely marks in that bar and was about to move on, when I showed up—"

"Looking a little more prosperous than any other pedestrian she'd seen down there," said Galeano. "You took a chance, Tom."

"Well, nobody had said he was going armed. It didn't turn out just exactly the way I thought—but anyway, we've got them. I wonder if any of the marks will identify them—that Dakin— Oh, and Barney had that Lambert's diamond ring on him, by the description. Hadn't got round to fencing it yet."

"And you are going to scare both our girls by tomorrow night," said Conway. "That eye's going to be all colors of the rainbow."

Landers laughed. "Good thing they're both LAPD officers too, isn't it? They won't scare so easy, Rich."

Mendoza read the condensed report on that at eight o'clock Tuesday morning, and passed it on with a grin to Lake and the early arrivals— Glasser, Piggott, Shogart. It was Grace's day off. Hackett or Higgins would be at the U.S.C. College of Medicine play-acting at Dr. Loose's first class. Off the top of his mind, that one—Mendoza didn't know that it would produce any results, at that. First cast, he thought.

It was Higgins who had done that; Hackett came in and said he was going out to look for Tiger Faley. "If he isn't one of the gang, he knows about the hijackings. And if he's the bumbling lamebrain Donlevy says, he may come apart when we look at him."

"So go and look. John—" Palliser had just come in. "You're hot on Stover, I suppose."

"You're damn right. It's still all up in the air, but I'd like to hear what he has to say."

"So would I. If you find him, bring him in and we'll listen together." Palliser cocked his head at him. "You've had a hunch?"

"*Pues no.* I'd just like to—mmh—size him up for myself," said Mendoza.

"And there's an A.P.B. out on Fawkes," said Piggott. "It's a dead one for us, unless he turns up, but I'd like to get him if he's still here."

"You might," suggested Mendoza, "go and ask Perce Andrews about gambling dens."

"Vice? What—"

"The official description of Private Fawkes tells us he's a compulsive gambler. If he's still here, he'll be hunting games to sit in. Of course he might be down in Gardena gambling all legal— *¡Dios!* I'm going senile, why didn't I think of that before? Jimmy—"

"What?" asked Piggott.

"You upright moral Christians with no vices," said Mendoza. "I think it's a handicap to a law officer, Matt. Your minds just don't work the same way as the felons—"

"Well, I should hope not," said Piggott.

"Jimmy, get me somebody on the Gardena force, *por favor.*" He was handed around, finally got a Captain Fordyce. "I'll send the Army flyer on him down—" Fordyce said he'd seen the A.P.B. "Well, the Army wants him too, naturally, but we've got priority—robbery and assault with intent. He's said to be a compulsive gambler. It doesn't say what his preferences are, draw or dice or parchesi, but I just thought—"

"Sure," said Fordyce. "We try to keep an eye on the gambling houses anyway." It wasn't always too careful an eye, thought Mendoza cynically, thinking back to that peculiar case when he'd been hanging around down there himself, playing the pro sharp. "We'll have a look around."

"Thanks very much."

And the first call of the day came in. An accident down at the Stack, one D.O.A. Shogart went out on that.

*   *   *

Palliser was due to have another frustrating day. Stettin had given him an address on Romaine in Hollywood for Stover; it turned out to be one of the new, square, ugly eight-unit apartments going up everywhere in mid-Hollywood these days. But apartment four was not responsive to its bell. There was a sign in front of the place, Apartment for rent, 2-bedrm., $195. The hell of a lot of money to pay out every four weeks, thought Palliser, shoving the bell marked *manageress*. "Mr. Stover," he said when the door opened. "I'm looking for—"

"Oh, Mr. Kemp got married," said the woman in the doorway. She wasn't very old, in her forties possibly, but she was thin and gray and anxious-looking, without makeup. The word *dreep* slid into Palliser's mind.

"I'm looking for Mr. Gene Stover—"

"Yes, that's what I said. Mr. Kemp got married," she said. "Last month. The rent was paid to the end of December. Mr. Stover moved because it was too high for him alone and I guess he couldn't find somebody else to share with."

"Oh." Palliser was annoyed. "Did he leave a forwarding address?"

"Oh, yes, sir. He moved to La Crescenta. They're buying a house there. It's so nice to see young people starting out, and I'm sure she's a very nice girl, he introduced me to her once, her name's Doreen."

"Mr. *Stover*," said Palliser. "Did he leave a forwarding—"

"Oh, him. No, he didn't. They never got much mail anyway."

"He didn't mention to you where he was moving?"

"No, he never. He wasn't as friendly as Mr. Kemp, and in and out a lot."

Well, thought Palliser, if Kemp and Stover had shared an apartment, Kemp ought to know Stover's present address. "May I have Mr. Kemp's new address, please?"

She took some time to find it, and apologized. "I made sure I put it right by the phone, but then I recalled I'd just started a new phonebook and I was still copying numbers in—"

Palliser thanked her, walked back to the Rambler down the block and started for La Crescenta.

It was a very new house, frame-stucco-redwood, on one of the newest curving streets up there. It was L-shaped, and sat above a steep terrace very newly seeded with variegated ivy, and there was a wide paved apron beyond a very steep driveway. Palliser was absently thankful, trudging up it, that they hadn't bought a house in the hills.

The new Mrs. Kemp was a pretty girl, brown-haired and brown-eyed, in a neat housedress. She looked at the badge in surprise and curiosity. "For heaven's sake," she said. "What do the police want with us?"

"LAPD," said Palliser, "not local. I'm trying to find a man named Gene Stover. I understand your husband once shared an apartment with him."

"That's right," she said. "Until Walter and I were married. What do you want Gene for? Don't tell me he's—"

"Just a few questions," said Palliser vaguely. "He's moved from the apartment."

"Yes, I know." She looked him over again, and said, "You'd better come in."

Everything in the living room looked spanking new, all early American. "So, do you know Stover's new address?" Palliser sat down on the couch.

Her eyes were still curious. "Well, Walter will be interested in this. Police asking for Gene. And I know you won't tell me why, but I'm dying to know what it's all about. Gene—well, no, we don't. That was the— Well, I suppose you'll have to hear about it. Or you'd think it was funny we didn't know, when Walter shared an apartment—" She sighed. "There was a row."

"A row?"

"A fight. And I don't flatter myself it was any compliment to me. Gene Stover thinks he's God's gift to all females. If you see what I mean. It's a—a kind of automatic reaction with him, make the pass at any girl who comes in ten feet of him."

"I see," said Palliser.

"He knew Walter and I were engaged. I don't think he *meant* anything by it, exactly, it's just how he is. But neither of us liked it. And—well, we were getting married in just a few days anyway, Walter'd be moving out, so it just—ended. When I said a fight, well, Walter told him off and"—she smiled faintly—"I told him off, and that was that."

"When was this?"

"About a week before we were married—call it five weeks ago. Walter said Gene wasn't there an awful lot anyway, mostly just to sleep, and he hardly saw him again. And you can see why we weren't interested in his new address. Walter had been getting pretty fed up with him anyway, he said, for a while before that. The way Gene was always boasting about—well, you can guess, I suppose. Girls."

"Where did they meet each other, do you know? Has your husband known him long?"

"Oh, when Walter was at the brokerage downtown—Stone, Fox and

Meyer. Only a couple of years. He's transferred to a better firm now. I'm just dying to know why the police are interested in Gene. I'll tell you—you might try his sister. I expect she'd know where he is."

"Do you know her address?"

"No, but she uses the name Rena Rowe. She's trying to break into TV, she's had just a few small bits."

Hackett, entering Pete's Gym out on Vermont, had met the expert eye of a beefy man in sweatshirt and shorts, who looked him up and down and said, "Haven't seen you here before. Want to work off some of that lard, hey?"

Annoyed, Hackett brought out the badge. He'd been up to two-sixteen this morning, but that was less than before he'd started the perennial diet. "I'm looking for a Daniel Faley."

"A cop," said the man, presumably Pete. "What the hell the cops want with Tiger? He's right over there working out with the weights."

Surveying Faley, Hackett thought that Mike Donlevy had summed him up to a T. He looked the prototype of the dimwitted third-rate profighter; and, confronted by the badge, he acted that way, saying all the usual things.

Economically, Hackett told him, "We picked up Kurt Kramer yesterday, Faley. For these hijacking jobs. What do you know about it? Who else is in on it?"

"What?" said Faley. "What? You got Kurt in jail—"

"That's right. I wonder," said Hackett, "if you were the strongarm that waited for the drivers. How about it?" Faley blinked at him. "And how long did it take Kurt to drive it into your head exactly what you were supposed to do?"

At this hour, Pete and Faley were the only men here, no crowd of physical-fitness nuts to interrupt and exclaim. Pete was listening openmouthed. Faley looked around wildly.

"I—how'd you pick up Kurt? I don't know nothin' about what you're talkin' about—" He wasn't quite as tall as Hackett, but carried as much weight or more; he had a forehead practically nonexistent, dull blue eyes, and a Prussian-cropped head. He looked about twenty-five.

"He left us some nice fingerprints on one of the trucks," said Hackett. He wondered, on second thought, if Faley had been the strongarm; if so, why had Kramer been driving that truck?

"So he thinks he's a brain," said Faley, astonished. "He did? He was allus tellin' me to be careful about that, an' then he goes an'—" he stopped.

"I thought you were in on it," said Hackett.

Faley swallowed. "I didn't do nothin' except hit them. When they come back to the truck."

"Is that so? You didn't drive the trucks?" asked Hackett gently.

"Oh, hell, I couldn't get the hang o' those things," said Faley. "Them air brakes an' the handle thing—"

"I see," said Hackett. "Was anybody in the deal besides you and Kurt?"

"It was Kurt's idea. He made the deals, sell all the stuff. He paid me fifty bucks every time I hit one of those guys."

"Yipes!" said Pete behind Hackett. "I knew he was dumb but I didn't think he was *that* dumb. This is the hijackings with all the liquor stole? Jee-sus Christ! The other guy conned this poor dumb Mick into— and what he musta took in profits— Yipes!"

Feeling a little tired of human nature, Hackett took Tiger Faley down to jail. He hadn't made any notes on it; he gave the gist to Wanda, who said she'd type it up. "You certainly make a difference around here, lady." Now to apply for a warrant on Tiger, and some time today talk to Kramer again, try for some kind of statement. And all those probable customers would have to be questioned, though it wasn't likely the D.A. could make any charges stick on them. "Where's the boss?"

He did his play-acting at the college at one o'clock, having conferred with Higgins. "How did it go?" Higgins had said, "I don't know, Art. I said a lot without saying anything. The sinister implications, just like Luis said. That we know more than we're telling. But the kids—I shouldn't call them that, they'll all be in the mid-twenties—they're poker-faced. I don't know. I talked about the break-in, told them about the exams being changed, and the murder—I'm not an actor, damn it," said Higgins plaintively. "It's making bricks without straw. I can say I jumped to the conclusion, the two things connected, but there's no evidence at all, and anybody can see that."

"Not everybody," said Hackett, "even the ones with the scientific minds, have to know as much about what constitutes legal evidence as we do, George." But now, having done his play-acting at that classroom of poker-faced young people, he was wondering. He sat over a late lunch (lunch: Ry Krisp and cottage cheese) and wondered.

"Sometimes Luis' ideas pay off," he said, finishing his black coffee. "It's a tricky one, George—even if there's anything in the connection at all. Wait and see."

*   *   *

NO HOLIDAY FOR CRIME

"And the sister is out of town on location for a TV part," said Palliser. "I found her agent. She'll be back on Thursday, he thought."

"Frustrating," agreed Mendoza. "Yes, I'd like to talk to Mr. Stover too. These things are sent to try us, so they say." He glanced at his watch: four-thirty. The routine getting cleared up; as usual, a couple of cases dragging on; and all too likely, new ones coming along.

CHAPTER 12

Hackett had spent a little while hunting for Al Dakin; when he finally located him, Dakin agreed amiably to take a look at Sue Carter. It had turned out that Sue and Barney were *bona fide* man and wife. It wouldn't be much of a charge but what evidence there was they wanted to get. No need to arrange a show-up; Hackett had her brought out to an interrogation room and Dakin identified her.

"That's her all right. The man I couldn't say about—I never saw him. Damn little cheapskate cheat," said Dakin. "I'm glad you got 'em."

Hackett went home to find that Angel had dismantled the Christmas tree. Mark was too engrossed with a new coloring set, and Sheila too young, to notice. "Don't tell me he's going to be an artist," said Hackett with misgivings.

"Heaven forbid, let's hope it's just a phase. I found a new low-calorie salad dressing for you," said Angel.

Hackett, thinking of Pete, scowled.

Mendoza, wandering into the living room after dinner, vaguely missed something and discovered that the tall Christmas tree had disappeared. The holidays were officially over; and up to five years back he hadn't gone in for the decorations and festivities, but—being domesticated—he thought they were nice to have. A lot of work, he supposed —"I could have helped you with that," he said to Alison, nodding to where it had stood.

"*¡Qué disparate!* Máiri and I managed fine—and you should have heard the wails of protest over it. Thank heaven it was warm enough to chase them out in the back yard, and *el pájaro* distracted their attention."

"That creature. This early—"

"Well, at least he's still alone," said Alison. "No sign of the Missus yet. And if it turns cooler—and heaven knows we're due more rain before the end of the season—"

Bast floated up into Mendoza's lap and he stroked her sleek Abyssinian head. "All your fault, niña—you brought him here to begin with," he reminded her.

"I think it was more Máiri's," said Alison thoughtfully, "dosing el pájaro with your whiskey until he recovered."

The waiter at The Castaways looked at Landers doubtfully and went away for menus. "You really are a sight," said Phil. "That eye is just like an Italian sunset."

Landers felt it gingerly. "I noticed it."

"I'll say one thing. It makes you look five years older." Landers, who was always being told he didn't look old enough to be a cop, grinned reluctantly.

"I think," said Margot Swain, "the cuts are quite distinguished—if she'd only alternated sides, you'd look like a Prussian officer."

"That's why he did it," said Conway, "to get all the attention. Intrepid they call him—venture down a dark alley with a beautiful brunette—the female of the species being, as we all know, more deadly—"

"All right, all right," said Landers. He looked at the girls. It was all right; they were going to like each other. Margot was a brunette, not much bigger than Phil, and she had an infectious chuckle and bright brown eyes.

She said now to Phil, "I never realized—"

"Just what I was thinking. It's one of the standard techniques we get told about in unarmed defense," said Phil, "but I never realized how much damage an innocent shoe could—"

"Look," said Landers, "there's a lot prettier view out the window, girls."

Schenke and Galeano had sat alone on night watch quite a while together, and unless it turned out to be a busy night they wouldn't miss Conway and Landers. No calls came in the first hour, and then the desk relayed one from Central Receiving that sent Galeano over there in a hurry, to Emergency and Dr. Emmanuel in charge of that wing.

"So what's the story, Doctor?"

Emmanuel took off his glasses, pinched the bridge of his nose; he was half-sitting on the corner of his desk. "These things," he said. "We never do quite get used to it, do we? The woman brought the child in about half an hour ago—little girl about three. Interns called me, but it was too late. Woman says she's the mother, says the child fell downstairs. Well, the child was beaten, of course—actual cause of death a fractured skull, I think."

"That's definite?"

"Absolutely. Mrs. Sardo is in the waiting room out there."

Galeano talked to her; she was sullen and tearful at once, and went on denying that anybody had done anything to Rosa. Galeano took her home and talked to her husband, a hulk of a man who smelled of stale wine and sweat, and refused to talk to any cop. It was a thing they saw, and the beat didn't matter: it happened in Beverly Hills too. Galeano went back to the office and filed a report on it for the day watch. They'd check with Welfare, Social Services, for any back record on the Sardos; apply for a warrant if the D.A. thought a charge would stick.

The next call came in at ten-forty, and it was—"He was about due," said Schenke—another burglary. Another old apartment with useless locks, and again the burglar had pried open a back window. Mr. and Mrs. Clifford were alternately bewailing losses and blaming the landlord for not installing decent locks and bolts.

"I know they cost something, but damn it, we pay a good rent—"

"And my mother's opal ring—and my pearl earrings—"

"Damn it, we were just out to the movies! You'd think—"

It wouldn't be much use to get the lab men up tomorrow, dust the place; he hadn't left any latents yet. It was a funny mixture of amateurishness—he wasn't getting much in the way of loot—and cunning. They got a list of what was missing, and left the day watch to do any follow-up.

They were sitting there talking desultorily at eleven-forty when a new call came in, reported routinely by a Traffic unit. Attempted suicide. Galeano went out on that. In legal terms, suicide was a felony, but an attempt was as a rule only prosecuted in theory: as a rule the probation would be tied to psychiatric examination. It wasn't anything much for their office, but as always the paperwork had to be done.

The address was Mariposa Avenue, toward Hollywood. When Galeano pulled up in front, in a red zone, the ambulance was just pulling away. A little gathering of people stood just inside the open front door, and Galeano went up and produced the badge. "Can anyone tell me what happened here?"

Most of them were in night clothes, dressing gowns: a thin gray-haired woman just outside the door labeled *manageress*, a man behind her, another couple hovering outside the open door across the hall. The exception was a very smartly dressed young woman who looked extremely shaken, white-faced and trembling. She had neat dark hair cut short, a triangular kitten face, and big brown eyes, and she was wearing an ankle-length royal blue evening dress, a little velvet cape, one long white glove, and high-heeled gold slippers. She kept clutching the long fashionable rope of fake pearls that hung to her waist. "Miss? Could you tell me—"

"But it isn't anything that *happens,*" she said. Suddenly she began to sag, and Galeano got hold of her and guided her to sit on the first step of the stairs, got her head down between her knees. The other women rushed to support her.

"You poor dear—" "But that nice Miss Baker, it doesn't seem possible—"

"I'm all right," she said after a minute, and sat up. "Really I am. And they—they have to ask questions. I k-kept my head all right—until just now. I'm sorry. Are you from the hospital?"

"No, miss, police." He showed the badge. "Can you tell me what happened?"

She nodded. "It's my—roommate. Pat Baker. I can't understand it, and oh, my God, I've got to call her mother and father—"

"Take it easy now, Miss—"

"Cerny. Evelyn Cerny. I just got home—from a date with Bill—we're engaged. And of course I thought Pat'd be asleep—I was quiet, but I turned on one lamp—in the bedroom—and she didn't look right, she was —like snoring and she doesn't—and there was the empty bottle marked morph— I don't believe it, it just couldn't—*Pat!* I c-called an ambulance, and the police— But why? Pat? There's no reason—"

"Her parents live here in town?"

She nodded. "I'll call them. I—Pat and I've been all through school together—"

"Was there a note?"

"I don't know. I didn't notice . . . Yes, you can look. Apartment six."

It was a small one-bedroom place, nicely furnished, neat and clean. In the bedroom was a pair of twin beds, one on the window side unmade and much rumpled. Nothing on the bedside table but the lamp and the empty bottle, with the label on it: Morphine all right. No note. Galeano looked around: there was a female handbag on the chest on that side of the room. It was a large pouch bag, gaping open. He looked, and reached in. On top of everything else there, an envelope. He took it out and lifted its flap.

No suicide note emerged, but four long brown cigarettes, looking home-made. "Well, well," said Galeano. He wondered if the Cerny girl knew that her roommate had been using the Mary Jane.

Mendoza was scanning the list of the night's happenings, as related to Robbery-Homicide, as the men drifted in. He frowned over the attempted suicide: a tiresome piece of routine, all the paperwork to bog down their private secretary. He tossed the report to Higgins, who made a little grunting sound, reading it.

"What?" said Hackett, peering over his shoulder.

"I—well, I don't know, the name rang a little bell. Baker—I don't know why, it doesn't—"

"And our burglar has struck again," said Mendoza. "Him and his fixed income . . . *¡Diez millones de demonios!* Here's one we follow up hard, boys." He gave them Galeano's report on the Sardo child. "Neanderthal—a thing you never quite believe. George, you'd better run a check on the Sardos—if they're on Welfare, see what Social Services knows about them. See if he's got a rap sheet of any kind. Bring him in and we'll lean on him—I don't suppose he's any brain."

"God, no," said Higgins. "I'd better check with the hospital on the suicide try first."

Private Fawkes hadn't turned up yet. There were inquests scheduled today and tomorrow, on the bodies piled up the last week or so, the accidents on the freeways. Police evidence would be taken at all of them. The Askell thing—that was bothering Mendoza by its very shapelessness, and the frustrating fact that there was nowhere to look on it. Until Palliser located this Stover—and that very small lead could collapse when he did.

"Where's John?" he asked Lake.

"Oh, he came in early and got a call right off. I don't know where."

"Don't tell me, something new. I—Art? Now what has struck you?" Hackett was standing gazing into space, a forgotten cigarette in one hand. "*¿Qué ocurre, hermano?*"

"I just," said Hackett, his eyes slowly focusing, "I just remembered— or seemed to remember—they were out at the movies. The Purdys. And —I wasn't on all of them, of course, but I think Matt said—and it just occurs to me, I wonder—because it'd be very funny—"

"Pull yourself together and make sense, Arturo. What are you talking about?"

"Well, I suppose it'd be in the reports." Hackett turned and went into the inner office, to Wanda Larsen. She was already busy at the typewriter. "Our copies of all the first reports on the burglar, lady. Got 'em handy?"

"Oh, certainly." She and Shogart were weeding out dead wood from the old Robbery files in their spare time, but she had started a new set of filing cases for the new bureau. She produced ten reports all filed together, and Hackett started to go through them.

"Just what is the brainwave?" asked Mendoza.

"Well, I will be damned," said Hackett two minutes later. "I will be— And what the hell can it say? They were all at the movies, Luis. The burglar's victims. Every single one of them. When the burglary occurred."

Mendoza reached for the reports, making for his office. Then he looked over the reports, sat back and lit a cigarette. "Is it a little funny, or just coincidence? I didn't think the silver screen was all that popular these days. And most of these people are middle-aged—not the audience producers aim for now, ¿cómo no? It does seem—mmh—a little too coincidental. But on the other hand—"

"On the other hand be damned," said Hackett. He was taking down phone numbers from the reports. "Let's ask. Just for fun." He took up the outside phone and at random called the Purdys.

"Now what do you want?" asked Purdy ungraciously. "You caught that thief yet?"

"Well, no, I'm afraid not. You were out at the movies the night of the burglary, you said—"

"And what about it? Entitled to a night out once in a while, not that we can afford much, prices so high even for movies now."

"Er—which one had you gone to?"

"Now what in the name of goodness you want to know that for? I don't recall the name of the picture, it wasn't very good, but it was the Bijou up on Broadway. We hadn't been to a movie in a year or better, but when the tickets came—"

"The tickets?"

"Yeah, yeah, complimentary from the manager, the note said. Advertising stunt of some kind, I—"

"Thanks very much." Hackett put the phone down and dialed again. This time he talked to Mr. Jarvis, who told him that they hadn't been to a movie in a couple of years, just bad luck they'd been out that night when the burglar—but of course when they were sent the complimentary tickets by the manager—

"I will be *damned!*" he said at the end of the fourth call. "Do we need to check it further, Luis? They were all sent tickets through the mail! They all—"

"But it's beautiful," said Mendoza, fascinated. "So simple and so human, Art. I like this fellow. That's very psychologically sound, you know. You get sent free tickets to something, the chances are you'll use them. Especially—mmh, yes—especially people like these, without much money to squander for entertainment. It's a beautiful piece of logic. The tickets sent for a certain evening, so he could be practically certain they were out, he could walk right in at his leisure. For the price of a pair of movie tickets."

"But how the hell can we follow it up? Would the girl in the ticket-booth notice if somebody bought a couple of tickets and then didn't—but wait a minute, that's wrong, because if there was a date on them—"

"Yes," said Mendoza. "And another thing—he's kept to that general area. Of the four couples you called, three were sent tickets to the Bijou, the other to a theatre not far off. ¡Vaya! I don't know about this, but if there are dates on the tickets, I should think it'd be fairly unusual— Let's see what we can turn on this, Arturo." Fired with sudden interest, he put out his cigarette and got up, reaching for his hat.

Palliser had noted the address of the urgent first call with surprise. It was the third time he'd been here: that chain market out on Third.

When he got there, the Traffic unit was just pulling off. In the big parking lot, empty except for two cars and a tall van, Raymond Osney was talking with angry gestures to two other men. Palliser parked beside the van and went up to them.

"Well, Mr. Osney—don't tell me you've had any more trouble here? I thought you said the district manager—"

"Me," said the shorter of the other two sadly. "Ames. Bill Ames."

"—That you were going to have the guard dogs here at—"

"That's right," said the third man gloomily. "Protection Service, Incorporated. Rent guaranteed protection day or night."

"But if—"

Osney looked ready to burst into tears. "Now they've stolen the dog!" he said.

Before he could stop himself Palliser began to laugh. "I'm sorry," he said, "but it just— How in hell could anybody steal a trained guard dog? A—what did you say—"

"Dobie," said the third man. "*My* Dobie. Eric von Rothenburg,

NO HOLIDAY FOR CRIME 693

Ricky for short. I ask you. I just ask you—" he raised eyebrows at
Palliser

"Sergeant Palliser."

"I just ask you. They got you coming and going. So you train guard
logs, for protection. I was with the K-nine corps, Army. There's a call
or more guard dogs every day, and you want to breed from the best to
et the best, no? So how can you spay and neuter all your best dogs? It
sn't feasible. You also want 'em to breed more good guard dogs." He
pat aside.

"But what—"

"Well, that's how they did it, of course. Ricky's three years old and a
ood stud. As well as a good guard. If somebody fetched a bitch in
eat and broke in a door—it was the back stockroom door, matter of
uct—any idea of bein' on guard'd fly right out of his mind, and you
an't blame the dog for that. It's nature."

"Yes, I see—" Palliser nearly dissolved in mirth again, but saved him-
elf.

"A mess—just a mess," said Osney. "All the liquor and cigarettes
gain—we'd just got new stock in—"

"*And* my dog," said the third man.

"Excuse me, I don't think I heard your name—"

"Katz. Al Katz."

This time Palliser managed to turn the laugh into a cough. "Well,
e'll get the lab up here and see if they can find any evidence—" He
idn't suppose it would be much use, but you never knew. "What about
ie dog, Mr. Katz? Would they have—er—hurt him, or—"

"Where's the need? Let the bitch lead him off, he won't remember he
'as on guard for quite a spell. God knows where he might've got to,
own here. Running the streets, and worth five hundred at least—not
iat it's all the money. He's a damn good dog. I'll take the van and tool
round awhile—he'll come to a silent whistle, and it carries quite a
ay." Katz swung over to the van in the lot. They watched it out.

Palliser called up a lab truck and they looked at the mess and clutter
i the stockroom. The lab men didn't look hopeful, but got out their
its and started to work.

Just as Palliser was starting back for his car, a dog came loping up
ie side street and turned hesitantly into the parking lot. He was a
oodsized dog, long and lean, black and tan, with ears laid despon-
ently against his head. His long tongue drooled out of his mouth, and
e was covered with dust and wild-mustard blossoms from some empty
t. His chain collar chinked.

"Ricky?" said Palliser doubtfully. "Come here, boy." The dog came over to him and plopped down, panting. He looked tired. "Well, at least you're all right," said Palliser. Thinking of Osney's expression, he began to laugh again.

Higgins had checked Central Receiving on the suicide attempt. The girl had been pulled through, the family was there; she could probably be talked to this afternoon. Higgins put the phone down, wondering why the ordinary name had rung a little bell in his mind; if it was important it would come to him. He went on to start the follow-up routine on the Sardo child.

And for once he was inclined to agree with Matt about the devil. If not an active force for evil driving a man, how could there be a thing like this, the tiny corpse with the bruises and cuts—the child hardly in the world before she was brutally sent out of it by her begetter? Inevitably Higgins thought of Margaret Emily at home, his new darling—and Mary was just teasing him, saying he'd spoil her. . . . The Sardos were on Welfare; according to Social Services, she had twice accused him of beating her, beating the children, and then refused to sign a complaint. And God knew that in a democratic republic the Sardos had rights like everybody else, but Higgins wondered if Bruno Sardo understood the recited ritual.

Shogart sat in on the questioning. They didn't get anywhere. "The baby, she fell downstairs," was all they got out of Sardo. But the medical evidence was firm.

They talked to the mother alone, and she finally broke down and admitted that Bruno had done it. "She's crying, he don't like it, he tell her stop, but she don't, an' he—" And she might retract that later, but they had it on record. They applied for the warrant.

"And only manslaughter," said Shogart. "Have they got any other kids?"

"Three, according to Nick."

"People," said Shogart. "That's a thing I guess a normal man couldn't ever understand, any more than suicide."

And a little bell rang again in Higgins' mind. Suicide, he thought. Now why—

Hackett sometimes felt a little superstitious about Mendoza. He'd seen the thing happen before, and wondered if among the unknown ancestors that had gone to produce Luis Rodolfo Vicente Mendoza there had been any warlocks. Mendoza would sit there at his desk, covering the routine like the well-trained detective he was, and occasionally watch his boys sweating out the offbeat tough one, throwing out suggestions that might or might not be helpful. But let him get really interested in a thing, go out on the legwork himself, and all of a sudden—as if his guardian angel was leading the way—something would turn up.

He had ruminated about the burglar, but now with the simplistic little cunning of the movie tickets turned up, he was fascinated. He took Hackett out Broadway to the Bijou Theatre, which of course was closed, but the required sign on the door gave him an emergency number. By ten o'clock they were sitting in the living room of the theatre's manager, Mr. Edward Rea, in a modest house in Hollywood. Mr. Rea was looking rather bewildered at this invasion of the law, but answered questions docilely. He was a little man with a bald head and horn-rimmed glasses.

"Dates?" he said. "Dates on the tickets? Why, yes, of course. To give us some check on attendance. And the prices—if any loges are— But really I don't understand why you're asking all this—"

Mendoza smiled at him. "Each day's tickets are in the ticket booth just that one day? But you do have—mmh—tickets ahead, as it were? That is, I could come and ask to buy a ticket for next Friday?"

"Well, you *could*," said Rea.

"But that'd be sort of unusual, wouldn't it?" asked Hackett. "The girl in the booth couldn't—the tickets wouldn't be there yet, if I understand you." He felt a little confused about it. "Where would they be?"

"I beg your pardon, where would what be?"

"The tickets ahead. For the next week, say."

"Oh, in my office, of course. At the theatre. They come in rolls, for the machine—"

"So," said Mendoza, "if I wanted a ticket for next Friday, I'd have to come to you?"

"Well, or the ticket girl would ask me— As a matter of fact," and Rea emitted a shrill tenor laugh, "we have one faithful patron who does buy tickets ahead, and heaven forgive me for laughing at the poor soul. She—"

"Who's that?" asked Hackett interestedly.

"Mrs. Devlin. Dora Devlin. She never misses a change of feature. She's on Social Security, and she always buys her tickets a month ahead because otherwise it'd all go for cheap *vino*. Poor soul."

"Oh," said Hackett. "But you'd know, that is there'd be a way of checking, on tickets sold for a showing several days later?"

"Certainly. But what is this all about?" asked Rea. "Really, I'd like to help the police, but I don't see what you're driving at—"

"He took the chance," said Mendoza softly to himself. "That we wouldn't notice. Yes. Movies—do you get much of an audience, on the average, any more?" It was an absent question; it opened the floodgates. Rea deplored the films being made today, the unrealistic ratings. "It's all but killed the medium. People simply don't go to movies any more—except the young people, and not too many of them. And what with union wages, and inflation, prices have gone up so— Why, I don't know why the owners keep the theatres open afternoons! If we have twenty people in between one and six— But I mustn't bore you with all that. Twenty years ago, when I took over the Bijou, it was a great deal different, I can tell you that. A lovely theatre, it was, and the crowds—I tell you, gentlemen, to those of us who can remember when there were films that were genuine artistic productions—some of the great pictures and great stars, you know—the stuff turned out today is—is—" He had no words for it; he gestured angrily. "It's a crying shame! I tell you, I've been sorry to see the Bijou run down the way it has—but at the same time, I'm just as happy that we don't often get the first-run stuff any more. Once in a while we'll get one of the great old ones, from the forties—but even the ones ten years old are better than the stuff they're turning out now. To think how they've cheapened the medium—I was saying to Mr. Pollock only the other day—"

"Yes, yes," said Hackett. "But these tickets—can you tell us who did buy any ahead"—he reckoned the days—"for last night? It'd have been on Saturday, probably—" Because he'd have had to have time to get them sent by mail.

"—And of course he agreed. Mr. Pollock is a real connoisseur of films. I suppose he's seen every film ever made—a projectionist for nearly fifty years, a remarkable record when you stop to think. Of course these days even that is getting automated," said Rea mournfully. "And he's retired now, of course, he must be seventy-five or so. But he still appreciates the good old ones. As I say, we sometimes get the great ones to run, and always, or mostly, the older ones, and the old man— Well, that's a case in point, just what you were asking, gentlemen. I always give him a discount, of course. You could say he served the industry long and faithfully. He does occasionally like to send out tickets to friends—and I'm glad to oblige him, of course. Such a fine old fellow—"

"Now you don't tell me," said Mendoza gently.

"Oh, now, Luis," said Hackett. "It can't fall into our laps from heaven like that."

"Where," said Mendoza, "does old Mr. Pollock live, do you know?"

"Why, he's only got a small pension, he has a couple of rooms over a store near the theatre—but really I don't understand what this is all about," said Rea. "The address? Mr. Pollock? Really I can't make out why the *police*—"

Higgins had given the gist of the Sardo case to Wanda to put in a formal report. Piggott and Glasser were out seeing those supposed customers of Kramer's. That would be a dead-end: no charge.

Grace had some more snapshots. "But you're right about that camera, you know. The film pack—it mounts up. Jimmy said Hackett had a brainstorm, and he and the boss went out on it. Something about that burglar."

"Burglars," said Higgins morosely. "Set us hunting for small-time burglars yet. Damn it. Damn it, I can't—it's something to do with— No, it's gone."

"You having a brainstorm now?"

"It's something right on the tip of my mind, sort of," said Higgins, "and I can't put a finger on it."

"If it's important it'll come to you."

"Yes, I keep telling myself."

There were always the routine things to do. He could help out Piggott and Glasser on that thankless job, or—Higgins lit another cigarette, sitting at his desk, and thought coldly about the Sardo baby and fondly of Margaret Emily, who would be four months old on the fifteenth of this month. The new year officially under way—and probably it would bring all the same things with it that the old year had. Nothing new or different or unexpectable about human nature.

"You seem to be the only one in," said Sergeant Lake. "Teletype from Communications. Just the routine thing."

"What?" Higgins started and looked up.

Lake repeated that. "Fellow committed suicide—this is from the chief down in New Orleans. A William Howerton—the suicide, I mean—and his father lives here, address up in Monterey Park. Will we please notify and ask about disposition of body, etcetera. The routine."

"Break the bad news," said Higgins with a sigh. And then he said, "By God! By God, but that was why— By God!"

"Something hit you?" said Lake.

"By God—Pat Baker," said Higgins. "Patricia Baker. Out of seventy-one names—but I swear she was on that list of Loose's— Where's Art? By God—"

CHAPTER 13

Along this block of Second Street the buildings were old, two- and three-storied, of dirty dark brick. There were small shops on the ground floor, and windows above gave vague clues as to what lay behind them: dirty white curtains, plain windowshades, nothing at all. Mendoza had parked the Ferrari down the block; they walked up past a dingy men's clothing store, a shop displaying Mexican silver jewelry, a shop advertising *Sandals made to measure,* a pawnshop. "How the hell do you get upstairs?" asked Hackett.

At the corner, there was a somewhat larger place: a doll factory. Hackett averted his eyes from the collection of torsos, arms, and heads in the window, and Mendoza said, *"Aquí está."* Almost hidden in a recess between this door and the corner of the building was a single narrow door. A small sign on it read, *Rooms By Week or Month, call Mr. Adams,* and a phone number.

They climbed rickety old stairs. At the top was a narrow hall, unlighted, leading left and right. Mendoza flicked his lighter at the nearest door, which bore the single numeral nine. *"Sí,"* he said, and knocked on it loudly. There was a step inside and the door opened. "Mr. Pollock? Mr. Roger Pollock?"

"That's who I am. And you, sir?" Light streamed out from the room; as he stepped back in tacit invitation, and they went in, they saw that this was one very large room, the three windows to their right looking out on Second. It was a tired old room, here and there plaster cracked, but very neat and clean. It was arranged in sections: up near the windows was a daybed, neatly made up, with a screen beside it. Farther down, against the inner wall, was a built-in sink with a table beside it holding stacked dishes. Out from that was a kitchen table with a chair, an electric hot plate on its own metal stand. Opposite the door was a tall bookshelf full of what looked like either photographic albums or scrapbooks, and nicely arranged before it an old leather armchair with a table beside it holding one dimestore glass ashtray, and an old standing lamp.

Mendoza had the badge out. "Lieutenant Mendoza—Sergeant Hackett. You took the chance that nobody would connect the complimentary theatre tickets. I'm afraid we're a little smarter than that."

"Well, you didn't do so for some time," said Pollock in a mild voice. He was a tall spare old man with thin white hair carefully plastered over a pink scalp. "I'm not sure of the etiquette involved—do I ask you to sit down?"

"Certainly." Mendoza sat down in the old leather armchair and lit a cigarette. "You know, Mr. Pollock, you shouldn't have done it. Taken to burglary at your time of life."

"Ah, it wouldn't have been my choice," said Pollock. He pulled the kitchen chair around and sat on it. "But I do not believe in forcing my fellow citizens to support me, which is what public welfare amounts to. I have supported myself since I was twelve years old, Lieutenant, and it would have been very distasteful to me to take money I had not earned."

"But the welfare—" began Hackett, and was quelled by a look.

"Money forcibly extorted from honest citizens by compulsory taxes is not true charity. I wanted no part of it. When I found, what with the increasing inflation, I simply had not enough for necessities, I said to myself, I would rather steal. For by doing that, you must admit, I was at least expending some labor for the—ah—return."

Mendoza laughed. "Well, it's a way to look at it."

"Life," said Pollock, and sighed, "plays tricks on us, gentlemen. I was a saving man, and I always earned steady money. I had quite a nice little nest egg—in a savings and loan company. But my wife's last illness —we hadn't any family, only ourselves to rely on—Parkinson's disease and then cancer—when she died I hadn't much left at all. All the doctors' bills, the hospital—I have only the Social Security now. And what with the rising inflation—" He shrugged. "I've lived here twenty years, I know this part of town very well. And the people. The idea—er—came to me in a flash, you could say. Of course it was natural in a way, my having been connected with the industry, in a sense, nearly all my working life. I suppose you have a warrant for my arrest?"

"Not yet. We just heard of you a short while ago. But you'll come back to headquarters now and I'll apply for one."

"Yes, I see. Dear me, I suppose I won't be allowed to take all my scrapbooks—" Pollock looked anxious. "Am I allowed to telephone a friend?"

"Certainly. And an attorney—"

"Oh, I don't think that's necessary. But I must ask Mr. Rea if he will kindly take care of all my scrapbooks. They go back a long way—really a miniature history of the industry. And Mr. Rea properly understands —I have left them to him in my will, of course." He blinked at the bookshelves lovingly. "One thing I can be grateful for, you know—I've lived through a great era of entertainment. I'm afraid the industry is committing suicide these days, the completely valueless material it's turning out—but ah, in the early and middle years, we had some great talents with us—really great! I do believe, one or two of them, the greatest ever among us. It's sad to compare what is offered today—you know, gentlemen, I find one can live a little too long." He stood up. "I suppose you could say," he added reflectively, "about the burglaries, that I was only acting by my lifelong conviction in the superiority of the free-enterprise system. Up to a *point*." And he laughed, a genuinely mirthful chuckle. "I am also aware that such a comparison of—ah—theft with capitalism is entirely fallacious, as these muddleheaded youngsters may one day find out, let's hope. But at least I—I paid my own way for a little time after—there simply wasn't enough to do that any more."

"Mr. Pollock," said Hackett, "your pawnbroker's receipt made our day. We appreciated it."

Pollock chuckled again. "A—ah—small commentary on this end of the twentieth century, Sergeant. And yet—in the middle years there was such promise, such fun, such talent, such memories in the making! Well, the memories one can keep. What will I be allowed to take, Lieutenant?"

Mendoza smiled at him. "We'll see that Mr. Rea looks after your things here. Not much, I'm afraid. Cigarettes—a book—you won't need clothes."

"I just wondered—" Pollock glanced at the wall beside the bookshelves, and went over there. Mendoza shrugged and nodded. They could argue about it at the jail.

Two framed photographs hung there: the only two pictures in the room. They were autographed black and white photographs, in cheap gold frames. Pollock took them down. The first showed a slim young man very dapper in the white flannels and navy blazer of the early thirties, smiling broadly into the camera. It was autographed in a scrawl at the right bottom edge. *Stan Laurel.*

"The very greatest," said Pollock, touching it. "Infinitely a superior pantomimist to Chaplin."

The other was a photograph of John Wayne which must have been taken twenty-five years ago.

"Well—" said Pollock, and looked around his home, "I'm quite ready. . . . And it did take you quite some time to find me, didn't it?"

Palliser, having shared the joke about the dog with Lake and Grace, was about to share it with Wanda, just back from a coffee break, when a new call came in: a head-on down at the Stack with one D.O.A. He went out on it, annoyed.

Even the out-of-state tourists these days mostly came from places where there were also freeways, and should be used to them. The L.A. Traffic Bureau prided itself on the placing, clarity and convenience of its freeway markings, and—always barring the drunks, of course—it was hard to see how drivers could get confused, try to enter on off-ramps and vice versa, causing the accidents. But while the signs were nearly infallible, the people were not.

When he got to it—traffic tied up on the inbound Santa Monica freeway, two squad cars, an ambulance, and a crowd of ghouls—it was, of course, a mess. The D.O.A., by what the Traffic men had sorted out, was the guilty party; he'd managed to get an old beat-up Dodge going west on the eastbound side, and rammed into a brand new Impala with Arizona plates. There had been a woman alone in the Impala, and the ambulance men had her on a stretcher. She was moaning, "No, no, no, where's Azzie? Azzie—please, is he all right? You can't take me anywhere until—please where's—"

Palliser squatted over the stretcher and one of the ambulance men said kindly, "You're not bad, ma'am, you've got a broken leg and probably some ribs, but you'll be O.K., don't worry—"

"No, no—" she moaned. She was a nice-looking woman about forty, with dark hair and a good complexion. "My dog—please find him, is he all right? Please—"

"Oh," said Palliser. He stood up. "Any sign of a dog around?"

"I got it," called a voice from the little crowd. "Big savage dog, I can't hardly hold—" And the dog came through the crowd, towing a citizen, tugging at a braided leather leash. He flashed up to the stretcher, tongue out frantically.

"Oh, Azzie! Oh, thank God you're all right— Please," and her gaze fastened on Palliser, "please will you see he's taken—some good boarding place, where he'll—I don't know anybody here, I can pay—please—"

"I'll see to it," said Palliser soothingly.

"I'm Madge Borman—the address is in the car—now, Azzie, you go with him. Go with the man here—it's all right, darling." The stretcher went into the ambulance, and it purred off quickly; Traffic wanted to get the freeway unjammed. Palliser stood there with the dog's leash in his hand. The dog was the biggest black German Shepherd he'd ever seen. He went to look in the Impala, and rescued Miss Borman's handbag from the front seat, together with a wooden box bearing a printed label: *Borman's Dark Angel of Langley*. Inside the box were several brushes, a hard rubber ball covered with teeth marks, and a box of Dog Yummies. "I guess this belongs to you," he said to the dog, and the dog moved his tail politely. He had strained after the ambulance, but seemed to understand that he was in Palliser's charge. He was a very handsome dog. Palliser put him in the Rambler, and after getting the names of the D.O.A. and a couple of witnesses, drove off the freeway and stopped along Venice Boulevard, wondering what to do with the dog. He didn't know anything about boarding kennels at all.

Mendoza, however, would. Palliser found a public phone and called in, explained his predicament to Sergeant Lake. "Well, this and that's been happening, John. They got the burglar—nicest old chap you'd want to meet—the warrant's applied for—and then Higgins— Well, just a minute. I'll see—"

There was silence, and then Mendoza's voice. "John? I understand you've acquired a dog. Why?"

Palliser told him. "A Miss Borman, from Arizona. She doesn't know anybody here. By the tag on his collar, the dog is Borman's Dark Angel, but she called him—"

"What is it?"

"What—oh, a great big black German Shepherd."

"Not that it matters. Evidently a show dog. Well, you take the dog up to the Los Feliz Small Animal Hospital on Los Feliz, and tell Dr. Douthit—"

"Dr. who?"

"Douthit. Tell him the circumstances, and that I'll guarantee the bill. And then you'd better come in."

"Yes, thanks," said Palliser. He drove across town to the hospital and left the dog; a brisk Dr. Douthit said he was a fine specimen. The dog licked Palliser's hand politely, and Palliser thought about what Roberta had said. That was quite a dog. And with the crime rate up—

But it bothered him a little, all the way back downtown, as to why she called the dog Azzie.

* * *

Higgins had got sidetracked. The routine was there to be done. And the LAPD liked to do it right. The LAPD did not call people on the telephone to tell them about sudden death to family members. Higgins drove out to Monterey Park to break the bad news, as requested by New Orleans, and gave the elder Mr. Howerton the addresses and phone numbers to use, making the arrangements. He then came back to the office hunting for Hackett, and Lake told him about Roger Pollock. "Funny, the things we run into," he said. "The nicest old fellow—" But Hackett and Mendoza had gone to see Pollock into jail. They'd be back shortly.

He was still thinking about that girl, Pat Baker. He'd been a little surprised to find several young women in Loose's first class; he shouldn't have been, girls went in for a lot of professions these days. Attempted suicide—and Galeano had said, the marijuana cigarettes. Higgins wondered more about that. A *medical* student—you'd think if anybody should know the truth about that, it would be—

He was surprised to find it was ten past twelve. He didn't know where the morning had gone. He went on out North Broadway to Federico's, and found Mendoza, Hackett, Grace and Glasser just sitting down at the big table.

"And wait until you hear about the burglar," said Grace. "Art had the hunch this time."

"Not a hunch. I just remembered about the movies."

Higgins listened impatiently. "A very funny little thing, yes. Listen—it just came to me a while ago—that attempted suicide last night. Girl named Pat Baker. I'm pretty sure she was on that list, in Loose's classes."

"What?" said Hackett. "It's an ordinary name, George." Palliser wandered up and sat down beside him.

"Yes, I know, but I'm sure. We can check. I think we'd better check. I called the hospital on it this morning, and we can talk to her this afternoon."

"Coincidence—"

"Once, not twice," said Mendoza. "*¿Cuánto apuestas?*—how much do you bet? Stir up the animals, I said, didn't I? I wonder—I do wonder—if you stirred that up, boys, or if she was already thinking about it."

"Talk about reaching—oh, we'd better see her," agreed Hackett.

"I hear you got the burglar," said Palliser, and heard about that. "Very funny. *I* can't make out about that dog. His name is Dark Angel of Langley, and she called him Azzie. A funny sort of name—"

"Most show dogs have names for short," said Mendoza.

"Yes, and others too—like Ricky. Did I tell you about Ricky?" He did so. "And you should have seen Osney's face—"

"That old devil sex," grinned Mendoza. *"De veras."* He put out his cigarette as the waiter came up with a tray, "And after lunch, I think we go and ask Miss Baker why she tried to take the hard way out."

All three of them had been cops a long time, Mendoza and his two senior sergeants, and they had for their sins seen a lot of people like Dr. and Mrs. James Baker. The kind of people, happy, successful, with the good life, suddenly seeing their world fall apart as Fate—or whatever it was decided such things—took a hand.

He was in general practice in Hollywood, distinguished looking, upright; she was the typical well-groomed efficient housewife. And they were saying to the police officers what they had been saying, probably to hospital staff and to each other, all night and day.

"But all of a sudden—there wasn't any hint of anything wrong—" "—Living with Evelyn, old friends and good experience for her—" "—Never any trouble with Pat, a good quiet girl—" "And she won't talk, she won't tell us what—just thank God they pulled her through, but—"

Mendoza listened to that a little while: the background. The girl had her own money; a grandmother had left her a trust fund. She hadn't been pressured to study for an M.D. degree, it was her own ambition. She was twenty-three, in her second year as a med student. She hadn't any steady boyfriend, dated sometimes. She'd always been a responsible girl, affectionate, steady, and she was home for dinner at least once a week, there hadn't been any hint of worry—

"Yes, well, it could be she'll talk to us," said Mendoza. They looked at him doubtfully; but he had the doctors' permission.

When they went into the little single hospital room she was lying flat in the high bed, her face turned toward the window. She turned slowly to look at them. She might be a middling pretty girl, made up and happy; she had a round face, very fine white skin, blue eyes and dark hair, uncombed and tousled now. Her voice was thin and listless. She looked at the dapper slim Mendoza between the two bigger men looming, and she said, "You're the police. I knew you'd come."

"That's right, Miss Baker," said Mendoza.

"They kept—asking and asking. About why, you know. Mother and Daddy and the doctor, and they got Evelyn to come and try to—and it was all just too long to explain, to make them understand—because it was all just one thing leading—I just thought I'd wait till you came, because you—already know—some of it."

"Miss Baker," said Hackett, exchanging a glance with Mendoza, "before you tell us anything we have to inform you about all your rights." He recited that.

She waited patiently, and nodded. "Yes—I know about that. You see, I never *meant*—any of it. I didn't know—things could happen like that—without your meaning it. But they do. And it was—all—just too much. Too *much*. All at once." She stopped there, turning her head restlessly.

Mendoza waited and then said quietly, "You broke into Dr. Loose's office?"

"Yes. I'd been worried—I suppose I ought to start from there—I'd been worried about grades. My—papers. I got A's and B's mostly all last year, but it was—harder, this year—and then—and then Donny gave me some of those cigarettes—" She swallowed and said, "But everybody knows—he said, everybody knows—marijuana isn't dangerous—like the other things. It'll be legal pretty soon, everybody says—just like ordinary cigarettes. And it seemed to help, sort of. I felt—"

None of them looked at each other, but Higgins gave an expressive sigh. As law-men they had to keep up with all sorts of things; some of what they knew wasn't general knowledge, but that recent story had been carried by the wire services to most newspapers: the painstaking research turning up the interesting fact that prolonged use of marijuana had the effect of physically shrinking the brain. And a medical student—but maybe the operative word was *student*. She was twenty-three, and on almost any campus these days, the silly, sordid, and dangerous talk was loud.

"—Felt better about it, as if I was doing fine—but then I went on getting bad marks, and I—was worried. Daddy—so proud—all last year, and I wanted— But along in November, I got to thinking—about the end-of-year exams—I tried to study, but then there was Christmas coming—presents to think about, things to—Mother's party, I had to—pretend there wasn't anything wrong—and it got harder and harder—"

"Miss Baker. How often were you using marijuana then?"

She looked up vaguely. "I don't know, when I tried to study—sometimes. I haven't now for about a month. I got—scared. I got scared one night about it. It was—way before Christmas. Evelyn was going out on a date. I was trying—memorize—for Anatomy class. And I—she'd just left, I *thought*, and then all of a sudden she came home and it was—one in the morning and I didn't know what had happened, what I'd been doing—all that time. I got scared. I haven't—had any since."

That was one effect it had, of course.

"And Daddy *would*—all through Christmas, people coming in—boasting about me—and I wasn't any good! I couldn't do the work— And there were exams coming up— You know about that. *That* was why. You know."

"We'd like to hear it from you, Miss Baker."

After silence, she said, "It's so long. Telling about it. I—I don't want —to see them when you tell them. You'll—tell them, won't you? Mother and Daddy. I never *meant* anything—it just happened. The exams—I got to thinking, if I just knew what *some* of the questions—it'd be a help. Dr. Loose's office—" She moved restlessly. "I read detective stories sometimes, I knew about deadbolts and all, and I looked at the door one day when I'd been up there—you could get in *there* easy enough. The building—and then—I thought—about the cleaning men. You see? It was just getting *in*. You could get out—easy enough—after they'd gone, the front doors open from inside with one of those bars even if the lock's thrown—I was there late one day—and—Dr. Loose showed me—"

"Go on, Miss Baker."

"I—got there just after they did. The cleaning men. That night. They were all—working down the hall, in the classrooms—I got upstairs right away, they never saw me. It was all right to turn on a light up there, if anybody saw it they'd just think—Dr. Loose—working late. And I found the exam questions—and—I was going to wait till the men left. And then one of them—came up to that floor, I heard him on the stairs and I was —so terribly scared—all I could see, all of a sudden, was them finding me and an awful scandal about the exams and me expelled and Daddy so ashamed, after—and I wanted to get *away!* I just wanted to get *away!* I—I grabbed up something from the desk, I thought a ruler or—just any way, I wanted to get *out* of there— But I didn't know he was so close! I ran out the door, I thought—the back stairs, before—but the man was right *there!* A man—I hit out at him, I didn't know what I did, I just— and I ran. I just threw that thing away—and I ran. Down the back stairs —and out the side door. And—"

They waited. "I didn't know—until I heard—people talking about it. I don't see a newspaper much. But Donny said—and everybody—about that man there. That poor man—dead. Murdered, they said. And some scissors—" Her voice dropped to a near whisper. "I don't *remember* any scissors. I turned the light off—when I heard him on the stairs—and I grabbed up a ruler or something—I thought. But when I knew—I knew that was *me*. Had done that. Not meaning anything—I was—just scared. I've been scared—ever since." She looked up at Higgins' craggy tough-looking face, and closed her eyes. "You came—yesterday morning—and I thought—I thought you knew, looking right at me. And it just seemed better not to—have it all open and in the papers and Mother and Daddy so—" And after a long silence she said, "I got the morphine from Daddy's bag. The office is closed till next week, he wouldn't find out right away. They were going to a party last night, and I've got a key to the house, of course."

"I see," said Mendoza quietly.

"And—that's—all. You can go and tell them now. And—and do whatever you have to do to me. But I'm so tired. I just wish Evelyn hadn't—found me so soon."

"Maybe you'll feel different about that some day," said Mendoza.

They went out, first to tell the story to the parents. Who asked numb questions, and said all the inevitable things. And the D.A. might call it manslaughter or murder two; she might get three-to-five, she might get a suspended sentence and probation; it was anybody's guess. It would probably drag on in the courts for some time; and by the time a judge and/or a jury decided Pat Baker's immediate fate, everybody would have forgotten who Joe Daly was, except the family that mourned him.

"Just the random chance really," said Higgins on the way back to the office. He sounded uneasy. "I'd hate to think it was my ugly puss scared her enough to push her over the edge."

Hackett laughed sharply. "Say it was cumulative, George."

"And I'm the one who told you to try to scare them," Mendoza reminded them. "I wonder if anything new's gone down. Woman's work —we get one cleared up, we get something else coming in."

Palliser, at loose ends, told Wanda and Shogart about the dog. "That's the funniest name for a dog I ever heard," said Wanda.

"We had a dog once named Dog," said Shogart.

Grace came back from a session with a couple of the supposed customers of Kramer's. "All up in the air," said Grace. "We'll never prove it."

Palliser told him about the dog. "Well, that is a funny name," said Grace. "I've heard some peculiar names for dogs, but that takes the cake."

Hackett and Higgins came in, looking rather glum, and told them about Pat Baker. "My successful play-acting," said Higgins. "Scaring the girl into—my God, if I'd had any inkling—"

"I did some of it too," said Hackett.

"And do we say," said Grace, "there but for the grace of God?"

"No," said Higgins, "because most people with any grain of common sense know better than to experiment with the Mary Jane."

"Most people," said Grace. "Who aren't twenty-three and hearing all the fool talk from—"

"Oh, Art," said Sergeant Lake from the anteroom. "Call for you."

Hackett picked up the phone on his desk and punched the outside button. "Robbery-Homicide, Sergeant Hackett."

"Are you *telling* me," said an outraged voice, "are you telling me—I just saw it in the *Herald*—arrested for complicity in those hijackings— Are you *telling* me it was *Tiger Faley* knocked me out cold? Me? *Me!* —that—that tanglefooted lout who hasn't got a punch to lick a bantam with any science—that it was *Faley*—"

"I'm afraid so, Mr. Donlevy," said Hackett, choking back a laugh.

The silence at the other end was eloquent. Then Donlevy said hollowly, "My God. My God. Faley—that damn punchdrunk— My God, I'll never live it down. Me! Basher Donlevy—"

"Well, you weren't expecting it," said Hackett.

"Expecting be damned. I'll never live it down. *Faley!*" said Donlevy, as if it was the worst cussword he knew, and the line went dead. Hackett sat back and laughed.

Piggott and Glasser came back at four-thirty and Glasser went to hand Wanda a couple of pages of notes.

"The devil," said Piggott, "is busy these days. Going up and down. All those customers of Kramer's, and absolutely no proof. We may as well forget it."

"Waste of time, I said so," said Grace. He was leafing fondly through the batch of snapshots. "And I should have listened to you," he added to Higgins. "You did warn me. The film pack for his camera—even if it is convenient, getting the picture right away—"

"And you haven't heard," said Higgins moodily, "about my ugly mug scaring that girl—" He started to tell them about that.

"If the head doctors are right," said Hackett, "he'll be growing a trauma about his looks."

"Oh, don't be a damn fool," said Higgins. "Though I will say, I hope Margaret takes after Mary instead of me. But—"

"I," said Palliser to Piggott, "seem to have got mixed up with dogs today. You didn't hear about Ricky—speaking of cameras, if I could have a shot of Osney's expression! And—"

Glasser was laughing over something with Wanda.

"And the thing on the freeway," said Palliser. "It beats me, with all the signs posted, how anybody with common sense could—but there was this dog. A show dog I suppose. With another name for short, but such a funny name. Azzie, she called him."

"Azzie," said Piggott, yawning.

"The tag on his collar said Dark Angel of Langley. A great big dog," said Palliser. "A good watchdog, a German Shepherd would be. And he'd been a smart dog, understanding he should cooperate with a strange man. A good watchdog for the baby, a dog like that would be."

"Oh," said Piggott. "Oh, well, that explains it."

"What?"

"The Dark Angel," said Piggott. "Didn't you ever read the Bible? Azrael, the Dark Angel. Probably—"

"Well, I will be damned," said Palliser. "I never heard—" And Lake broke in urgently.

"Heist at the Federal Savings and Loan, Wilshire and Rampart—"

Mendoza came out to join them as they all got up. A bank job—the Feds would be alerted and on the way too.

And irrelevantly Palliser thought, not a bank job. The banks were all closed by now, it was long after three. But the savings and loan associations would be open till six.

There was always something new coming along to make work for the law-men.

CHAPTER 14

The Feds were of the opinion, after listening to what the tellers and patrons at the savings and loan branch had to say, that the three heist-men were the same gang that had done a job on a bank in Pasadena last month and Stockton the month before that. "All we need," said Mendoza. It had been a professional job: ski-masks, a lookout at the door, very businesslike. The first estimate was that they'd got away with about eleven grand. There wasn't even a close make on the car; several people had seen them get away, but their descriptions varied from a tan Dodge to a white Ford, and nobody had seen any part of the plate-number.

"It's what we usually get, isn't it?" said Bright of the local FBI. "Bricks without straw."

"Fortunately there aren't too many bright ones," said Mendoza.

They were all late getting away, and met the night watch coming on. Landers' eye was still colorful, but fading. Grace stopped to pass a few snapshots around. "How you doing with that blonde, Tom?"

"I think I'm making an impression, but she's a damn level-headed girl," said Landers.

As Palliser sat over the warmed-up and savory beef stew, he told Roberta he supposed he ought to go and tell Miss Borman where her dog was. Roberta had heard all about the dog, and said he certainly had. "She'll be worried to death. Of course they're nice dogs, but too big for the city. And you needn't help with the dishes—you'll just about make visiting-hour at the hospital." Roberta smiled at him. She was looking—his normally svelte and slim Robin—fairly rotund these days, with David Andrew (or possibly Margaret).

He found Madge Borman in a four-bed room, propped up against the pillow. Her face cleared when he told her about the dog, and Lieutenant Mendoza knowing about the boarding place, and Dr. Douthit; she thanked him warmly. "I don't know a soul here, I don't know what would have happened—we were on our way to the Pasadena show. I'll never forget how kind you've been—"

"Well, the LAPD tries to do its best for everybody, Miss Borman. He's a fine dog. My wife's been saying we ought to get a dog after the baby—but of course not—"

"You shall have one of Azzie's pups, Sergeant. No, I insist! I'm breeding Marla to him next month, just say which you'd like and you shall—of course the bitches are better watchdogs if that's what you were thinking of—"

"Well, but they're—" *Too big for the city* was lost in the volume of her gratitude.

"You shall have one of the girls. I just don't know what I'd have done if you hadn't been so kind."

Miss Borman had a strong personality. Uneasily Palliser wondered how to tell Robin, and decided to put it off. Possibly Miss Borman would forget all about it once she was back in Arizona.

Hackett, Higgins and Shogart were off on Thursday.

The night watch had left them a legacy: a break-in at a big pharmacy on Beverly Boulevard. The pharmacist and his employees would be taking stock this morning, to reckon what was missing, but not until the lab men had been there; Mendoza chased them out on that early. There had also been a mugging near MacArthur Park, and a new body reported by Traffic about midnight. The body, found in the street on Temple, was described as male, Caucasian, late twenties, probable overdose. Mendoza knew how that would go. If they didn't identify it from prints, sooner or later some relative would come in—or maybe not. Once in a long while they got a body they never could put a name to.

Piggott and Glasser went out to talk to the pharmacist. Mendoza wandered out of his office and said to Palliser, "You said something about that Gene Stover—his sister, who ought to know where he is—"

"Yes, I'm going to do something about it right now," said Palliser, picking up the phone. "I told you I found her agent. These boys so damned upstage—all they can think of—"

"I don't," said Mendoza, "like the ones like Lila Askell. No handle. No shape. *No sirve—es difícil.* Witnesses—too many witnesses, John."

"What?" Palliser was dialing.

"Down there. Broadway and Seventh, the day before Christmas. How many people saw Lila and the strange young man?—but never saw them at all. To notice. Only Louise Chaffee—and she couldn't say at all where they went after they had that—mm—peculiar lunch. An Orange Julius bar, *Dios*. And the cotoneaster leaves— Who are you calling?"

"The damn agent. Rena Rowe's. There's no—"

"At this hour? Show biz people don't keep our hours, John. He won't be in his office until eleven at least."

"But he was so damn worried about publicity, he wouldn't give me the address—"

"Who is she? . . . bit parts, on the make for the big time and all the odds against her if she hasn't strings to pull. Mmh," said Mendoza. "*¡Ca! Esto me da en que pensar.*" He started back for his office with Palliser trailing him. At the desk, he flipped over the pages of the phone-list rapidly. "Maybe we'll pull some strings ourselves. It's always helpful to have friends in exalted places."

"I didn't know you had," said Palliser.

"Oh, that was before you made rank and joined us, now I think. I had—mmh—occasion to oblige that well-known producer Mr. Toby Pickering in a rather delicate personal matter—" He had dialed rapidly and now said, "Lieutenant Mendoza, if Mr. Pickering has a moment, please . . ." Within three minutes he was apologizing for disturbing the great man. "I'm trying to get in touch with a would-be starlet, she's had bits and pieces I understand—one Rena Rowe. Would you have any idea how to locate her? . . . Oh. Well, I would appreciate it. Thanks very much." He put the phone down, circled thumb and forefinger at Palliser. "He can demand the head powers at Central Casting and bully an address out of them. A mere LAPD officer, not a hope in hell."

"It's nice to have friends in high places," said Palliser.

Grace came back from a routine check at nine-fifty. Five minutes later R. and I. called in the crisp voice of Policewoman Phil O'Neill. "That new body of yours," she said. "S.I.D. sent its prints up, and the computer made them. In our records. William Francis Jay, little record of possession. Do you want his package?"

"Well," said Lake, "if there's any relative listed—"

"Wife. St. Andrews Place, but this is two years back."

"Give it to me, " said Lake resignedly. "We'd better check."

He handed the address to Grace, who went back downstairs. The job could get boring. But as he drove he thought fondly of their very own family—now all the red tape had got cut—plump brown Celia Ann, such a good baby. Only, of course, that camera—he wondered what it might cost him to turn it in on the same kind Higgins had.

At the old brick apartment house on St. Andrews Place, he found Linda Jay still listed on a mailbox. When she finally opened the door to him, she looked blearily at him around it—slim brown Grace nearly as dapper as Mendoza—and peered at the badge. "For God's sake," she said. "Come around at *this* hour—cops! What you want with me? I haven't even had a traffic ticket lately." She wasn't bad-looking, blonde by request, clutching a terry bathrobe around her tightly.

"It's your husband, Mrs. Jay. I'm sorry to have to tell you he's dead. He was found last night—"

"Dead?" she said. "Bill? Well, goody-goody! I've been saving up for a divorce, and now I can blow it. Is that for real, it's really Bill? In your morgue?"

"By his fingerprints, yes—"

"Thank *you*, mister! This really makes my day!" she said, and banged the door in his face.

People, people, thought Grace. They did come all sorts forever.

Within five minutes Pickering got back to Mendoza on the phone. "It's Sweetzer Avenue off the Strip," he said tersely. "Never heard of the girl myself, but Central Casting had her down all right. Not at all, glad to oblige. Any time."

Mendoza put out his cigarette and looked at Palliser thoughtfully. "How do you feel about this Stover?"

"Any hunches, you mean? No. But he's the only thing, and the last thing that showed at all on Lila, and I just want to see him," said Palliser, "to—round it out, do I mean? To—feel as if we'd done everything we damn well could on it, if it has to wind up in Pending."

"Yes. I don't like shoving cases into Pending, but once in a while there's just no handle. So, good luck on finding him. If it was anybody else," said Mendoza, "I might come along for the ride in case you do find him. But if so, I'll trust you to size him up."

"Well, a compliment from the maestro himself." Palliser went out past the switchboard.

On the way to Sweetzer Avenue, which was out in county territory in west Hollywood, Palliser thought again about that dog. Or rather pup. He had the feeling that Robin might go straight up in the air. Well, nice dogs, but in town—they'd been talking about a chain-link fence, or some kind of fence round the yard, on account of the baby. If Madge Borman remembered about that pup, and Palliser thought she wasn't a woman to forget promises, there'd have to be some kind of fence.

Well, there was time—the baby due in April. Just about, he reckoned up hastily, the time those pups would be due, by what she said. . . .

The address was one of the stark square new apartments. The rent would be median out here, near fashionable areas but not of them; exactly the sort of address a girl like this would have. He wondered as he climbed the front steps what delicate service Mendoza had performed for the exalted Mr. Pickering.

Eight mailboxes. Rena Rowe was listed at apartment six upstairs. They were uncarpeted cement stairs; above, a narrow hall with four doors. Six was at the left rear. He pushed the bell.

When the door opened he had the badge out. She was a tall girl, perhaps five-seven, a natural blonde, leggy and very much a Hollywood type, almost oozing synthetic glamor. "Who the hell are you?" she said in a throaty voice. "Where'd you get my address? I'm not listed—what's that?" She looked at the badge. "A cop? Where'd you get my—"

Palliser was tempted to tell her; the mention of Pickering's name would doubtless earn him instant welcome. "We're trying to locate your brother, Miss Rowe—Gene Stover. It's nothing to do with you. Do you know where he's living?"

"What's it about? Is Gene in some kind of cop trouble?"

"We just want to ask him some questions," said Palliser.

"Oh." She thought that over. "Oh, well, if it gets in the papers, any publicity's good. Sure. Come on in. He always runs to big sister, he's broke. But you aren't going to get any willing answers to your questions at this hour, before he's had some coffee."

"He's here?"

"Sure. The other bedroom." She gestured, uncaring that the nylon peignoir over very little underwear slid open revealingly. She walked over to the coffee table, bent to light a cigarette. It was an ugly square room, painted stark white, furnished in violent modern, with two surrealist prints on the walls.

Palliser knocked on the indicated door. "Mr. Stover! Police! I'd like to talk to you, please."

"You won't get anywhere that way," she said. She went past him, opening the door. "Gene? You up yet? Come and see the nice handsome cop, dear. I don't know if it's a traffic ticket or what, but he wants to talk to you."

"What the hell?" It was a high tenor, sounding boyish. He came out to the living room slowly, with her prodding him behind. Gene Stover would be at least Stettin's age, twenty-five or so, but he looked younger. He was also too good-looking for a man. Only his sister's height, he was a little stocky, very blond. He had regular cameo features, the fair skin that showed blood easily, very white teeth, a mouth slightly too small. He was wrapping a white terry robe around him, and he looked at Palliser with dislike and a curious fury in his pale blue eyes.

"A cop!" he said. "What—do you want with me?"

And Palliser knew. In that split second, he knew and was sure. Whether it was a thing akin to Mendoza's *daemon* he didn't know, nor could he say exactly what told him. Little things: things not evidence, except to whatever it was in him which on occasion read between the lines about human nature. The hand clenched on the belt of the robe: the eyes: the mouth too taut.

"About Lila Askell, Mr. Stover," he said, and the warm satisfaction spread through him like light. "I think you can tell us something about Lila Askell."

"I can't. I don't know a damn thing about that," he said roughly. "That damned Ron Stettin! He said you'd come nosing around up there, and he had the nerve, tell you about that—just a joke, the note to tell me she— Well, like I told him, I never got it, so I never knew—and if you ask me it was slander, him even suggesting—"

"Hey, don't get worked up," said Rena. "You got some girl in trouble, Gene?"

Palliser eyed him interestedly, thinking. There were the two latents from Lila's necklace, not known to any records. Unfortunately, without much more legal cause than they had, they couldn't ask Gene Stover to let himself be printed. There wasn't any other solid evidence at all, so far. If Stover stuck to that story, and they couldn't prove he'd had Stettin's note—if Louise Chaffee couldn't identify him positively—there was nothing to tie him in.

"So what have you got to say to that, cop? Slander—try to make out— I want some coffee," he said querulously. He started for the kitchen at the other side of the apartment.

Palliser thought, this was January fourth. A week ago last Sunday, Lila Askell had been on her way home for Christmas, with a three-hour wait for her bus in Los Angeles. And she'd never made it home. Ten days. But the lab sometimes made miracles; and the average citizen didn't realize just what evidence the lab could turn up, when they went really looking. And then, of course, when it came to fingerprints, they *had* the two latents from the necklace, and if—

"Mr. Stover," he asked, "do you have a car?" Stover had just come back with a cup of well-creamed coffee.

"Well, of course I've got a car. Why?"

"Where is it?"

Stover looked at him narrowly. "Why?"

"Where?"

"It's in the alley at the back," said the girl. "There's only one carport, mine's in that. What's this all about?" It had penetrated her mind that this was about something more than a traffic ticket. "It's a Corvair. What's—"

"I'm afraid," said Palliser, "I'll have to ask you to get dressed, Mr. Stover. I'd like you to come back to headquarters to answer some questions. We'd also like to examine your car."

"But I *told* you! I don't know anything about that! I—I don't think I was even in town that day—"

"What day?"

"I don't *remember* what day it was! You can't make me—you can't—"

"Well, I'm afraid we can, Mr. Stover, when we have reason to think you might be able to help us. We'd prefer you to cooperate voluntarily, but—"

"I can't—all I can do is go on saying—I don't know anything about it," he said too breathlessly. "I—oh, damn it, that bastard Ron—"

Palliser asked to use the phone, got the Traffic garage, and asked that the Corvair be towed in at once for examination. "Priority," he added. "Tell Duke. . . . You'd better get dressed, Mr. Stover."

A new call came in at ten-thirty, just as Palliser came back with a blond fellow in tow. Grace and Piggott were in. "You'd better both roll on it," said Lake. "It sounds like a thing, what the uniformed branch had to say. It's Carroll Avenue—" He added the address.

It was a thing. It was going to be quite a thing to work, and was probably the next offbeat little mystery—sometimes they got the little mysteries—to occupy them for a while.

This street of modest old houses, a few apartments, close in to Echo Park Avenue, was rental-zoned, and most of the houses had smaller houses on the back of the lot. The address was one of those. The squad car was still there, and the two uniformed men were in the yard between the houses with a fat woman in a bright pink dress. The house was on a corner, and there was a chain-link fence round the yard with a gate open on the side. Grace and Piggott went through it.

"I didn't see her all yesterday, I told you that, I just saw she hadn't gone to work today, her car still there, I wondered was she sick, and when she didn't answer the door I just looked in the wind—" she'd been saying it over and over; and was crying a little, more in excitement and shock than sorrow.

"You'll want the lab boys on this pronto," said one of the patrolmen. "All we got so far is, she was a divorcée, Mrs. Ellen Reynolds, worked in an office somewhere. Lived here alone. The back door was forced—"

They went around the little house, which would contain about three rooms. There was a single step, to a narrow rear door; a screen hung half off its hinges, and there were savage pry-marks on the open inner door. It led to a tiny kitchen. In there was a body, and a good deal of blood.

In the middle of the floor, which wasn't more than six feet square, she was spread-eagled. By the dark hair, the slim figure, she was probably young; her face and upper body were so covered with long-dried dark blood, it was hard to say. She was naked except for a white lace brassiere tangled around one arm, stockings crumpled about her ankles. Things lay on the floor: a couple of broken dishes, in the opposite doorway a green ceramic vase, broken. Mutely they followed the trail to a tiny living room, where a chair was overturned, a love-seat pulled away from the wall, a scatter-rug wadded up. The telephone lay on the floor, its wire pulled out and broken. One high-heeled shoe lay upside down near another door.

"She put up a fight," said Grace. "It started in here." The tinier bedroom was a shambles—bedclothes on the floor, a straight chair broken in two parts, the big mirror over a vanity table shattered, half of it in shards on the table. There was probably, they could hope, a welter of scientific evidence here to be picked up.

They went, avoiding possible pieces of evidence, back to the kitchen.

"Did you see the note?" asked one of the patrolmen through the back door.

"Note?" said Piggott.

"On top of her handbag in the living room. We didn't touch it, there might be prints—"

They went to look. The handbag was a workaday affair, brown leather much worn. It was on the coffee table, neatly closed with the clasp fastened, as if it had been put there to be noticed. On top of it was an empty used envelope, with something scrawled on the wrong side.

"My God," said Grace. "My God, Matt."

It was a nearly illiterate scrawl: but it seemed to shout a certain lunatic arrogance into the silence. Crookedly across the back of the envelope it ran—*god bles th parol bord.*

"Satan," said Piggott, "getting around these days, Jase. And how the lieutenant is going to love this."

Palliser came into Mendoza's office alone and said tersely, "The long way round, but we do get there. Let's hope there'll be the lab evidence to prove it. I want to call Duke."

"*¡Parece mentira!*" said Mendoza. "Don't tell me—"

"Oh, you'll have the feeling about him too, I don't doubt. The trouble is, he's saying loud and clear, don't know nothing about it, and unless we do turn up the solid evidence—Jimmy, get me the lab," said Palliser. "Duke? That car just fetched in to the garage—blue Corvair—give it everything you've got. Now. I've got our man here, but we can't hold him, we haven't even got enough to warrant holding him overnight —and I have the definite feeling that if he slides out from under us now, he'll run. If there's any evidence we want it in the next hour."

"Fun and games," said Duke. "What are we looking for?"

"Some people," said Palliser, "always drive in gloves. Let's hope he's not one of them. Those latents you picked up from the Askell girl's necklace—if you get any liftable ones from the driver's side of the Corvair, run a comparison. I don't think it'd be much use to look for any of her prints, it's ten days back. And anything else interesting about the car—"

"O.K.," said Duke. "We're on it."

"So, elucidate," said Mendoza.

Palliser shook his head. "How do you know these things? You can't explain it. He's too handsome. His voice is too high. His clothes are a little too fancy."

Mendoza laughed. "*Como sí.* The little cold finger down the spine, saying the fellow across the table really does hold a full house. Well— where is he?"

"Interrogation room down the hall. But we can't stall him too long, he's already yelling about citizens' rights."

"Sometimes," said Mendoza, "they can yell too loud. And talk themselves into trouble. Let's let him sit for half an hour and then see."

And, in the interrogation room, he looked at Gene Stover and felt as Palliser had felt about him. "Who're you?" asked Stover angrily. "You can't keep me here for no reason—I *said* I didn't know anything about it and nobody can prove—"

Mendoza introduced himself. "What are you afraid of, Mr. Stover?" he asked blandly.

"I'm not afraid of anything, damn it! I don't know anything about all this," he said doggedly. "I told you I never got that crazy damn note Ron said—I told him—so I didn't know about her—I wasn't interested—"

He said it all over again, several different ways, to a few leading questions. He began to sweat, and Mendoza leaned on the wall smoking and watching him. Stover moved restlessly, sitting at the small table; he wasn't a smoker, and was unsure what to do with his hands. He folded them, unfolded them, scratched his cheek, and his pale eyes moved too. When at last a silence had held to tension, he sprang up and shouted, "Damn you, stop *looking* at me! Who the hell do you think you are, standing there *looking* at me—I told you I don't know anything—"

"About Lila Askell," said Mendoza gently, "who wanted to go home for Christmas." And he had wondered about the motive on Lila; they didn't have to show motive, legally, and often motive was very slight in any case. But when the girl hadn't been raped, he had wondered. Now, looking at Gene Stover, it came to him what the motive must have been, the very little, sordid, silly motive. Matt talking about the devil . . . "It rankled with you, didn't it, that she didn't fall for your masculine charms? That doesn't often happen to you, does it? If the girls don't fall for your pretty-boy looks, they'll feel motherly about you." That was the type. "And Lila annoyed you, didn't she? So obviously uninterested. Turning you down."

"I never— She was a nothing," he said. "Strictly from Boresville— why the hell should I—"

"But you called and asked her for dates, several times—after the double dates with Monica and Stettin," said Mendoza. "And she turned you down. The only reason you did ask her was to prove you could get to her, wasn't it? You were annoyed because she hadn't any use for Pretty Boy, weren't you?"

"You go to hell," said Stover furiously. "I never—and you can't make me say I did! I don't know anything about it!" But his hands were shaking.

It went on like that another ten minutes. A weak character can be very stubborn, and he had pinned his faith on the magic reiteration. The last time he said it, it was pure automatic reflex.

There was a gentle tap on the closed door. Palliser opened it and went out to the corridor, shutting it behind him. "So?" he said to Duke.

"Bingo. He doesn't," said Duke, "drive in gloves. Quite a few good prints on the steering wheel, dash, and rear view mirror. They match the prints off the necklace. But also—"

"We sometimes get lucky. Thanks, Duke."

"But also," said Duke, "people trying to wipe off fingerprints forget he most obvious places. You thought that was the car the Askell girl ode in. None of her prints on the dash, passenger's door. But he forgot he seat. Where it curves under at the front. It's vinyl upholstery, takes rints medium well. You watch a woman in a car, if she's not driving, he'll take hold there round a curve, keeping her balance, you know? Ve got two dandy prints off that spot, on the passenger's side. They're ila Askell's."

"Bingo," said Palliser. He went back into the interrogation room and odded at Mendoza, smiling. Mendoza came away from the wall, up- ight.

"So let's stop hearing the broken record, Stover, and get the truth. It ad rankled with you—Lila so uninterested, turning you down. A girl ke that too," said Mendoza softly. "Not bad-looking, but in the slang dog—a boring girl, a very normal and respectable girl, a girl all rapped up in her dull little job, helping the hospital patients. A stupid irl like that, turning *you* down. Good-looking Gene, all the girls falling or him—"

"Damn you! No—I never saw that girl here—"

"Then how," asked Palliser, "did her fingerprints get inside your car? nd how did yours get on that necklace she was wearing? That's nice olid physical evidence, Stover, and it's going to send you up on murder ne."

Stover went muddy gray. He said wildly, "But I wiped all the places he—her *necklace*—" And then he put his head on his arms across the ble and moaned, "No. No. I didn't mean to *hurt* her. Like that." fter a long silence he sat up a little, huddled miserably in the straight hair. "Yes, I was mad about it—damn her—that stupid boring small- wn *thing*—going to church and talking about her silly job—and turning e down as if I was—as if I wasn't— And Ron's note. Damn it, damn it, was all Ron's fault—like a joke, saying she'd be here then, I should ake another try at her—and she didn't want to go with me, but I—and fter we had lunch, I thought about Echo Park—nobody there then and ere's shrubbery—but she got mad again when I tried to kiss her, she it me, and I was so damn mad—treating me as if I smelled bad or—me! nd I—all of a sudden she just—" He shook his head. "I don't know ow it happened." But it was a very easy way to kill somebody without eaning to. "I didn't know what—I nearly left her there, but I was fraid, I thought some place even—emptier, and I got her back in the ar— She might have been *nice* to me!" he said. "She might have been— ut that stupid, stupid girl—"

* * *

"Stupid is a word for it," said Mendoza. Palliser had just come back from booking him in. The warrant was applied for. "Human nature is damned monotonous, John." He was shuffling the deck dexterously.

The inside phone burred at him and he picked it up. "Mendoza. Oh, Saul. How're you doing, boy?"

"My sins are finding me out," said Goldberg. "This big Mick ordering me around. And no girls attached to Narco. Damn it, I haven't typed a report in years—" He sneezed.

Mendoza laughed. "So you're doing some work for a change. We appreciate the legacy, Saul. Very much."

"You'd better appreciate her. I just wondered if you ever caught up to the burglar."

"Oh, yes. We're just as efficient as ever. And it's my office now, *hermano*." He put the phone down, smiling.

And Piggott and Grace came in, with the details so far on the new one, Ellen Reynolds. "We got a lab truck up," said Grace, brushing his moustache in unconscious imitation of Mendoza. "But the queerest damn thing—and you're going to cuss—is the note." He produced it. "It's been printed. Nothing."

Mendoza looked at it and said loudly, "*¡Diez millones de demonios negros desde el infierno—Por el amor de Dios!* Why in hell's name I stay in this thankless job—"

Hackett and Higgins, and their new faithful plodder, Shogart, would hear about the new one tomorrow—the little offbeat one to give them the most work for a while.

Hackett was up to two-eighteen and feeling what-the-hell about it. Angel tried to stop him, but he had a piece of her latest devil's food cake.

Higgins was feeling adventurous, but only so far. "I tell you, Steve," he said, "suppose we try developing our own negatives first, see how that goes, and think about the enlarger later."

"O.K.," said Steve. Laura was at the piano again. Mary, scooping up Margaret Emily from the blanket on the floor, for bath and bed, smiled at her menfolk indulgently.

Glasser, unlocking the door of his apartment, thought dimly that it might be kind of nice to have somebody to come home to. Somebody there, when he came home. He hadn't any family but a couple of cousins back east.

*   *   *

Grace stopped on the way home and got a new film-pack for the camera. Higgins was right about that camera, but it was nice to get the prints right off. And very nice, at long last, to have their very own family—

When Piggot let himself into the apartment, thinking pessimistically about the new case (it did say that Satan should be loosed for a little time), Prudence was in the kitchen, her good contralto voice raised lustily on "Rock of Ages." He felt a little better, going out to kiss her. It was good to have a place of his own, and Prudence. And God would not be mocked; eventually the truth would prevail.

Palliser, thinking uneasily about Madge Borman, the chain-link fence, and that German Shepherd pup sometime around May, reflected suddenly that Robin shouldn't be upset. The baby due in April—David Andrew or possibly Margaret—and Robin shouldn't be annoyed. His conscience cleared slightly.

It would be time enough, after the baby was here, to tell her about Madge Borman's notions of gratitude.

It had, the last twenty-four hours, turned cool and gray: more like what January was supposed to be, even in southern California. Alison reported that the mockingbird had disappeared. "¡Gracias a Dios!" said Mendoza.

For a man who had walked alone so long, he had gone in for the domesticities with a vengeance. The Just-So Stories had been duly read to the twins, pink from their baths—El Gato who walked by himself, El Rinoceronte with his skin full of cake-crumbs—and Máiri MacTaggart would be lulling them to sleep with Jacobite fervor on "We're no awa' to bide awa'," the current demanded favorite.

Bast was coiled on the credenza, ruddy and plump; Nefertite was washing El Señor's ears on the sectional. Sheba was poised on top of the bookcase, and Alison said, "¡Cuidado!" too late. Sheba launched herself for his shoulder and Mendoza caught her and hauled her down to his arms. "Monstruoso . . . If I had a kind and generous nature, I should call Art and George, warn them about this new damned thing we've got . . . Mystery be damned. The parole board!" said Mendoza as if it was a new oath. "¡Dios! Letting the wild ones loose—" He put Sheba down on top of Nefertite, who spat amiably and started to wash her.

Cedric the hairy sheepdog marched in, jowls dripping from his water-bowl, and Mendoza said, "I need a drink. The damned thankless job—why I stay on at it, the dirt at the bottom—"

"*Amador*, you wouldn't know what to do with yourself," said Alison amusedly.

And El Señor understood English. He galloped after Mendoza and floated up to the drainboard for his half-ounce of rye.

"The parole board," said Mendoza balefully, pacing back to the living room with his drink. He had stripped off jacket and tie; he looked keyed-up and dangerous. "And God knows what else turning up?"

"Don't bring the office home, *amador*," said Alison. He looked at her, his lovely copper-haired girl who after too long had domesticated him, and he laughed, finished the drink and went to put his arms around her.

"You know me too well, *mi corazón. Y manaña es otro día*—tomorrow is also a day."